DUNGEONS & DRAGONS™

Forgotten Realms™:
The Legend of Drizzt™

OMNIBUS

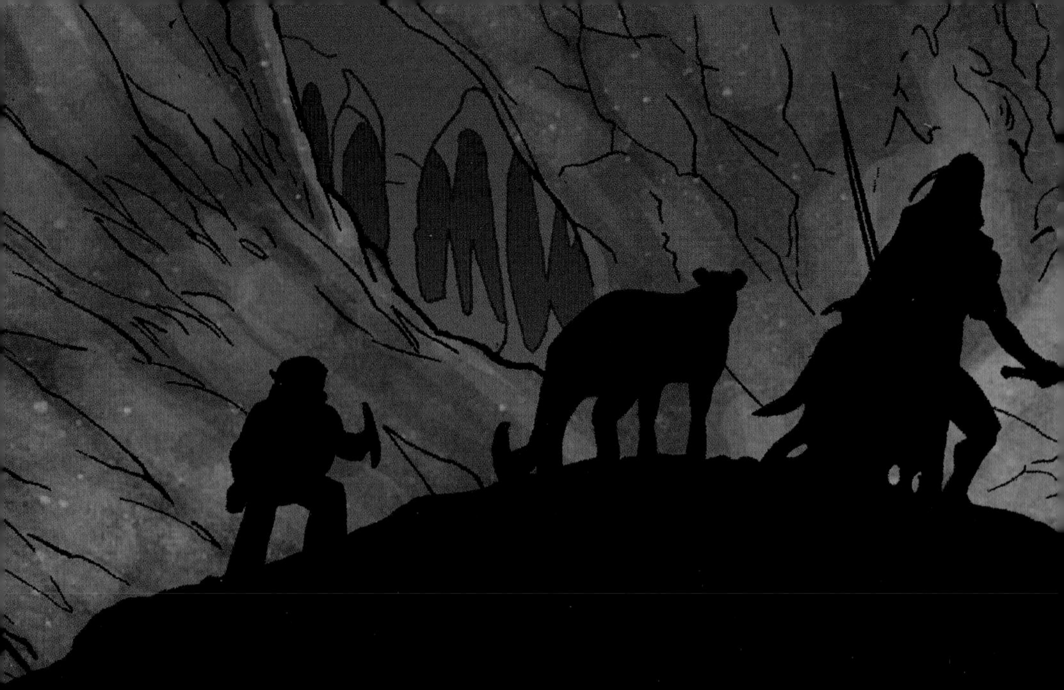

Original Series Edits by
Mark Powers

Collection Edits by
Justin Eisinger and Alonzo Simon

Cover by
Tyler Walpole

Collection Design by
Neil Uyetake

For international rights, contact **licensing@idwpublishing.com**

Special thanks to Hasbro's Michael Kelly and Val Roca, and Wizards of the Coast's Jon Schindehette, James Wyatt, Chris Perkins, Liz Schuh, Nathan Stewart, Laura Tommervik, Shelly Mazzanoble, Hilary Ross, and Chris Lindsay.

ISBN: 978-1-60010-997-3

22 21 20 19   8 9 10 11

IDW®

Licensed By:

www.IDWPUBLISHING.com

Chris Ryall, President & Publisher/CCO • **John Barber**, Editor-in-Chief • **Cara Morrison**, Chief Financial Officer • **Matthew Ruzicka**, Chief Accounting Officer • **David Hedgecock**, Associate Publisher • **Jerry Bennington**, VP of New Product Development • **Lorelei Bunjes**, VP of Digital Services • **Justin Eisinger**, Editorial Director, Graphic novels and Collections • **Eric Moss**, Sr. Director, Licensing & Business Development

Ted Adam and Robbie Robbins, IDW Founders

Facebook: **facebook.com/idwpublishing** • Twitter: **@idwpublishing**
YouTube: **youtube.com/idwpublishing** • Tumblr: **tumblr.idwpublishing.com**
Instagram: **instagram.com/idwpublishing**

Originally published by Devil's Due Publishing as HOMELAND Issues #1–3, EXILE Issues #1–3, and SOJOURN Issues #1–3.

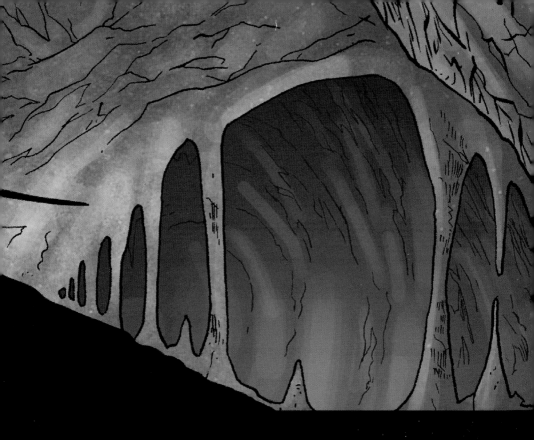

DUNGEONS & DRAGONS

**Forgotten Realms:
The Legend of Drizzt**

OMNIBUS
VOLUME 1

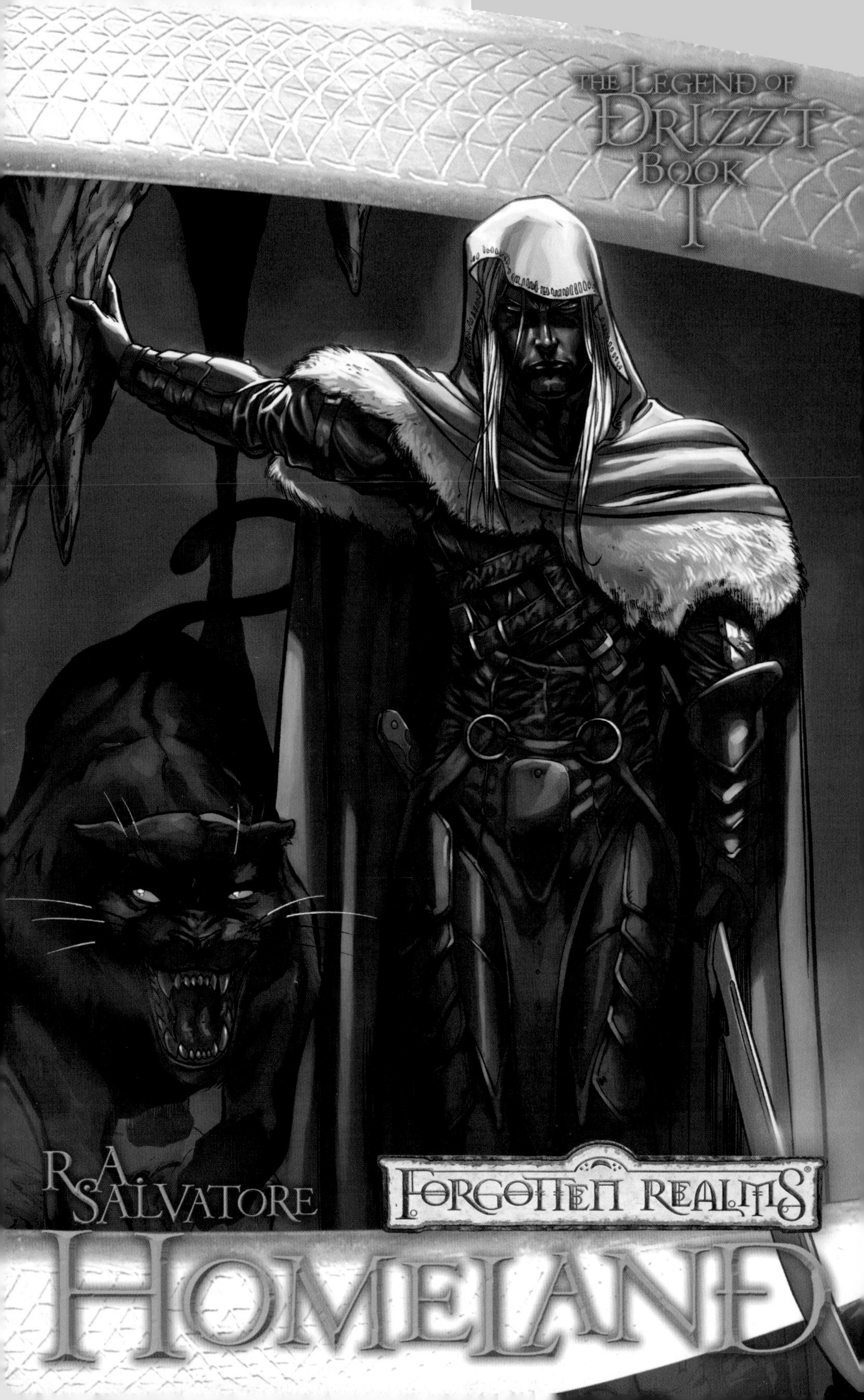
THE LEGEND OF
DRIZZT
BOOK
I
R.A.
SALVATORE
FORGOTTEN REALMS
HOMELAND

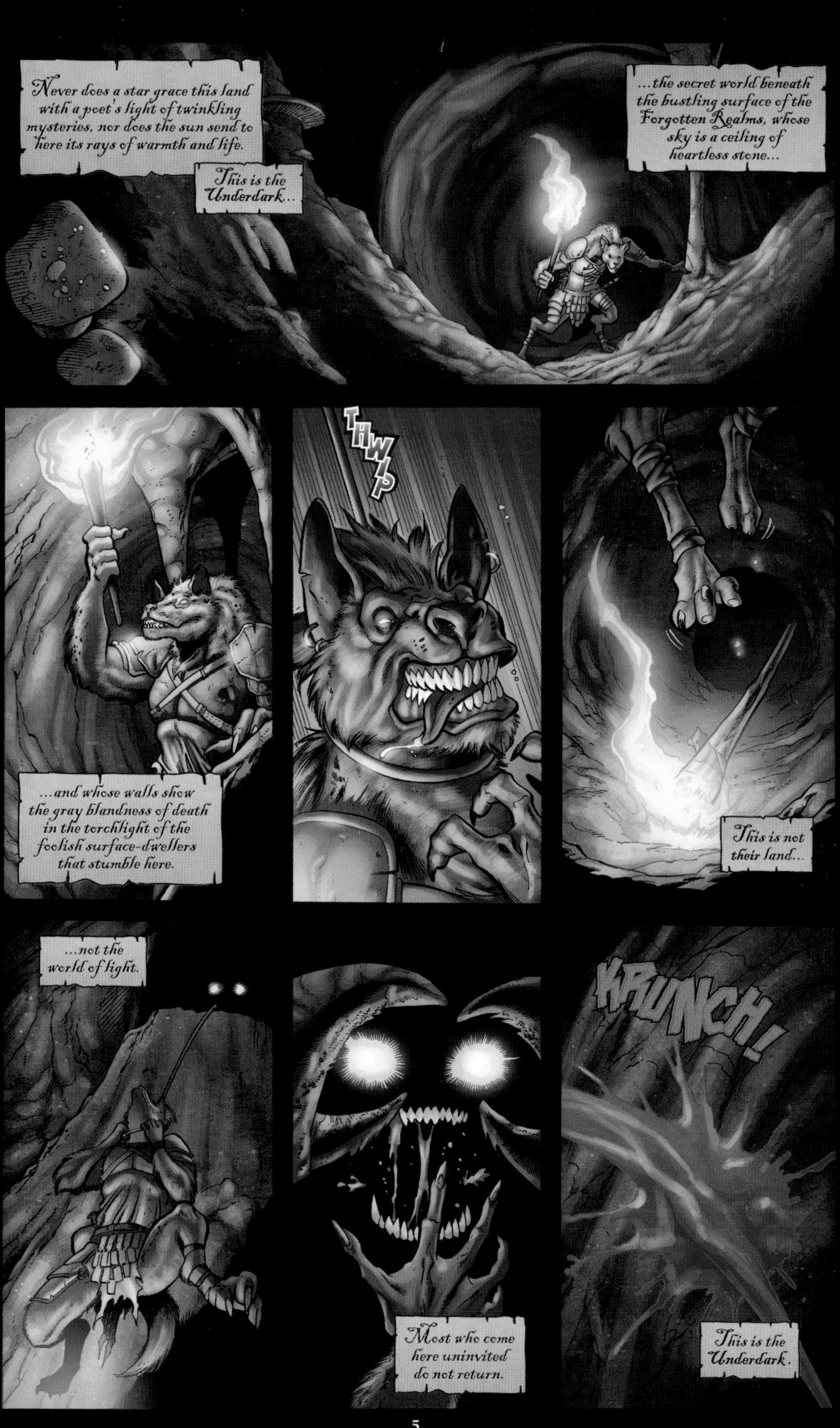
Never does a star grace this land with a poet's light of twinkling mysteries, nor does the sun send to here its rays of warmth and life.
This is the Underdark...
...the secret world beneath the bustling surface of the Forgotten Realms, whose sky is a ceiling of heartless stone...
...and whose walls show the gray blandness of death in the torchlight of the foolish surface-dwellers that stumble here.
THWIP
This is not their land...
...not the world of light.
Most who come here uninvited do not return.
KRUNCH!
This is the Underdark.

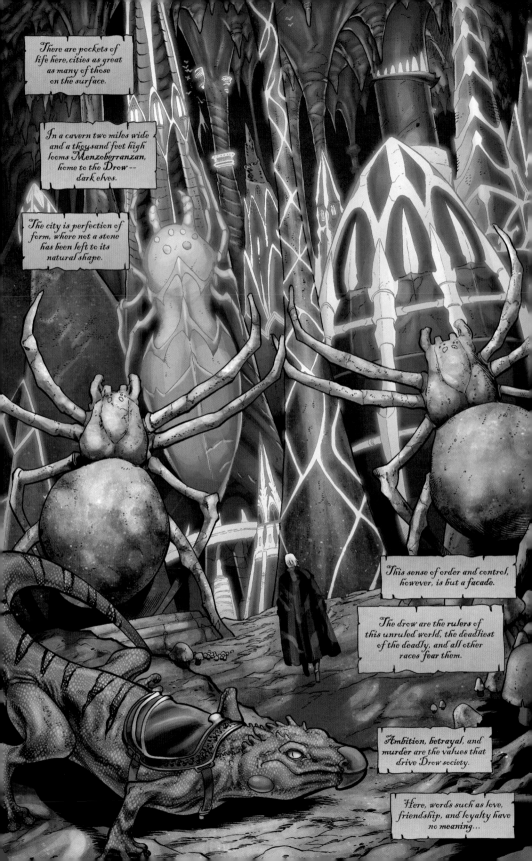

There are pockets of life here, cities as great as many of those on the surface.

In a cavern two miles wide and a thousand feet high looms Menzoberranzan, home to the Drow -- dark elves.

The city is perfection of form, where not a stone has been left to its natural shape.

This sense of order and control, however, is but a facade.

The drow are the rulers of this unruled world, the deadliest of the deadly, and all other races fear them.

Ambition, betrayal, and murder are the values that drive Drow society.

Here, words such as love, friendship, and loyalty have no meaning...

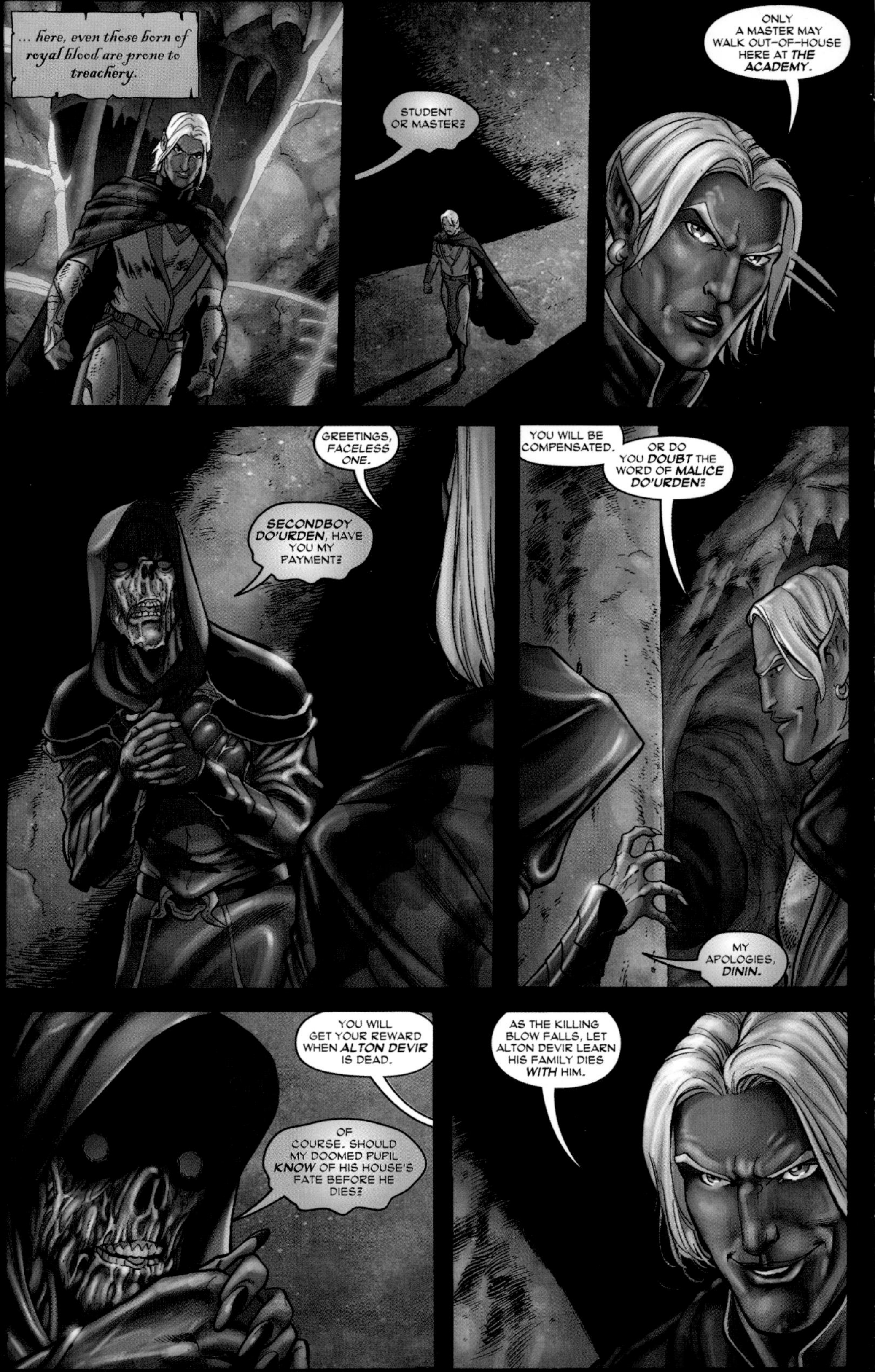
... here, even those born of royal blood are prone to treachery.
STUDENT OR MASTER?
ONLY A MASTER MAY WALK OUT-OF-HOUSE HERE AT THE ACADEMY.
GREETINGS, FACELESS ONE.
SECONDBOY DO'URDEN, HAVE YOU MY PAYMENT?
YOU WILL BE COMPENSATED.
OR DO YOU DOUBT THE WORD OF MALICE DO'URDEN?
MY APOLOGIES, DININ.
YOU WILL GET YOUR REWARD WHEN ALTON DEVIR IS DEAD.
OF COURSE. SHOULD MY DOOMED PUPIL KNOW OF HIS HOUSE'S FATE BEFORE HE DIES?
AS THE KILLING BLOW FALLS, LET ALTON DEVIR LEARN HIS FAMILY DIES WITH HIM.

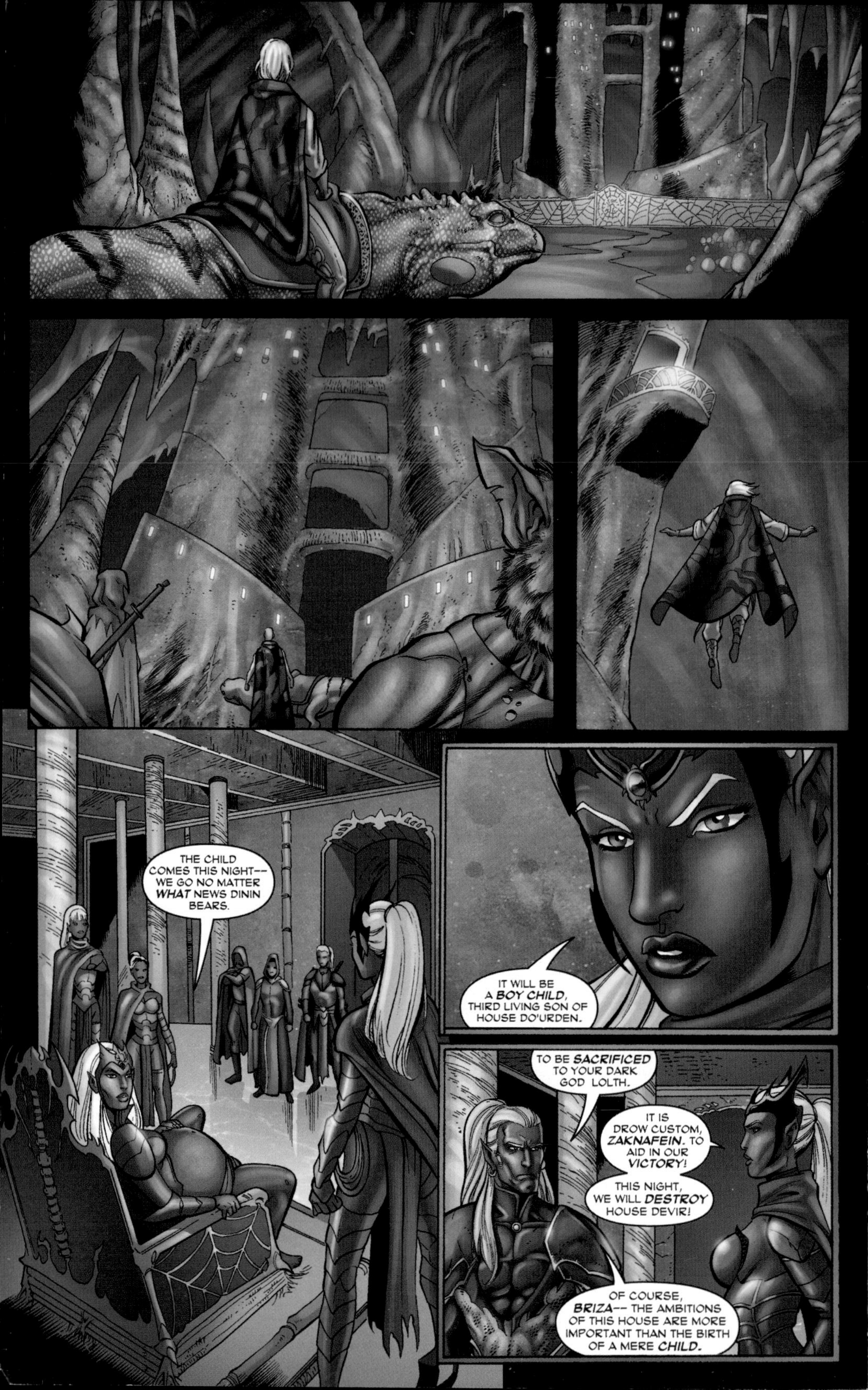
THE CHILD COMES THIS NIGHT-- WE GO NO MATTER WHAT NEWS DININ BEARS.
IT WILL BE A BOY CHILD, THIRD LIVING SON OF HOUSE DO'URDEN.
TO BE SACRIFICED TO YOUR DARK GOD LOLTH.
IT IS DROW CUSTOM, ZAKNAFEIN. TO AID IN OUR VICTORY!
THIS NIGHT, WE WILL DESTROY HOUSE DEVIR!
OF COURSE, BRIZA-- THE AMBITIONS OF THIS HOUSE ARE MORE IMPORTANT THAN THE BIRTH OF A MERE CHILD.

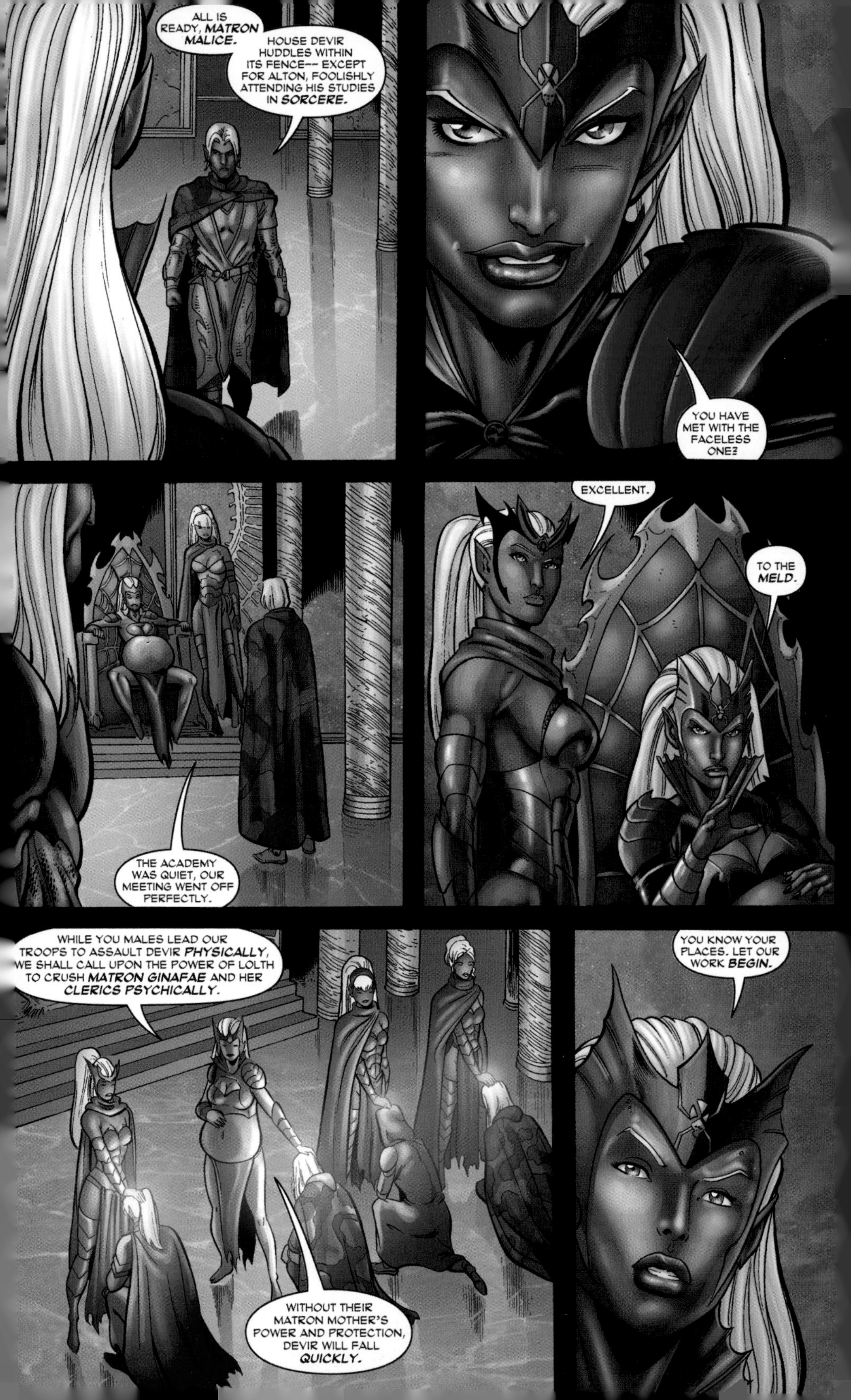
ALL IS READY, MATRON MALICE.
HOUSE DEVIR HUDDLES WITHIN ITS FENCE-- EXCEPT FOR ALTON, FOOLISHLY ATTENDING HIS STUDIES IN SORCERE.
YOU HAVE MET WITH THE FACELESS ONE?
THE ACADEMY WAS QUIET, OUR MEETING WENT OFF PERFECTLY.
EXCELLENT.
TO THE MELD.
WHILE YOU MALES LEAD OUR TROOPS TO ASSAULT DEVIR PHYSICALLY, WE SHALL CALL UPON THE POWER OF LOLTH TO CRUSH MATRON GINAFAE AND HER CLERICS PSYCHICALLY.
WITHOUT THEIR MATRON MOTHER'S POWER AND PROTECTION, DEVIR WILL FALL QUICKLY.
YOU KNOW YOUR PLACES. LET OUR WORK BEGIN.

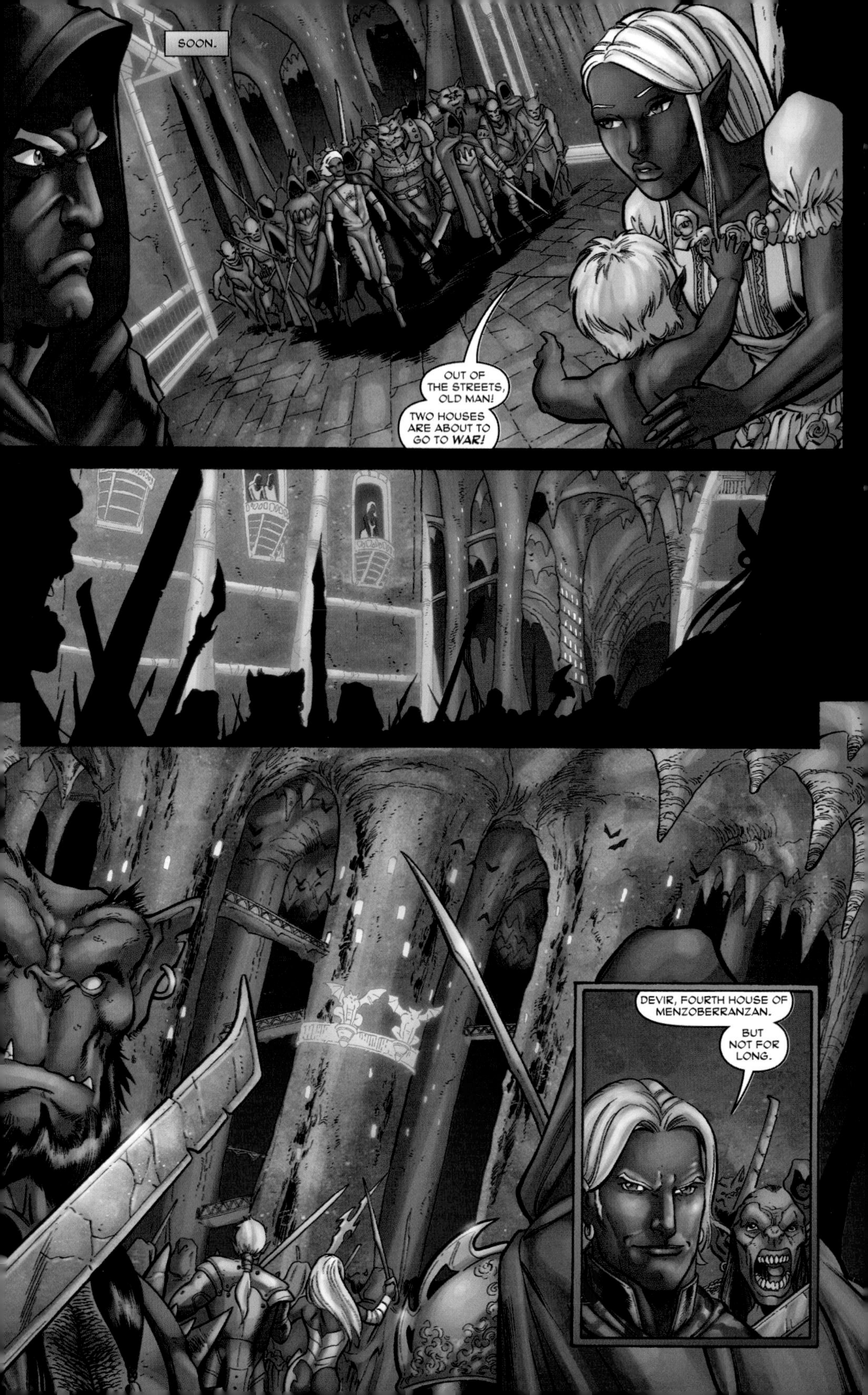
SOON.
OUT OF THE STREETS, OLD MAN!
TWO HOUSES ARE ABOUT TO GO TO WAR!
DEVIR, FOURTH HOUSE OF MENZOBERRANZAN.
BUT NOT FOR LONG.

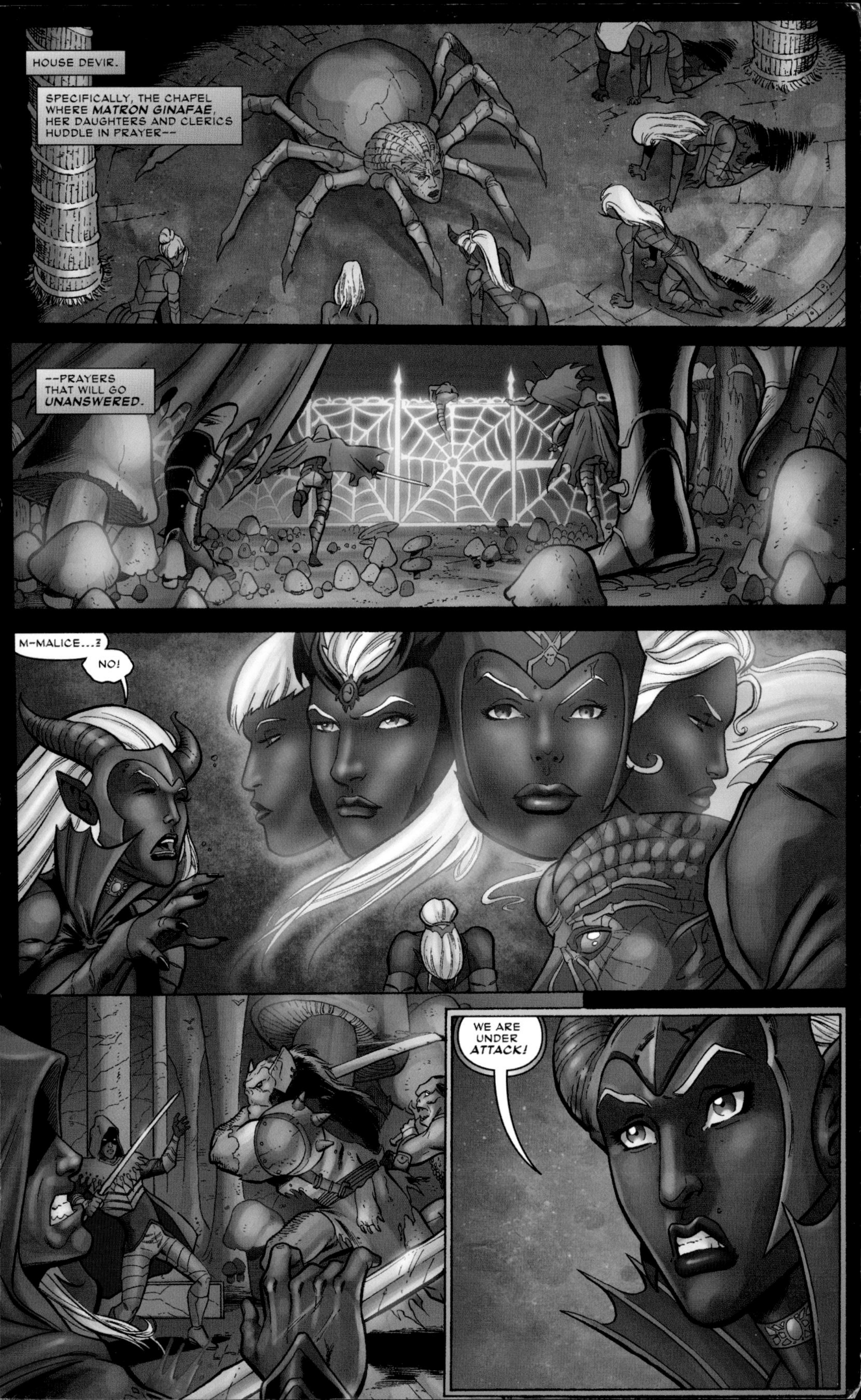

HOUSE DEVIR.
SPECIFICALLY, THE CHAPEL WHERE MATRON GINAFAE, HER DAUGHTERS AND CLERICS HUDDLE IN PRAYER--
--PRAYERS THAT WILL GO UNANSWERED.
M-MALICE...?
NO!
WE ARE UNDER ATTACK!

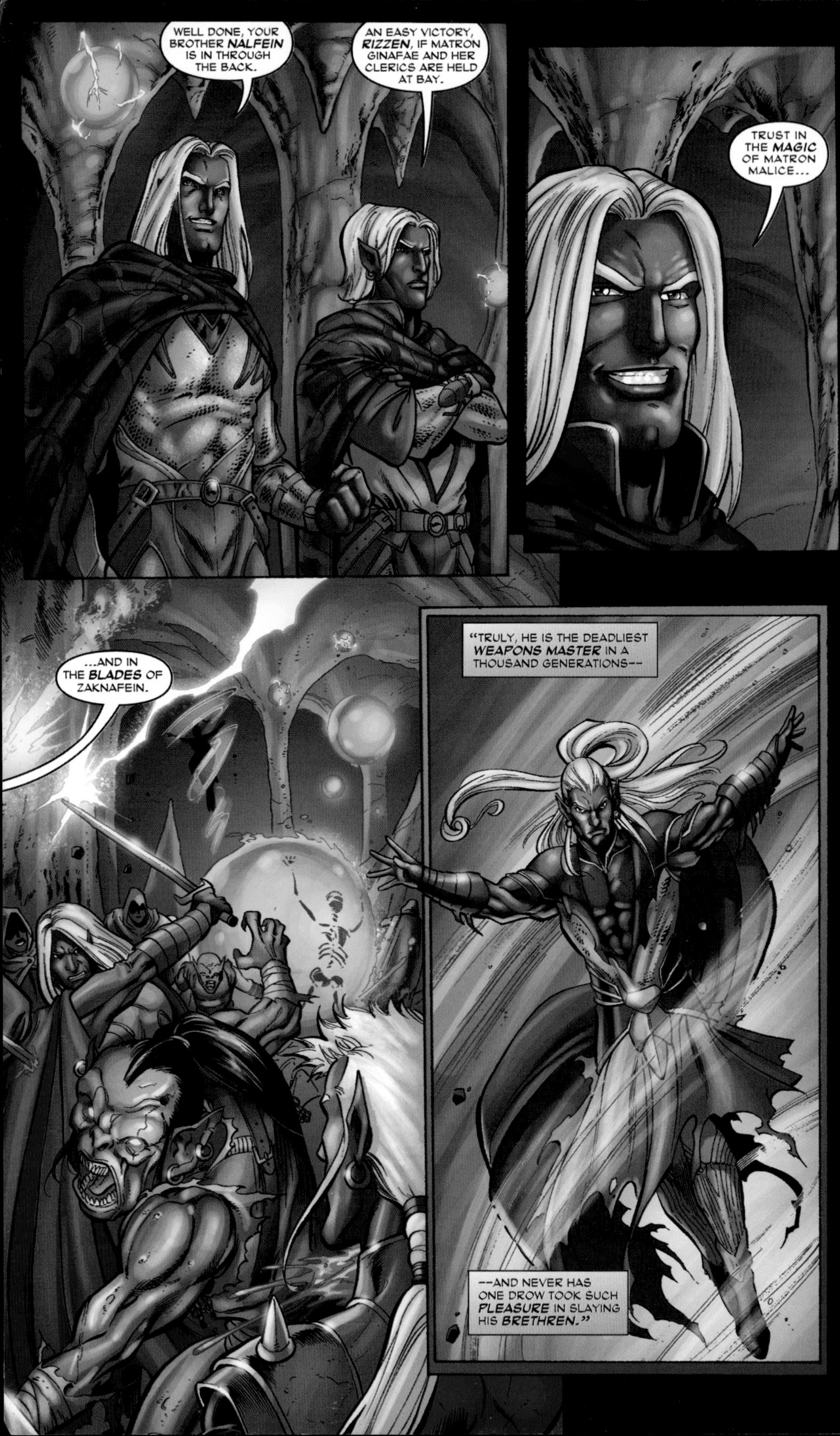
WELL DONE, YOUR BROTHER NALFEIN IS IN THROUGH THE BACK.
AN EASY VICTORY, RIZZEN, IF MATRON GINAFAE AND HER CLERICS ARE HELD AT BAY.
TRUST IN THE MAGIC OF MATRON MALICE...
...AND IN THE BLADES OF ZAKNAFEIN.
"TRULY, HE IS THE DEADLIEST WEAPONS MASTER IN A THOUSAND GENERATIONS--
--AND NEVER HAS ONE DROW TOOK SUCH PLEASURE IN SLAYING HIS BRETHREN."

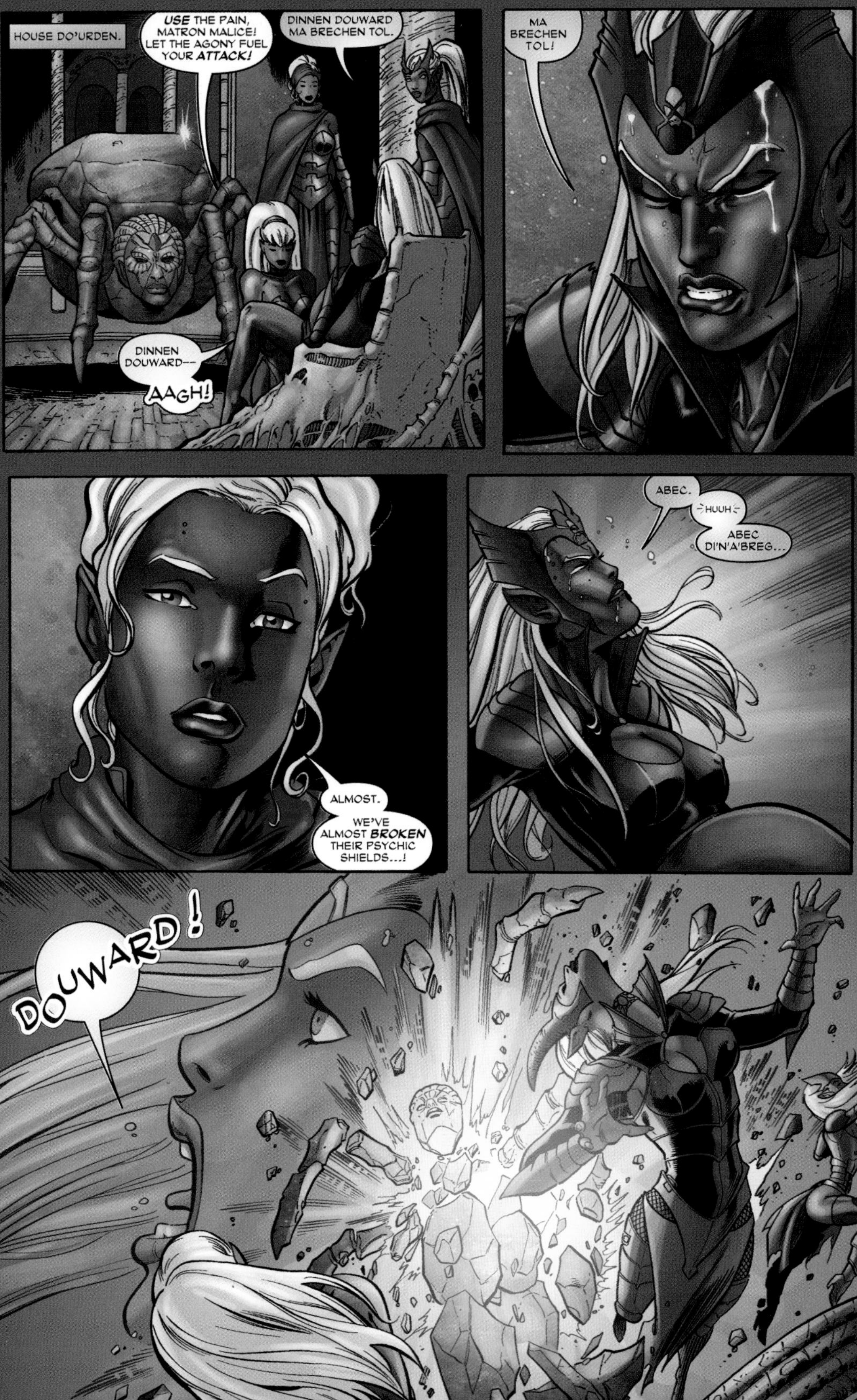
HOUSE DO'URDEN.
USE THE PAIN, MATRON MALICE! LET THE AGONY FUEL YOUR ATTACK!
DINNEN DOUWARD MA BRECHEN TOL.
DINNEN DOUWARD--
AAGH!
MA BRECHEN TOL!
ALMOST. WE'VE ALMOST BROKEN THEIR PSYCHIC SHIELDS...!
ABEC.
HUUH
ABEC DI'N'A'BREG...
DOUWARD!

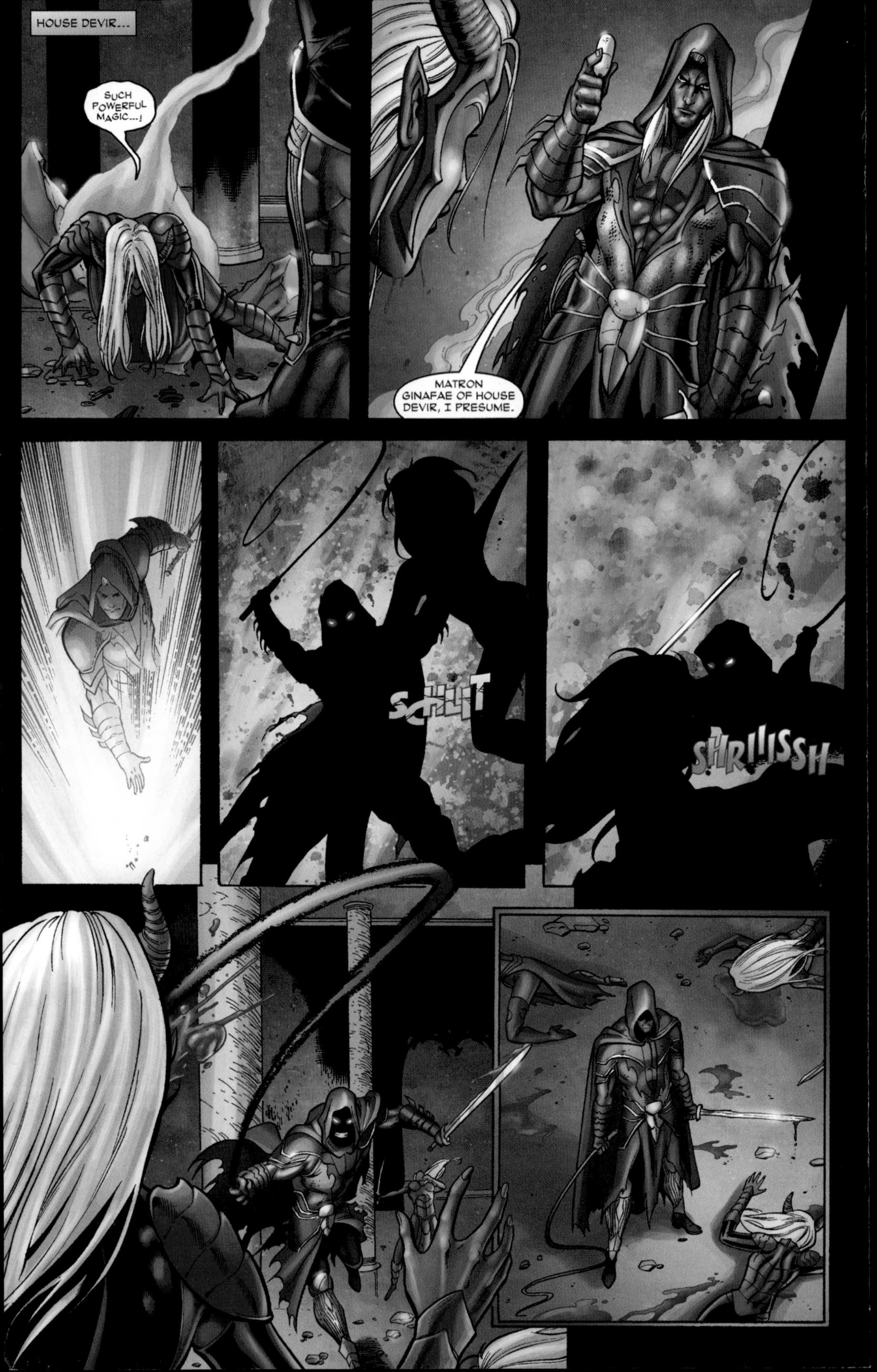
HOUSE DEVIR...
SUCH POWERFUL MAGIC...!
MATRON GINAFAE OF HOUSE DEVIR, I PRESUME.
SCHLIT
SHRIIISSH

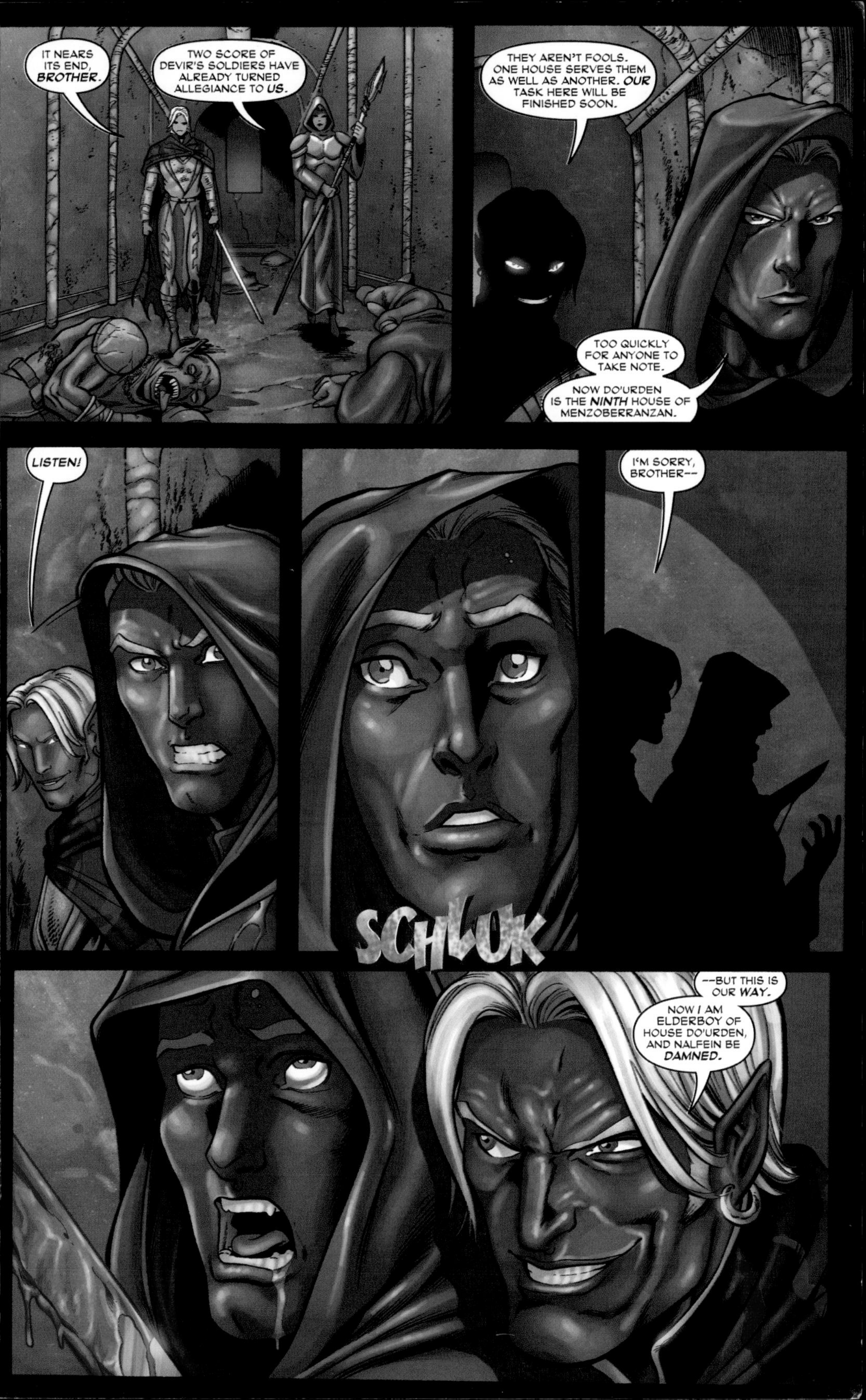
IT NEARS ITS END, BROTHER.
TWO SCORE OF DEVIR'S SOLDIERS HAVE ALREADY TURNED ALLEGIANCE TO US.
THEY AREN'T FOOLS. ONE HOUSE SERVES THEM AS WELL AS ANOTHER. OUR TASK HERE WILL BE FINISHED SOON.
TOO QUICKLY FOR ANYONE TO TAKE NOTE.
NOW DO'URDEN IS THE NINTH HOUSE OF MENZOBERRANZAN.
LISTEN!
I'M SORRY, BROTHER--
SCHLUK
--BUT THIS IS OUR WAY.
NOW I AM ELDERBOY OF HOUSE DO'URDEN, AND NALFEIN BE DAMNED.

HOUSE DO'URDEN.

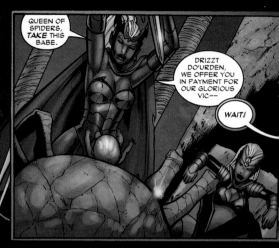

QUEEN OF SPIDERS, *TAKE* THIS BABE.

DRIZZT DO'URDEN, WE OFFER YOU IN PAYMENT FOR OUR GLORIOUS VIC--

WAIT!

DRIZZT.

THE CHILD'S NAME IS *DRIZZT.*

MAYA?!

DO YOU NOT *SENSE* IT? NALFEIN IS *DEAD!* THE BABY IS NO LONGER THE *THIRD* LIVING SON!

WE PROMISED THE SPIDER QUEEN A SON OF HOUSE DO'URDEN, AND IT HAS BEEN GIVEN.

BUT NOT IN SACRIFICE!

STAY YOUR HAND, BRIZA. LOLTH IS CONTENT; OUR VICTORY IS *WON.*

WELCOME, THEN, YOUR BROTHER.

LOOK AT HIS EYES... THEY'RE *PURPLE.* SUCH AN ODD COLOR.

⸮HRMPH⸮ IT'S JUST A *MALE,* VIERNA.

HE'D HAVE BEEN BETTER OFF *DEAD.*

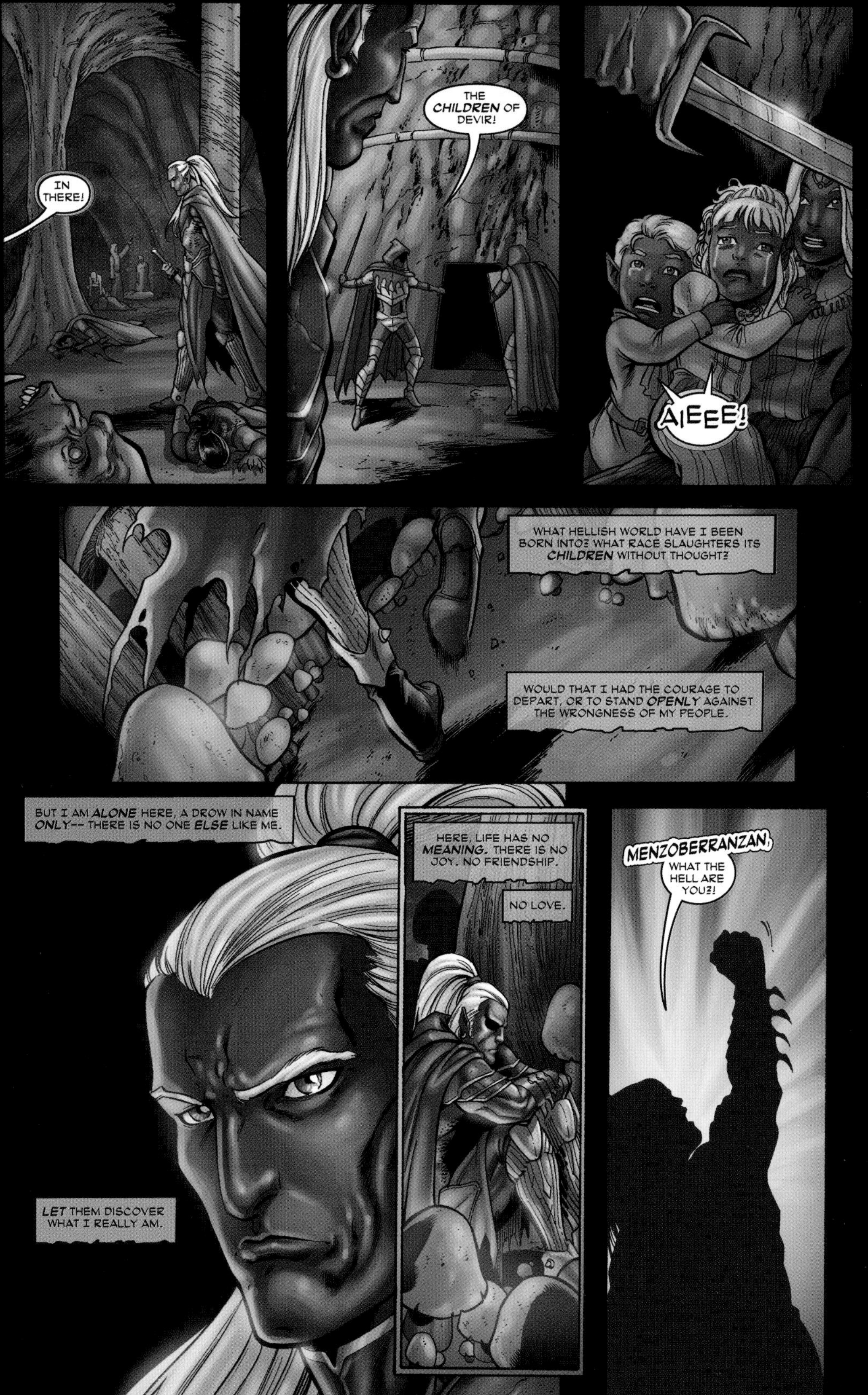
IN THERE!
THE CHILDREN OF DEVIR!
AIEEE!
WHAT HELLISH WORLD HAVE I BEEN BORN INTO? WHAT RACE SLAUGHTERS ITS CHILDREN WITHOUT THOUGHT?
WOULD THAT I HAD THE COURAGE TO DEPART, OR TO STAND OPENLY AGAINST THE WRONGNESS OF MY PEOPLE.
BUT I AM ALONE HERE, A DROW IN NAME ONLY-- THERE IS NO ONE ELSE LIKE ME.
LET THEM DISCOVER WHAT I REALLY AM.
HERE, LIFE HAS NO MEANING. THERE IS NO JOY. NO FRIENDSHIP.
NO LOVE.
MENZOBERRANZAN,
WHAT THE HELL ARE YOU?!

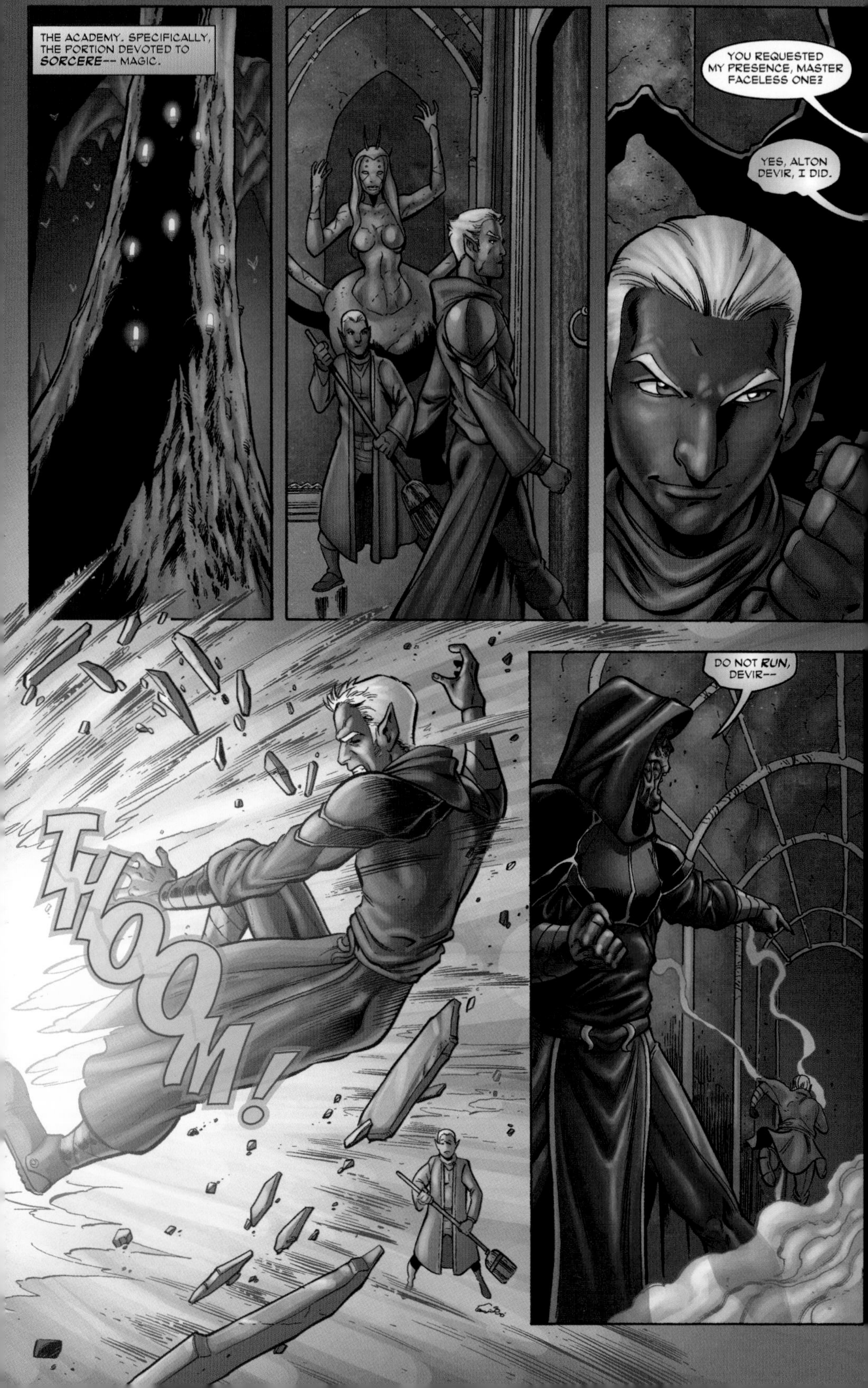
THE ACADEMY. SPECIFICALLY, THE PORTION DEVOTED TO SORCERE-- MAGIC.
YOU REQUESTED MY PRESENCE, MASTER FACELESS ONE?
YES, ALTON DEVIR, I DID.
THOOM!
DO NOT RUN, DEVIR--

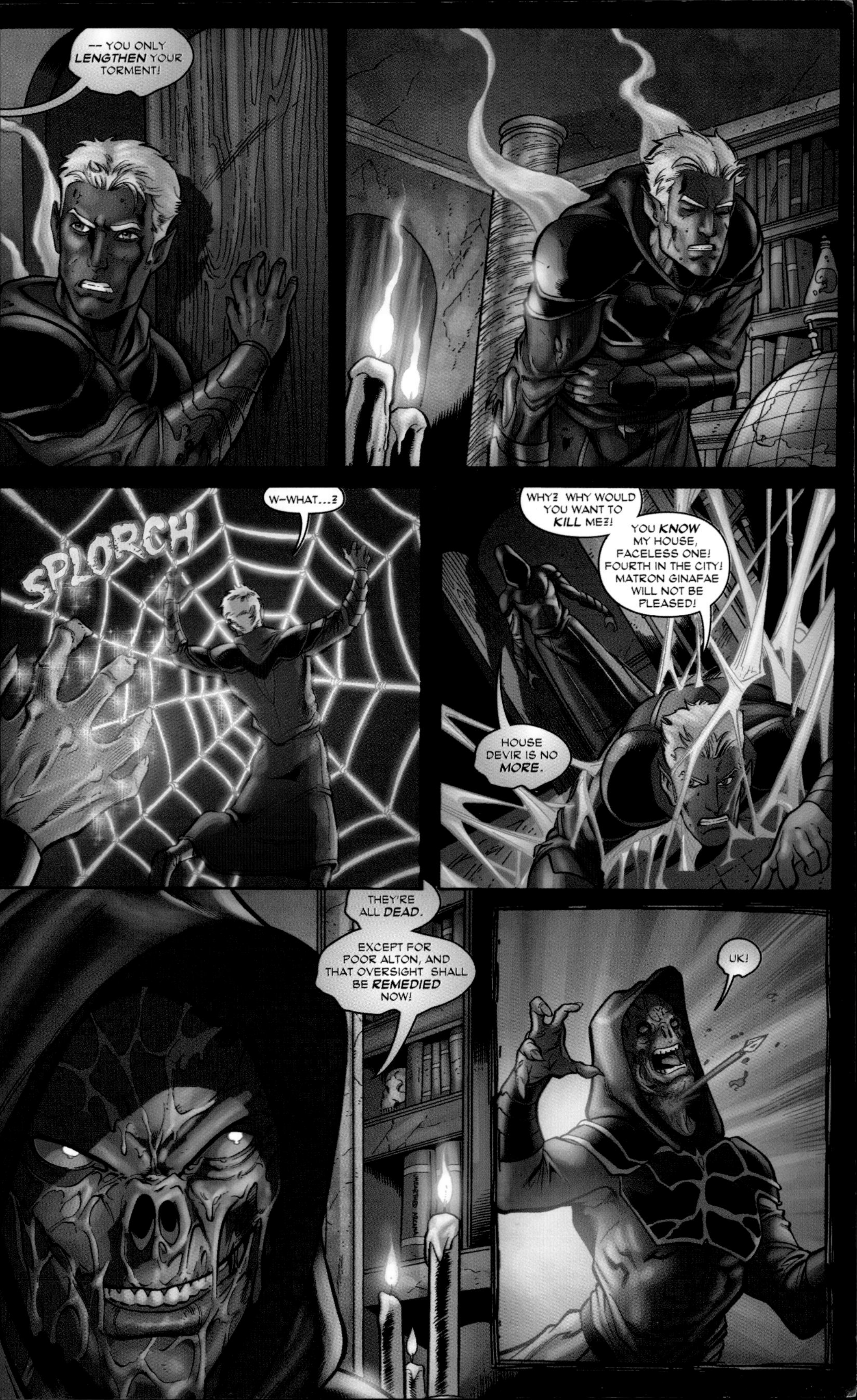
-- YOU ONLY LENGTHEN YOUR TORMENT!
W-WHAT...?
SPLORCH
WHY? WHY WOULD YOU WANT TO KILL ME?!
YOU KNOW MY HOUSE, FACELESS ONE! FOURTH IN THE CITY! MATRON GINAFAE WILL NOT BE PLEASED!
HOUSE DEVIR IS NO MORE.
THEY'RE ALL DEAD.
EXCEPT FOR POOR ALTON, AND THAT OVERSIGHT SHALL BE REMEDIED NOW!
UK!

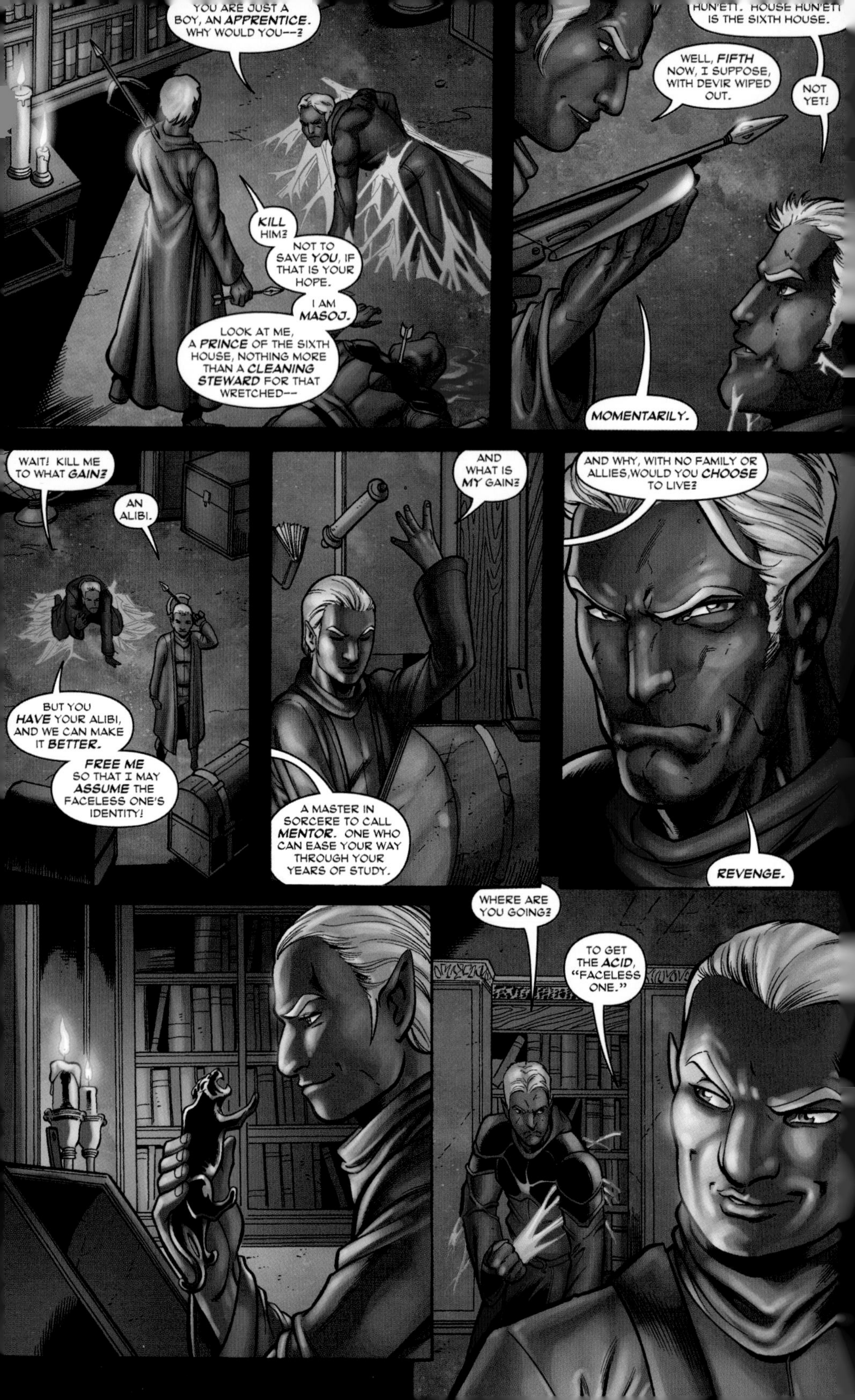
YOU ARE JUST A BOY, AN APPRENTICE. WHY WOULD YOU--?
KILL HIM? NOT TO SAVE YOU, IF THAT IS YOUR HOPE.
I AM MASOJ.
LOOK AT ME, A PRINCE OF THE SIXTH HOUSE, NOTHING MORE THAN A CLEANING STEWARD FOR THAT WRETCHED--
HUN'ETT. HOUSE HUN'ETT IS THE SIXTH HOUSE.
WELL, FIFTH NOW, I SUPPOSE, WITH DEVIR WIPED OUT.
NOT YET!
MOMENTARILY.
WAIT! KILL ME TO WHAT GAIN?
AN ALIBI.
BUT YOU HAVE YOUR ALIBI, AND WE CAN MAKE IT BETTER.
FREE ME SO THAT I MAY ASSUME THE FACELESS ONE'S IDENTITY!
AND WHAT IS MY GAIN?
A MASTER IN SORCERE TO CALL MENTOR. ONE WHO CAN EASE YOUR WAY THROUGH YOUR YEARS OF STUDY.
AND WHY, WITH NO FAMILY OR ALLIES,WOULD YOU CHOOSE TO LIVE?
REVENGE.
WHERE ARE YOU GOING?
TO GET THE ACID, "FACELESS ONE."

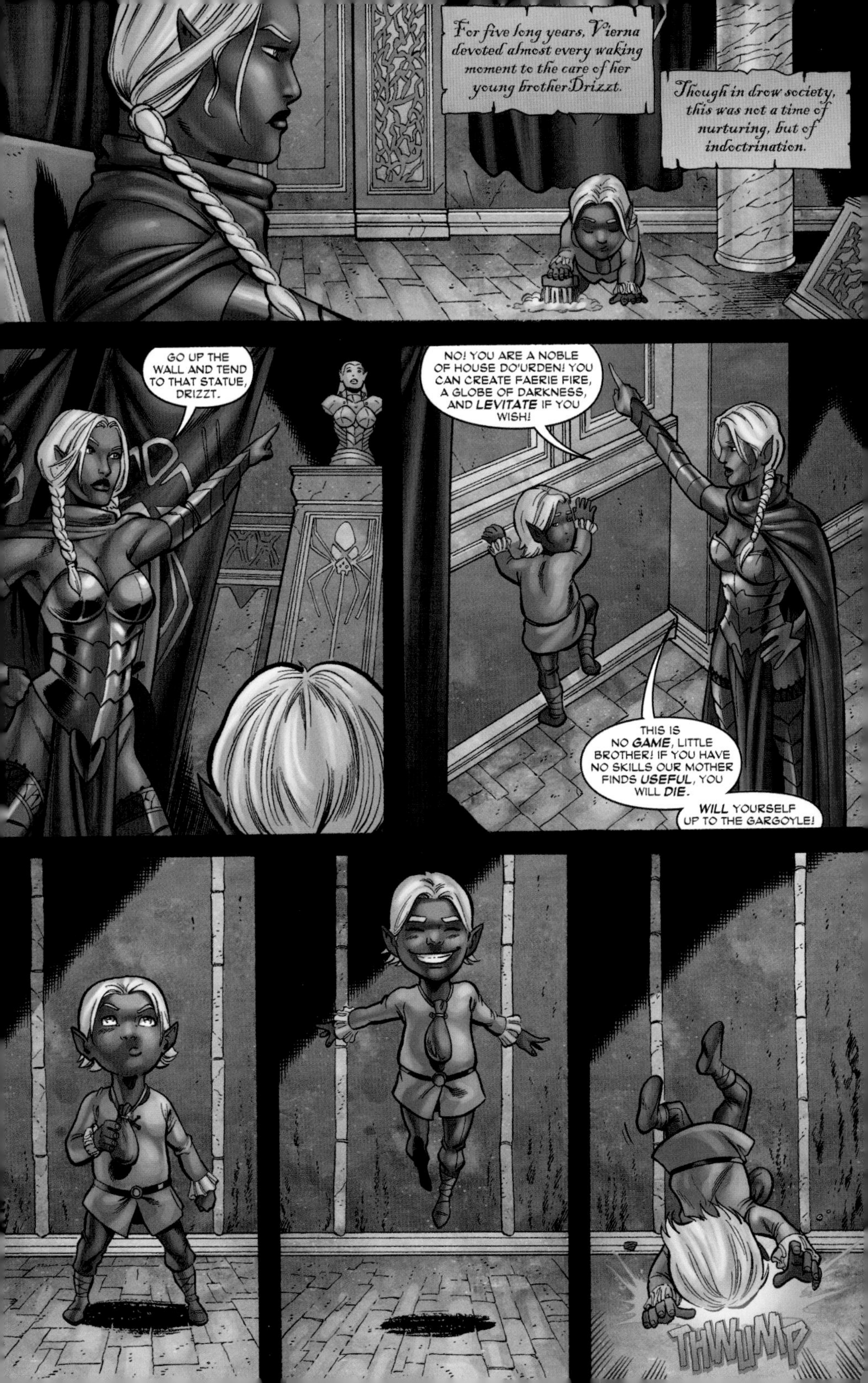
For five long years, Vierna devoted almost every waking moment to the care of her young brother Drizzt.
Though in drow society, this was not a time of nurturing, but of indoctrination.
GO UP THE WALL AND TEND TO THAT STATUE, DRIZZT.
NO! YOU ARE A NOBLE OF HOUSE DO'URDEN! YOU CAN CREATE FAERIE FIRE, A GLOBE OF DARKNESS, AND LEVITATE IF YOU WISH!
THIS IS NO GAME, LITTLE BROTHER! IF YOU HAVE NO SKILLS OUR MOTHER FINDS USEFUL, YOU WILL DIE.
WILL YOURSELF UP TO THE GARGOYLE!
THWUMP

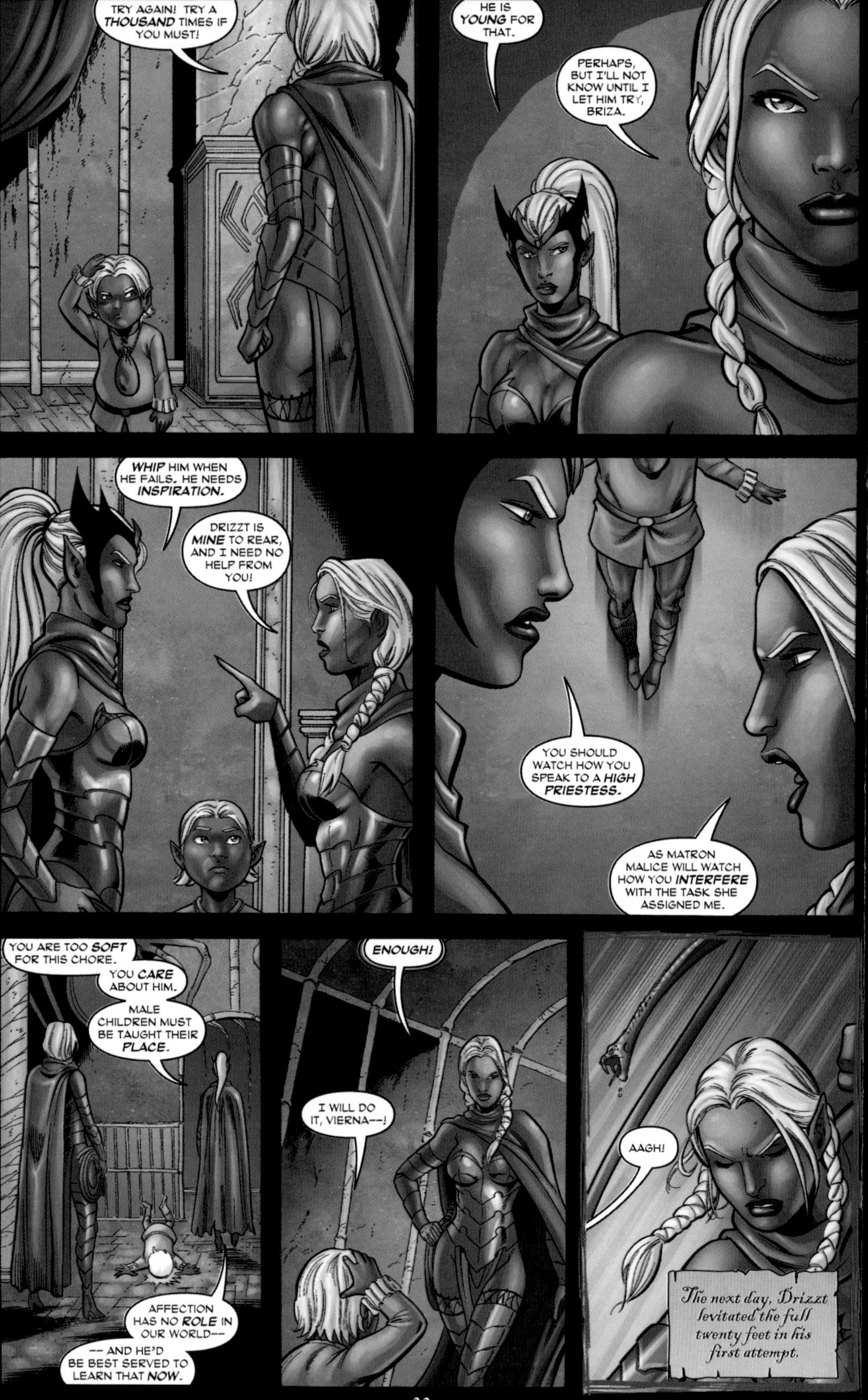
TRY AGAIN! TRY A THOUSAND TIMES IF YOU MUST!
HE IS YOUNG FOR THAT.
PERHAPS, BUT I'LL NOT KNOW UNTIL I LET HIM TRY, BRIZA.
WHIP HIM WHEN HE FAILS. HE NEEDS INSPIRATION.
DRIZZT IS MINE TO REAR, AND I NEED NO HELP FROM YOU!
YOU SHOULD WATCH HOW YOU SPEAK TO A HIGH PRIESTESS.
AS MATRON MALICE WILL WATCH HOW YOU INTERFERE WITH THE TASK SHE ASSIGNED ME.
YOU ARE TOO SOFT FOR THIS CHORE.
YOU CARE ABOUT HIM.
MALE CHILDREN MUST BE TAUGHT THEIR PLACE.
AFFECTION HAS NO ROLE IN OUR WORLD--
-- AND HE'D BE BEST SERVED TO LEARN THAT NOW.
ENOUGH!
I WILL DO IT, VIERNA--!
AAGH!
The next day, Drizzt levitated the full twenty feet in his first attempt.

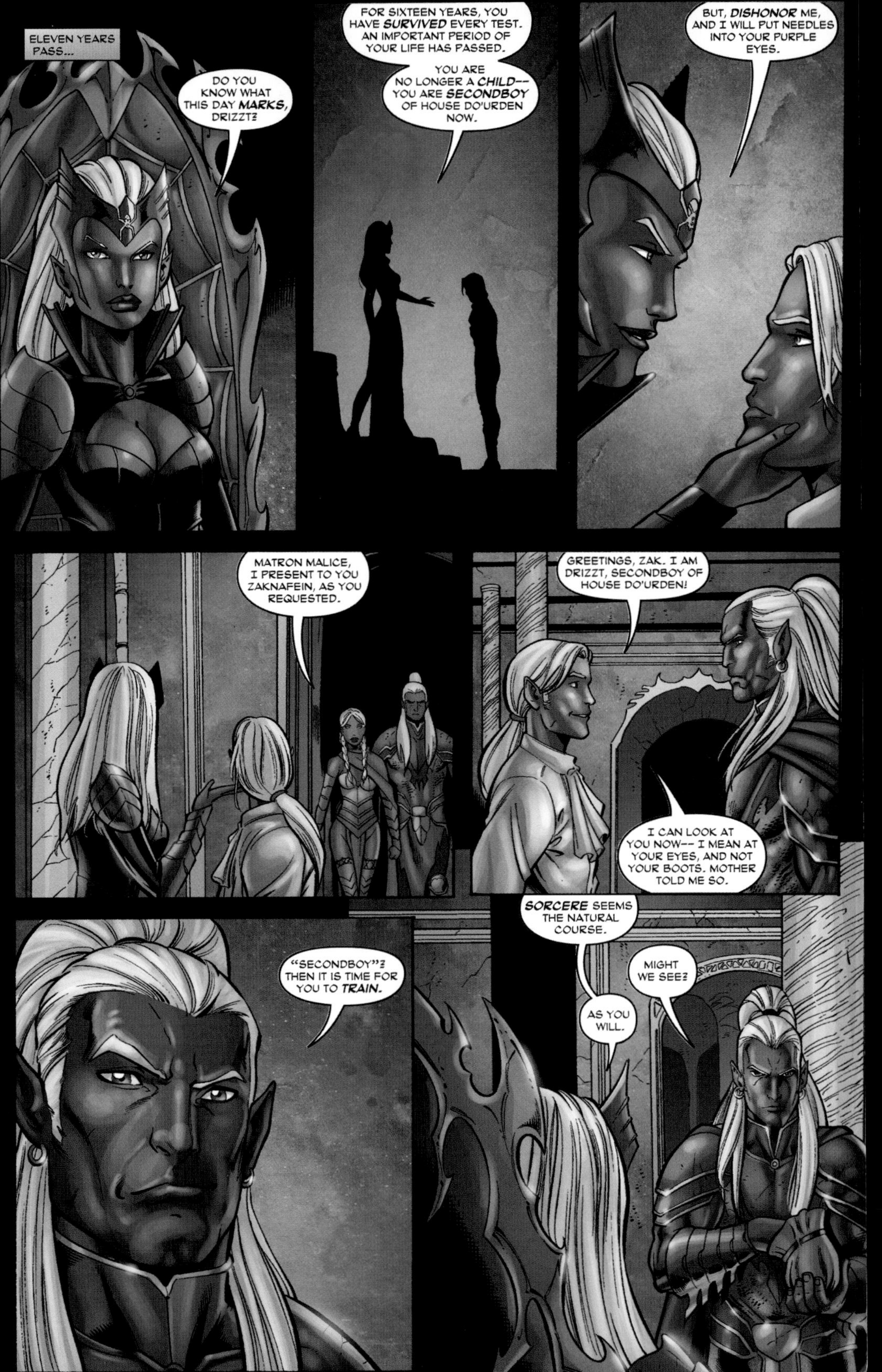
ELEVEN YEARS PASS...
DO YOU KNOW WHAT THIS DAY MARKS, DRIZZT?
FOR SIXTEEN YEARS, YOU HAVE SURVIVED EVERY TEST. AN IMPORTANT PERIOD OF YOUR LIFE HAS PASSED.
YOU ARE NO LONGER A CHILD-- YOU ARE SECONDBOY OF HOUSE DO'URDEN NOW.
BUT, DISHONOR ME, AND I WILL PUT NEEDLES INTO YOUR PURPLE EYES.
MATRON MALICE, I PRESENT TO YOU ZAKNAFEIN, AS YOU REQUESTED.
GREETINGS, ZAK. I AM DRIZZT, SECONDBOY OF HOUSE DO'URDEN!
I CAN LOOK AT YOU NOW-- I MEAN AT YOUR EYES, AND NOT YOUR BOOTS. MOTHER TOLD ME SO.
"SECONDBOY"? THEN IT IS TIME FOR YOU TO TRAIN.
SORCERE SEEMS THE NATURAL COURSE.
MIGHT WE SEE?
AS YOU WILL.

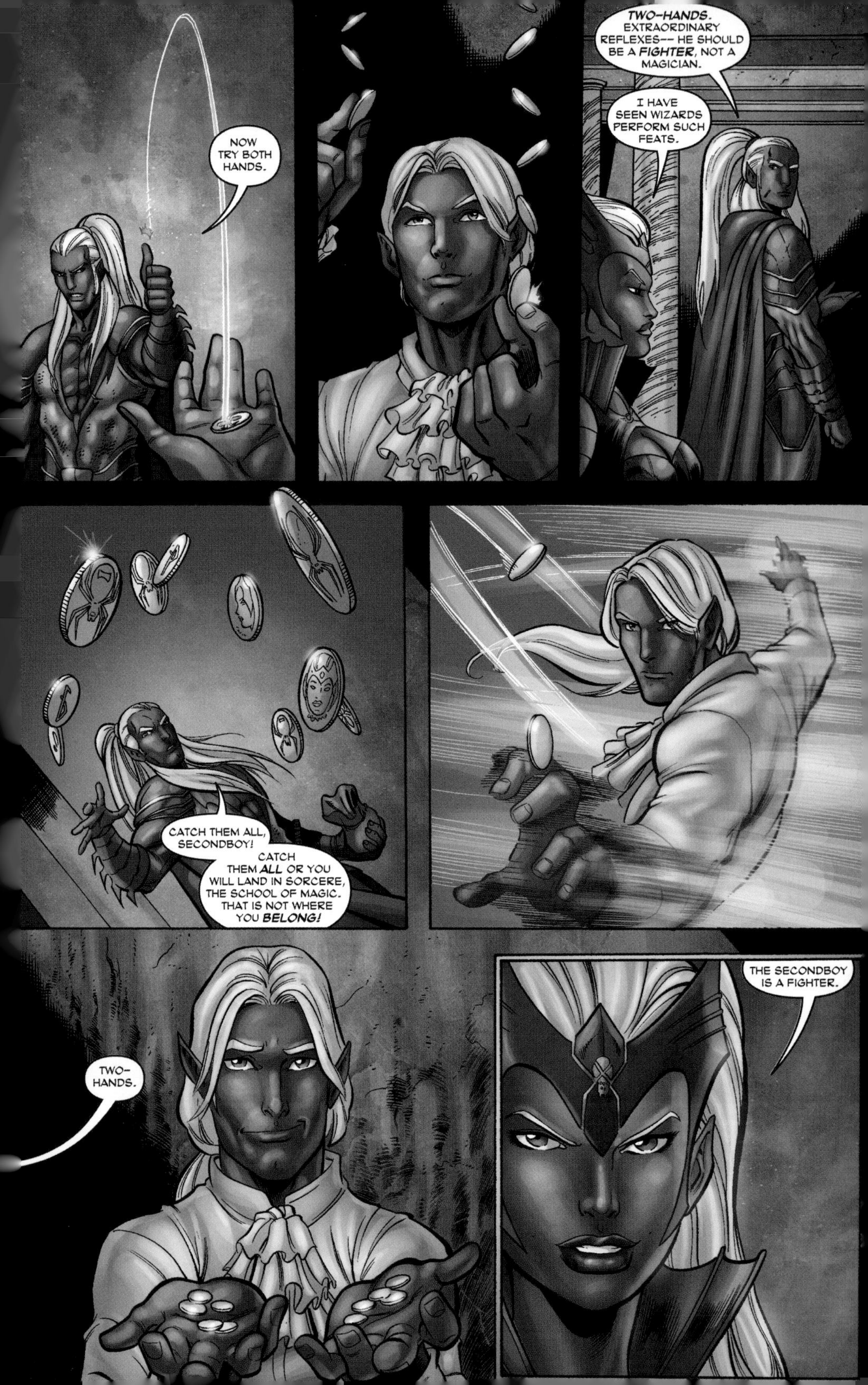
NOW TRY BOTH HANDS.
TWO-HANDS. EXTRAORDINARY REFLEXES-- HE SHOULD BE A FIGHTER, NOT A MAGICIAN.
I HAVE SEEN WIZARDS PERFORM SUCH FEATS.
CATCH THEM ALL, SECONDBOY!
CATCH THEM ALL OR YOU WILL LAND IN SORCERE, THE SCHOOL OF MAGIC. THAT IS NOT WHERE YOU BELONG!
TWO-HANDS.
THE SECONDBOY IS A FIGHTER.

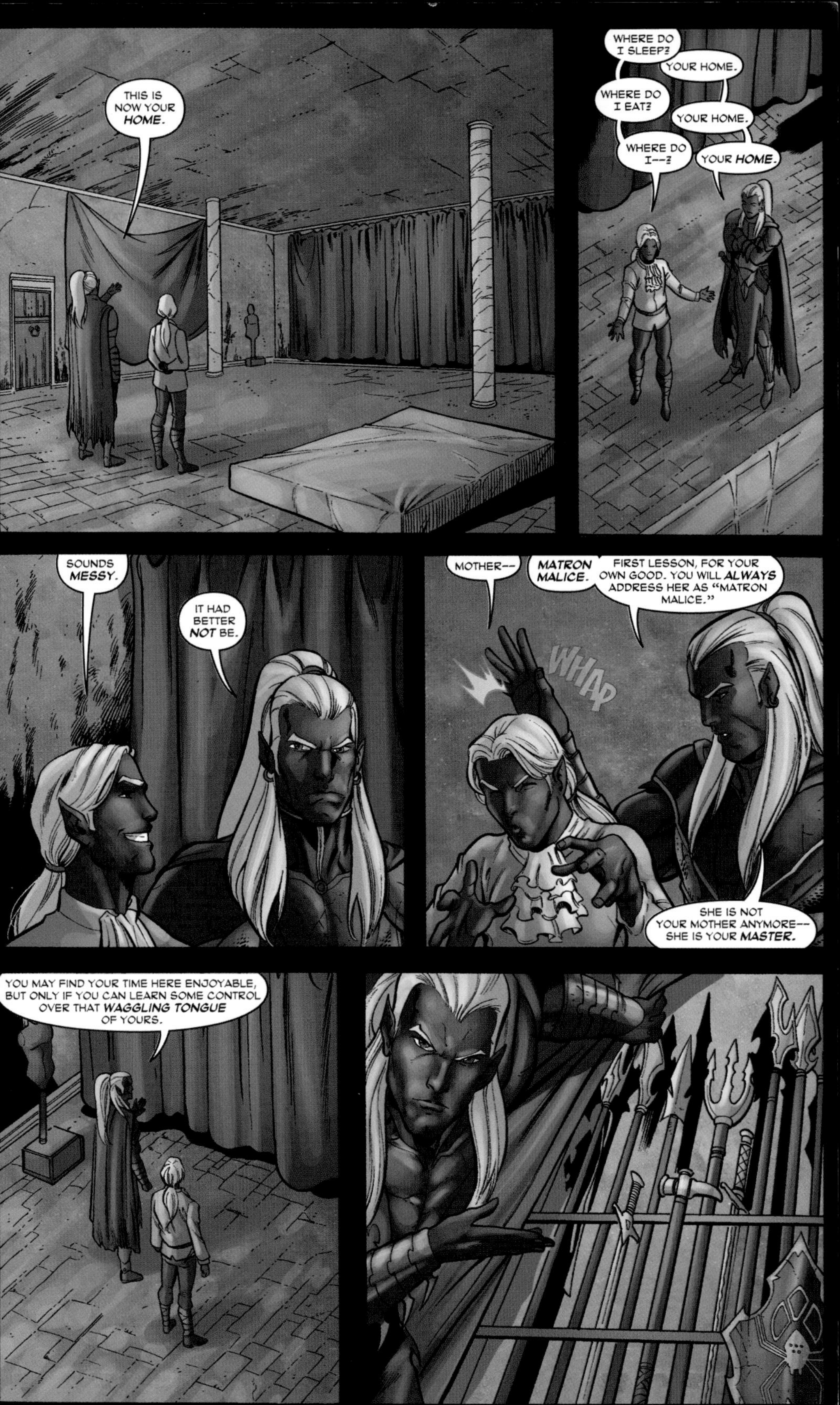

THIS IS NOW YOUR HOME.
WHERE DO I SLEEP?
YOUR HOME.
WHERE DO I EAT?
YOUR HOME.
WHERE DO I--?
YOUR HOME.
SOUNDS MESSY.
IT HAD BETTER NOT BE.
MOTHER--
MATRON MALICE.
FIRST LESSON, FOR YOUR OWN GOOD. YOU WILL ALWAYS ADDRESS HER AS "MATRON MALICE."
WHAP
SHE IS NOT YOUR MOTHER ANYMORE-- SHE IS YOUR MASTER.
YOU MAY FIND YOUR TIME HERE ENJOYABLE, BUT ONLY IF YOU CAN LEARN SOME CONTROL OVER THAT WAGGLING TONGUE OF YOURS.

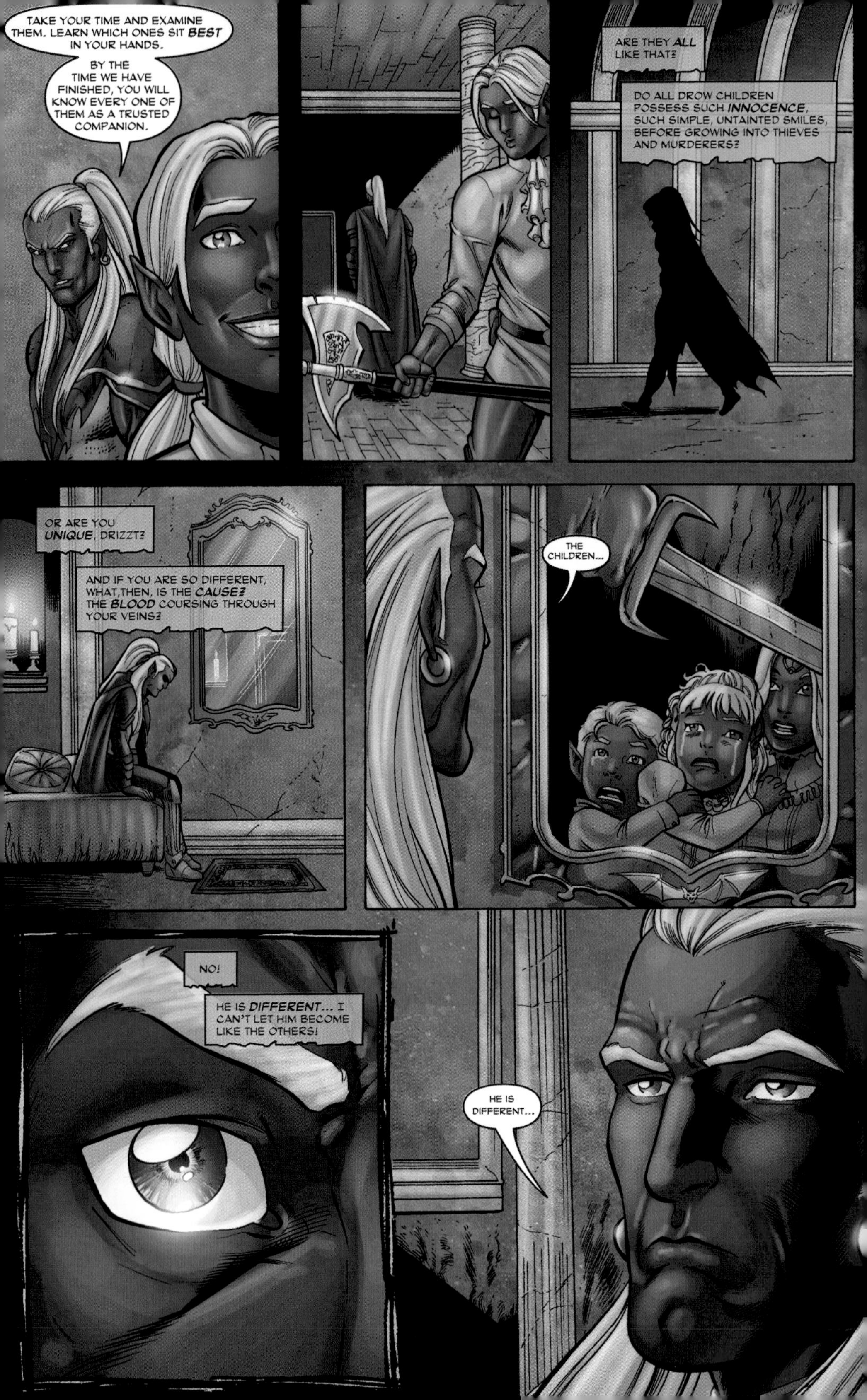
TAKE YOUR TIME AND EXAMINE THEM. LEARN WHICH ONES SIT BEST IN YOUR HANDS.
BY THE TIME WE HAVE FINISHED, YOU WILL KNOW EVERY ONE OF THEM AS A TRUSTED COMPANION.
ARE THEY ALL LIKE THAT?
DO ALL DROW CHILDREN POSSESS SUCH INNOCENCE, SUCH SIMPLE, UNTAINTED SMILES, BEFORE GROWING INTO THIEVES AND MURDERERS?
OR ARE YOU UNIQUE, DRIZZT?
AND IF YOU ARE SO DIFFERENT, WHAT,THEN, IS THE CAUSE? THE BLOOD COURSING THROUGH YOUR VEINS?
THE CHILDREN...
NO!
HE IS DIFFERENT... I CAN'T LET HIM BECOME LIKE THE OTHERS!
HE IS DIFFERENT...

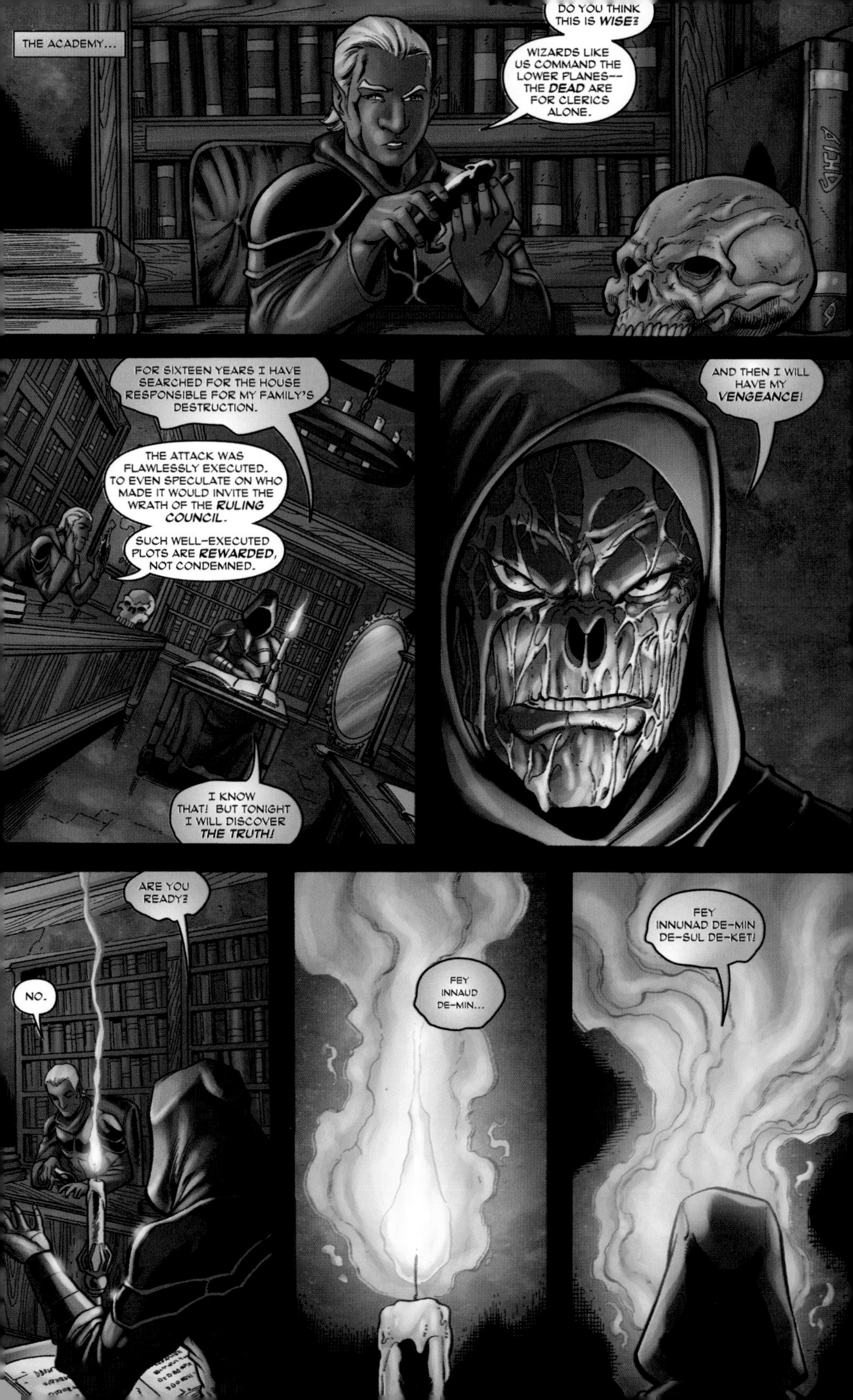
THE ACADEMY...
DO YOU THINK THIS IS WISE?
WIZARDS LIKE US COMMAND THE LOWER PLANES-- THE DEAD ARE FOR CLERICS ALONE.
FOR SIXTEEN YEARS I HAVE SEARCHED FOR THE HOUSE RESPONSIBLE FOR MY FAMILY'S DESTRUCTION.
THE ATTACK WAS FLAWLESSLY EXECUTED. TO EVEN SPECULATE ON WHO MADE IT WOULD INVITE THE WRATH OF THE RULING COUNCIL.
SUCH WELL-EXECUTED PLOTS ARE REWARDED, NOT CONDEMNED.
I KNOW THAT! BUT TONIGHT I WILL DISCOVER THE TRUTH!
AND THEN I WILL HAVE MY VENGEANCE!
ARE YOU READY?
NO.
FEY INNAUD DE-MIN...
FEY INNUNAD DE-MIN DE-SUL DE-KET!

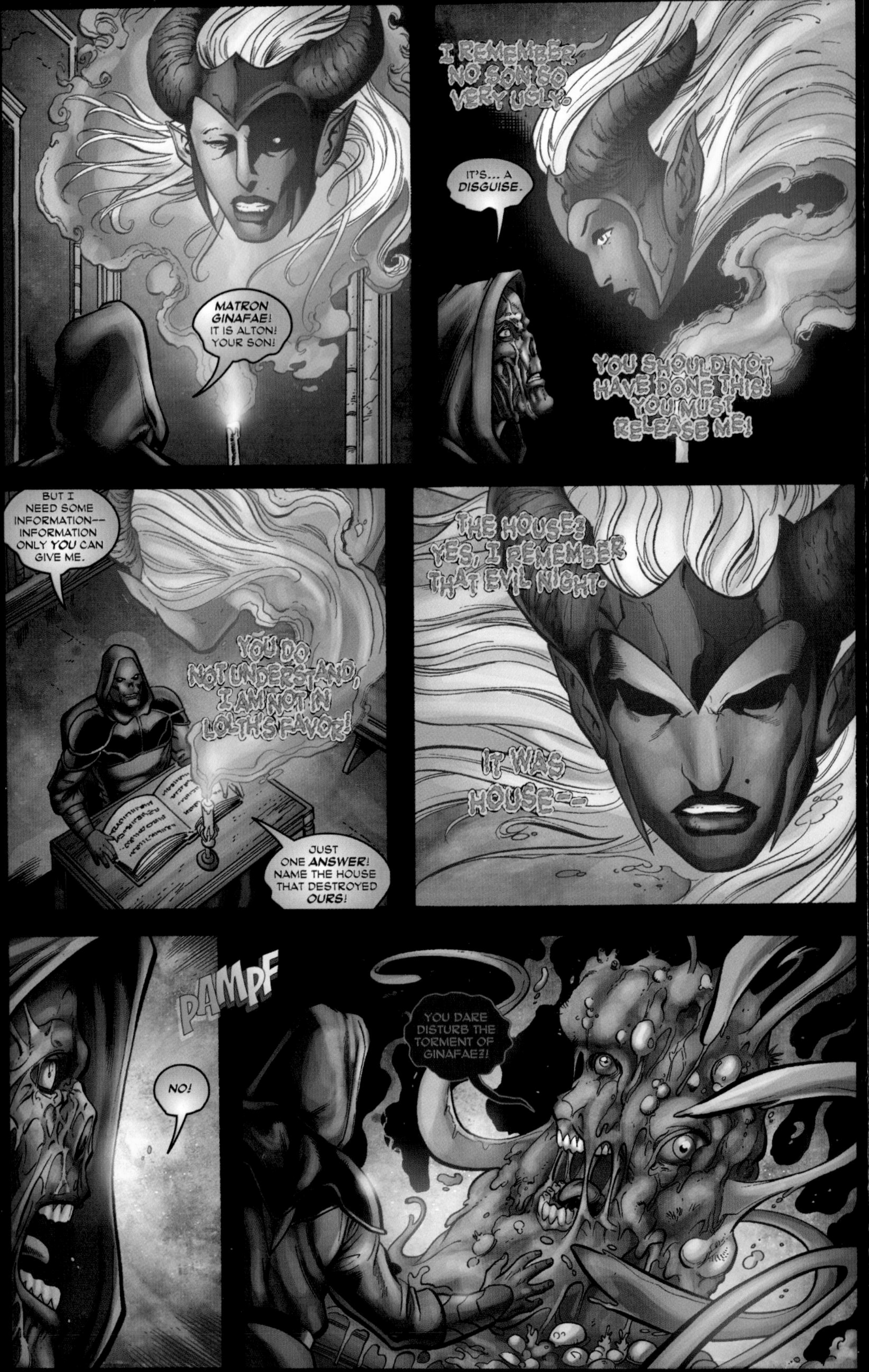

MATRON GINAFAE! IT IS ALTON! YOUR SON!
I REMEMBER NO SON SO VERY UGLY.
IT'S... A DISGUISE.
YOU SHOULD NOT HAVE DONE THIS! YOU MUST RELEASE ME!
BUT I NEED SOME INFORMATION-- INFORMATION ONLY YOU CAN GIVE ME.
YOU DO NOT UNDERSTAND, I AM NOT IN LOLTH'S FAVOR!
JUST ONE ANSWER! NAME THE HOUSE THAT DESTROYED OURS!
THE HOUSE? YES, I REMEMBER THAT EVIL NIGHT.
IT WAS HOUSE--
PAMPF
NO!
YOU DARE DISTURB THE TORMENT OF GINAFAE?!

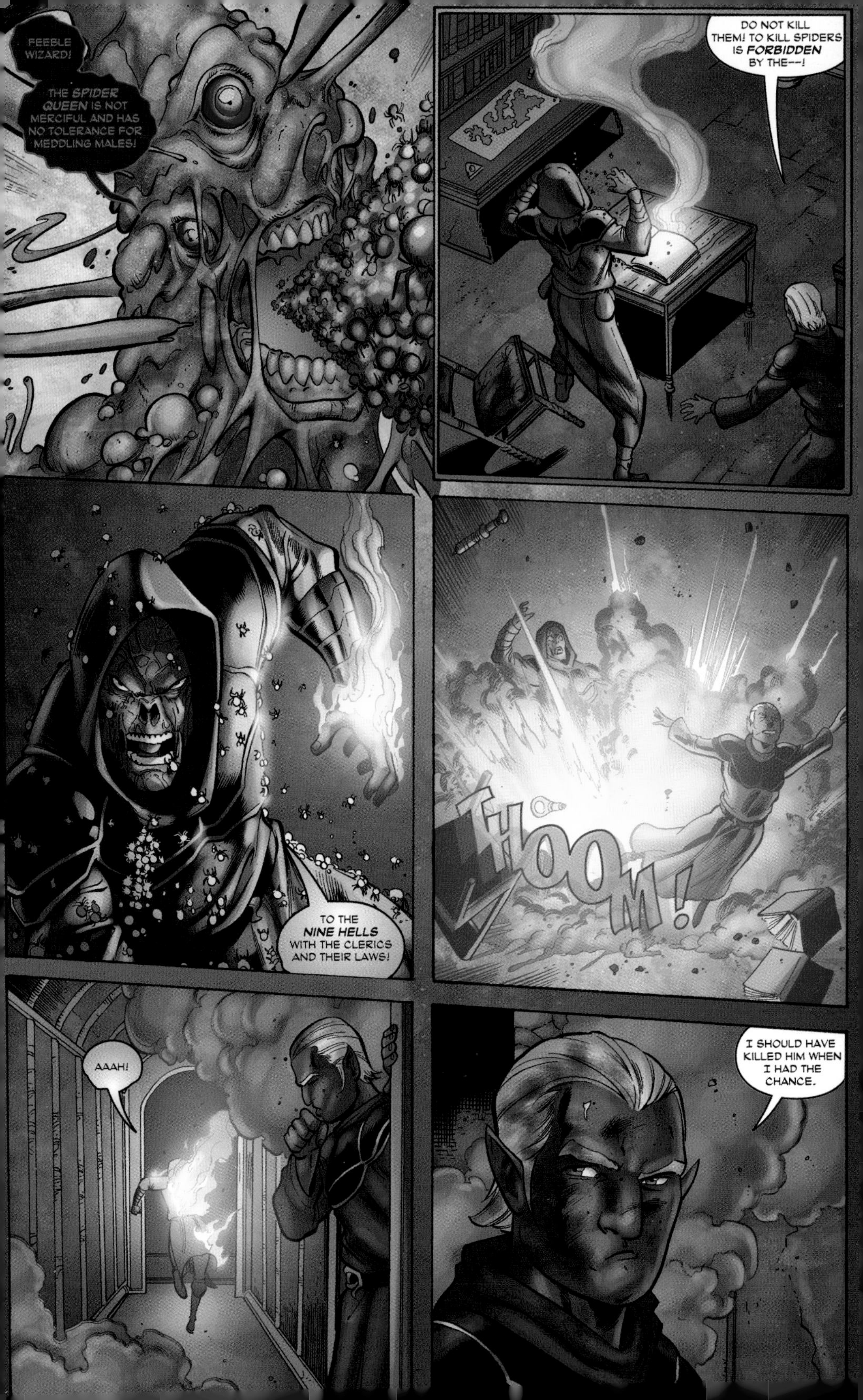
FEEBLE WIZARD!
THE SPIDER QUEEN IS NOT MERCIFUL AND HAS NO TOLERANCE FOR MEDDLING MALES!
DO NOT KILL THEM! TO KILL SPIDERS IS FORBIDDEN BY THE--!
TO THE NINE HELLS WITH THE CLERICS AND THEIR LAWS!
THOOOM!
AAAH!
I SHOULD HAVE KILLED HIM WHEN I HAD THE CHANCE.

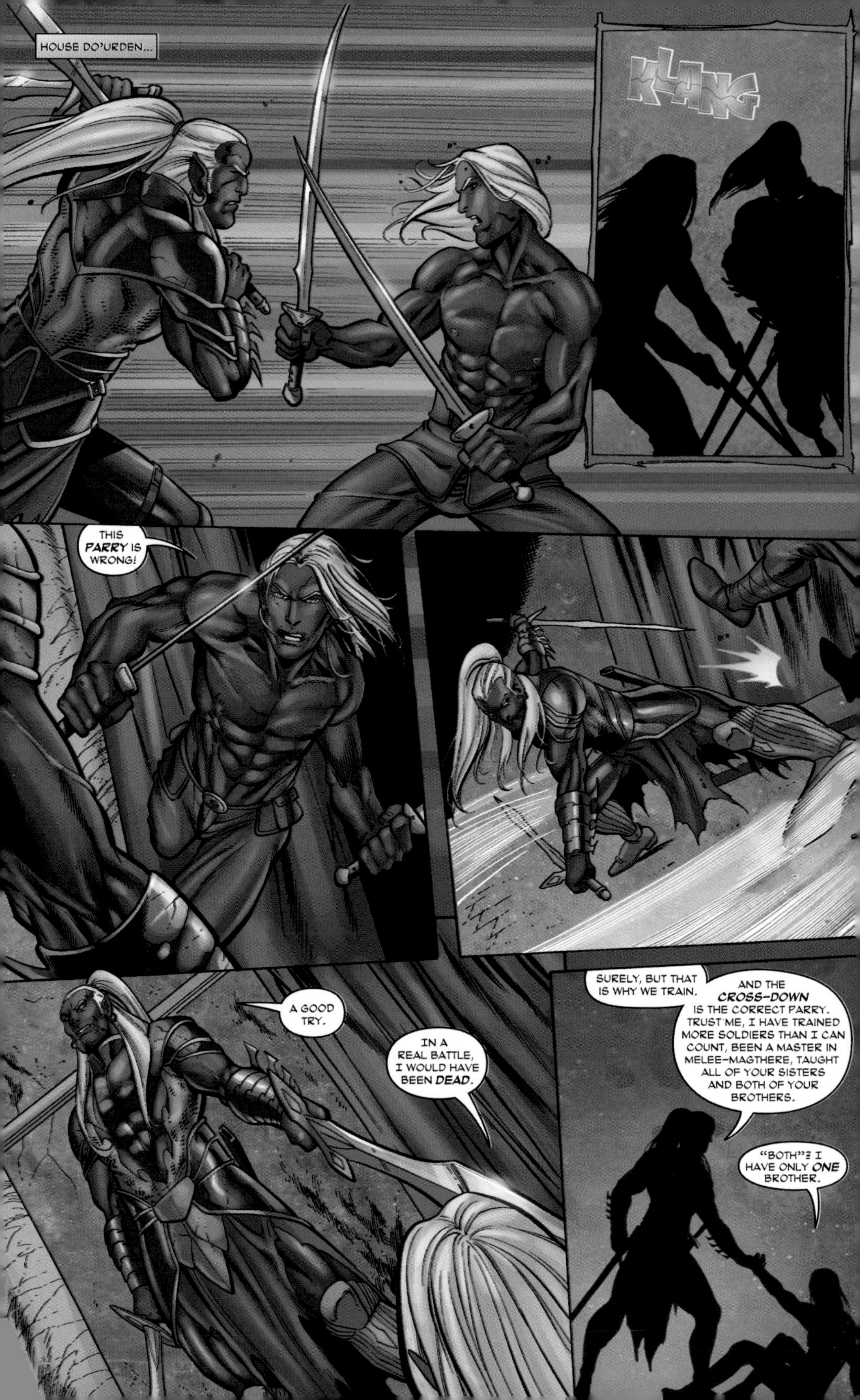
HOUSE DO'URDEN...
KLANG
THIS PARRY IS WRONG!
A GOOD TRY.
IN A REAL BATTLE, I WOULD HAVE BEEN DEAD.
SURELY, BUT THAT IS WHY WE TRAIN.
AND THE CROSS-DOWN IS THE CORRECT PARRY. TRUST ME, I HAVE TRAINED MORE SOLDIERS THAN I CAN COUNT, BEEN A MASTER IN MELEE-MAGTHERE, TAUGHT ALL OF YOUR SISTERS AND BOTH OF YOUR BROTHERS.
"BOTH"? I HAVE ONLY ONE BROTHER.

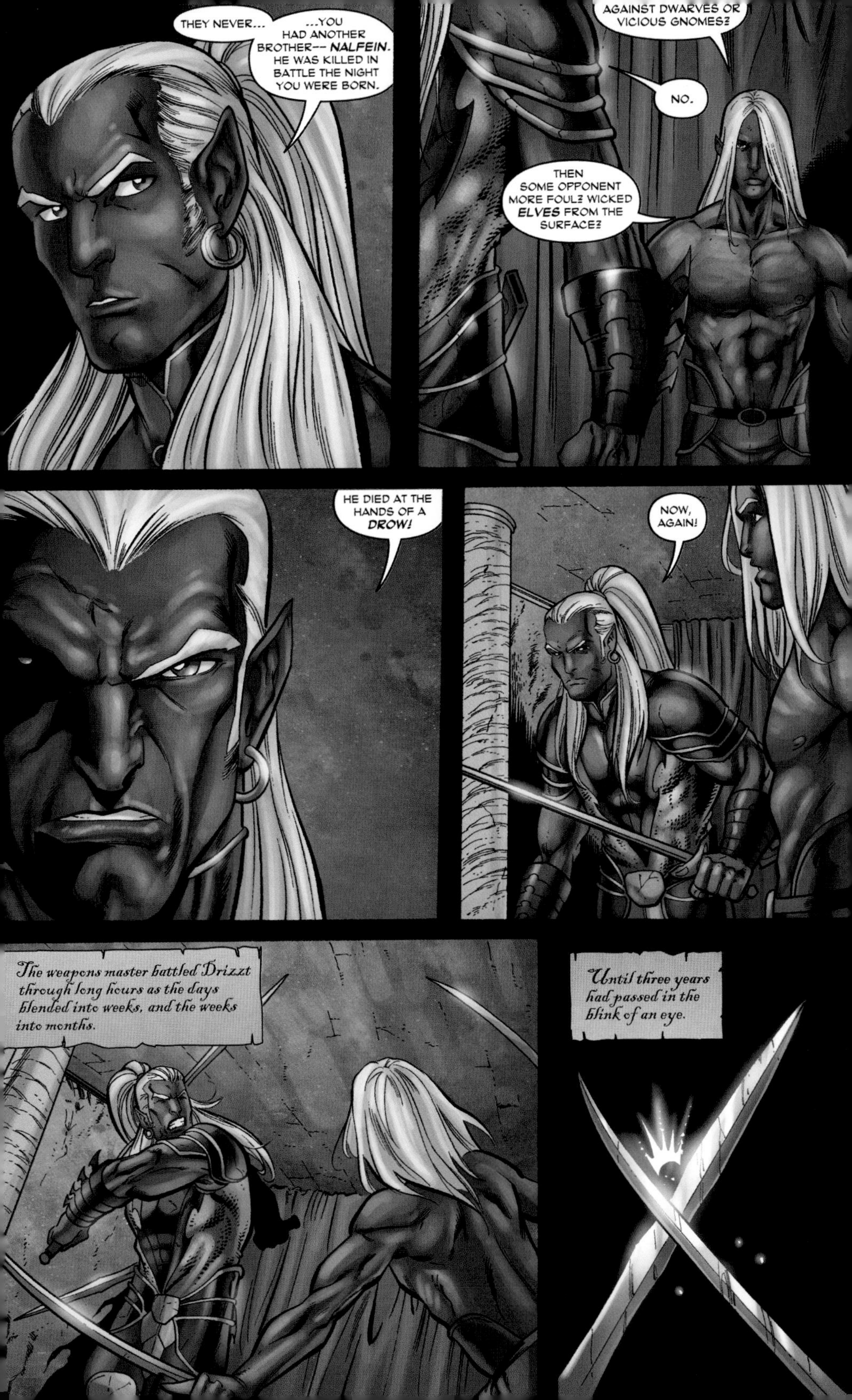
THEY NEVER...
...YOU HAD ANOTHER BROTHER-- NALFEIN. HE WAS KILLED IN BATTLE THE NIGHT YOU WERE BORN.
AGAINST DWARVES OR VICIOUS GNOMES?
NO.
THEN SOME OPPONENT MORE FOUL? WICKED ELVES FROM THE SURFACE?
HE DIED AT THE HANDS OF A DROW!
NOW, AGAIN!
The weapons master battled Drizzt through long hours as the days blended into weeks, and the weeks into months.
Until three years had passed in the blink of an eye.

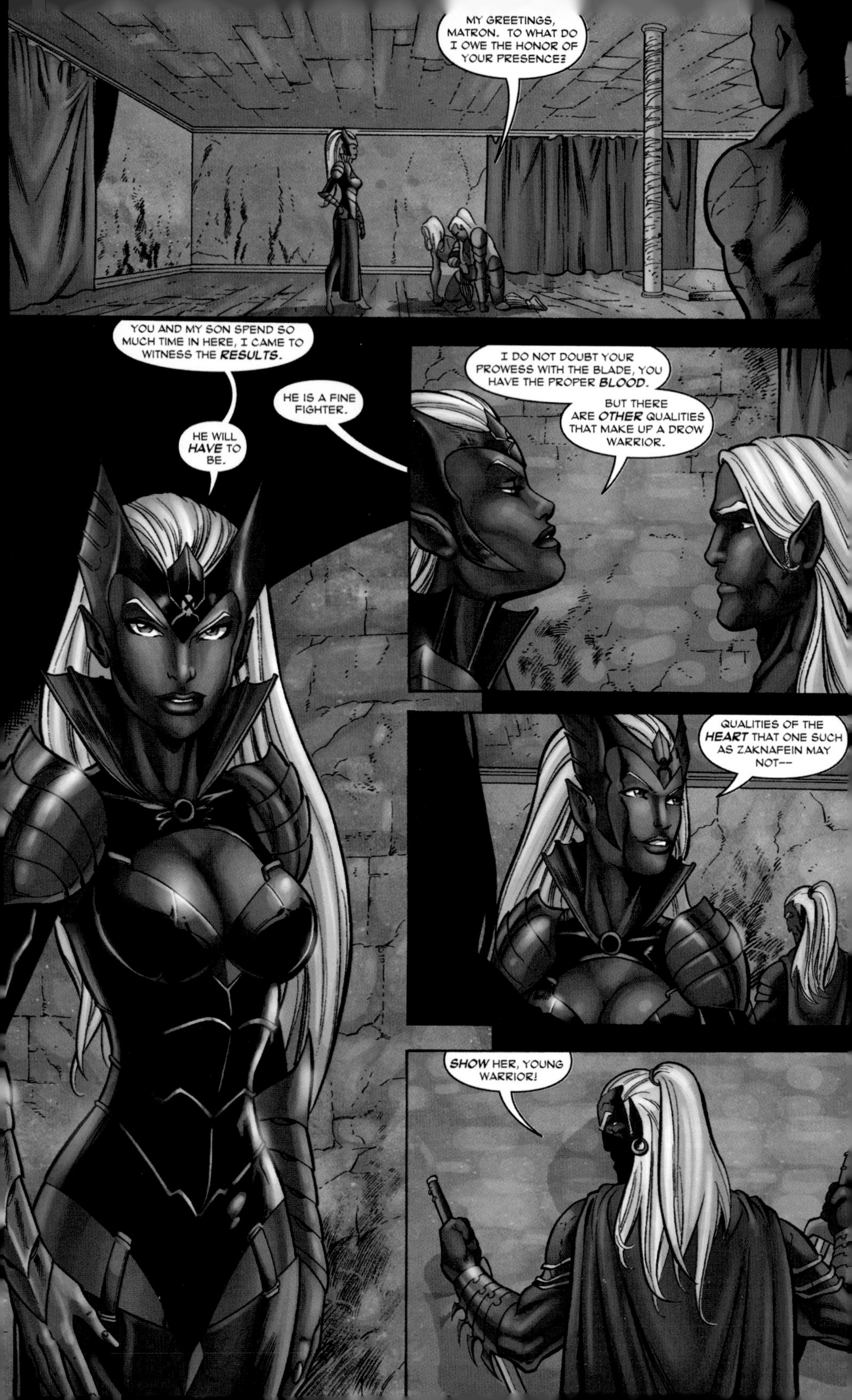
MY GREETINGS, MATRON. TO WHAT DO I OWE THE HONOR OF YOUR PRESENCE?
YOU AND MY SON SPEND SO MUCH TIME IN HERE, I CAME TO WITNESS THE RESULTS.
HE IS A FINE FIGHTER.
HE WILL HAVE TO BE.
I DO NOT DOUBT YOUR PROWESS WITH THE BLADE, YOU HAVE THE PROPER BLOOD.
BUT THERE ARE OTHER QUALITIES THAT MAKE UP A DROW WARRIOR.
QUALITIES OF THE HEART THAT ONE SUCH AS ZAKNAFEIN MAY NOT--
SHOW HER, YOUNG WARRIOR!

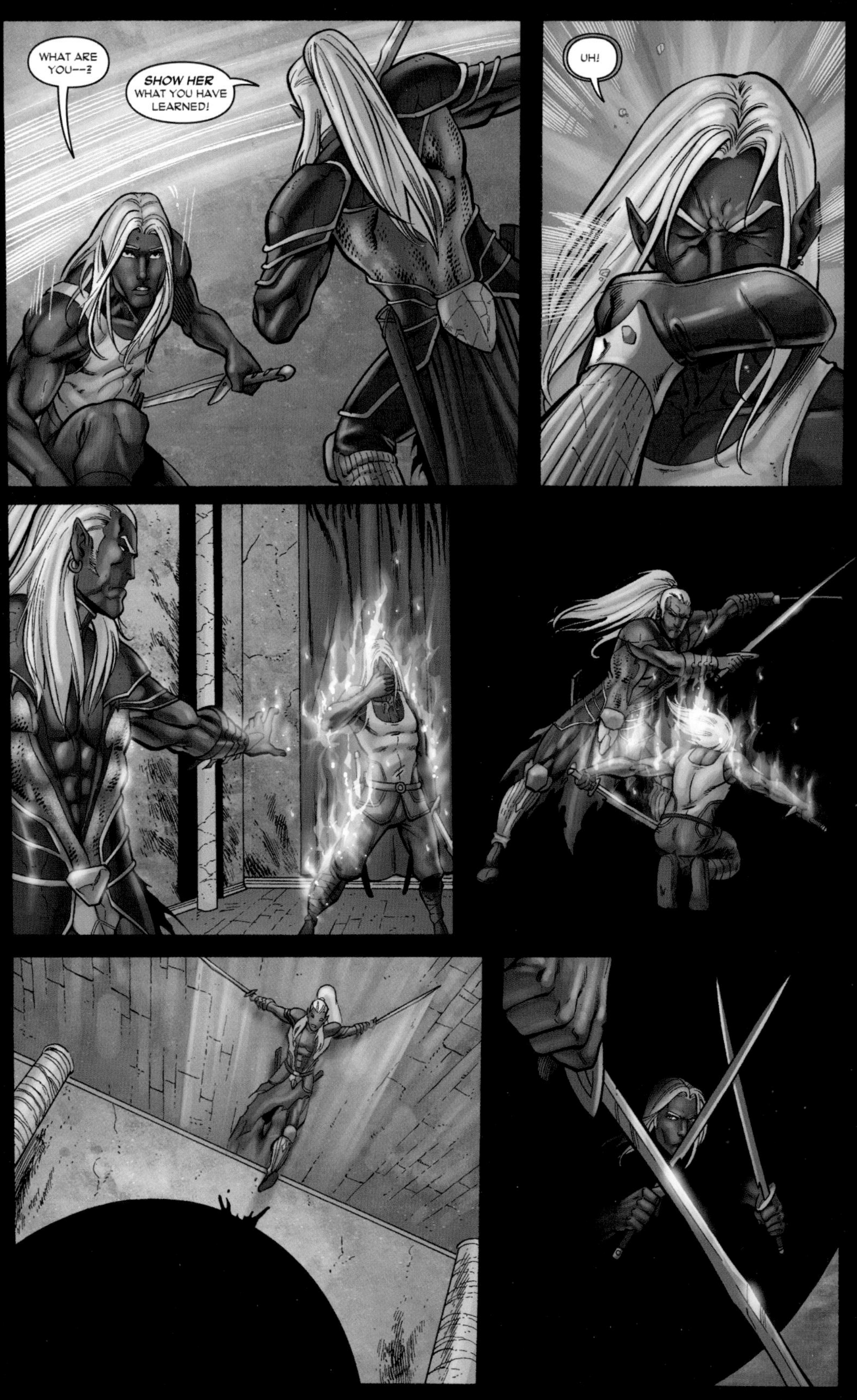
WHAT ARE YOU--?
SHOW HER WHAT YOU HAVE LEARNED!
UH!

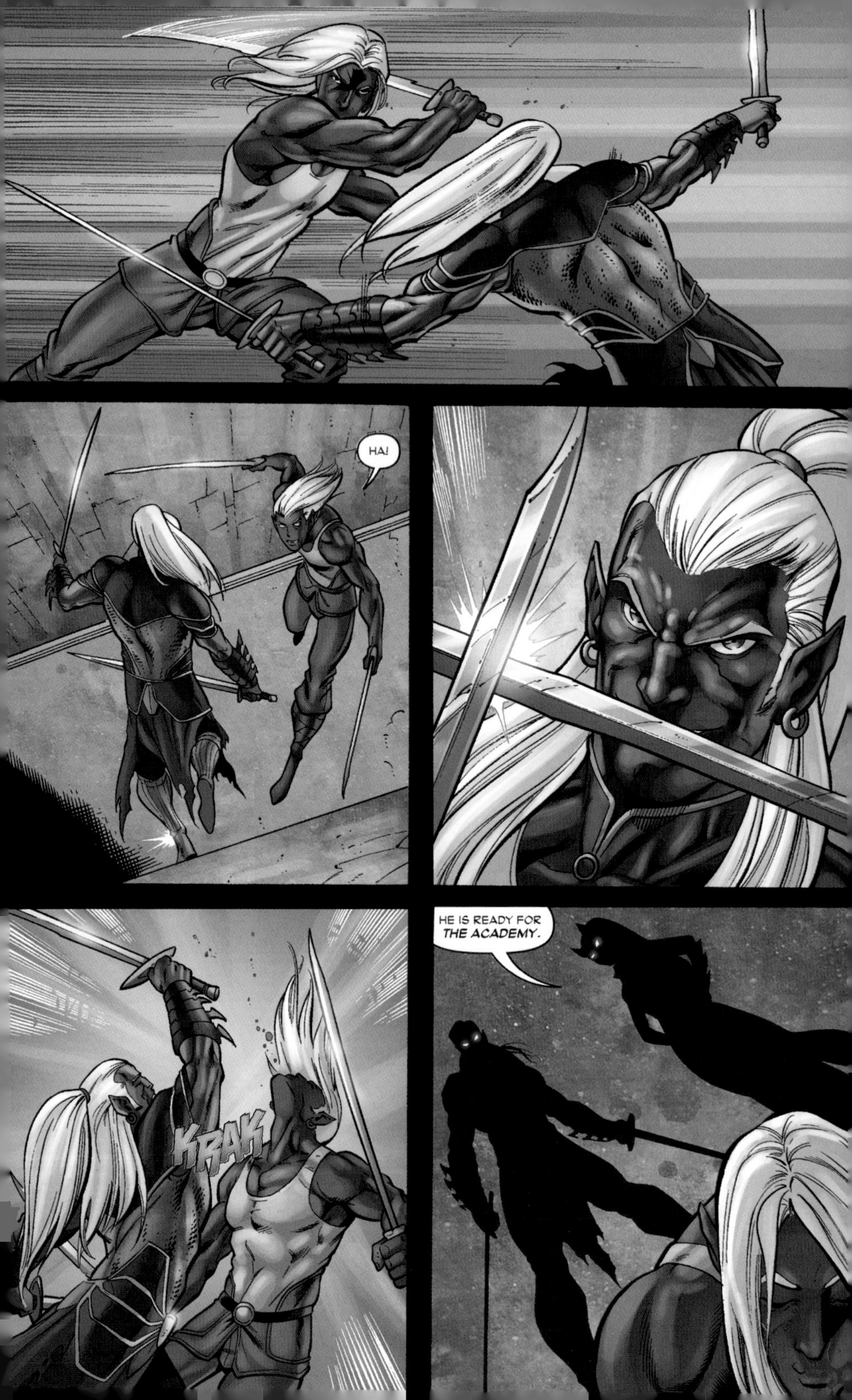
HA!
KRAK
HE IS READY FOR THE ACADEMY.

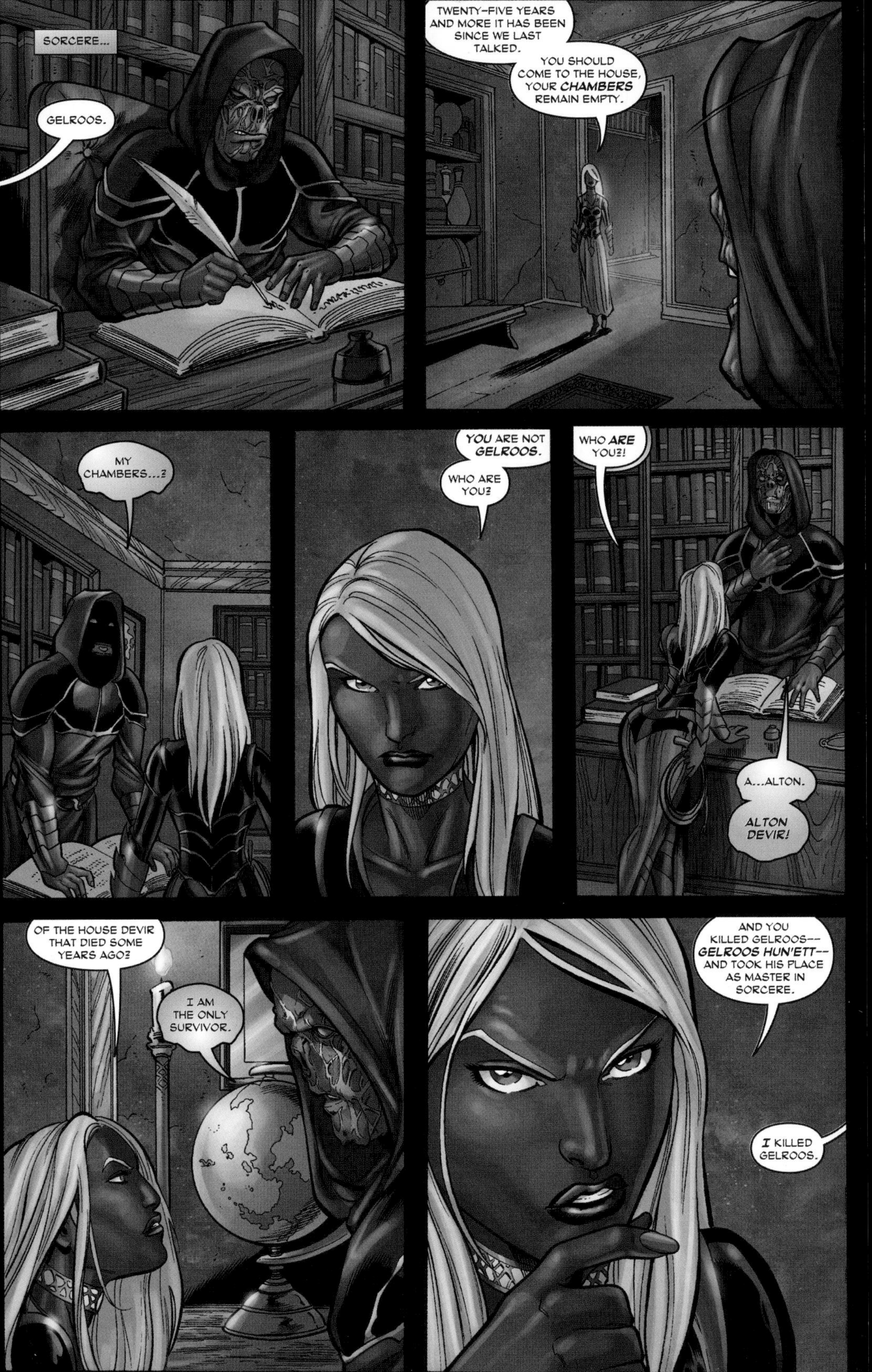
SORCERE...
GELROOS.
TWENTY-FIVE YEARS AND MORE IT HAS BEEN SINCE WE LAST TALKED.
YOU SHOULD COME TO THE HOUSE, YOUR **CHAMBERS** REMAIN EMPTY.
MY CHAMBERS...?
YOU ARE NOT **GELROOS.**
WHO ARE YOU?
WHO **ARE** YOU?!
A...ALTON.
ALTON DEVIR!
OF THE HOUSE DEVIR THAT DIED SOME YEARS AGO?
I AM THE ONLY SURVIVOR.
AND YOU KILLED GELROOS-- **GELROOS HUN'ETT**-- AND TOOK HIS PLACE AS MASTER IN SORCERE.
I KILLED GELROOS.

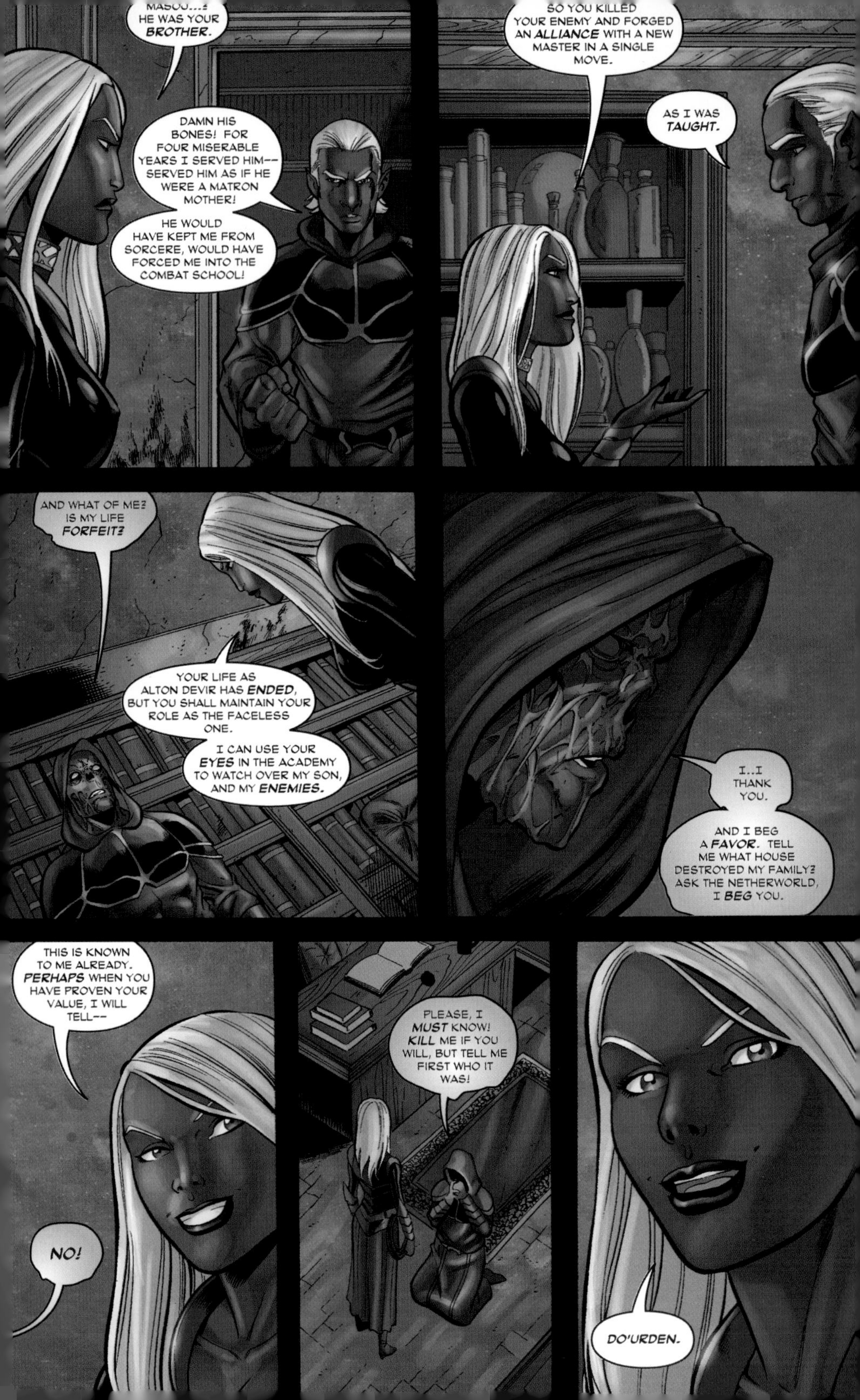
HE WAS YOUR BROTHER.
DAMN HIS BONES! FOR FOUR MISERABLE YEARS I SERVED HIM-- SERVED HIM AS IF HE WERE A MATRON MOTHER!
HE WOULD HAVE KEPT ME FROM SORCERE, WOULD HAVE FORCED ME INTO THE COMBAT SCHOOL!
SO YOU KILLED YOUR ENEMY AND FORGED AN ALLIANCE WITH A NEW MASTER IN A SINGLE MOVE.
AS I WAS TAUGHT.
AND WHAT OF ME? IS MY LIFE FORFEIT?
YOUR LIFE AS ALTON DEVIR HAS ENDED, BUT YOU SHALL MAINTAIN YOUR ROLE AS THE FACELESS ONE.
I CAN USE YOUR EYES IN THE ACADEMY TO WATCH OVER MY SON, AND MY ENEMIES.
I..I THANK YOU.
AND I BEG A FAVOR. TELL ME WHAT HOUSE DESTROYED MY FAMILY? ASK THE NETHERWORLD, I BEG YOU.
THIS IS KNOWN TO ME ALREADY. PERHAPS WHEN YOU HAVE PROVEN YOUR VALUE, I WILL TELL--
NO!
PLEASE, I MUST KNOW! KILL ME IF YOU WILL, BUT TELL ME FIRST WHO IT WAS!
DO'URDEN.

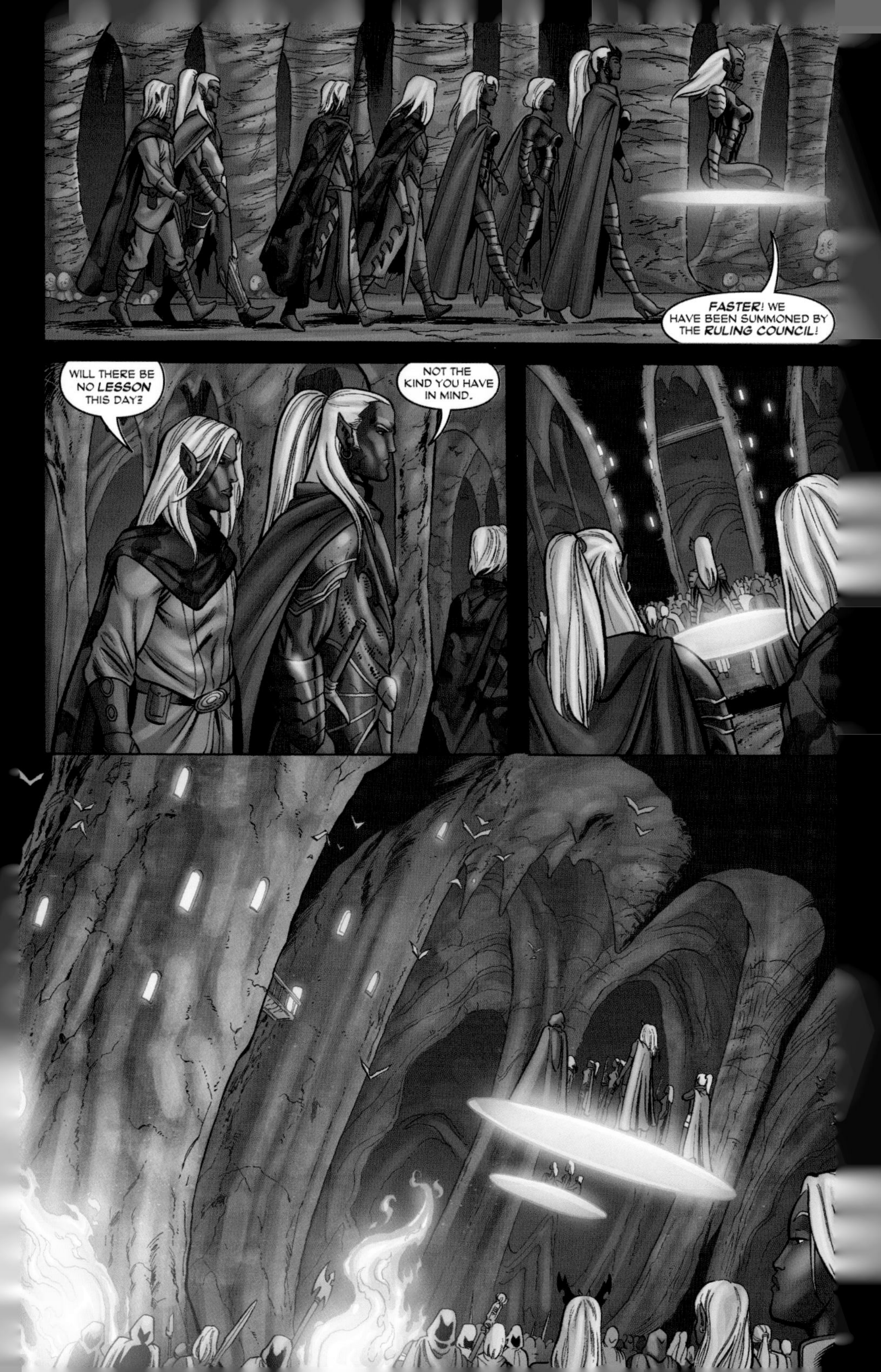
FASTER! WE HAVE BEEN SUMMONED BY THE RULING COUNCIL!
WILL THERE BE NO LESSON THIS DAY?
NOT THE KIND YOU HAVE IN MIND.

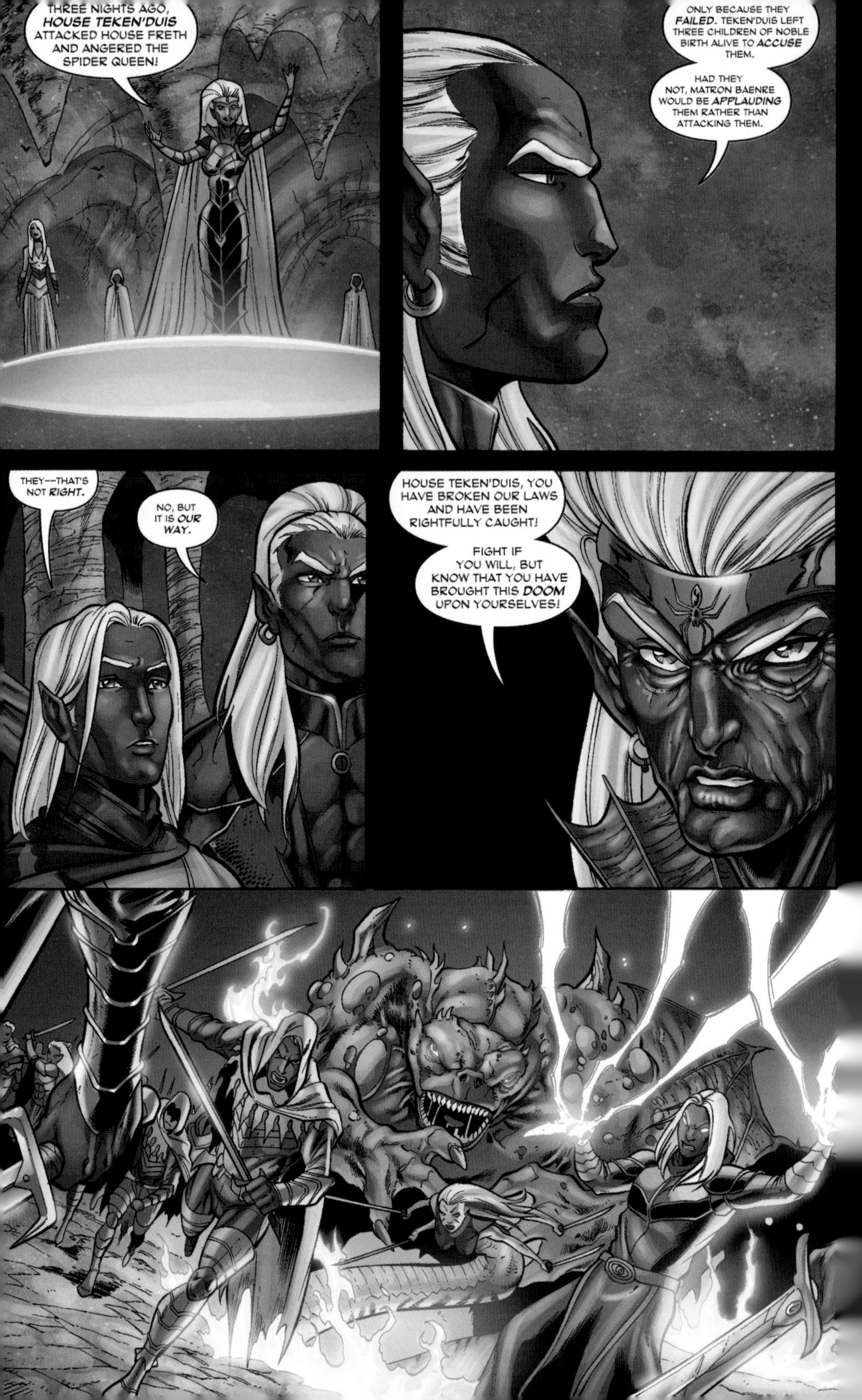
THREE NIGHTS AGO, HOUSE TEKEN'DUIS ATTACKED HOUSE FRETH AND ANGERED THE SPIDER QUEEN!
ONLY BECAUSE THEY FAILED. TEKEN'DUIS LEFT THREE CHILDREN OF NOBLE BIRTH ALIVE TO ACCUSE THEM.
HAD THEY NOT, MATRON BAENRE WOULD BE APPLAUDING THEM RATHER THAN ATTACKING THEM.
THEY--THAT'S NOT RIGHT.
NO, BUT IT IS OUR WAY.
HOUSE TEKEN'DUIS, YOU HAVE BROKEN OUR LAWS AND HAVE BEEN RIGHTFULLY CAUGHT!
FIGHT IF YOU WILL, BUT KNOW THAT YOU HAVE BROUGHT THIS DOOM UPON YOURSELVES!

THIS IS WHAT PASSES FOR DROW JUSTICE.

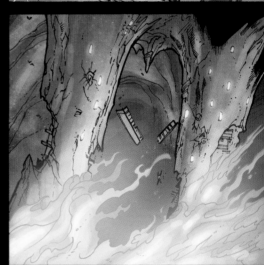

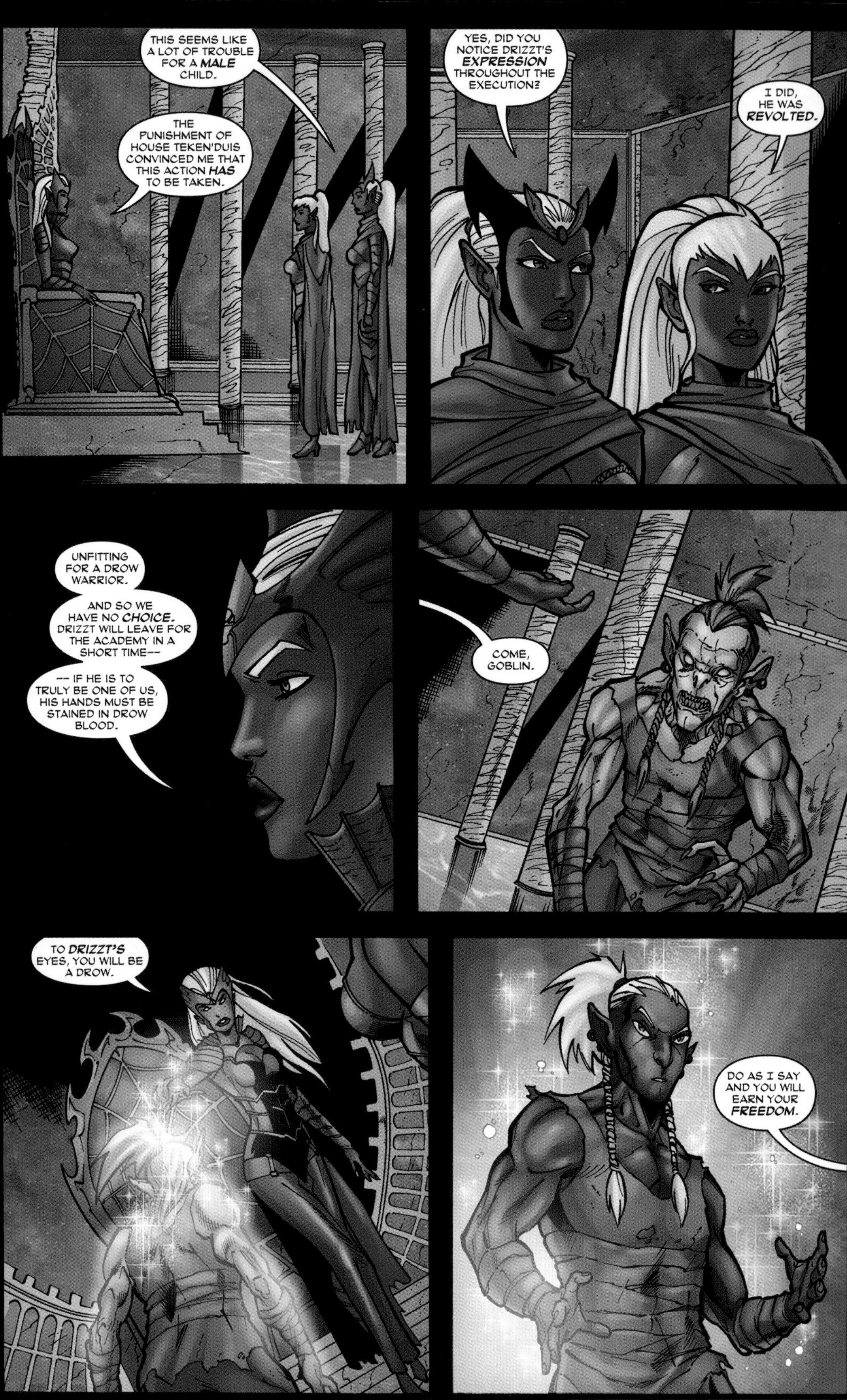
THIS SEEMS LIKE A LOT OF TROUBLE FOR A MALE CHILD.
THE PUNISHMENT OF HOUSE TEKEN'DUIS CONVINCED ME THAT THIS ACTION HAS TO BE TAKEN.
YES, DID YOU NOTICE DRIZZT'S EXPRESSION THROUGHOUT THE EXECUTION?
I DID, HE WAS REVOLTED.
UNFITTING FOR A DROW WARRIOR.
AND SO WE HAVE NO CHOICE. DRIZZT WILL LEAVE FOR THE ACADEMY IN A SHORT TIME--
-- IF HE IS TO TRULY BE ONE OF US, HIS HANDS MUST BE STAINED IN DROW BLOOD.
COME, GOBLIN.
TO DRIZZT'S EYES, YOU WILL BE A DROW.
DO AS I SAY AND YOU WILL EARN YOUR FREEDOM.

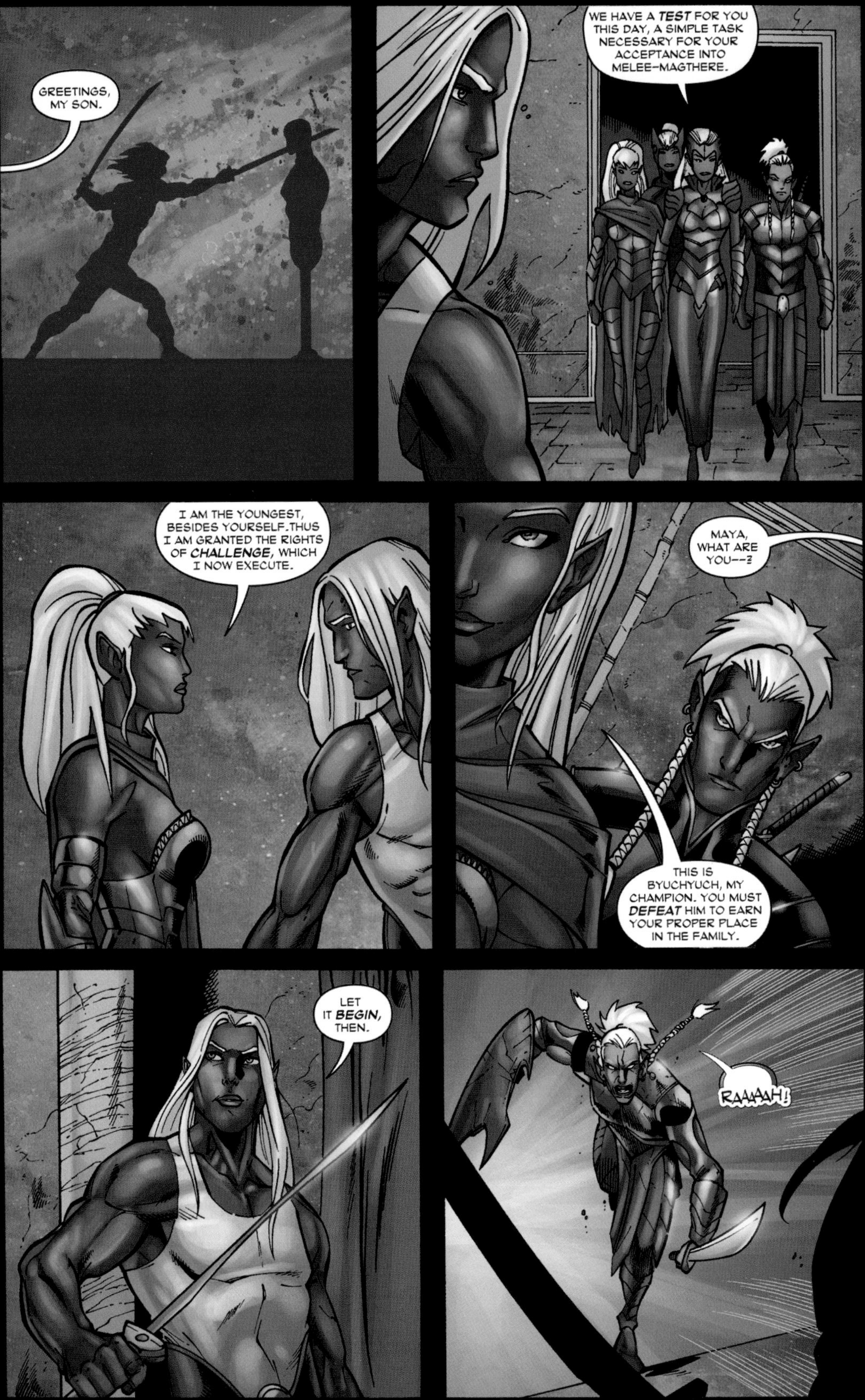
GREETINGS, MY SON.
WE HAVE A TEST FOR YOU THIS DAY, A SIMPLE TASK NECESSARY FOR YOUR ACCEPTANCE INTO MELEE-MAGTHERE.
I AM THE YOUNGEST, BESIDES YOURSELF. THUS I AM GRANTED THE RIGHTS OF CHALLENGE, WHICH I NOW EXECUTE.
MAYA, WHAT ARE YOU--?
THIS IS BYUCHYUCH, MY CHAMPION. YOU MUST DEFEAT HIM TO EARN YOUR PROPER PLACE IN THE FAMILY.
LET IT BEGIN, THEN.
RAAAAAH!

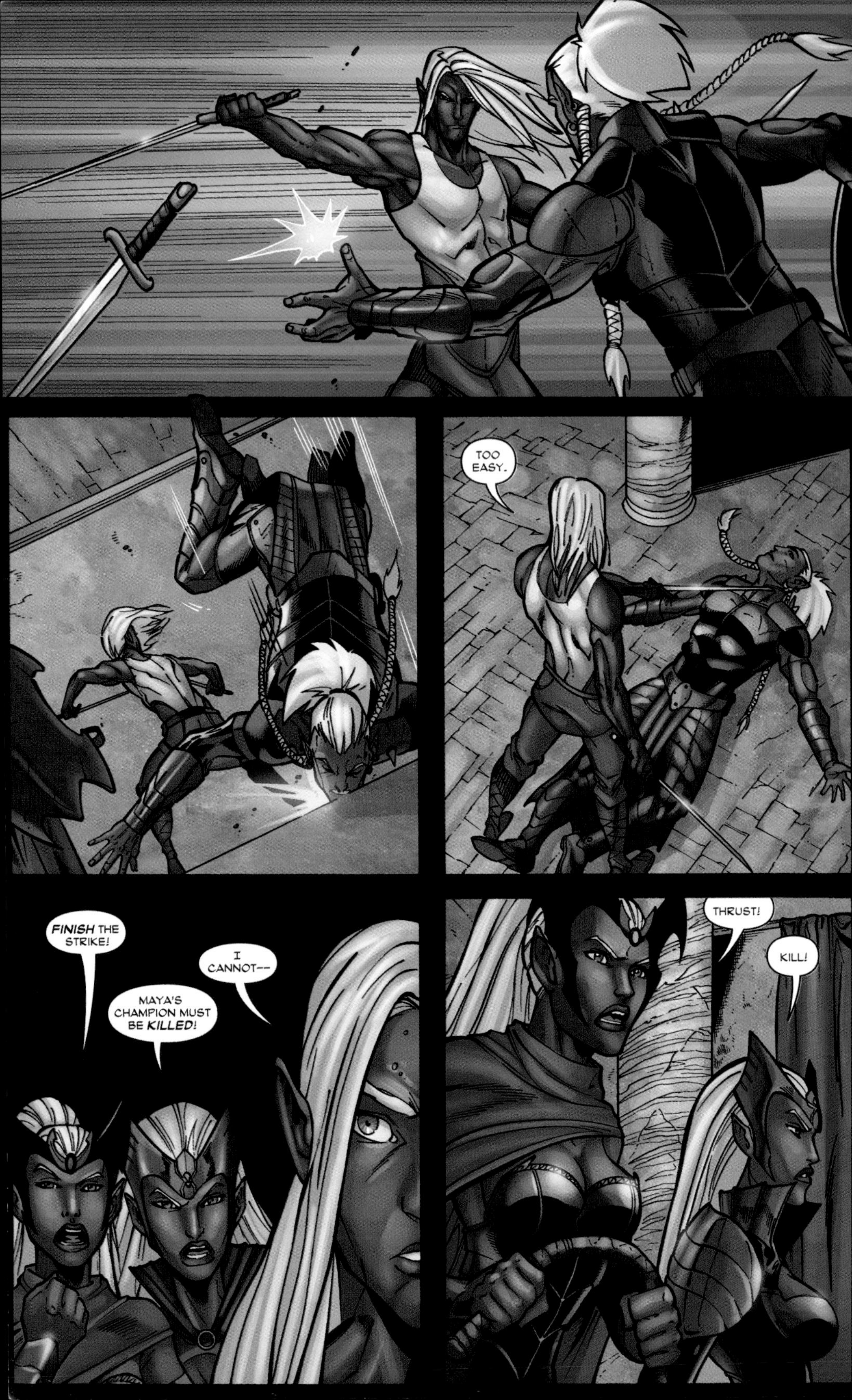
TOO EASY.
FINISH THE STRIKE!
MAYA'S CHAMPION MUST BE KILLED!
I CANNOT--
THRUST!
KILL!

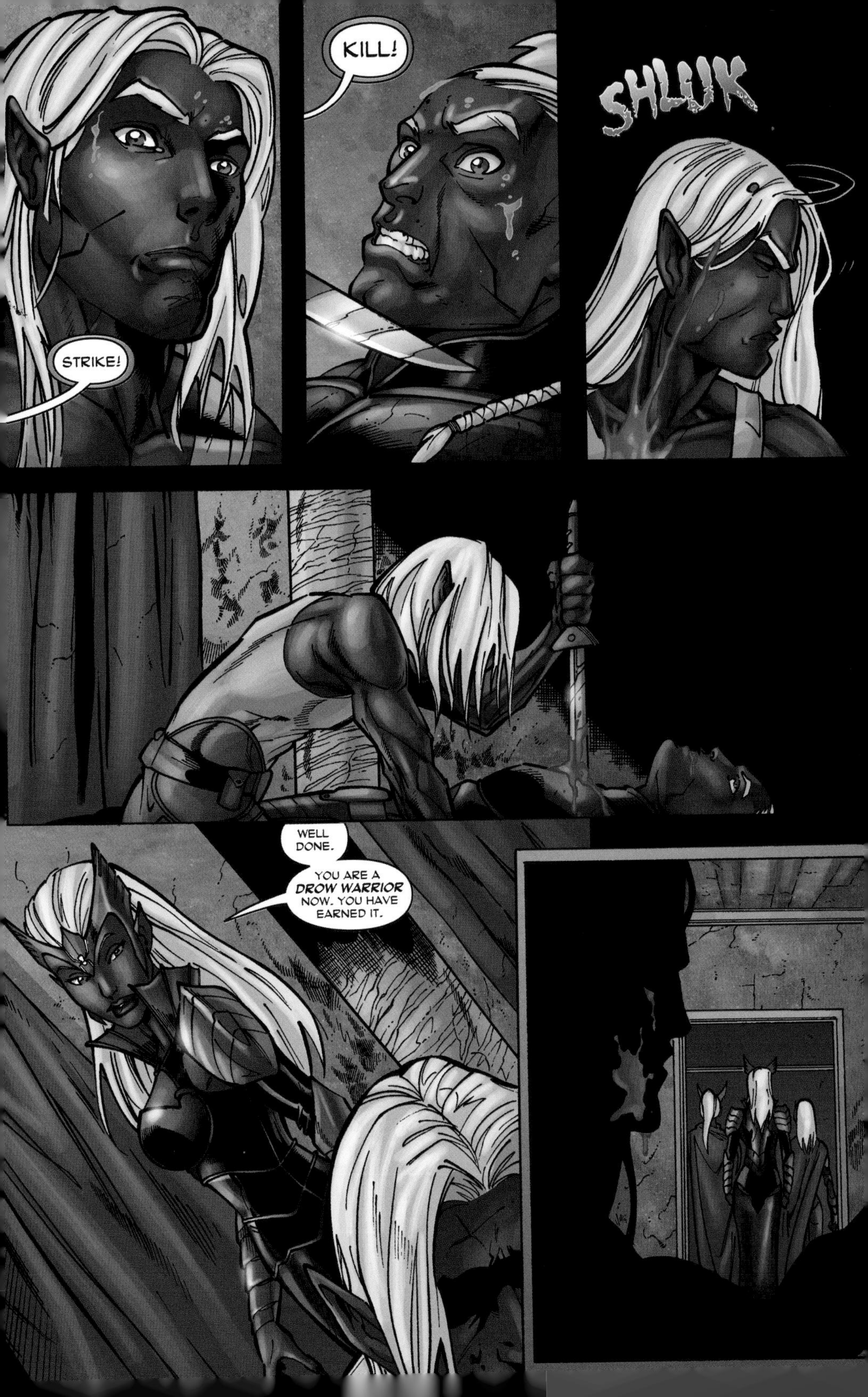
STRIKE!
KILL!
SHLUK
WELL DONE.
YOU ARE A DROW WARRIOR NOW. YOU HAVE EARNED IT.

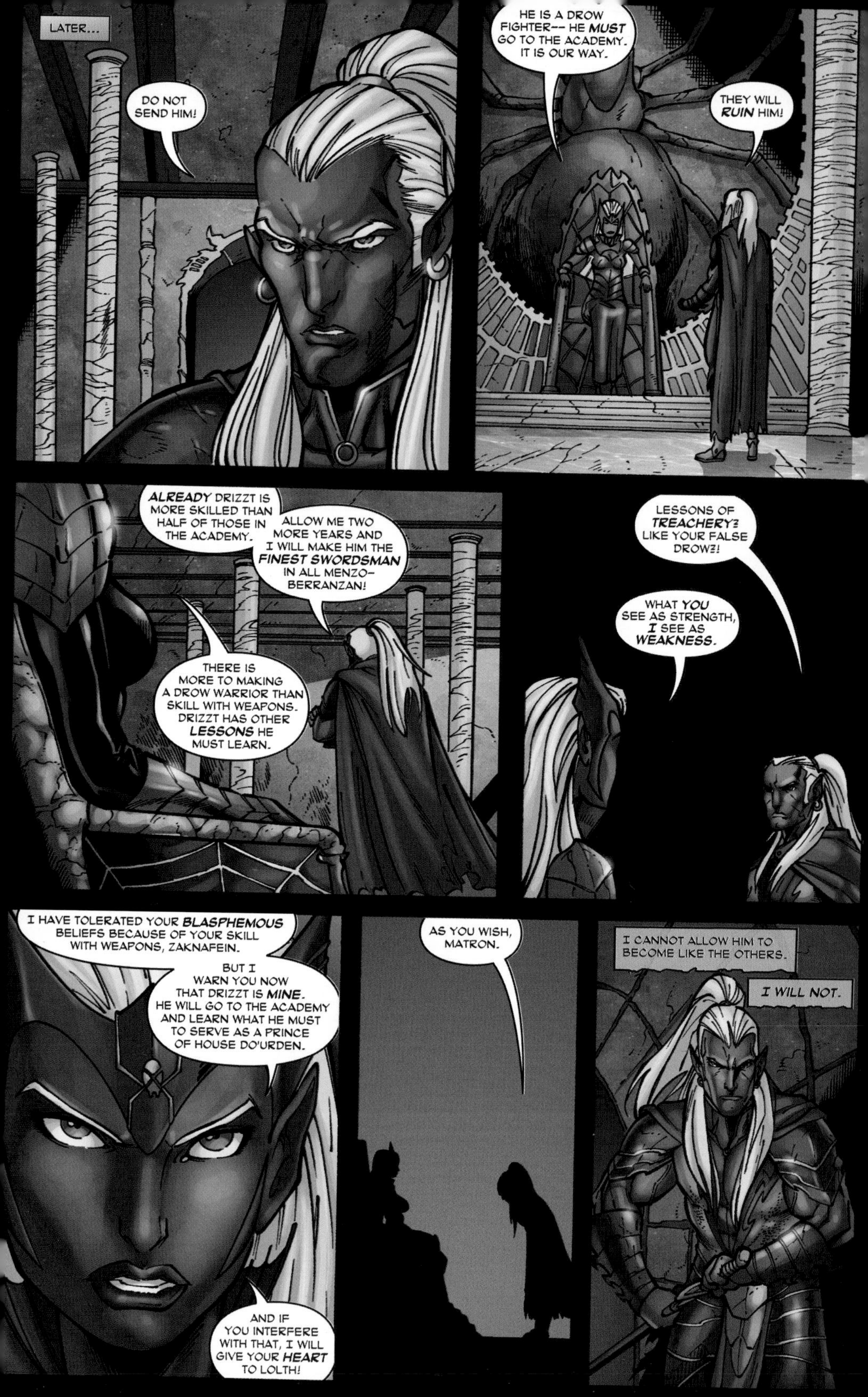
LATER...
DO NOT SEND HIM!
HE IS A DROW FIGHTER-- HE MUST GO TO THE ACADEMY. IT IS OUR WAY.
THEY WILL RUIN HIM!
ALREADY DRIZZT IS MORE SKILLED THAN HALF OF THOSE IN THE ACADEMY.
ALLOW ME TWO MORE YEARS AND I WILL MAKE HIM THE FINEST SWORDSMAN IN ALL MENZO-BERRANZAN!
THERE IS MORE TO MAKING A DROW WARRIOR THAN SKILL WITH WEAPONS. DRIZZT HAS OTHER LESSONS HE MUST LEARN.
LESSONS OF TREACHERY?! LIKE YOUR FALSE DROW?!
WHAT YOU SEE AS STRENGTH, I SEE AS WEAKNESS.
I HAVE TOLERATED YOUR BLASPHEMOUS BELIEFS BECAUSE OF YOUR SKILL WITH WEAPONS, ZAKNAFEIN.
BUT I WARN YOU NOW THAT DRIZZT IS MINE. HE WILL GO TO THE ACADEMY AND LEARN WHAT HE MUST TO SERVE AS A PRINCE OF HOUSE DO'URDEN.
AND IF YOU INTERFERE WITH THAT, I WILL GIVE YOUR HEART TO LOLTH!
AS YOU WISH, MATRON.
I CANNOT ALLOW HIM TO BECOME LIKE THE OTHERS.
I WILL NOT.

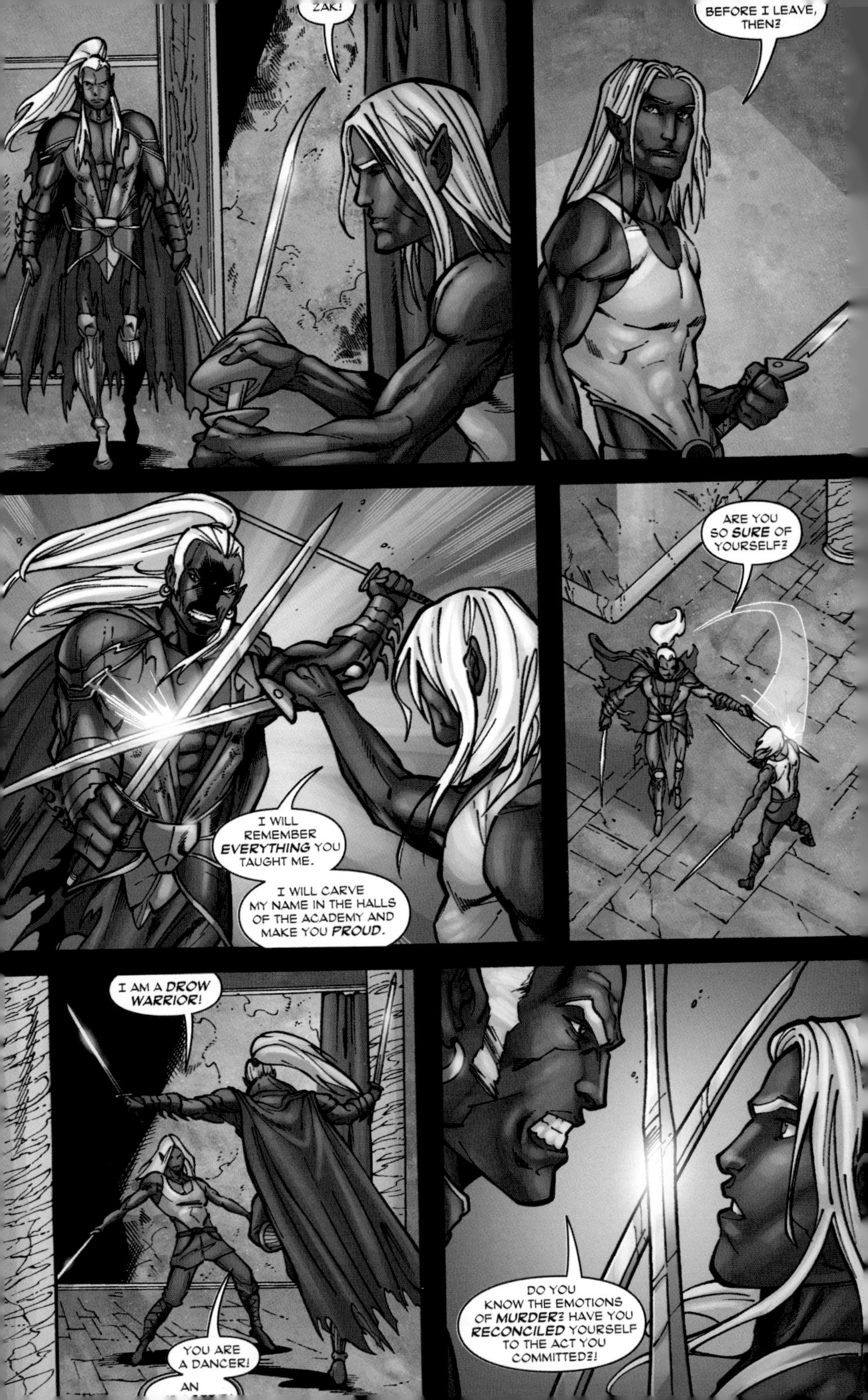
ZAK!
BEFORE I LEAVE, THEN?
ARE YOU SO SURE OF YOURSELF?
I WILL REMEMBER EVERYTHING YOU TAUGHT ME.
I WILL CARVE MY NAME IN THE HALLS OF THE ACADEMY AND MAKE YOU PROUD.
I AM A DROW WARRIOR!
YOU ARE A DANCER!
AN
DO YOU KNOW THE EMOTIONS OF MURDER? HAVE YOU RECONCILED YOURSELF TO THE ACT YOU COMMITTED?!

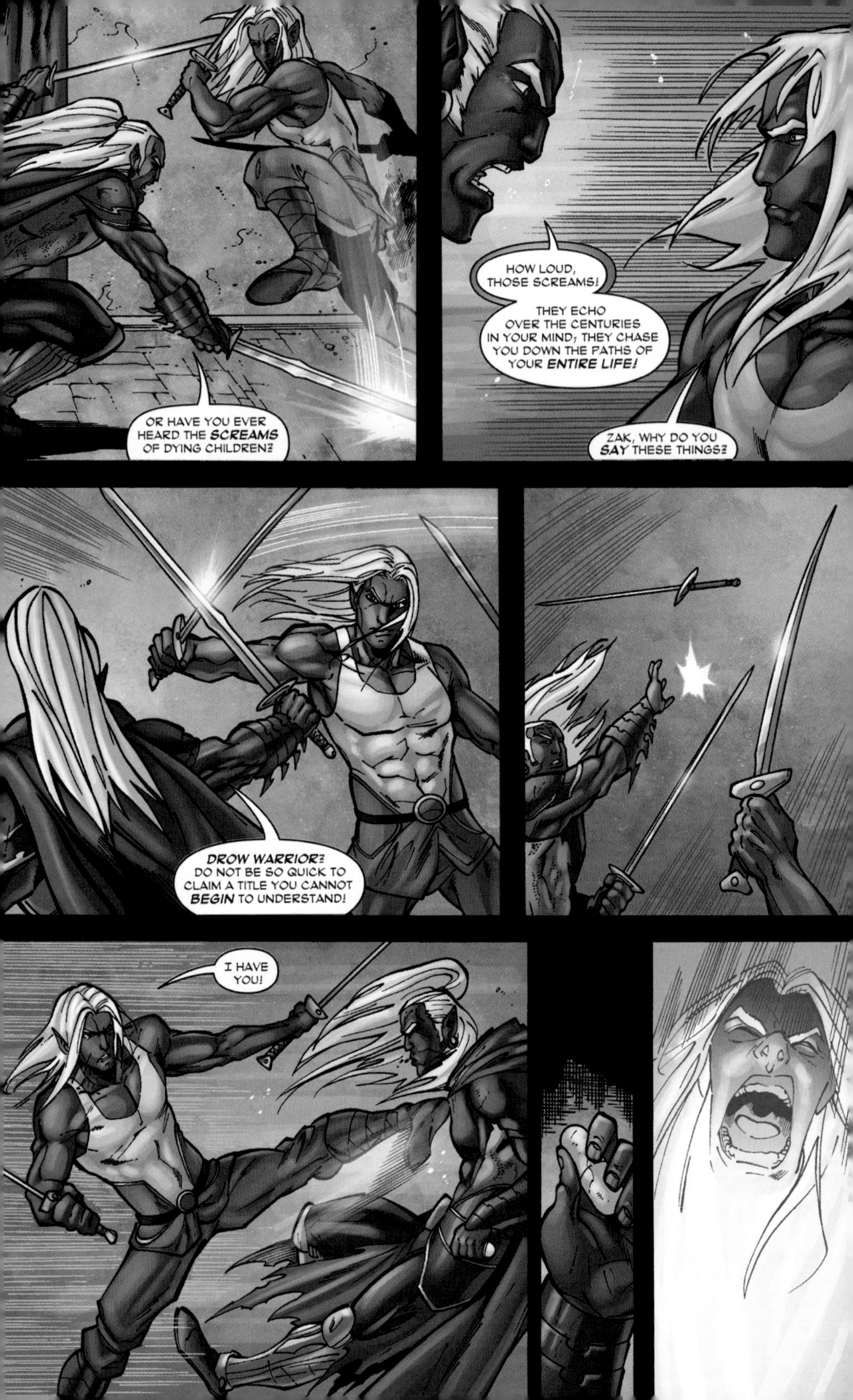
OR HAVE YOU EVER HEARD THE SCREAMS OF DYING CHILDREN?
HOW LOUD, THOSE SCREAMS!
THEY ECHO OVER THE CENTURIES IN YOUR MIND; THEY CHASE YOU DOWN THE PATHS OF YOUR ENTIRE LIFE!
ZAK, WHY DO YOU SAY THESE THINGS?
DROW WARRIOR? DO NOT BE SO QUICK TO CLAIM A TITLE YOU CANNOT BEGIN TO UNDERSTAND!
I HAVE YOU!

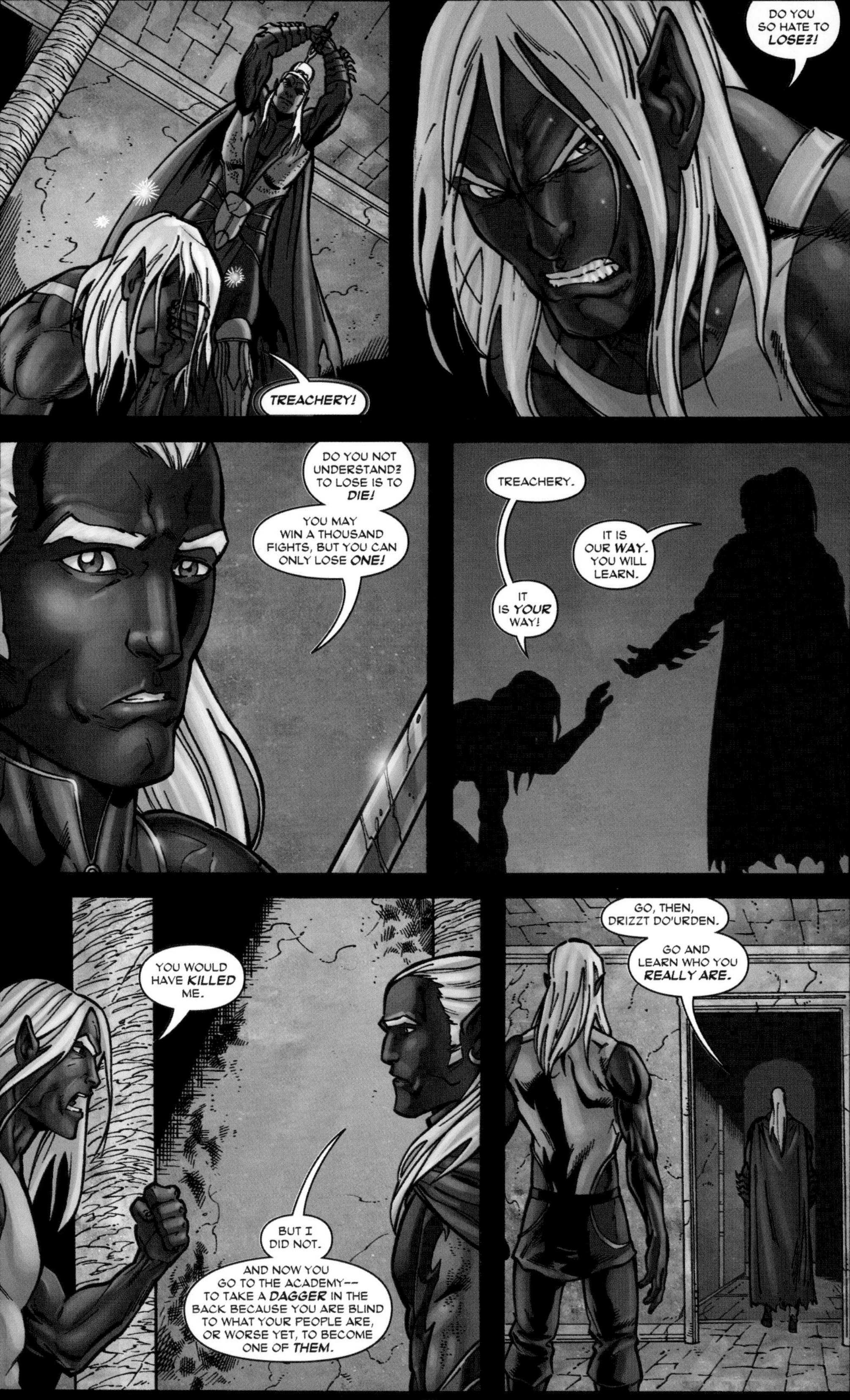
TREACHERY!
DO YOU SO HATE TO LOSE?!
DO YOU NOT UNDERSTAND? TO LOSE IS TO DIE!
YOU MAY WIN A THOUSAND FIGHTS, BUT YOU CAN ONLY LOSE ONE!
TREACHERY.
IT IS YOUR WAY!
IT IS OUR WAY. YOU WILL LEARN.
YOU WOULD HAVE KILLED ME.
BUT I DID NOT.
AND NOW YOU GO TO THE ACADEMY-- TO TAKE A DAGGER IN THE BACK BECAUSE YOU ARE BLIND TO WHAT YOUR PEOPLE ARE, OR WORSE YET, TO BECOME ONE OF THEM.
GO, THEN, DRIZZT DO'URDEN.
GO AND LEARN WHO YOU REALLY ARE.

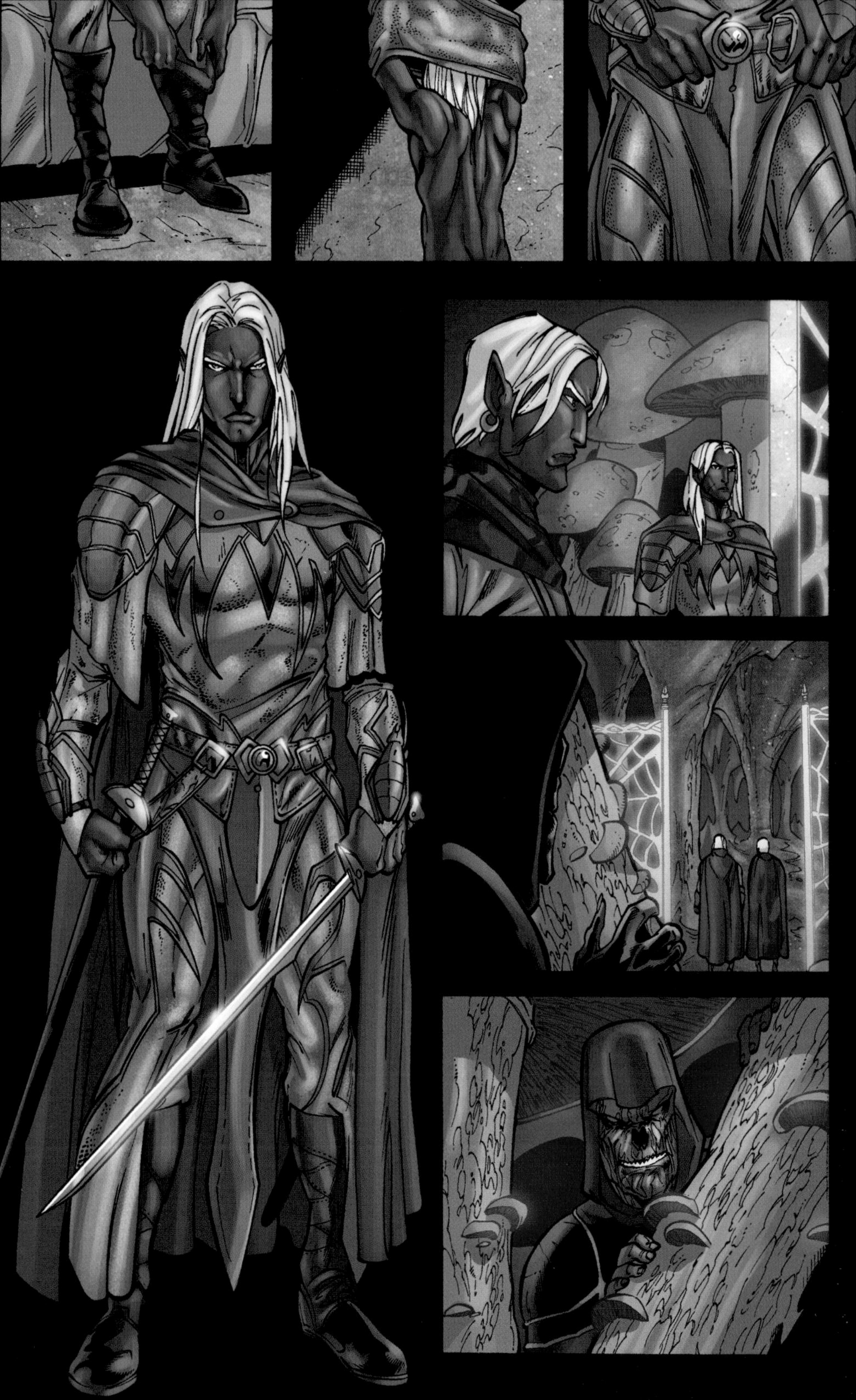

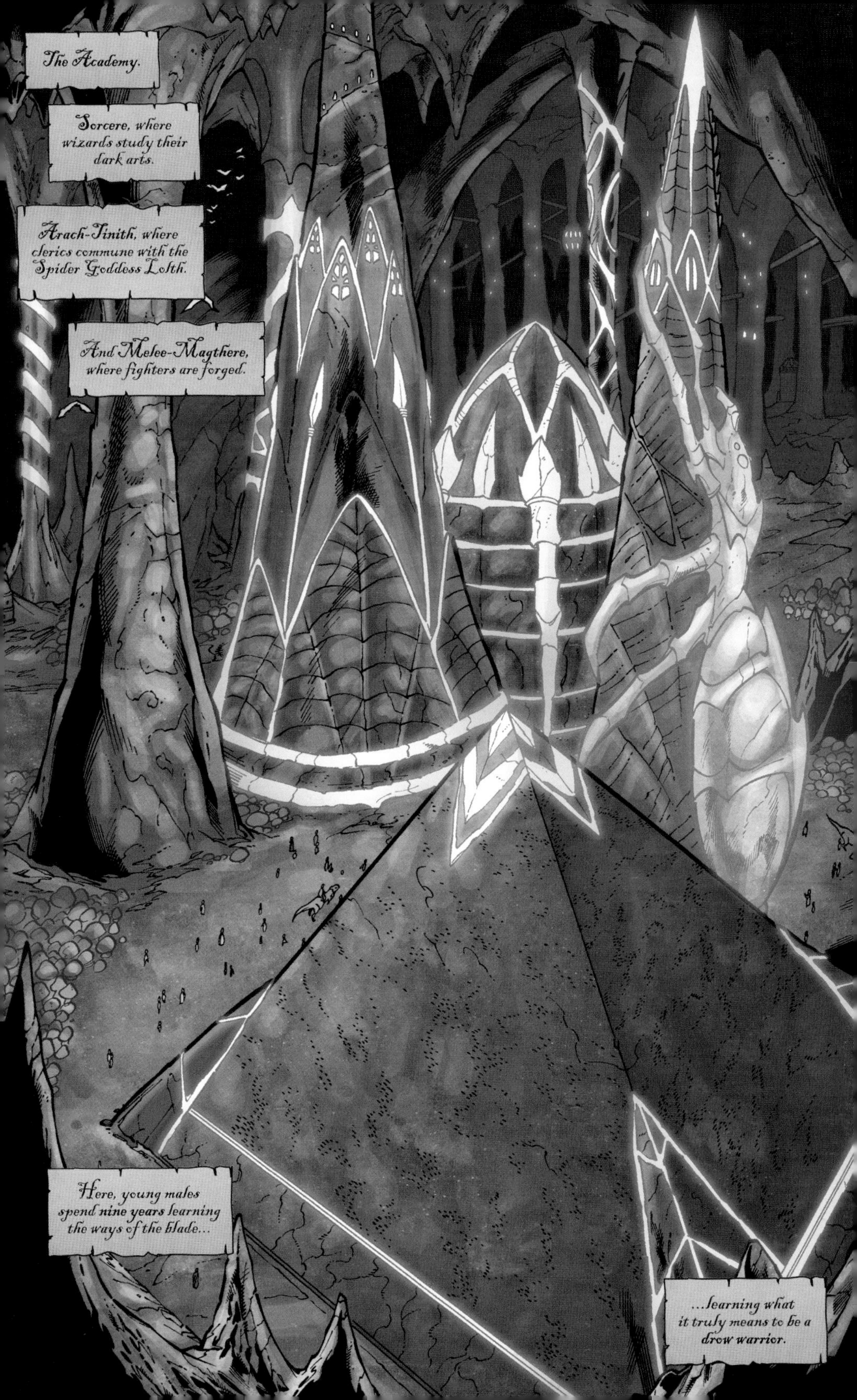
The Academy.
Sorcere, where wizards study their dark arts.
Arach-Tinith, where clerics commune with the Spider Goddess Lolth.
And Melee-Magthere, where fighters are forged.
Here, young males spend nine years learning the ways of the blade...
...learning what it truly means to be a drow warrior.

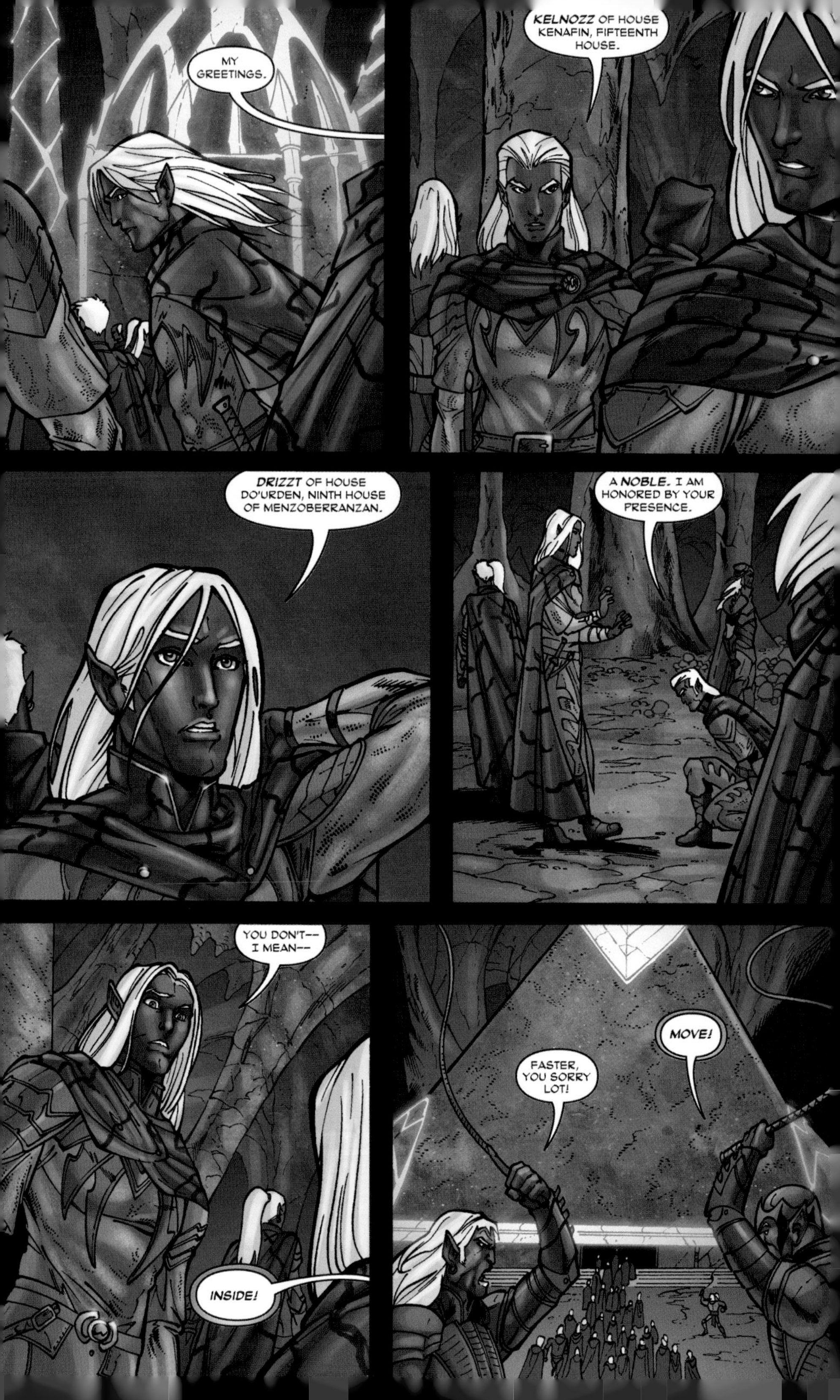
MY GREETINGS.
KELNOZZ OF HOUSE KENAFIN, FIFTEENTH HOUSE.
DRIZZT OF HOUSE DO'URDEN, NINTH HOUSE OF MENZOBERRANZAN.
A NOBLE. I AM HONORED BY YOUR PRESENCE.
YOU DON'T-- I MEAN--
INSIDE!
FASTER, YOU SORRY LOT!
MOVE!

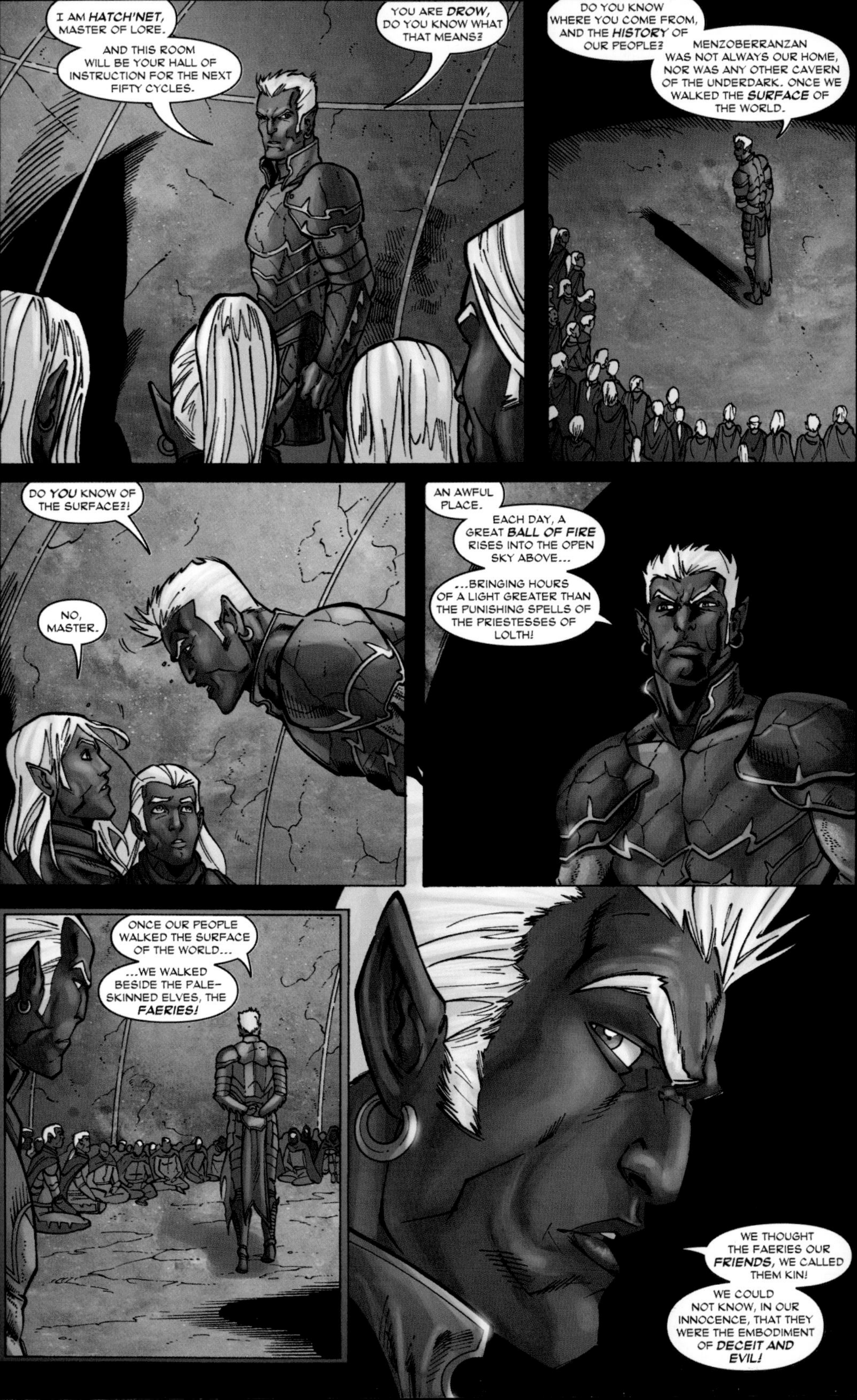
I AM HATCH'NET, MASTER OF LORE.
AND THIS ROOM WILL BE YOUR HALL OF INSTRUCTION FOR THE NEXT FIFTY CYCLES.
YOU ARE DROW, DO YOU KNOW WHAT THAT MEANS?
DO YOU KNOW WHERE YOU COME FROM, AND THE HISTORY OF OUR PEOPLE?
MENZOBERRANZAN WAS NOT ALWAYS OUR HOME, NOR WAS ANY OTHER CAVERN OF THE UNDERDARK. ONCE WE WALKED THE SURFACE OF THE WORLD.
DO YOU KNOW OF THE SURFACE?!
NO, MASTER.
AN AWFUL PLACE.
EACH DAY, A GREAT BALL OF FIRE RISES INTO THE OPEN SKY ABOVE...
...BRINGING HOURS OF A LIGHT GREATER THAN THE PUNISHING SPELLS OF THE PRIESTESSES OF LOLTH!
ONCE OUR PEOPLE WALKED THE SURFACE OF THE WORLD...
...WE WALKED BESIDE THE PALE-SKINNED ELVES, THE FAERIES!
WE THOUGHT THE FAERIES OUR FRIENDS, WE CALLED THEM KIN!
WE COULD NOT KNOW, IN OUR INNOCENCE, THAT THEY WERE THE EMBODIMENT OF DECEIT AND EVIL!

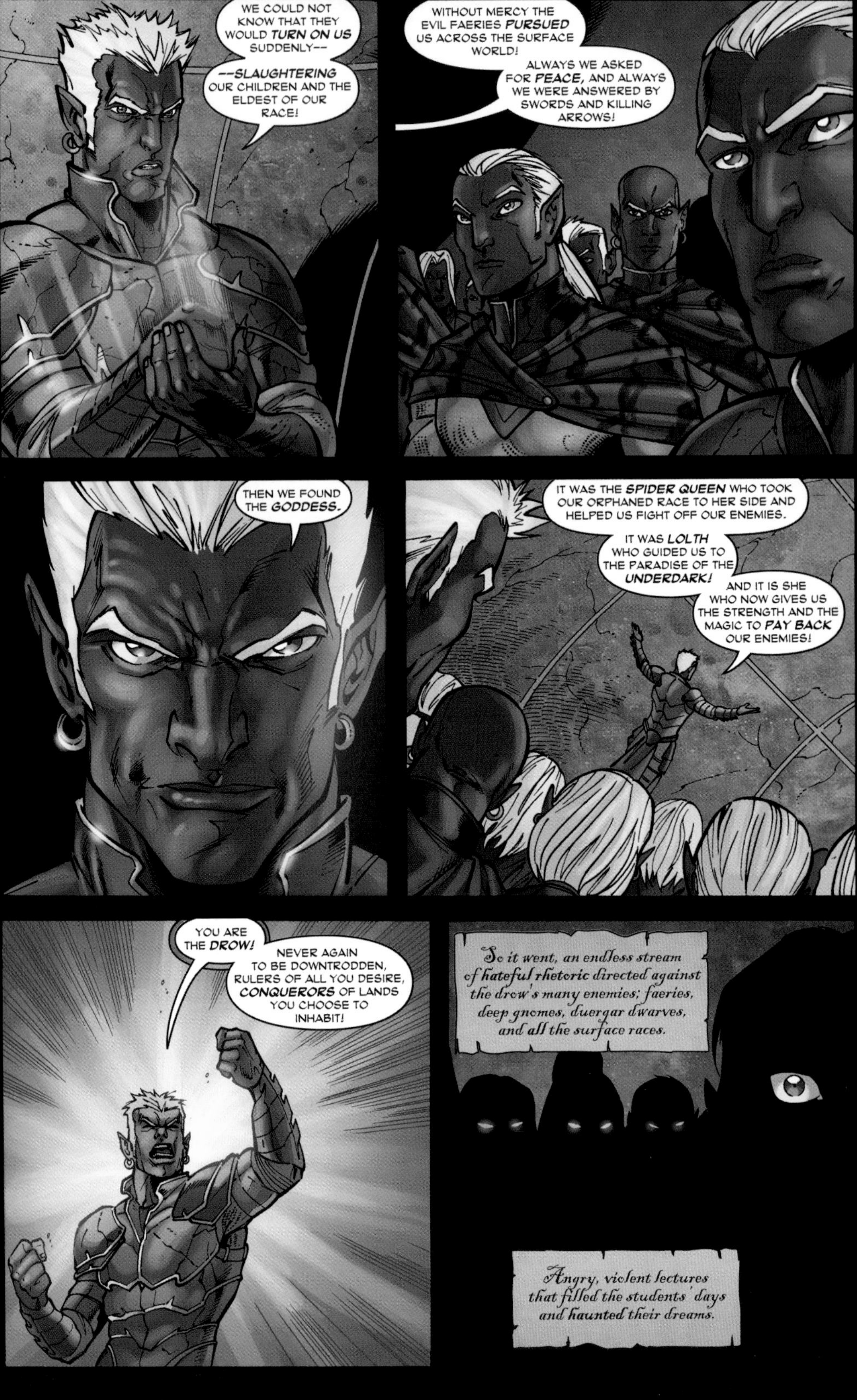
WE COULD NOT KNOW THAT THEY WOULD TURN ON US SUDDENLY--
--SLAUGHTERING OUR CHILDREN AND THE ELDEST OF OUR RACE!
WITHOUT MERCY THE EVIL FAERIES PURSUED US ACROSS THE SURFACE WORLD!
ALWAYS WE ASKED FOR PEACE, AND ALWAYS WE WERE ANSWERED BY SWORDS AND KILLING ARROWS!
THEN WE FOUND THE GODDESS.
IT WAS THE SPIDER QUEEN WHO TOOK OUR ORPHANED RACE TO HER SIDE AND HELPED US FIGHT OFF OUR ENEMIES.
IT WAS LOLTH WHO GUIDED US TO THE PARADISE OF THE UNDERDARK!
AND IT IS SHE WHO NOW GIVES US THE STRENGTH AND THE MAGIC TO PAY BACK OUR ENEMIES!
YOU ARE THE DROW!
NEVER AGAIN TO BE DOWNTRODDEN, RULERS OF ALL YOU DESIRE, CONQUERORS OF LANDS YOU CHOOSE TO INHABIT!
So it went, an endless stream of hateful rhetoric directed against the drow's many enemies; faeries, deep gnomes, duergar dwarves, and all the surface races.
Angry, violent lectures that filled the students' days and haunted their dreams.

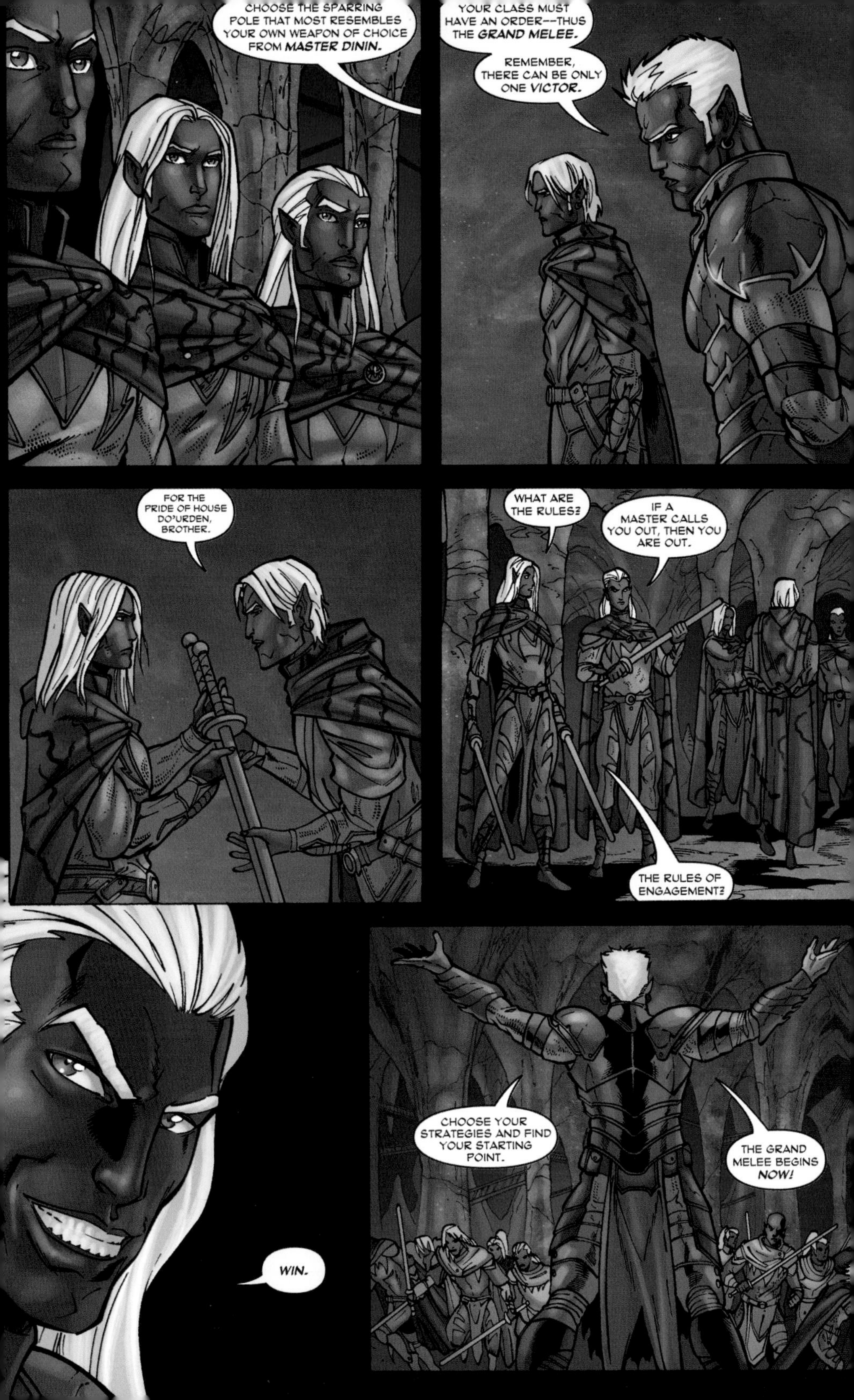
CHOOSE THE SPARRING POLE THAT MOST RESEMBLES YOUR OWN WEAPON OF CHOICE FROM MASTER DININ.
YOUR CLASS MUST HAVE AN ORDER--THUS THE GRAND MELEE.
REMEMBER, THERE CAN BE ONLY ONE VICTOR.
FOR THE PRIDE OF HOUSE DO'URDEN, BROTHER.
WHAT ARE THE RULES?
IF A MASTER CALLS YOU OUT, THEN YOU ARE OUT.
THE RULES OF ENGAGEMENT?
WIN.
CHOOSE YOUR STRATEGIES AND FIND YOUR STARTING POINT.
THE GRAND MELEE BEGINS NOW!

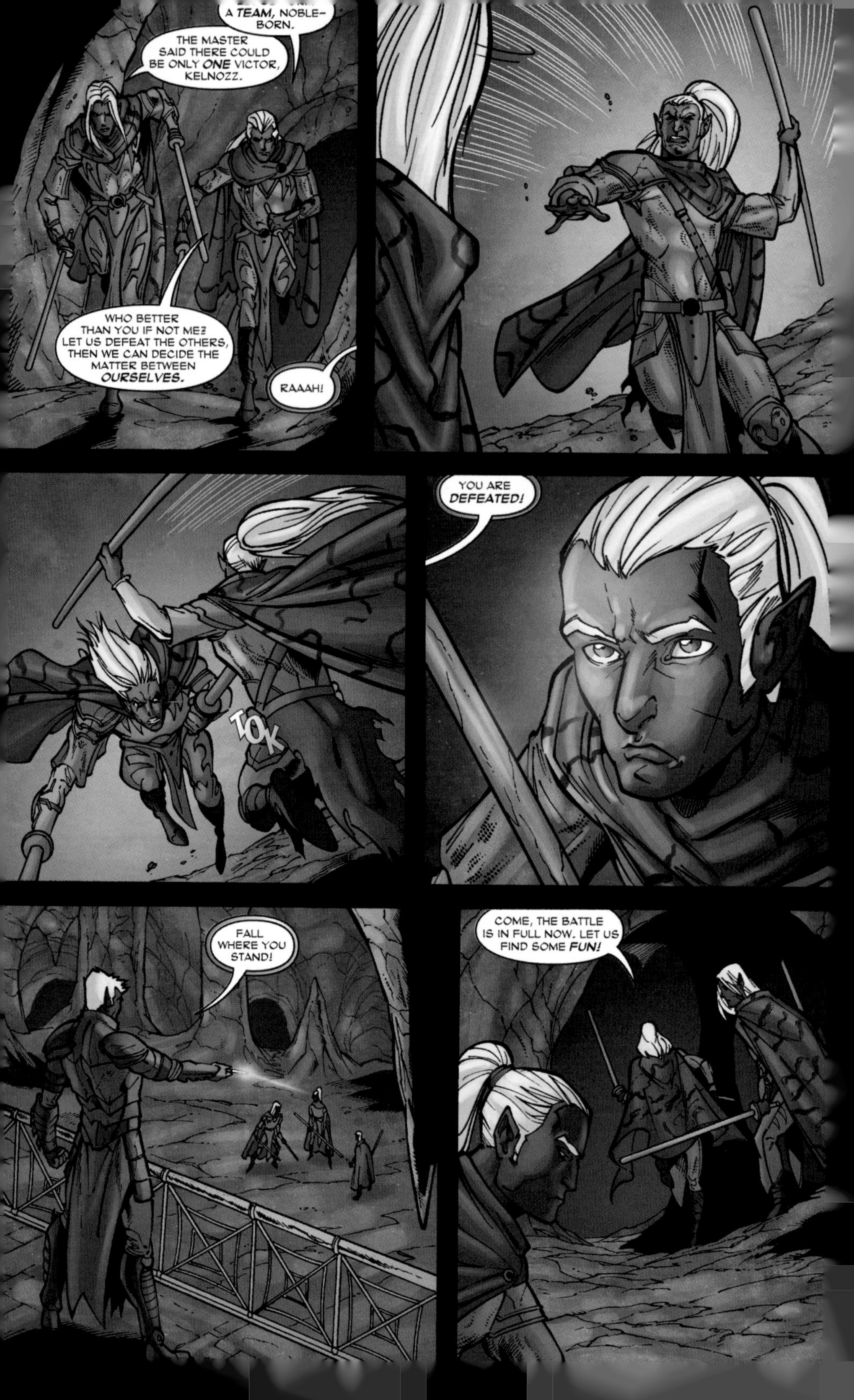
A TEAM, NOBLE-BORN.
THE MASTER SAID THERE COULD BE ONLY ONE VICTOR, KELNOZZ.
WHO BETTER THAN YOU IF NOT ME? LET US DEFEAT THE OTHERS, THEN WE CAN DECIDE THE MATTER BETWEEN OURSELVES.
RAAAH!
TOK
YOU ARE DEFEATED!
FALL WHERE YOU STAND!
COME, THE BATTLE IS IN FULL NOW. LET US FIND SOME FUN!

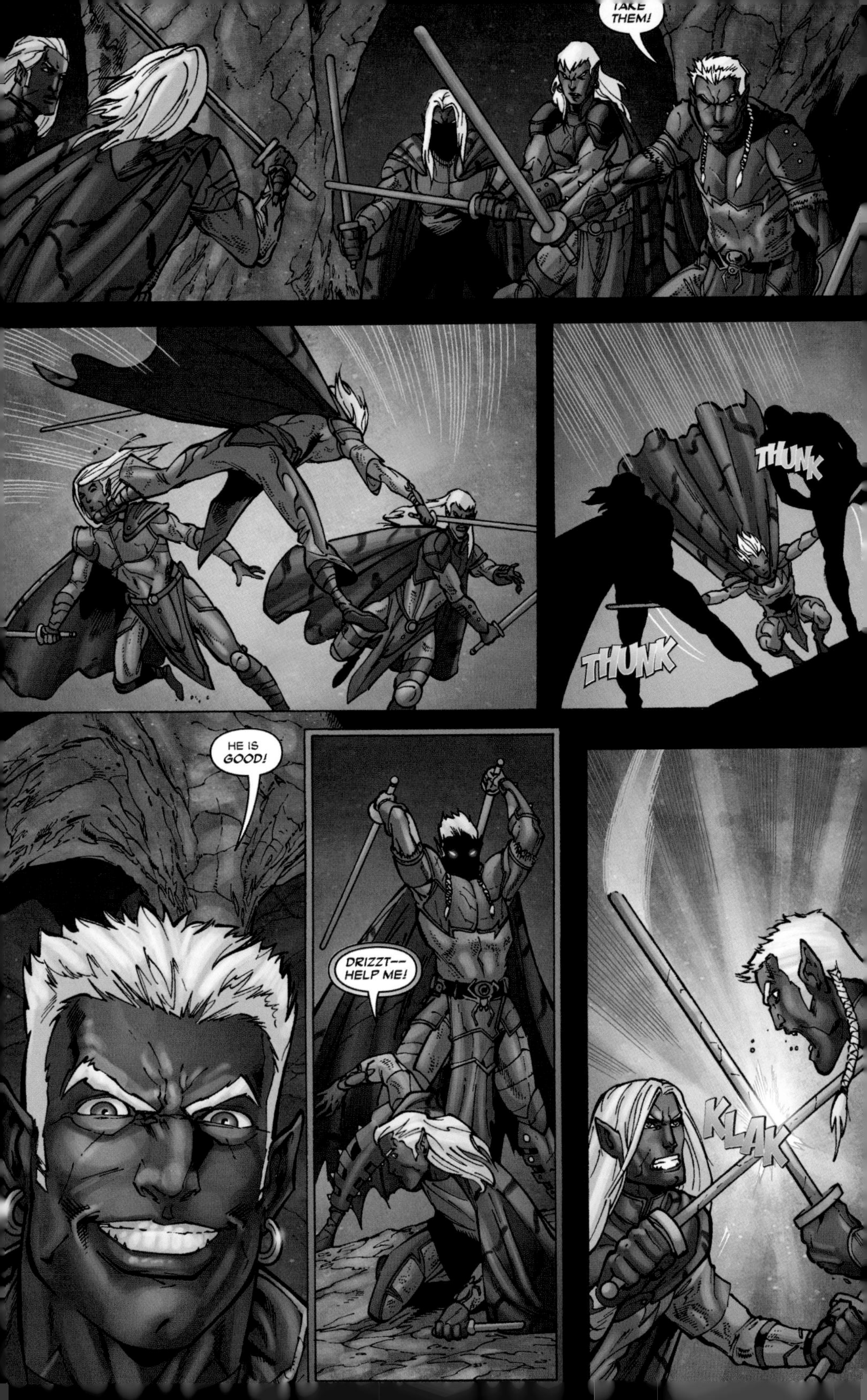
TAKE THEM!
THUNK
THUNK
HE IS GOOD!
DRIZZT-- HELP ME!
KLAK

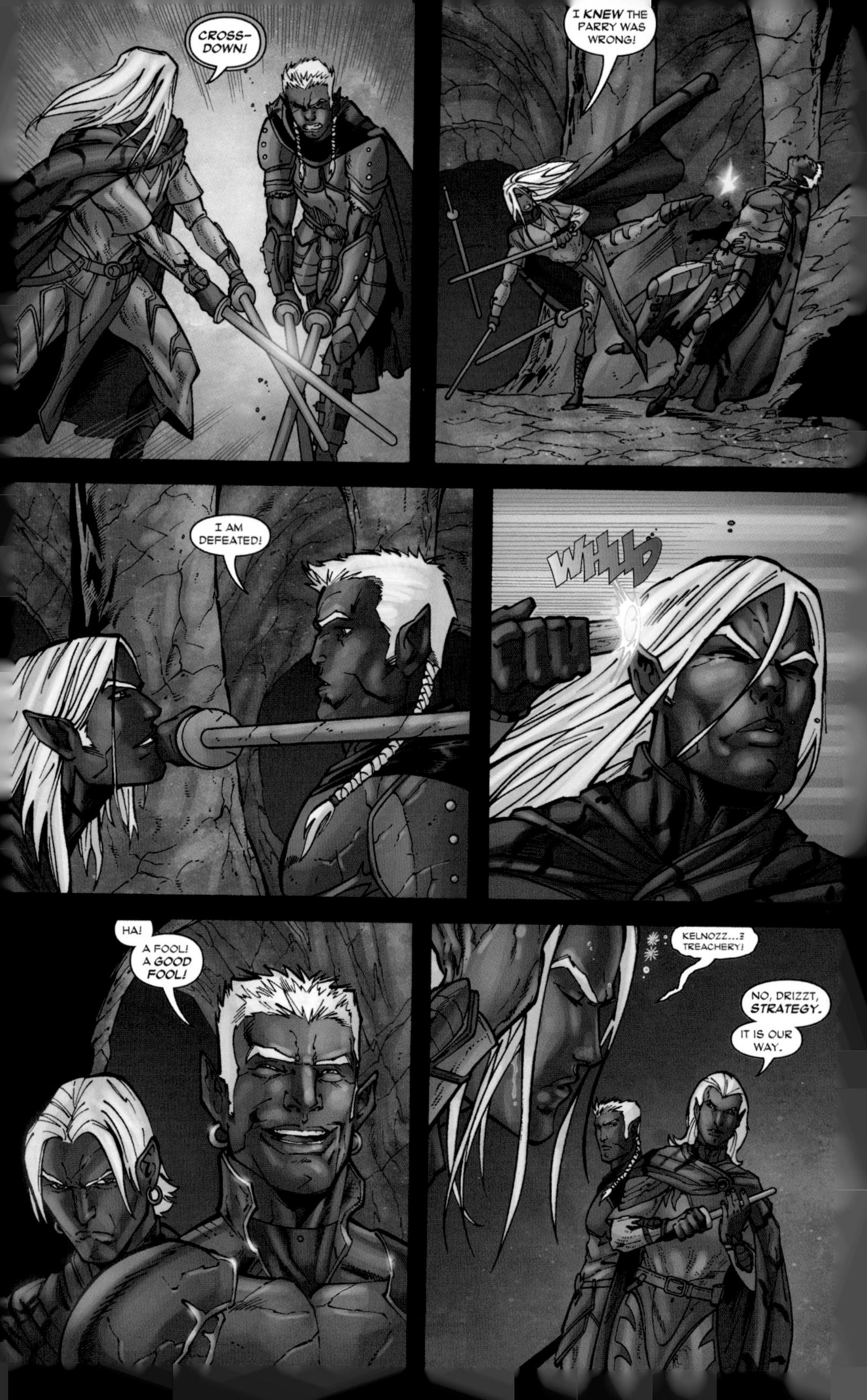
CROSS-DOWN!
I KNEW THE PARRY WAS WRONG!
I AM DEFEATED!
WHUD
HA!
A FOOL! A GOOD FOOL!
KELNOZZ...? TREACHERY!
NO, DRIZZT, STRATEGY.
IT IS OUR WAY.

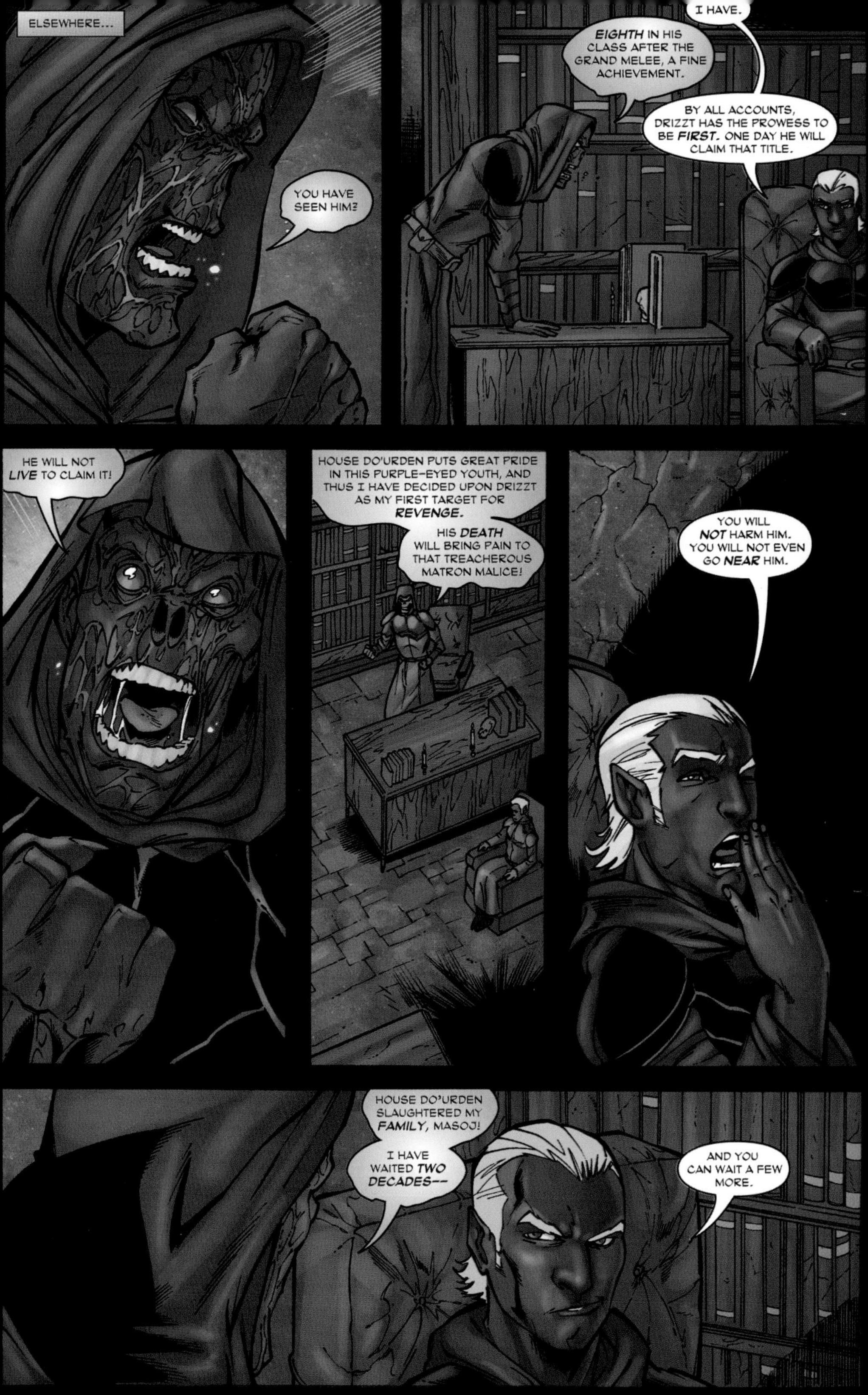
ELSEWHERE...
YOU HAVE SEEN HIM?
I HAVE.
EIGHTH IN HIS CLASS AFTER THE GRAND MELEE, A FINE ACHIEVEMENT.
BY ALL ACCOUNTS, DRIZZT HAS THE PROWESS TO BE FIRST. ONE DAY HE WILL CLAIM THAT TITLE.
HE WILL NOT LIVE TO CLAIM IT!
HOUSE DO'URDEN PUTS GREAT PRIDE IN THIS PURPLE-EYED YOUTH, AND THUS I HAVE DECIDED UPON DRIZZT AS MY FIRST TARGET FOR REVENGE.
HIS DEATH WILL BRING PAIN TO THAT TREACHEROUS MATRON MALICE!
YOU WILL NOT HARM HIM. YOU WILL NOT EVEN GO NEAR HIM.
HOUSE DO'URDEN SLAUGHTERED MY FAMILY, MASOJ!
I HAVE WAITED TWO DECADES--
AND YOU CAN WAIT A FEW MORE.

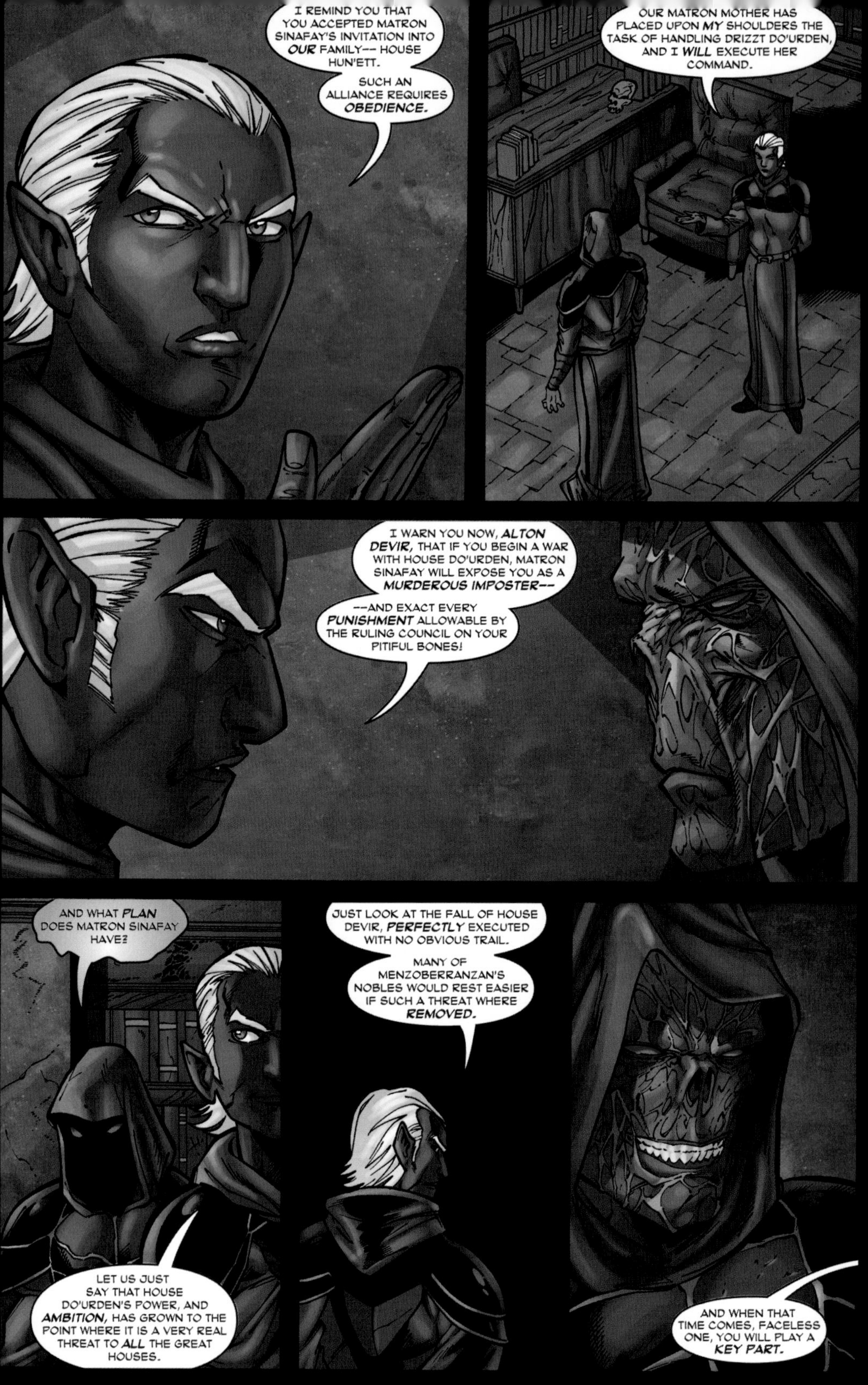
I REMIND YOU THAT YOU ACCEPTED MATRON SINAFAY'S INVITATION INTO *OUR* FAMILY-- HOUSE HUN'ETT.
SUCH AN ALLIANCE REQUIRES *OBEDIENCE.*
OUR MATRON MOTHER HAS PLACED UPON *MY* SHOULDERS THE TASK OF HANDLING DRIZZT DO'URDEN, AND I *WILL* EXECUTE HER COMMAND.
I WARN YOU NOW, *ALTON DEVIR,* THAT IF YOU BEGIN A WAR WITH HOUSE DO'URDEN, MATRON SINAFAY WILL EXPOSE YOU AS A *MURDEROUS IMPOSTER--*
--AND EXACT EVERY *PUNISHMENT* ALLOWABLE BY THE RULING COUNCIL ON YOUR PITIFUL BONES!
AND WHAT *PLAN* DOES MATRON SINAFAY HAVE?
LET US JUST SAY THAT HOUSE DO'URDEN'S POWER, AND *AMBITION,* HAS GROWN TO THE POINT WHERE IT IS A VERY REAL THREAT TO *ALL* THE GREAT HOUSES.
JUST LOOK AT THE FALL OF HOUSE DEVIR, *PERFECTLY* EXECUTED WITH NO OBVIOUS TRAIL.
MANY OF MENZOBERRANZAN'S NOBLES WOULD REST EASIER IF SUCH A THREAT WHERE *REMOVED.*
AND WHEN THAT TIME COMES, FACELESS ONE, YOU WILL PLAY A *KEY PART.*

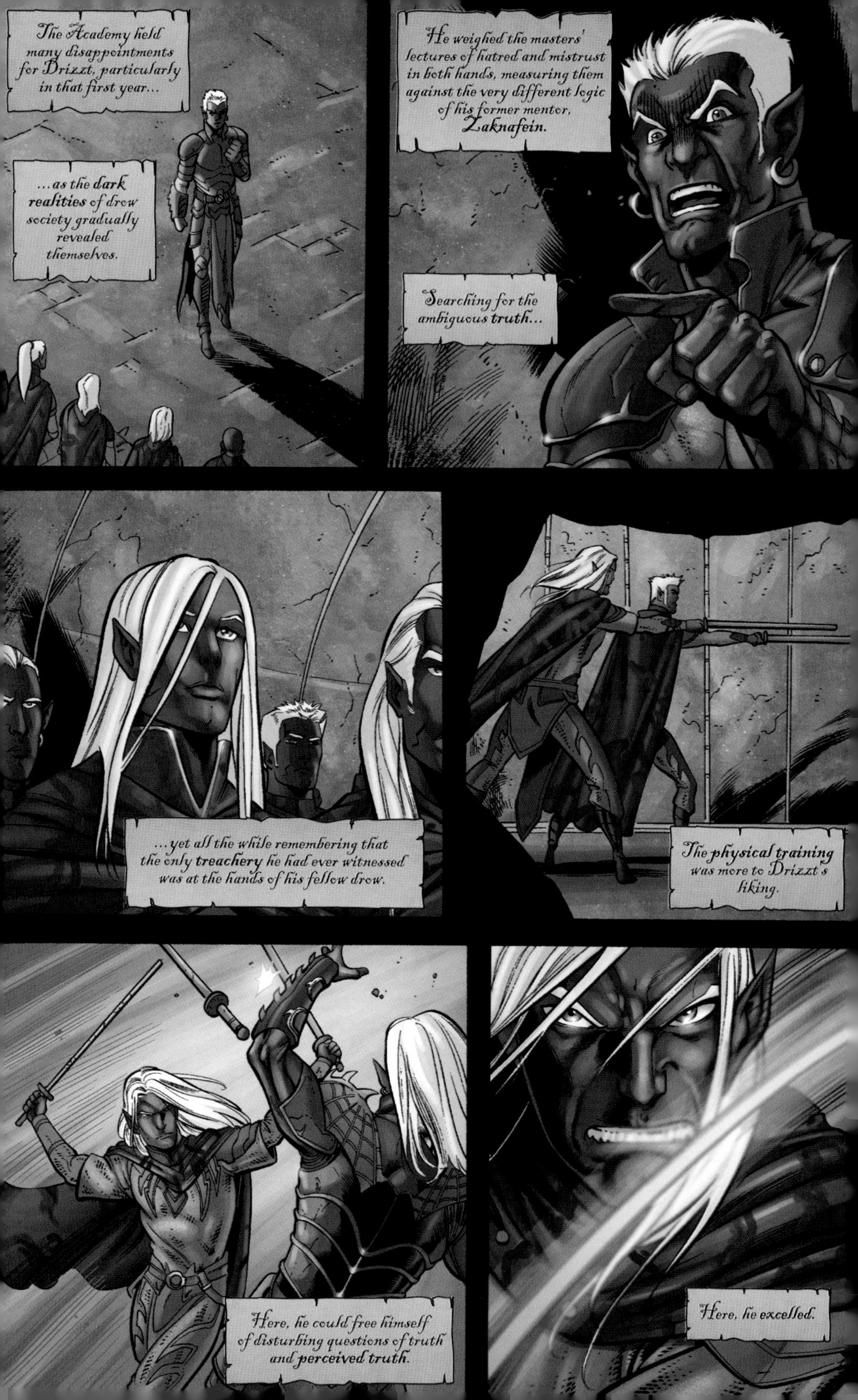
The Academy held many disappointments for Drizzt, particularly in that first year...
...as the dark realities of drow society gradually revealed themselves.
He weighed the masters' lectures of hatred and mistrust in both hands, measuring them against the very different logic of his former mentor, Zaknafein.
Searching for the ambiguous truth...
...yet all the while remembering that the only treachery he had ever witnessed was at the hands of his fellow drow.
The physical training was more to Drizzt's liking.
Here, he could free himself of disturbing questions of truth and perceived truth.
Here, he excelled.

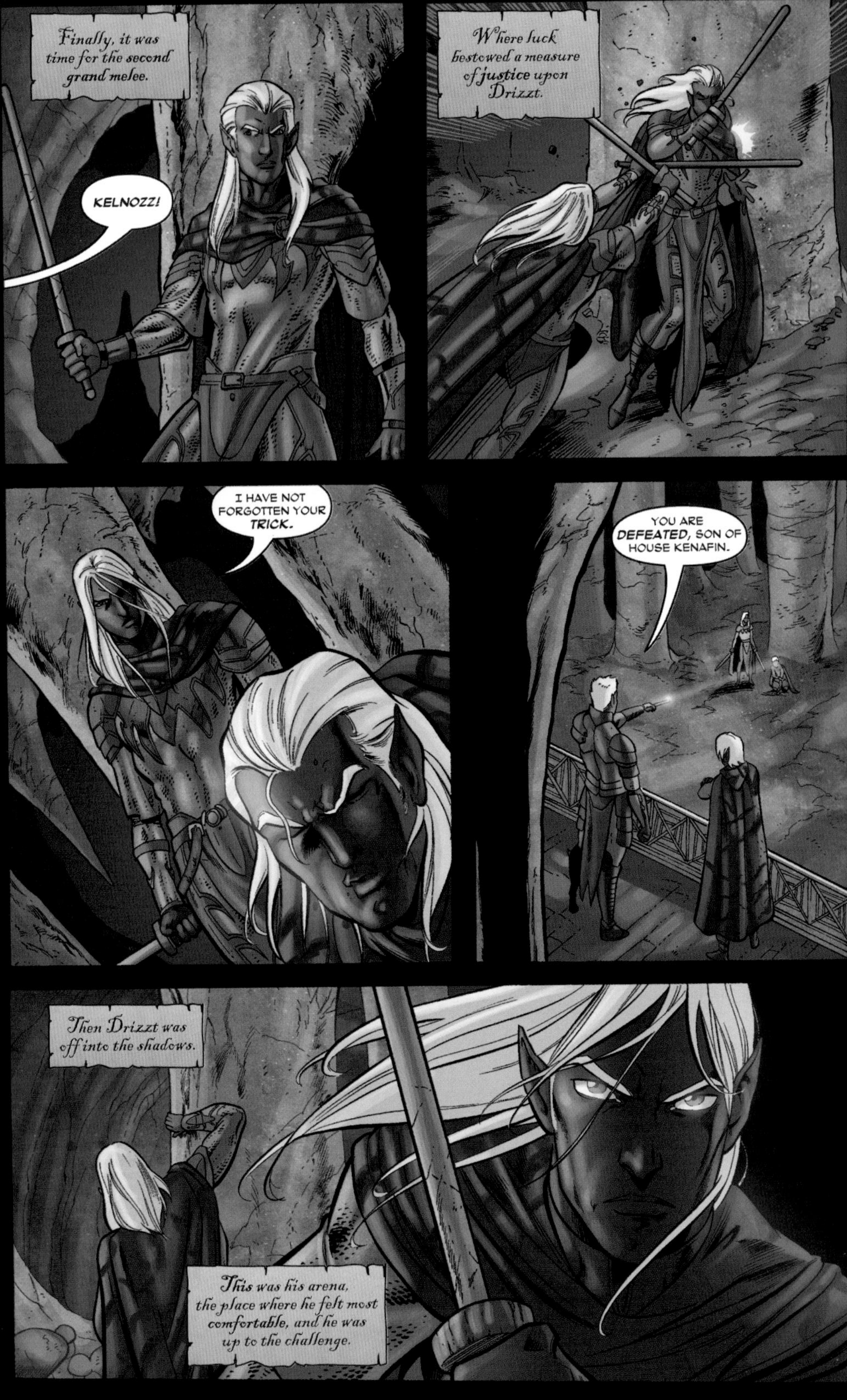
Finally, it was time for the second grand melee.
KELNOZZ!
Where luck bestowed a measure of justice upon Drizzt.
I HAVE NOT FORGOTTEN YOUR TRICK.
YOU ARE DEFEATED, SON OF HOUSE KENAFIN.
Then Drizzt was off into the shadows.
This was his arena, the place where he felt most comfortable, and he was up to the challenge.

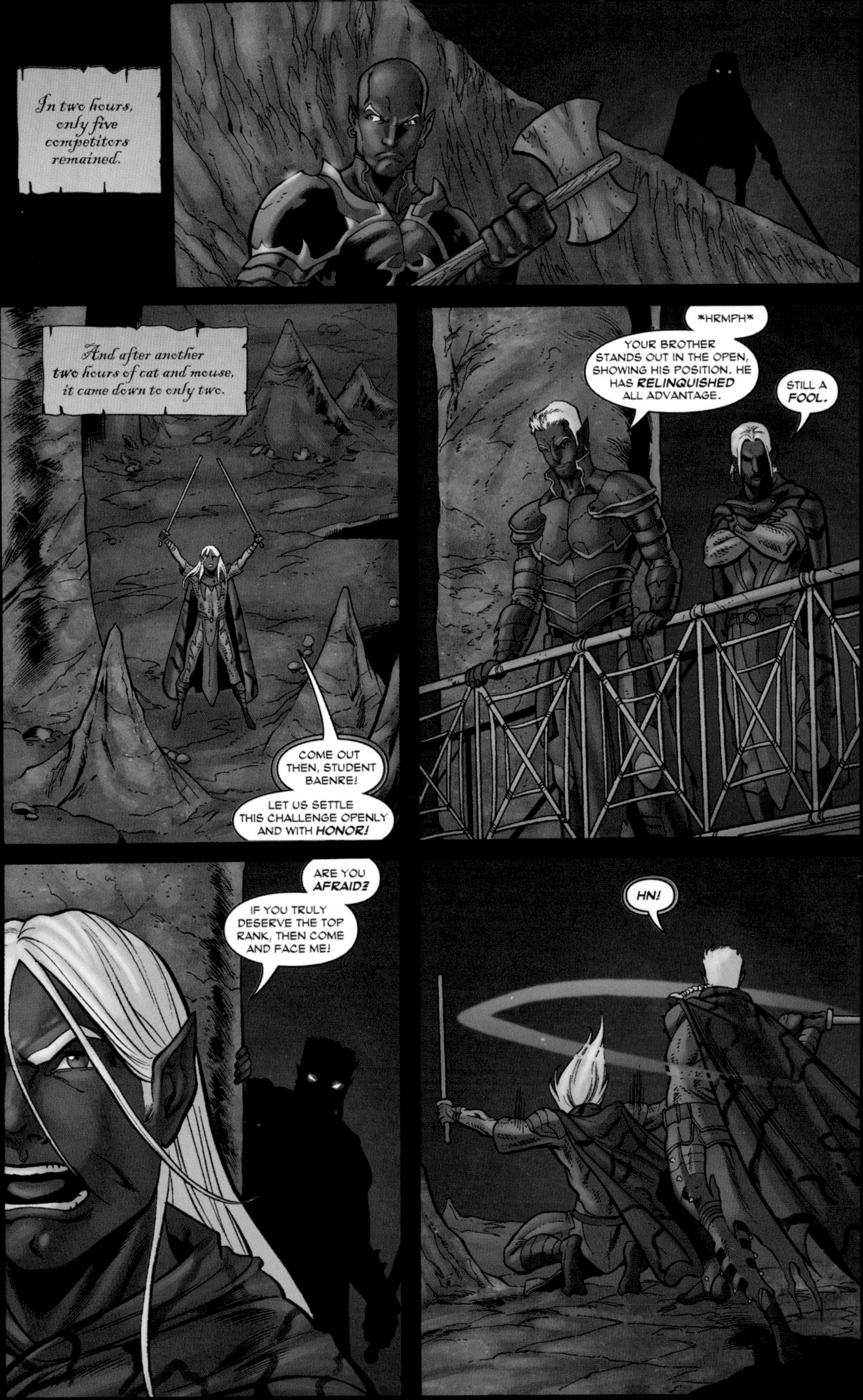
In two hours, only five competitors remained.
And after another two hours of cat and mouse, it came down to only two.
COME OUT THEN, STUDENT BAENRE!
LET US SETTLE THIS CHALLENGE OPENLY AND WITH HONOR!
HRMPH
YOUR BROTHER STANDS OUT IN THE OPEN, SHOWING HIS POSITION. HE HAS RELINQUISHED ALL ADVANTAGE.
STILL A FOOL.
ARE YOU AFRAID?
IF YOU TRULY DESERVE THE TOP RANK, THEN COME AND FACE ME!
HN!

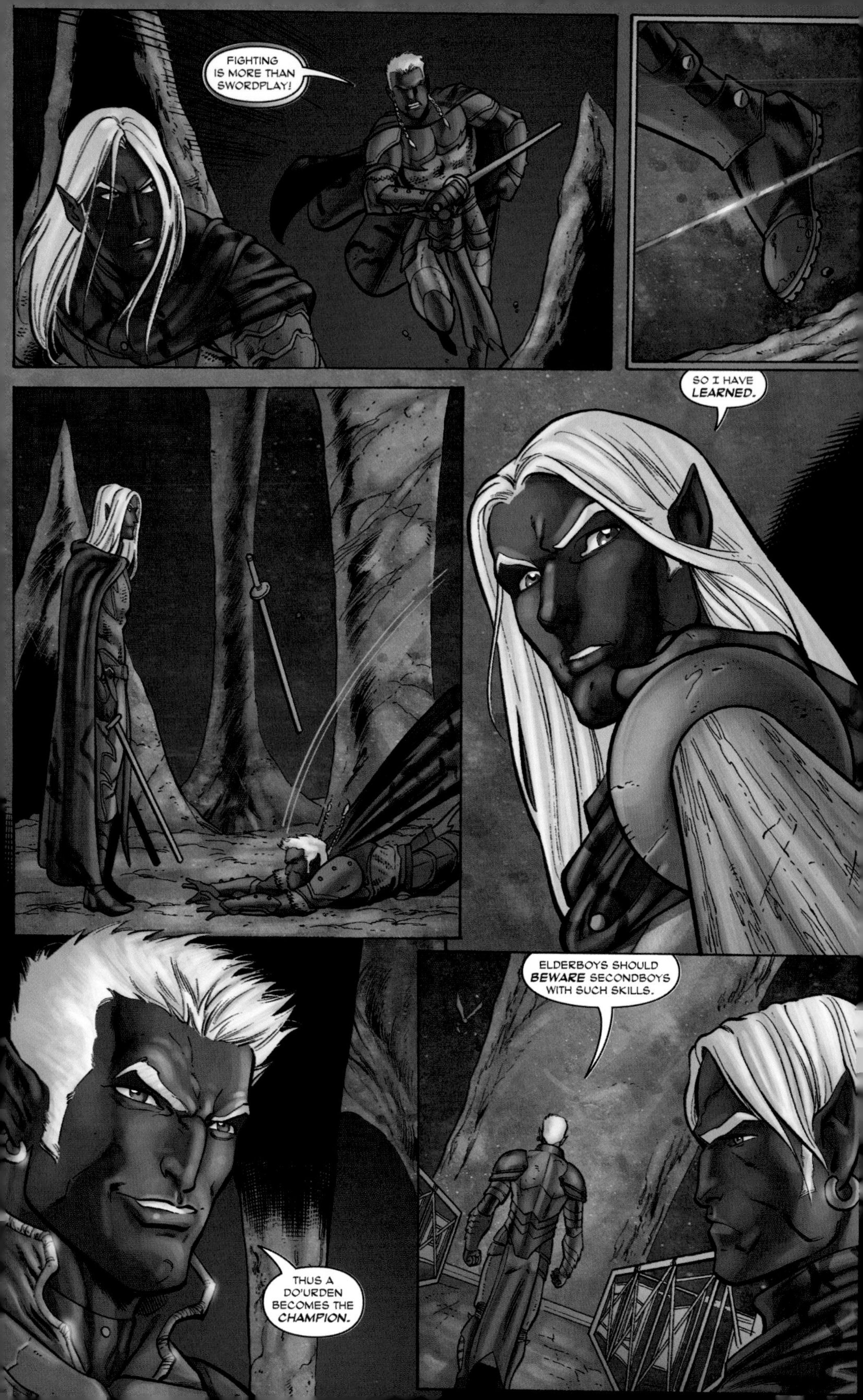
FIGHTING IS MORE THAN SWORDPLAY!
SO I HAVE LEARNED.
THUS A DO'URDEN BECOMES THE CHAMPION.
ELDERBOYS SHOULD BEWARE SECONDBOYS WITH SUCH SKILLS.

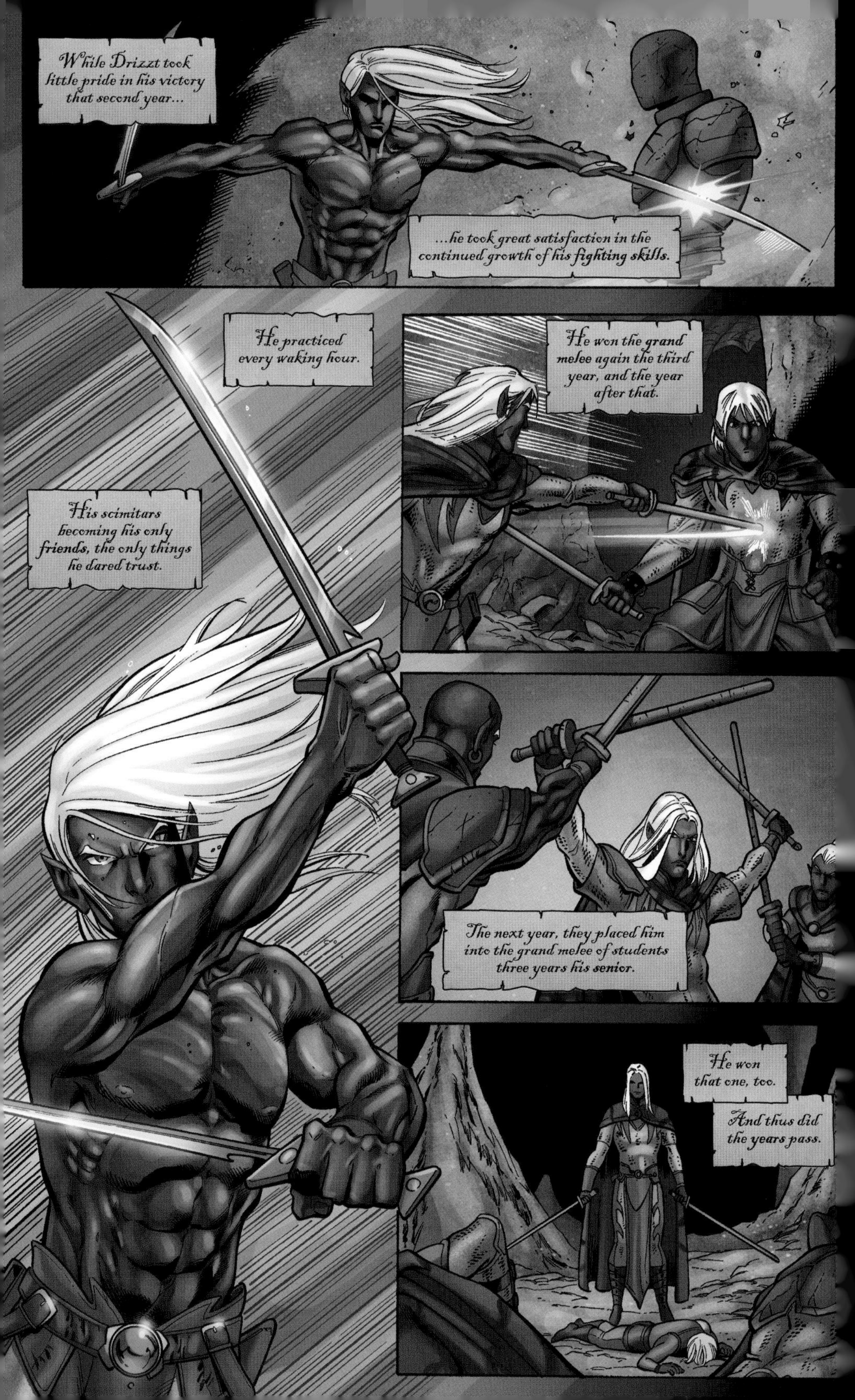
While Drizzt took little pride in his victory that second year...
...he took great satisfaction in the continued growth of his fighting skills.
He practiced every waking hour.
His scimitars becoming his only friends, the only things he dared trust.
He won the grand melee again the third year, and the year after that.
The next year, they placed him into the grand melee of students three years his senior.
He won that one, too.
And thus did the years pass.

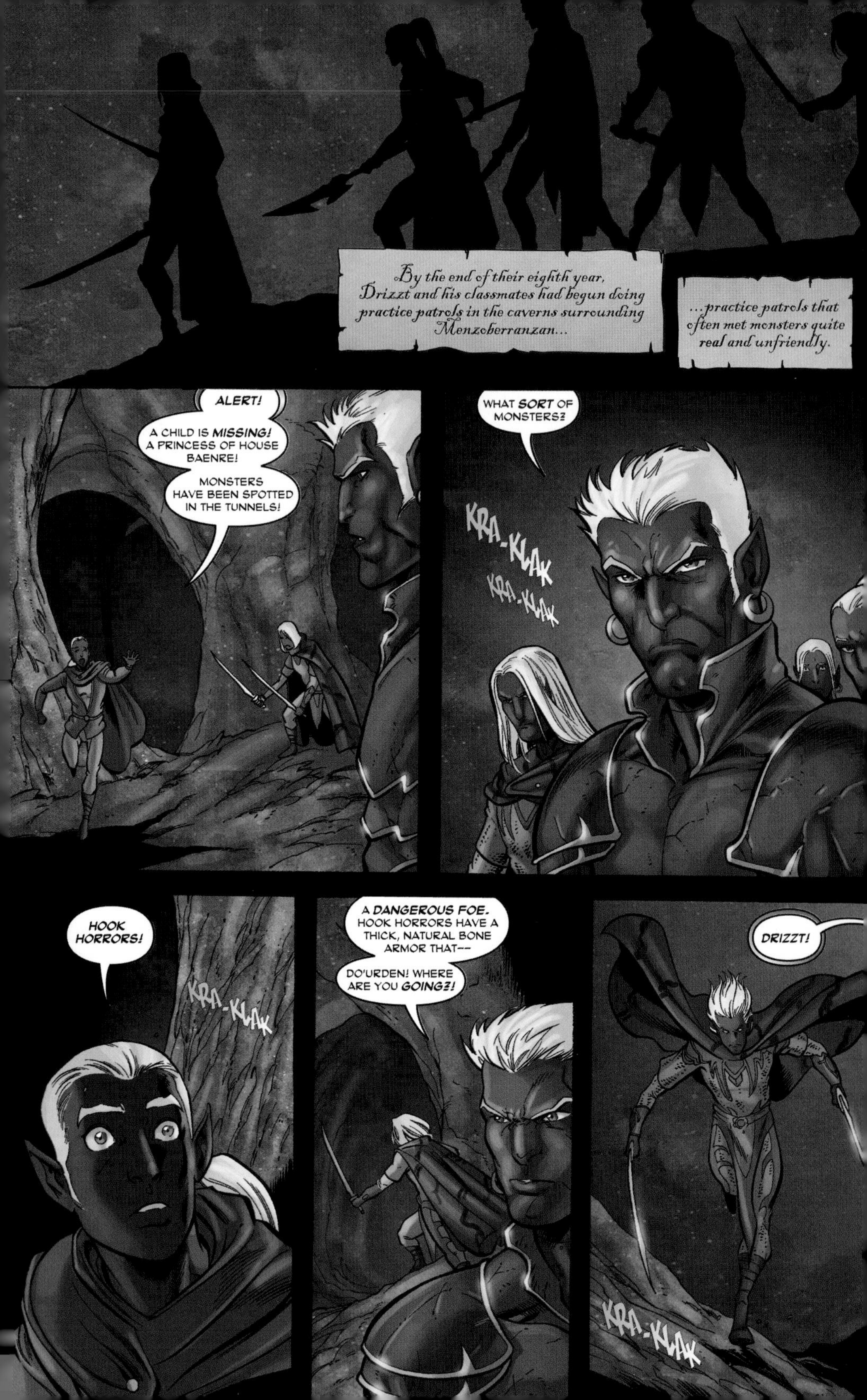
By the end of their eighth year, Drizzt and his classmates had begun doing practice patrols in the caverns surrounding Menzoberranzan...
...practice patrols that often met monsters quite real and unfriendly.
ALERT!
A CHILD IS MISSING! A PRINCESS OF HOUSE BAENRE!
MONSTERS HAVE BEEN SPOTTED IN THE TUNNELS!
WHAT SORT OF MONSTERS?
KRA-KLAK
KRA-KLAK
HOOK HORRORS!
KRA-KLAK
A DANGEROUS FOE. HOOK HORRORS HAVE A THICK, NATURAL BONE ARMOR THAT--
DO'URDEN! WHERE ARE YOU GOING?!
DRIZZT!
KRA-KLAK

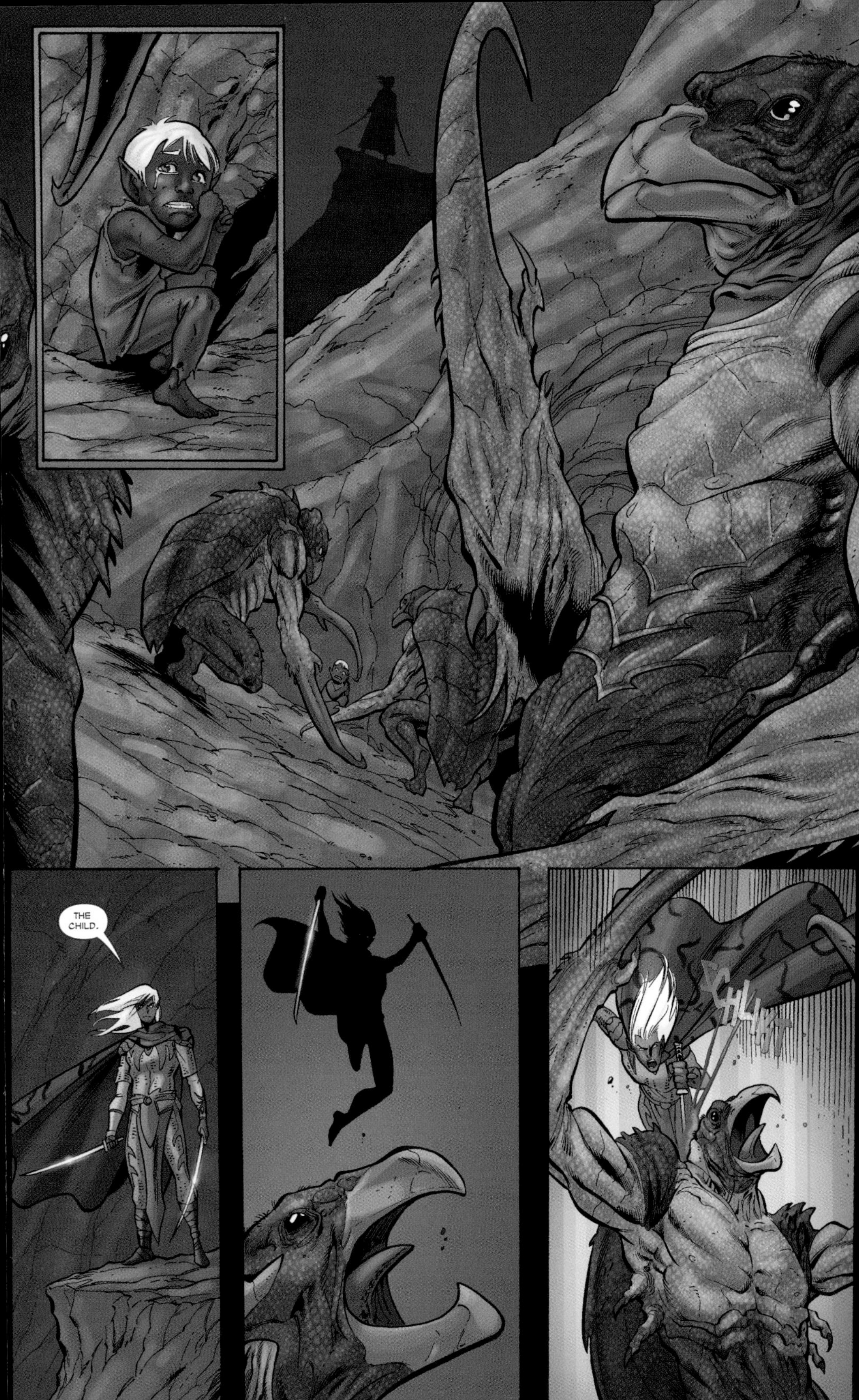
THE CHILD.
SCHLIKT

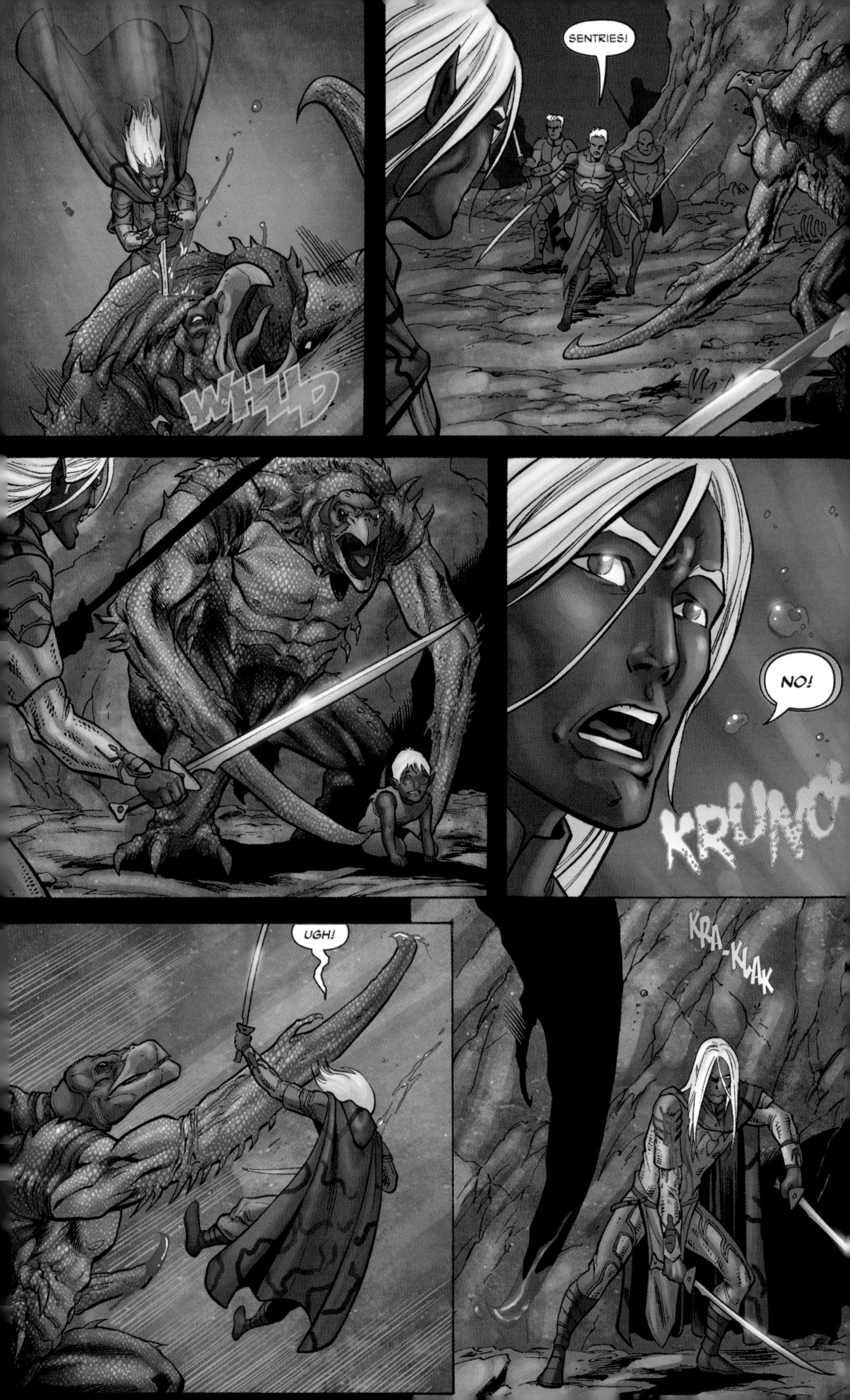
WHUD
SENTRIES!
NO!
KRUNQ
UGH!
KRA-KWAK

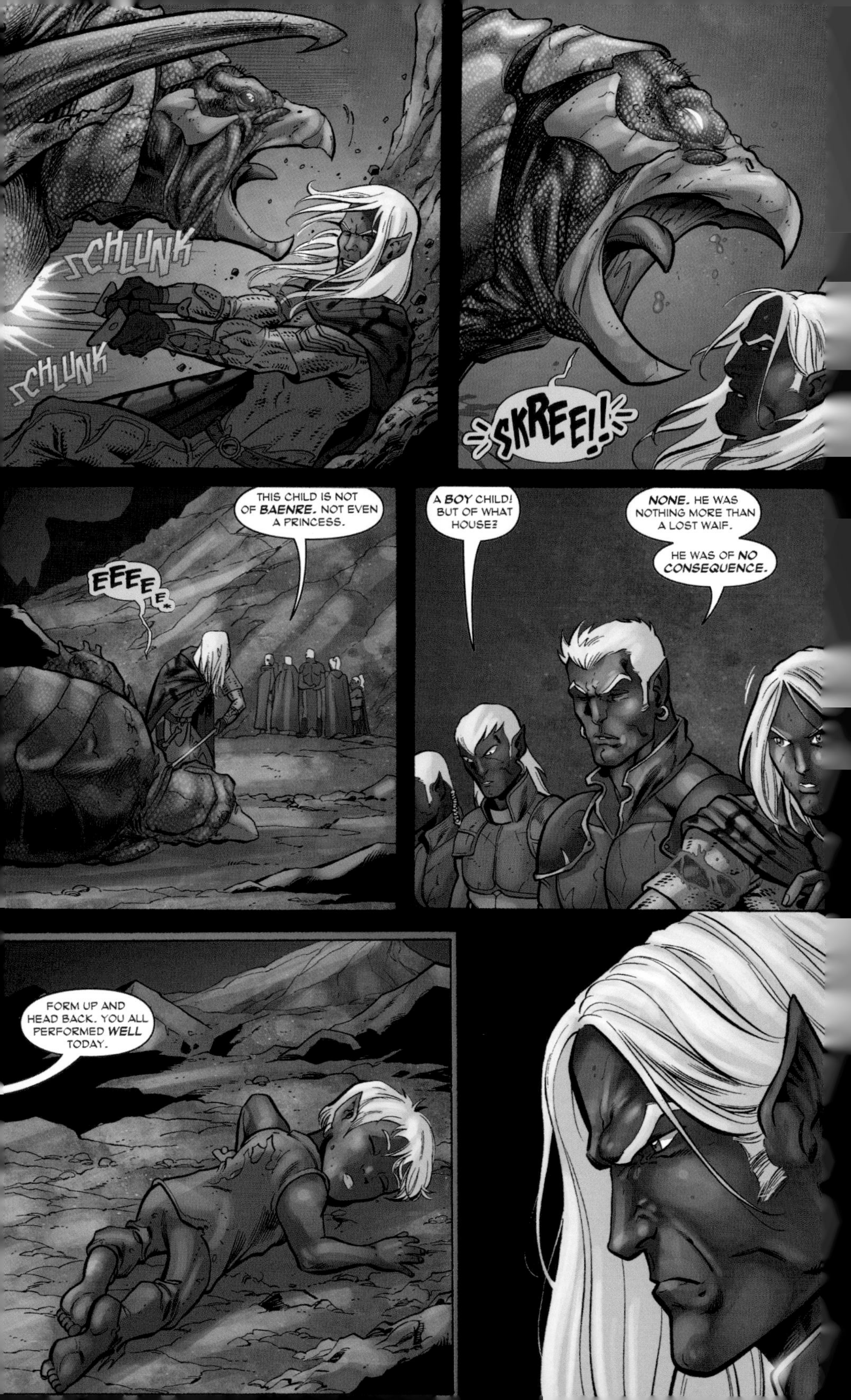
SCHLUNK
SCHLUNK
SKREE!!
THIS CHILD IS NOT OF BAENRE. NOT EVEN A PRINCESS.
EEEEE
A BOY CHILD! BUT OF WHAT HOUSE?
NONE. HE WAS NOTHING MORE THAN A LOST WAIF.
HE WAS OF NO CONSEQUENCE.
FORM UP AND HEAD BACK. YOU ALL PERFORMED WELL TODAY.

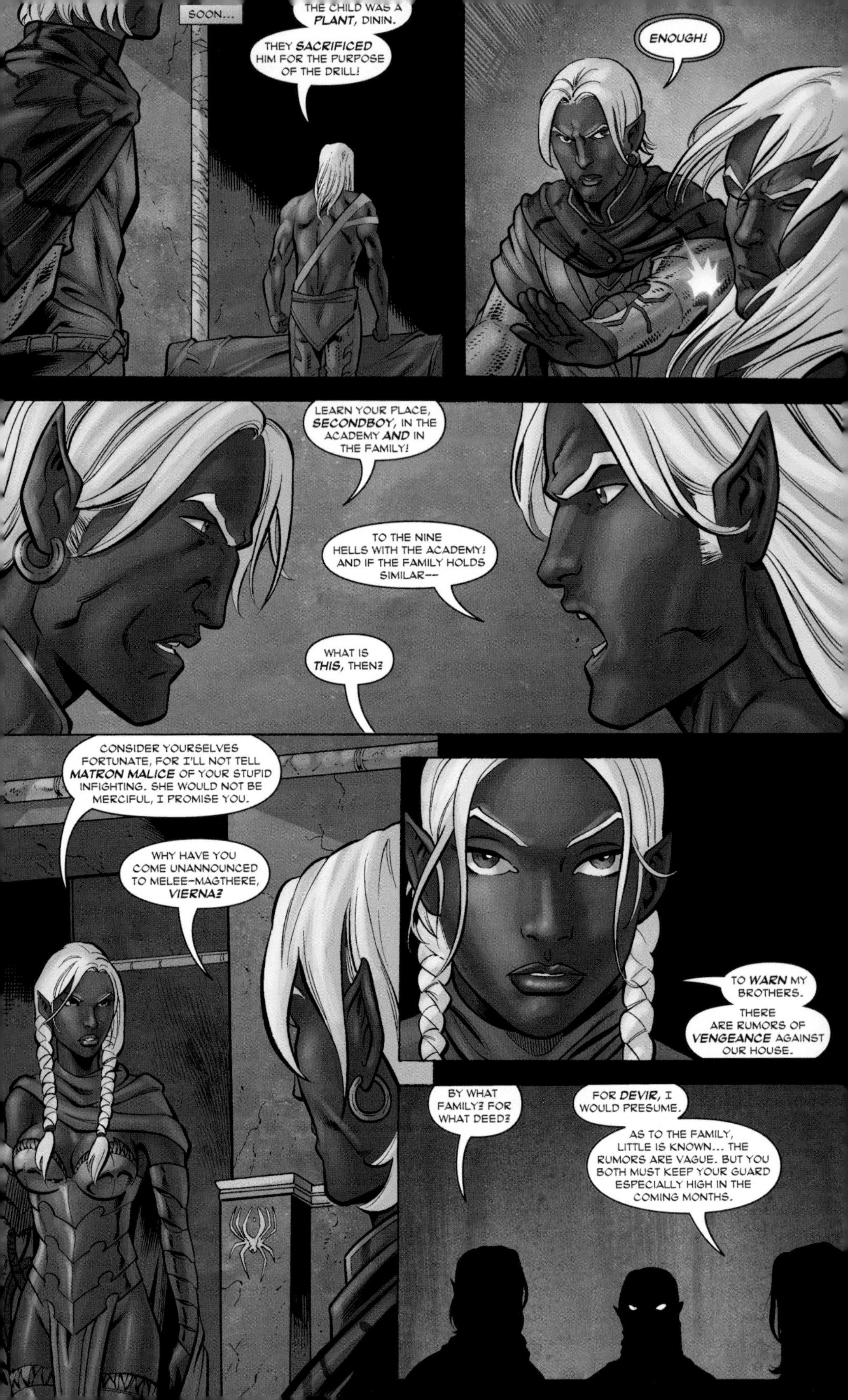
SOON...
THE CHILD WAS A PLANT, DININ.
THEY SACRIFICED HIM FOR THE PURPOSE OF THE DRILL!
ENOUGH!
LEARN YOUR PLACE, SECONDBOY, IN THE ACADEMY AND IN THE FAMILY!
TO THE NINE HELLS WITH THE ACADEMY! AND IF THE FAMILY HOLDS SIMILAR--
WHAT IS THIS, THEN?
CONSIDER YOURSELVES FORTUNATE, FOR I'LL NOT TELL MATRON MALICE OF YOUR STUPID INFIGHTING. SHE WOULD NOT BE MERCIFUL, I PROMISE YOU.
WHY HAVE YOU COME UNANNOUNCED TO MELEE-MAGTHERE, VIERNA?
TO WARN MY BROTHERS.
THERE ARE RUMORS OF VENGEANCE AGAINST OUR HOUSE.
BY WHAT FAMILY? FOR WHAT DEED?
FOR DEVIR, I WOULD PRESUME.
AS TO THE FAMILY, LITTLE IS KNOWN... THE RUMORS ARE VAGUE. BUT YOU BOTH MUST KEEP YOUR GUARD ESPECIALLY HIGH IN THE COMING MONTHS.

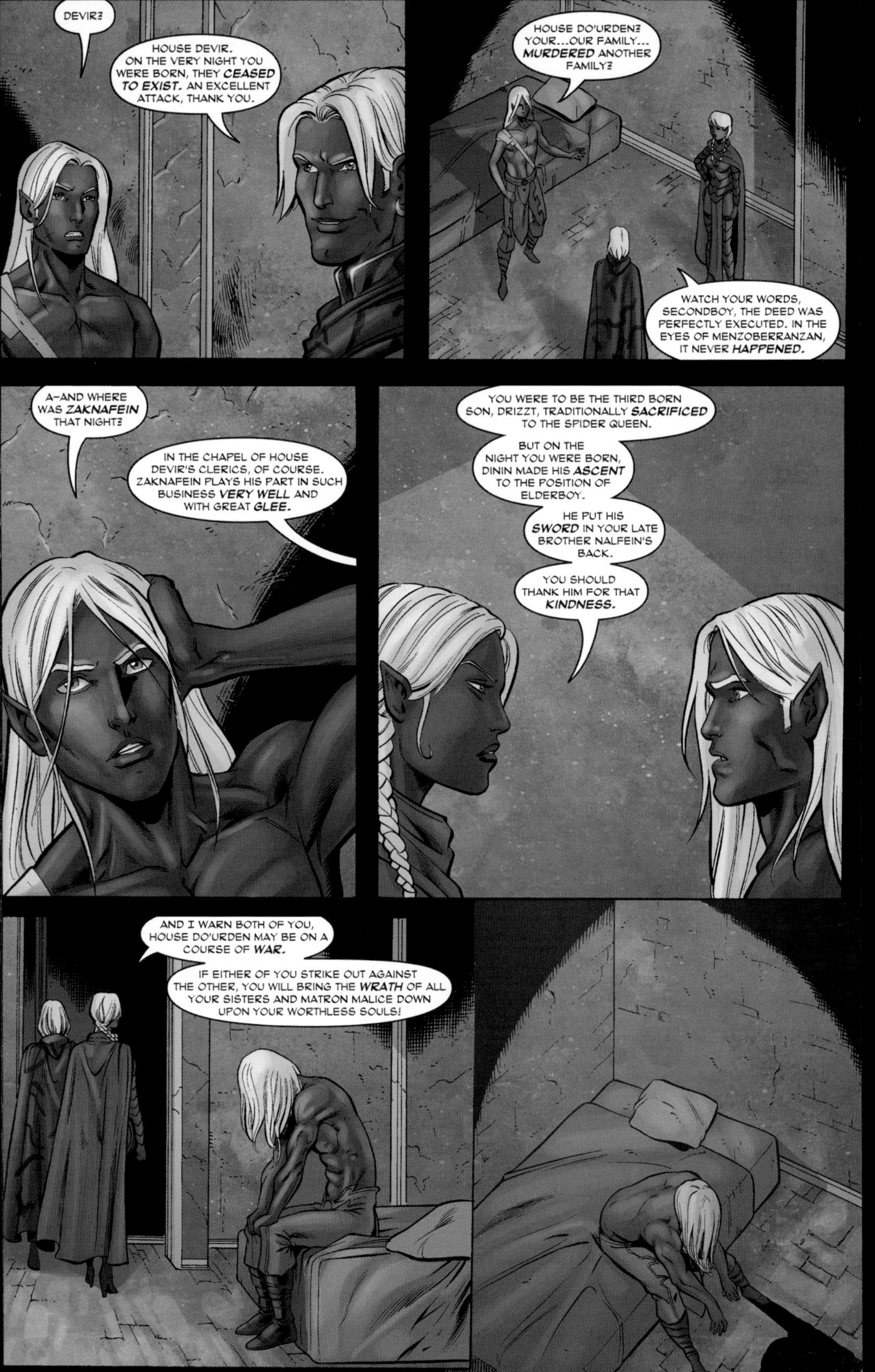
DEVIR?
HOUSE DEVIR. ON THE VERY NIGHT YOU WERE BORN, THEY CEASED TO EXIST. AN EXCELLENT ATTACK, THANK YOU.
HOUSE DO'URDEN? YOUR...OUR FAMILY... MURDERED ANOTHER FAMILY?
WATCH YOUR WORDS, SECONDBOY, THE DEED WAS PERFECTLY EXECUTED. IN THE EYES OF MENZOBERRANZAN, IT NEVER HAPPENED.
A-AND WHERE WAS ZAKNAFEIN THAT NIGHT?
IN THE CHAPEL OF HOUSE DEVIR'S CLERICS, OF COURSE. ZAKNAFEIN PLAYS HIS PART IN SUCH BUSINESS VERY WELL AND WITH GREAT GLEE.
YOU WERE TO BE THE THIRD BORN SON, DRIZZT, TRADITIONALLY SACRIFICED TO THE SPIDER QUEEN.
BUT ON THE NIGHT YOU WERE BORN, DININ MADE HIS ASCENT TO THE POSITION OF ELDERBOY.
HE PUT HIS SWORD IN YOUR LATE BROTHER NALFEIN'S BACK.
YOU SHOULD THANK HIM FOR THAT KINDNESS.
AND I WARN BOTH OF YOU, HOUSE DO'URDEN MAY BE ON A COURSE OF WAR.
IF EITHER OF YOU STRIKE OUT AGAINST THE OTHER, YOU WILL BRING THE WRATH OF ALL YOUR SISTERS AND MATRON MALICE DOWN UPON YOUR WORTHLESS SOULS!

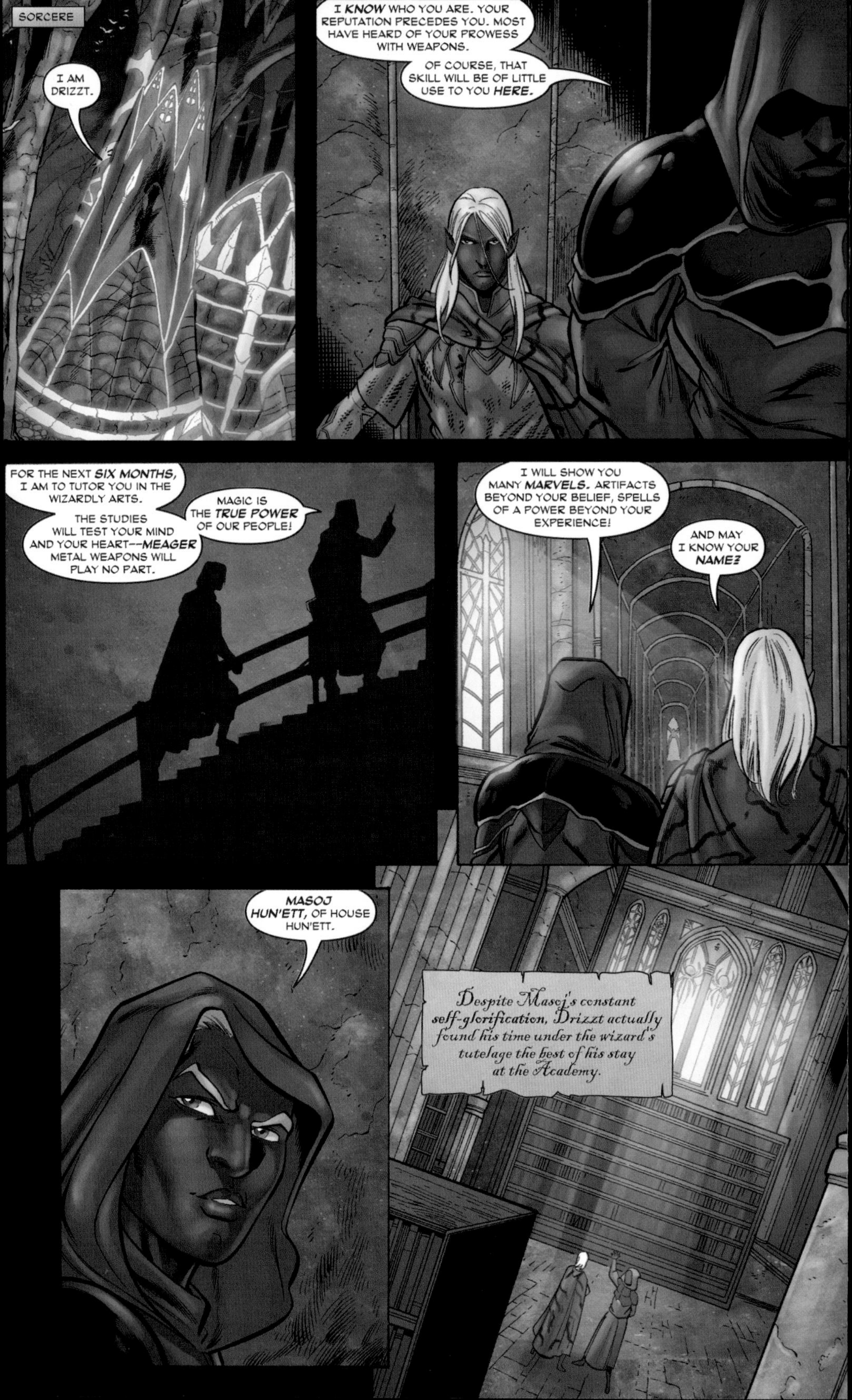
SORCERE
I AM DRIZZT.
I KNOW WHO YOU ARE. YOUR REPUTATION PRECEDES YOU. MOST HAVE HEARD OF YOUR PROWESS WITH WEAPONS.
OF COURSE, THAT SKILL WILL BE OF LITTLE USE TO YOU HERE.
FOR THE NEXT SIX MONTHS, I AM TO TUTOR YOU IN THE WIZARDLY ARTS.
THE STUDIES WILL TEST YOUR MIND AND YOUR HEART--MEAGER METAL WEAPONS WILL PLAY NO PART.
MAGIC IS THE TRUE POWER OF OUR PEOPLE!
I WILL SHOW YOU MANY MARVELS. ARTIFACTS BEYOND YOUR BELIEF, SPELLS OF A POWER BEYOND YOUR EXPERIENCE!
AND MAY I KNOW YOUR NAME?
MASOJ HUN'ETT, OF HOUSE HUN'ETT.
Despite Masoj's constant self-glorification, Drizzt actually found his time under the wizard's tutelage the best of his stay at the Academy.

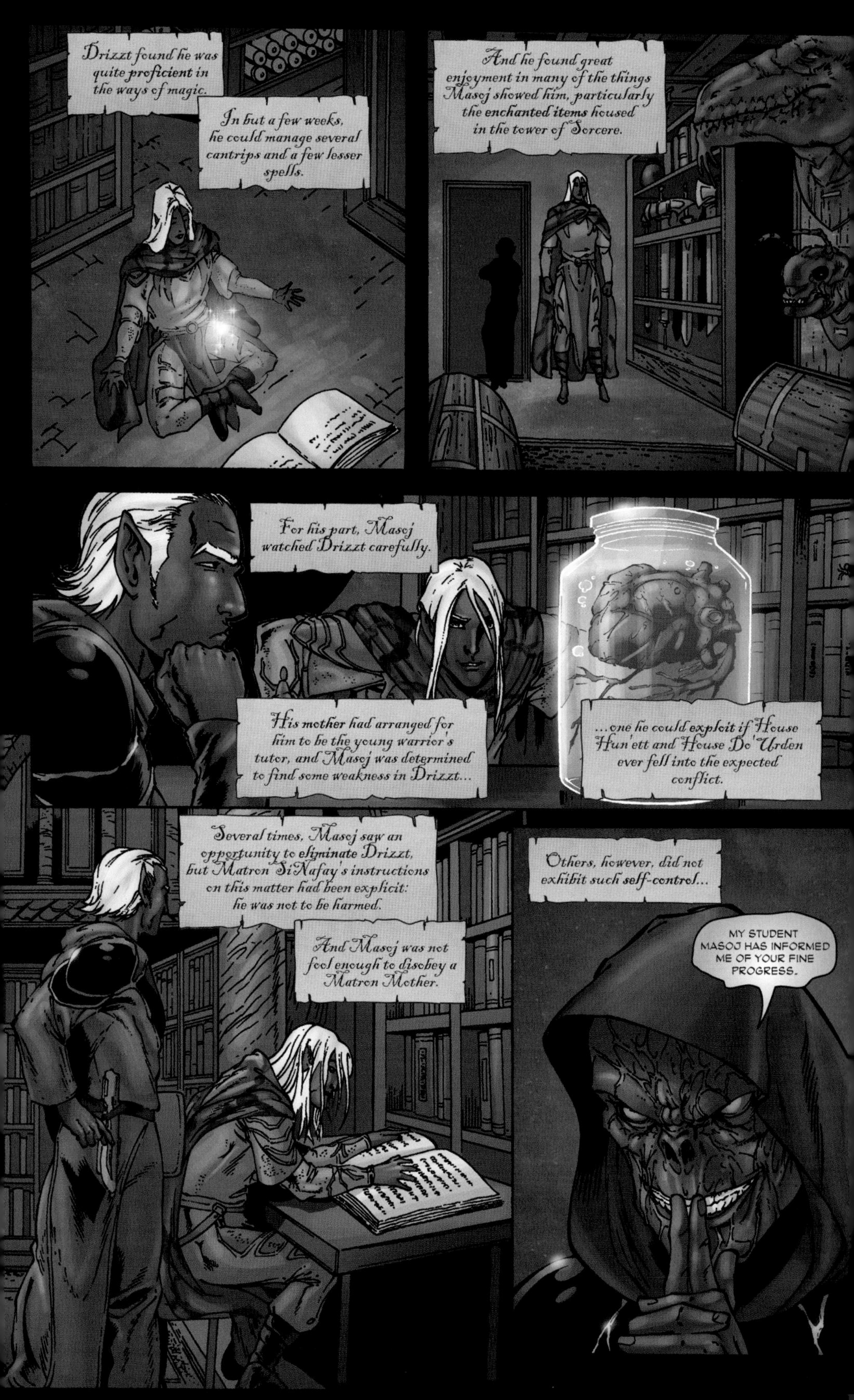

Drizzt found he was quite proficient in the ways of magic.
In but a few weeks, he could manage several cantrips and a few lesser spells.
And he found great enjoyment in many of the things Masoj showed him, particularly the enchanted items housed in the tower of Sorcere.
For his part, Masoj watched Drizzt carefully.
His mother had arranged for him to be the young warrior's tutor, and Masoj was determined to find some weakness in Drizzt...
...one he could exploit if House Hun'ett and House Do'Urden ever fell into the expected conflict.
Several times, Masoj saw an opportunity to eliminate Drizzt, but Matron SiNafay's instructions on this matter had been explicit: he was not to be harmed.
And Masoj was not fool enough to disobey a Matron Mother.
Others, however, did not exhibit such self-control...
MY STUDENT MASOJ HAS INFORMED ME OF YOUR FINE PROGRESS.

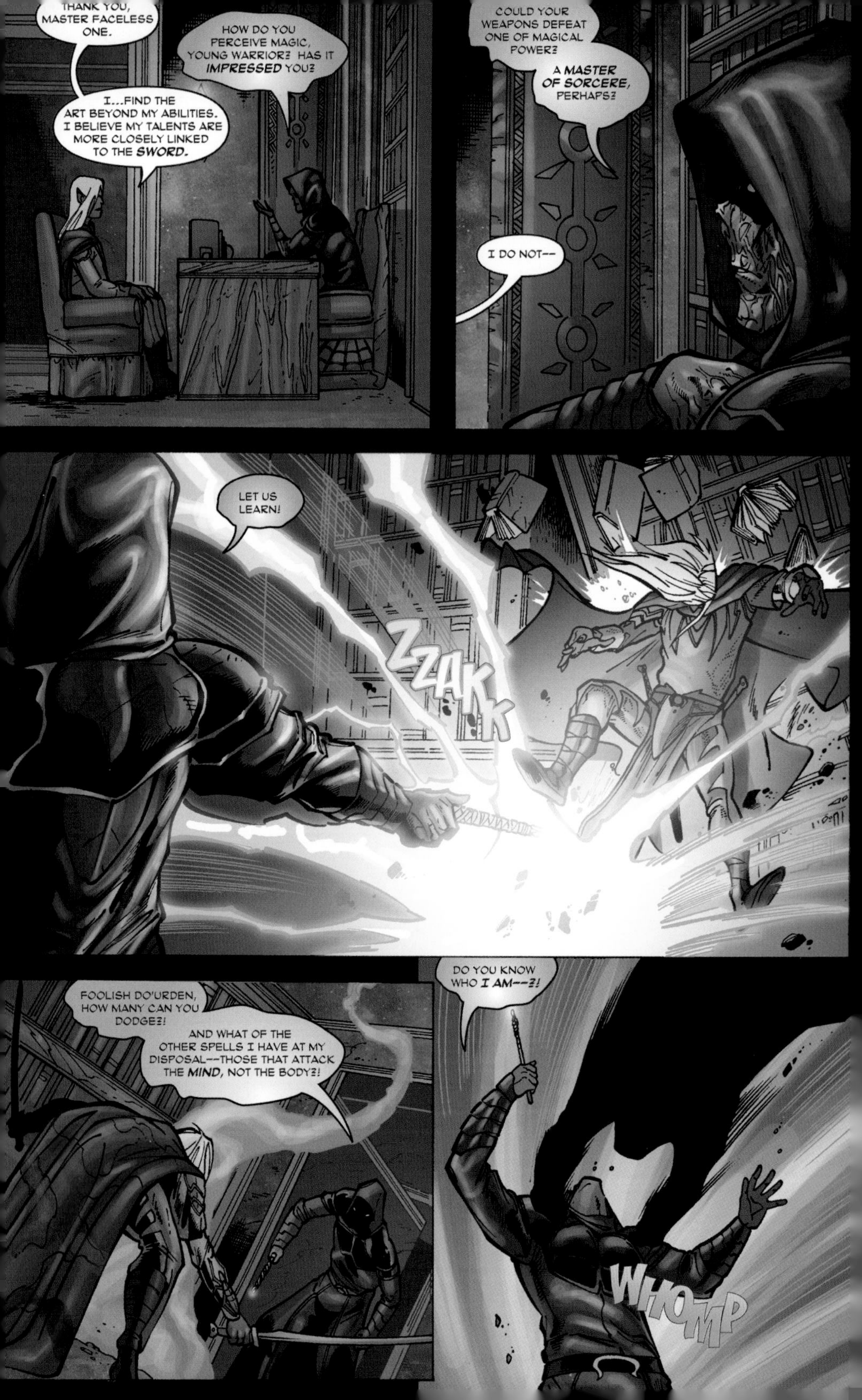
THANK YOU, MASTER FACELESS ONE.
HOW DO YOU PERCEIVE MAGIC, YOUNG WARRIOR? HAS IT IMPRESSED YOU?
I...FIND THE ART BEYOND MY ABILITIES. I BELIEVE MY TALENTS ARE MORE CLOSELY LINKED TO THE SWORD.
COULD YOUR WEAPONS DEFEAT ONE OF MAGICAL POWER?
A MASTER OF SORCERE, PERHAPS?
I DO NOT--
LET US LEARN!
ZZAKKK
FOOLISH DO'URDEN, HOW MANY CAN YOU DODGE?!
AND WHAT OF THE OTHER SPELLS I HAVE AT MY DISPOSAL--THOSE THAT ATTACK THE MIND, NOT THE BODY?!
DO YOU KNOW WHO I AM--?!
WHOMP

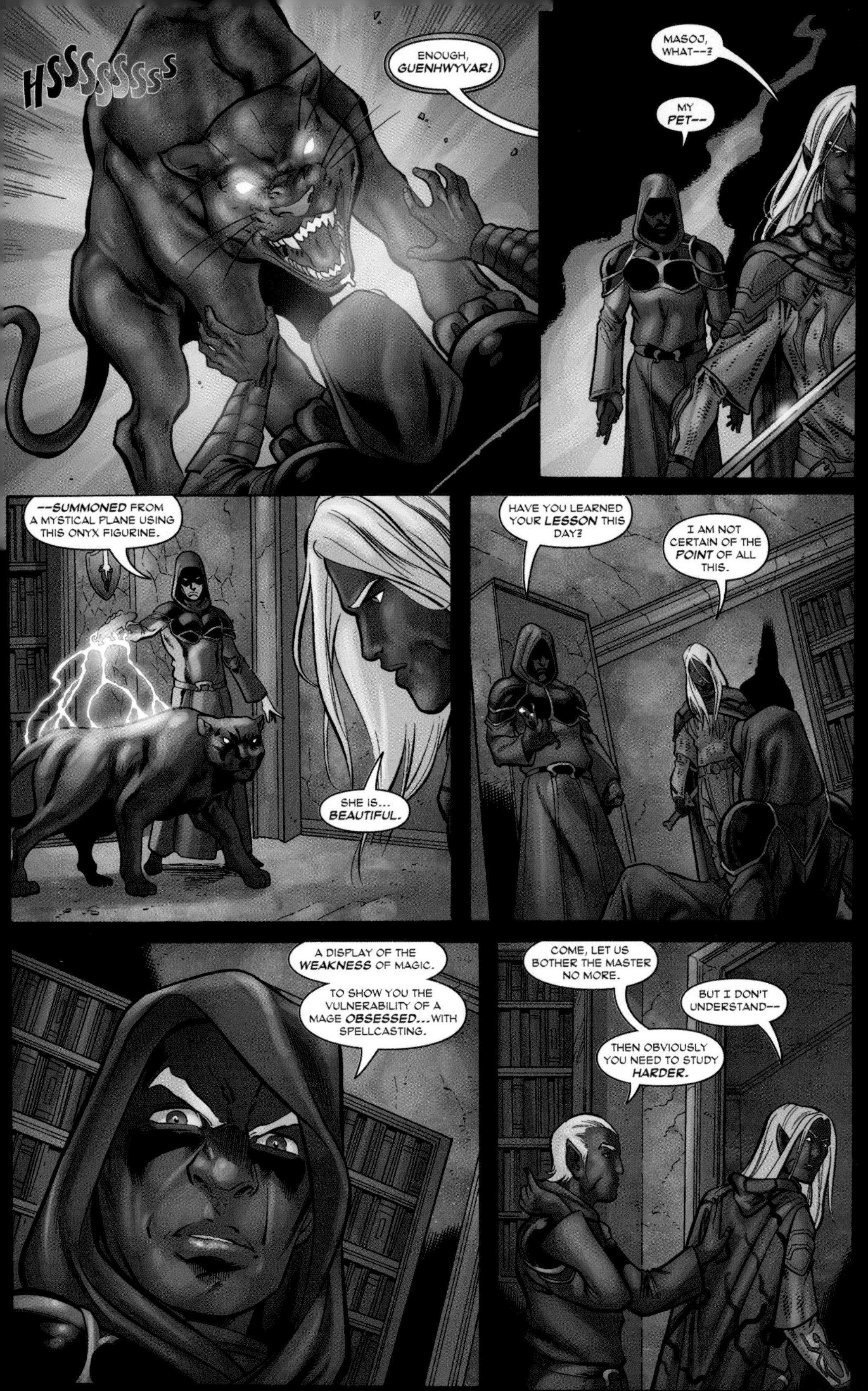
HSSSSSSSSS
ENOUGH, GUENHWYVAR!
MASOJ, WHAT--?
MY PET--
--SUMMONED FROM A MYSTICAL PLANE USING THIS ONYX FIGURINE.
SHE IS... BEAUTIFUL.
HAVE YOU LEARNED YOUR LESSON THIS DAY?
I AM NOT CERTAIN OF THE POINT OF ALL THIS.
A DISPLAY OF THE WEAKNESS OF MAGIC.
TO SHOW YOU THE VULNERABILITY OF A MAGE OBSESSED...WITH SPELLCASTING.
COME, LET US BOTHER THE MASTER NO MORE.
BUT I DON'T UNDERSTAND--
THEN OBVIOUSLY YOU NEED TO STUDY HARDER.

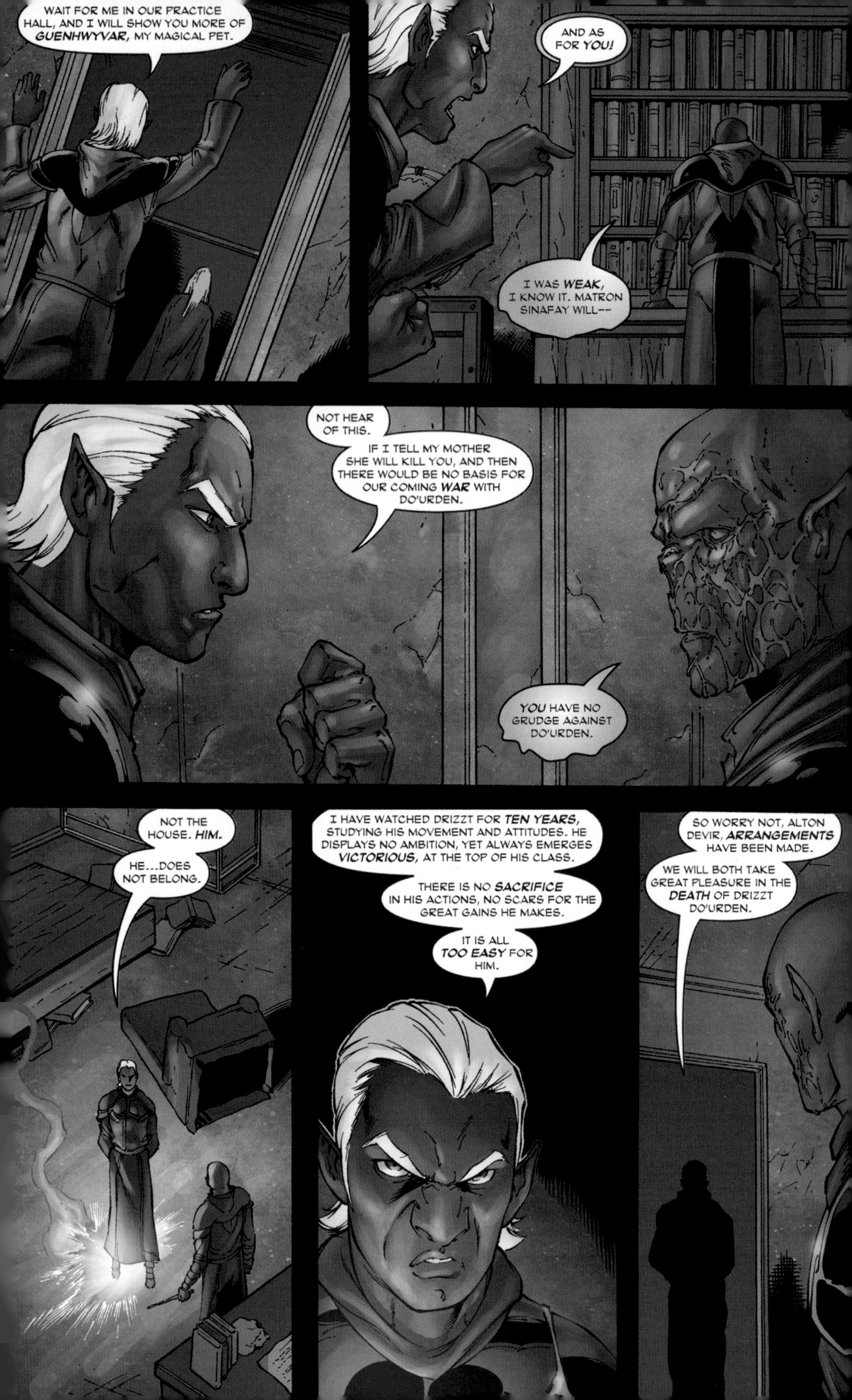
WAIT FOR ME IN OUR PRACTICE HALL, AND I WILL SHOW YOU MORE OF GUENHWYVAR, MY MAGICAL PET.
AND AS FOR YOU!
I WAS WEAK, I KNOW IT. MATRON SINAFAY WILL--
NOT HEAR OF THIS.
IF I TELL MY MOTHER SHE WILL KILL YOU, AND THEN THERE WOULD BE NO BASIS FOR OUR COMING WAR WITH DO'URDEN.
YOU HAVE NO GRUDGE AGAINST DO'URDEN.
NOT THE HOUSE. HIM.
HE...DOES NOT BELONG.
I HAVE WATCHED DRIZZT FOR TEN YEARS, STUDYING HIS MOVEMENT AND ATTITUDES. HE DISPLAYS NO AMBITION, YET ALWAYS EMERGES VICTORIOUS, AT THE TOP OF HIS CLASS.
THERE IS NO SACRIFICE IN HIS ACTIONS, NO SCARS FOR THE GREAT GAINS HE MAKES.
IT IS ALL TOO EASY FOR HIM.
SO WORRY NOT, ALTON DEVIR, ARRANGEMENTS HAVE BEEN MADE.
WE WILL BOTH TAKE GREAT PLEASURE IN THE DEATH OF DRIZZT DO'URDEN.

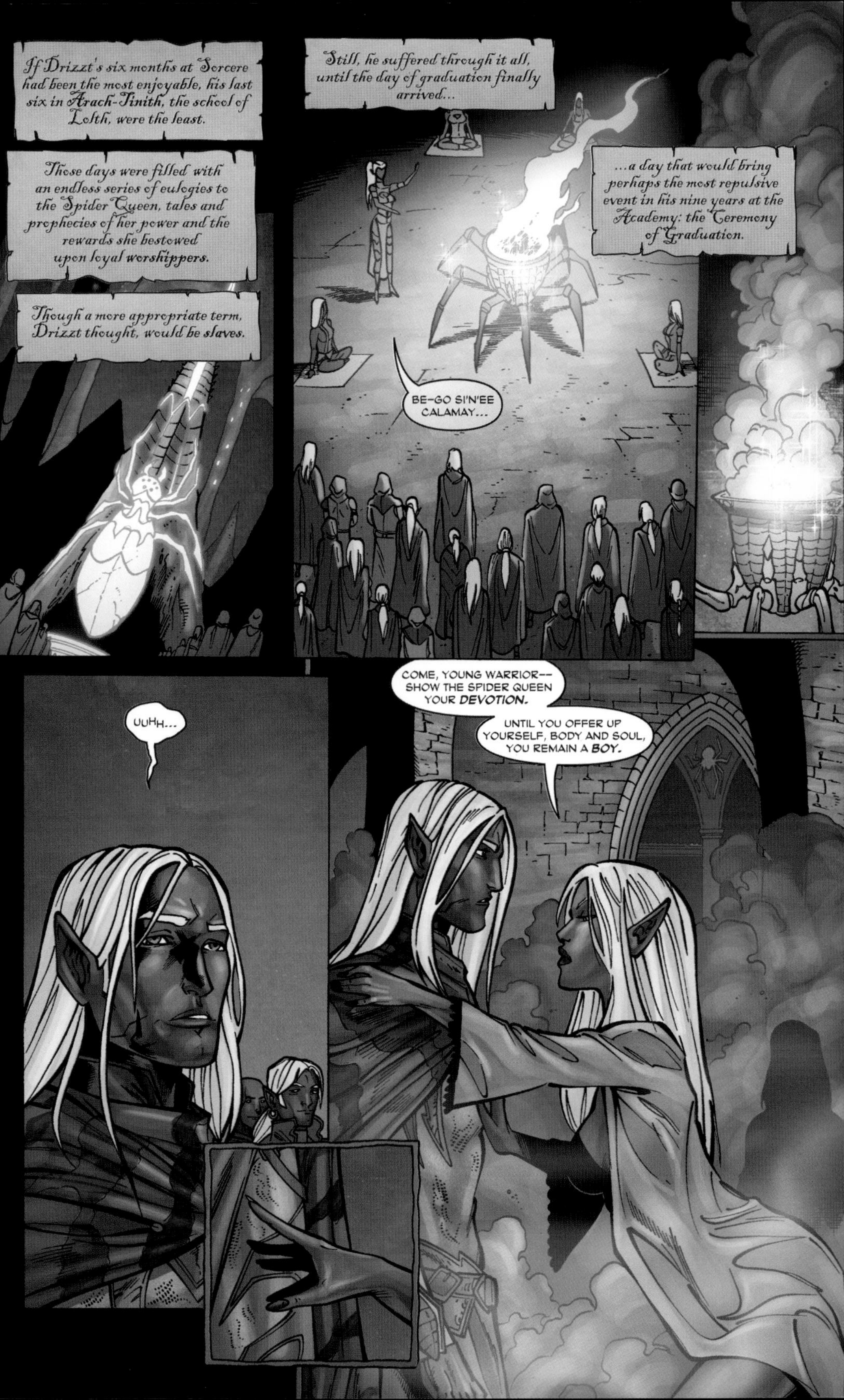
If Drizzt's six months at Sorcere had been the most enjoyable, his last six in Arach-Tinith, the school of Lolth, were the least.
Those days were filled with an endless series of eulogies to the Spider Queen, tales and prophecies of her power and the rewards she bestowed upon loyal worshippers.
Though a more appropriate term, Drizzt thought, would be slaves.
Still, he suffered through it all, until the day of graduation finally arrived...
...a day that would bring perhaps the most repulsive event in his nine years at the Academy: the Ceremony of Graduation.
BE-GO SI'N'EE CALAMAY...
COME, YOUNG WARRIOR-- SHOW THE SPIDER QUEEN YOUR DEVOTION.
UNTIL YOU OFFER UP YOURSELF, BODY AND SOUL, YOU REMAIN A BOY.
UUHH...

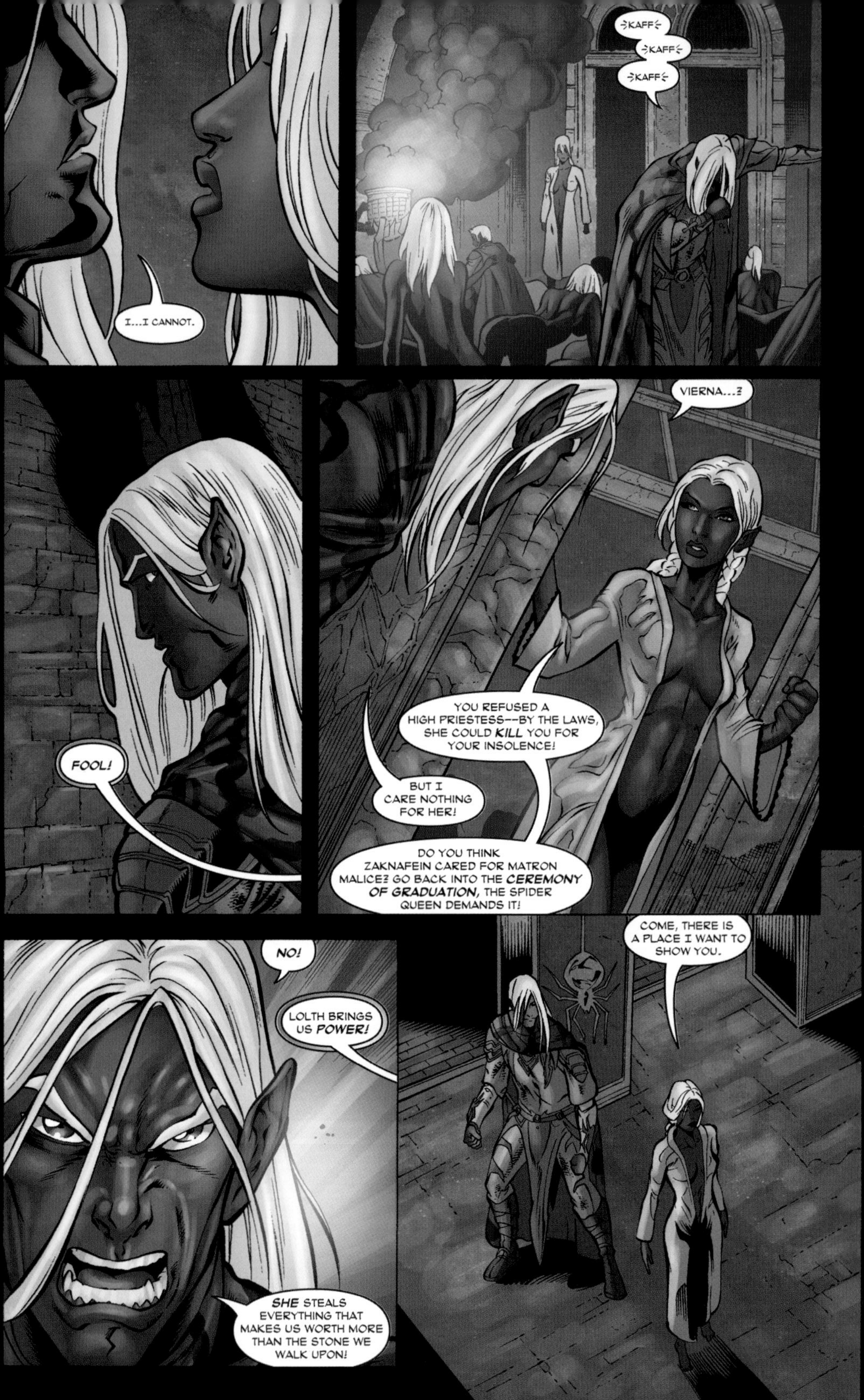
I...I CANNOT.
KAFF
KAFF
KAFF
VIERNA...?
FOOL!
YOU REFUSED A HIGH PRIESTESS--BY THE LAWS, SHE COULD *KILL* YOU FOR YOUR INSOLENCE!
BUT I CARE NOTHING FOR HER!
DO YOU THINK ZAKNAFEIN CARED FOR MATRON MALICE? GO BACK INTO THE *CEREMONY OF GRADUATION*, THE SPIDER QUEEN DEMANDS IT!
NO!
LOLTH BRINGS US *POWER!*
SHE STEALS EVERYTHING THAT MAKES US WORTH MORE THAN THE STONE WE WALK UPON!
COME, THERE IS A PLACE I WANT TO SHOW YOU.

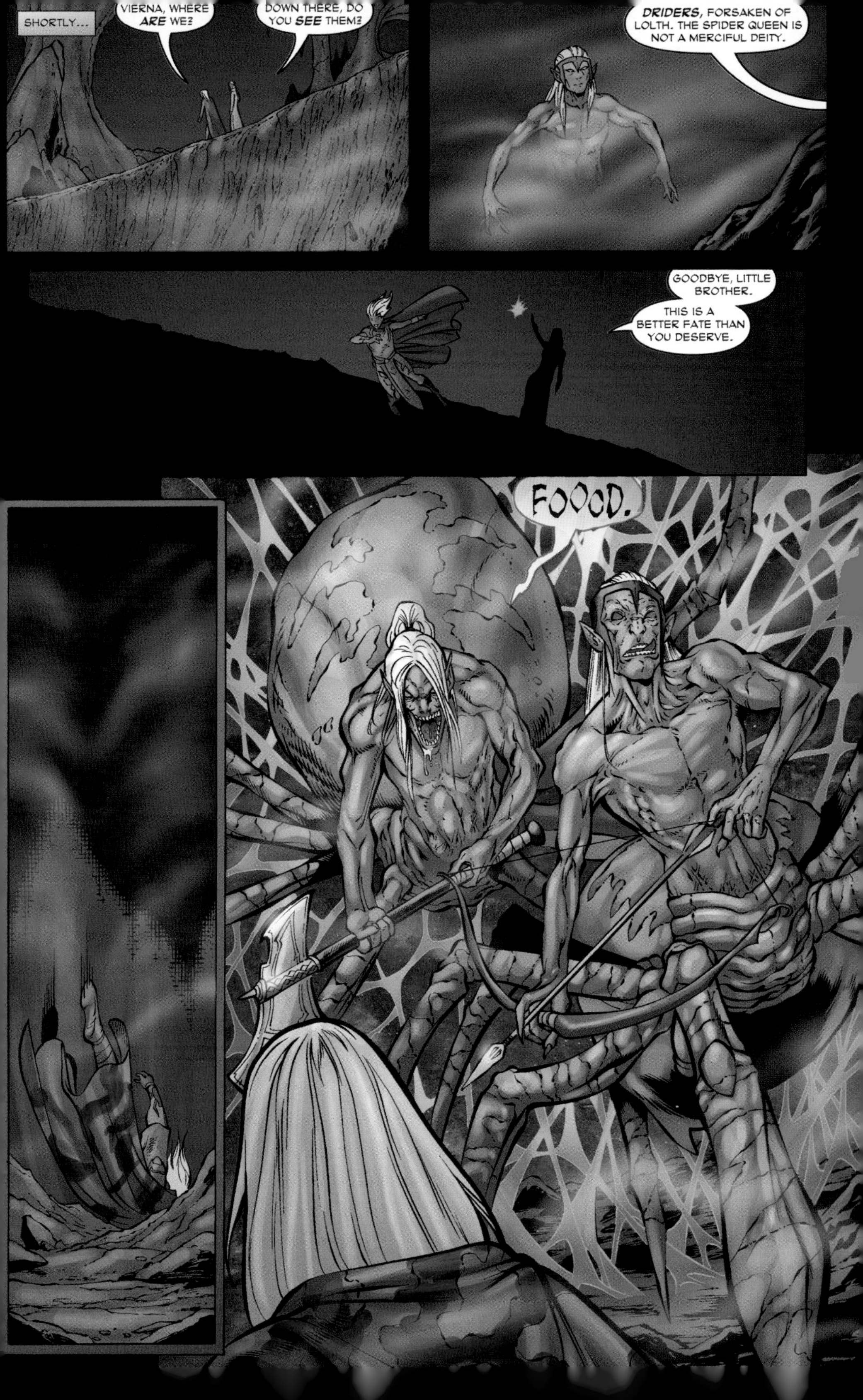
SHORTLY...
VIERNA, WHERE ARE WE?
DOWN THERE, DO YOU SEE THEM?
DRIDERS, FORSAKEN OF LOLTH. THE SPIDER QUEEN IS NOT A MERCIFUL DEITY.
GOODBYE, LITTLE BROTHER.
THIS IS A BETTER FATE THAN YOU DESERVE.
FOOOD.

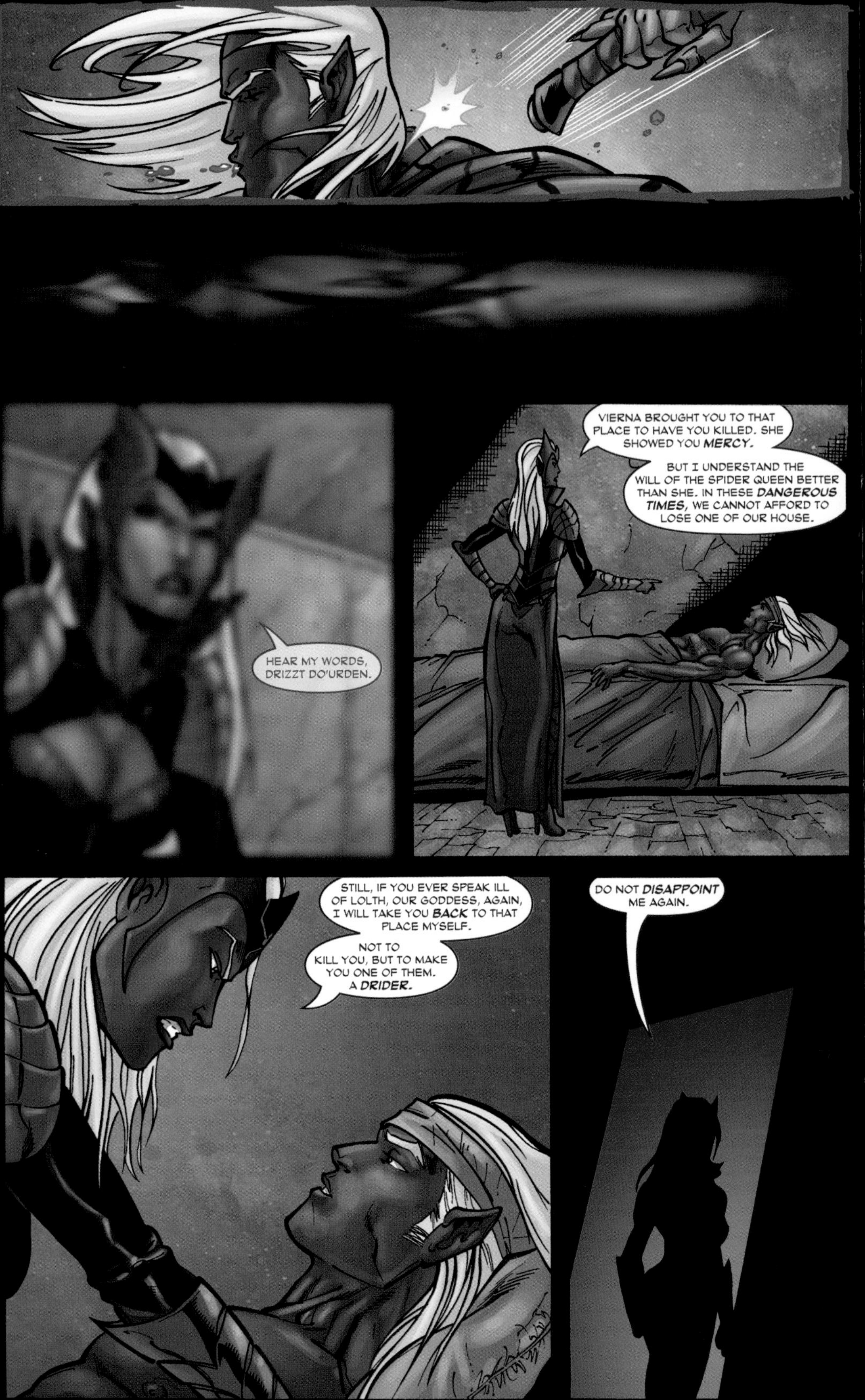
HEAR MY WORDS, DRIZZT DO'URDEN.
VIERNA BROUGHT YOU TO THAT PLACE TO HAVE YOU KILLED. SHE SHOWED YOU MERCY.
BUT I UNDERSTAND THE WILL OF THE SPIDER QUEEN BETTER THAN SHE. IN THESE DANGEROUS TIMES, WE CANNOT AFFORD TO LOSE ONE OF OUR HOUSE.
STILL, IF YOU EVER SPEAK ILL OF LOLTH, OUR GODDESS, AGAIN, I WILL TAKE YOU BACK TO THAT PLACE MYSELF.
NOT TO KILL YOU, BUT TO MAKE YOU ONE OF THEM. A DRIDER.
DO NOT DISAPPOINT ME AGAIN.

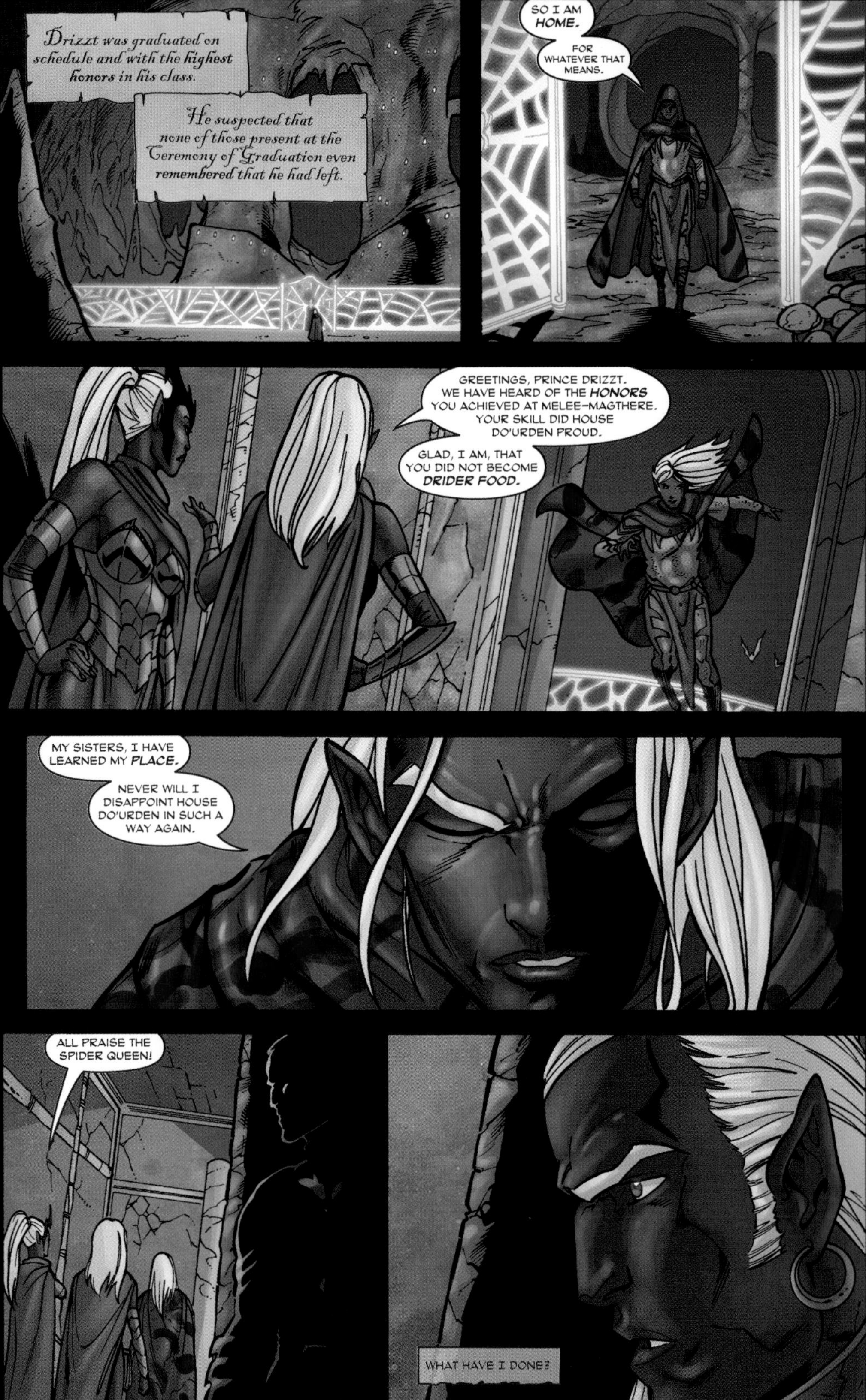
Drizzt was graduated on schedule and with the highest honors in his class.
He suspected that none of those present at the Ceremony of Graduation even remembered that he had left.
SO I AM HOME.
FOR WHATEVER THAT MEANS.
GREETINGS, PRINCE DRIZZT. WE HAVE HEARD OF THE HONORS YOU ACHIEVED AT MELEE-MAGTHERE. YOUR SKILL DID HOUSE DO'URDEN PROUD.
GLAD, I AM, THAT YOU DID NOT BECOME DRIDER FOOD.
MY SISTERS, I HAVE LEARNED MY PLACE.
NEVER WILL I DISAPPOINT HOUSE DO'URDEN IN SUCH A WAY AGAIN.
ALL PRAISE THE SPIDER QUEEN!
WHAT HAVE I DONE?

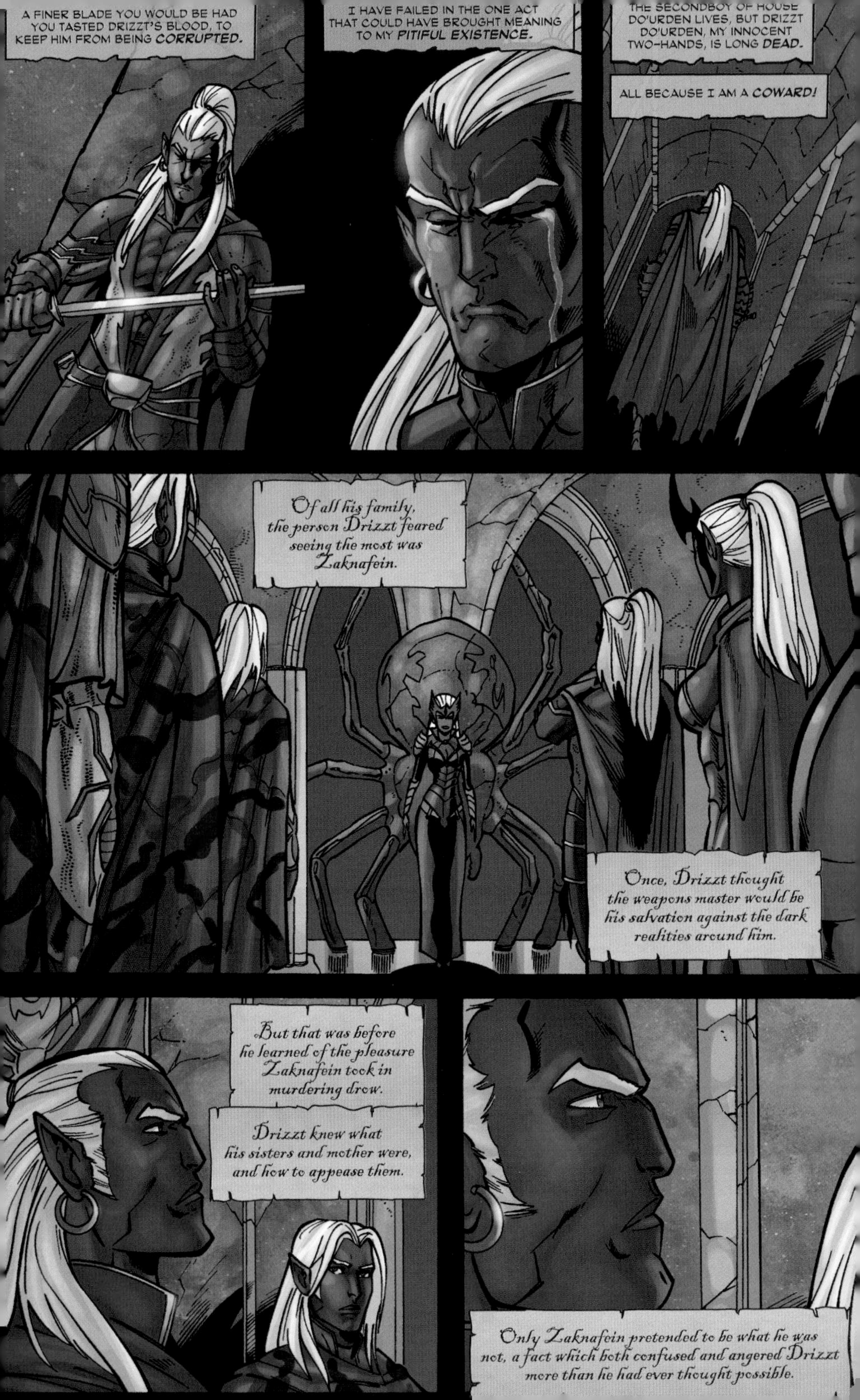
A FINER BLADE YOU WOULD BE HAD YOU TASTED DRIZZT'S BLOOD, TO KEEP HIM FROM BEING CORRUPTED.
I HAVE FAILED IN THE ONE ACT THAT COULD HAVE BROUGHT MEANING TO MY PITIFUL EXISTENCE.
THE SECONDBOY OF HOUSE DO'URDEN LIVES, BUT DRIZZT DO'URDEN, MY INNOCENT TWO-HANDS, IS LONG DEAD.
ALL BECAUSE I AM A COWARD!
Of all his family, the person Drizzt feared seeing the most was Zaknafein.
Once, Drizzt thought the weapons master would be his salvation against the dark realities around him.
But that was before he learned of the pleasure Zaknafein took in murdering drow.
Drizzt knew what his sisters and mother were, and how to appease them.
Only Zaknafein pretended to be what he was not, a fact which both confused and angered Drizzt more than he had ever thought possible.

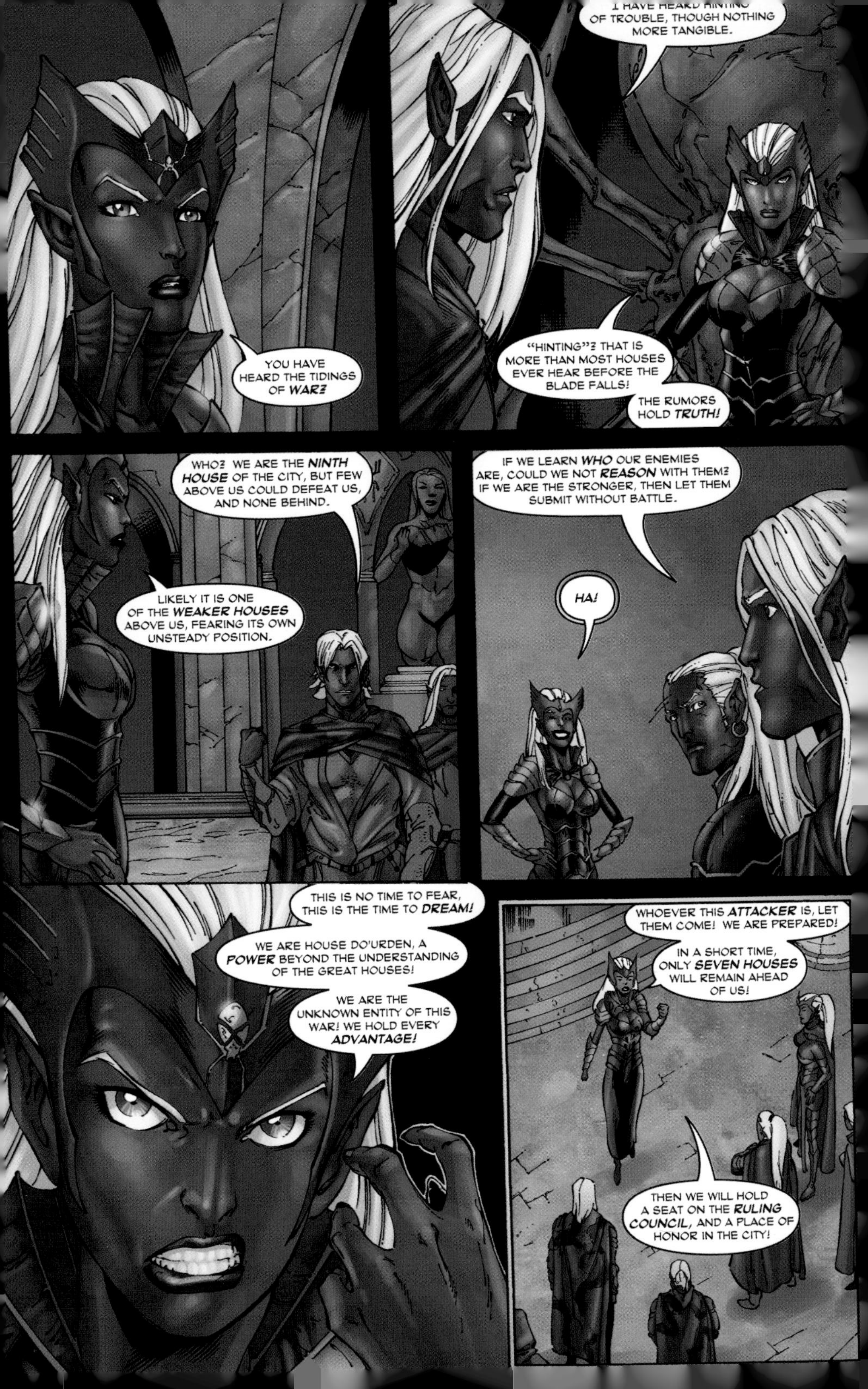
YOU HAVE HEARD THE TIDINGS OF WAR?
OF TROUBLE, THOUGH NOTHING MORE TANGIBLE.
"HINTING"? THAT IS MORE THAN MOST HOUSES EVER HEAR BEFORE THE BLADE FALLS!
THE RUMORS HOLD TRUTH!
WHO? WE ARE THE NINTH HOUSE OF THE CITY, BUT FEW ABOVE US COULD DEFEAT US, AND NONE BEHIND.
LIKELY IT IS ONE OF THE WEAKER HOUSES ABOVE US, FEARING ITS OWN UNSTEADY POSITION.
IF WE LEARN WHO OUR ENEMIES ARE, COULD WE NOT REASON WITH THEM? IF WE ARE THE STRONGER, THEN LET THEM SUBMIT WITHOUT BATTLE.
HA!
THIS IS NO TIME TO FEAR, THIS IS THE TIME TO DREAM!
WE ARE HOUSE DO'URDEN, A POWER BEYOND THE UNDERSTANDING OF THE GREAT HOUSES!
WE ARE THE UNKNOWN ENTITY OF THIS WAR! WE HOLD EVERY ADVANTAGE!
WHOEVER THIS ATTACKER IS, LET THEM COME! WE ARE PREPARED!
IN A SHORT TIME, ONLY SEVEN HOUSES WILL REMAIN AHEAD OF US!
THEN WE WILL HOLD A SEAT ON THE RULING COUNCIL, AND A PLACE OF HONOR IN THE CITY!

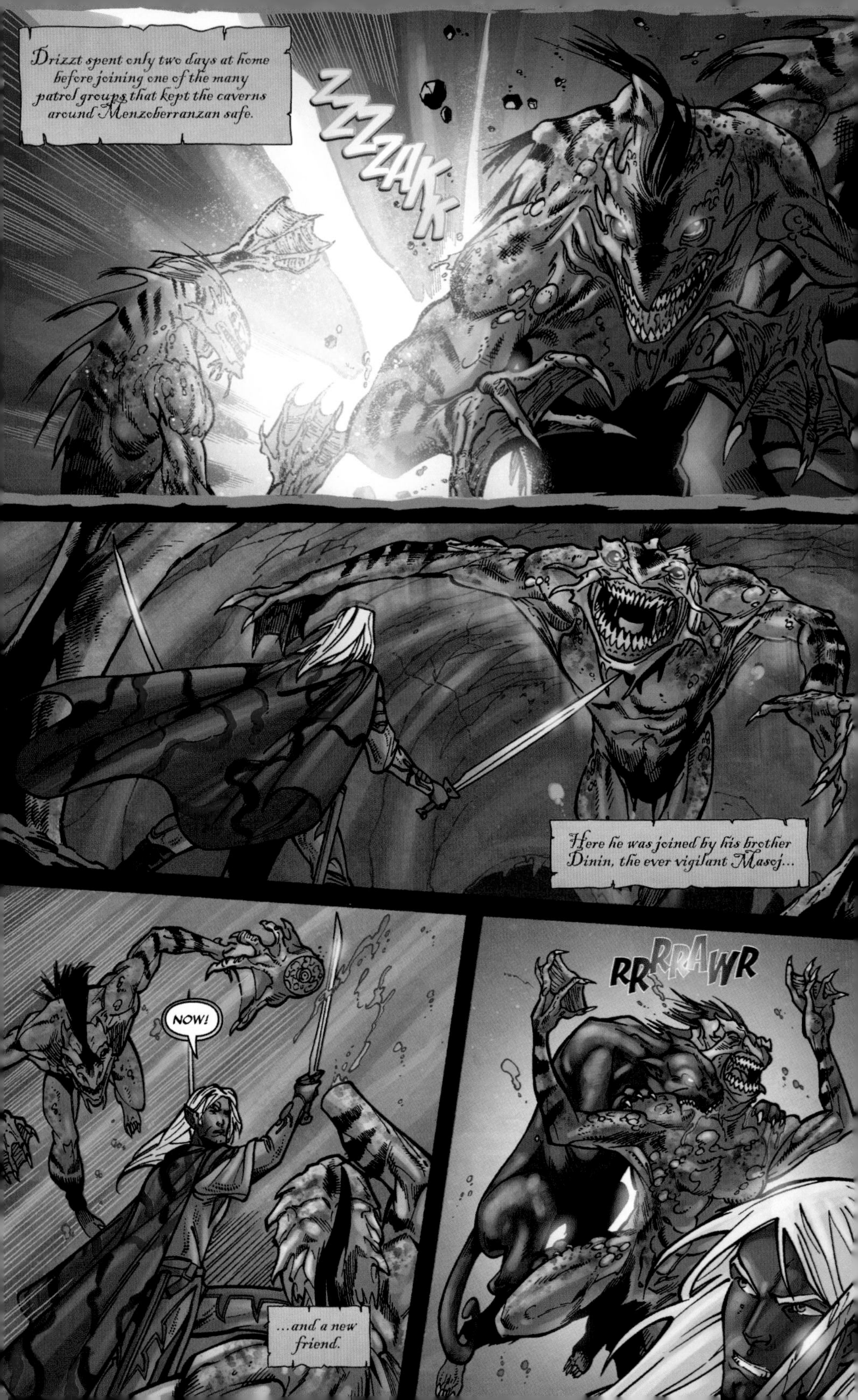
Drizzt spent only two days at home before joining one of the many patrol groups that kept the caverns around Menzoberranzan safe.
ZZZZAKK
Here he was joined by his brother Dinin, the ever vigilant Masoj...
NOW!
...and a new friend.
RRRRAWR

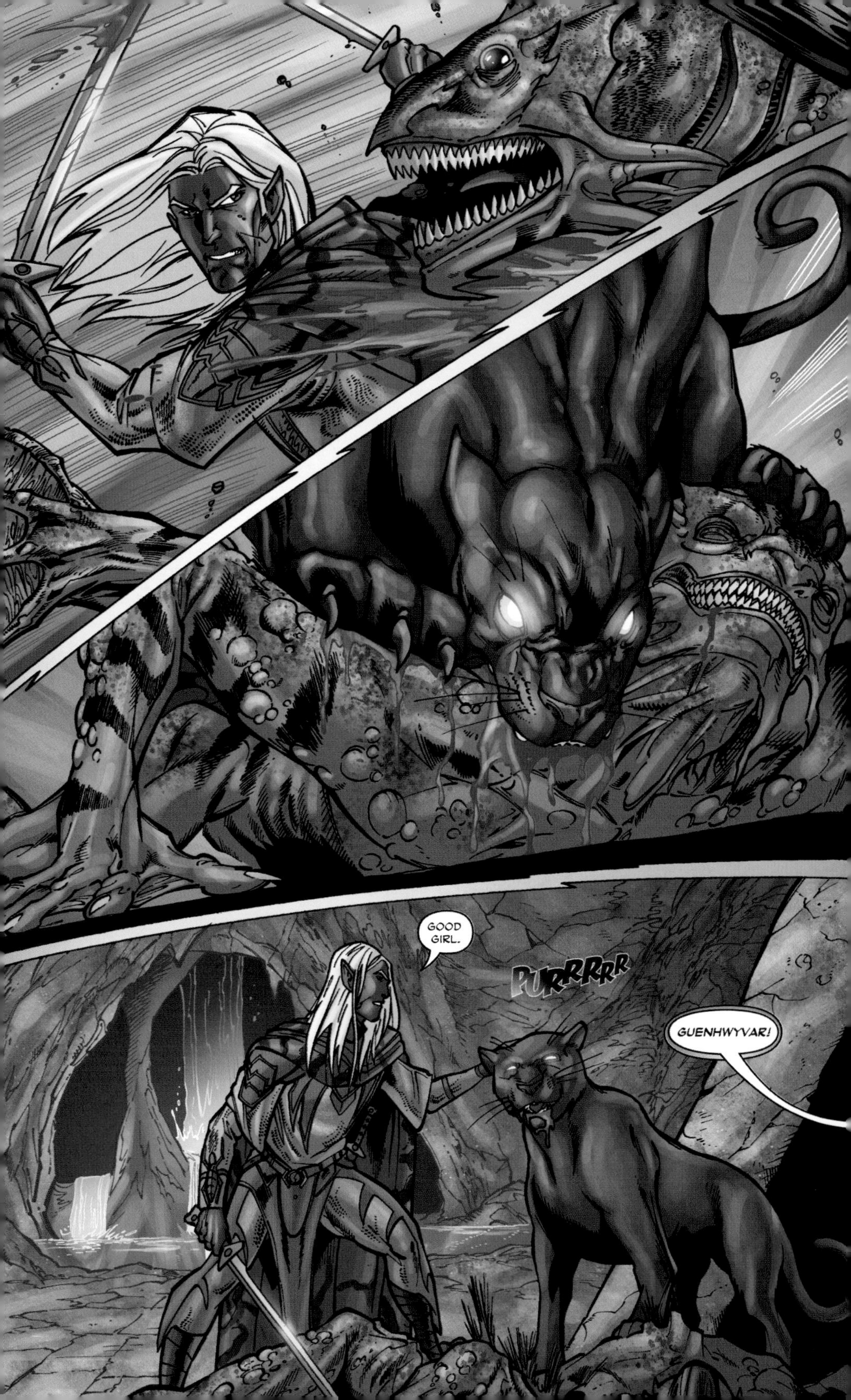
GOOD GIRL.
PURRRRR
GUENHWYVAR!

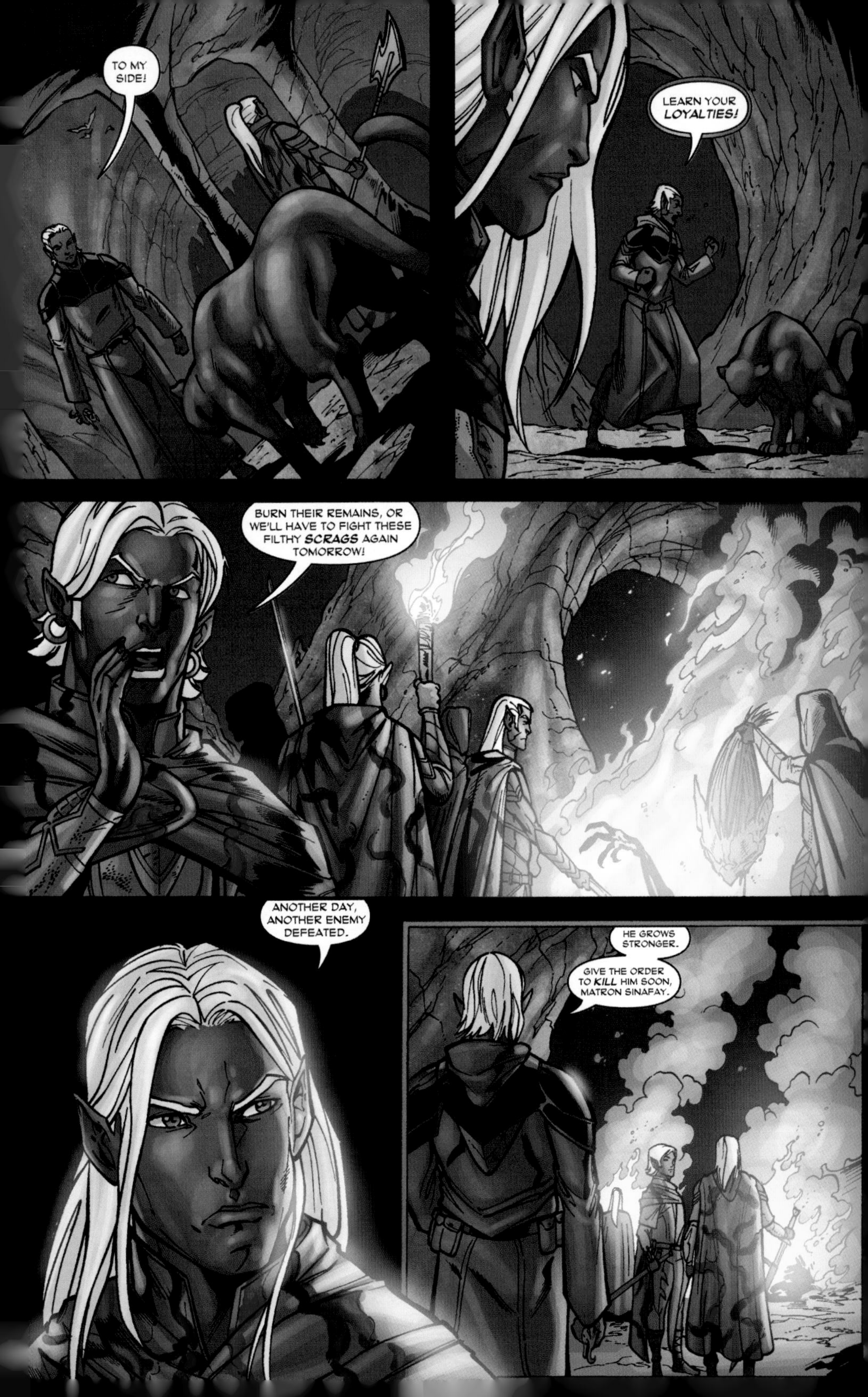
TO MY SIDE!
LEARN YOUR LOYALTIES!
BURN THEIR REMAINS, OR WE'LL HAVE TO FIGHT THESE FILTHY SCRAGS AGAIN TOMORROW!
ANOTHER DAY, ANOTHER ENEMY DEFEATED.
HE GROWS STRONGER.
GIVE THE ORDER TO KILL HIM SOON, MATRON SINAFAY.

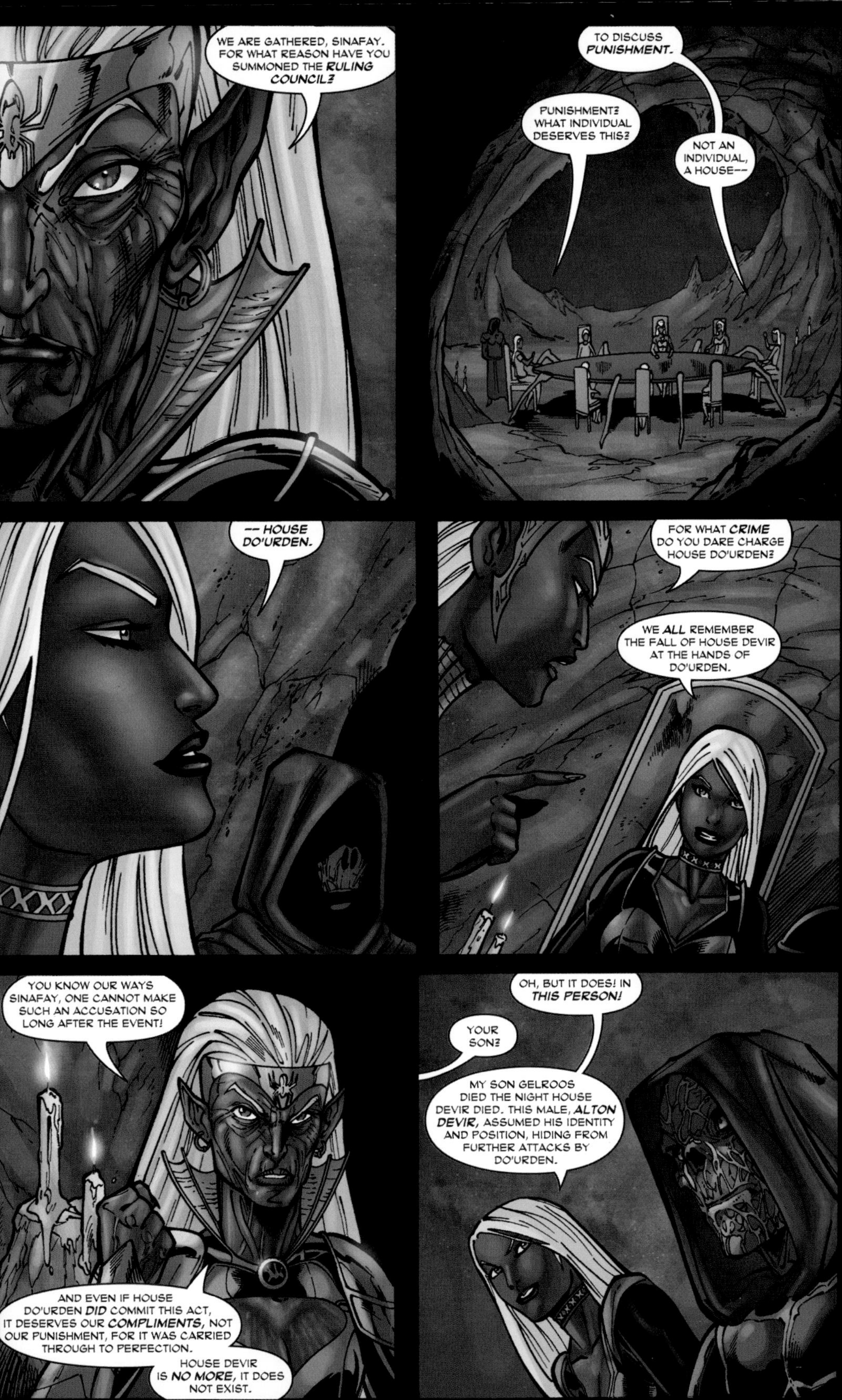
WE ARE GATHERED, SINAFAY. FOR WHAT REASON HAVE YOU SUMMONED THE RULING COUNCIL?
TO DISCUSS PUNISHMENT.
PUNISHMENT? WHAT INDIVIDUAL DESERVES THIS?
NOT AN INDIVIDUAL, A HOUSE--
-- HOUSE DO'URDEN.
FOR WHAT CRIME DO YOU DARE CHARGE HOUSE DO'URDEN?
WE ALL REMEMBER THE FALL OF HOUSE DEVIR AT THE HANDS OF DO'URDEN.
YOU KNOW OUR WAYS SINAFAY, ONE CANNOT MAKE SUCH AN ACCUSATION SO LONG AFTER THE EVENT!
AND EVEN IF HOUSE DO'URDEN DID COMMIT THIS ACT, IT DESERVES OUR COMPLIMENTS, NOT OUR PUNISHMENT, FOR IT WAS CARRIED THROUGH TO PERFECTION.
HOUSE DEVIR IS NO MORE, IT DOES NOT EXIST.
OH, BUT IT DOES! IN THIS PERSON!
YOUR SON?
MY SON GELROOS DIED THE NIGHT HOUSE DEVIR DIED. THIS MALE, ALTON DEVIR, ASSUMED HIS IDENTITY AND POSITION, HIDING FROM FURTHER ATTACKS BY DO'URDEN.

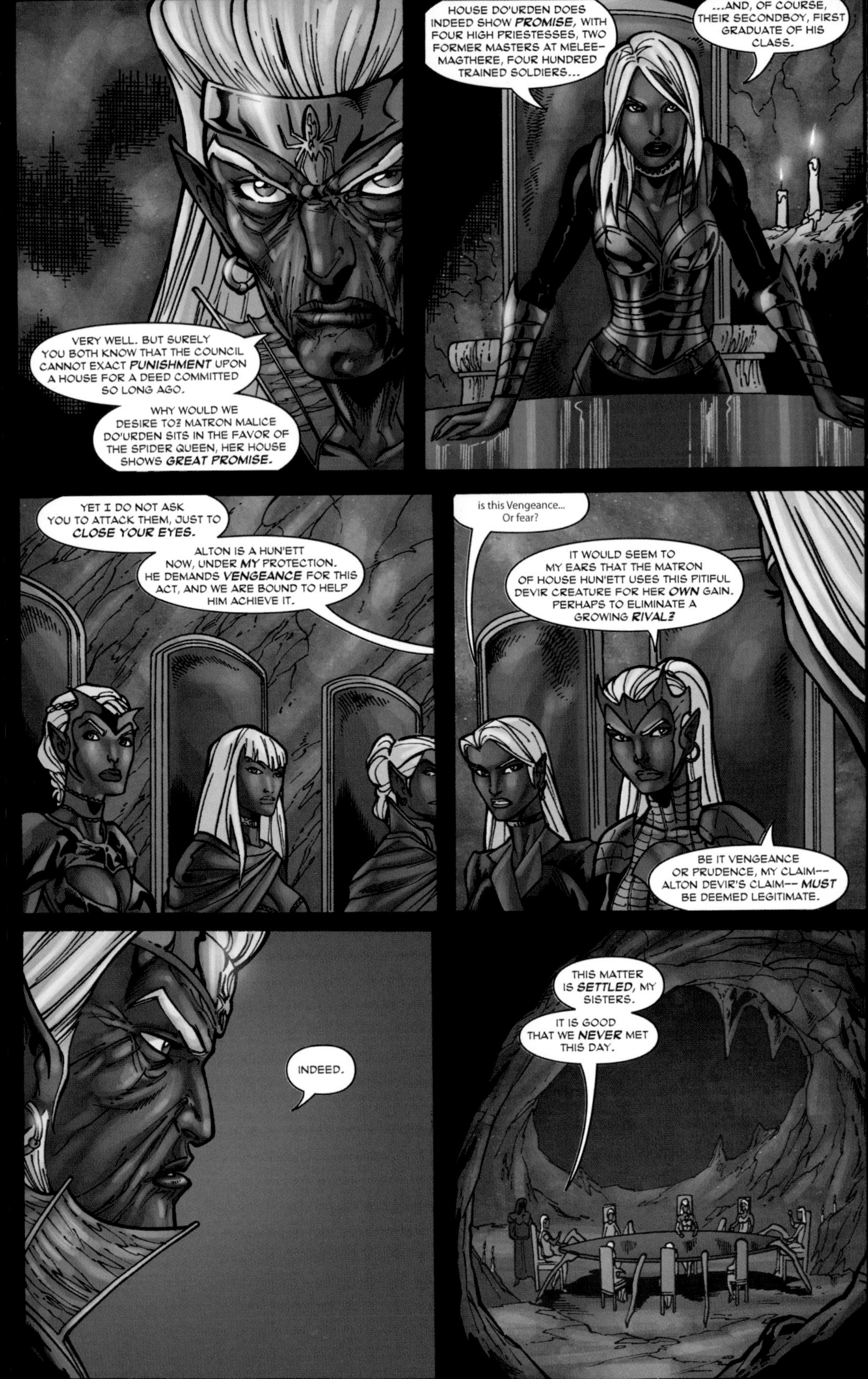

VERY WELL. BUT SURELY YOU BOTH KNOW THAT THE COUNCIL CANNOT EXACT PUNISHMENT UPON A HOUSE FOR A DEED COMMITTED SO LONG AGO.
WHY WOULD WE DESIRE TO? MATRON MALICE DO'URDEN SITS IN THE FAVOR OF THE SPIDER QUEEN, HER HOUSE SHOWS GREAT PROMISE.
HOUSE DO'URDEN DOES INDEED SHOW PROMISE, WITH FOUR HIGH PRIESTESSES, TWO FORMER MASTERS AT MELEE-MAGTHERE, FOUR HUNDRED TRAINED SOLDIERS...
...AND, OF COURSE, THEIR SECONDBOY, FIRST GRADUATE OF HIS CLASS.
YET I DO NOT ASK YOU TO ATTACK THEM, JUST TO CLOSE YOUR EYES.
ALTON IS A HUN'ETT NOW, UNDER MY PROTECTION. HE DEMANDS VENGEANCE FOR THIS ACT, AND WE ARE BOUND TO HELP HIM ACHIEVE IT.
is this Vengeance... Or fear?
IT WOULD SEEM TO MY EARS THAT THE MATRON OF HOUSE HUN'ETT USES THIS PITIFUL DEVIR CREATURE FOR HER OWN GAIN. PERHAPS TO ELIMINATE A GROWING RIVAL?
BE IT VENGEANCE OR PRUDENCE, MY CLAIM-- ALTON DEVIR'S CLAIM-- MUST BE DEEMED LEGITIMATE.
INDEED.
THIS MATTER IS SETTLED, MY SISTERS.
IT IS GOOD THAT WE NEVER MET THIS DAY.

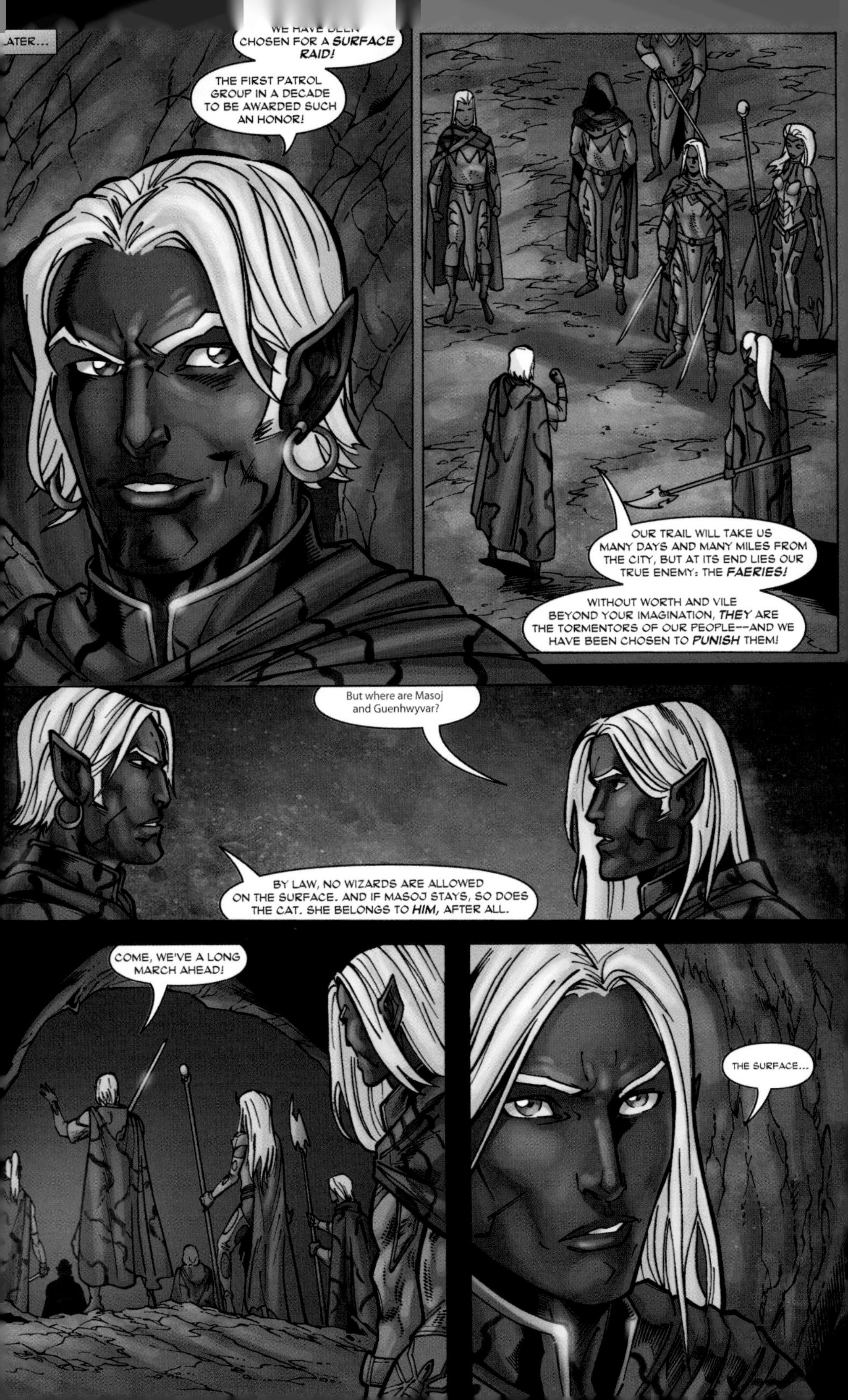
LATER...
WE HAVE BEEN CHOSEN FOR A SURFACE RAID!
THE FIRST PATROL GROUP IN A DECADE TO BE AWARDED SUCH AN HONOR!
OUR TRAIL WILL TAKE US MANY DAYS AND MANY MILES FROM THE CITY, BUT AT ITS END LIES OUR TRUE ENEMY: THE FAERIES!
WITHOUT WORTH AND VILE BEYOND YOUR IMAGINATION, THEY ARE THE TORMENTORS OF OUR PEOPLE--AND WE HAVE BEEN CHOSEN TO PUNISH THEM!
But where are Masoj and Guenhwyvar?
BY LAW, NO WIZARDS ARE ALLOWED ON THE SURFACE. AND IF MASOJ STAYS, SO DOES THE CAT. SHE BELONGS TO HIM, AFTER ALL.
COME, WE'VE A LONG MARCH AHEAD!
THE SURFACE...

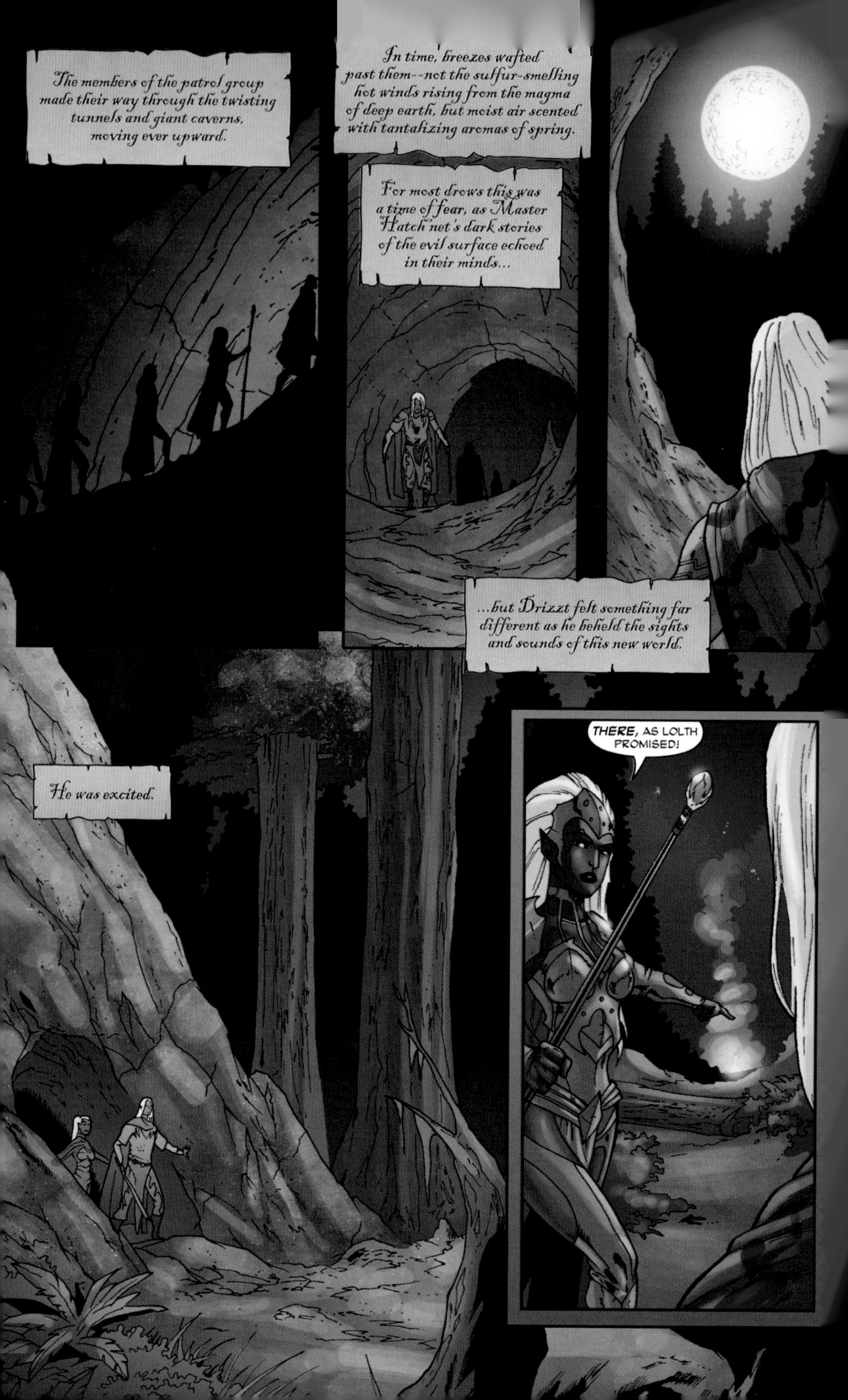

The members of the patrol group made their way through the twisting tunnels and giant caverns, moving ever upward.
In time, breezes wafted past them--not the sulfur-smelling hot winds rising from the magma of deep earth, but moist air scented with tantalizing aromas of spring.
For most drows this was a time of fear, as Master Hatch'net's dark stories of the evil surface echoed in their minds...
...but Drizzt felt something far different as he beheld the sights and sounds of this new world.
He was excited.
THERE, AS LOLTH PROMISED!

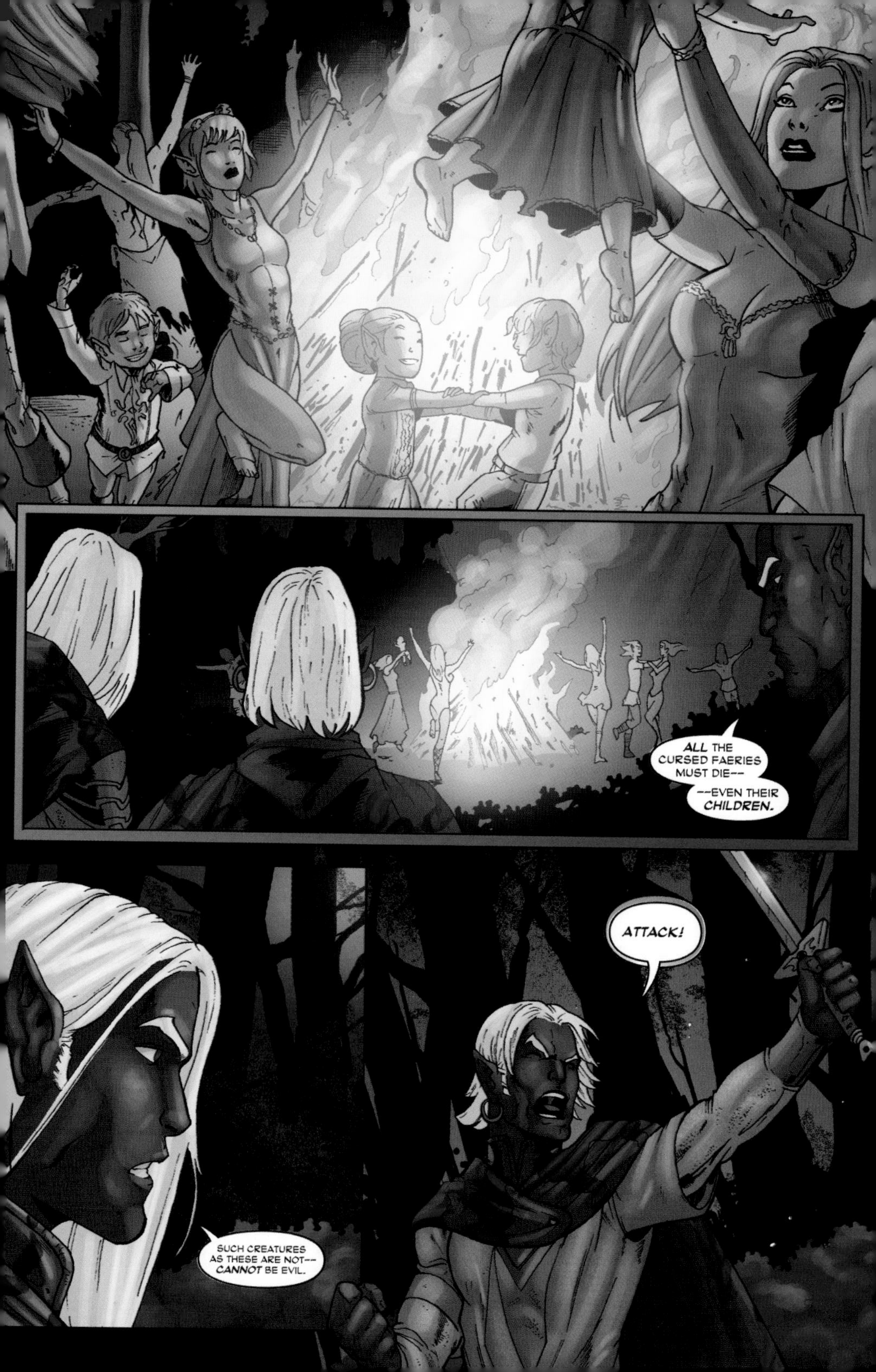
ALL THE CURSED FAERIES MUST DIE--
--EVEN THEIR CHILDREN.
ATTACK!
SUCH CREATURES AS THESE ARE NOT-- CANNOT BE EVIL.

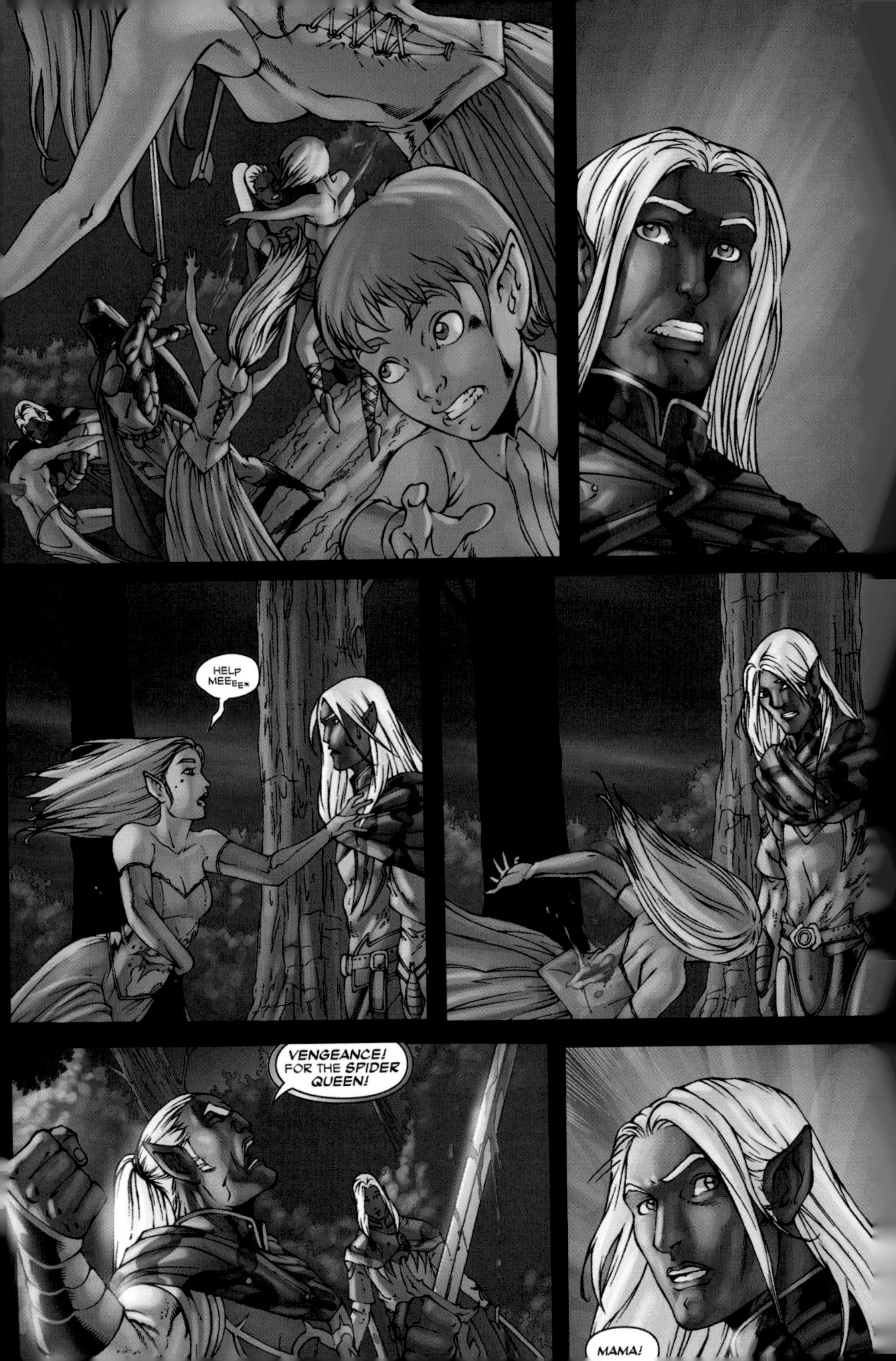
HELP MEEEEE*
VENGEANCE! FOR THE SPIDER QUEEN!
MAMA!

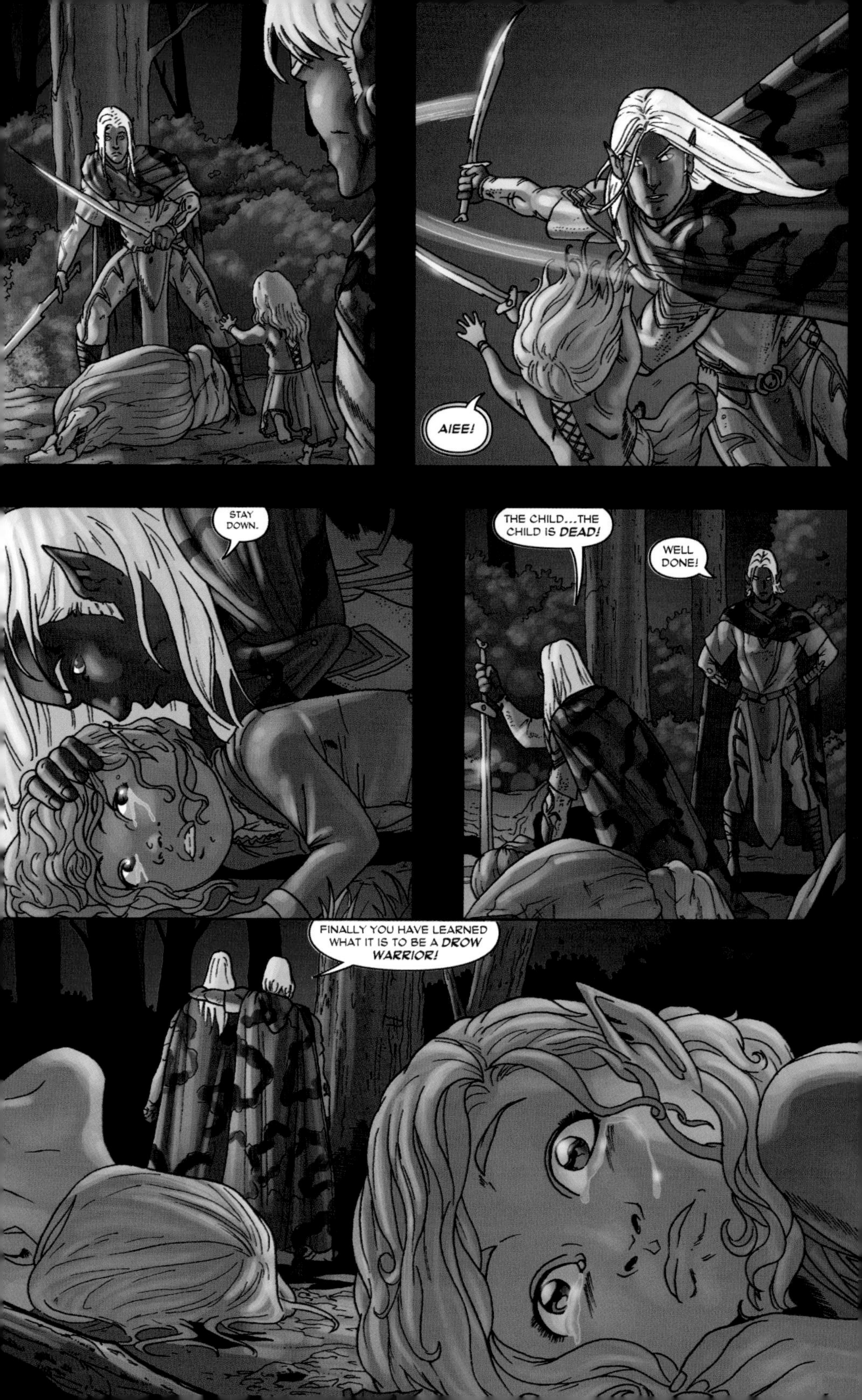
AIEE!
STAY DOWN.
THE CHILD...THE CHILD IS *DEAD!*
WELL DONE!
FINALLY YOU HAVE LEARNED WHAT IT IS TO BE A *DROW WARRIOR!*

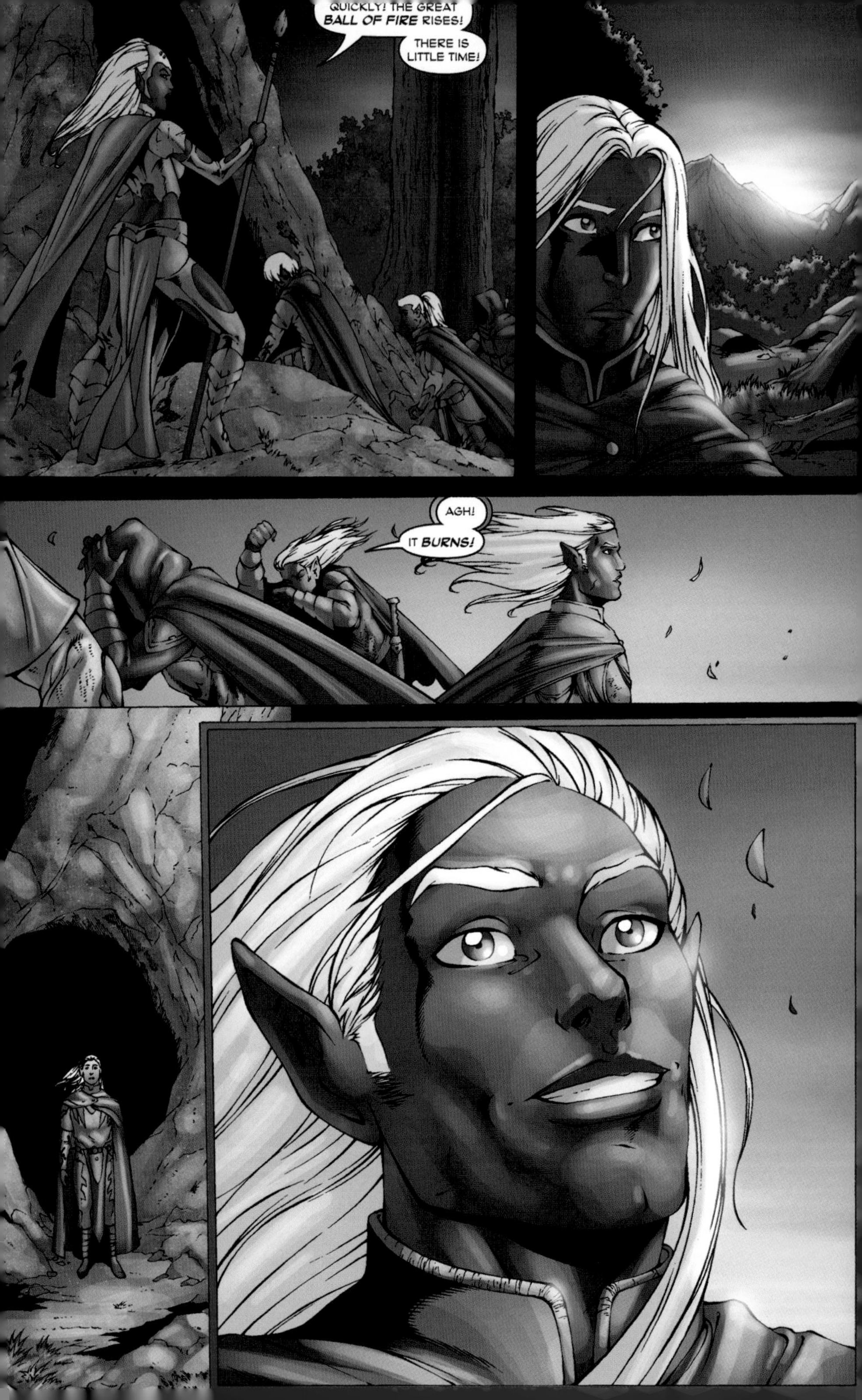
QUICKLY! THE GREAT BALL OF FIRE RISES!
THERE IS LITTLE TIME!
AGH!
IT BURNS!

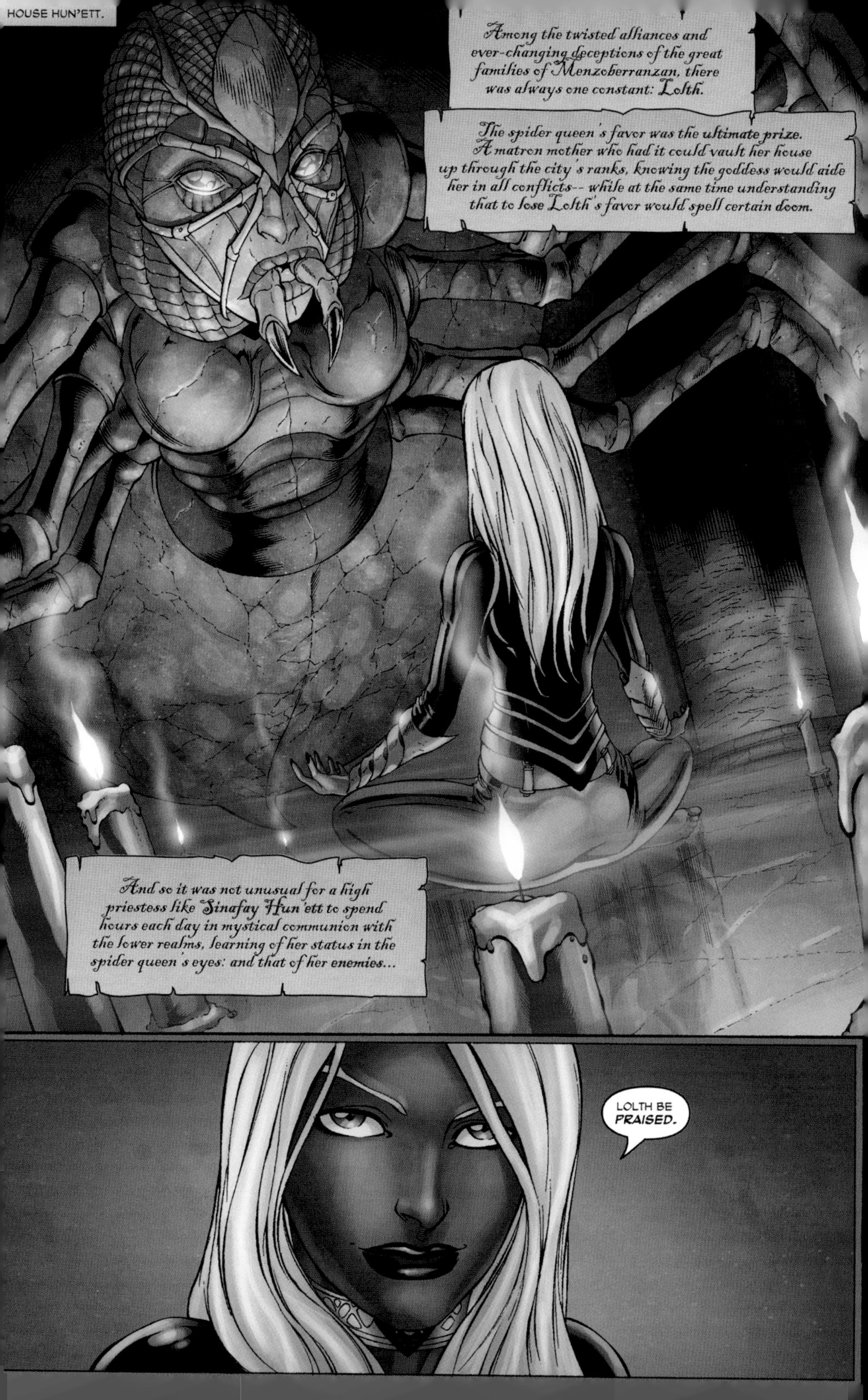
HOUSE HUN'ETT.
Among the twisted alliances and ever-changing deceptions of the great families of Menzoberranzan, there was always one constant: Lolth.
The spider queen's favor was the ultimate prize. A matron mother who had it could vault her house up through the city's ranks, knowing the goddess would aide her in all conflicts-- while at the same time understanding that to lose Lolth's favor would spell certain doom.
And so it was not unusual for a high priestess like Sinafay Hun'ett to spend hours each day in mystical communion with the lower realms, learning of her status in the spider queen's eyes: and that of her enemies...
LOLTH BE PRAISED.

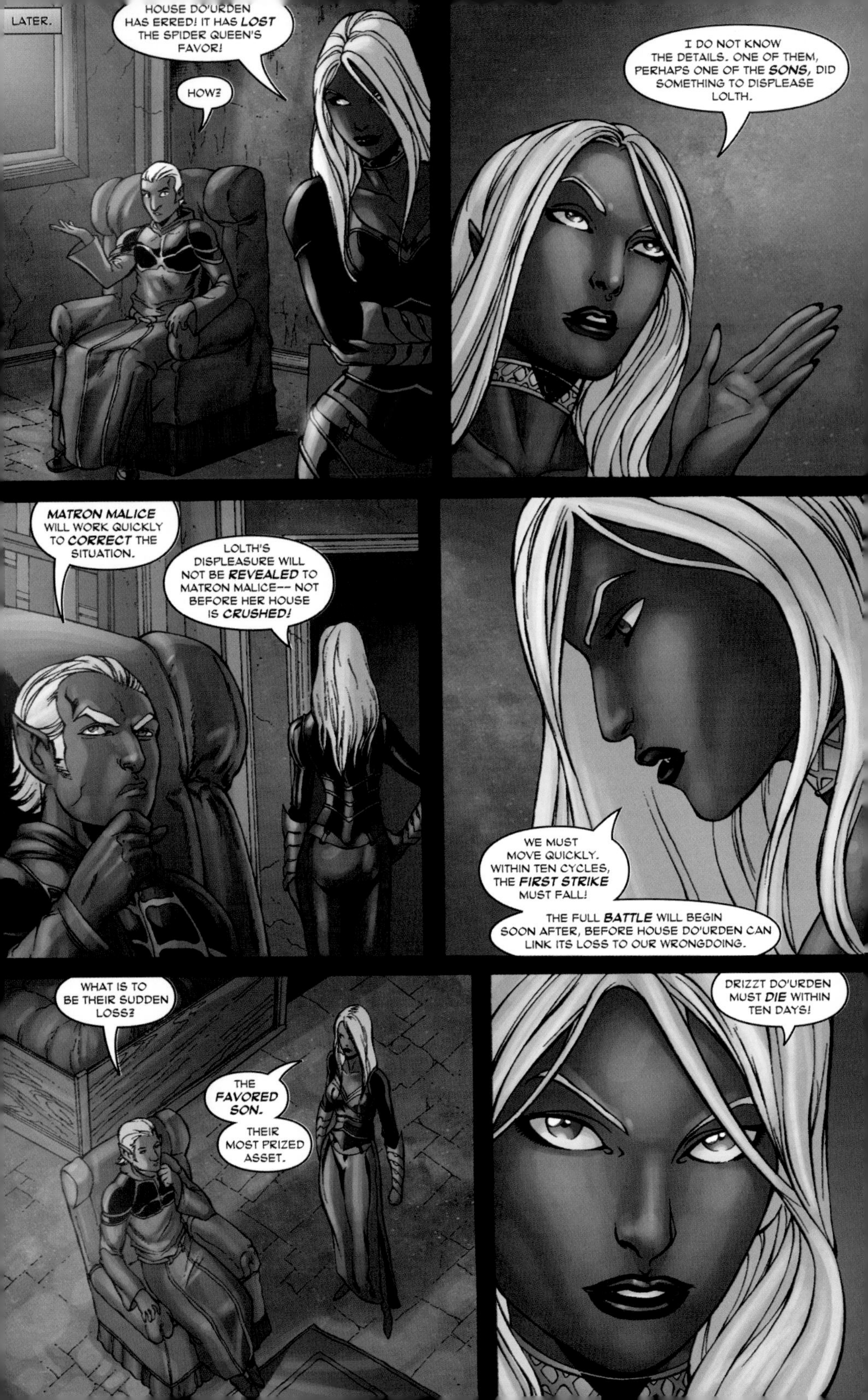

LATER.
HOUSE DO'URDEN HAS ERRED! IT HAS LOST THE SPIDER QUEEN'S FAVOR!
HOW?
I DO NOT KNOW THE DETAILS. ONE OF THEM, PERHAPS ONE OF THE SONS, DID SOMETHING TO DISPLEASE LOLTH.
MATRON MALICE WILL WORK QUICKLY TO CORRECT THE SITUATION.
LOLTH'S DISPLEASURE WILL NOT BE REVEALED TO MATRON MALICE-- NOT BEFORE HER HOUSE IS CRUSHED!
WE MUST MOVE QUICKLY. WITHIN TEN CYCLES, THE FIRST STRIKE MUST FALL!
THE FULL BATTLE WILL BEGIN SOON AFTER, BEFORE HOUSE DO'URDEN CAN LINK ITS LOSS TO OUR WRONGDOING.
WHAT IS TO BE THEIR SUDDEN LOSS?
THE FAVORED SON.
THEIR MOST PRIZED ASSET.
DRIZZT DO'URDEN MUST DIE WITHIN TEN DAYS!

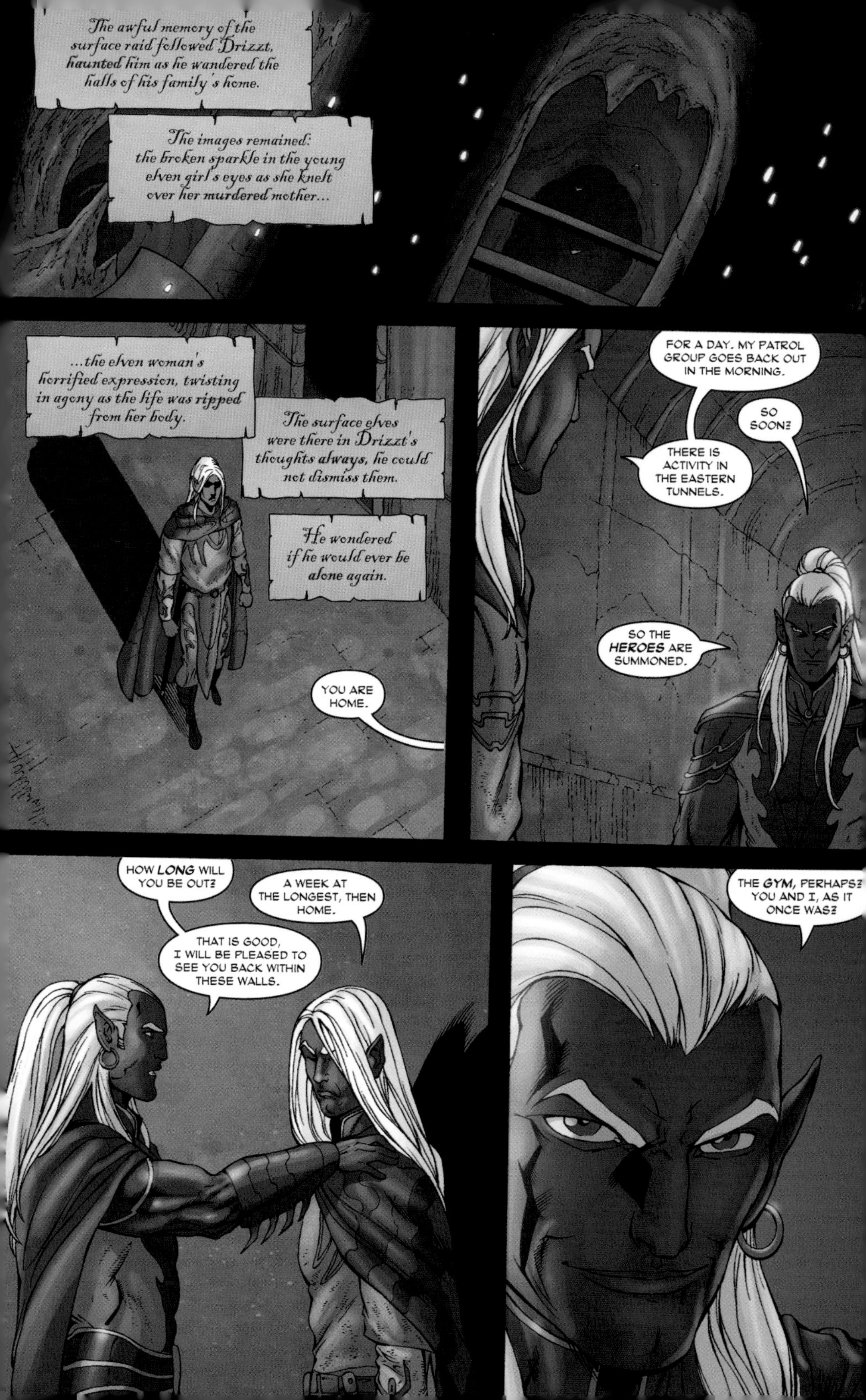
The awful memory of the surface raid followed Drizzt, haunted him as he wandered the halls of his family's home.
The images remained: the broken sparkle in the young elven girl's eyes as she knelt over her murdered mother...
...the elven woman's horrified expression, twisting in agony as the life was ripped from her body.
The surface elves were there in Drizzt's thoughts always, he could not dismiss them.
He wondered if he would ever be alone again.
YOU ARE HOME.
FOR A DAY. MY PATROL GROUP GOES BACK OUT IN THE MORNING.
SO SOON?
THERE IS ACTIVITY IN THE EASTERN TUNNELS.
SO THE HEROES ARE SUMMONED.
HOW LONG WILL YOU BE OUT?
A WEEK AT THE LONGEST, THEN HOME.
THAT IS GOOD, I WILL BE PLEASED TO SEE YOU BACK WITHIN THESE WALLS.
THE GYM, PERHAPS? YOU AND I, AS IT ONCE WAS?

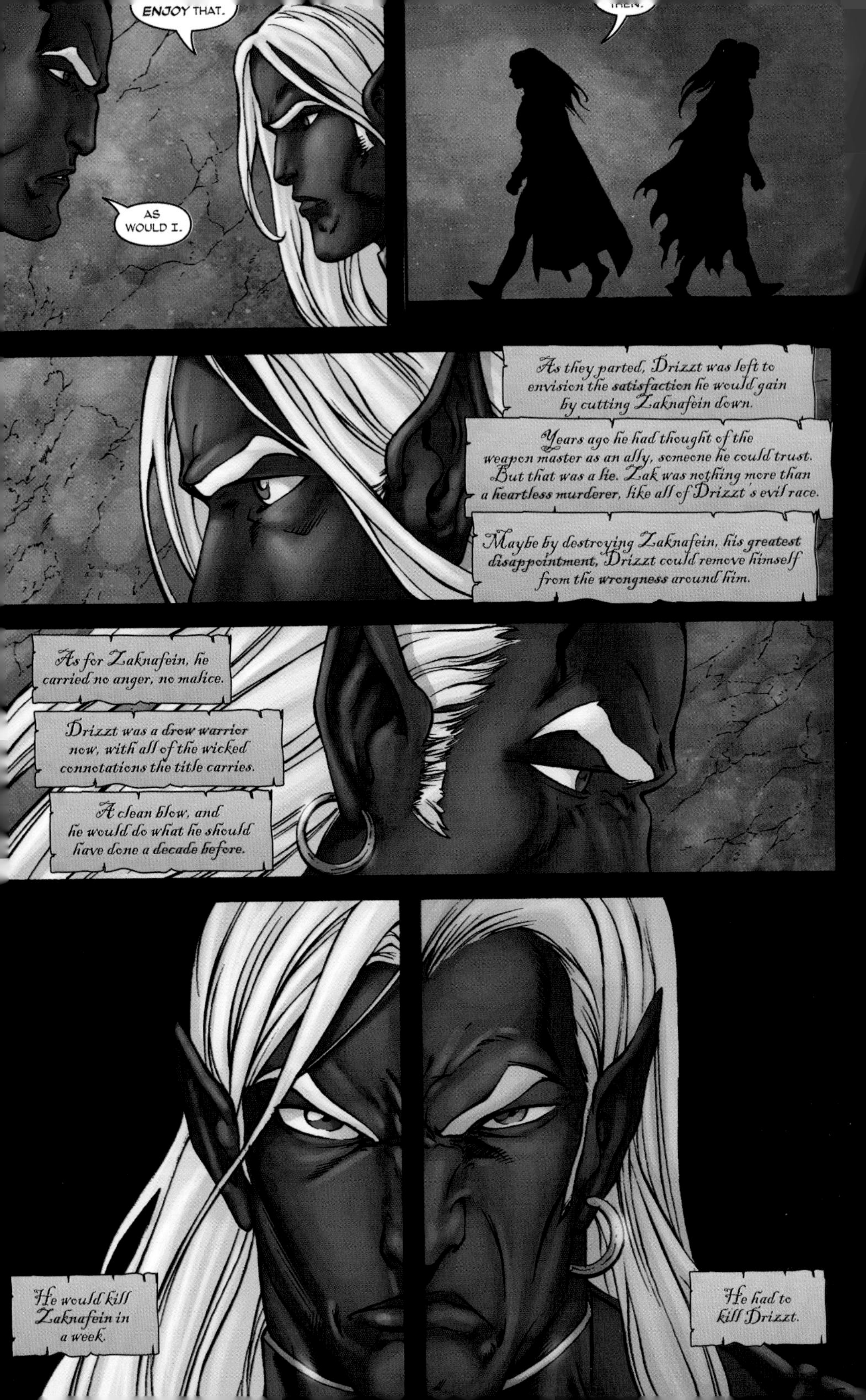
ENJOY THAT.
AS WOULD I.
As they parted, Drizzt was left to envision the satisfaction he would gain by cutting Zaknafein down.
Years ago he had thought of the weapon master as an ally, someone he could trust. But that was a lie. Zak was nothing more than a heartless murderer, like all of Drizzt's evil race.
Maybe by destroying Zaknafein, his greatest disappointment, Drizzt could remove himself from the wrongness around him.
As for Zaknafein, he carried no anger, no malice.
Drizzt was a drow warrior now, with all of the wicked connotations the title carries.
A clean blow, and he would do what he should have done a decade before.
He would kill Zaknafein in a week.
He had to kill Drizzt.

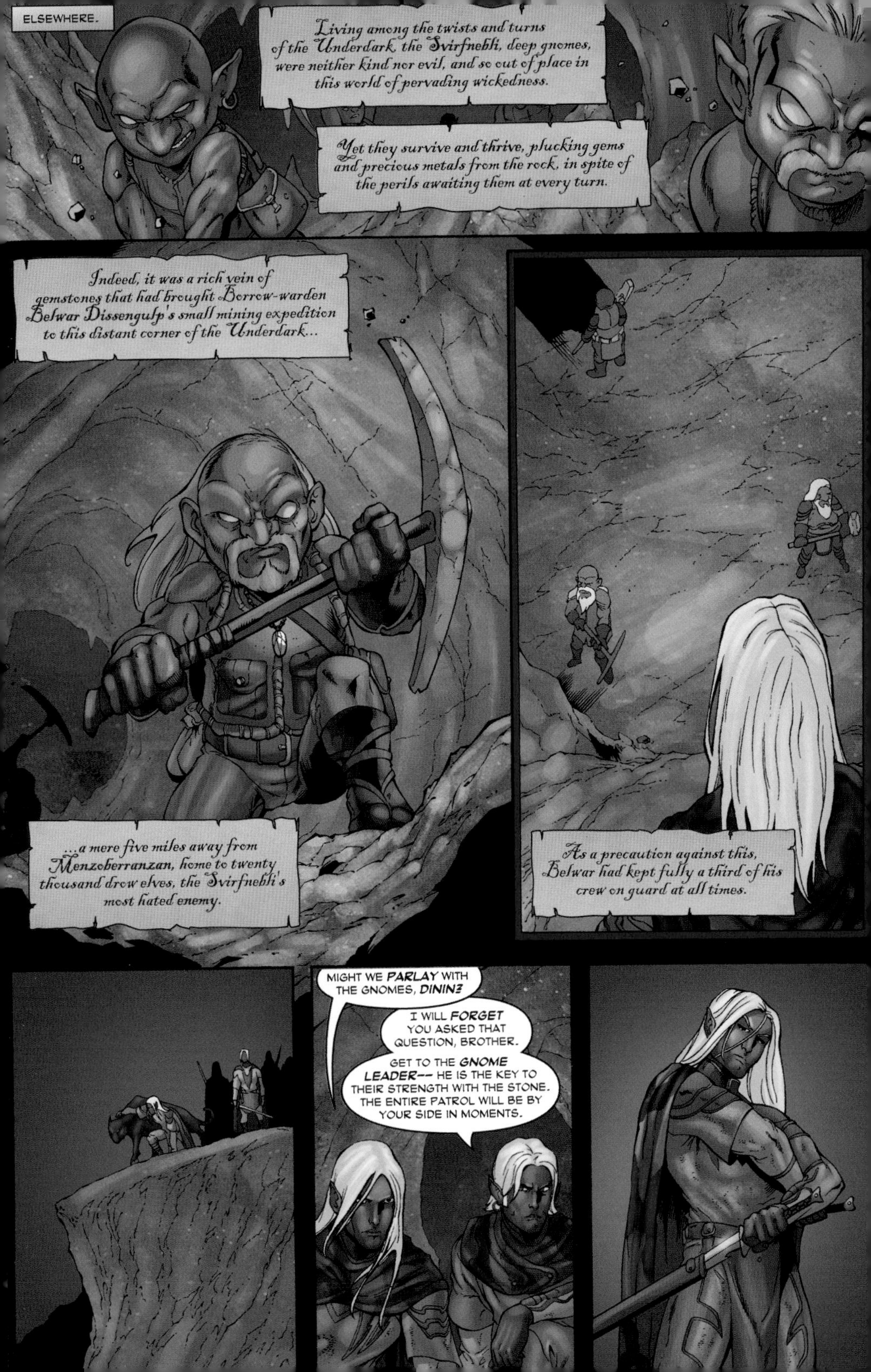
ELSEWHERE.
Living among the twists and turns of the Underdark, the Svirfnebli, deep gnomes, were neither kind nor evil, and so out of place in this world of pervading wickedness.
Yet they survive and thrive, plucking gems and precious metals from the rock, in spite of the perils awaiting them at every turn.
Indeed, it was a rich vein of gemstones that had brought Borrow-warden Belwar Dissengulp's small mining expedition to this distant corner of the Underdark...
...a mere five miles away from Menzoberranzan, home to twenty thousand drow elves, the Svirfnebli's most hated enemy.
As a precaution against this, Belwar had kept fully a third of his crew on guard at all times.
MIGHT WE PARLAY WITH THE GNOMES, DININ?
I WILL FORGET YOU ASKED THAT QUESTION, BROTHER.
GET TO THE GNOME LEADER-- HE IS THE KEY TO THEIR STRENGTH WITH THE STONE. THE ENTIRE PATROL WILL BE BY YOUR SIDE IN MOMENTS.

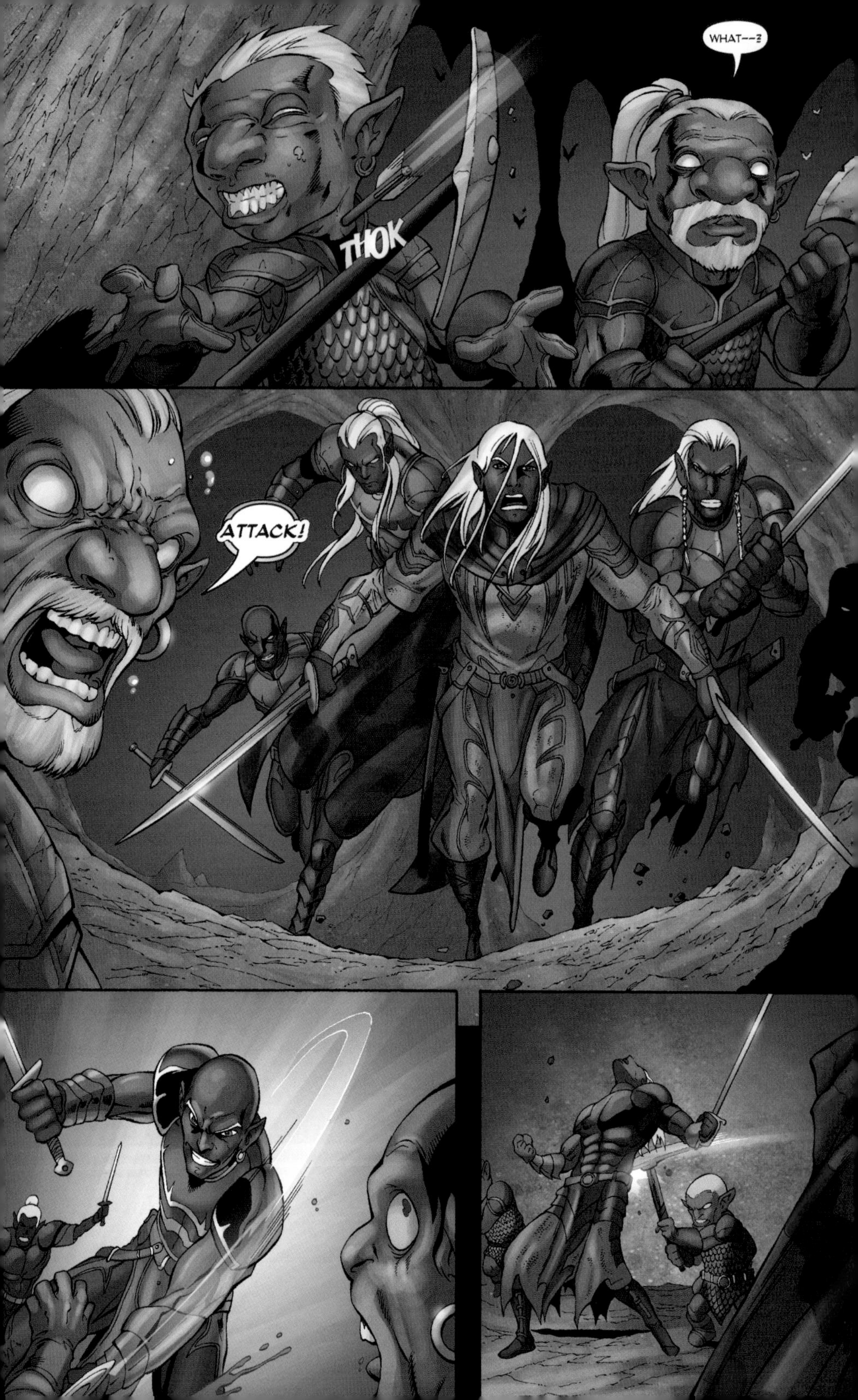
THOK
WHAT--?
ATTACK!

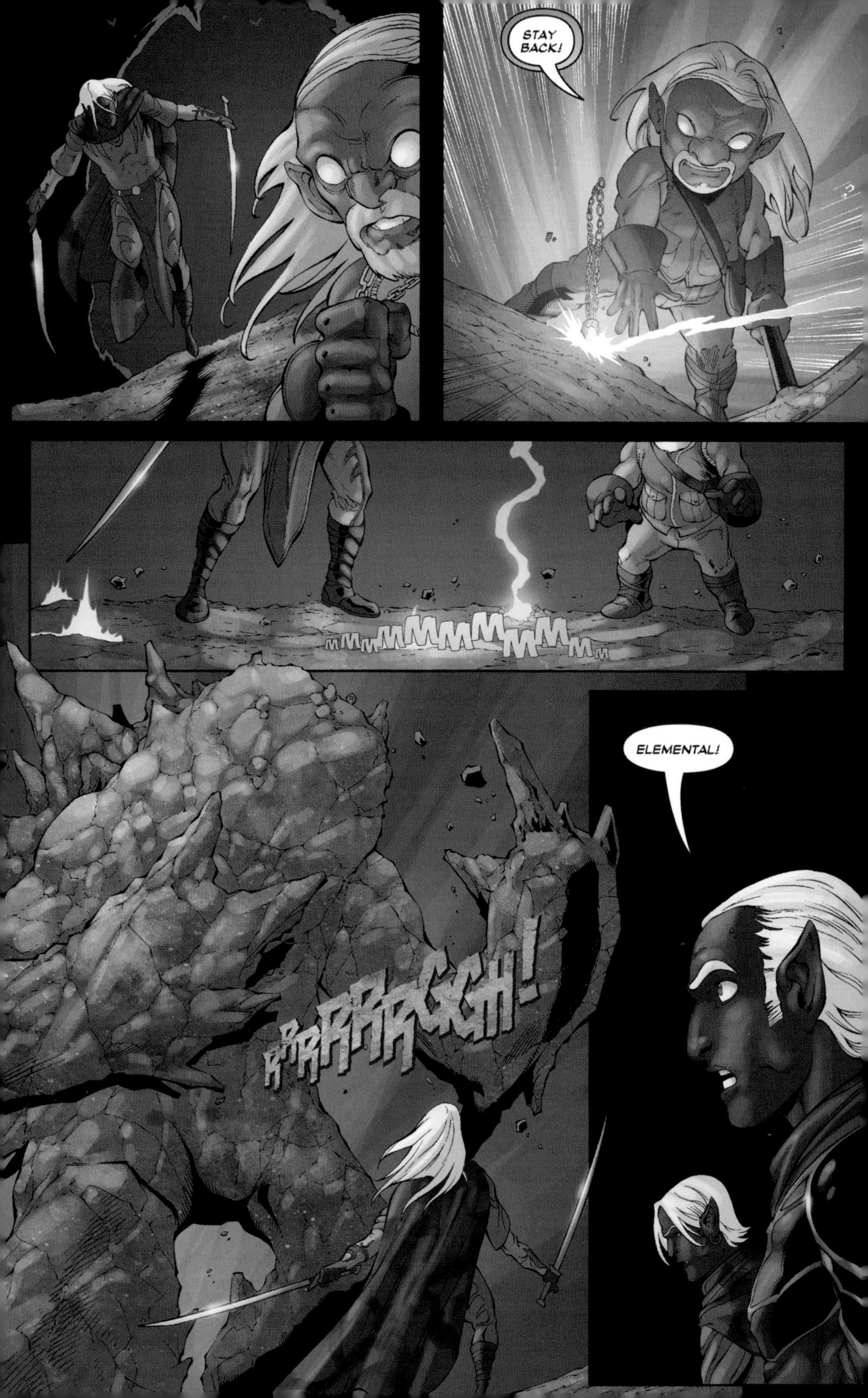
STAY BACK!
MMMMMMMMMMMMMMMMMM
ELEMENTAL!
RRRRRRGGH!

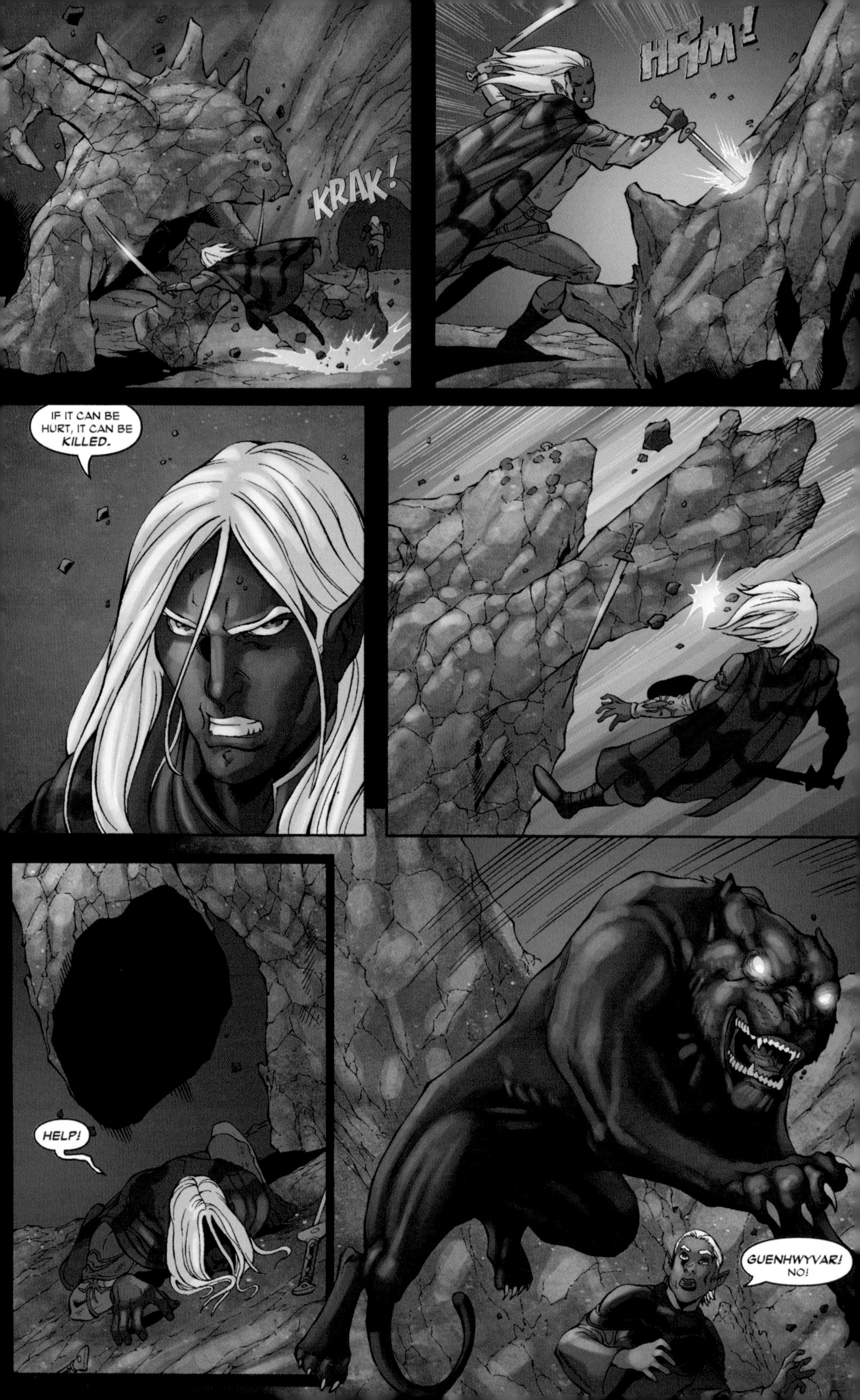
KRAK!
HRM!
IF IT CAN BE HURT, IT CAN BE KILLED.
HELP!
GUENHWYVAR! NO!

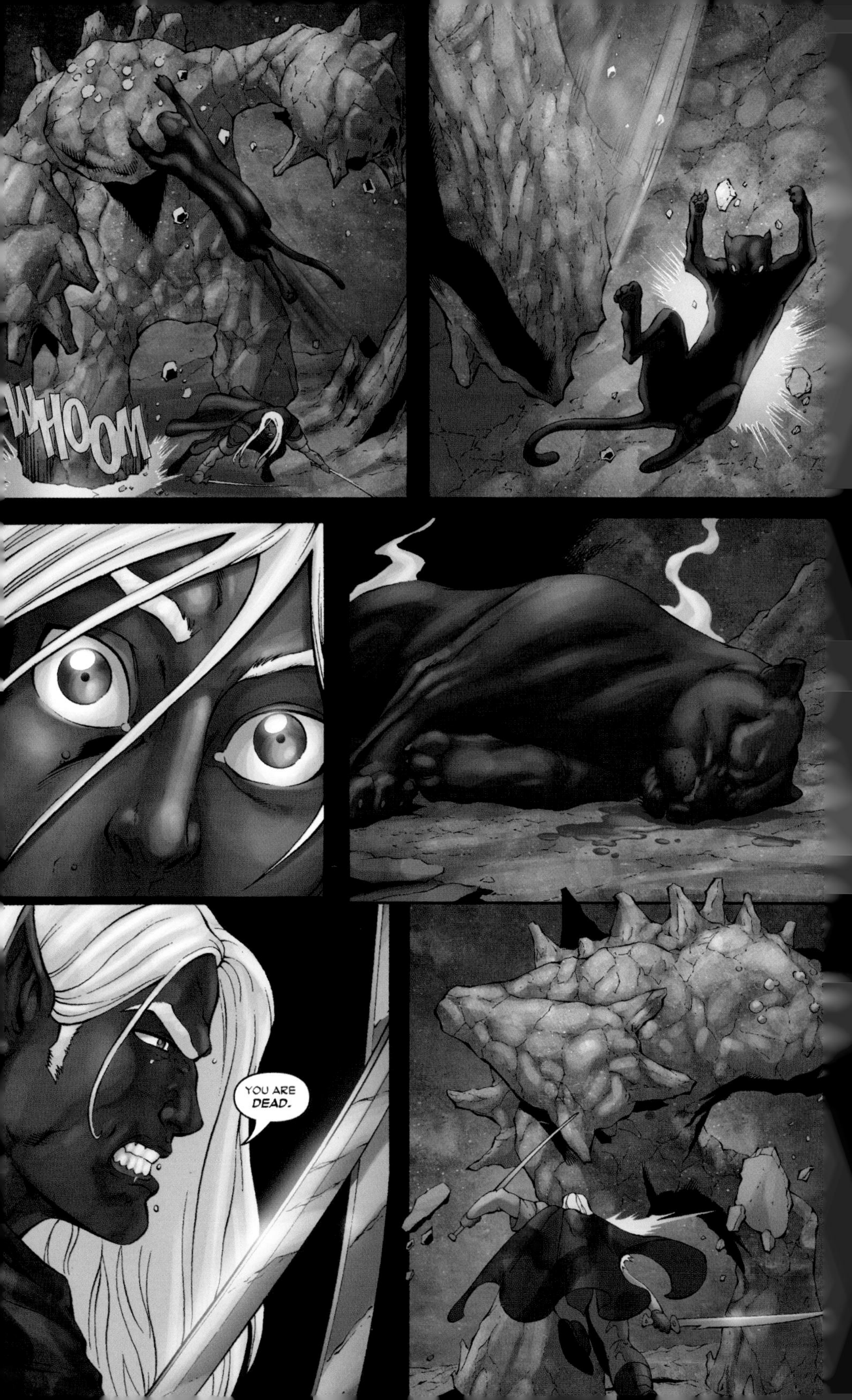

WHOOM
YOU ARE DEAD.

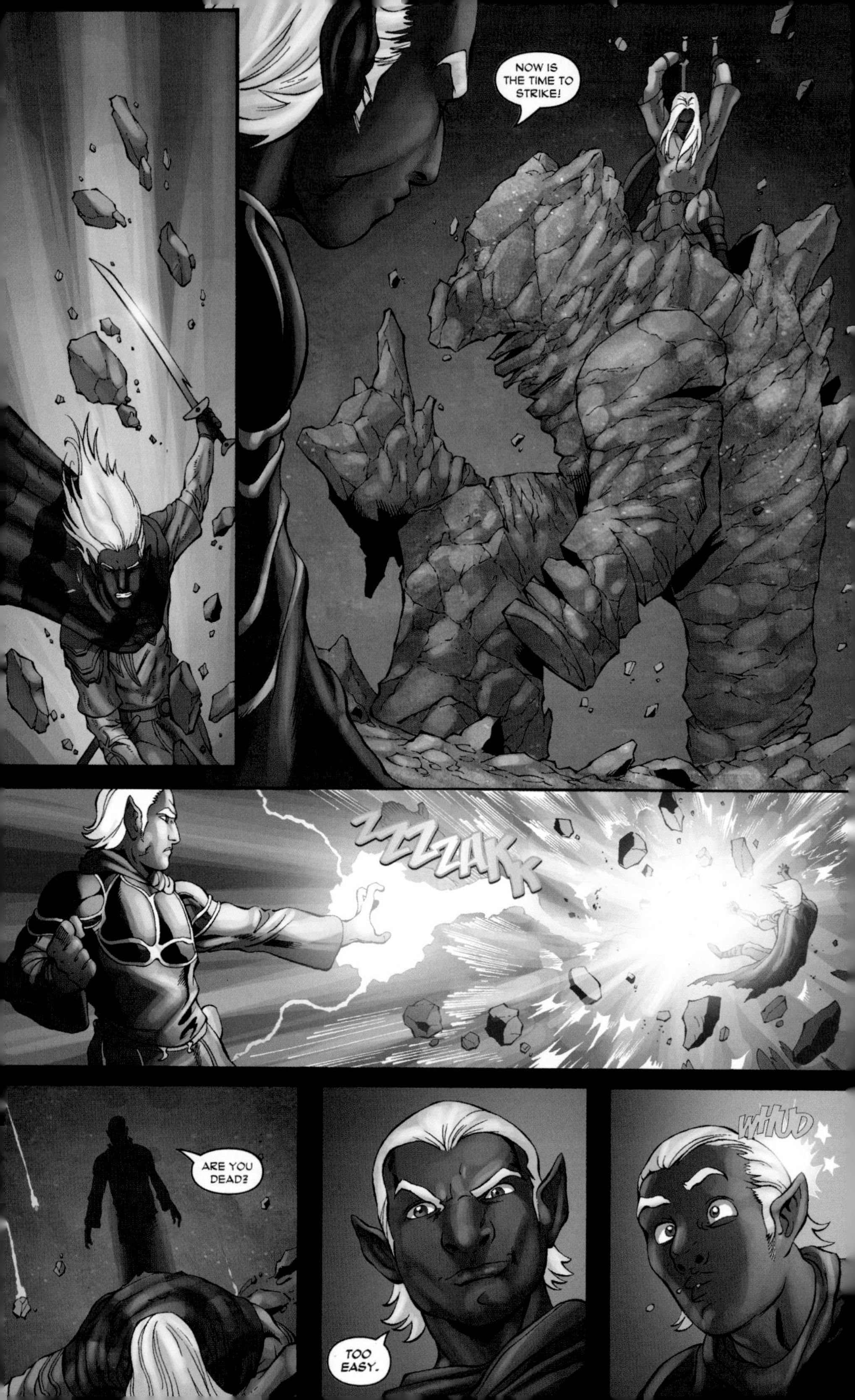
NOW IS THE TIME TO STRIKE!
ZZZZAKK
ARE YOU DEAD?
TOO EASY.
WHUD

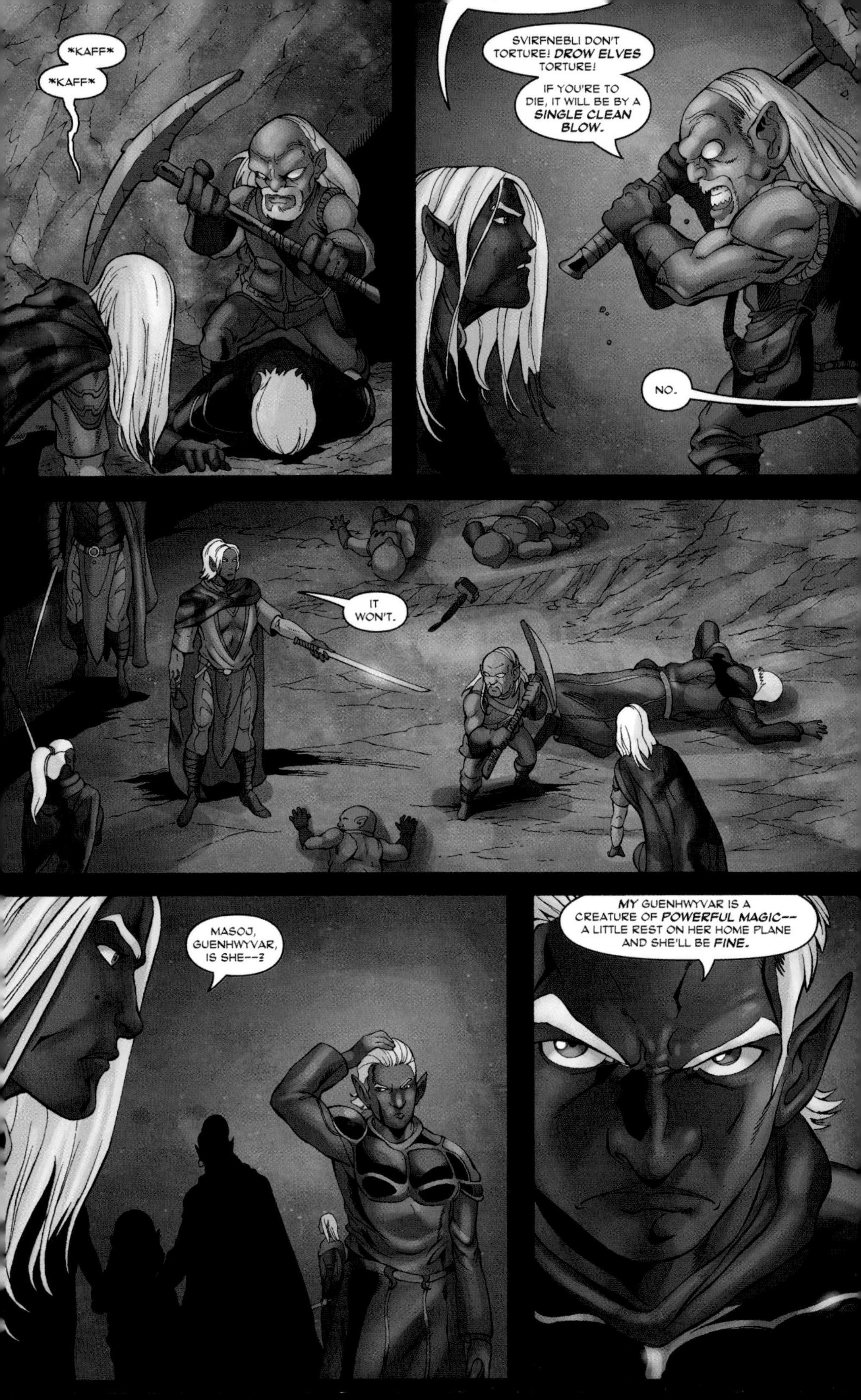
KAFF
KAFF
SVIRFNEBLI DON'T TORTURE! *DROW ELVES* TORTURE!
IF YOU'RE TO DIE, IT WILL BE BY A *SINGLE CLEAN BLOW.*
NO.
IT WON'T.
MASOJ, GUENHWYVAR, IS SHE--?
MY GUENHWYVAR IS A CREATURE OF *POWERFUL MAGIC--* A LITTLE REST ON HER HOME PLANE AND SHE'LL BE *FINE.*

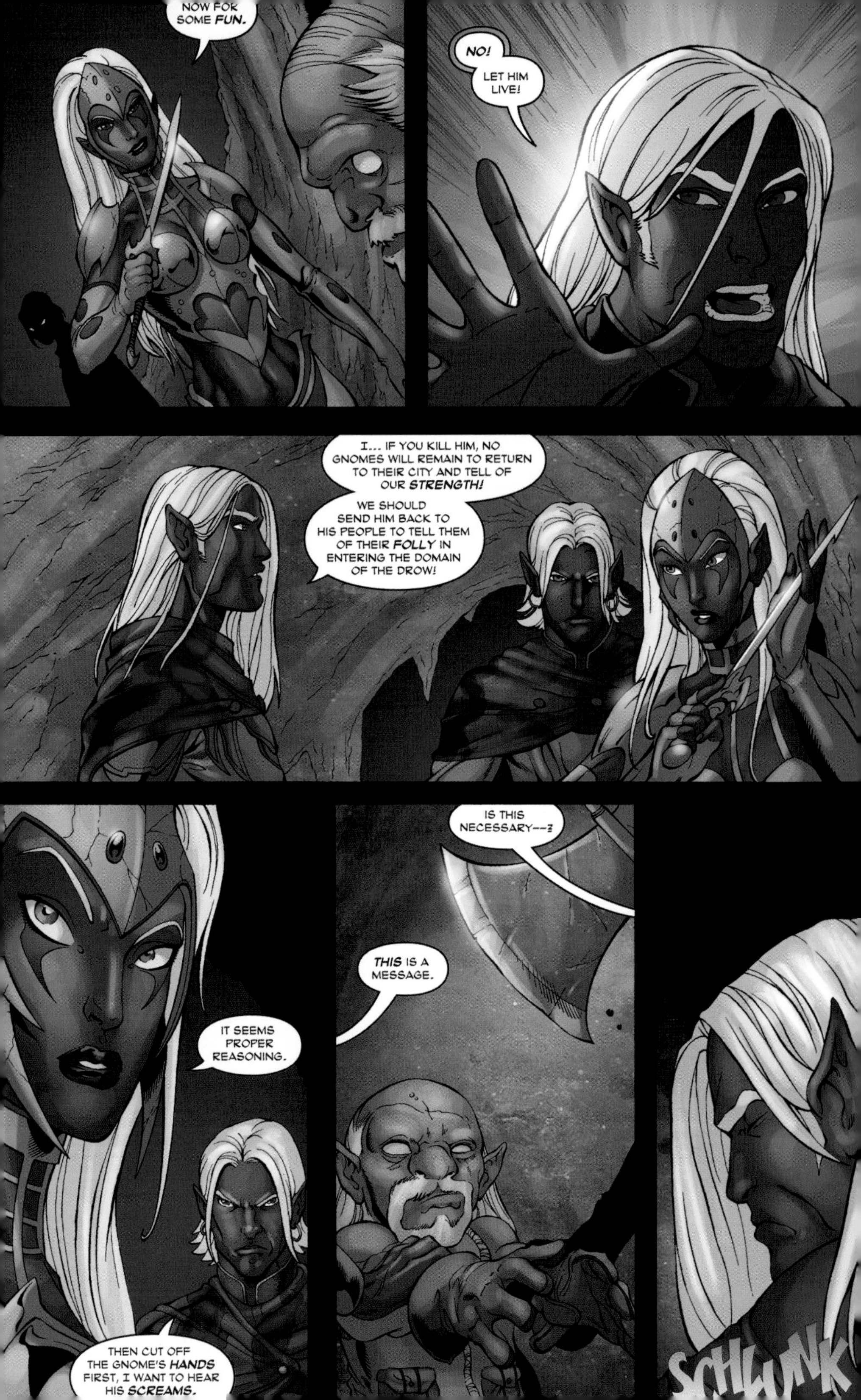
NOW FOR SOME FUN.
NO! LET HIM LIVE!
I... IF YOU KILL HIM, NO GNOMES WILL REMAIN TO RETURN TO THEIR CITY AND TELL OF OUR STRENGTH!
WE SHOULD SEND HIM BACK TO HIS PEOPLE TO TELL THEM OF THEIR FOLLY IN ENTERING THE DOMAIN OF THE DROW!
IT SEEMS PROPER REASONING.
THEN CUT OFF THE GNOME'S HANDS FIRST, I WANT TO HEAR HIS SCREAMS.
IS THIS NECESSARY--?
THIS IS A MESSAGE.
SCHLUNK

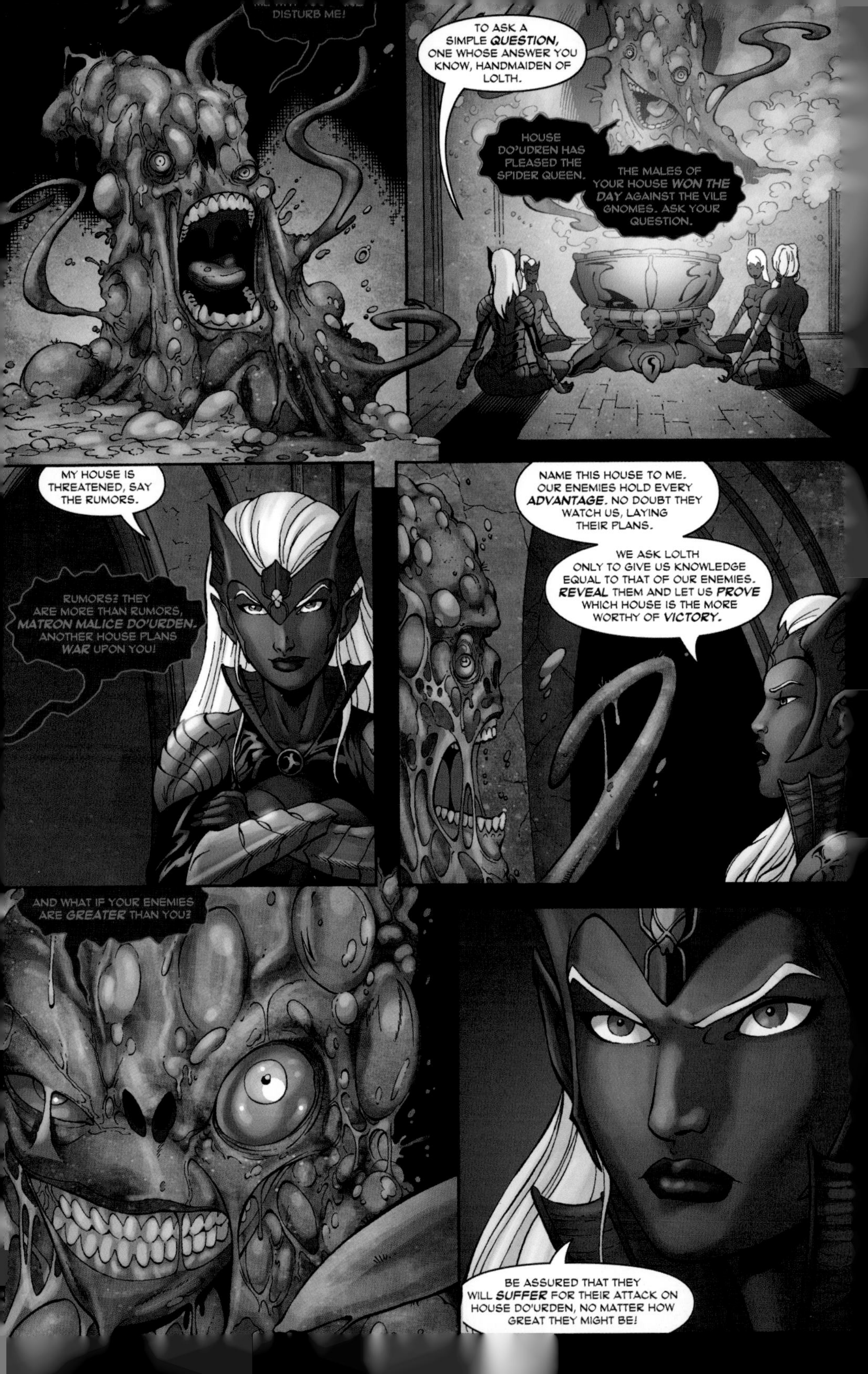
DISTURB ME!
TO ASK A SIMPLE QUESTION, ONE WHOSE ANSWER YOU KNOW, HANDMAIDEN OF LOLTH.
HOUSE DO'UDREN HAS PLEASED THE SPIDER QUEEN.
THE MALES OF YOUR HOUSE WON THE DAY AGAINST THE VILE GNOMES. ASK YOUR QUESTION.
MY HOUSE IS THREATENED, SAY THE RUMORS.
RUMORS? THEY ARE MORE THAN RUMORS, MATRON MALICE DO'URDEN. ANOTHER HOUSE PLANS WAR UPON YOU!
NAME THIS HOUSE TO ME. OUR ENEMIES HOLD EVERY ADVANTAGE. NO DOUBT THEY WATCH US, LAYING THEIR PLANS.
WE ASK LOLTH ONLY TO GIVE US KNOWLEDGE EQUAL TO THAT OF OUR ENEMIES. REVEAL THEM AND LET US PROVE WHICH HOUSE IS THE MORE WORTHY OF VICTORY.
AND WHAT IF YOUR ENEMIES ARE GREATER THAN YOU?
BE ASSURED THAT THEY WILL SUFFER FOR THEIR ATTACK ON HOUSE DO'URDEN, NO MATTER HOW GREAT THEY MIGHT BE!

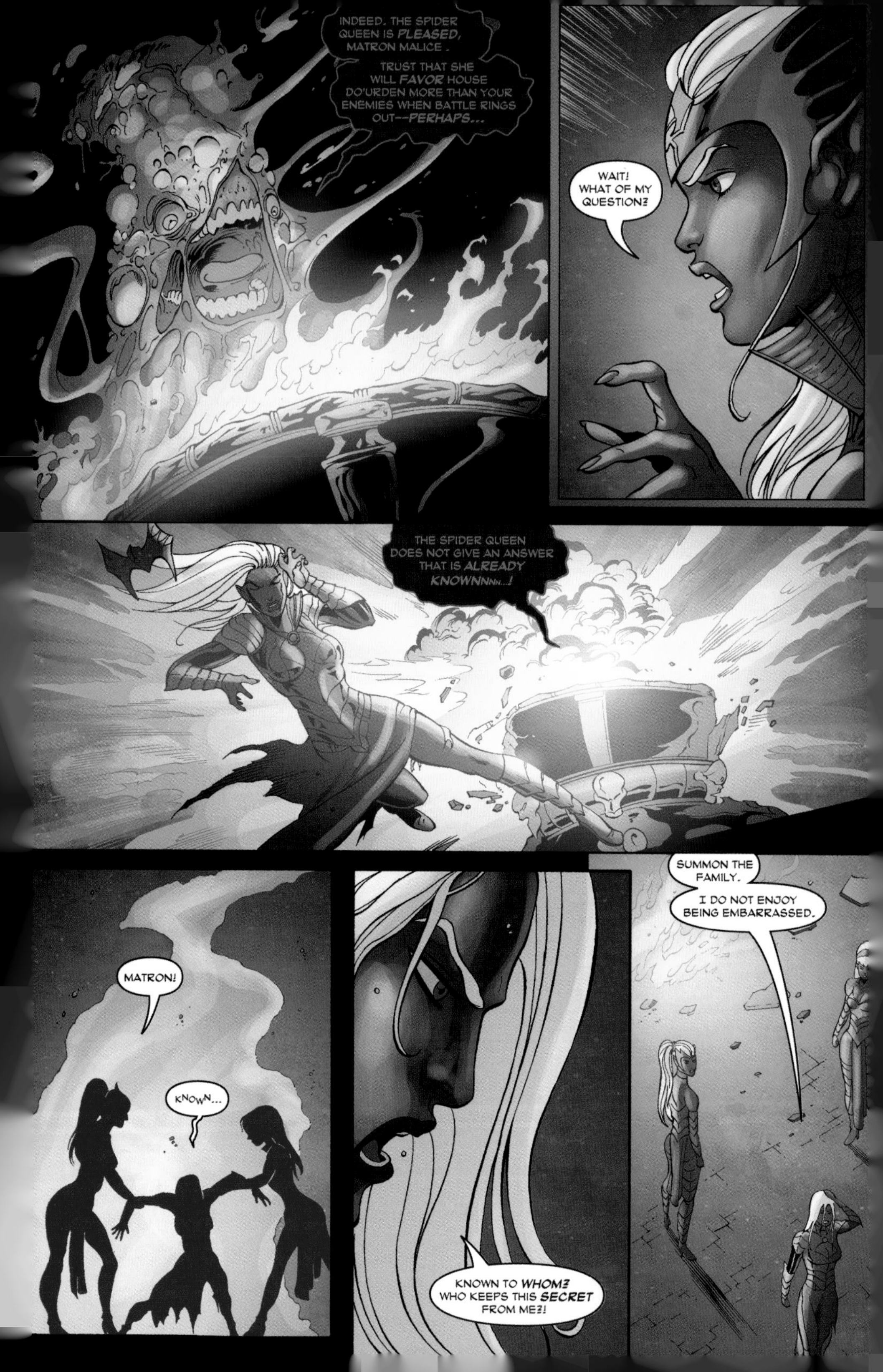
INDEED. THE SPIDER QUEEN IS PLEASED, MATRON MALICE.
TRUST THAT SHE WILL FAVOR HOUSE DO'URDEN MORE THAN YOUR ENEMIES WHEN BATTLE RINGS OUT--PERHAPS...
WAIT! WHAT OF MY QUESTION?
THE SPIDER QUEEN DOES NOT GIVE AN ANSWER THAT IS ALREADY KNOWNNNN...!
MATRON!
KNOWN...
KNOWN TO WHOM? WHO KEEPS THIS SECRET FROM ME?!
SUMMON THE FAMILY.
I DO NOT ENJOY BEING EMBARRASSED.

YOU LET HIM *ESCAPE!*

NO, MY MATRON! I HIT HIM SQUARELY WITH A *LIGHTNING BOLT.* HE NEVER EVEN SUSPECTED THE BLOW TO BE AIMED AT HIM!

YET HE STILL *LIVES.*

I WILL GET HIM. I HAVE THE WEAPON READIED; DRIZZT WILL BE *DEAD* BEFORE THE TENTH CYCLE, AS YOU COMMANDED.

WHY SHOULD I GRANT YOU ANOTHER CHANCE?

BECAUSE I WANT HIM DEAD! I WANT TO *TEAR* THE LIFE FROM DRIZZT DO'URDEN! WHEN HE IS DEAD, I WANT TO RIP OUT HIS *HEART* AND DISPLAY IT AS A TROPHY!

YOU WILL HAVE YOUR SECOND CHANCE, MASOJ, BUT NOT ALONE. *ALTON* WILL ACCOMPANY YOU.

PERHAPS THE TWO OF YOU CAN ACCOMPLISH TOGETHER WHAT YOU BOTH *FAILED* TO DO ALONE.

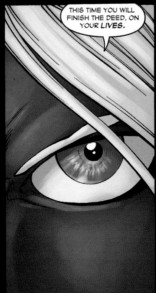

THIS TIME YOU WILL FINISH THE DEED, ON YOUR *LIVES.*

COULD IT BE ANY OTHER WAY?

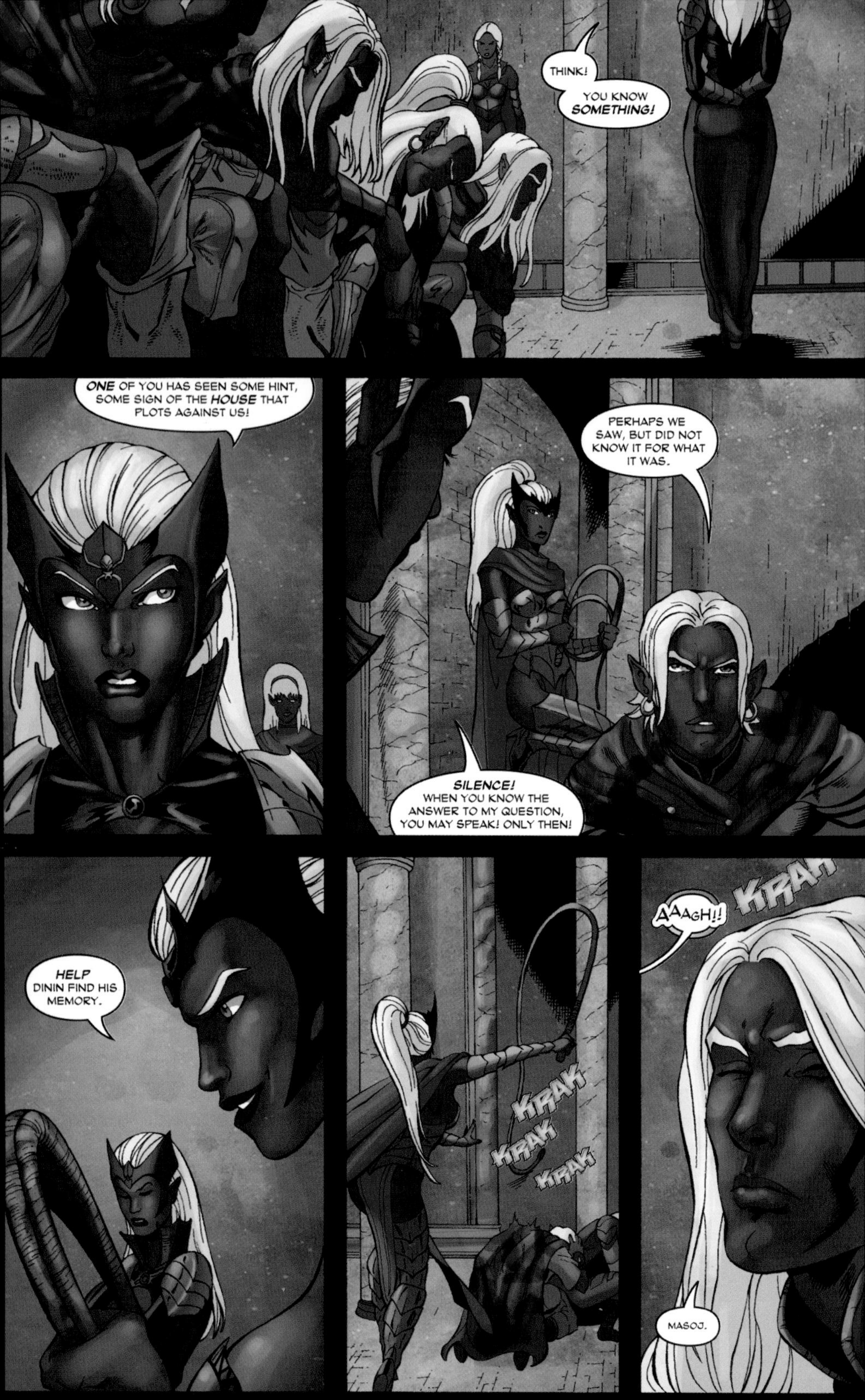
THINK!
YOU KNOW SOMETHING!
ONE OF YOU HAS SEEN SOME HINT, SOME SIGN OF THE HOUSE THAT PLOTS AGAINST US!
PERHAPS WE SAW, BUT DID NOT KNOW IT FOR WHAT IT WAS.
SILENCE! WHEN YOU KNOW THE ANSWER TO MY QUESTION, YOU MAY SPEAK! ONLY THEN!
HELP DININ FIND HIS MEMORY.
KRAK
KRAK
KRAK
AAAGH!!
KRAK
MASOJ.

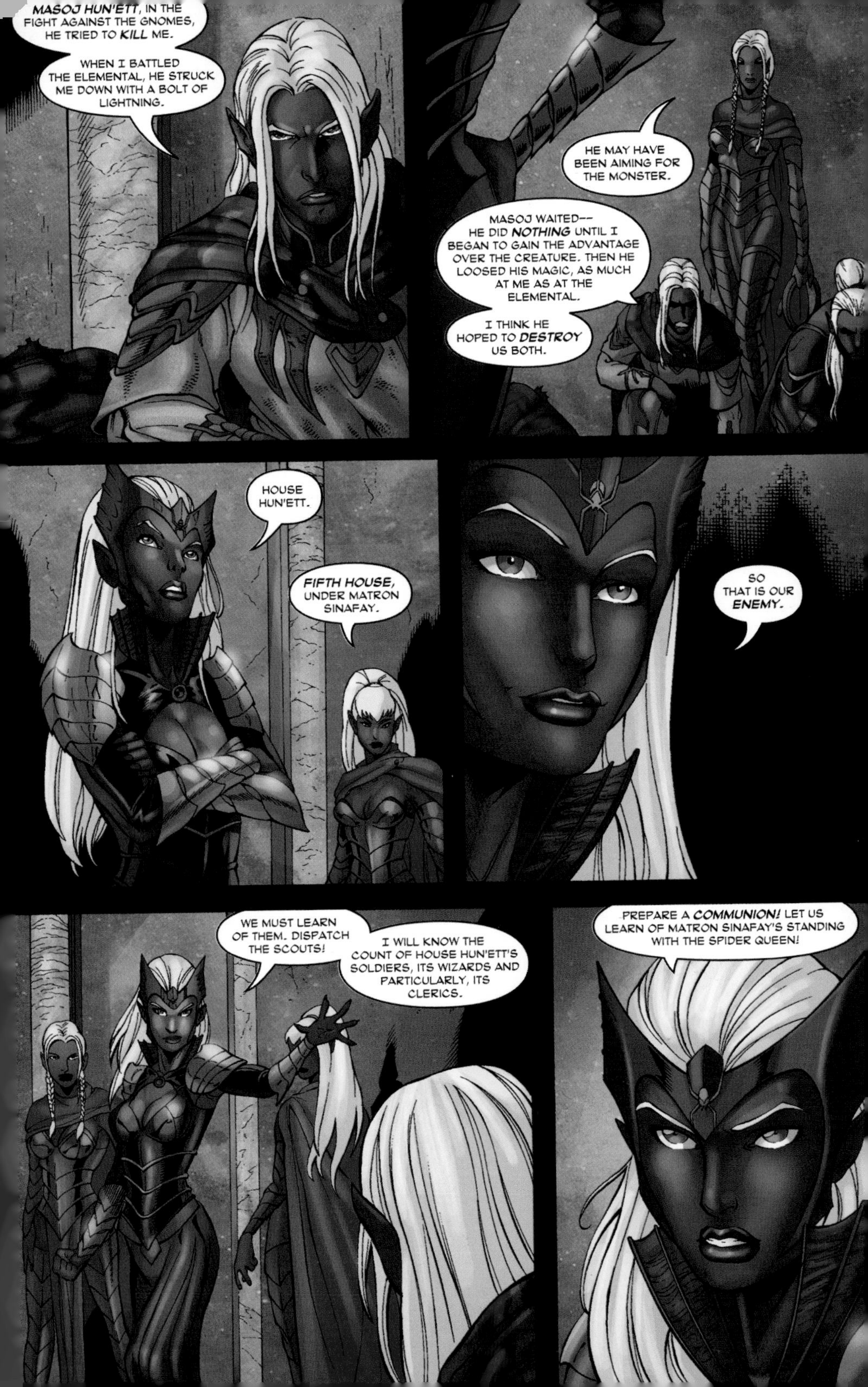
MASOJ HUN'ETT, IN THE FIGHT AGAINST THE GNOMES, HE TRIED TO KILL ME.
WHEN I BATTLED THE ELEMENTAL, HE STRUCK ME DOWN WITH A BOLT OF LIGHTNING.
HE MAY HAVE BEEN AIMING FOR THE MONSTER.
MASOJ WAITED-- HE DID NOTHING UNTIL I BEGAN TO GAIN THE ADVANTAGE OVER THE CREATURE. THEN HE LOOSED HIS MAGIC, AS MUCH AT ME AS AT THE ELEMENTAL.
I THINK HE HOPED TO DESTROY US BOTH.
HOUSE HUN'ETT.
FIFTH HOUSE, UNDER MATRON SINAFAY.
SO THAT IS OUR ENEMY.
WE MUST LEARN OF THEM. DISPATCH THE SCOUTS!
I WILL KNOW THE COUNT OF HOUSE HUN'ETT'S SOLDIERS, ITS WIZARDS AND PARTICULARLY, ITS CLERICS.
PREPARE A COMMUNION! LET US LEARN OF MATRON SINAFAY'S STANDING WITH THE SPIDER QUEEN!

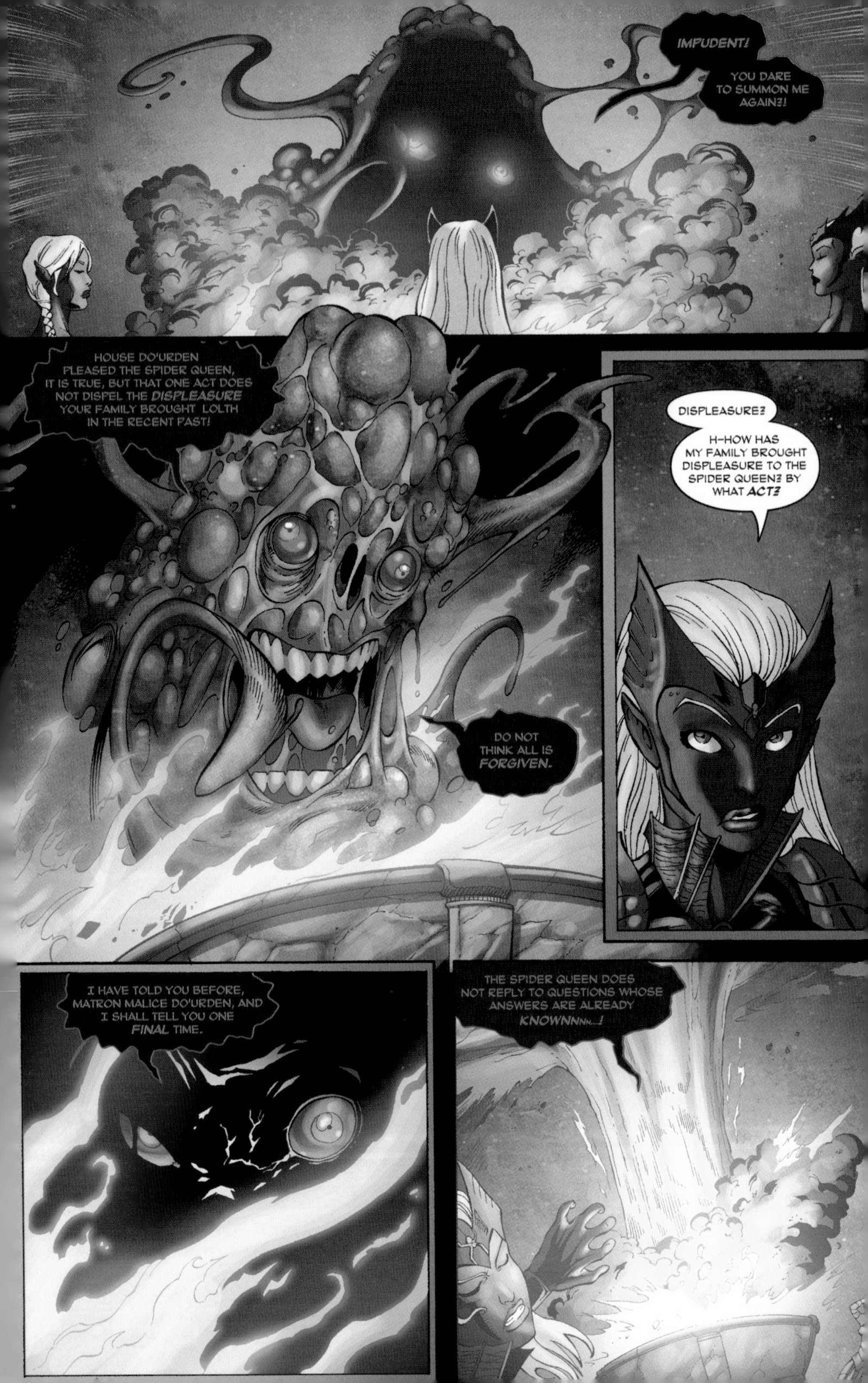

IMPUDENT!
YOU DARE TO SUMMON ME AGAIN?!
HOUSE DO'URDEN PLEASED THE SPIDER QUEEN, IT IS TRUE, BUT THAT ONE ACT DOES NOT DISPEL THE DISPLEASURE YOUR FAMILY BROUGHT LOLTH IN THE RECENT PAST!
DISPLEASURE?
H-HOW HAS MY FAMILY BROUGHT DISPLEASURE TO THE SPIDER QUEEN? BY WHAT ACT?
DO NOT THINK ALL IS FORGIVEN.
I HAVE TOLD YOU BEFORE, MATRON MALICE DO'URDEN, AND I SHALL TELL YOU ONE FINAL TIME.
THE SPIDER QUEEN DOES NOT REPLY TO QUESTIONS WHOSE ANSWERS ARE ALREADY KNOWNNNnn...!

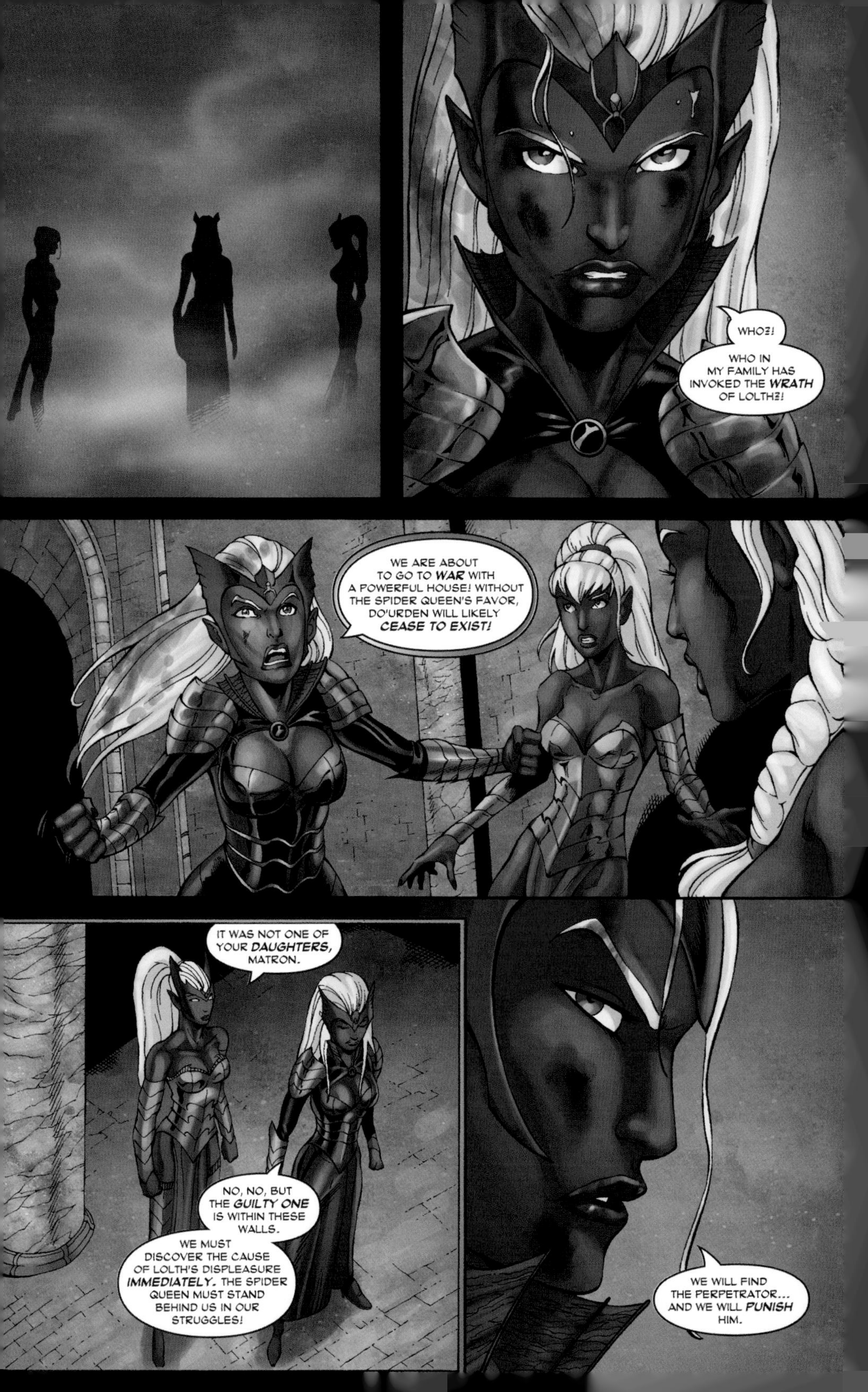
WHO?!
WHO IN MY FAMILY HAS INVOKED THE WRATH OF LOLTH?!
WE ARE ABOUT TO GO TO WAR WITH A POWERFUL HOUSE! WITHOUT THE SPIDER QUEEN'S FAVOR, DO'URDEN WILL LIKELY CEASE TO EXIST!
IT WAS NOT ONE OF YOUR DAUGHTERS, MATRON.
NO, NO, BUT THE GUILTY ONE IS WITHIN THESE WALLS.
WE MUST DISCOVER THE CAUSE OF LOLTH'S DISPLEASURE IMMEDIATELY. THE SPIDER QUEEN MUST STAND BEHIND US IN OUR STRUGGLES!
WE WILL FIND THE PERPETRATOR... AND WE WILL PUNISH HIM.

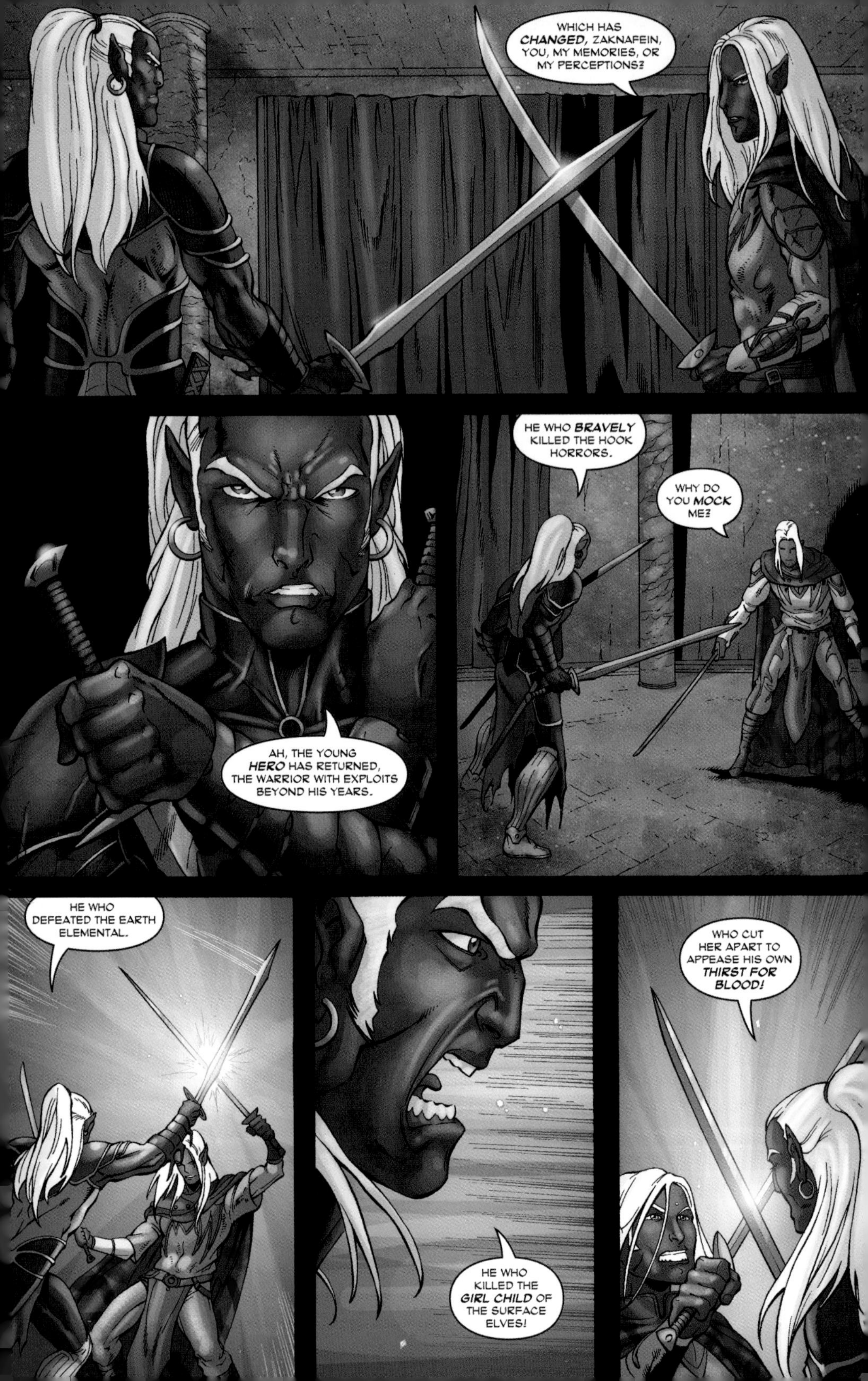

WHICH HAS CHANGED, ZAKNAFEIN, YOU, MY MEMORIES, OR MY PERCEPTIONS?
AH, THE YOUNG HERO HAS RETURNED, THE WARRIOR WITH EXPLOITS BEYOND HIS YEARS.
HE WHO BRAVELY KILLED THE HOOK HORRORS.
WHY DO YOU MOCK ME?
HE WHO DEFEATED THE EARTH ELEMENTAL.
HE WHO KILLED THE GIRL CHILD OF THE SURFACE ELVES!
WHO CUT HER APART TO APPEASE HIS OWN THIRST FOR BLOOD!

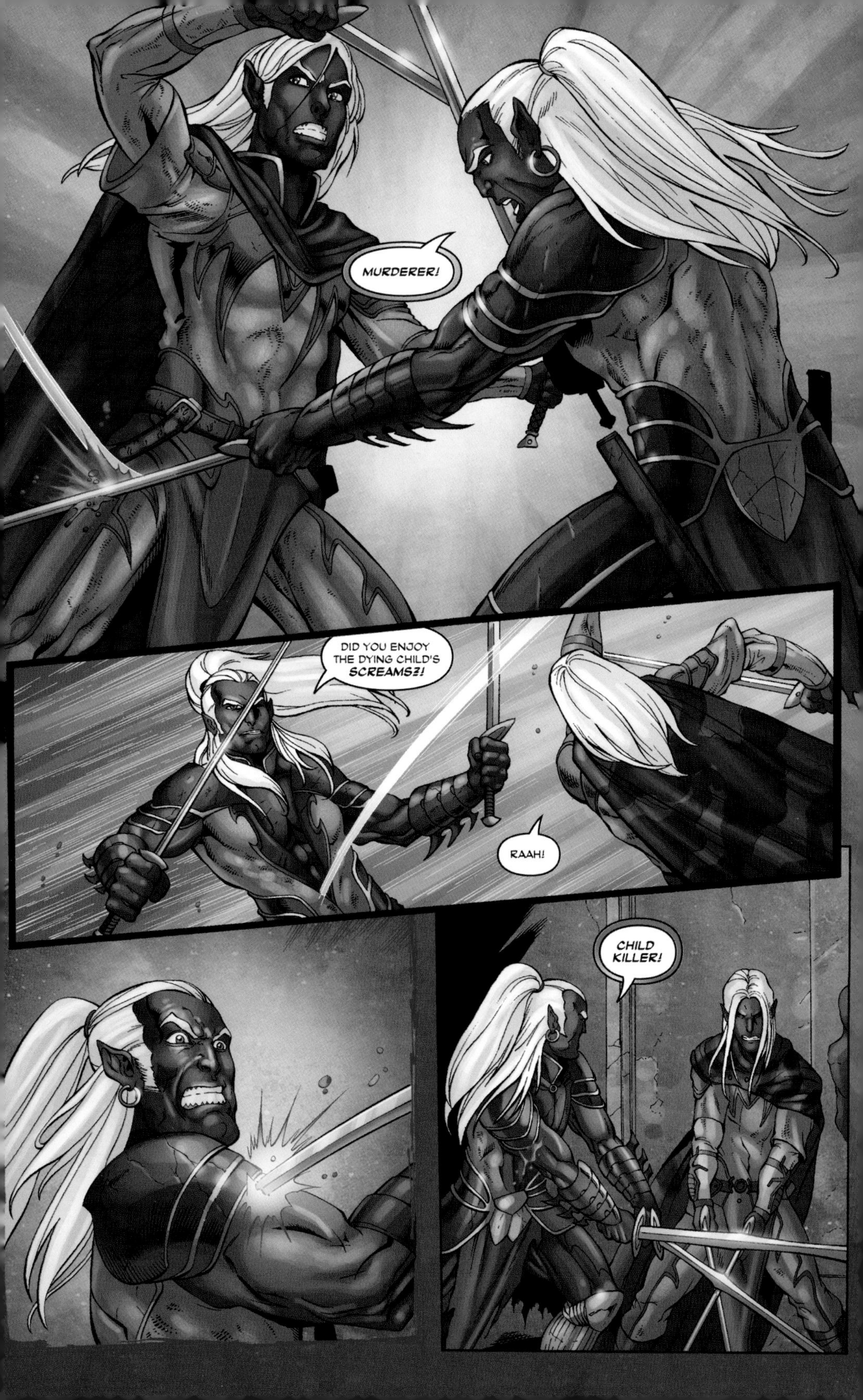
MURDERER!
DID YOU ENJOY THE DYING CHILD'S SCREAMS?!
RAAH!
CHILD KILLER!

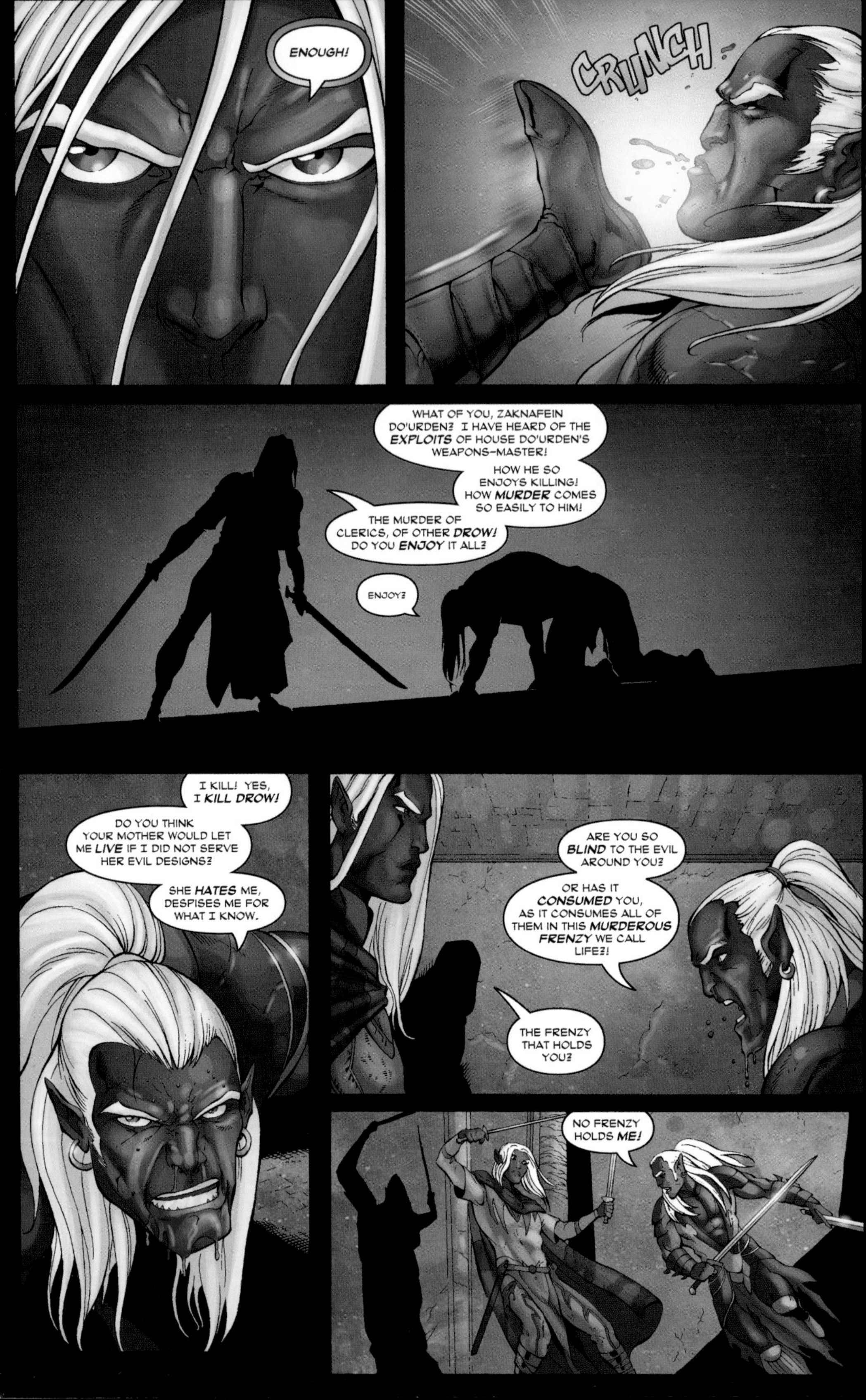
ENOUGH!
CRUNCH
WHAT OF YOU, ZAKNAFEIN DO'URDEN? I HAVE HEARD OF THE EXPLOITS OF HOUSE DO'URDEN'S WEAPONS-MASTER!
HOW HE SO ENJOYS KILLING! HOW MURDER COMES SO EASILY TO HIM!
THE MURDER OF CLERICS, OF OTHER DROW! DO YOU ENJOY IT ALL?
ENJOY?
I KILL! YES, I KILL DROW!
DO YOU THINK YOUR MOTHER WOULD LET ME LIVE IF I DID NOT SERVE HER EVIL DESIGNS?
SHE HATES ME, DESPISES ME FOR WHAT I KNOW.
ARE YOU SO BLIND TO THE EVIL AROUND YOU?
OR HAS IT CONSUMED YOU, AS IT CONSUMES ALL OF THEM IN THIS MURDEROUS FRENZY WE CALL LIFE?!
THE FRENZY THAT HOLDS YOU?
NO FRENZY HOLDS ME!

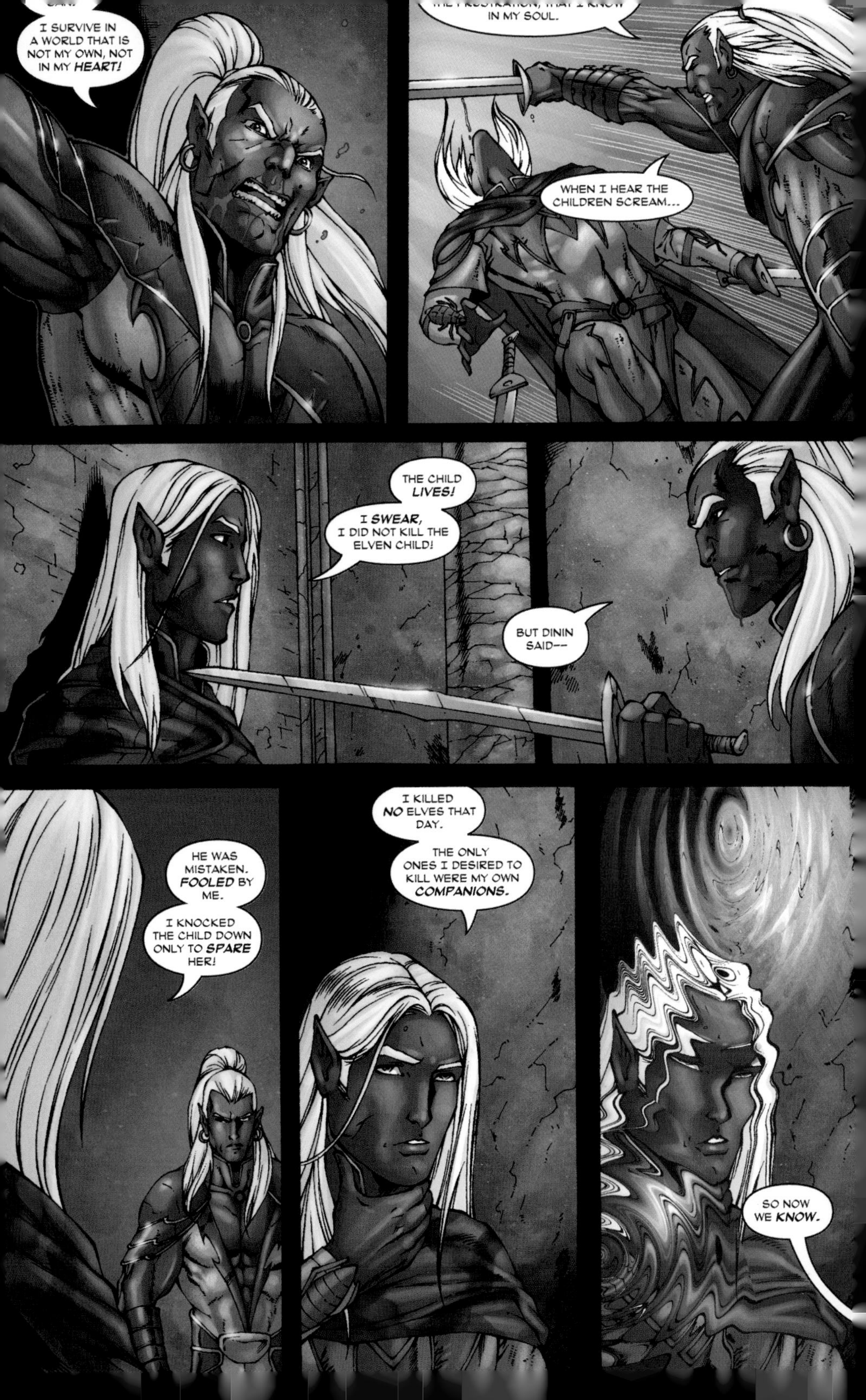

I SURVIVE IN A WORLD THAT IS NOT MY OWN, NOT IN MY **HEART!**
IN MY SOUL.
WHEN I HEAR THE CHILDREN SCREAM...
THE CHILD **LIVES!**
I **SWEAR,** I DID NOT KILL THE ELVEN CHILD!
BUT DININ SAID--
HE WAS MISTAKEN. **FOOLED** BY ME.
I KNOCKED THE CHILD DOWN ONLY TO **SPARE** HER!
I KILLED **NO** ELVES THAT DAY.
THE ONLY ONES I DESIRED TO KILL WERE MY OWN **COMPANIONS.**
SO NOW WE **KNOW.**

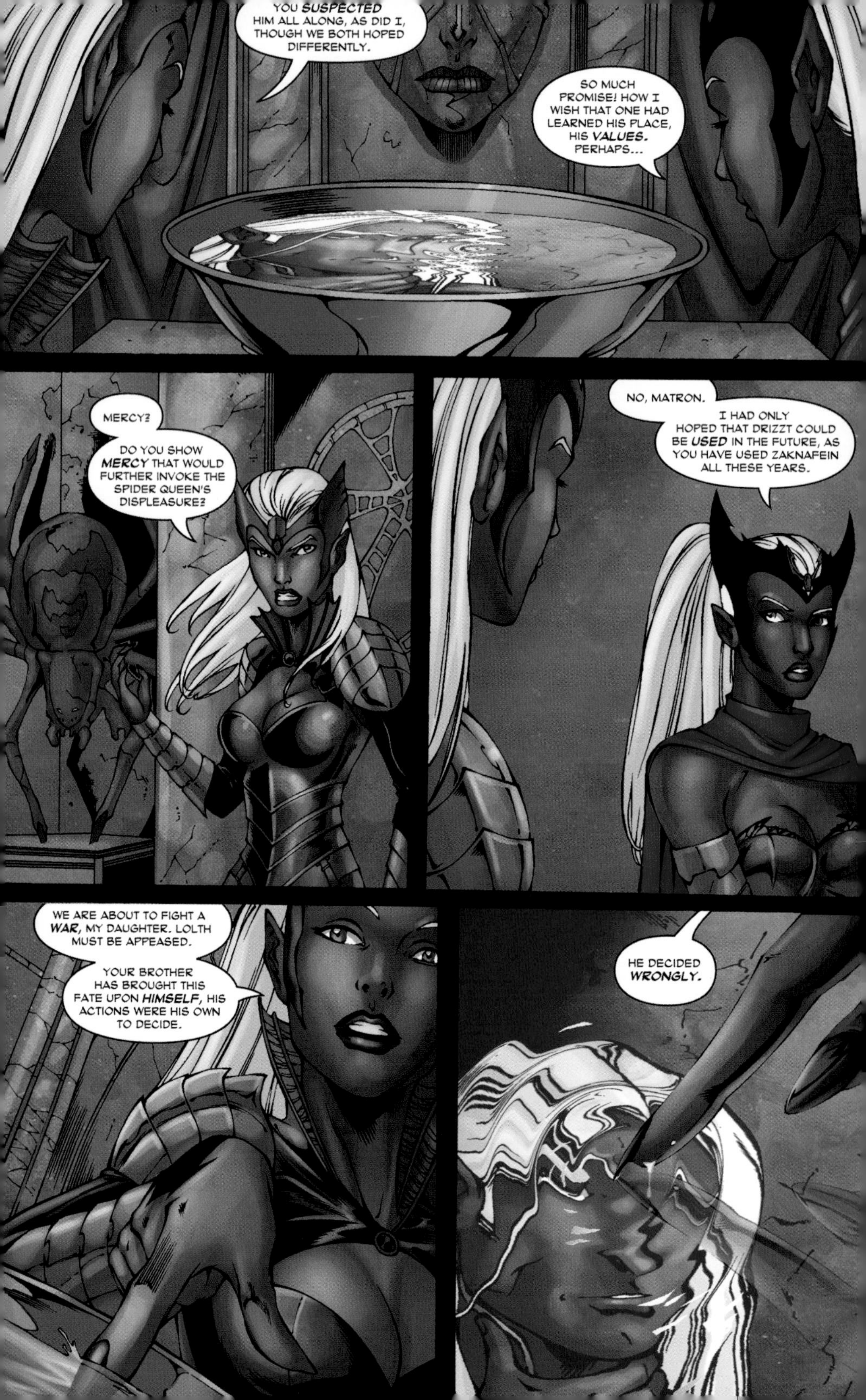
YOU SUSPECTED HIM ALL ALONG, AS DID I, THOUGH WE BOTH HOPED DIFFERENTLY.
SO MUCH PROMISE! HOW I WISH THAT ONE HAD LEARNED HIS PLACE, HIS VALUES. PERHAPS...
MERCY?
DO YOU SHOW MERCY THAT WOULD FURTHER INVOKE THE SPIDER QUEEN'S DISPLEASURE?
NO, MATRON.
I HAD ONLY HOPED THAT DRIZZT COULD BE USED IN THE FUTURE, AS YOU HAVE USED ZAKNAFEIN ALL THESE YEARS.
WE ARE ABOUT TO FIGHT A WAR, MY DAUGHTER. LOLTH MUST BE APPEASED.
YOUR BROTHER HAS BROUGHT THIS FATE UPON HIMSELF, HIS ACTIONS WERE HIS OWN TO DECIDE.
HE DECIDED WRONGLY.

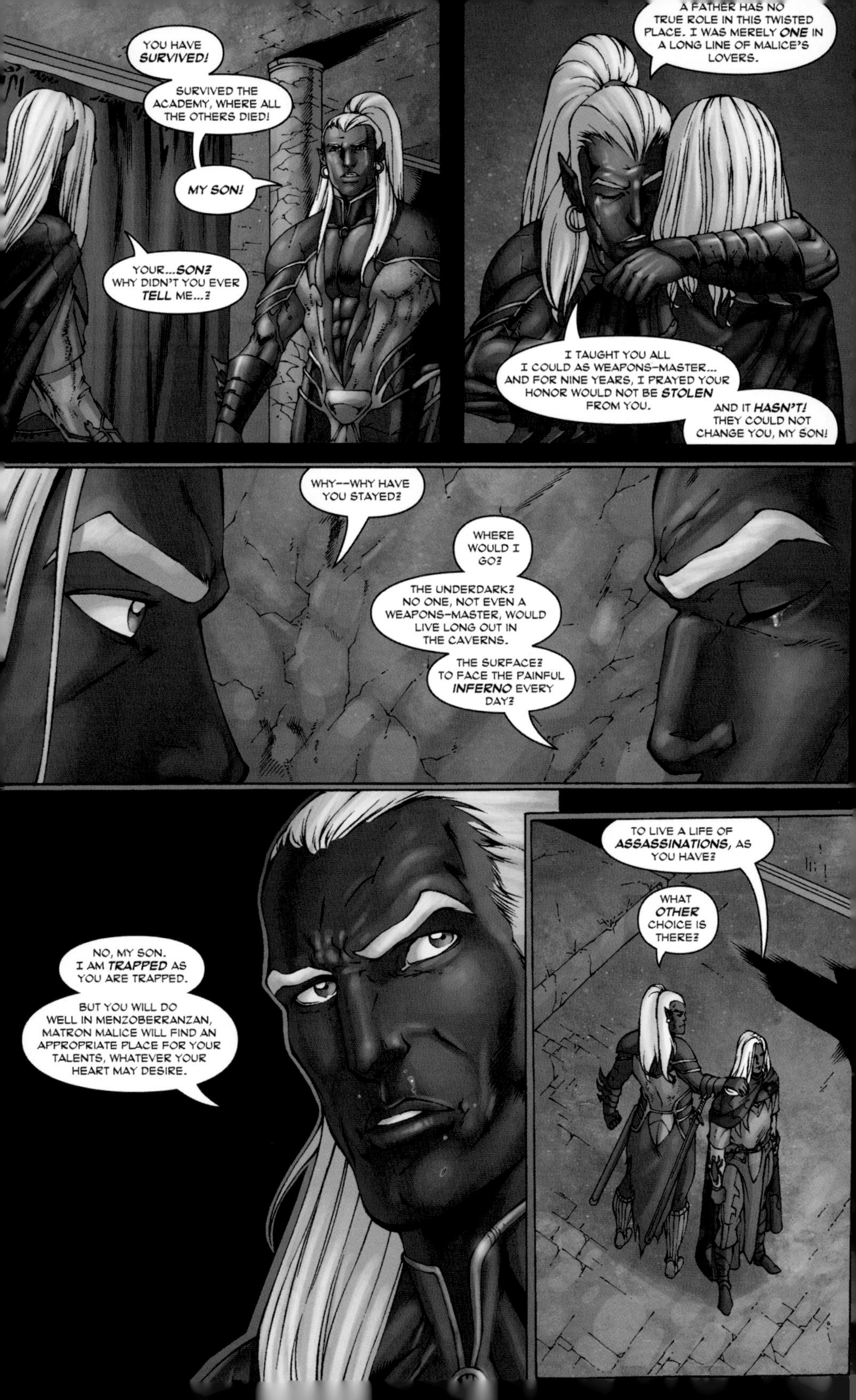
YOU HAVE SURVIVED!
SURVIVED THE ACADEMY, WHERE ALL THE OTHERS DIED!
MY SON!
YOUR...SON? WHY DIDN'T YOU EVER TELL ME...?
A FATHER HAS NO TRUE ROLE IN THIS TWISTED PLACE. I WAS MERELY ONE IN A LONG LINE OF MALICE'S LOVERS.
I TAUGHT YOU ALL I COULD AS WEAPONS-MASTER... AND FOR NINE YEARS, I PRAYED YOUR HONOR WOULD NOT BE STOLEN FROM YOU.
AND IT HASN'T! THEY COULD NOT CHANGE YOU, MY SON!
WHY--WHY HAVE YOU STAYED?
WHERE WOULD I GO?
THE UNDERDARK? NO ONE, NOT EVEN A WEAPONS-MASTER, WOULD LIVE LONG OUT IN THE CAVERNS.
THE SURFACE? TO FACE THE PAINFUL INFERNO EVERY DAY?
NO, MY SON. I AM TRAPPED AS YOU ARE TRAPPED.
BUT YOU WILL DO WELL IN MENZOBERRANZAN, MATRON MALICE WILL FIND AN APPROPRIATE PLACE FOR YOUR TALENTS, WHATEVER YOUR HEART MAY DESIRE.
TO LIVE A LIFE OF ASSASSINATIONS, AS YOU HAVE?
WHAT OTHER CHOICE IS THERE?

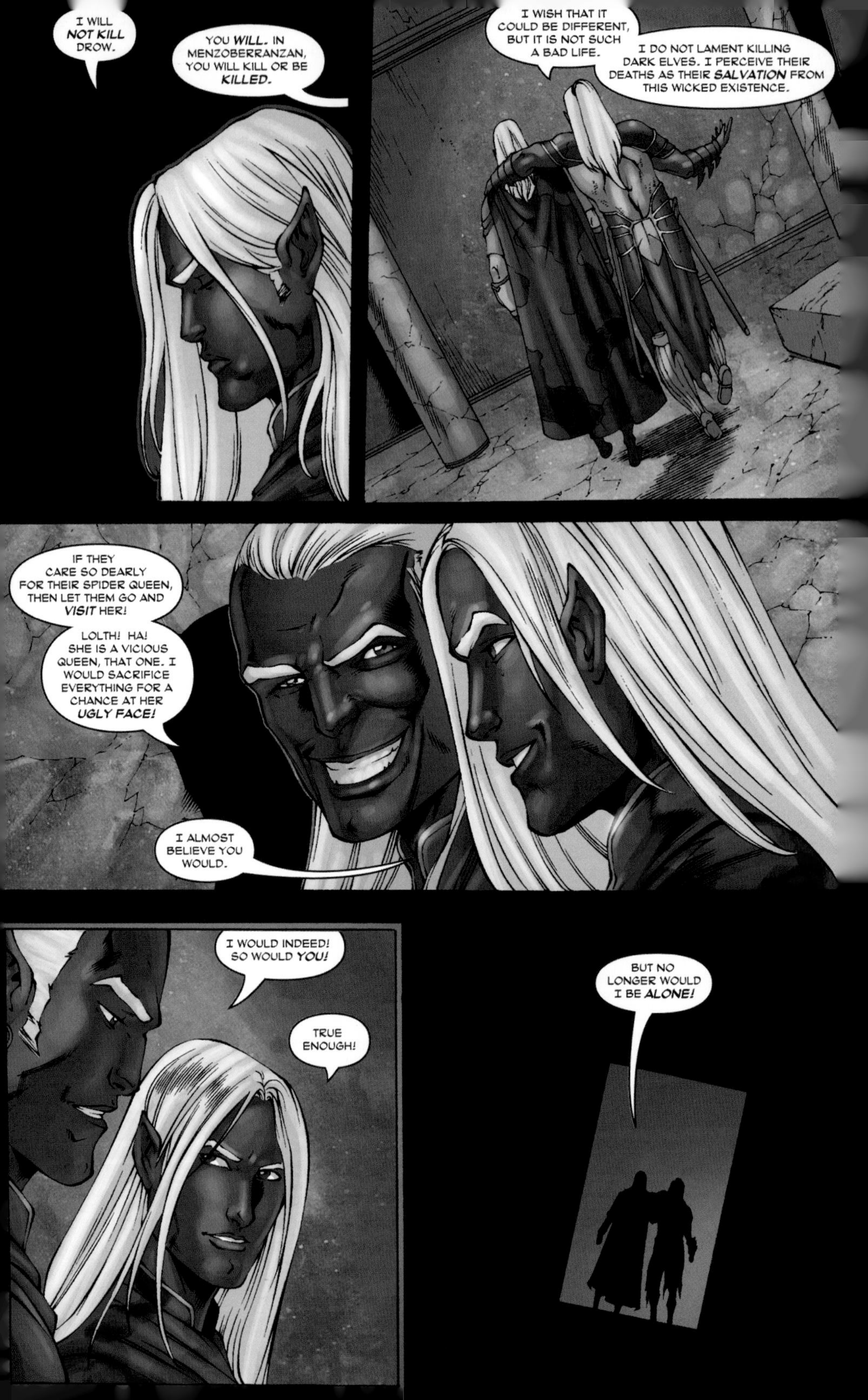
I WILL NOT KILL DROW.
YOU WILL. IN MENZOBERRANZAN, YOU WILL KILL OR BE KILLED.
I WISH THAT IT COULD BE DIFFERENT, BUT IT IS NOT SUCH A BAD LIFE.
I DO NOT LAMENT KILLING DARK ELVES. I PERCEIVE THEIR DEATHS AS THEIR SALVATION FROM THIS WICKED EXISTENCE.
IF THEY CARE SO DEARLY FOR THEIR SPIDER QUEEN, THEN LET THEM GO AND VISIT HER!
LOLTH! HA! SHE IS A VICIOUS QUEEN, THAT ONE. I WOULD SACRIFICE EVERYTHING FOR A CHANCE AT HER UGLY FACE!
I ALMOST BELIEVE YOU WOULD.
I WOULD INDEED! SO WOULD YOU!
TRUE ENOUGH!
BUT NO LONGER WOULD I BE ALONE!

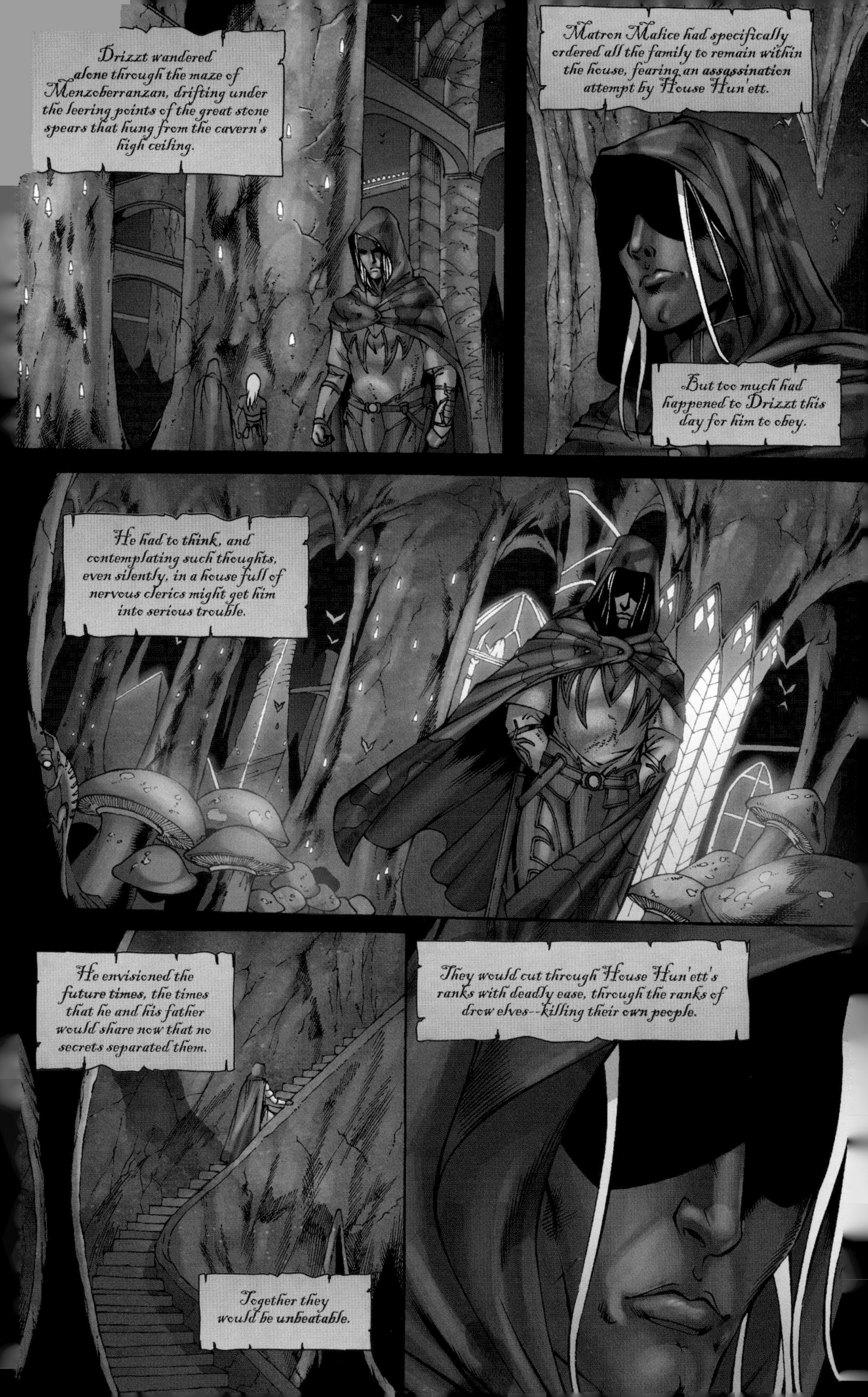
Drizzt wandered alone through the maze of Menzoberranzan, drifting under the leering points of the great stone spears that hung from the cavern's high ceiling.
Matron Malice had specifically ordered all the family to remain within the house, fearing an assassination attempt by House Hun'ett.
But too much had happened to Drizzt this day for him to obey.
He had to think, and contemplating such thoughts, even silently, in a house full of nervous clerics might get him into serious trouble.
He envisioned the future times, the times that he and his father would share now that no secrets separated them.
Together they would be unbeatable.
They would cut through House Hun'ett's ranks with deadly ease, through the ranks of drow elves--killing their own people.

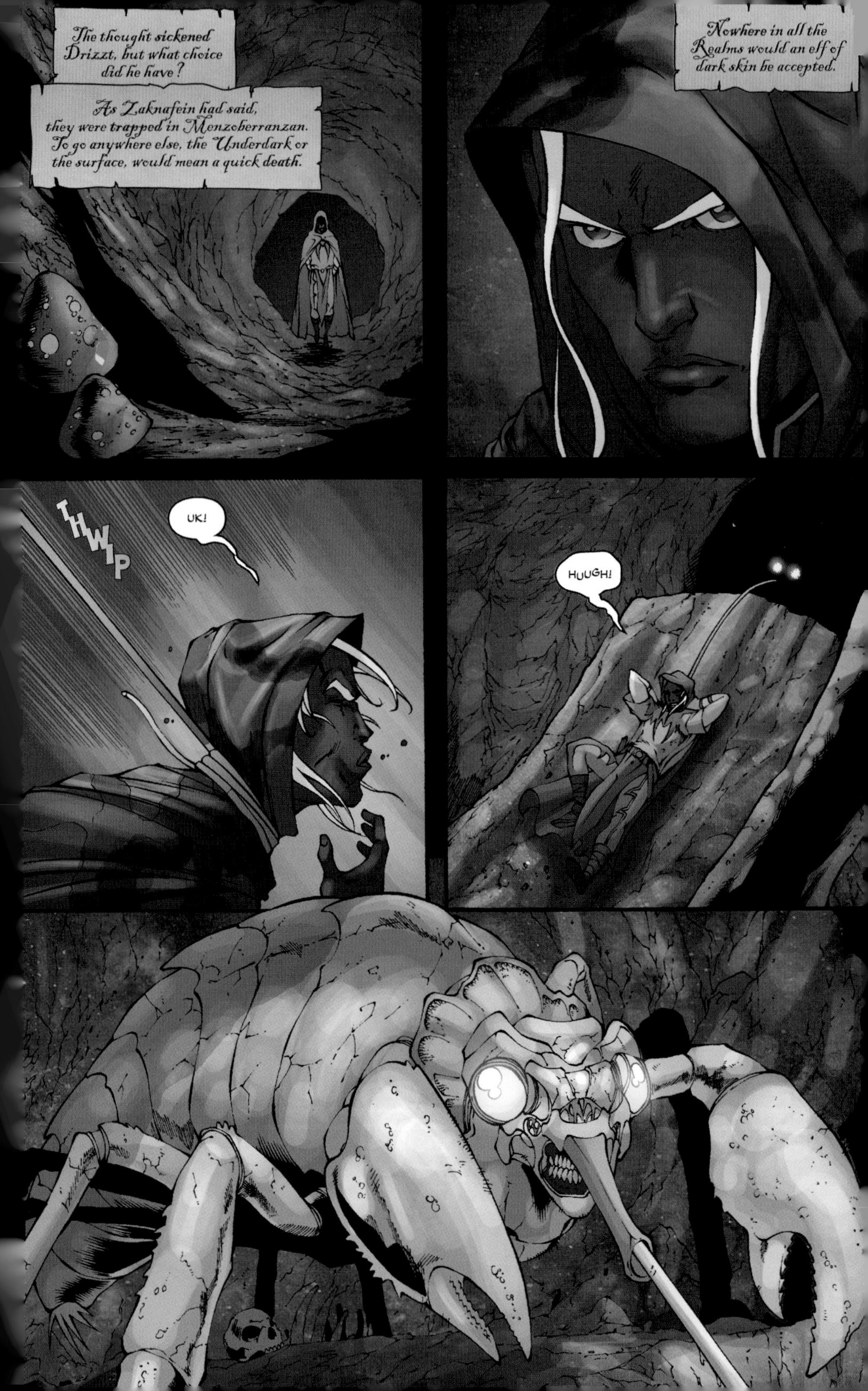
The thought sickened Drizzt, but what choice did he have?
As Zaknafein had said, they were trapped in Menzoberranzan. To go anywhere else, the Underdark or the surface, would mean a quick death.
Nowhere in all the Realms would an elf of dark skin be accepted.
THWIP
UK!
HUUGH!

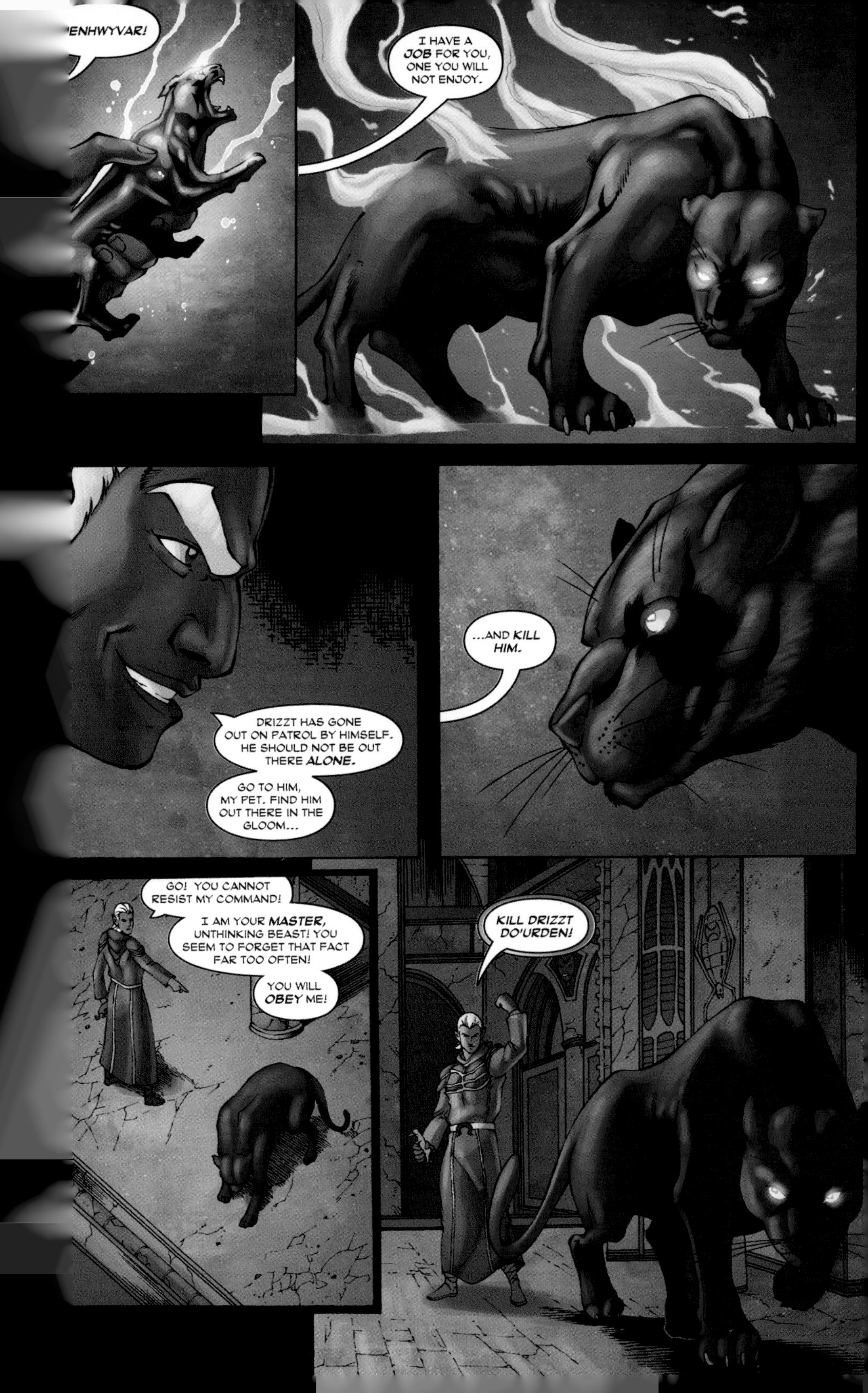

ENHWYVAR!
I HAVE A JOB FOR YOU, ONE YOU WILL NOT ENJOY.
DRIZZT HAS GONE OUT ON PATROL BY HIMSELF. HE SHOULD NOT BE OUT THERE ALONE.
GO TO HIM, MY PET. FIND HIM OUT THERE IN THE GLOOM...
...AND KILL HIM.
GO! YOU CANNOT RESIST MY COMMAND!
I AM YOUR MASTER, UNTHINKING BEAST! YOU SEEM TO FORGET THAT FACT FAR TOO OFTEN!
YOU WILL OBEY ME!
KILL DRIZZT DO'URDEN!

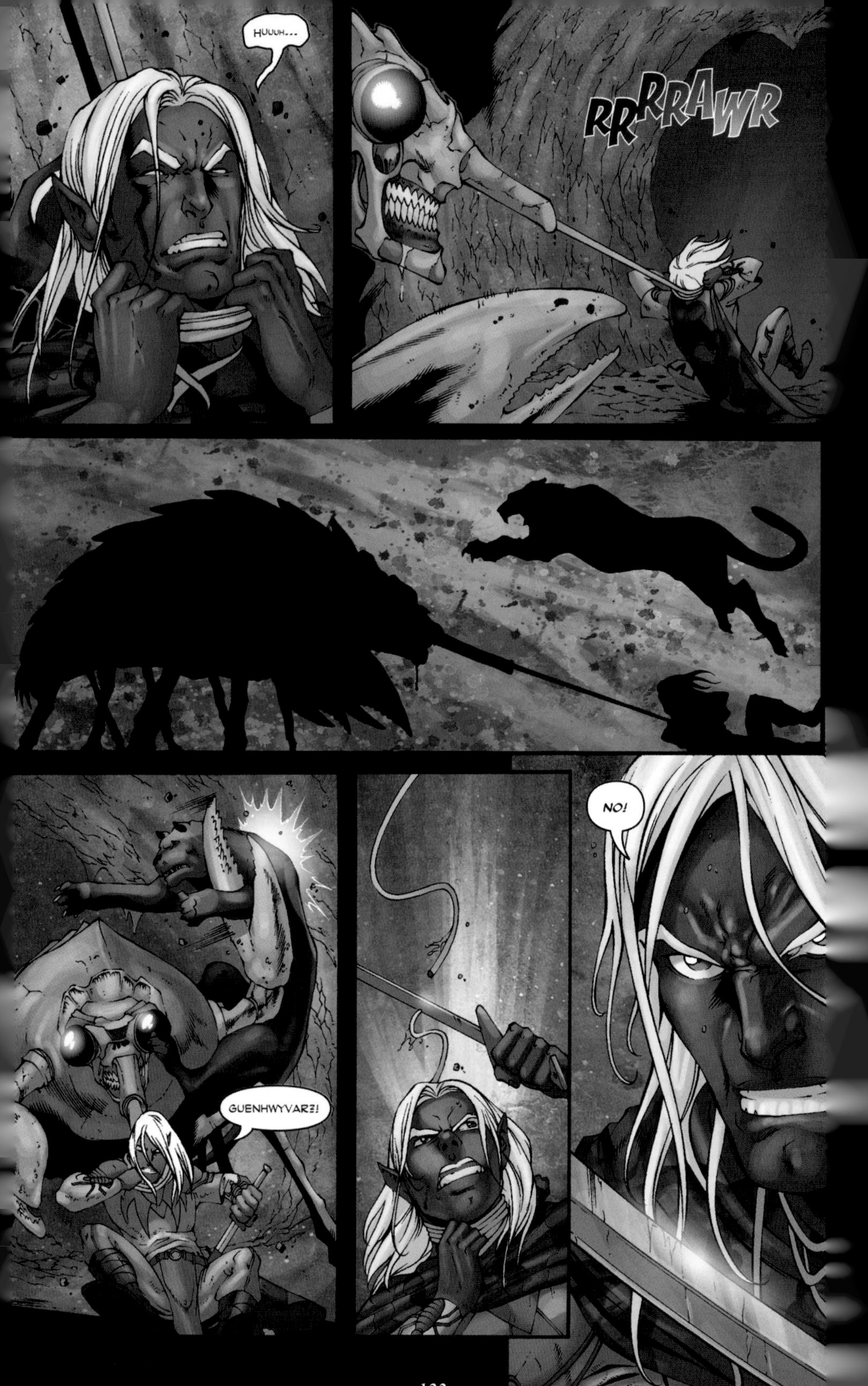
HUUUH...
RRRRRAWR
GUENHWYVAR!
NO!

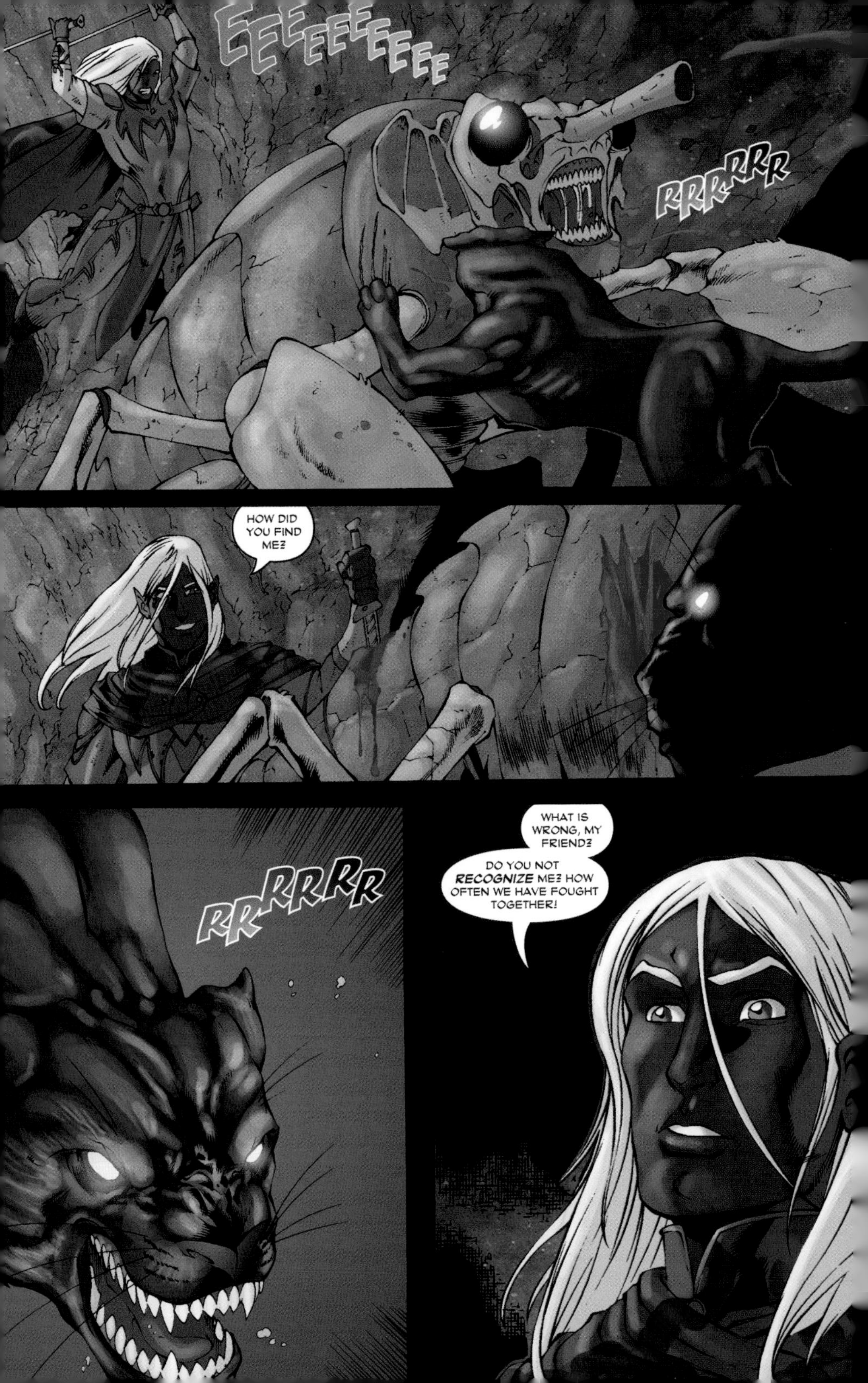
EEEEEEEEEE
RRRRRR
HOW DID YOU FIND ME?
RRRRRR
WHAT IS WRONG, MY FRIEND?
DO YOU NOT RECOGNIZE ME? HOW OFTEN WE HAVE FOUGHT TOGETHER!

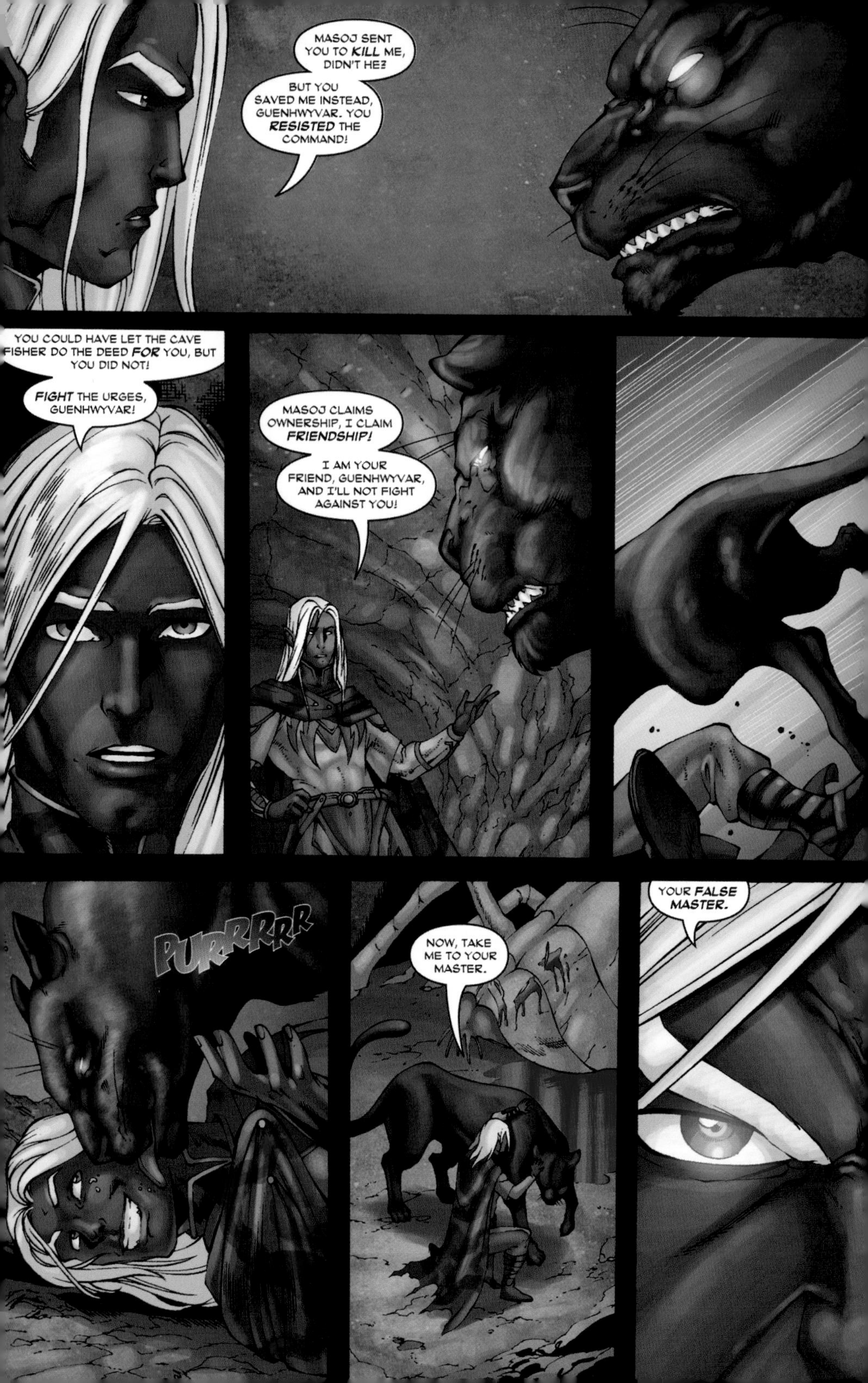
MASOJ SENT YOU TO KILL ME, DIDN'T HE?
BUT YOU SAVED ME INSTEAD, GUENHWYVAR. YOU RESISTED THE COMMAND!
YOU COULD HAVE LET THE CAVE FISHER DO THE DEED FOR YOU, BUT YOU DID NOT!
FIGHT THE URGES, GUENHWYVAR!
MASOJ CLAIMS OWNERSHIP, I CLAIM FRIENDSHIP!
I AM YOUR FRIEND, GUENHWYVAR, AND I'LL NOT FIGHT AGAINST YOU!
PURRRRR
NOW, TAKE ME TO YOUR MASTER.
YOUR FALSE MASTER.

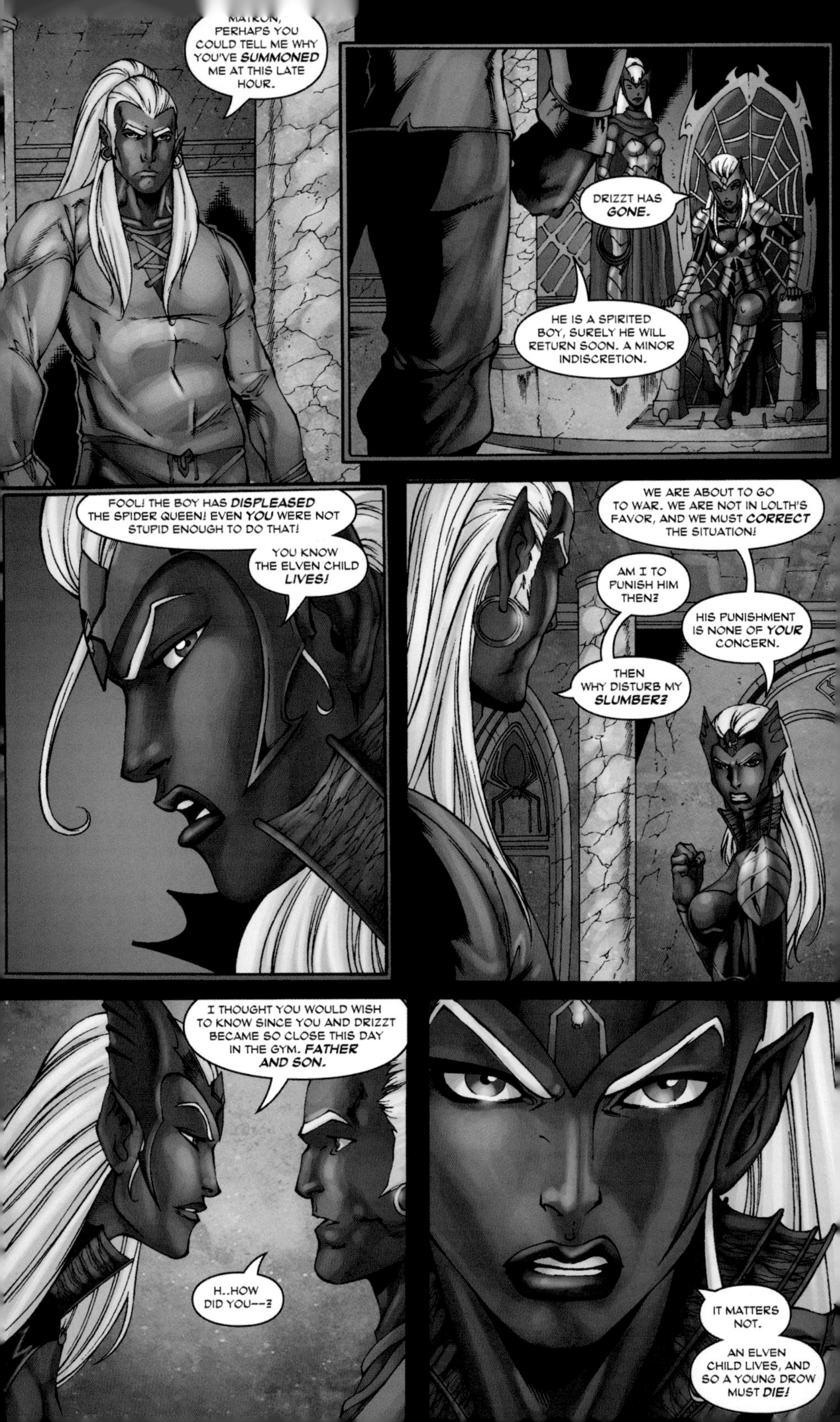
MATRON, PERHAPS YOU COULD TELL ME WHY YOU'VE SUMMONED ME AT THIS LATE HOUR.
DRIZZT HAS GONE.
HE IS A SPIRITED BOY, SURELY HE WILL RETURN SOON. A MINOR INDISCRETION.
FOOL! THE BOY HAS DISPLEASED THE SPIDER QUEEN! EVEN YOU WERE NOT STUPID ENOUGH TO DO THAT!
YOU KNOW THE ELVEN CHILD LIVES!
WE ARE ABOUT TO GO TO WAR. WE ARE NOT IN LOLTH'S FAVOR, AND WE MUST CORRECT THE SITUATION!
AM I TO PUNISH HIM THEN?
HIS PUNISHMENT IS NONE OF YOUR CONCERN.
THEN WHY DISTURB MY SLUMBER?
I THOUGHT YOU WOULD WISH TO KNOW SINCE YOU AND DRIZZT BECAME SO CLOSE THIS DAY IN THE GYM. FATHER AND SON.
H..HOW DID YOU--?
IT MATTERS NOT.
AN ELVEN CHILD LIVES, AND SO A YOUNG DROW MUST DIE!

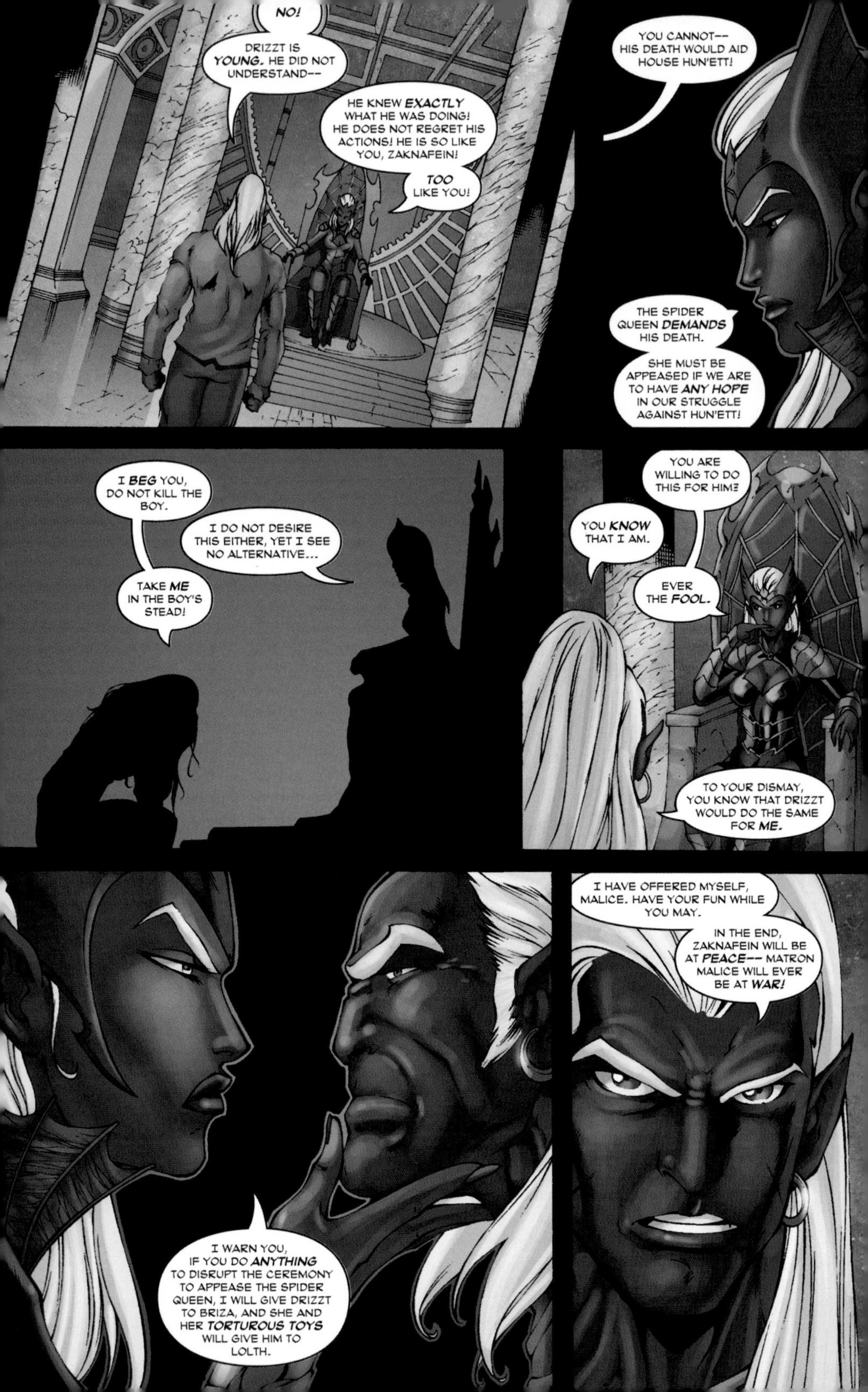
NO!
DRIZZT IS YOUNG. HE DID NOT UNDERSTAND--
HE KNEW EXACTLY WHAT HE WAS DOING! HE DOES NOT REGRET HIS ACTIONS! HE IS SO LIKE YOU, ZAKNAFEIN!
TOO LIKE YOU!
YOU CANNOT-- HIS DEATH WOULD AID HOUSE HUN'ETT!
THE SPIDER QUEEN DEMANDS HIS DEATH.
SHE MUST BE APPEASED IF WE ARE TO HAVE ANY HOPE IN OUR STRUGGLE AGAINST HUN'ETT!
I BEG YOU, DO NOT KILL THE BOY.
I DO NOT DESIRE THIS EITHER, YET I SEE NO ALTERNATIVE...
TAKE ME IN THE BOY'S STEAD!
YOU ARE WILLING TO DO THIS FOR HIM?
YOU KNOW THAT I AM.
EVER THE FOOL.
TO YOUR DISMAY, YOU KNOW THAT DRIZZT WOULD DO THE SAME FOR ME.
I WARN YOU, IF YOU DO ANYTHING TO DISRUPT THE CEREMONY TO APPEASE THE SPIDER QUEEN, I WILL GIVE DRIZZT TO BRIZA, AND SHE AND HER TORTUROUS TOYS WILL GIVE HIM TO LOLTH.
I HAVE OFFERED MYSELF, MALICE. HAVE YOUR FUN WHILE YOU MAY.
IN THE END, ZAKNAFEIN WILL BE AT PEACE-- MATRON MALICE WILL EVER BE AT WAR!

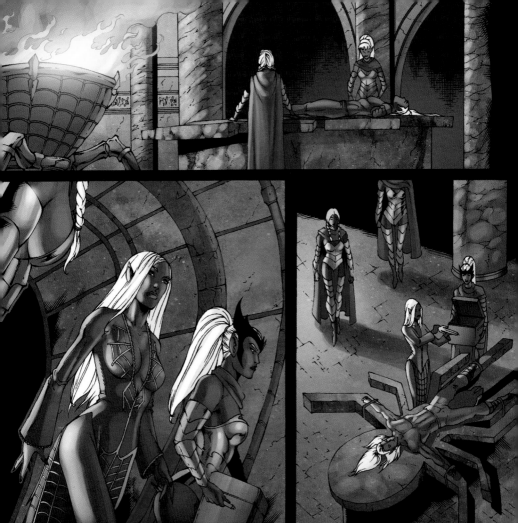

BEAT THEM ALL, MY SON. DO MORE THAN SURVIVE, AS I HAVE SURVIVED.

LIVE! BE TRUE TO THE CALLINGS OF YOUR HEART!

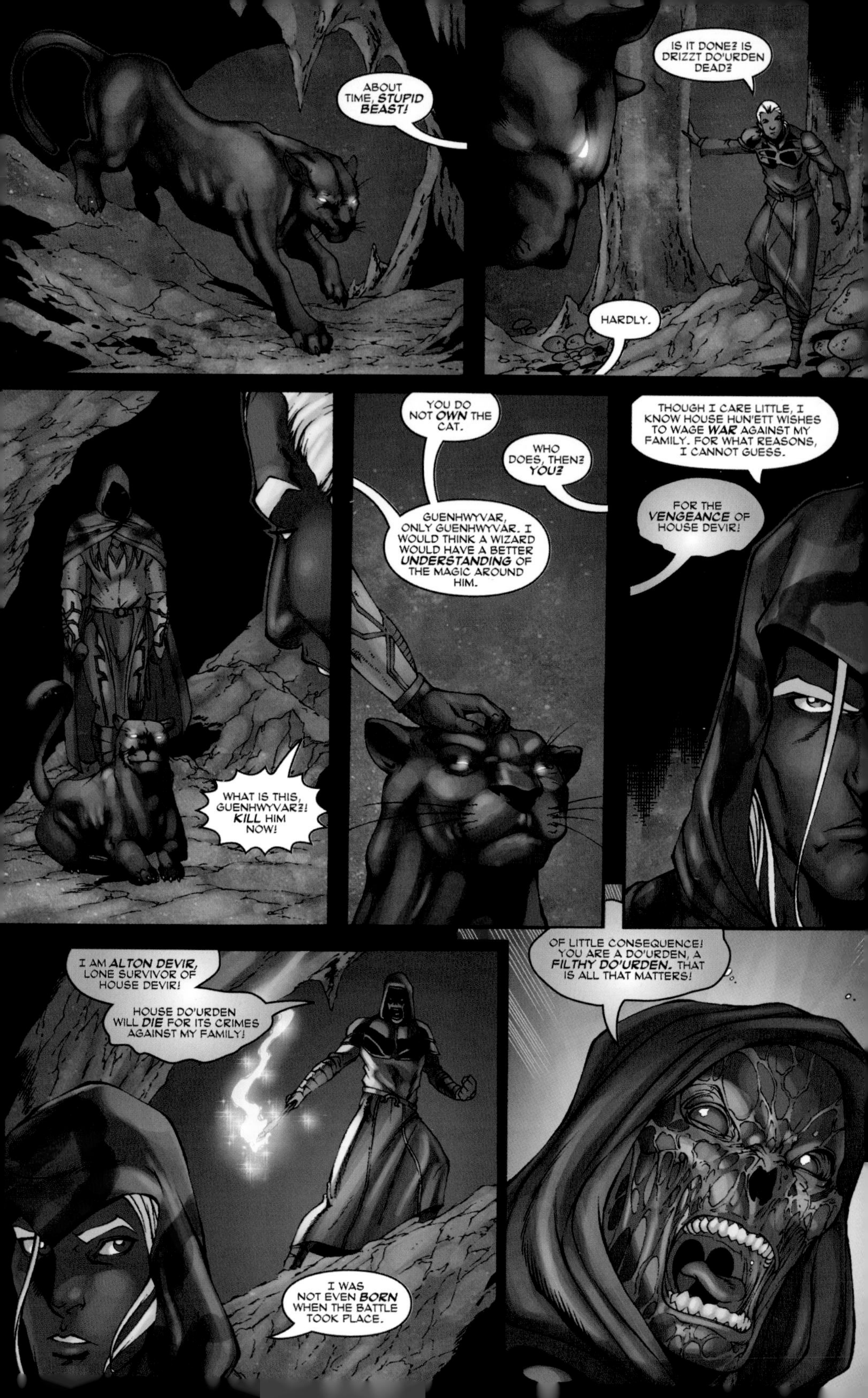
ABOUT TIME, STUPID BEAST!
IS IT DONE? IS DRIZZT DO'URDEN DEAD?
HARDLY.
WHAT IS THIS, GUENHWYVAR?! KILL HIM NOW!
YOU DO NOT OWN THE CAT.
WHO DOES, THEN? YOU?
GUENHWYVAR, ONLY GUENHWYVAR. I WOULD THINK A WIZARD WOULD HAVE A BETTER UNDERSTANDING OF THE MAGIC AROUND HIM.
THOUGH I CARE LITTLE, I KNOW HOUSE HUN'ETT WISHES TO WAGE WAR AGAINST MY FAMILY. FOR WHAT REASONS, I CANNOT GUESS.
FOR THE VENGEANCE OF HOUSE DEVIR!
I AM ALTON DEVIR, LONE SURVIVOR OF HOUSE DEVIR!
HOUSE DO'URDEN WILL DIE FOR ITS CRIMES AGAINST MY FAMILY!
I WAS NOT EVEN BORN WHEN THE BATTLE TOOK PLACE.
OF LITTLE CONSEQUENCE! YOU ARE A DO'URDEN, A FILTHY DO'URDEN. THAT IS ALL THAT MATTERS!

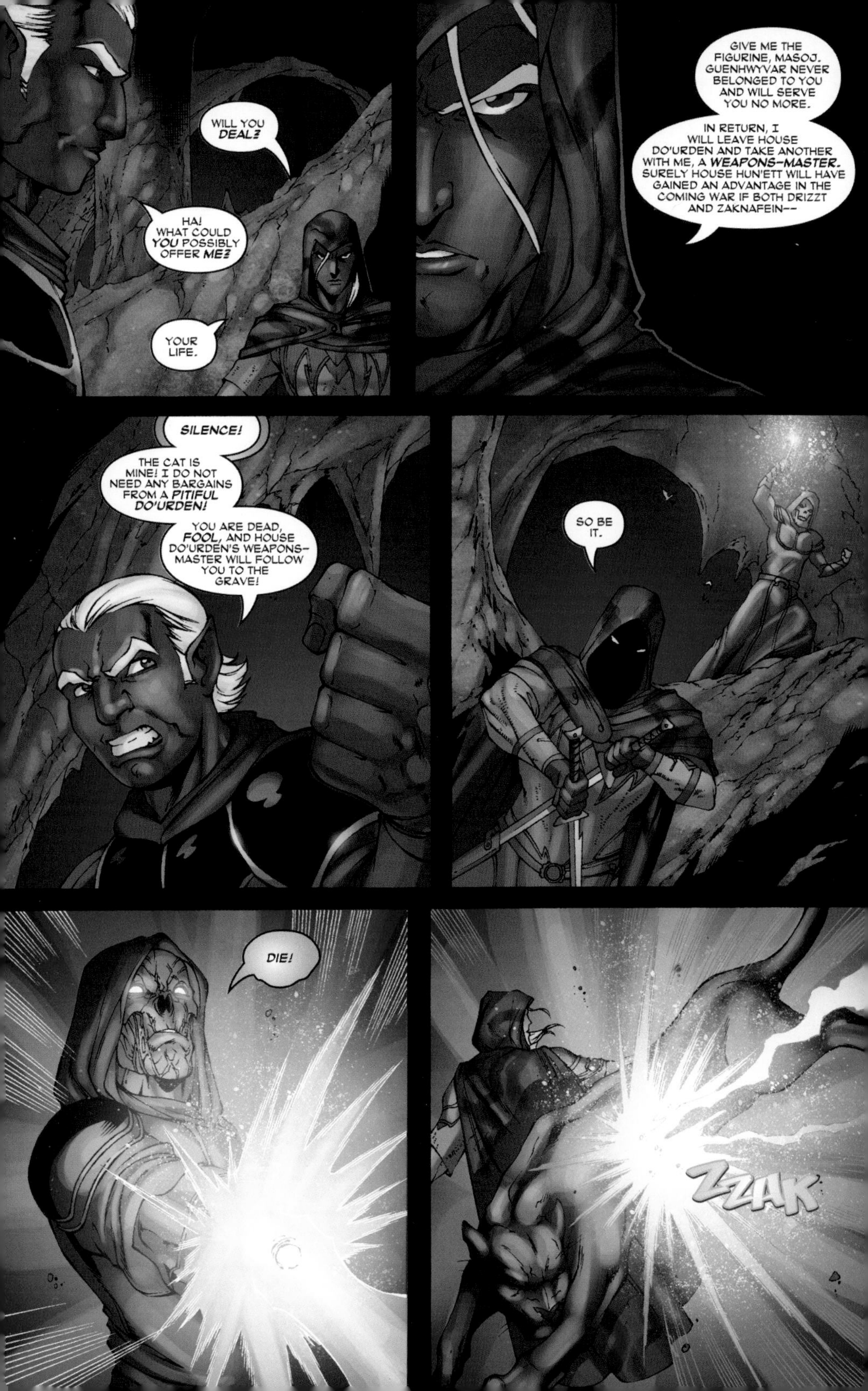
WILL YOU DEAL?
HA! WHAT COULD YOU POSSIBLY OFFER ME?
YOUR LIFE.
GIVE ME THE FIGURINE, MASOJ. GUENHWYVAR NEVER BELONGED TO YOU AND WILL SERVE YOU NO MORE.
IN RETURN, I WILL LEAVE HOUSE DO'URDEN AND TAKE ANOTHER WITH ME, A WEAPONS-MASTER. SURELY HOUSE HUN'ETT WILL HAVE GAINED AN ADVANTAGE IN THE COMING WAR IF BOTH DRIZZT AND ZAKNAFEIN--
SILENCE!
THE CAT IS MINE! I DO NOT NEED ANY BARGAINS FROM A PITIFUL DO'URDEN!
YOU ARE DEAD, FOOL, AND HOUSE DO'URDEN'S WEAPONS-MASTER WILL FOLLOW YOU TO THE GRAVE!
SO BE IT.
DIE!
ZZZAK

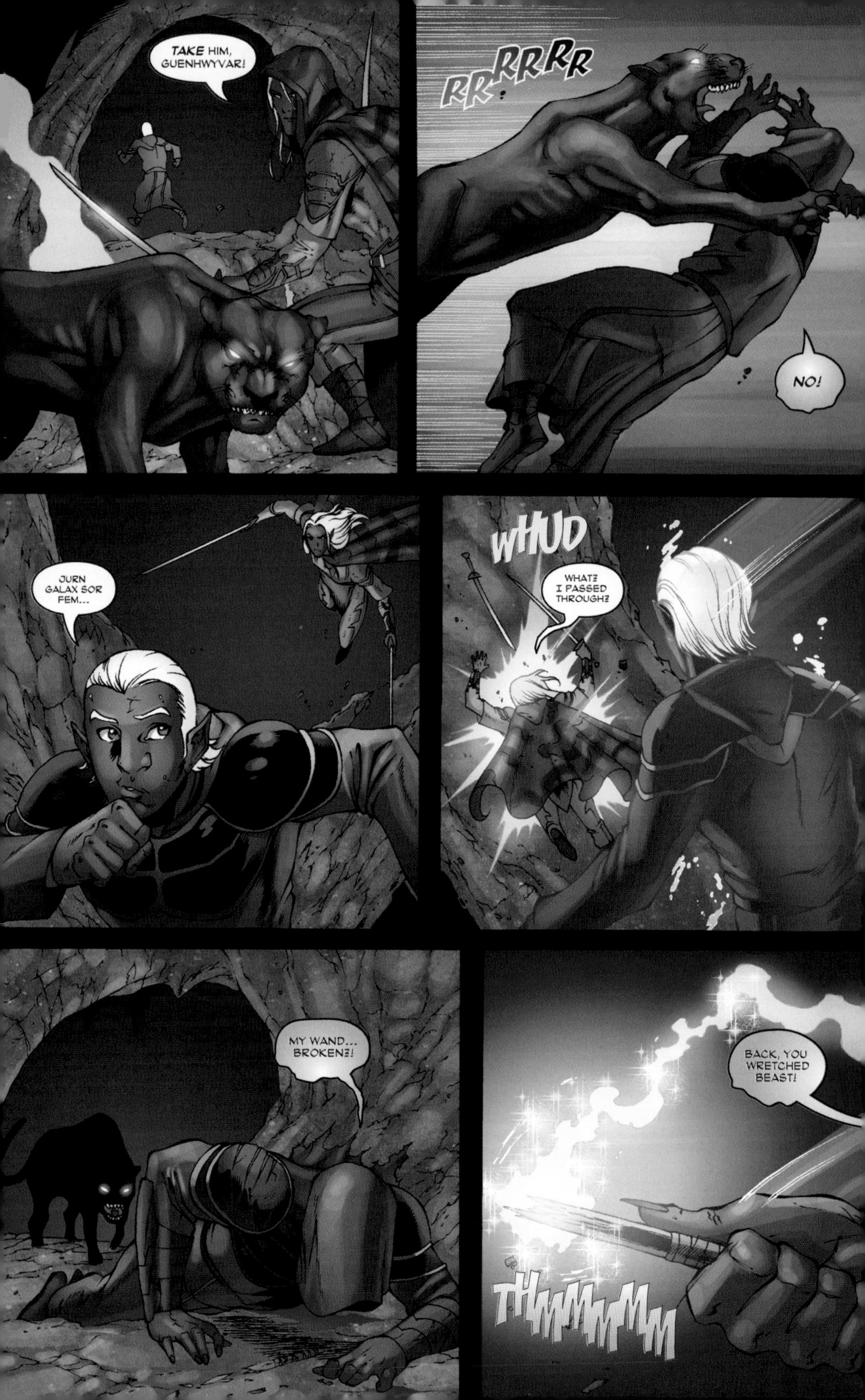
TAKE HIM, GUENHWYVAR!
RRRRRRR
NO!
JURN GALAX SOR FEM...
WHUD
WHAT? I PASSED THROUGH?
MY WAND... BROKEN?!
BACK, YOU WRETCHED BEAST!
THMMMMMM

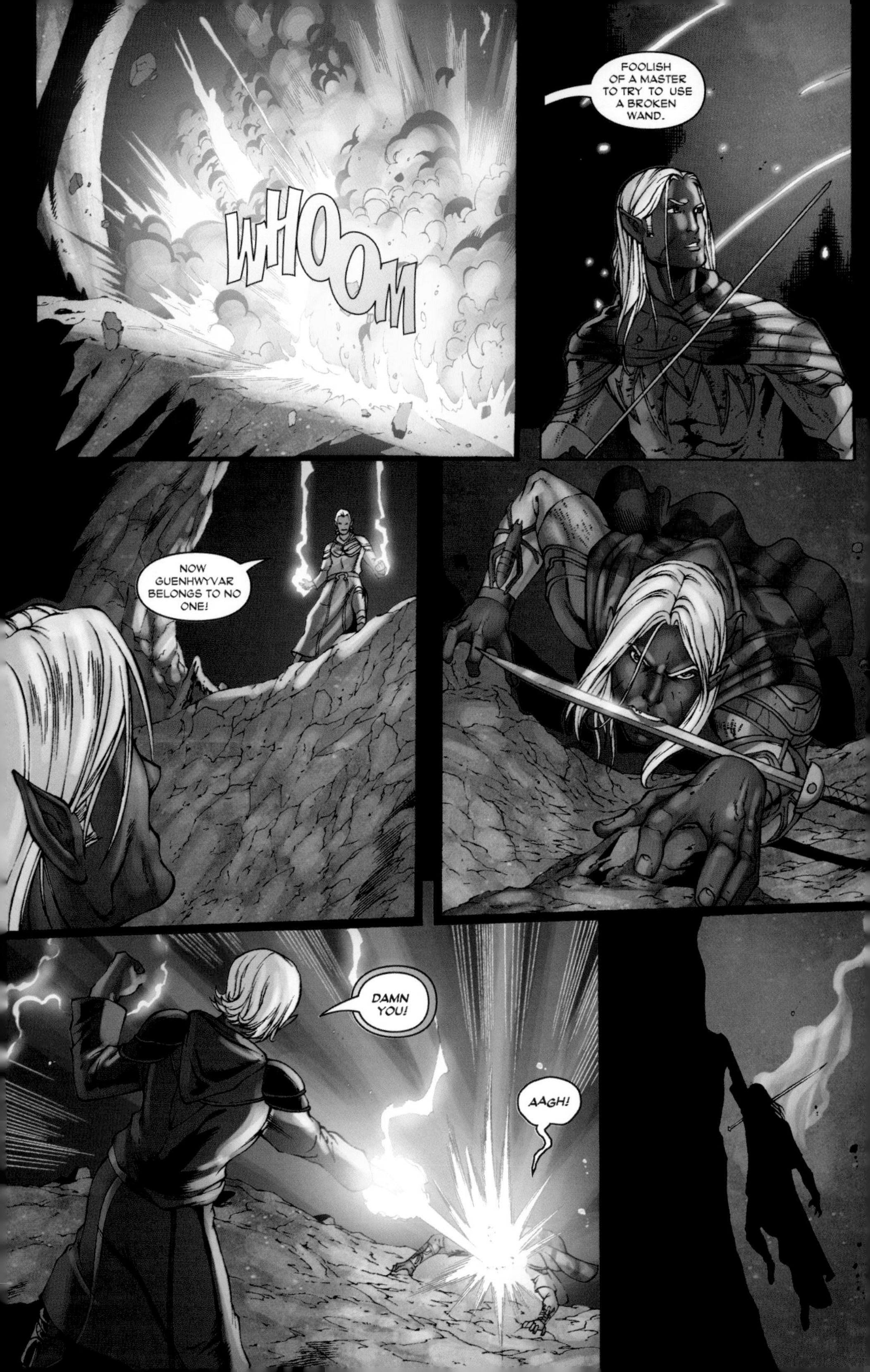
WHOOM
FOOLISH OF A MASTER TO TRY TO USE A BROKEN WAND.
NOW GUENHWYVAR BELONGS TO NO ONE!
DAMN YOU!
AAGH!

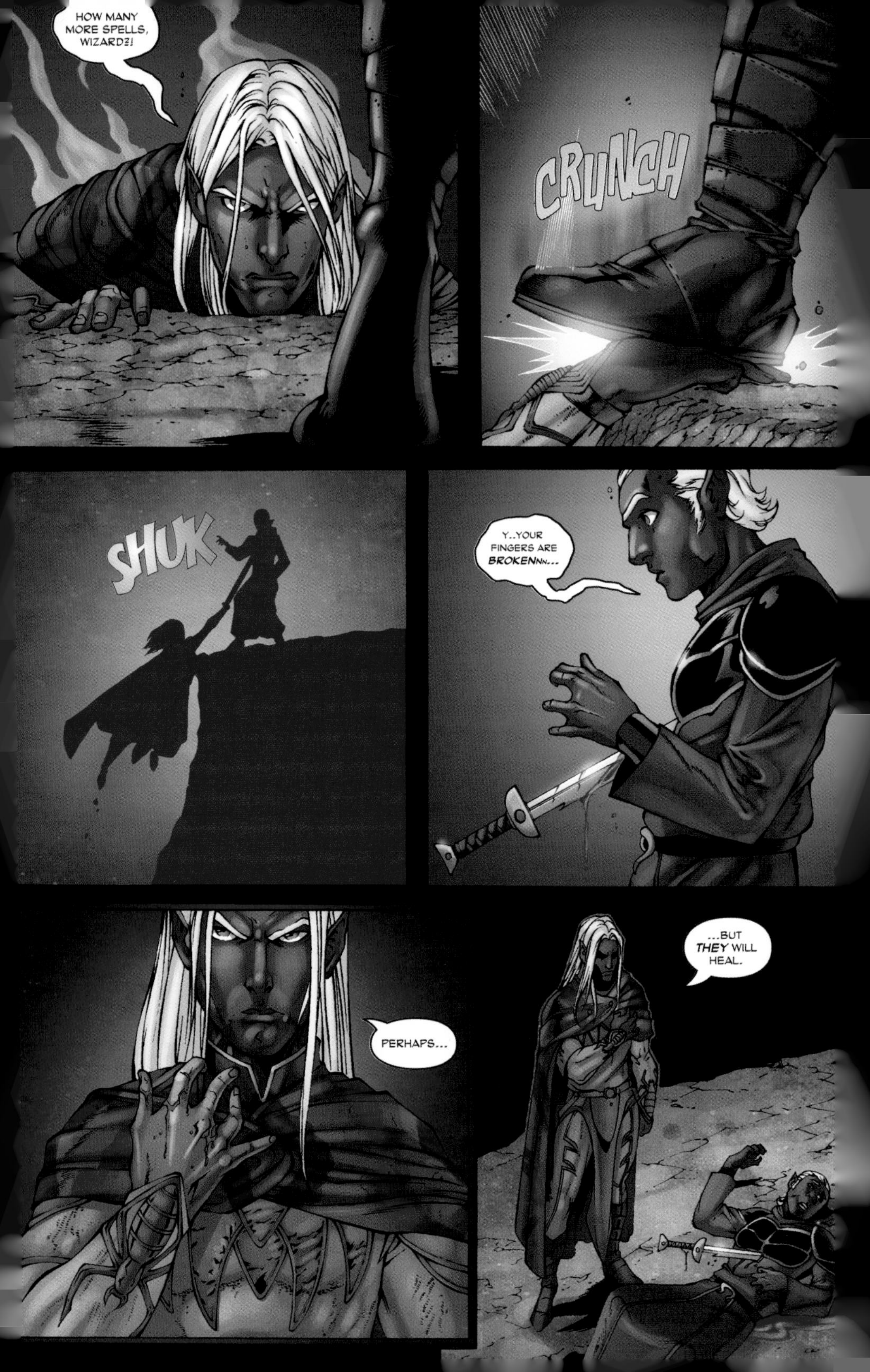
HOW MANY MORE SPELLS, WIZARD?!
CRUNCH
SHUK
Y..YOUR FINGERS ARE BROKENNN...
PERHAPS...
...BUT THEY WILL HEAL.

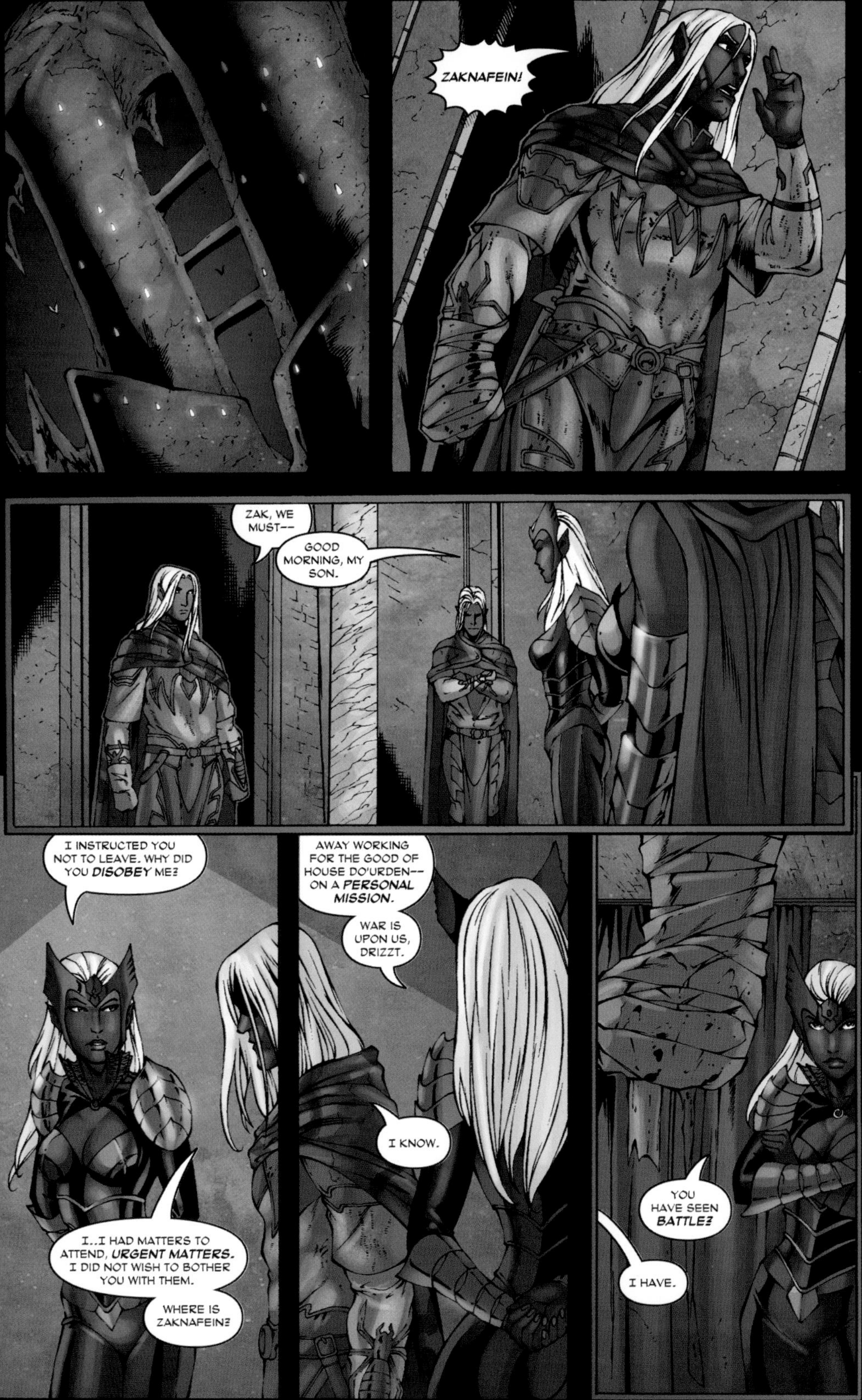
ZAKNAFEIN!
ZAK, WE MUST--
GOOD MORNING, MY SON.
I INSTRUCTED YOU NOT TO LEAVE. WHY DID YOU DISOBEY ME?
I..I HAD MATTERS TO ATTEND, URGENT MATTERS. I DID NOT WISH TO BOTHER YOU WITH THEM.
WHERE IS ZAKNAFEIN?
AWAY WORKING FOR THE GOOD OF HOUSE DO'URDEN-- ON A PERSONAL MISSION.
WAR IS UPON US, DRIZZT.
I KNOW.
YOU HAVE SEEN BATTLE?
I HAVE.

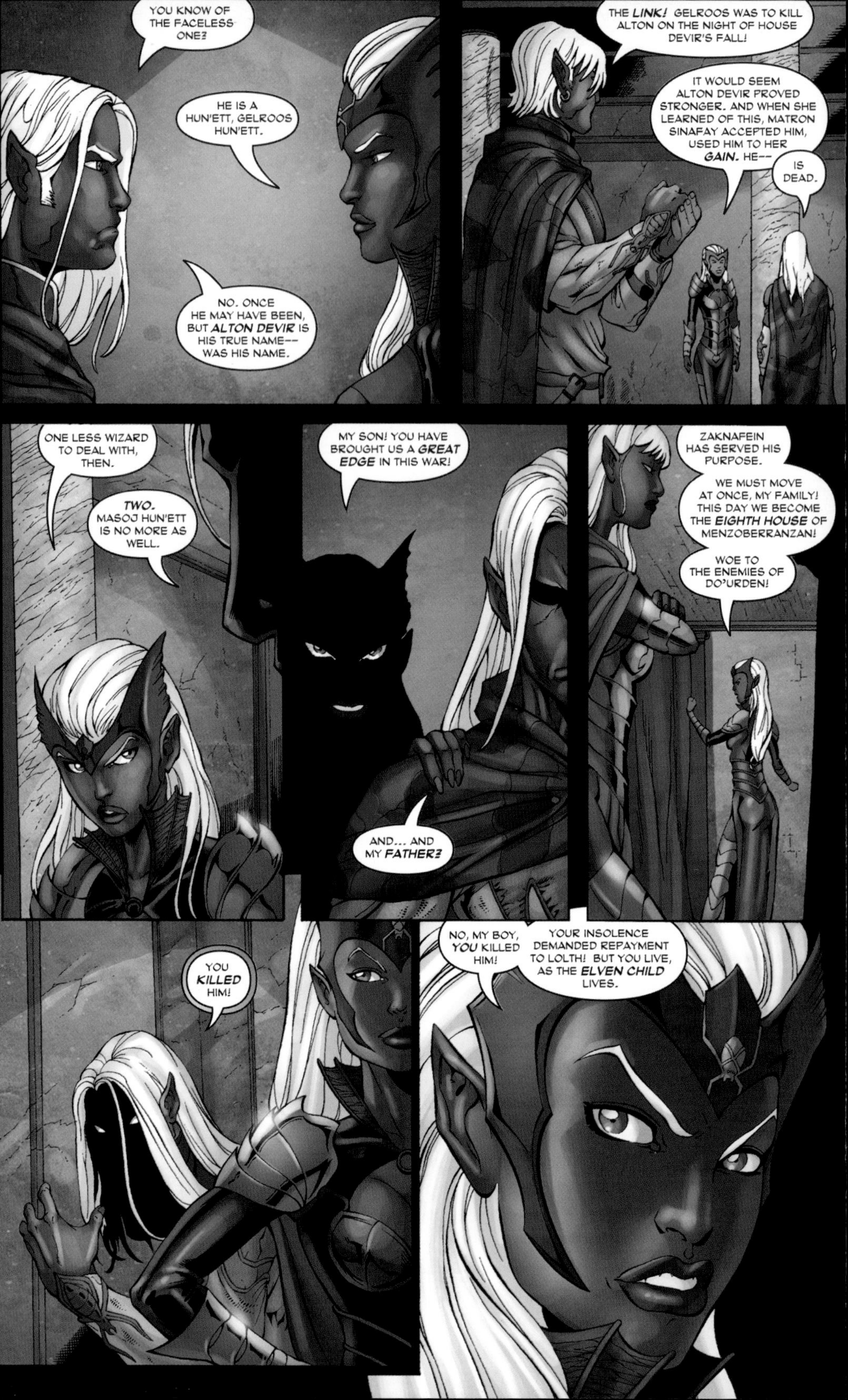
YOU KNOW OF THE FACELESS ONE?
HE IS A HUN'ETT, GELROOS HUN'ETT.
NO. ONCE HE MAY HAVE BEEN, BUT ALTON DEVIR IS HIS TRUE NAME-- WAS HIS NAME.
THE LINK! GELROOS WAS TO KILL ALTON ON THE NIGHT OF HOUSE DEVIR'S FALL!
IT WOULD SEEM ALTON DEVIR PROVED STRONGER. AND WHEN SHE LEARNED OF THIS, MATRON SINAFAY ACCEPTED HIM, USED HIM TO HER GAIN. HE--
IS DEAD.
ONE LESS WIZARD TO DEAL WITH, THEN.
TWO. MASOJ HUN'ETT IS NO MORE AS WELL.
MY SON! YOU HAVE BROUGHT US A GREAT EDGE IN THIS WAR!
AND... AND MY FATHER?
ZAKNAFEIN HAS SERVED HIS PURPOSE.
WE MUST MOVE AT ONCE, MY FAMILY! THIS DAY WE BECOME THE EIGHTH HOUSE OF MENZOBERRANZAN!
WOE TO THE ENEMIES OF DO'URDEN!
YOU KILLED HIM!
NO, MY BOY, YOU KILLED HIM!
YOUR INSOLENCE DEMANDED REPAYMENT TO LOLTH! BUT YOU LIVE, AS THE ELVEN CHILD LIVES.

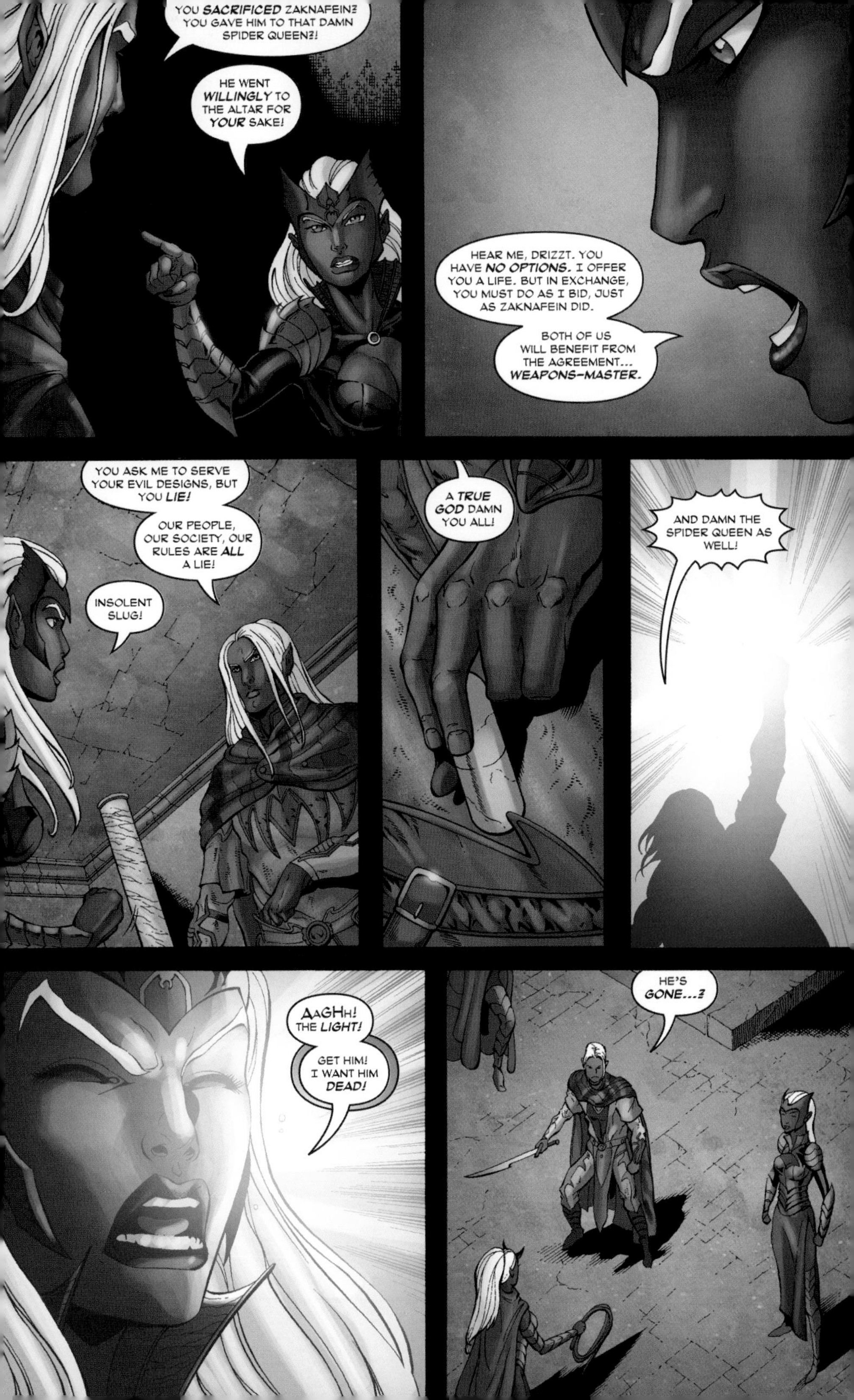
YOU SACRIFICED ZAKNAFEIN? YOU GAVE HIM TO THAT DAMN SPIDER QUEEN?!
HE WENT WILLINGLY TO THE ALTAR FOR YOUR SAKE!
HEAR ME, DRIZZT. YOU HAVE NO OPTIONS. I OFFER YOU A LIFE. BUT IN EXCHANGE, YOU MUST DO AS I BID, JUST AS ZAKNAFEIN DID.
BOTH OF US WILL BENEFIT FROM THE AGREEMENT... WEAPONS-MASTER.
YOU ASK ME TO SERVE YOUR EVIL DESIGNS, BUT YOU LIE!
OUR PEOPLE, OUR SOCIETY, OUR RULES ARE ALL A LIE!
INSOLENT SLUG!
A TRUE GOD DAMN YOU ALL!
AND DAMN THE SPIDER QUEEN AS WELL!
AAGHH! THE LIGHT!
GET HIM! I WANT HIM DEAD!
HE'S GONE...?

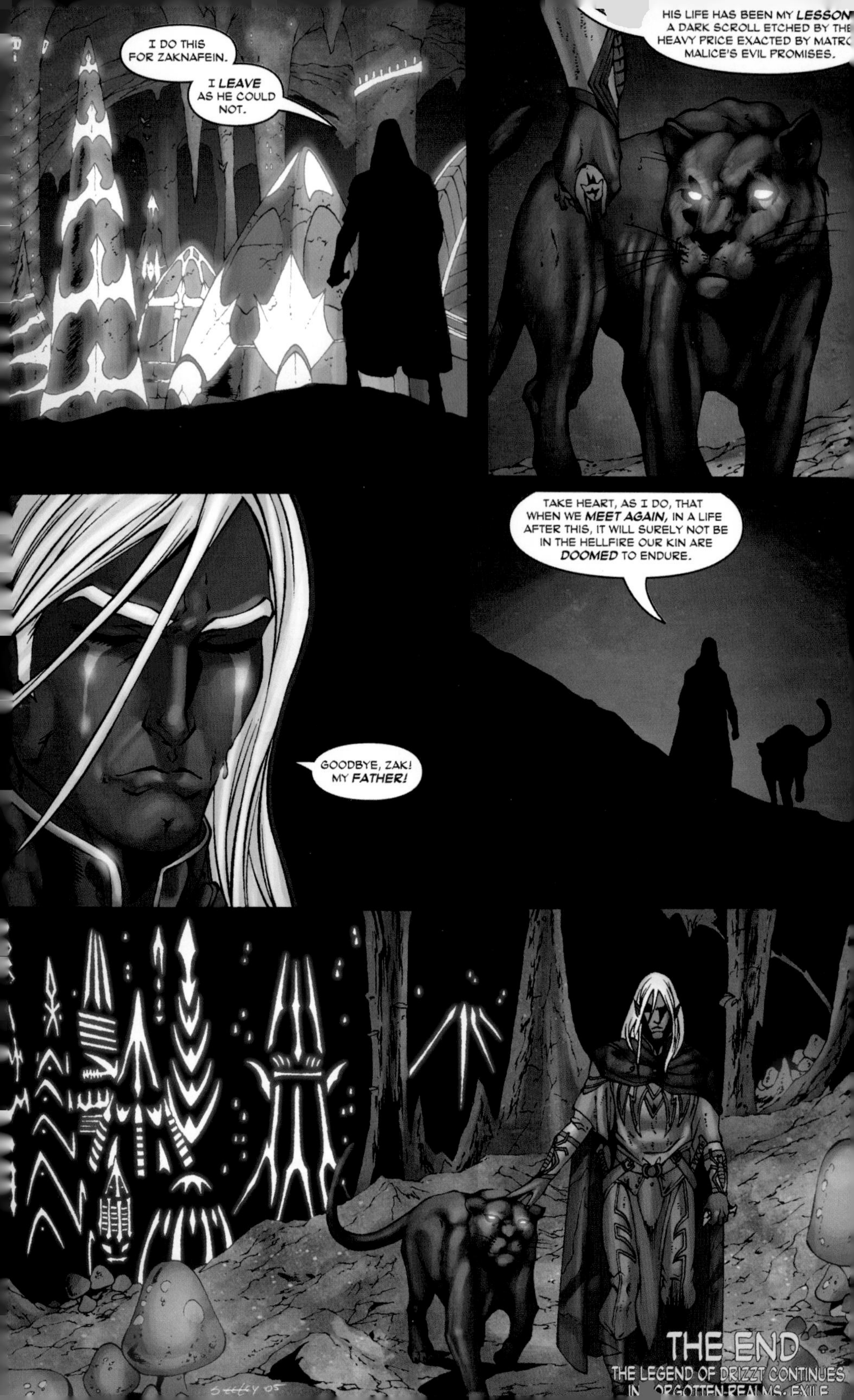

I DO THIS FOR ZAKNAFEIN.
I LEAVE AS HE COULD NOT.
HIS LIFE HAS BEEN MY LESSON A DARK SCROLL ETCHED BY THE HEAVY PRICE EXACTED BY MATRO MALICE'S EVIL PROMISES.
TAKE HEART, AS I DO, THAT WHEN WE MEET AGAIN, IN A LIFE AFTER THIS, IT WILL SURELY NOT BE IN THE HELLFIRE OUR KIN ARE DOOMED TO ENDURE.
GOODBYE, ZAK! MY FATHER!
THE END
THE LEGEND OF DRIZZT CONTINUES

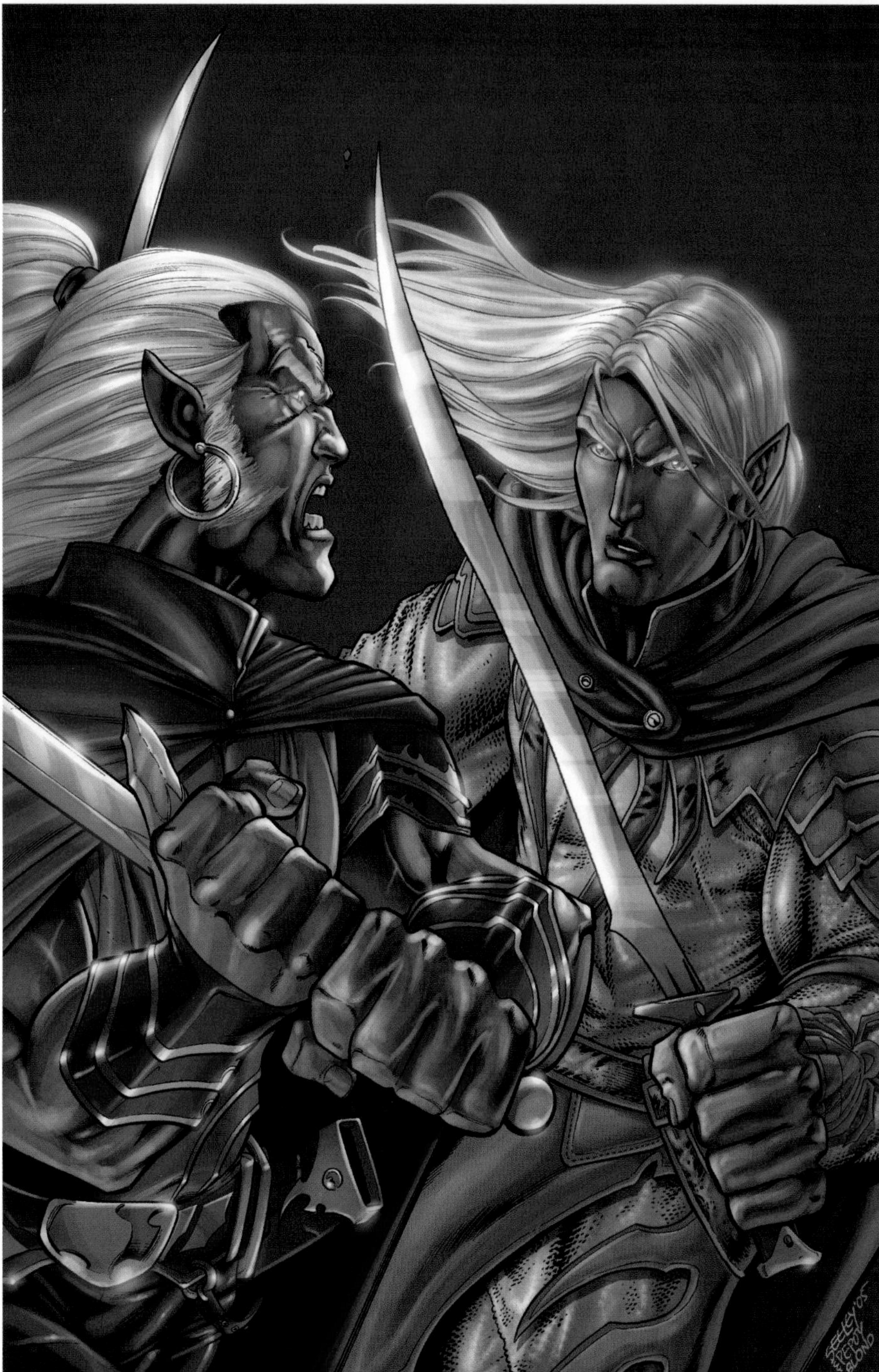

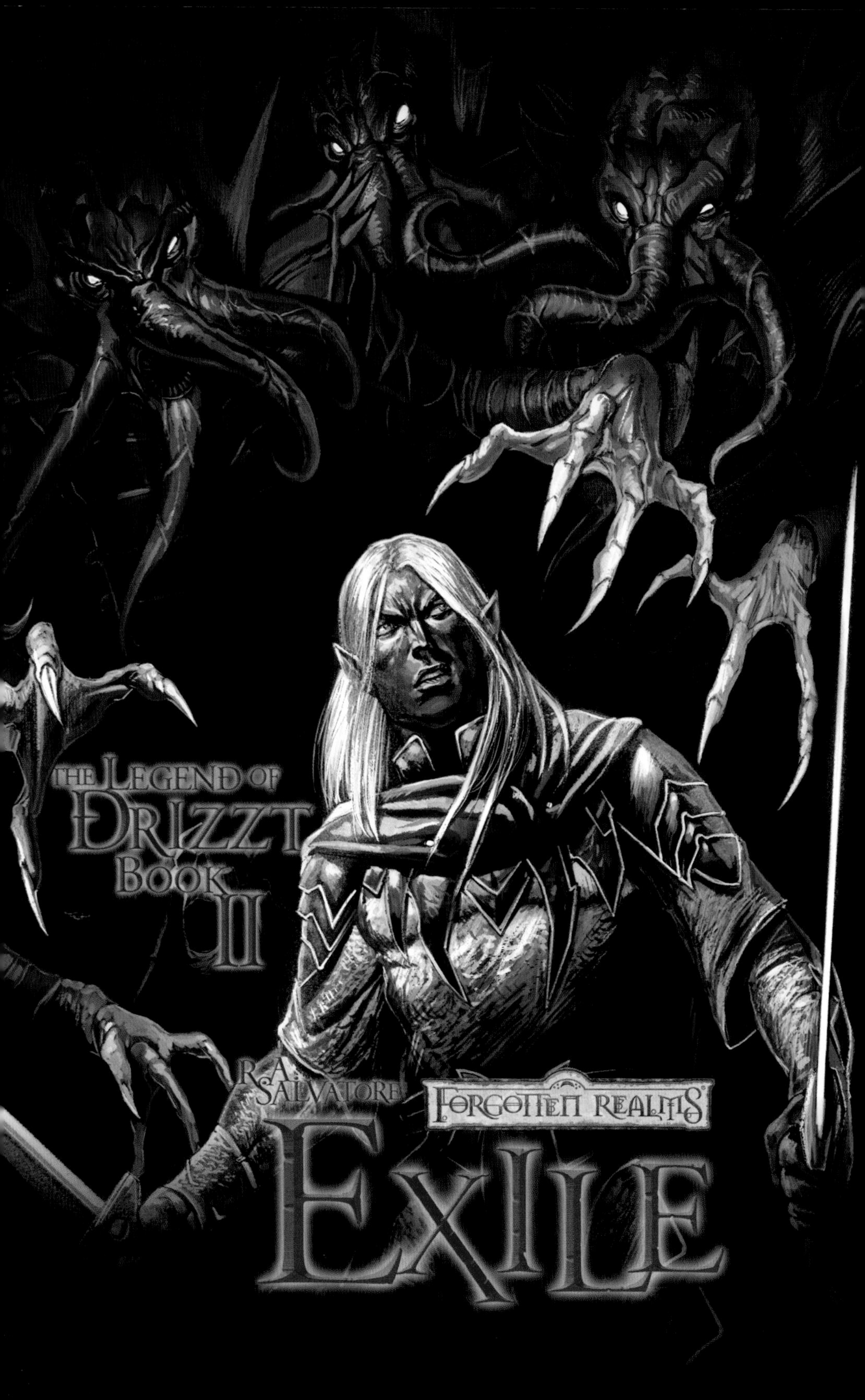
THE LEGEND OF
DRIZZT
BOOK
II
R.A.
SALVATORE
FORGOTTEN REALMS
EXILE

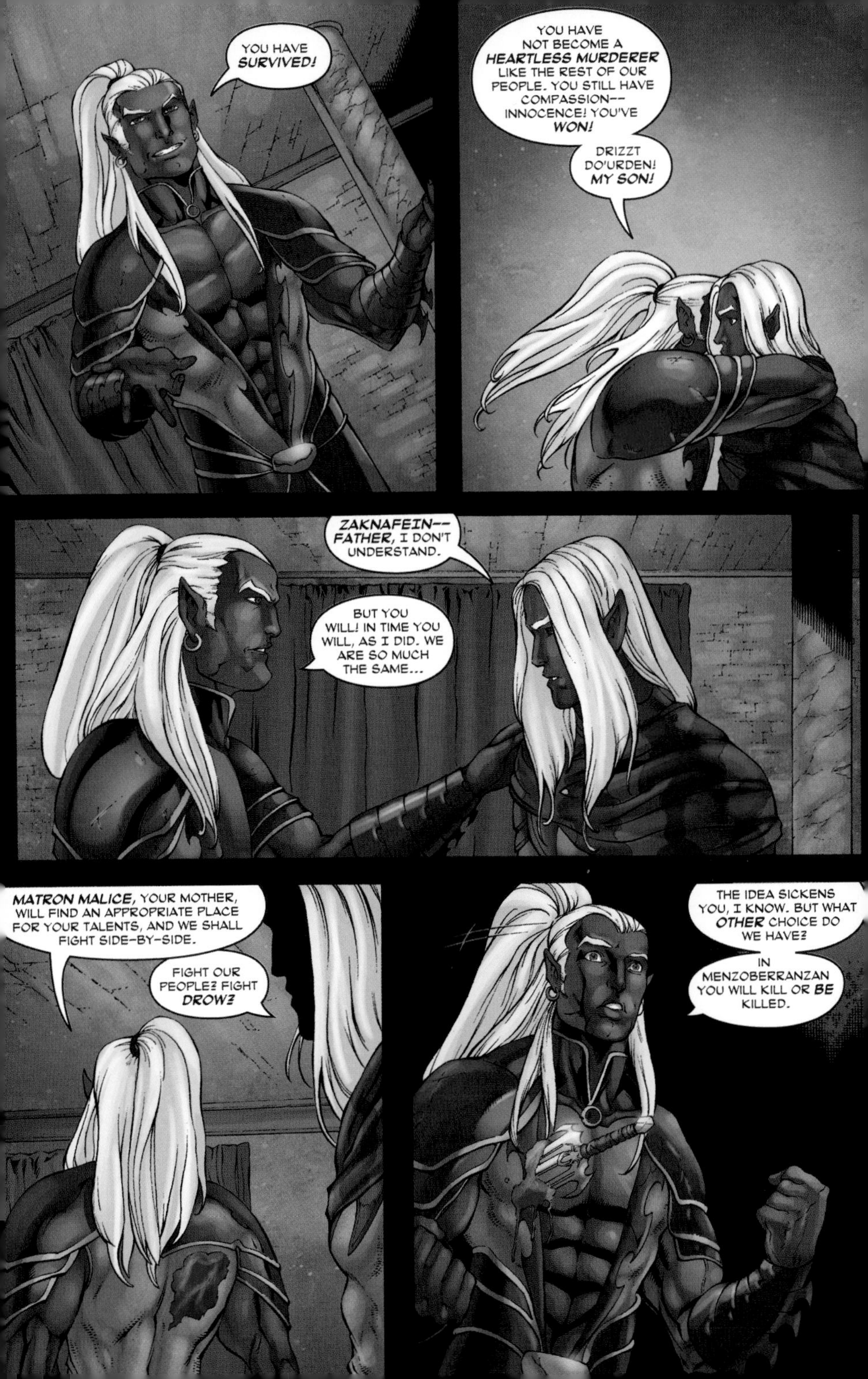
YOU HAVE **SURVIVED!**
YOU HAVE NOT BECOME A **HEARTLESS MURDERER** LIKE THE REST OF OUR PEOPLE. YOU STILL HAVE COMPASSION-- INNOCENCE! YOU'VE **WON!**
DRIZZT DO'URDEN! **MY SON!**
ZAKNAFEIN-- **FATHER,** I DON'T UNDERSTAND.
BUT YOU WILL! IN TIME YOU WILL, AS I DID. WE ARE SO MUCH THE SAME...
MATRON MALICE, YOUR MOTHER, WILL FIND AN APPROPRIATE PLACE FOR YOUR TALENTS, AND WE SHALL FIGHT SIDE-BY-SIDE.
FIGHT OUR PEOPLE? FIGHT **DROW?**
THE IDEA SICKENS YOU, I KNOW. BUT WHAT **OTHER** CHOICE DO WE HAVE?
IN MENZOBERRANZAN YOU WILL KILL OR **BE** KILLED.

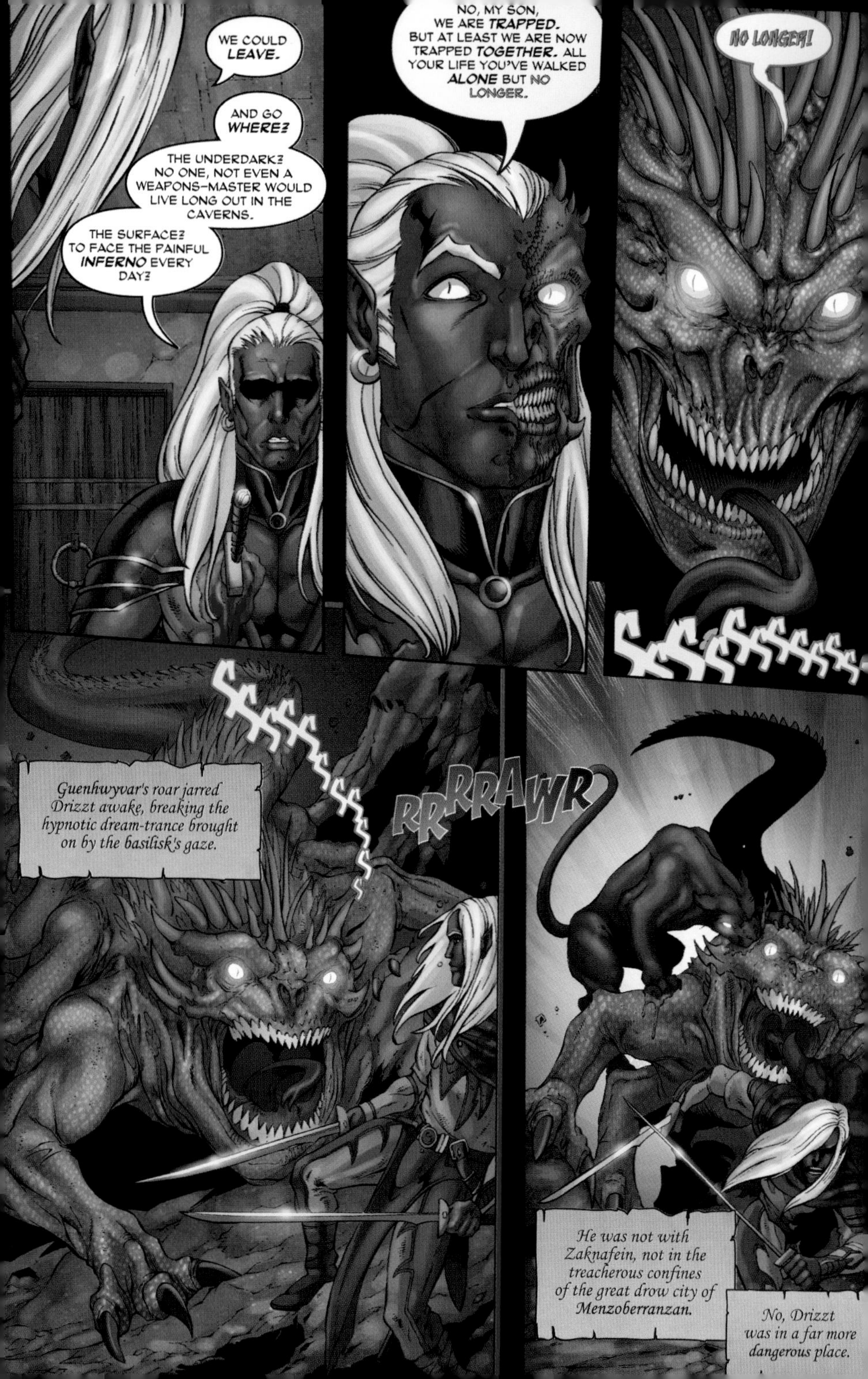
WE COULD LEAVE.
AND GO WHERE?
THE UNDERDARK? NO ONE, NOT EVEN A WEAPONS-MASTER WOULD LIVE LONG OUT IN THE CAVERNS.
THE SURFACE? TO FACE THE PAINFUL INFERNO EVERY DAY?
NO, MY SON, WE ARE TRAPPED. BUT AT LEAST WE ARE NOW TRAPPED TOGETHER. ALL YOUR LIFE YOU'VE WALKED ALONE BUT NO LONGER.
NO LONGER!
SSSSSSSSSSS
SSSSSSSSS
Guenhwyvar's roar jarred Drizzt awake, breaking the hypnotic dream-trance brought on by the basilisk's gaze.
RRRRAWR
He was not with Zaknafein, not in the treacherous confines of the great drow city of Menzoberranzan.
No, Drizzt was in a far more dangerous place.

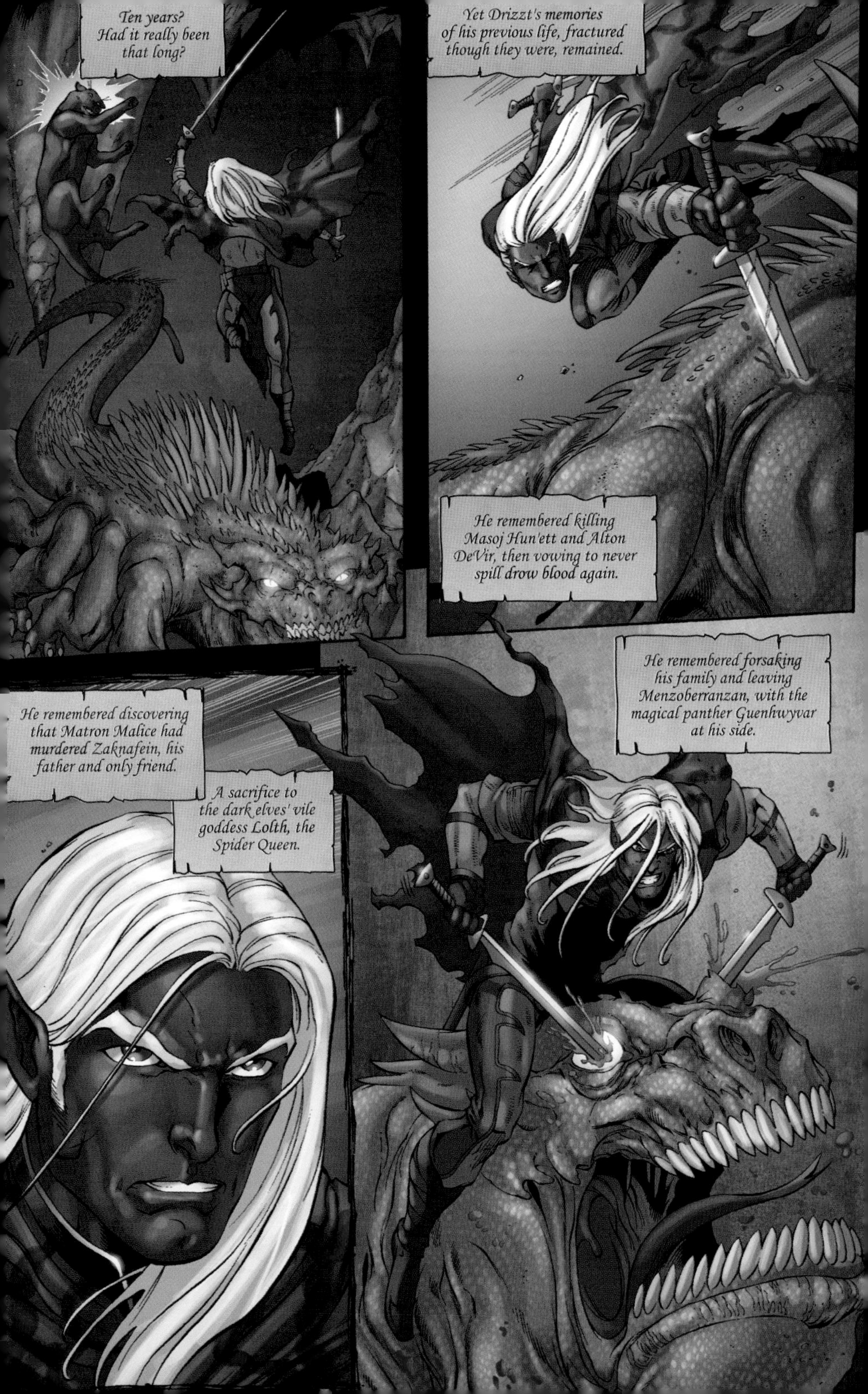
Ten years? Had it really been that long?
Yet Drizzt's memories of his previous life, fractured though they were, remained.
He remembered killing Masoj Hun'ett and Alton DeVir, then vowing to never spill drow blood again.
He remembered discovering that Matron Malice had murdered Zaknafein, his father and only friend.
A sacrifice to the dark elves' vile goddess Lolth, the Spider Queen.
He remembered forsaking his family and leaving Menzoberranzan, with the magical panther Guenhwyvar at his side.

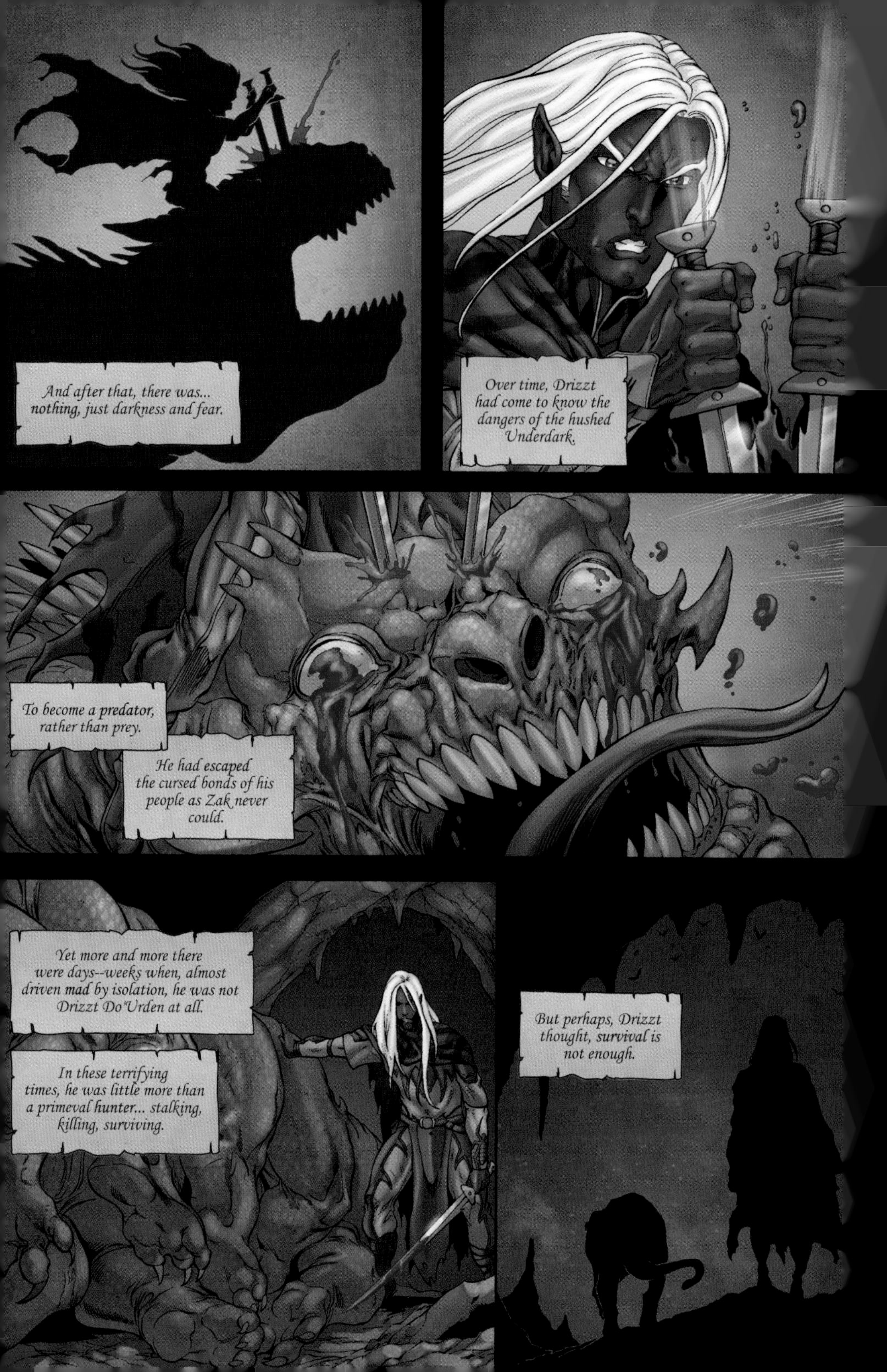
And after that, there was... nothing, just darkness and fear.
Over time, Drizzt had come to know the dangers of the hushed Underdark.
To become a predator, rather than prey.
He had escaped the cursed bonds of his people as Zak never could.
Yet more and more there were days--weeks when, almost driven mad by isolation, he was not Drizzt Do'Urden at all.
In these terrifying times, he was little more than a primeval hunter... stalking, killing, surviving.
But perhaps, Drizzt thought, survival is not enough.

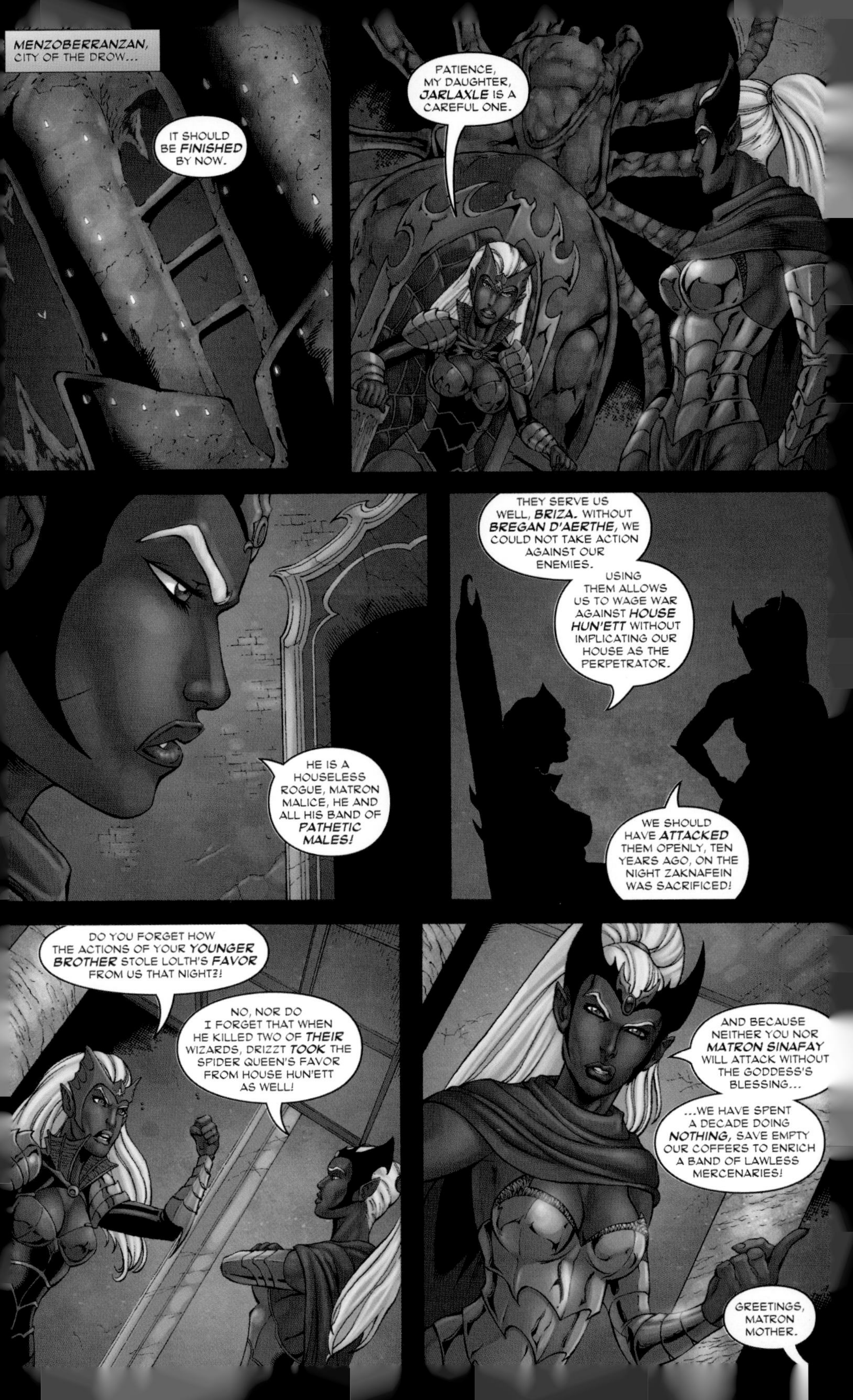
MENZOBERRANZAN, CITY OF THE DROW...
IT SHOULD BE FINISHED BY NOW.
PATIENCE, MY DAUGHTER, JARLAXLE IS A CAREFUL ONE.
HE IS A HOUSELESS ROGUE, MATRON MALICE, HE AND ALL HIS BAND OF PATHETIC MALES!
THEY SERVE US WELL, BRIZA. WITHOUT BREGAN D'AERTHE, WE COULD NOT TAKE ACTION AGAINST OUR ENEMIES.
USING THEM ALLOWS US TO WAGE WAR AGAINST HOUSE HUN'ETT WITHOUT IMPLICATING OUR HOUSE AS THE PERPETRATOR.
WE SHOULD HAVE ATTACKED THEM OPENLY, TEN YEARS AGO, ON THE NIGHT ZAKNAFEIN WAS SACRIFICED!
DO YOU FORGET HOW THE ACTIONS OF YOUR YOUNGER BROTHER STOLE LOLTH'S FAVOR FROM US THAT NIGHT?!
NO, NOR DO I FORGET THAT WHEN HE KILLED TWO OF THEIR WIZARDS, DRIZZT TOOK THE SPIDER QUEEN'S FAVOR FROM HOUSE HUN'ETT AS WELL!
AND BECAUSE NEITHER YOU NOR MATRON SINAFAY WILL ATTACK WITHOUT THE GODDESS'S BLESSING...
...WE HAVE SPENT A DECADE DOING NOTHING, SAVE EMPTY OUR COFFERS TO ENRICH A BAND OF LAWLESS MERCENARIES!
GREETINGS, MATRON MOTHER.

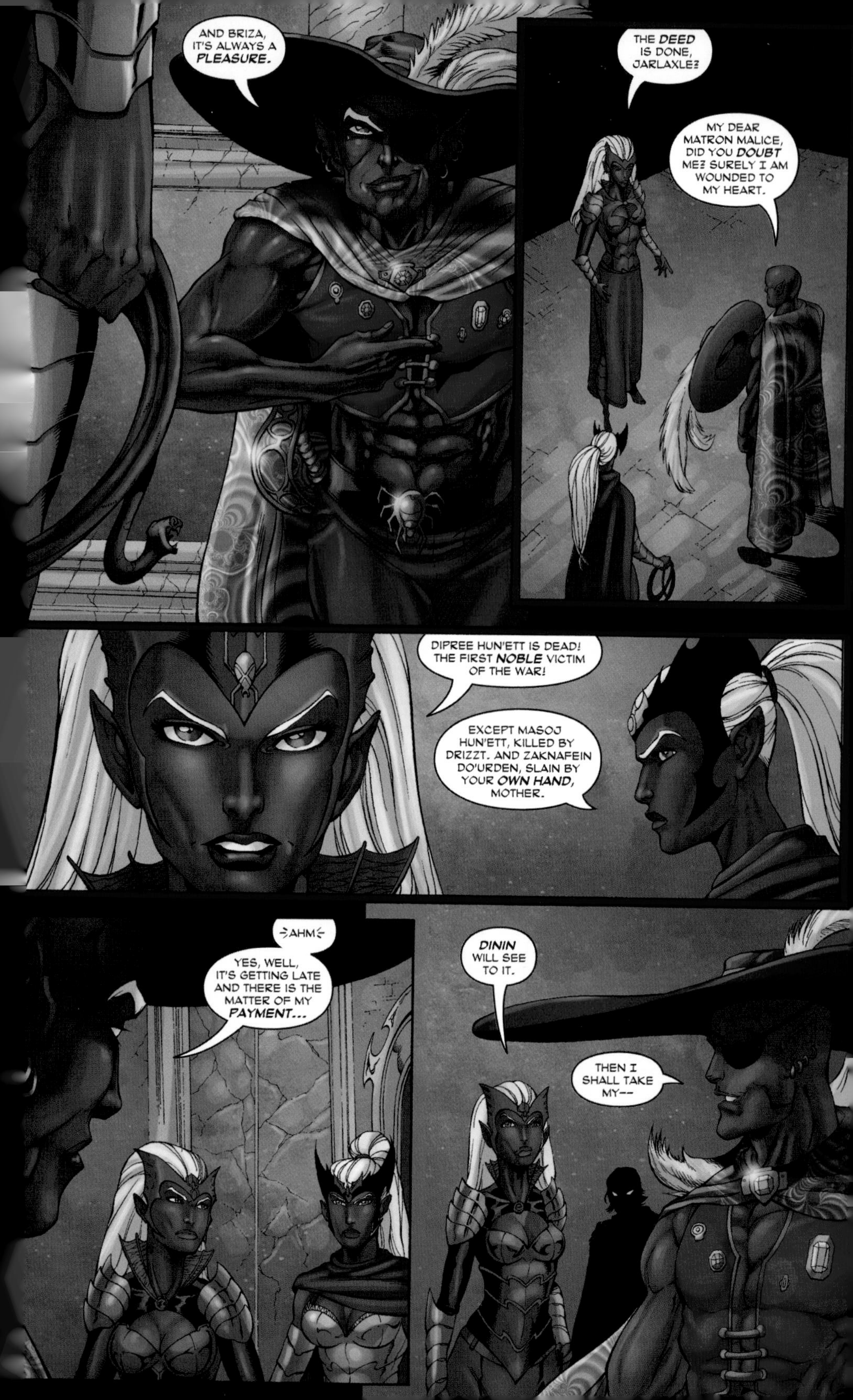
AND BRIZA, IT'S ALWAYS A PLEASURE.
THE DEED IS DONE, JARLAXLE?
MY DEAR MATRON MALICE, DID YOU DOUBT ME? SURELY I AM WOUNDED TO MY HEART.
DIPREE HUN'ETT IS DEAD! THE FIRST NOBLE VICTIM OF THE WAR!
EXCEPT MASOJ HUN'ETT, KILLED BY DRIZZT. AND ZAKNAFEIN DO'URDEN, SLAIN BY YOUR OWN HAND, MOTHER.
AHM
YES, WELL, IT'S GETTING LATE AND THERE IS THE MATTER OF MY PAYMENT...
DININ WILL SEE TO IT.
THEN I SHALL TAKE MY--

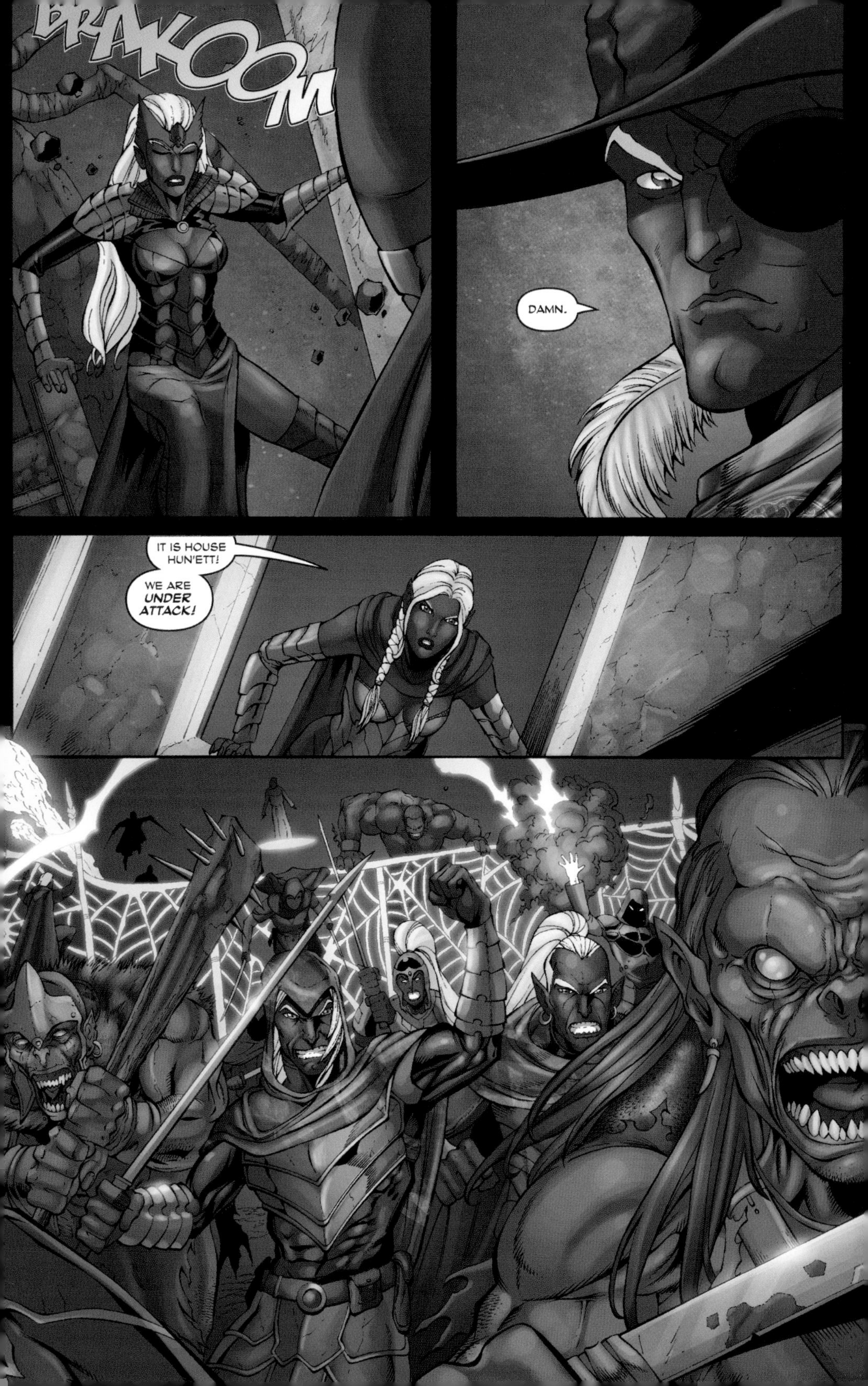
BRAKOOM
DAMN.
IT IS HOUSE HUN'ETT!
WE ARE UNDER ATTACK!

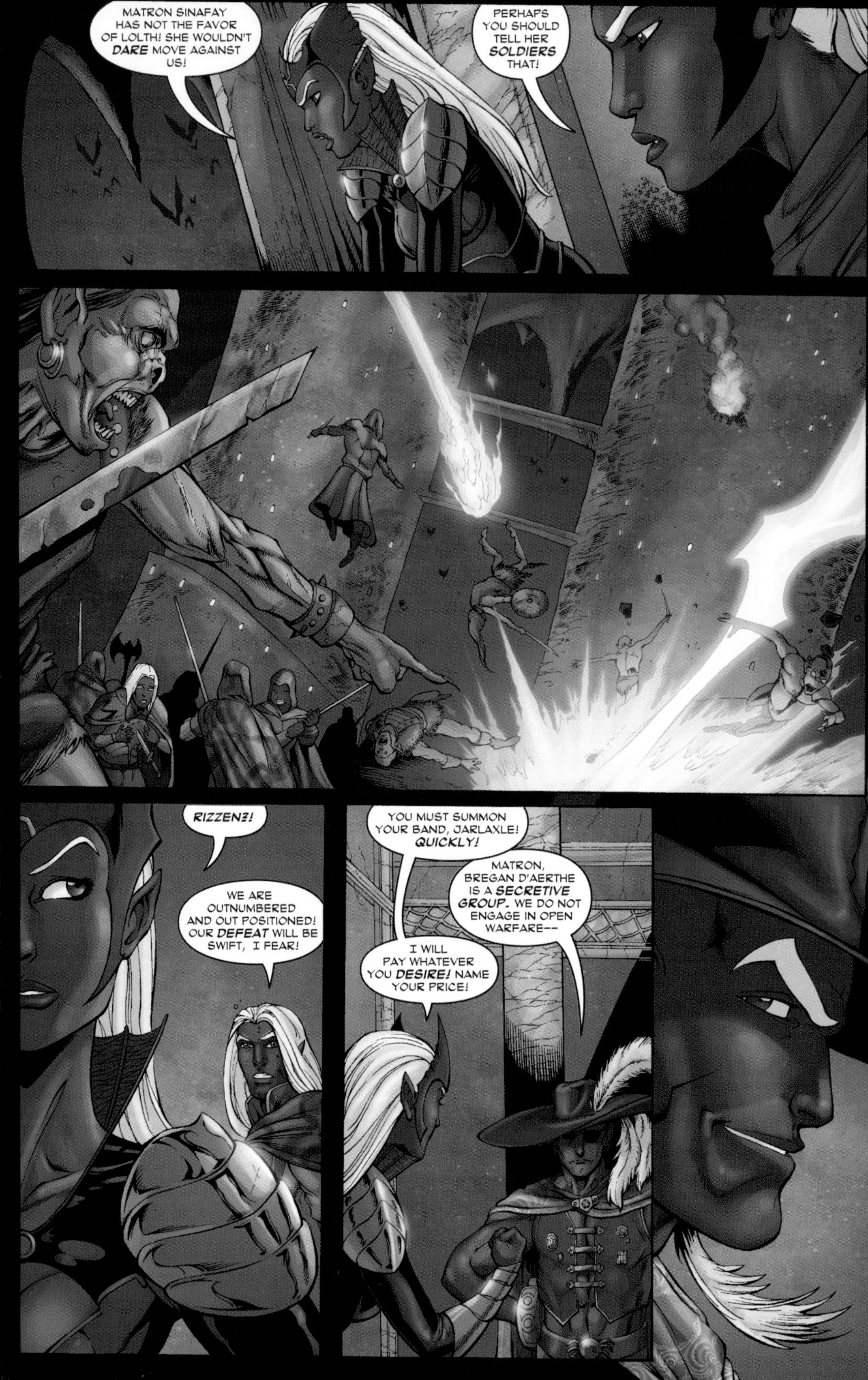
MATRON SINAFAY HAS NOT THE FAVOR OF LOLTH! SHE WOULDN'T DARE MOVE AGAINST US!
PERHAPS YOU SHOULD TELL HER SOLDIERS THAT!
RIZZEN?!
WE ARE OUTNUMBERED AND OUT POSITIONED! OUR DEFEAT WILL BE SWIFT, I FEAR!
YOU MUST SUMMON YOUR BAND, JARLAXLE! QUICKLY!
MATRON, BREGAN D'AERTHE IS A SECRETIVE GROUP. WE DO NOT ENGAGE IN OPEN WARFARE--
I WILL PAY WHATEVER YOU DESIRE! NAME YOUR PRICE!

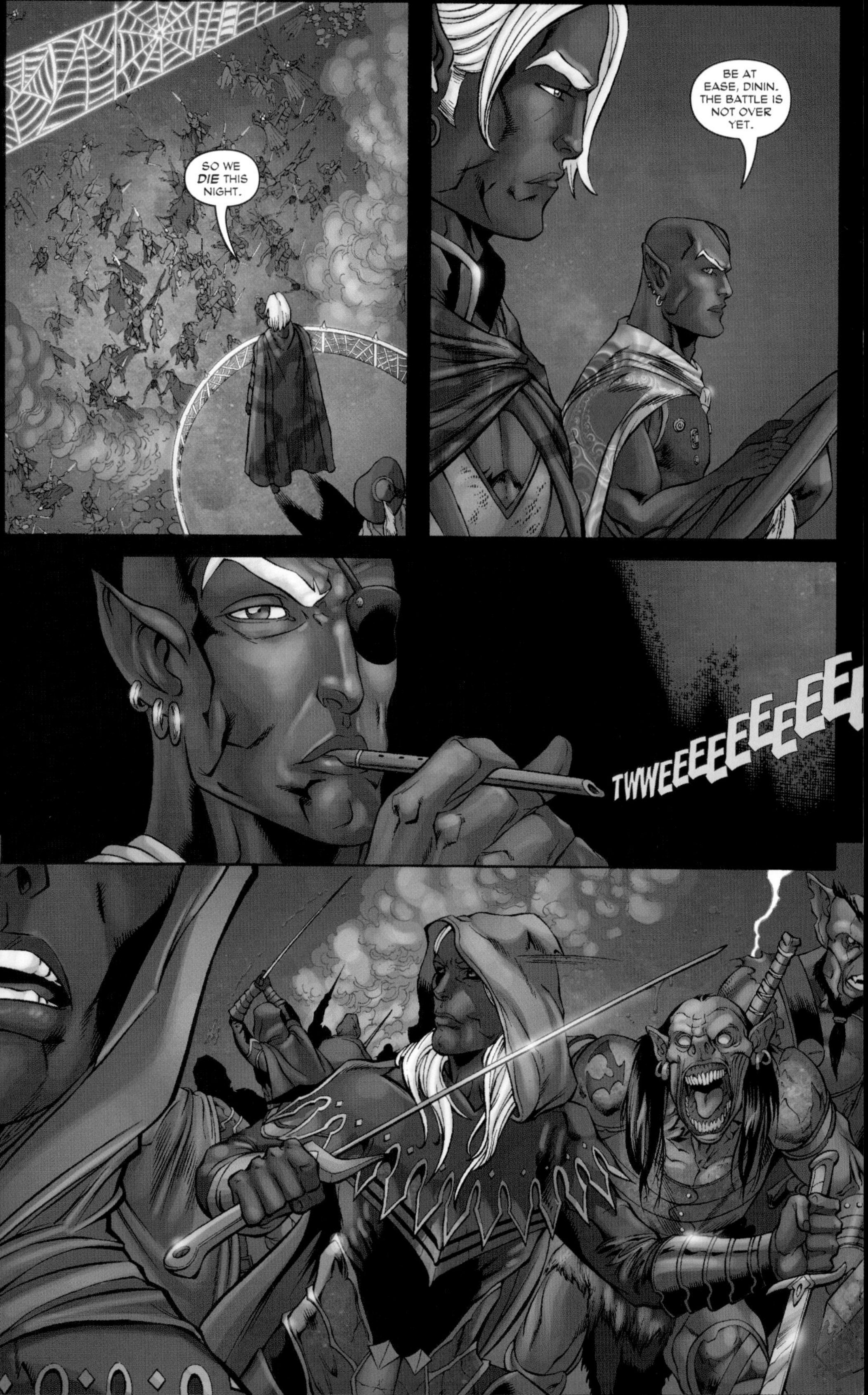
SO WE DIE THIS NIGHT.
BE AT EASE, DININ. THE BATTLE IS NOT OVER YET.
TWWEEEEEEEEEE

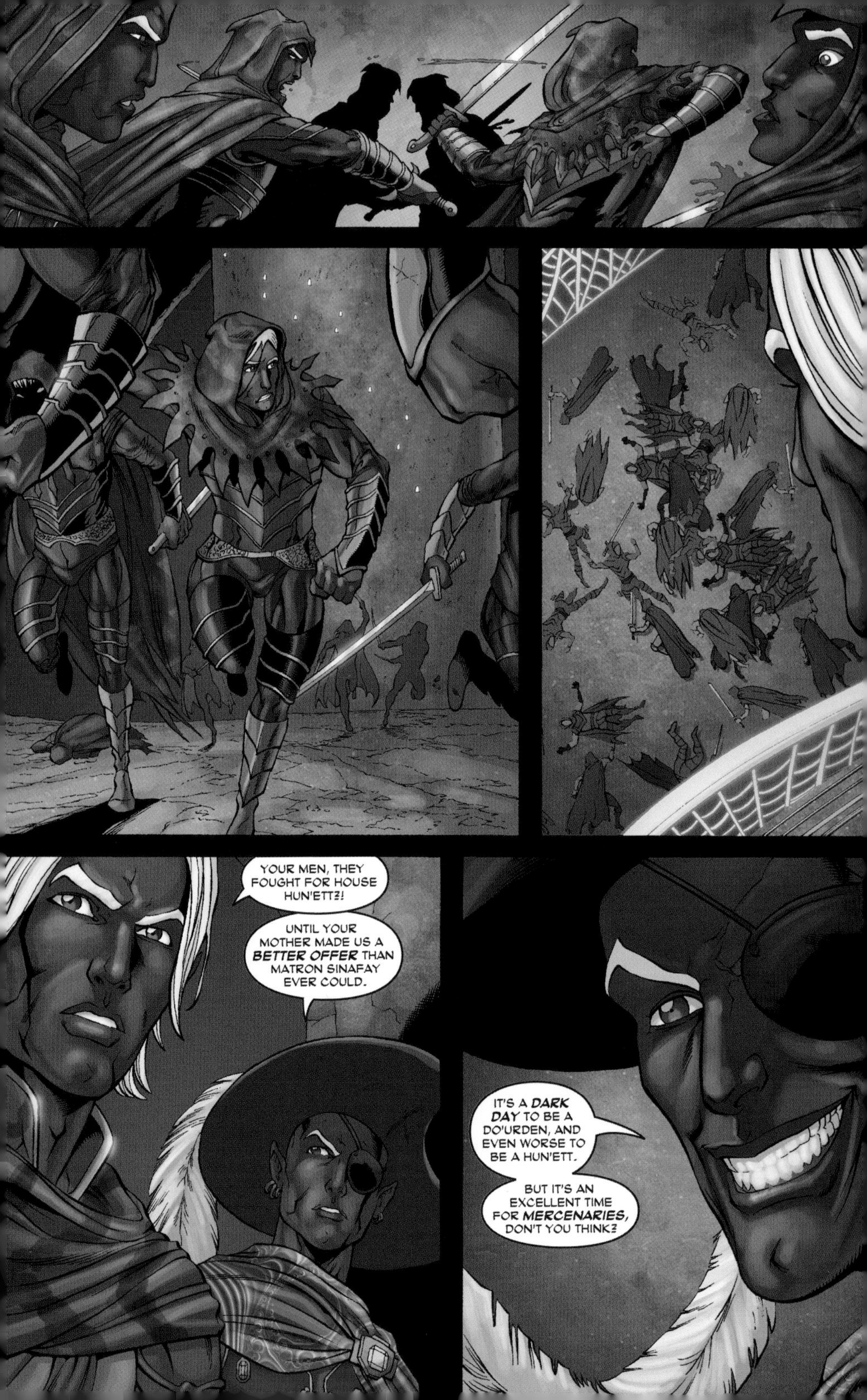
YOUR MEN, THEY FOUGHT FOR HOUSE HUN'ETT?!
UNTIL YOUR MOTHER MADE US A BETTER OFFER THAN MATRON SINAFAY EVER COULD.
IT'S A DARK DAY TO BE A DO'URDEN, AND EVEN WORSE TO BE A HUN'ETT.
BUT IT'S AN EXCELLENT TIME FOR MERCENARIES, DON'T YOU THINK?

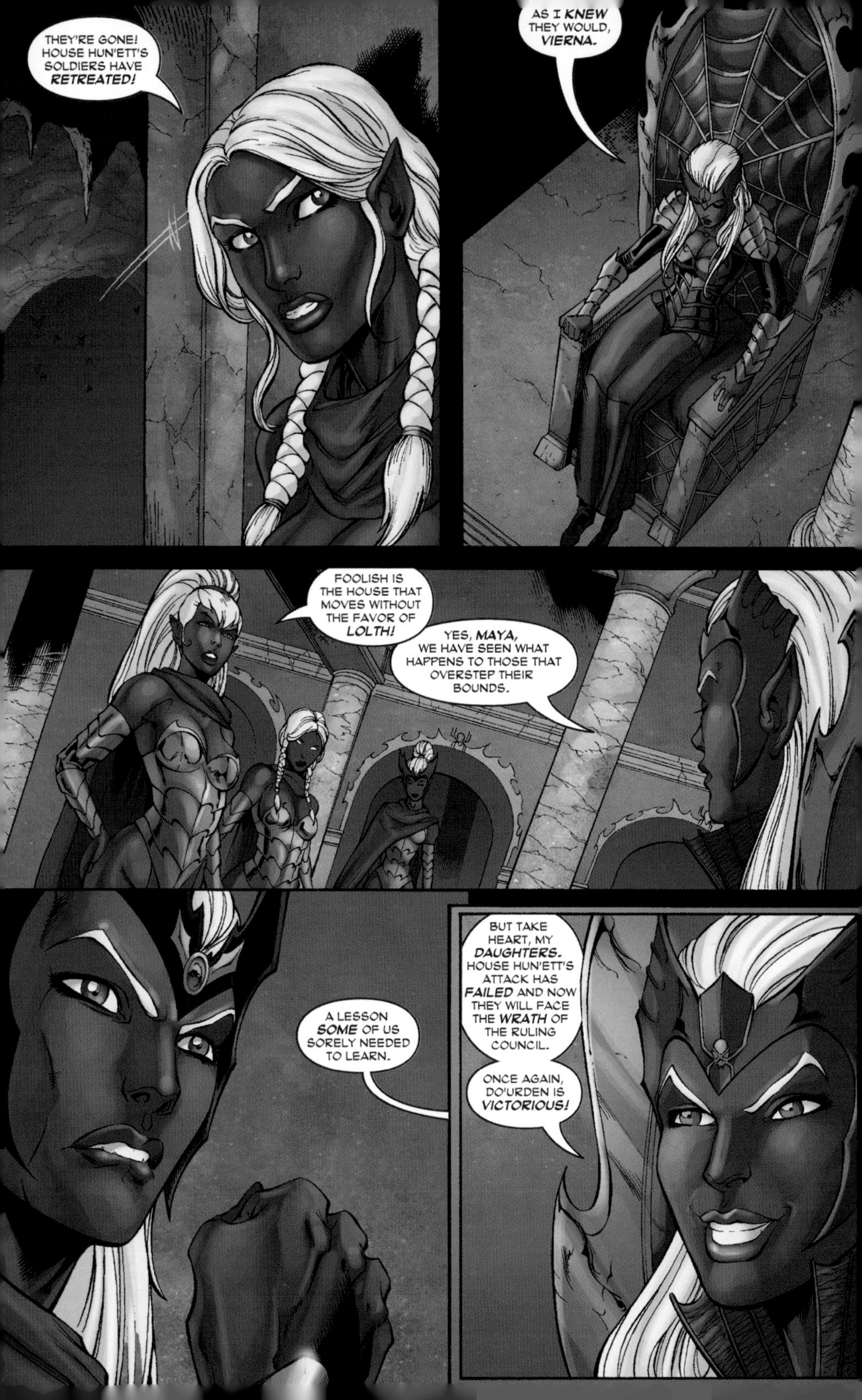
THEY'RE GONE! HOUSE HUN'ETT'S SOLDIERS HAVE RETREATED!
AS I KNEW THEY WOULD, VIERNA.
FOOLISH IS THE HOUSE THAT MOVES WITHOUT THE FAVOR OF LOLTH!
YES, MAYA, WE HAVE SEEN WHAT HAPPENS TO THOSE THAT OVERSTEP THEIR BOUNDS.
A LESSON SOME OF US SORELY NEEDED TO LEARN.
BUT TAKE HEART, MY DAUGHTERS. HOUSE HUN'ETT'S ATTACK HAS FAILED AND NOW THEY WILL FACE THE WRATH OF THE RULING COUNCIL.
ONCE AGAIN, DO'URDEN IS VICTORIOUS!

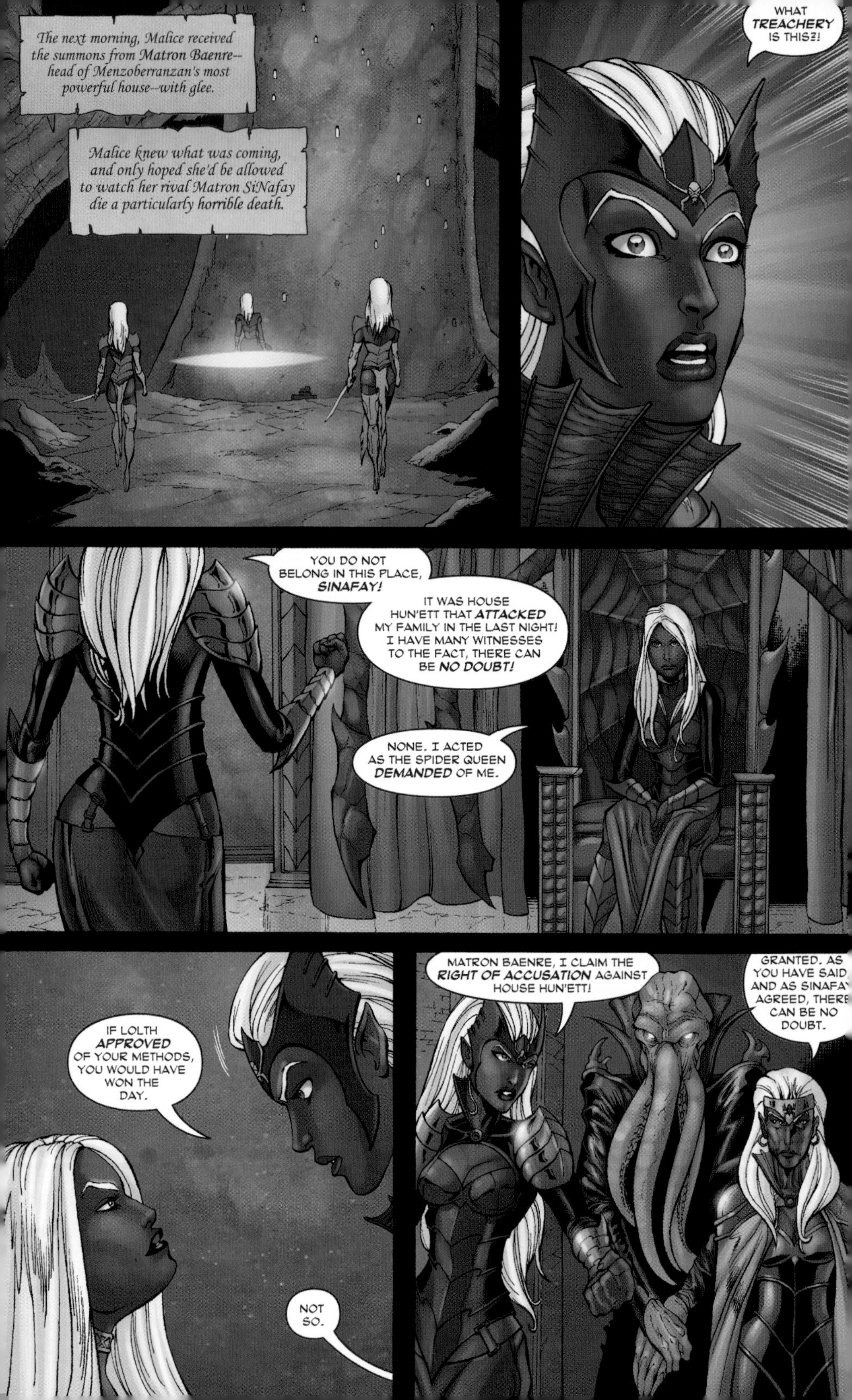
The next morning, Malice received the summons from Matron Baenre--head of Menzoberranzan's most powerful house--with glee.
Malice knew what was coming, and only hoped she'd be allowed to watch her rival Matron SiNafay die a particularly horrible death.
WHAT TREACHERY IS THIS?!
YOU DO NOT BELONG IN THIS PLACE, SINAFAY!
IT WAS HOUSE HUN'ETT THAT ATTACKED MY FAMILY IN THE LAST NIGHT! I HAVE MANY WITNESSES TO THE FACT, THERE CAN BE NO DOUBT!
NONE. I ACTED AS THE SPIDER QUEEN DEMANDED OF ME.
IF LOLTH APPROVED OF YOUR METHODS, YOU WOULD HAVE WON THE DAY.
NOT SO.
MATRON BAENRE, I CLAIM THE RIGHT OF ACCUSATION AGAINST HOUSE HUN'ETT!
GRANTED. AS YOU HAVE SAID AND AS SINAFAY AGREED, THERE CAN BE NO DOUBT.

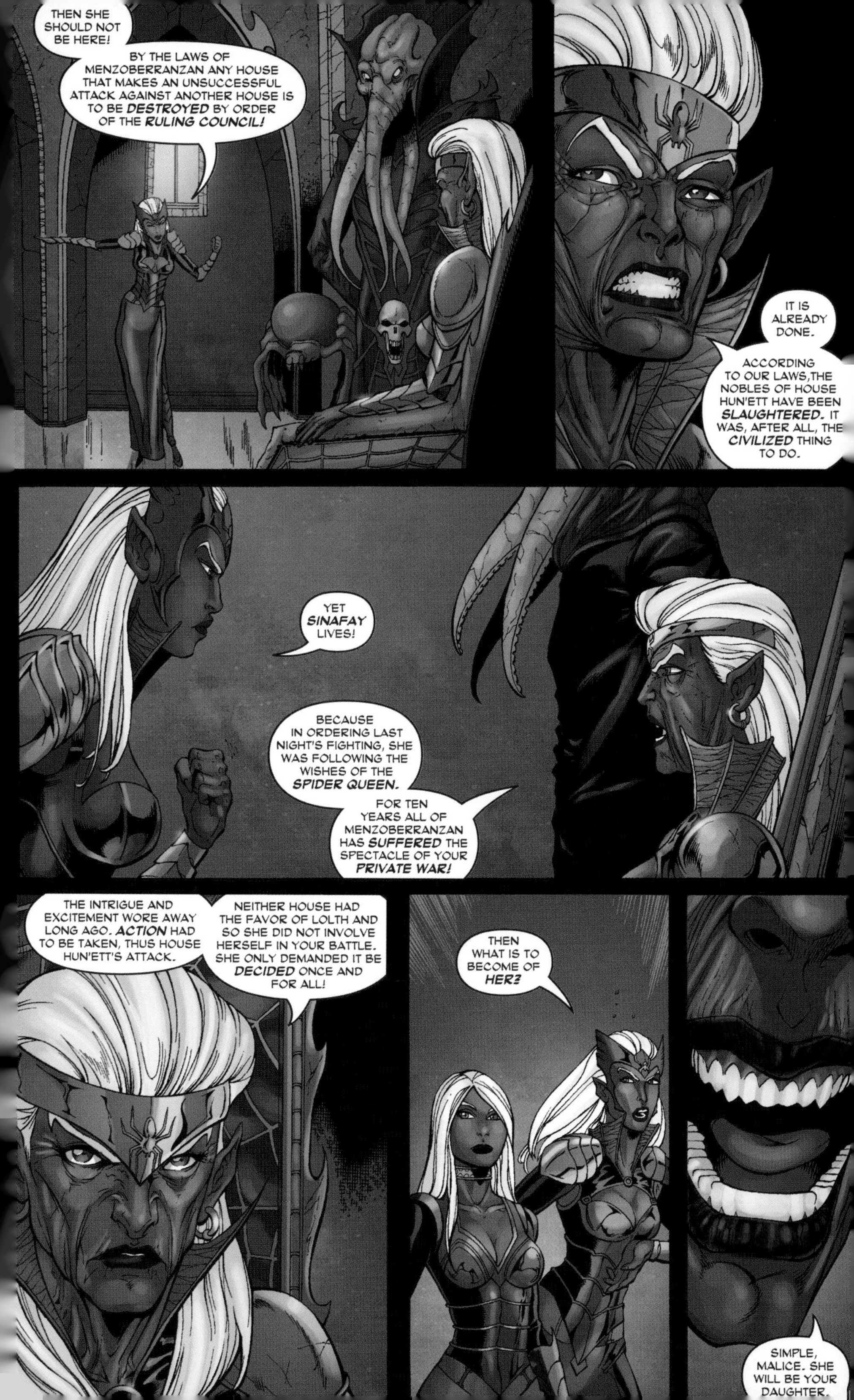
THEN SHE SHOULD NOT BE HERE!
BY THE LAWS OF MENZOBERRANZAN ANY HOUSE THAT MAKES AN UNSUCCESSFUL ATTACK AGAINST ANOTHER HOUSE IS TO BE DESTROYED BY ORDER OF THE RULING COUNCIL!
IT IS ALREADY DONE.
ACCORDING TO OUR LAWS, THE NOBLES OF HOUSE HUN'ETT HAVE BEEN SLAUGHTERED. IT WAS, AFTER ALL, THE CIVILIZED THING TO DO.
YET SINAFAY LIVES!
BECAUSE IN ORDERING LAST NIGHT'S FIGHTING, SHE WAS FOLLOWING THE WISHES OF THE SPIDER QUEEN.
FOR TEN YEARS ALL OF MENZOBERRANZAN HAS SUFFERED THE SPECTACLE OF YOUR PRIVATE WAR!
THE INTRIGUE AND EXCITEMENT WORE AWAY LONG AGO. ACTION HAD TO BE TAKEN, THUS HOUSE HUN'ETT'S ATTACK.
NEITHER HOUSE HAD THE FAVOR OF LOLTH AND SO SHE DID NOT INVOLVE HERSELF IN YOUR BATTLE. SHE ONLY DEMANDED IT BE DECIDED ONCE AND FOR ALL!
THEN WHAT IS TO BECOME OF HER?
SIMPLE, MALICE. SHE WILL BE YOUR DAUGHTER.

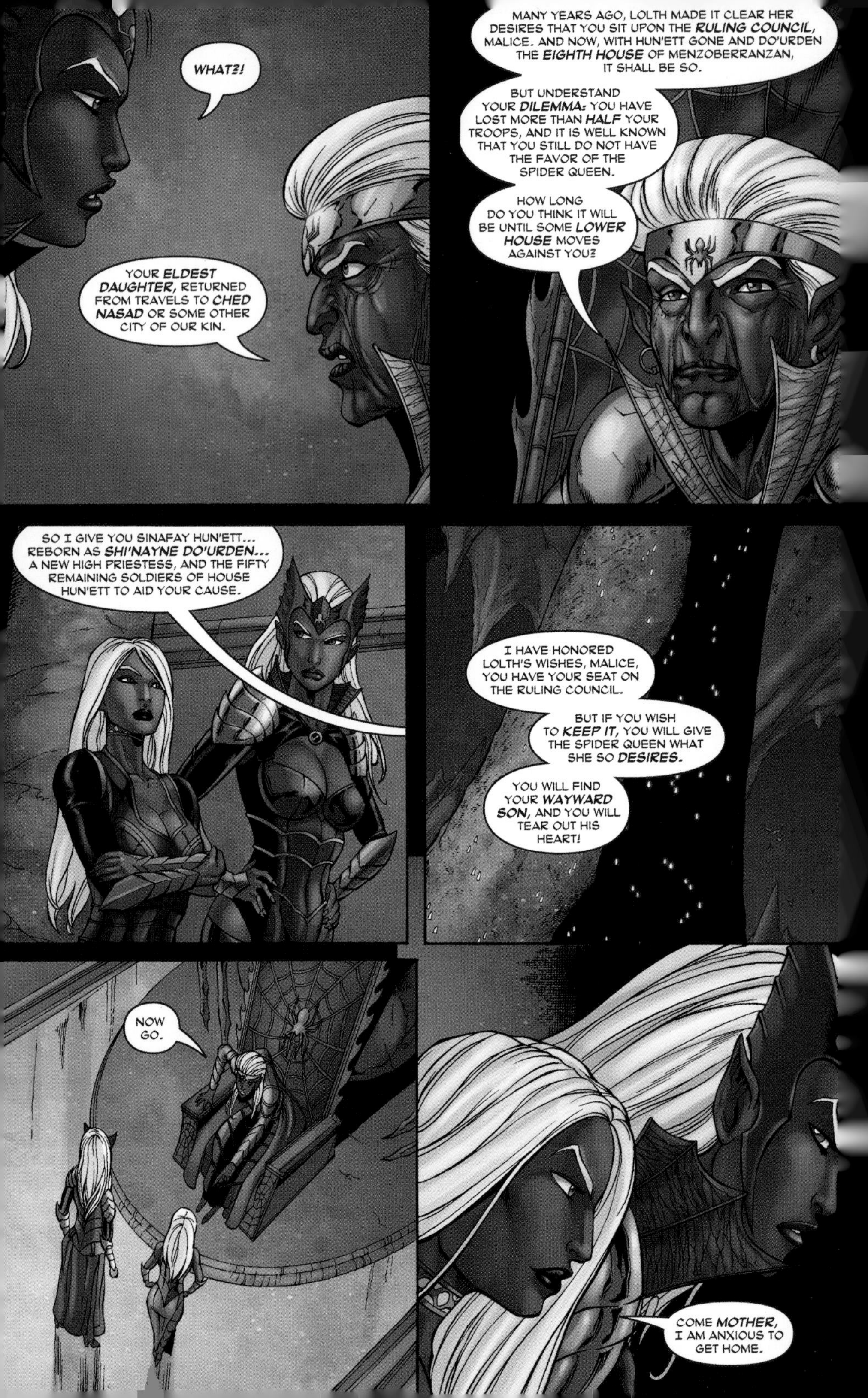
WHAT?!
YOUR ELDEST DAUGHTER, RETURNED FROM TRAVELS TO CHED NASAD OR SOME OTHER CITY OF OUR KIN.
MANY YEARS AGO, LOLTH MADE IT CLEAR HER DESIRES THAT YOU SIT UPON THE RULING COUNCIL, MALICE. AND NOW, WITH HUN'ETT GONE AND DO'URDEN THE EIGHTH HOUSE OF MENZOBERRANZAN, IT SHALL BE SO.
BUT UNDERSTAND YOUR DILEMMA: YOU HAVE LOST MORE THAN HALF YOUR TROOPS, AND IT IS WELL KNOWN THAT YOU STILL DO NOT HAVE THE FAVOR OF THE SPIDER QUEEN.
HOW LONG DO YOU THINK IT WILL BE UNTIL SOME LOWER HOUSE MOVES AGAINST YOU?
SO I GIVE YOU SINAFAY HUN'ETT... REBORN AS SHI'NAYNE DO'URDEN... A NEW HIGH PRIESTESS, AND THE FIFTY REMAINING SOLDIERS OF HOUSE HUN'ETT TO AID YOUR CAUSE.
I HAVE HONORED LOLTH'S WISHES, MALICE. YOU HAVE YOUR SEAT ON THE RULING COUNCIL.
BUT IF YOU WISH TO KEEP IT, YOU WILL GIVE THE SPIDER QUEEN WHAT SHE SO DESIRES.
YOU WILL FIND YOUR WAYWARD SON, AND YOU WILL TEAR OUT HIS HEART!
NOW GO.
COME MOTHER, I AM ANXIOUS TO GET HOME.

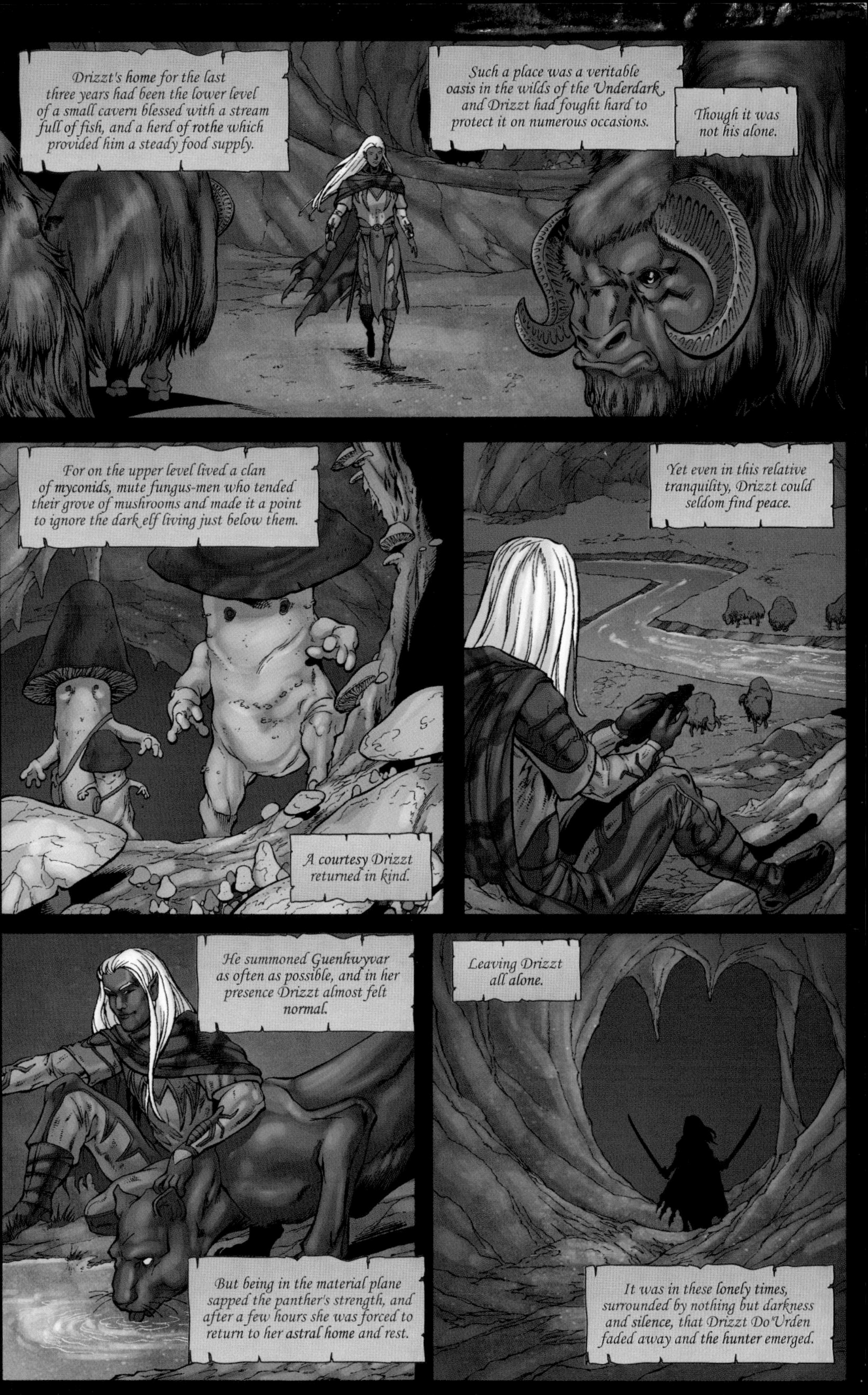
Drizzt's home for the last three years had been the lower level of a small cavern blessed with a stream full of fish, and a herd of rothe which provided him a steady food supply.
Such a place was a veritable oasis in the wilds of the Underdark, and Drizzt had fought hard to protect it on numerous occasions.
Though it was not his alone.
For on the upper level lived a clan of myconids, mute fungus-men who tended their grove of mushrooms and made it a point to ignore the dark elf living just below them.
A courtesy Drizzt returned in kind.
Yet even in this relative tranquility, Drizzt could seldom find peace.
He summoned Guenhwyvar as often as possible, and in her presence Drizzt almost felt normal.
But being in the material plane sapped the panther's strength, and after a few hours she was forced to return to her astral home and rest.
Leaving Drizzt all alone.
It was in these lonely times, surrounded by nothing but darkness and silence, that Drizzt Do'Urden faded away and the hunter emerged.

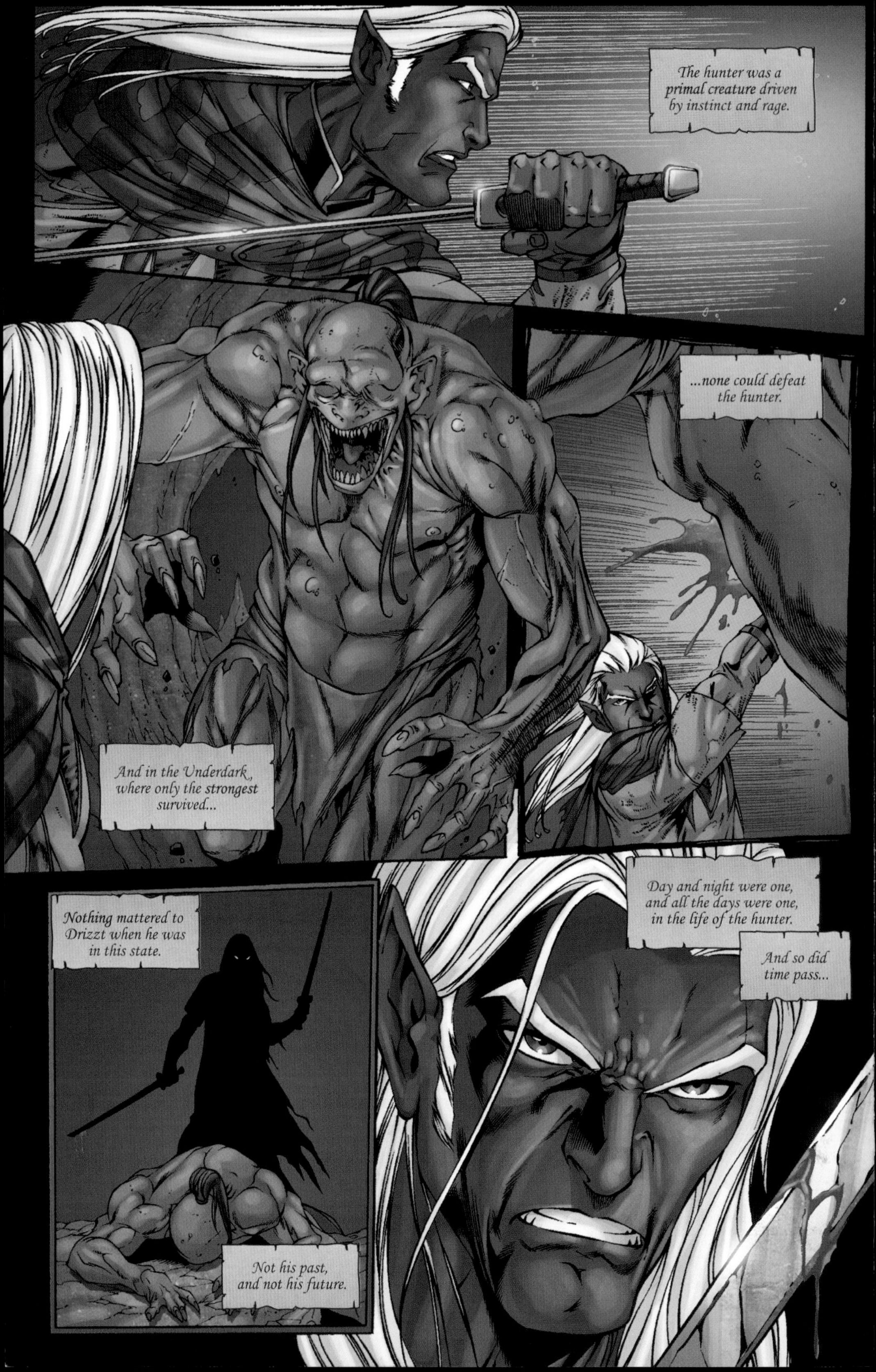
The hunter was a primal creature driven by instinct and rage.
And in the Underdark, where only the strongest survived...
...none could defeat the hunter.
Nothing mattered to Drizzt when he was in this state.
Not his past, and not his future.
Day and night were one, and all the days were one, in the life of the hunter.
And so did time pass...

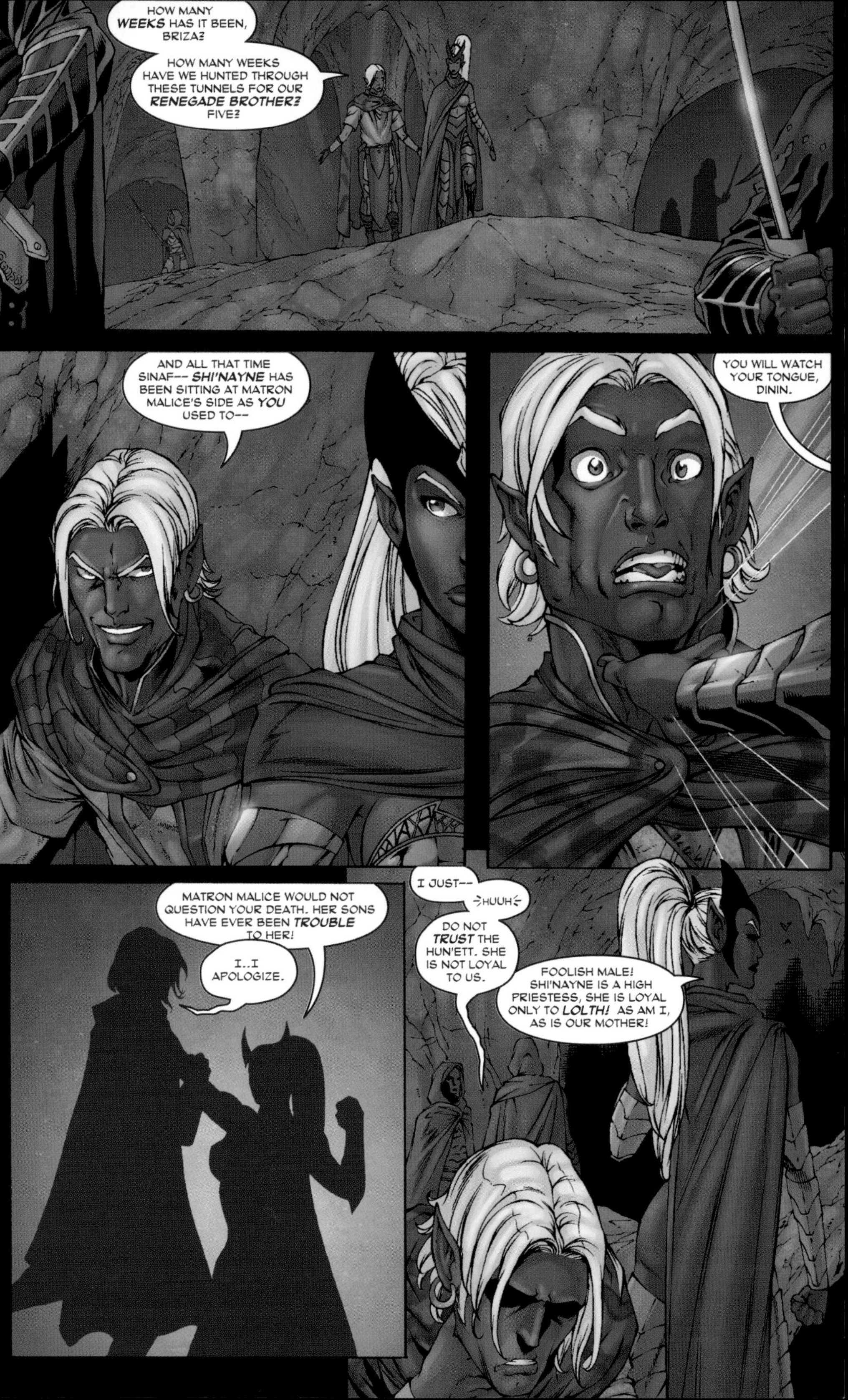
HOW MANY WEEKS HAS IT BEEN, BRIZA?
HOW MANY WEEKS HAVE WE HUNTED THROUGH THESE TUNNELS FOR OUR RENEGADE BROTHER? FIVE?
AND ALL THAT TIME SINAF-- SHI'NAYNE HAS BEEN SITTING AT MATRON MALICE'S SIDE AS YOU USED TO--
YOU WILL WATCH YOUR TONGUE, DININ.
MATRON MALICE WOULD NOT QUESTION YOUR DEATH. HER SONS HAVE EVER BEEN TROUBLE TO HER!
I..I APOLOGIZE.
I JUST--
HUUH
DO NOT TRUST THE HUN'ETT. SHE IS NOT LOYAL TO US.
FOOLISH MALE! SHI'NAYNE IS A HIGH PRIESTESS, SHE IS LOYAL ONLY TO LOLTH! AS AM I, AS IS OUR MOTHER!

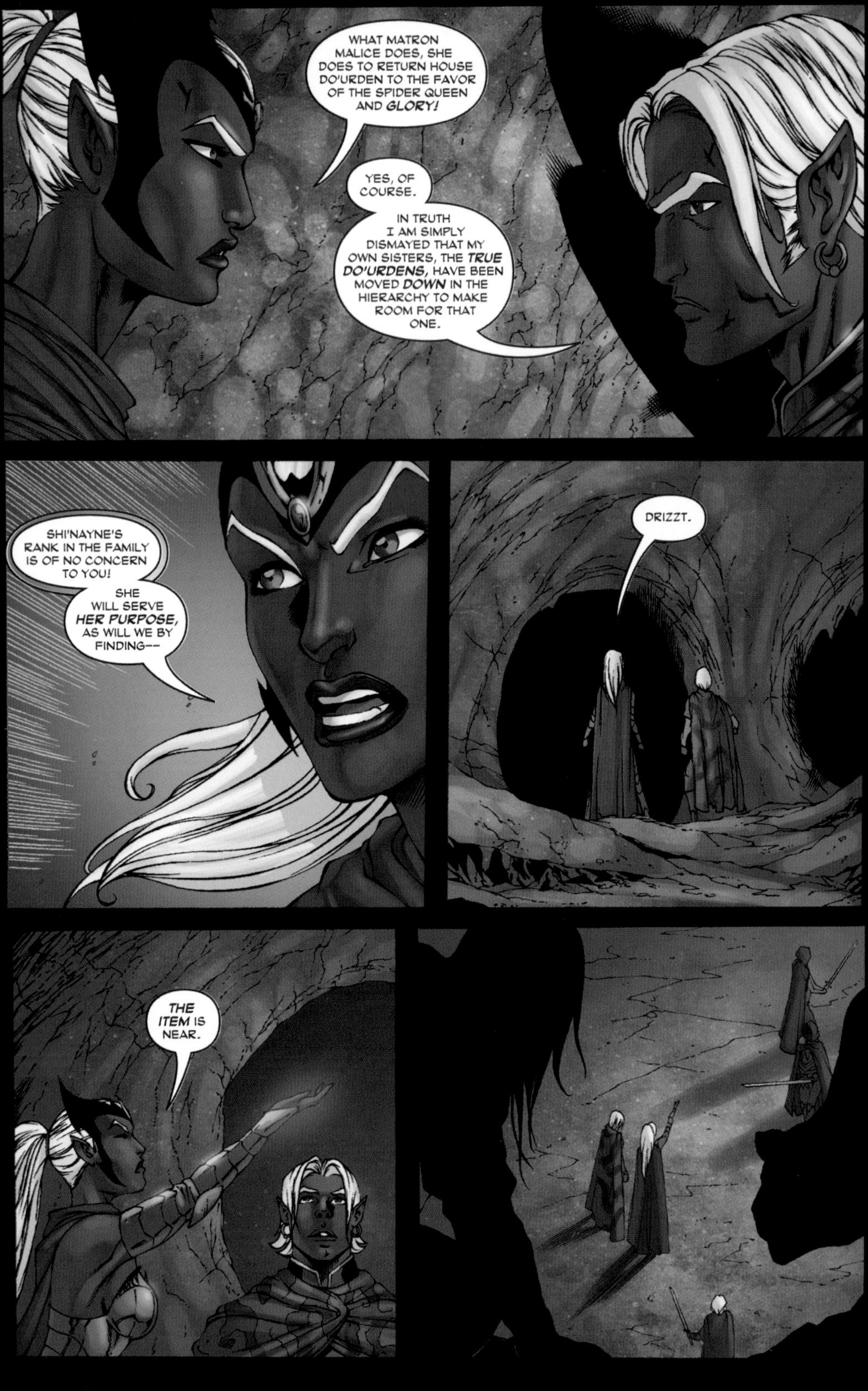
WHAT MATRON MALICE DOES, SHE DOES TO RETURN HOUSE DO'URDEN TO THE FAVOR OF THE SPIDER QUEEN AND GLORY!
YES, OF COURSE.
IN TRUTH I AM SIMPLY DISMAYED THAT MY OWN SISTERS, THE TRUE DO'URDENS, HAVE BEEN MOVED DOWN IN THE HIERARCHY TO MAKE ROOM FOR THAT ONE.
SHI'NAYNE'S RANK IN THE FAMILY IS OF NO CONCERN TO YOU!
SHE WILL SERVE HER PURPOSE, AS WILL WE BY FINDING---
DRIZZT.
THE ITEM IS NEAR.

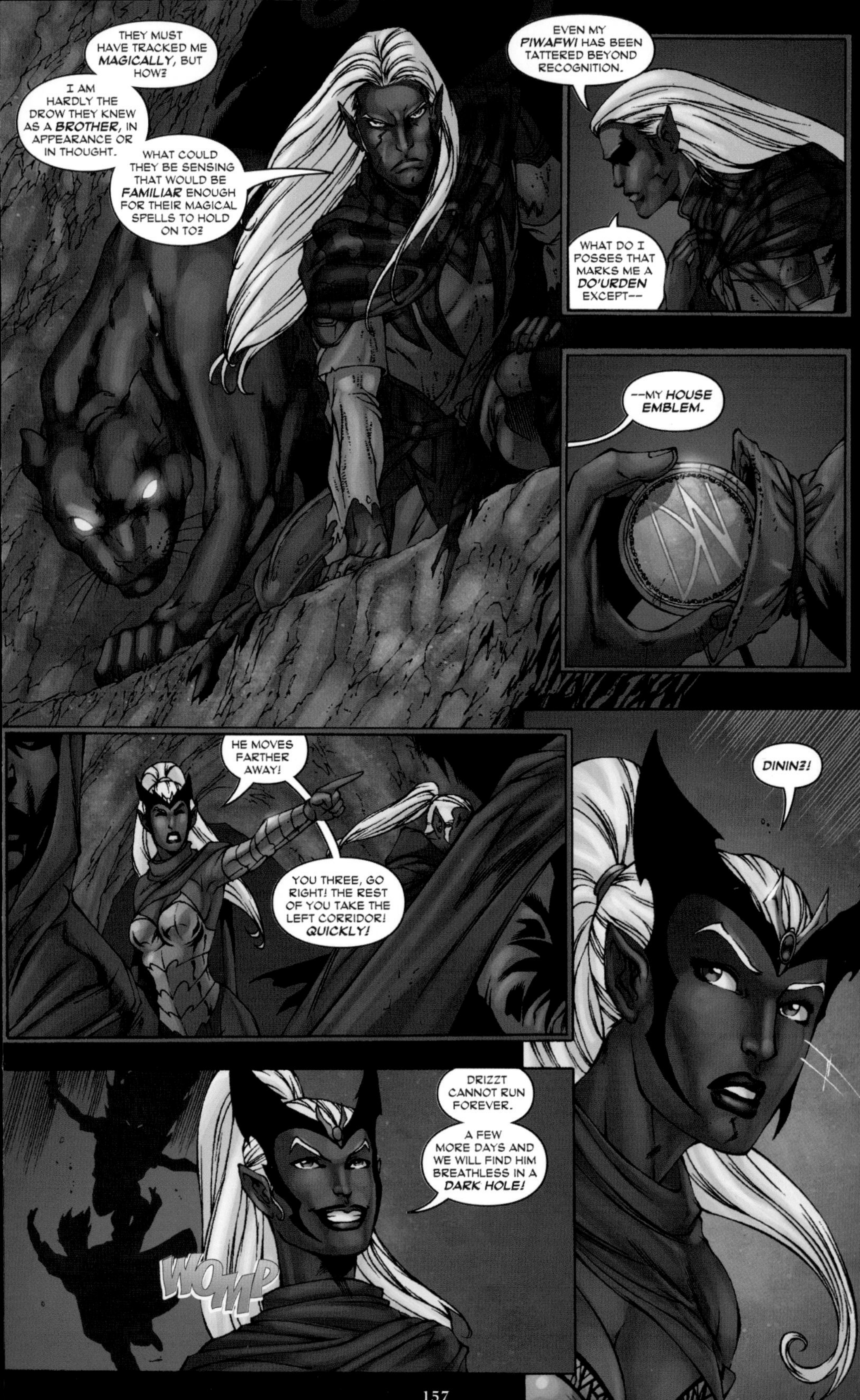
THEY MUST HAVE TRACKED ME MAGICALLY, BUT HOW?
I AM HARDLY THE DROW THEY KNEW AS A BROTHER, IN APPEARANCE OR IN THOUGHT.
WHAT COULD THEY BE SENSING THAT WOULD BE FAMILIAR ENOUGH FOR THEIR MAGICAL SPELLS TO HOLD ON TO?
EVEN MY PIWAFWI HAS BEEN TATTERED BEYOND RECOGNITION.
WHAT DO I POSSES THAT MARKS ME A DO'URDEN EXCEPT--
--MY HOUSE EMBLEM.
HE MOVES FARTHER AWAY!
YOU THREE, GO RIGHT! THE REST OF YOU TAKE THE LEFT CORRIDOR! QUICKLY!
DININ?!
DRIZZT CANNOT RUN FOREVER.
A FEW MORE DAYS AND WE WILL FIND HIM BREATHLESS IN A DARK HOLE!
WOMP

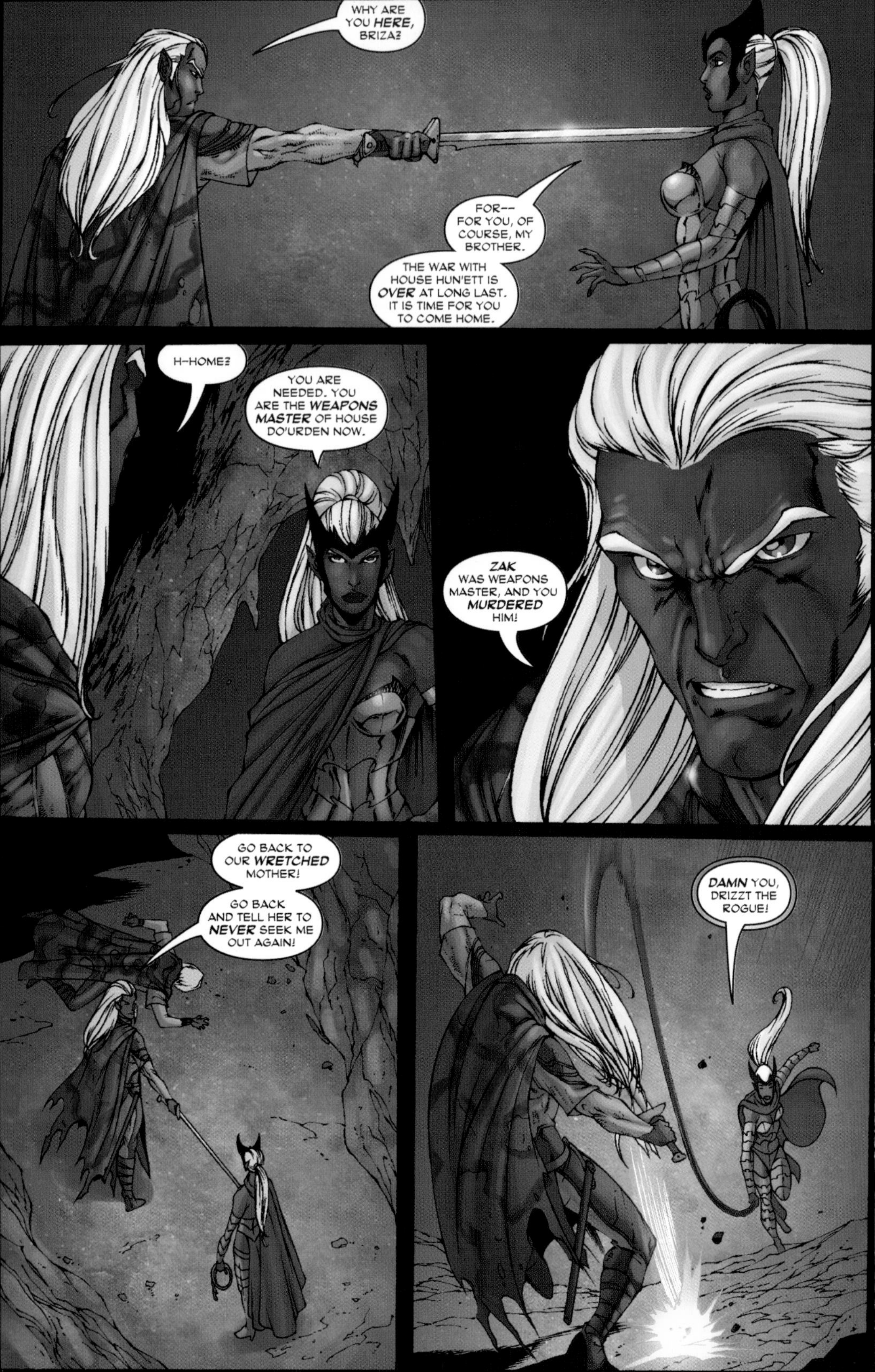
WHY ARE YOU HERE, BRIZA?
FOR-- FOR YOU, OF COURSE, MY BROTHER.
THE WAR WITH HOUSE HUN'ETT IS OVER AT LONG LAST. IT IS TIME FOR YOU TO COME HOME.
H-HOME?
YOU ARE NEEDED. YOU ARE THE WEAPONS MASTER OF HOUSE DO'URDEN NOW.
ZAK WAS WEAPONS MASTER, AND YOU MURDERED HIM!
GO BACK TO OUR WRETCHED MOTHER!
GO BACK AND TELL HER TO NEVER SEEK ME OUT AGAIN!
DAMN YOU, DRIZZT THE ROGUE!

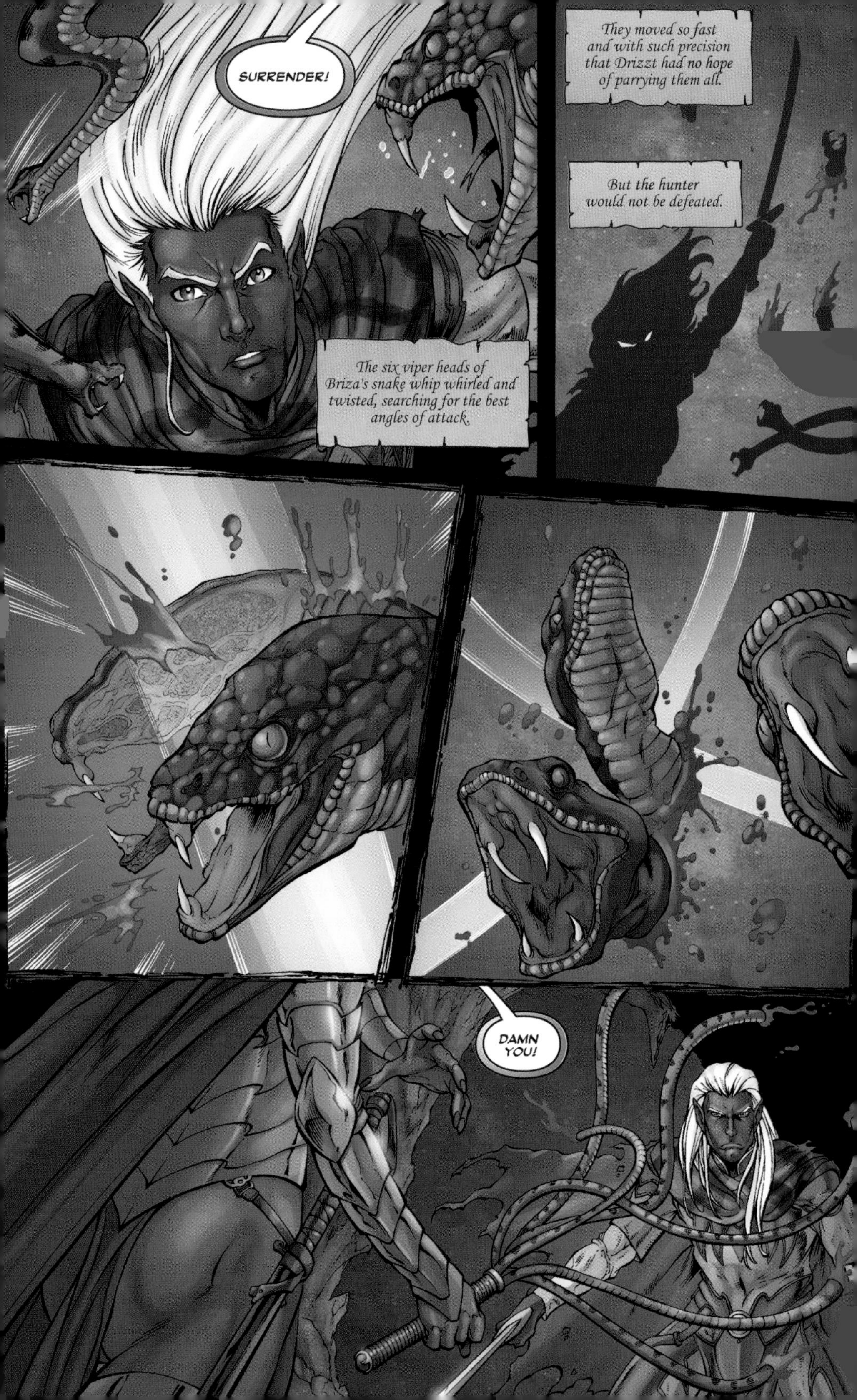
SURRENDER!
They moved so fast and with such precision that Drizzt had no hope of parrying them all.
But the hunter would not be defeated.
The six viper heads of Briza's snake whip whirled and twisted, searching for the best angles of attack.
DAMN YOU!

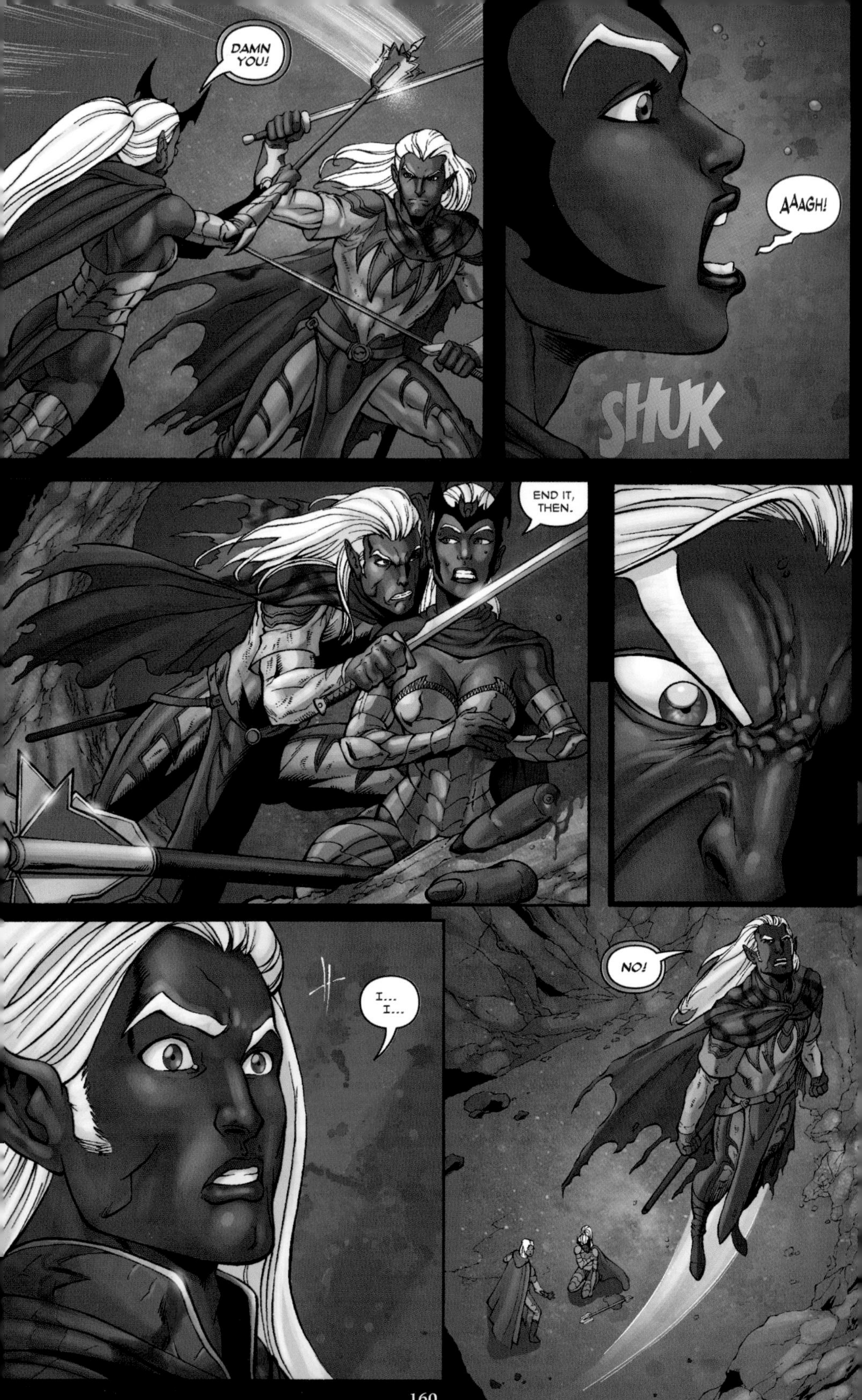
DAMN YOU!
AAAGH!
SHUK
END IT, THEN.
I... I...
NO!

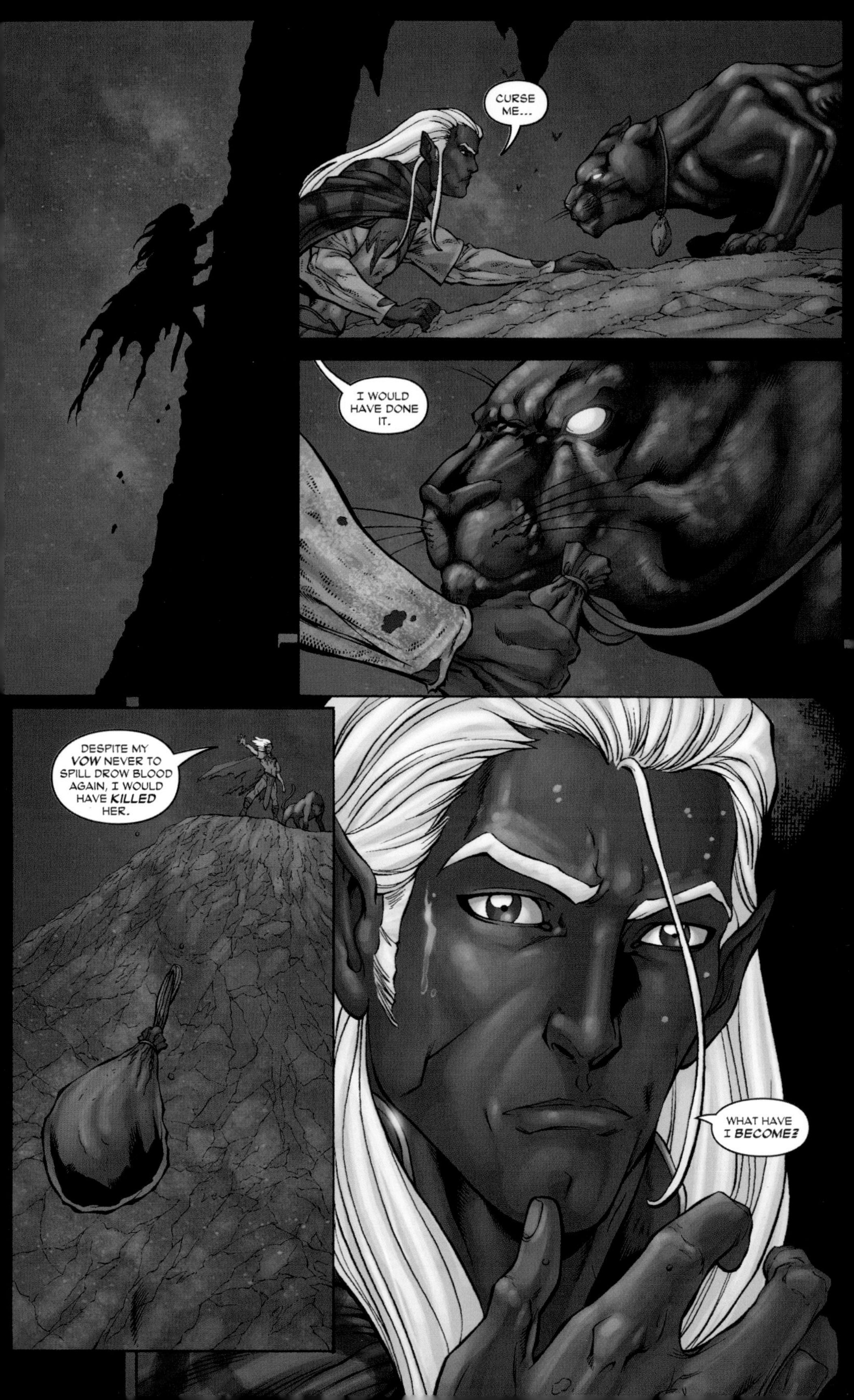
CURSE ME...
I WOULD HAVE DONE IT.
DESPITE MY VOW NEVER TO SPILL DROW BLOOD AGAIN, I WOULD HAVE KILLED HER.
WHAT HAVE I BECOME?

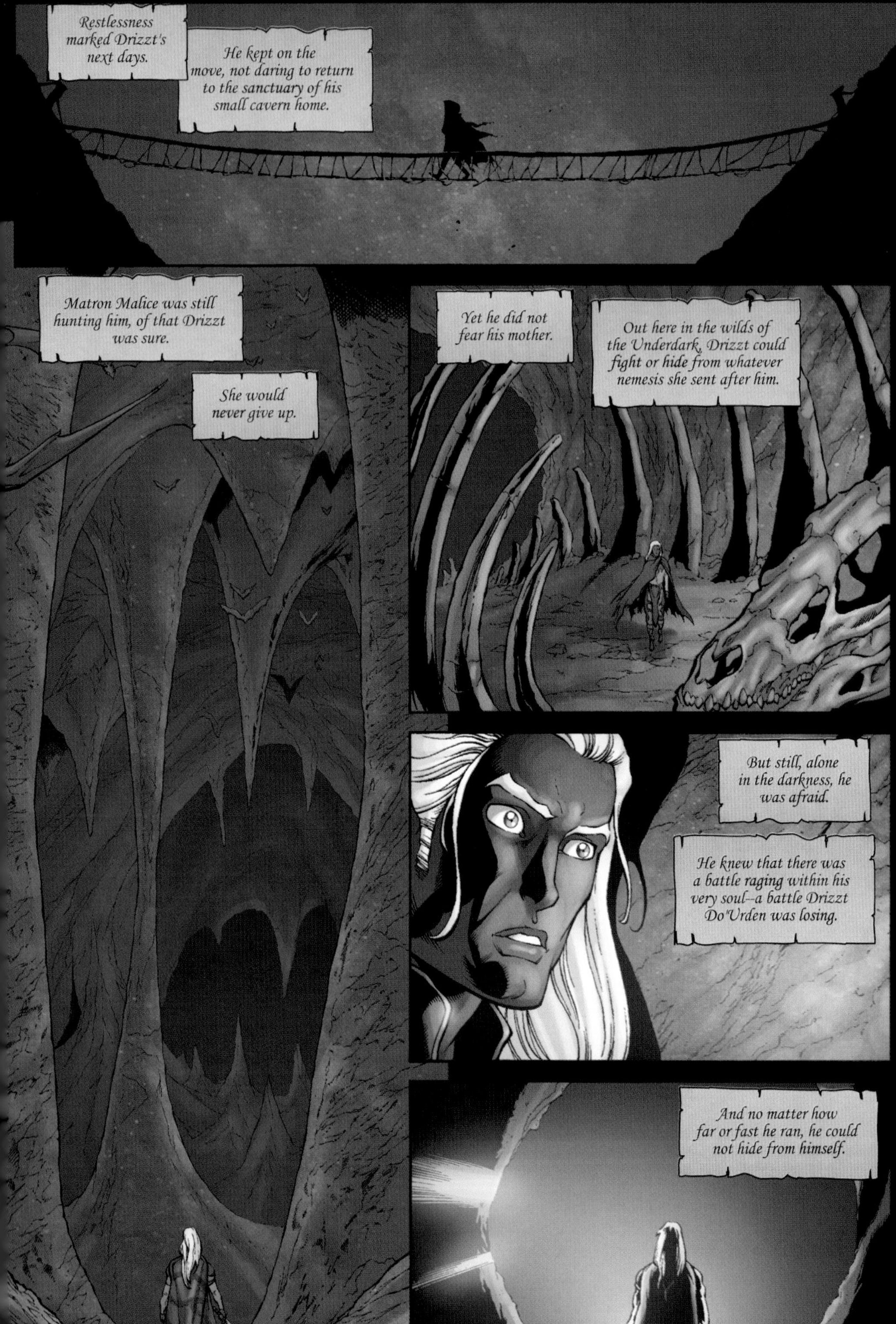
Restlessness marked Drizzt's next days.
He kept on the move, not daring to return to the sanctuary of his small cavern home.
Matron Malice was still hunting him, of that Drizzt was sure.
She would never give up.
Yet he did not fear his mother.
Out here in the wilds of the Underdark, Drizzt could fight or hide from whatever nemesis she sent after him.
But still, alone in the darkness, he was afraid.
He knew that there was a battle raging within his very soul--a battle Drizzt Do'Urden was losing.
And no matter how far or fast he ran, he could not hide from himself.

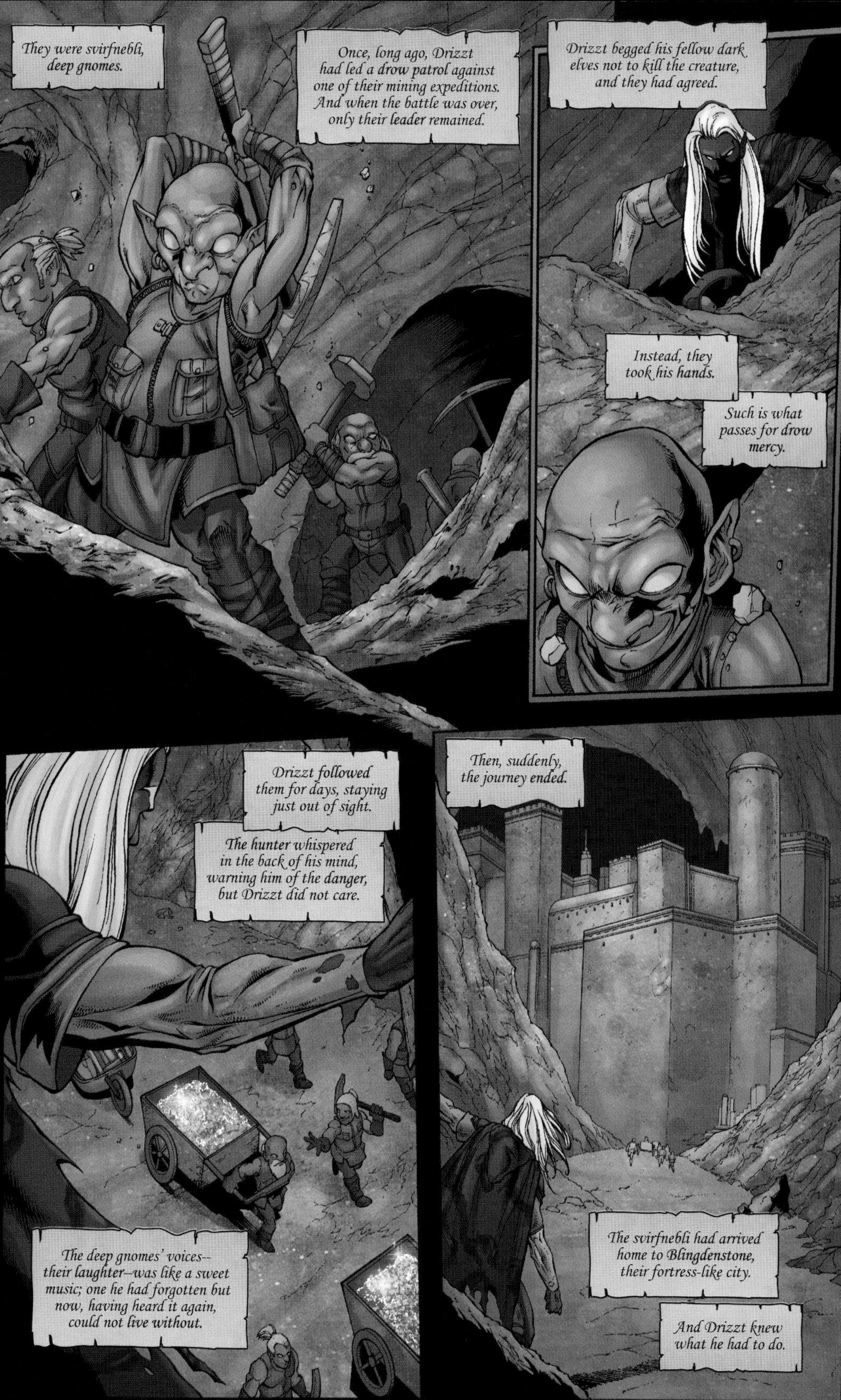
They were svirfnebli, deep gnomes.
Once, long ago, Drizzt had led a drow patrol against one of their mining expeditions. And when the battle was over, only their leader remained.
Drizzt begged his fellow dark elves not to kill the creature, and they had agreed.
Instead, they took his hands.
Such is what passes for drow mercy.
Drizzt followed them for days, staying just out of sight.
The hunter whispered in the back of his mind, warning him of the danger, but Drizzt did not care.
The deep gnomes' voices--their laughter--was like a sweet music; one he had forgotten but now, having heard it again, could not live without.
Then, suddenly, the journey ended.
The svirfnebli had arrived home to Blingdenstone, their fortress-like city.
And Drizzt knew what he had to do.

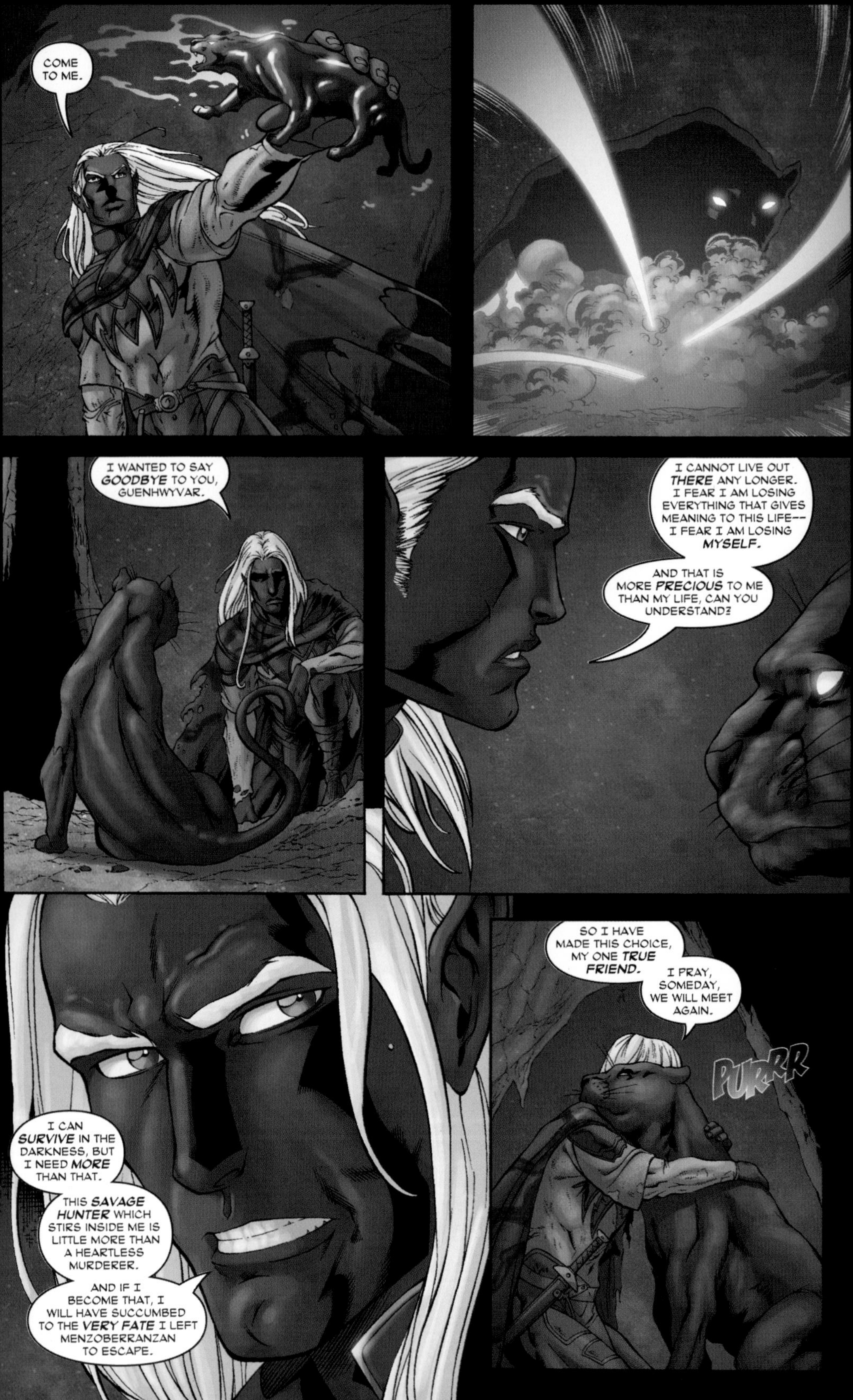
COME TO ME.
I WANTED TO SAY GOODBYE TO YOU, GUENHWYVAR.
I CANNOT LIVE OUT THERE ANY LONGER. I FEAR I AM LOSING EVERYTHING THAT GIVES MEANING TO THIS LIFE-- I FEAR I AM LOSING MYSELF.
AND THAT IS MORE PRECIOUS TO ME THAN MY LIFE, CAN YOU UNDERSTAND?
I CAN SURVIVE IN THE DARKNESS, BUT I NEED MORE THAN THAT.
THIS SAVAGE HUNTER WHICH STIRS INSIDE ME IS LITTLE MORE THAN A HEARTLESS MURDERER.
AND IF I BECOME THAT, I WILL HAVE SUCCUMBED TO THE VERY FATE I LEFT MENZOBERRANZAN TO ESCAPE.
SO I HAVE MADE THIS CHOICE, MY ONE TRUE FRIEND.
I PRAY, SOMEDAY, WE WILL MEET AGAIN.
PURRR

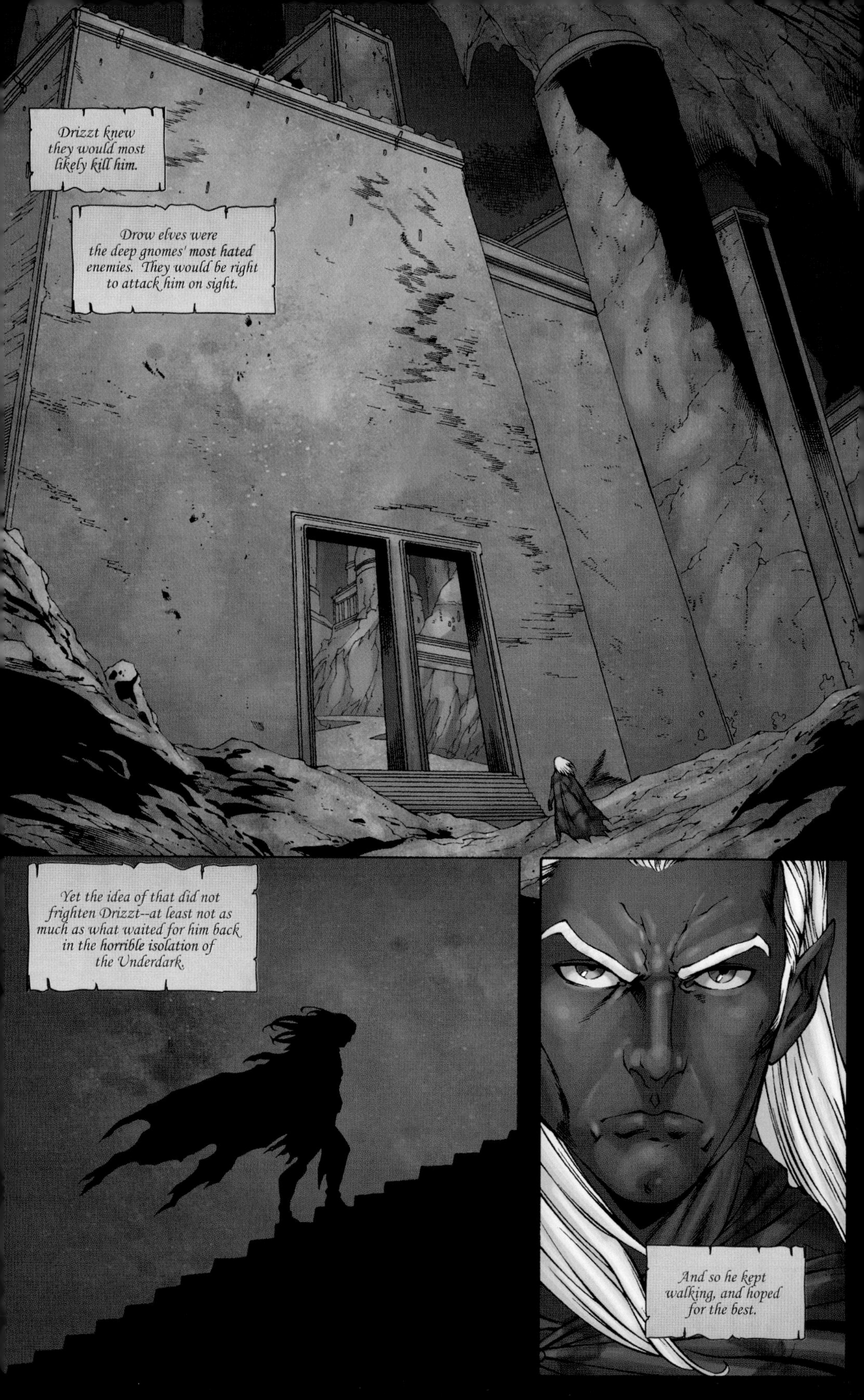
Drizzt knew they would most likely kill him.
Drow elves were the deep gnomes' most hated enemies. They would be right to attack him on sight.
Yet the idea of that did not frighten Drizzt--at least not as much as what waited for him back in the horrible isolation of the Underdark.
And so he kept walking, and hoped for the best.

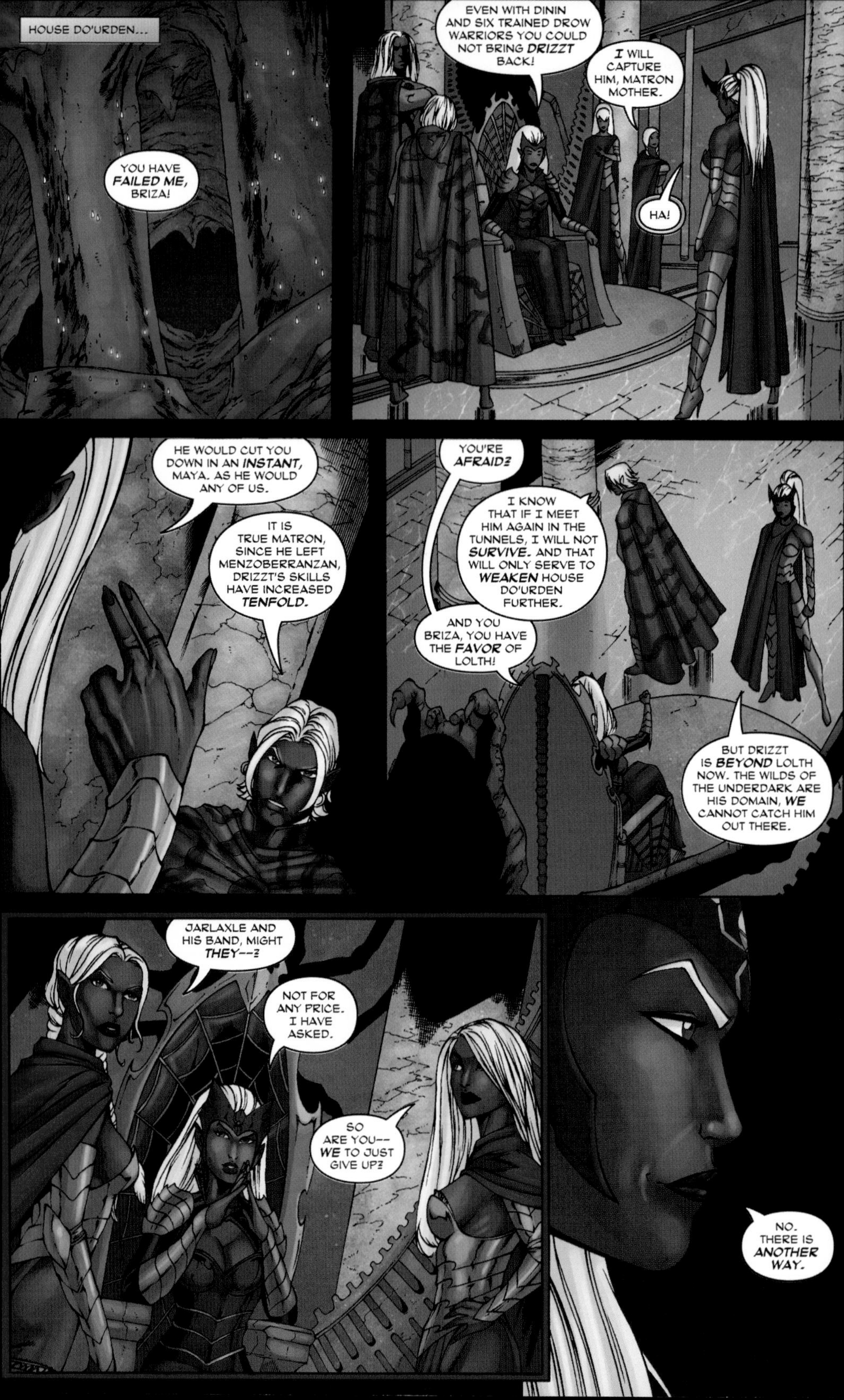
HOUSE DO'URDEN...
YOU HAVE FAILED ME, BRIZA!
EVEN WITH DININ AND SIX TRAINED DROW WARRIORS YOU COULD NOT BRING DRIZZT BACK!
I WILL CAPTURE HIM, MATRON MOTHER.
HA!
HE WOULD CUT YOU DOWN IN AN INSTANT, MAYA. AS HE WOULD ANY OF US.
IT IS TRUE MATRON, SINCE HE LEFT MENZOBERRANZAN, DRIZZT'S SKILLS HAVE INCREASED TENFOLD.
YOU'RE AFRAID?
I KNOW THAT IF I MEET HIM AGAIN IN THE TUNNELS, I WILL NOT SURVIVE. AND THAT WILL ONLY SERVE TO WEAKEN HOUSE DO'URDEN FURTHER.
AND YOU BRIZA, YOU HAVE THE FAVOR OF LOLTH!
BUT DRIZZT IS BEYOND LOLTH NOW. THE WILDS OF THE UNDERDARK ARE HIS DOMAIN, WE CANNOT CATCH HIM OUT THERE.
JARLAXLE AND HIS BAND, MIGHT THEY--?
NOT FOR ANY PRICE. I HAVE ASKED.
SO ARE YOU-- WE TO JUST GIVE UP?
NO. THERE IS ANOTHER WAY.

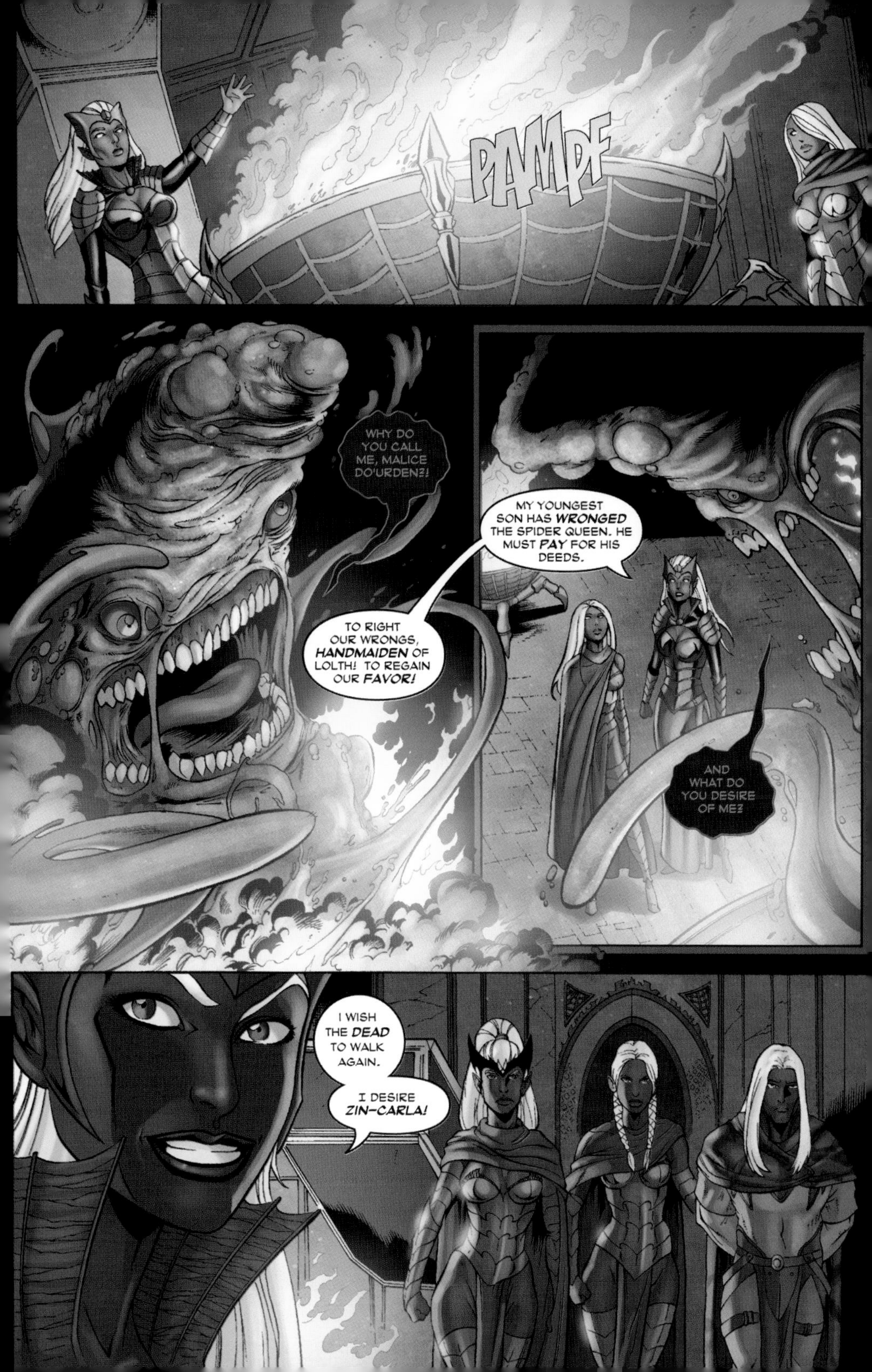
PAMPF
WHY DO YOU CALL ME, MALICE DO'URDEN?!
MY YOUNGEST SON HAS WRONGED THE SPIDER QUEEN. HE MUST PAY FOR HIS DEEDS.
TO RIGHT OUR WRONGS, HANDMAIDEN OF LOLTH! TO REGAIN OUR FAVOR!
AND WHAT DO YOU DESIRE OF ME?
I WISH THE DEAD TO WALK AGAIN.
I DESIRE ZIN-CARLA!

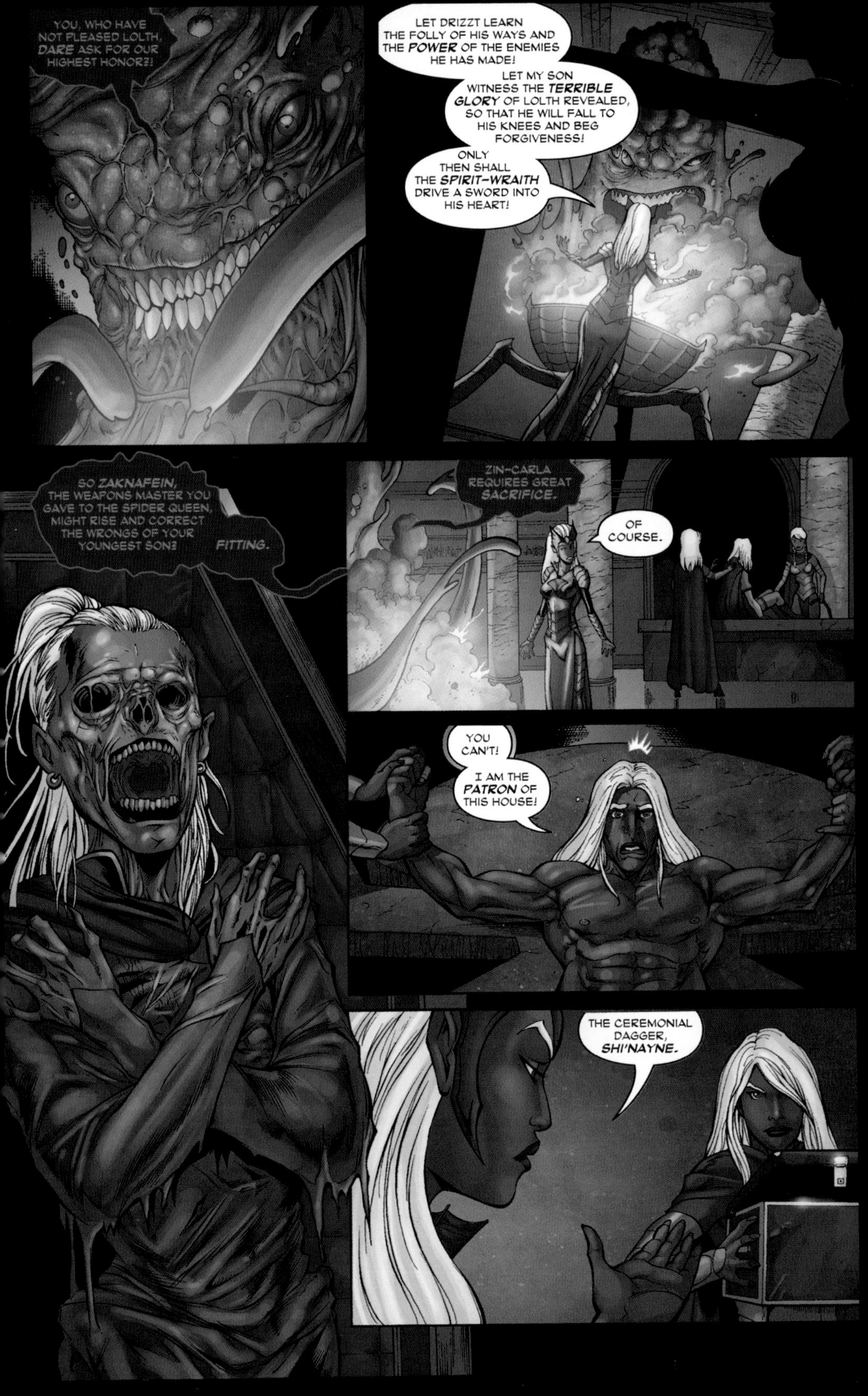
YOU, WHO HAVE NOT PLEASED LOLTH, DARE ASK FOR OUR HIGHEST HONOR?!
LET DRIZZT LEARN THE FOLLY OF HIS WAYS AND THE POWER OF THE ENEMIES HE HAS MADE!
LET MY SON WITNESS THE TERRIBLE GLORY OF LOLTH REVEALED, SO THAT HE WILL FALL TO HIS KNEES AND BEG FORGIVENESS!
ONLY THEN SHALL THE SPIRIT-WRAITH DRIVE A SWORD INTO HIS HEART!
SO ZAKNAFEIN, THE WEAPONS MASTER YOU GAVE TO THE SPIDER QUEEN, MIGHT RISE AND CORRECT THE WRONGS OF YOUR YOUNGEST SON?
FITTING.
ZIN-CARLA REQUIRES GREAT SACRIFICE.
OF COURSE.
YOU CAN'T!
I AM THE PATRON OF THIS HOUSE!
THE CEREMONIAL DAGGER, SHI'NAYNE.

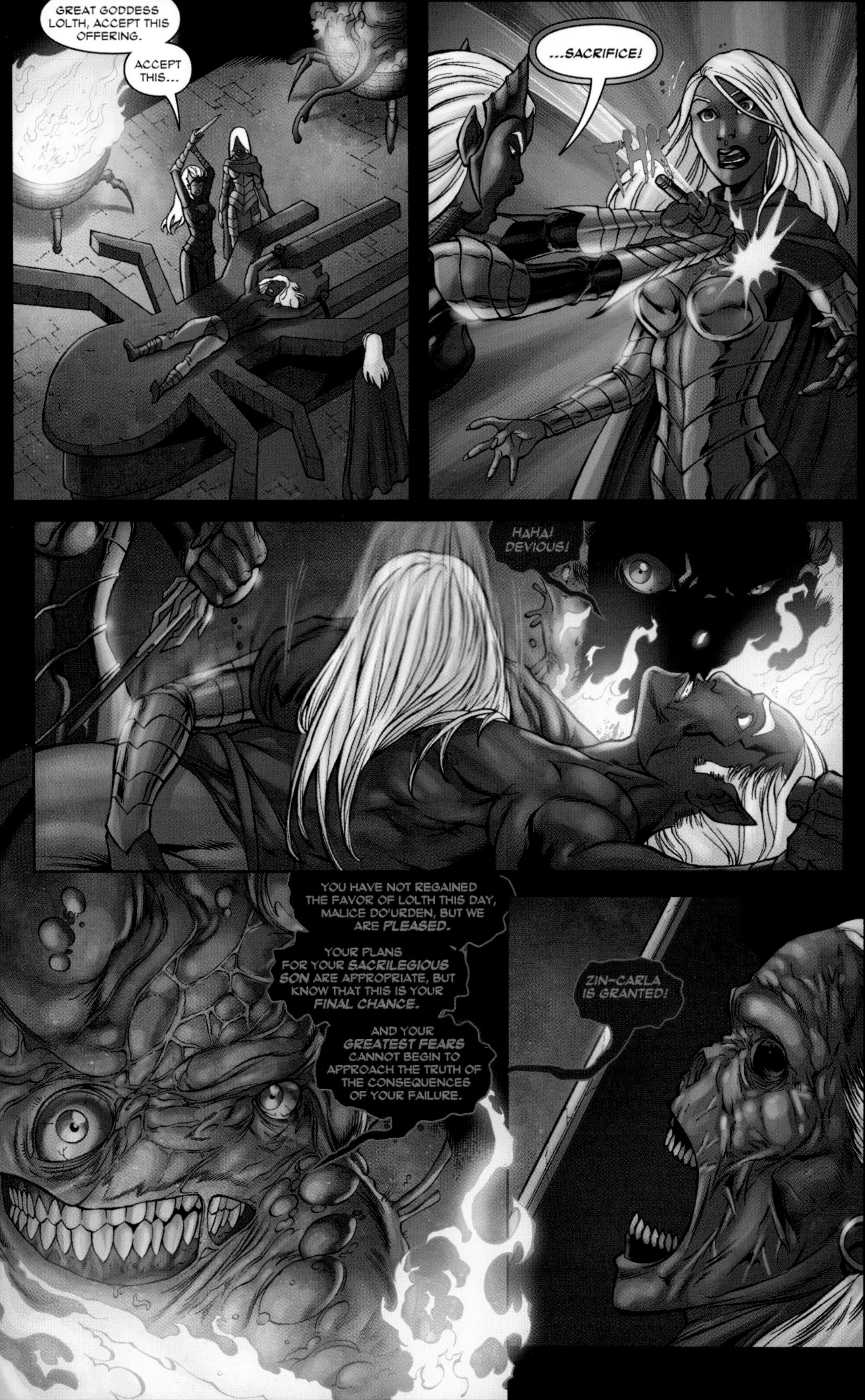
GREAT GODDESS LOLTH, ACCEPT THIS OFFERING.
ACCEPT THIS...
...SACRIFICE!
THK
HAHA! DEVIOUS!
YOU HAVE NOT REGAINED THE FAVOR OF LOLTH THIS DAY, MALICE DO'URDEN, BUT WE ARE PLEASED.
YOUR PLANS FOR YOUR SACRILEGIOUS SON ARE APPROPRIATE, BUT KNOW THAT THIS IS YOUR FINAL CHANCE.
AND YOUR GREATEST FEARS CANNOT BEGIN TO APPROACH THE TRUTH OF THE CONSEQUENCES OF YOUR FAILURE.
ZIN-CARLA IS GRANTED!

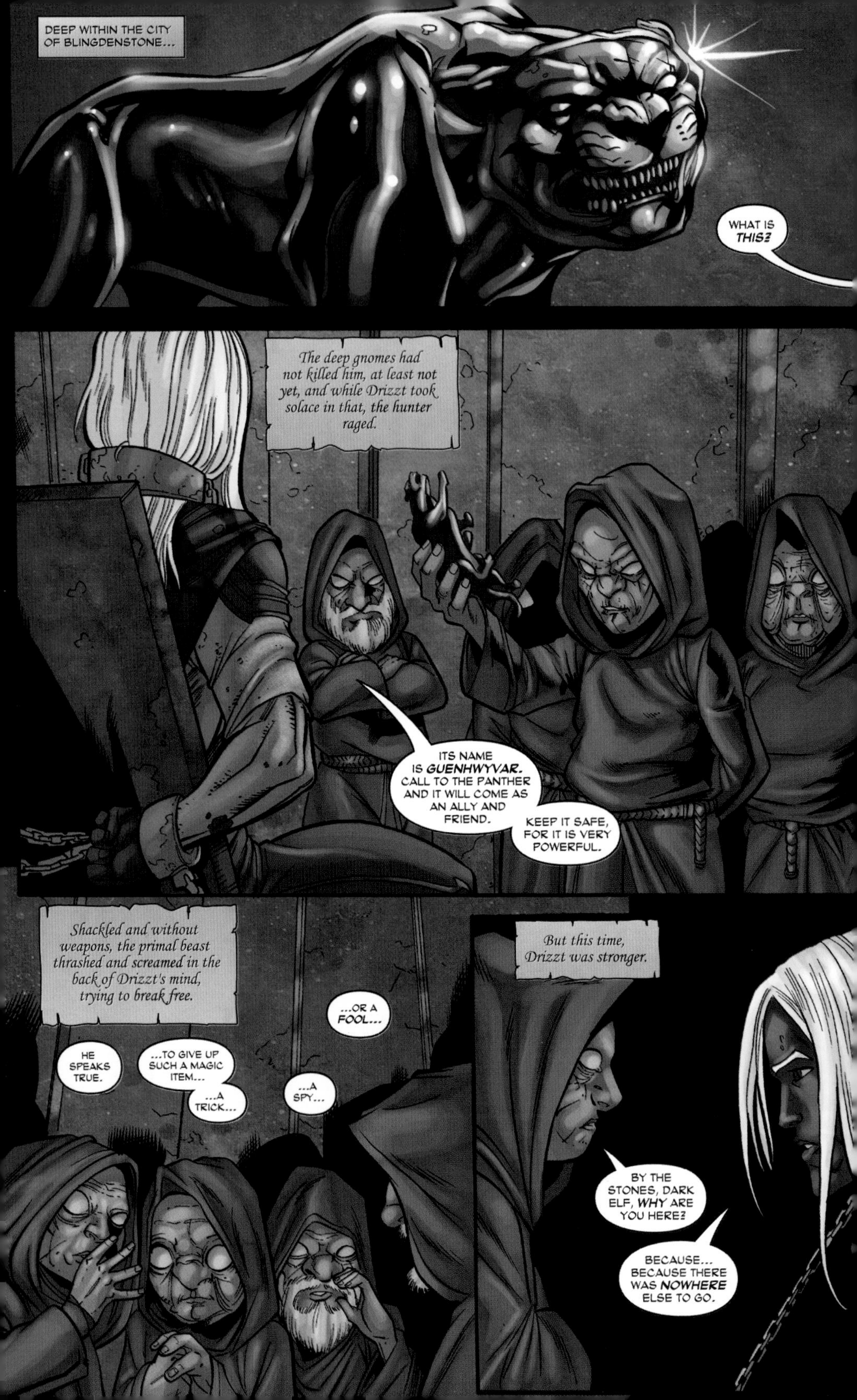
DEEP WITHIN THE CITY OF BLINGDENSTONE...
WHAT IS THIS?
The deep gnomes had not killed him, at least not yet, and while Drizzt took solace in that, the hunter raged.
ITS NAME IS GUENHWYVAR. CALL TO THE PANTHER AND IT WILL COME AS AN ALLY AND FRIEND.
KEEP IT SAFE, FOR IT IS VERY POWERFUL.
Shackled and without weapons, the primal beast thrashed and screamed in the back of Drizzt's mind, trying to break free.
HE SPEAKS TRUE.
...TO GIVE UP SUCH A MAGIC ITEM...
...A TRICK...
...A SPY...
...OR A FOOL...
But this time, Drizzt was stronger.
BY THE STONES, DARK ELF, WHY ARE YOU HERE?
BECAUSE... BECAUSE THERE WAS NOWHERE ELSE TO GO.

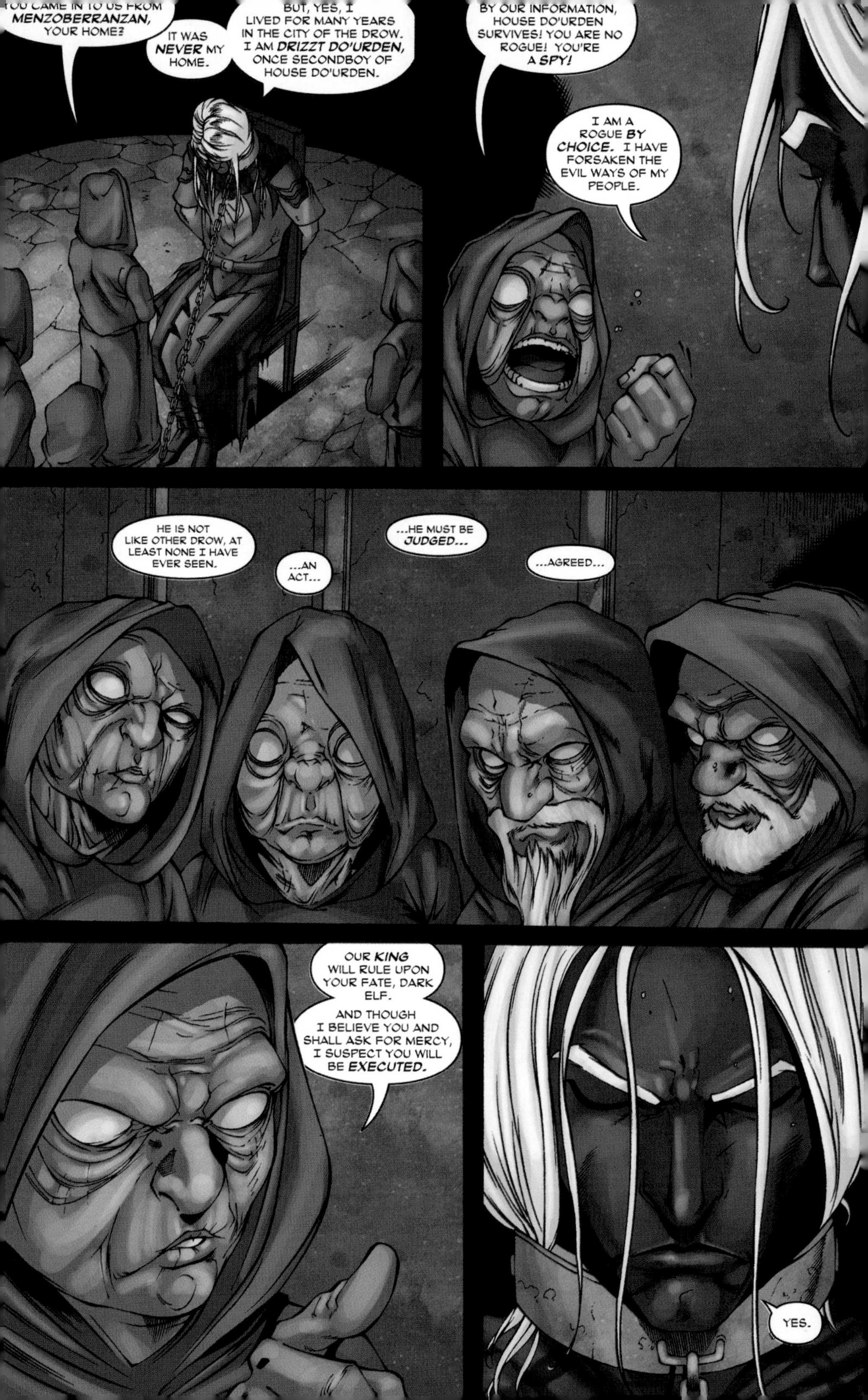
YOU CAME IN TO US FROM MENZOBERRANZAN, YOUR HOME?
IT WAS NEVER MY HOME.
BUT, YES, I LIVED FOR MANY YEARS IN THE CITY OF THE DROW. I AM DRIZZT DO'URDEN, ONCE SECONDBOY OF HOUSE DO'URDEN.
BY OUR INFORMATION, HOUSE DO'URDEN SURVIVES! YOU ARE NO ROGUE! YOU'RE A SPY!
I AM A ROGUE BY CHOICE. I HAVE FORSAKEN THE EVIL WAYS OF MY PEOPLE.
HE IS NOT LIKE OTHER DROW, AT LEAST NONE I HAVE EVER SEEN.
...AN ACT...
...HE MUST BE JUDGED...
...AGREED...
OUR KING WILL RULE UPON YOUR FATE, DARK ELF.
AND THOUGH I BELIEVE YOU AND SHALL ASK FOR MERCY, I SUSPECT YOU WILL BE EXECUTED.
YES.

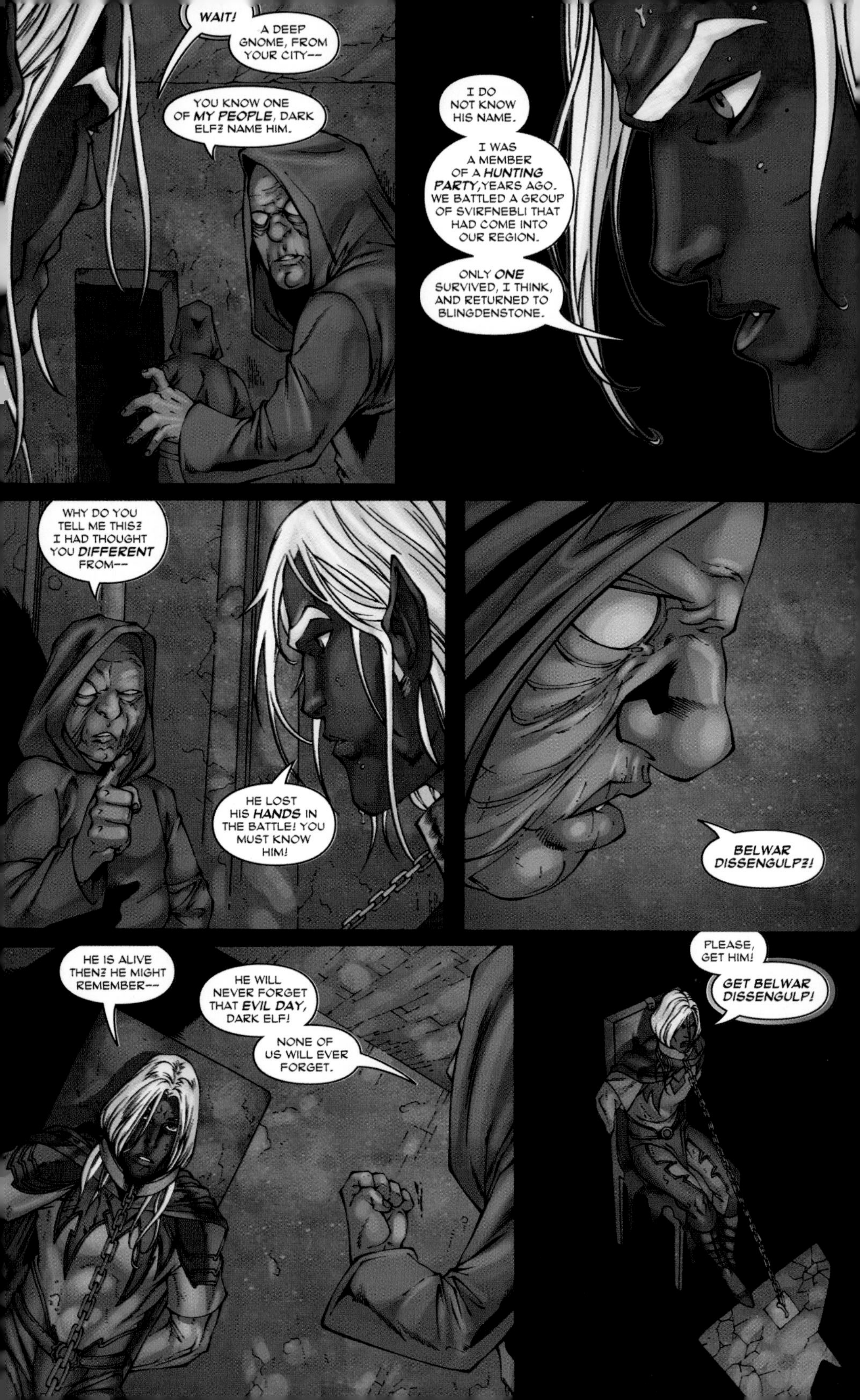
WAIT!
A DEEP GNOME, FROM YOUR CITY--
YOU KNOW ONE OF MY PEOPLE, DARK ELF? NAME HIM.
I DO NOT KNOW HIS NAME.
I WAS A MEMBER OF A HUNTING PARTY, YEARS AGO. WE BATTLED A GROUP OF SVIRFNEBLI THAT HAD COME INTO OUR REGION.
ONLY ONE SURVIVED, I THINK, AND RETURNED TO BLINGDENSTONE.
WHY DO YOU TELL ME THIS? I HAD THOUGHT YOU DIFFERENT FROM--
HE LOST HIS HANDS IN THE BATTLE! YOU MUST KNOW HIM!
BELWAR DISSENGULP?!
HE IS ALIVE THEN? HE MIGHT REMEMBER--
HE WILL NEVER FORGET THAT EVIL DAY, DARK ELF!
NONE OF US WILL EVER FORGET.
PLEASE, GET HIM!
GET BELWAR DISSENGULP!

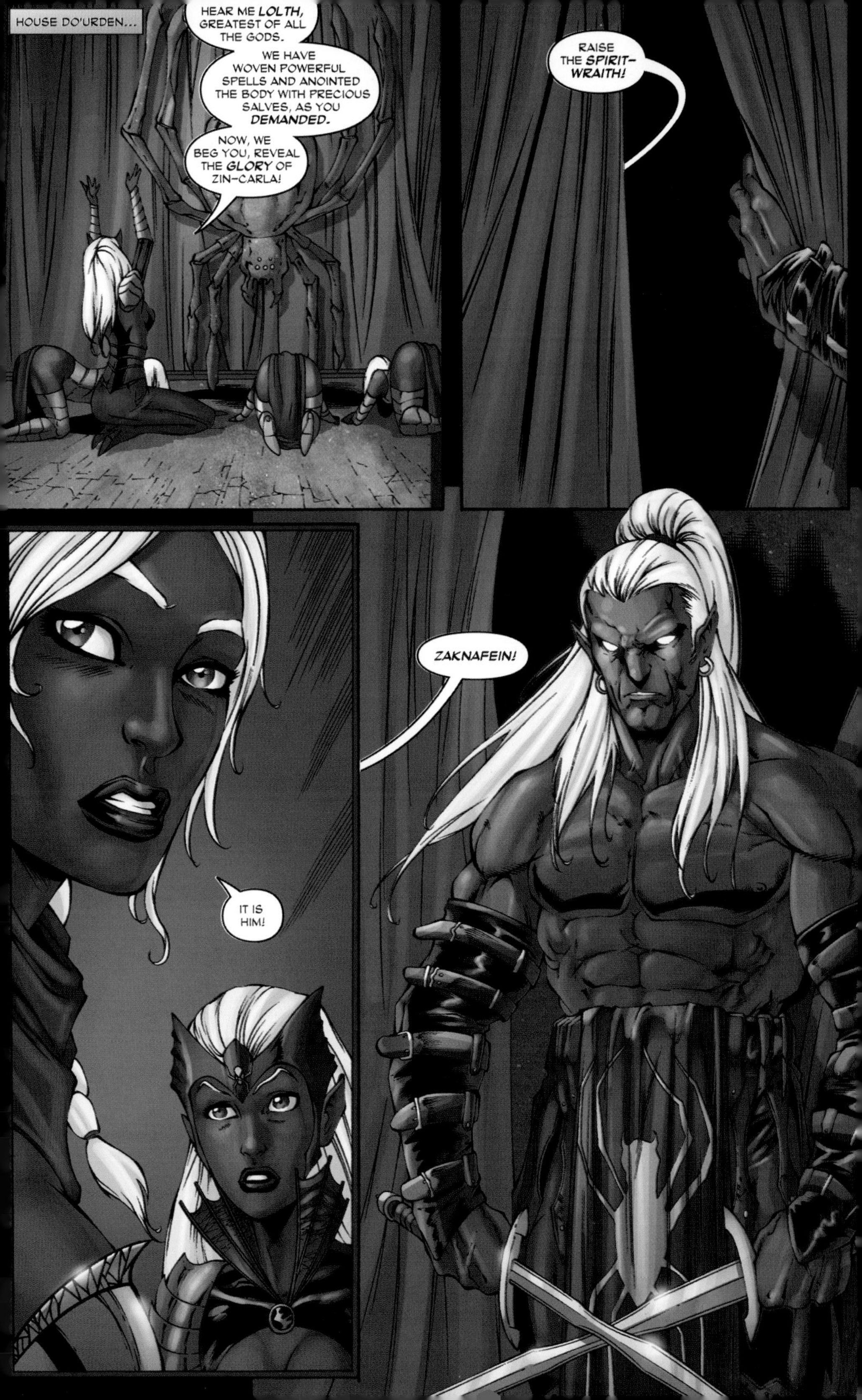
HOUSE DO'URDEN...
HEAR ME LOLTH, GREATEST OF ALL THE GODS.
WE HAVE WOVEN POWERFUL SPELLS AND ANOINTED THE BODY WITH PRECIOUS SALVES, AS YOU DEMANDED.
NOW, WE BEG YOU, REVEAL THE GLORY OF ZIN-CARLA!
RAISE THE SPIRIT-WRAITH!
ZAKNAFEIN!
IT IS HIM!

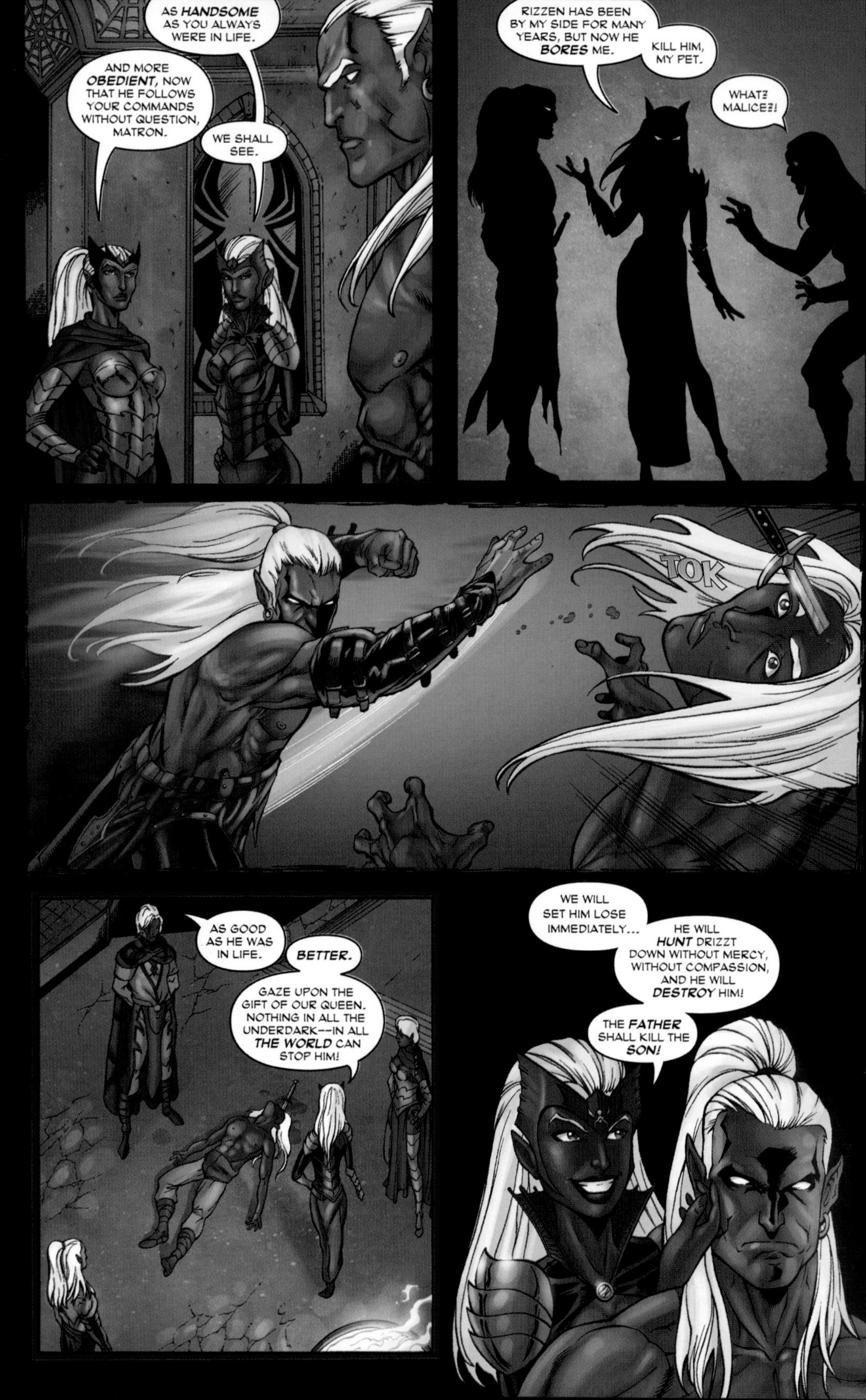
AS HANDSOME AS YOU ALWAYS WERE IN LIFE.
AND MORE OBEDIENT, NOW THAT HE FOLLOWS YOUR COMMANDS WITHOUT QUESTION, MATRON.
WE SHALL SEE.
RIZZEN HAS BEEN BY MY SIDE FOR MANY YEARS, BUT NOW HE BORES ME.
KILL HIM, MY PET.
WHAT? MALICE?!
TOK
AS GOOD AS HE WAS IN LIFE.
BETTER.
GAZE UPON THE GIFT OF OUR QUEEN. NOTHING IN ALL THE UNDERDARK--IN ALL THE WORLD CAN STOP HIM!
WE WILL SET HIM LOSE IMMEDIATELY...
HE WILL HUNT DRIZZT DOWN WITHOUT MERCY, WITHOUT COMPASSION, AND HE WILL DESTROY HIM!
THE FATHER SHALL KILL THE SON!

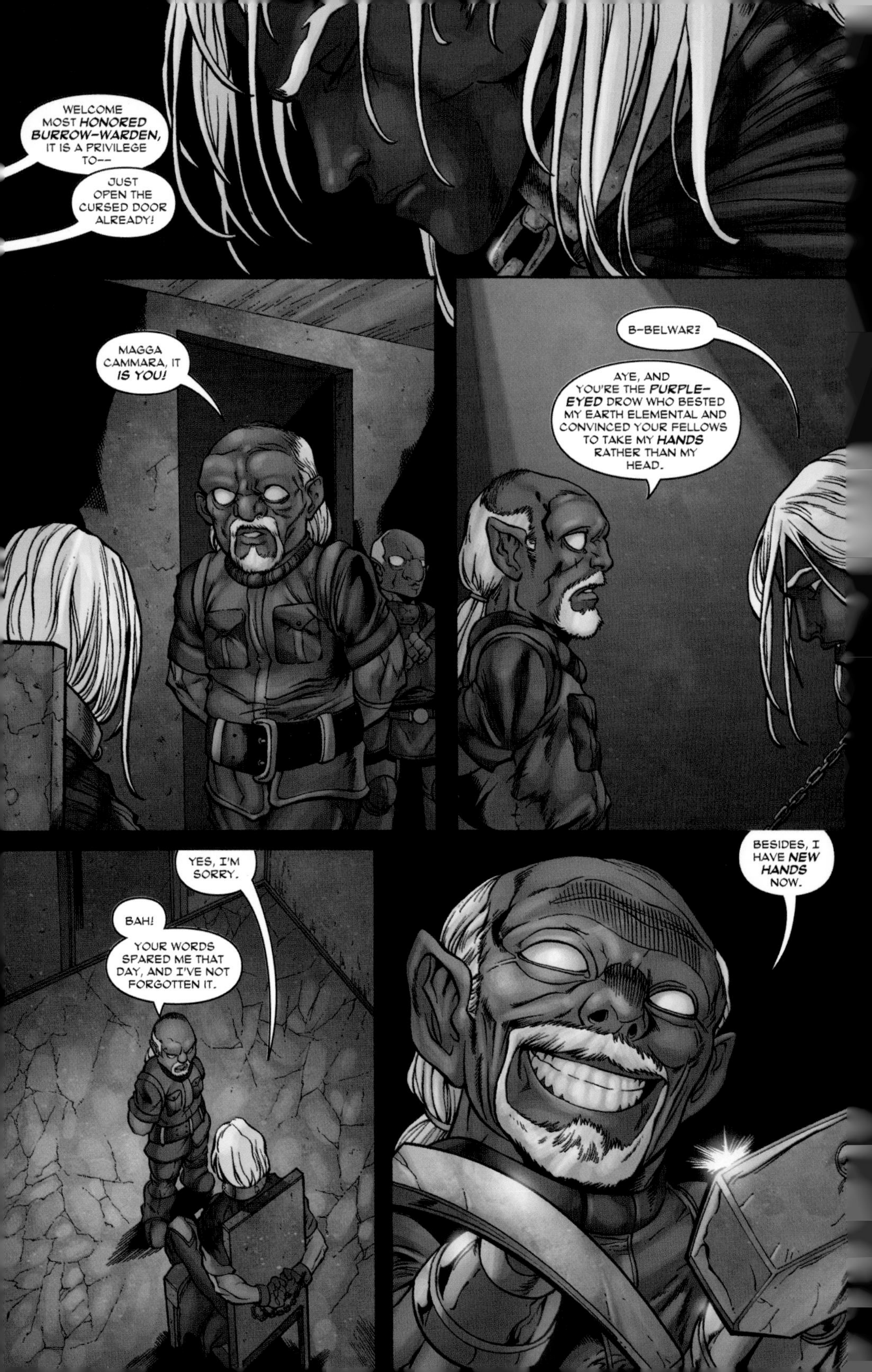
WELCOME MOST HONORED BURROW-WARDEN, IT IS A PRIVILEGE TO--
JUST OPEN THE CURSED DOOR ALREADY!
MAGGA CAMMARA, IT IS YOU!
B-BELWAR?
AYE, AND YOU'RE THE PURPLE-EYED DROW WHO BESTED MY EARTH ELEMENTAL AND CONVINCED YOUR FELLOWS TO TAKE MY HANDS RATHER THAN MY HEAD.
YES, I'M SORRY.
BAH! YOUR WORDS SPARED ME THAT DAY, AND I'VE NOT FORGOTTEN IT.
BESIDES, I HAVE NEW HANDS NOW.

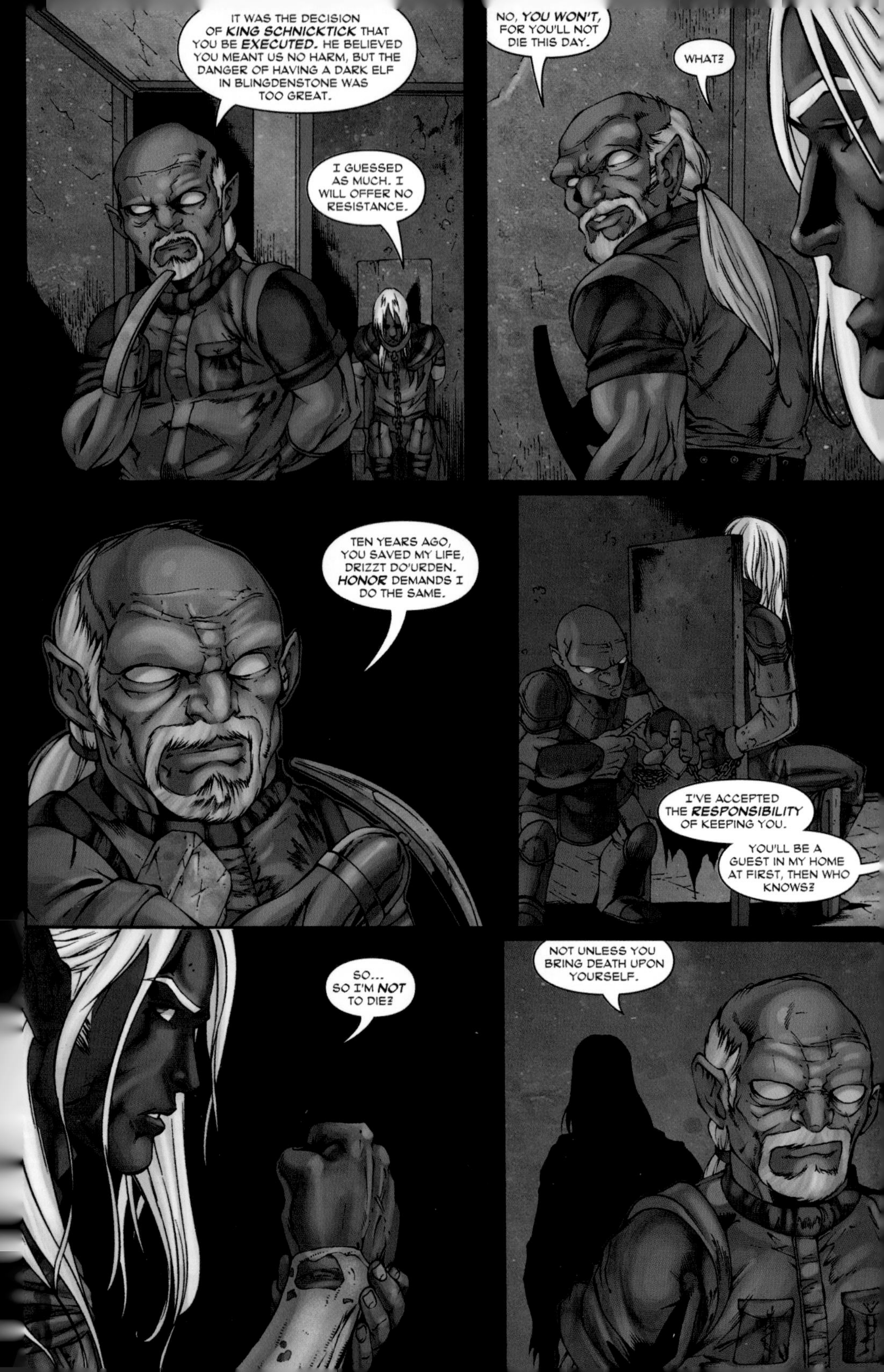
IT WAS THE DECISION OF KING SCHNICKTICK THAT YOU BE EXECUTED. HE BELIEVED YOU MEANT US NO HARM, BUT THE DANGER OF HAVING A DARK ELF IN BLINGDENSTONE WAS TOO GREAT.
I GUESSED AS MUCH. I WILL OFFER NO RESISTANCE.
NO, YOU WON'T, FOR YOU'LL NOT DIE THIS DAY.
WHAT?
TEN YEARS AGO, YOU SAVED MY LIFE, DRIZZT DO'URDEN. HONOR DEMANDS I DO THE SAME.
I'VE ACCEPTED THE RESPONSIBILITY OF KEEPING YOU.
YOU'LL BE A GUEST IN MY HOME AT FIRST, THEN WHO KNOWS?
SO... SO I'M NOT TO DIE?
NOT UNLESS YOU BRING DEATH UPON YOURSELF.

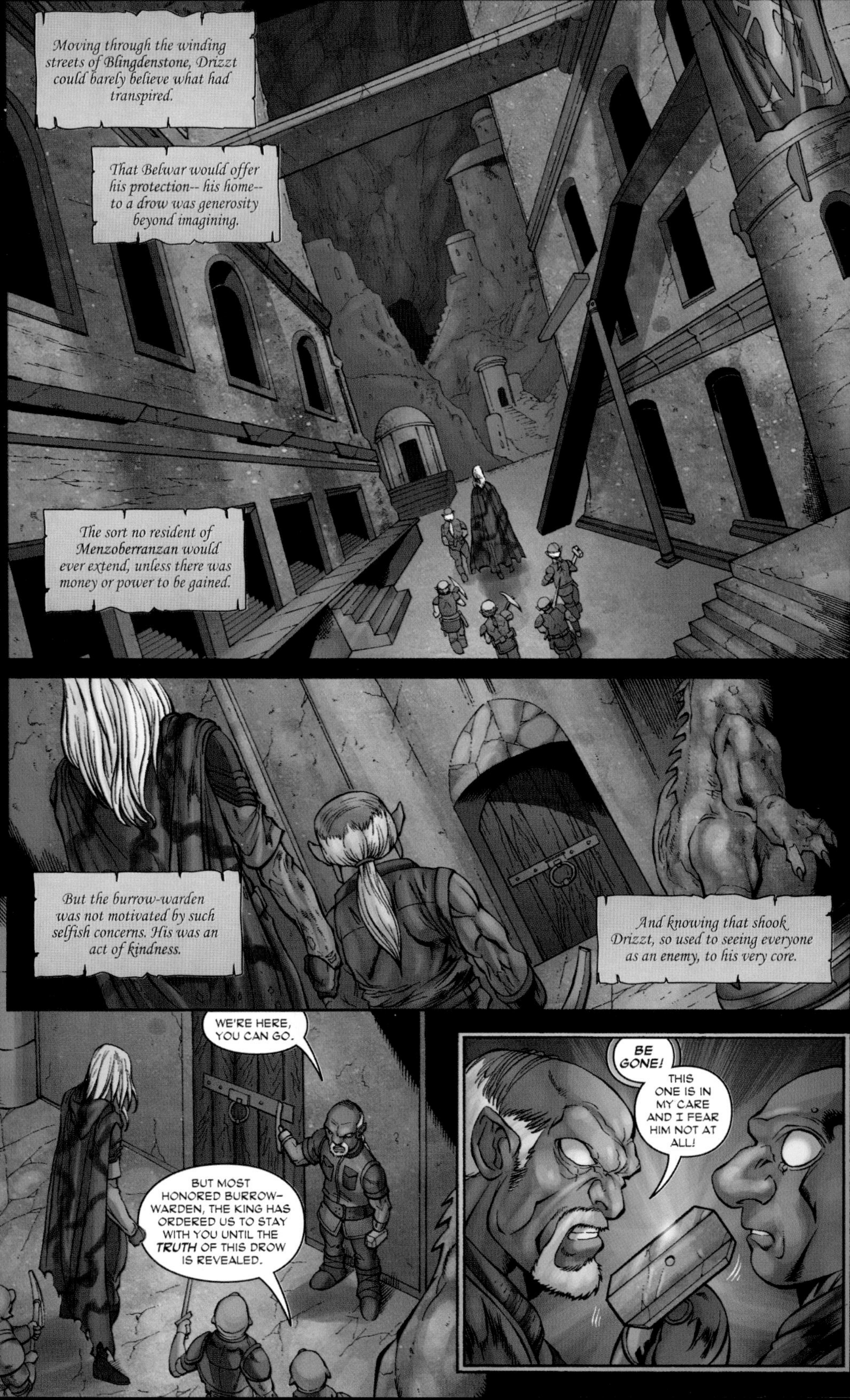
Moving through the winding streets of Blingdenstone, Drizzt could barely believe what had transpired.
That Belwar would offer his protection-- his home-- to a drow was generosity beyond imagining.
The sort no resident of Menzoberranzan would ever extend, unless there was money or power to be gained.
But the burrow-warden was not motivated by such selfish concerns. His was an act of kindness.
And knowing that shook Drizzt, so used to seeing everyone as an enemy, to his very core.
WE'RE HERE, YOU CAN GO.
BUT MOST HONORED BURROW-WARDEN, THE KING HAS ORDERED US TO STAY WITH YOU UNTIL THE TRUTH OF THIS DROW IS REVEALED.
BE GONE!
THIS ONE IS IN MY CARE AND I FEAR HIM NOT AT ALL!

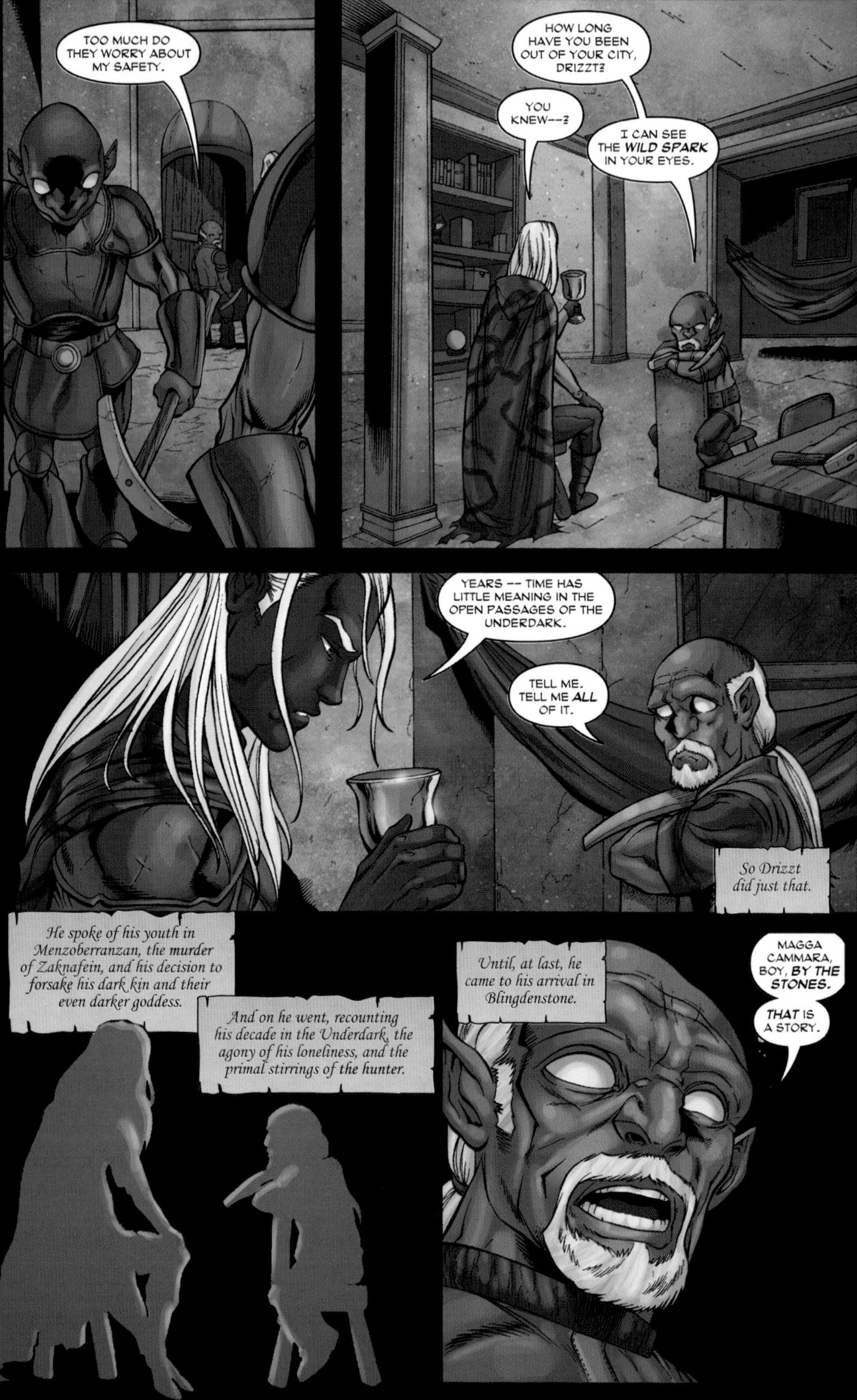
TOO MUCH DO THEY WORRY ABOUT MY SAFETY.
HOW LONG HAVE YOU BEEN OUT OF YOUR CITY, DRIZZT?
YOU KNEW--?
I CAN SEE THE WILD SPARK IN YOUR EYES.
YEARS -- TIME HAS LITTLE MEANING IN THE OPEN PASSAGES OF THE UNDERDARK.
TELL ME. TELL ME ALL OF IT.
So Drizzt did just that.
He spoke of his youth in Menzoberranzan, the murder of Zaknafein, and his decision to forsake his dark kin and their even darker goddess.
And on he went, recounting his decade in the Underdark, the agony of his loneliness, and the primal stirrings of the hunter.
Until, at last, he came to his arrival in Blingdenstone.
MAGGA CAMMARA, BOY, BY THE STONES.
THAT IS A STORY.

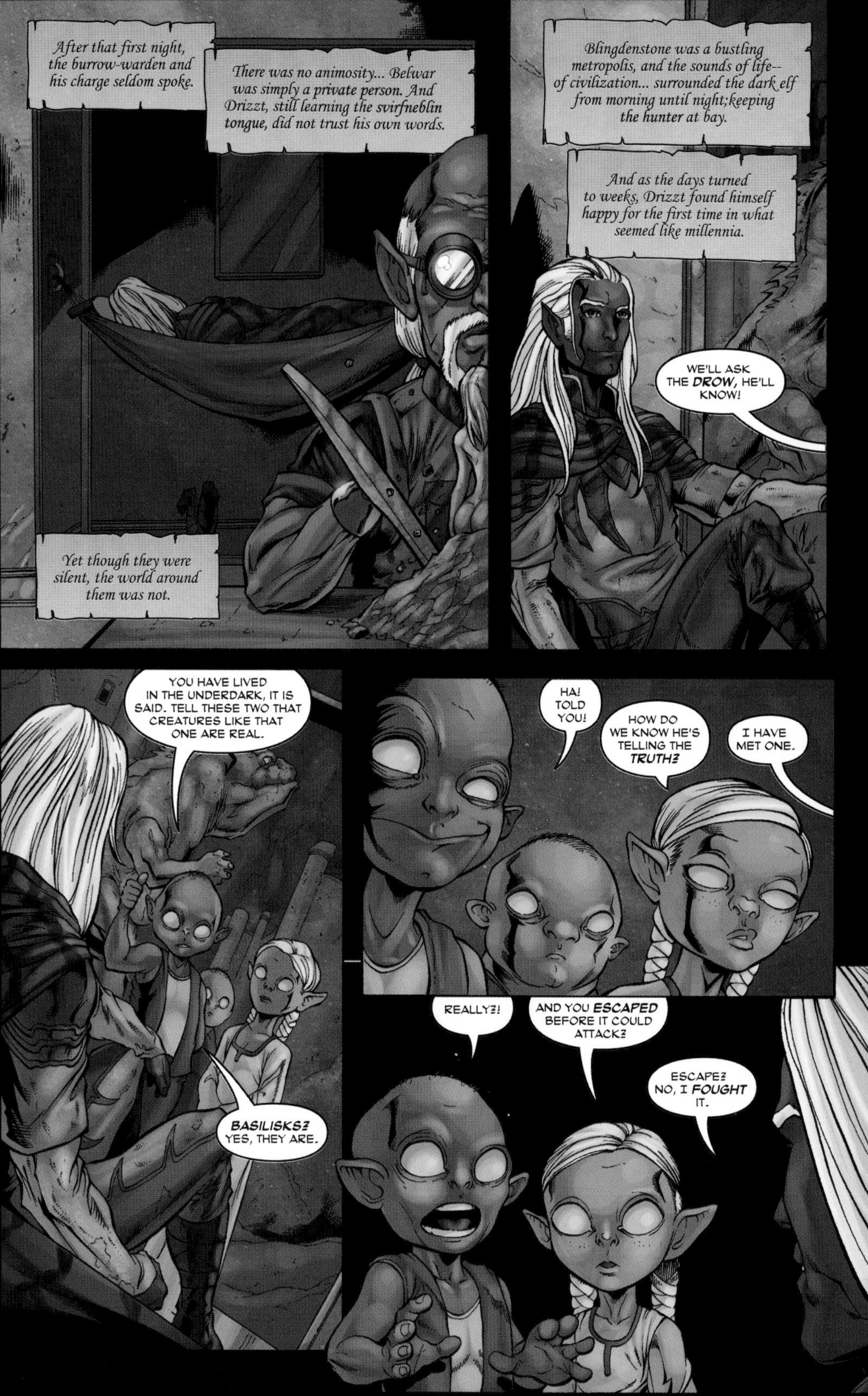

After that first night, the burrow-warden and his charge seldom spoke.
There was no animosity... Belwar was simply a private person. And Drizzt, still learning the svirfneblin tongue, did not trust his own words.
Yet though they were silent, the world around them was not.
Blingdenstone was a bustling metropolis, and the sounds of life--of civilization... surrounded the dark elf from morning until night; keeping the hunter at bay.
And as the days turned to weeks, Drizzt found himself happy for the first time in what seemed like millennia.
WE'LL ASK THE DROW, HE'LL KNOW!
YOU HAVE LIVED IN THE UNDERDARK, IT IS SAID. TELL THESE TWO THAT CREATURES LIKE THAT ONE ARE REAL.
BASILISKS? YES, THEY ARE.
HA! TOLD YOU!
HOW DO WE KNOW HE'S TELLING THE TRUTH?
I HAVE MET ONE.
REALLY?!
AND YOU ESCAPED BEFORE IT COULD ATTACK?
ESCAPE? NO, I FOUGHT IT.

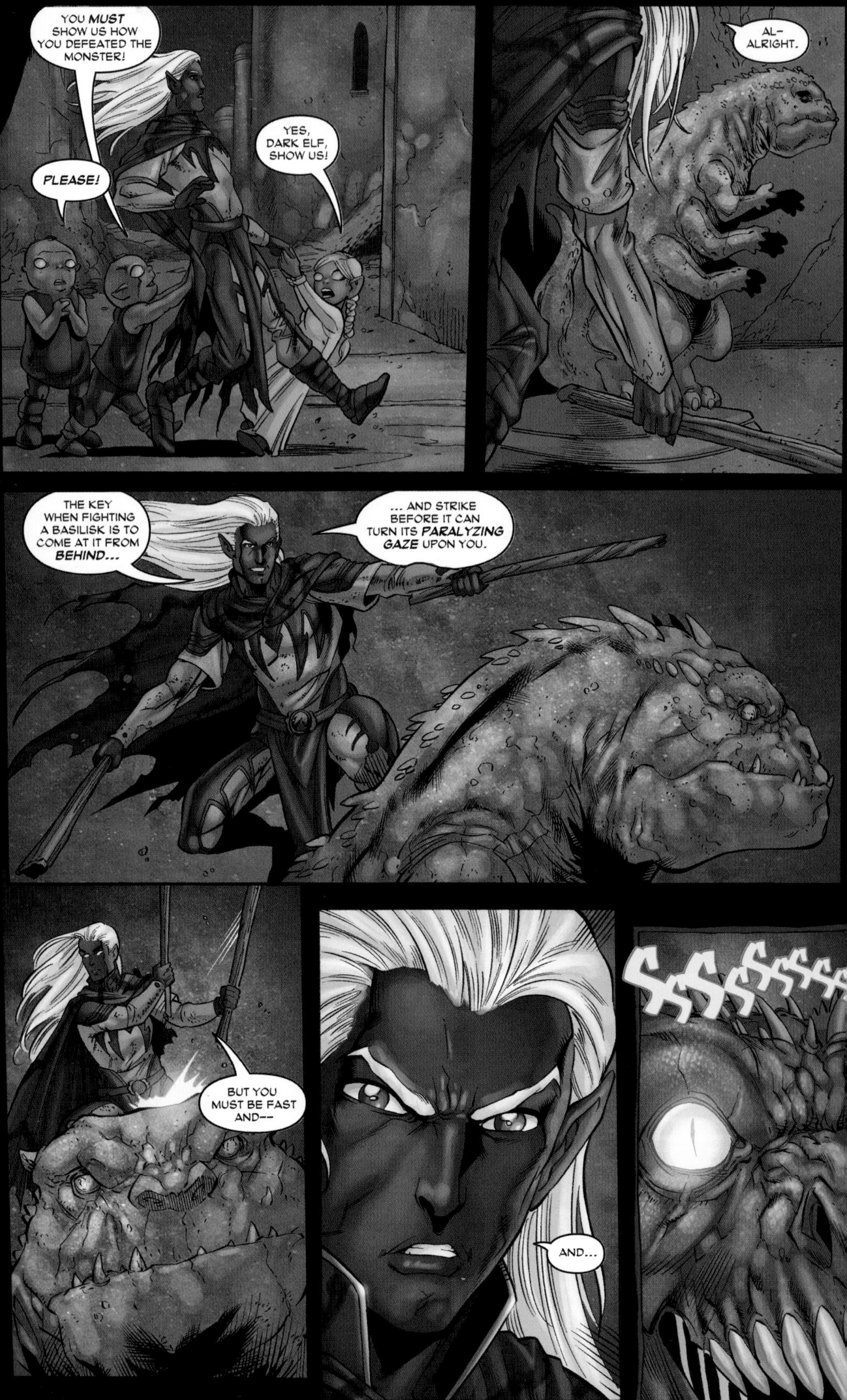
YOU **MUST** SHOW US HOW YOU DEFEATED THE MONSTER!
PLEASE!
YES, DARK ELF, SHOW US!
AL-ALRIGHT.
THE KEY WHEN FIGHTING A BASILISK IS TO COME AT IT FROM **BEHIND...**
... AND STRIKE BEFORE IT CAN TURN ITS **PARALYZING GAZE** UPON YOU.
BUT YOU MUST BE FAST AND--
AND...
SSSSSSS

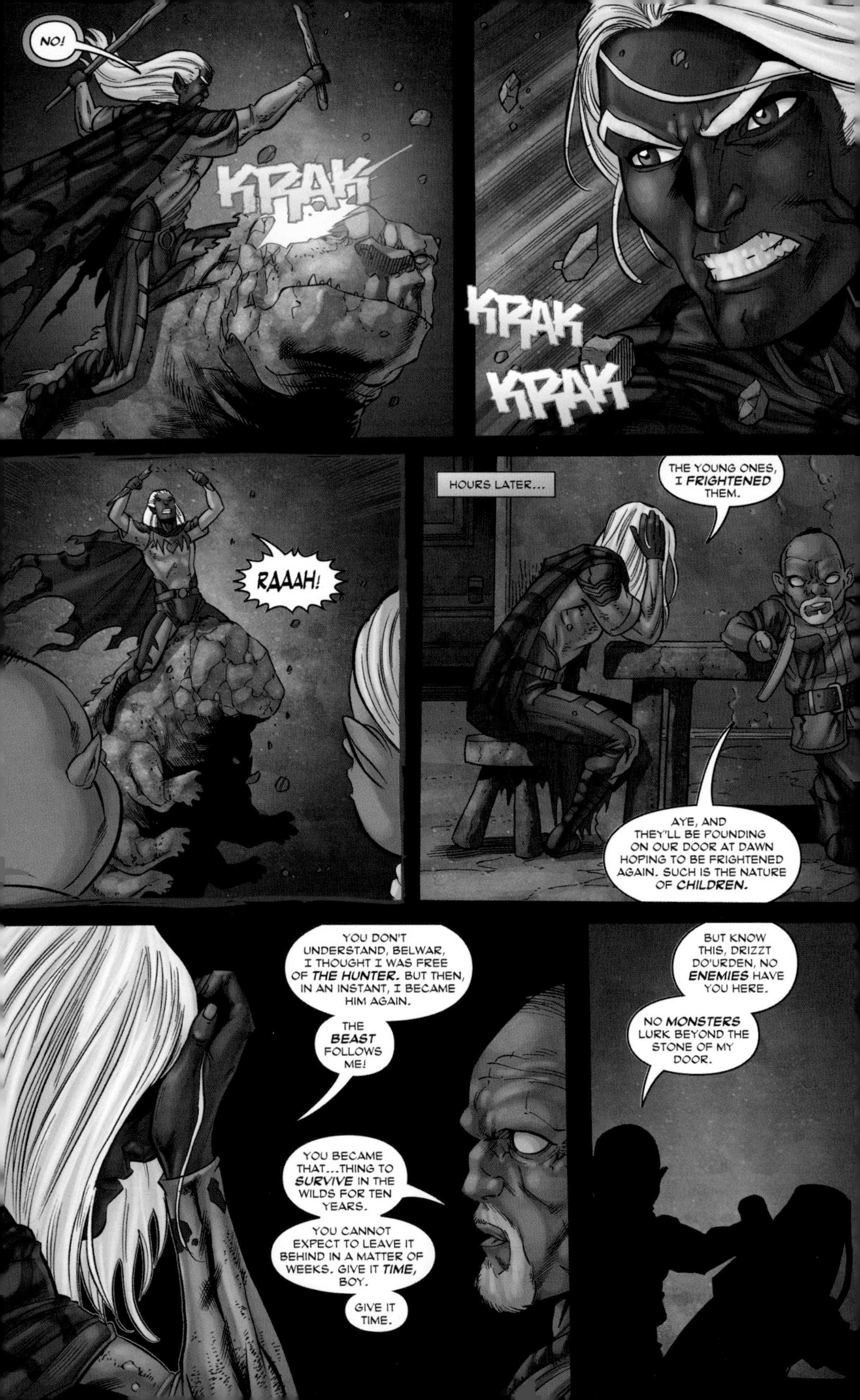
NO!
KRAK
KRAK
KRAK
RAAAH!
HOURS LATER...
THE YOUNG ONES, I FRIGHTENED THEM.
AYE, AND THEY'LL BE POUNDING ON OUR DOOR AT DAWN HOPING TO BE FRIGHTENED AGAIN. SUCH IS THE NATURE OF CHILDREN.
YOU DON'T UNDERSTAND, BELWAR, I THOUGHT I WAS FREE OF THE HUNTER. BUT THEN, IN AN INSTANT, I BECAME HIM AGAIN.
THE BEAST FOLLOWS ME!
YOU BECAME THAT...THING TO SURVIVE IN THE WILDS FOR TEN YEARS.
YOU CANNOT EXPECT TO LEAVE IT BEHIND IN A MATTER OF WEEKS. GIVE IT TIME, BOY.
GIVE IT TIME.
BUT KNOW THIS, DRIZZT DO'URDEN, NO ENEMIES HAVE YOU HERE.
NO MONSTERS LURK BEYOND THE STONE OF MY DOOR.

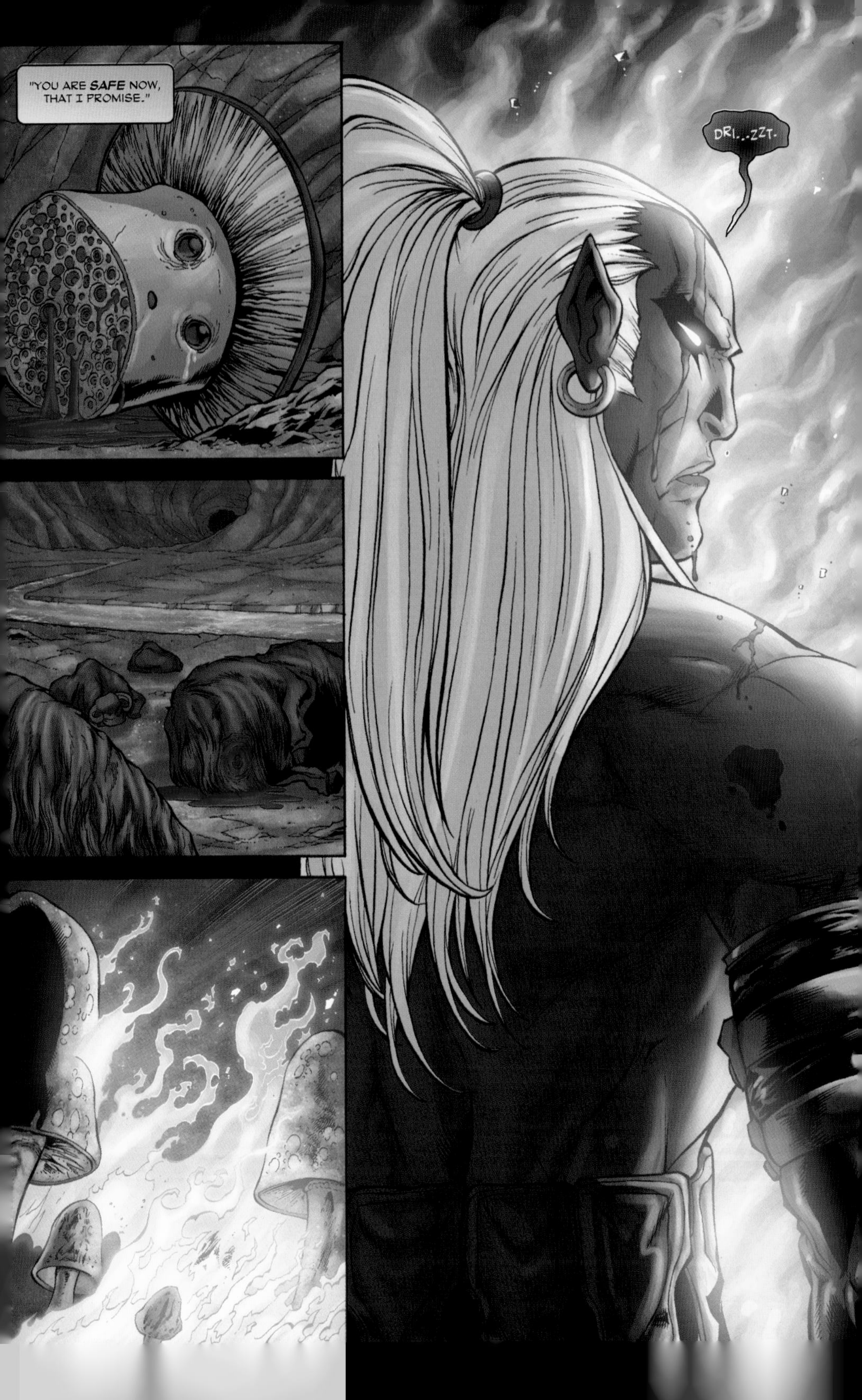
"YOU ARE SAFE NOW, THAT I PROMISE."
DRI...ZZT.

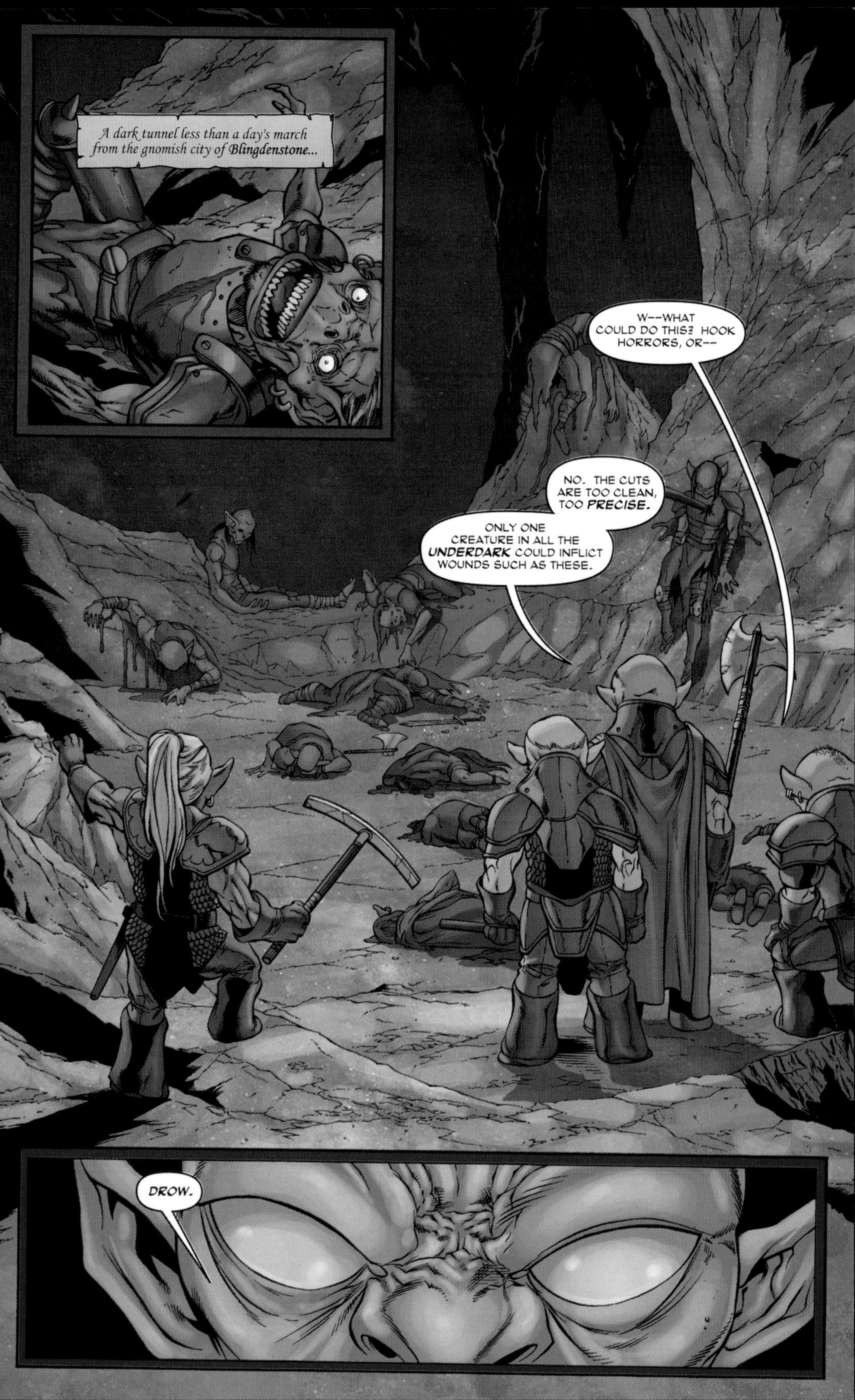
A dark tunnel less than a day's march from the gnomish city of Blingdenstone...
W--WHAT COULD DO THIS? HOOK HORRORS, OR--
NO. THE CUTS ARE TOO CLEAN, TOO PRECISE.
ONLY ONE CREATURE IN ALL THE UNDERDARK COULD INFLICT WOUNDS SUCH AS THESE.
DROW.

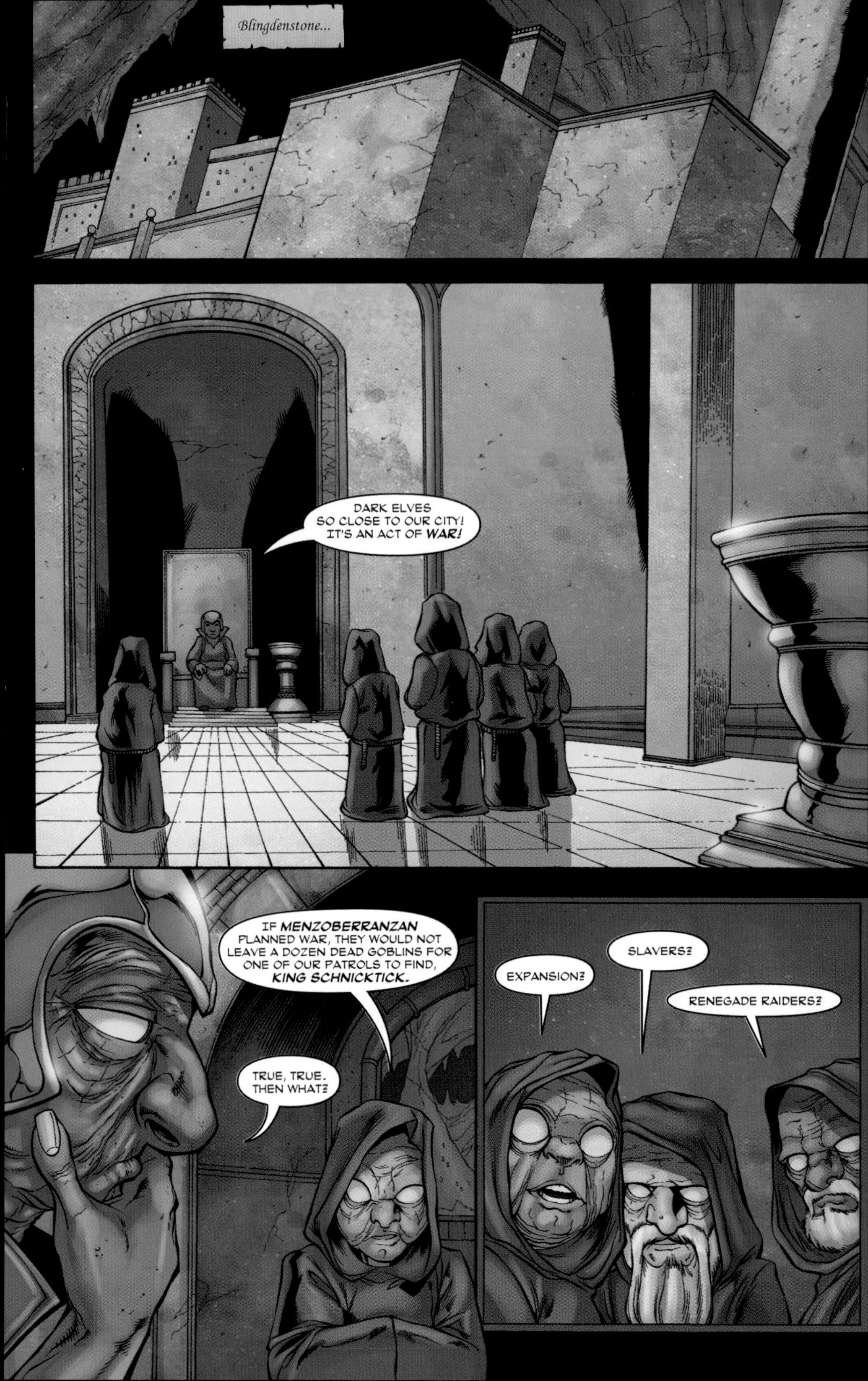
Blingdenstone...
DARK ELVES SO CLOSE TO OUR CITY! IT'S AN ACT OF WAR!
IF MENZOBERRANZAN PLANNED WAR, THEY WOULD NOT LEAVE A DOZEN DEAD GOBLINS FOR ONE OF OUR PATROLS TO FIND, KING SCHNICKTICK.
TRUE, TRUE. THEN WHAT?
EXPANSION?
SLAVERS?
RENEGADE RAIDERS?

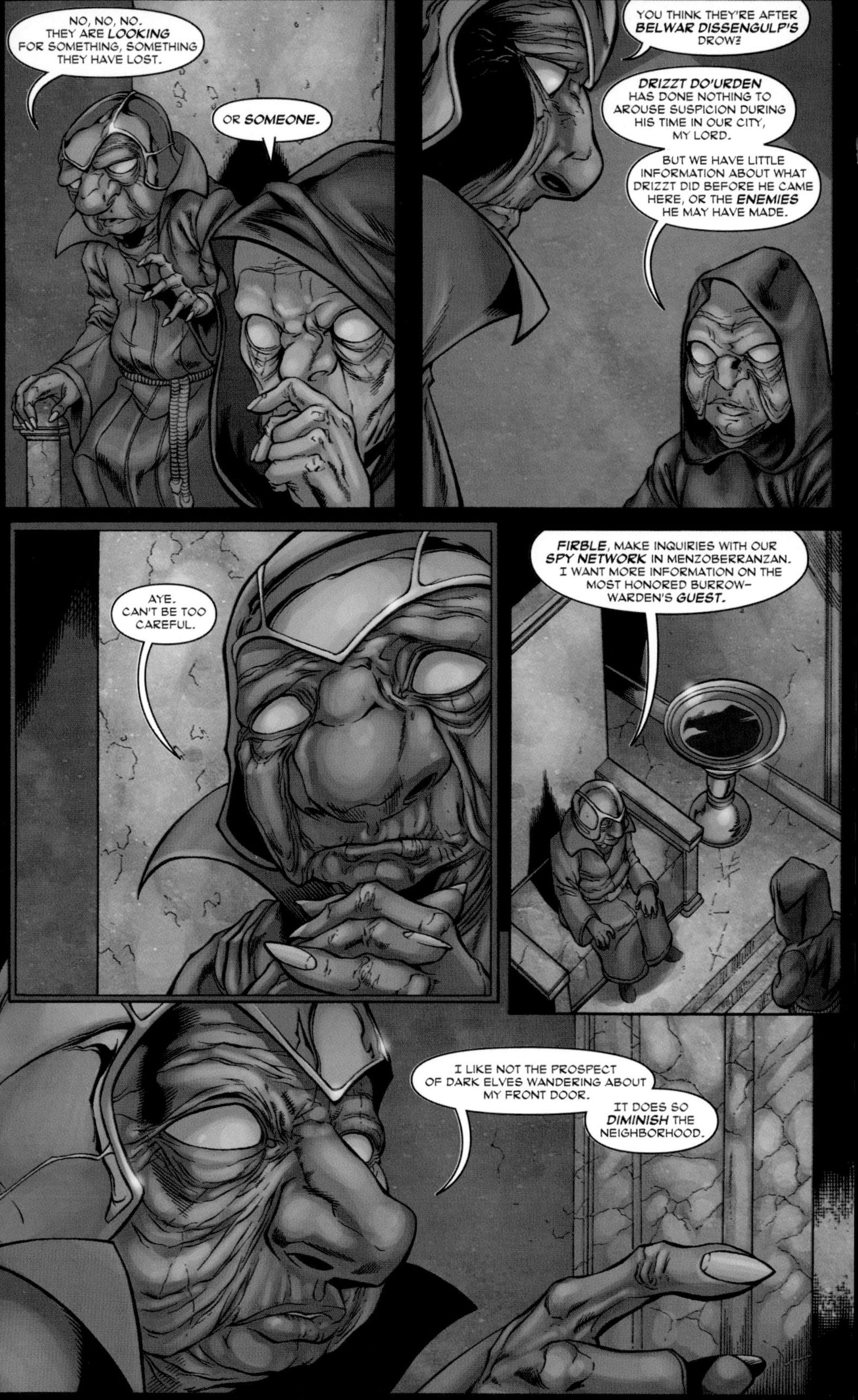

NO, NO, NO. THEY ARE LOOKING FOR SOMETHING, SOMETHING THEY HAVE LOST.
OR SOMEONE.
YOU THINK THEY'RE AFTER BELWAR DISSENGULP'S DROW?
DRIZZT DO'URDEN HAS DONE NOTHING TO AROUSE SUSPICION DURING HIS TIME IN OUR CITY, MY LORD.
BUT WE HAVE LITTLE INFORMATION ABOUT WHAT DRIZZT DID BEFORE HE CAME HERE, OR THE ENEMIES HE MAY HAVE MADE.
AYE. CAN'T BE TOO CAREFUL.
FIRBLE, MAKE INQUIRIES WITH OUR SPY NETWORK IN MENZOBERRANZAN. I WANT MORE INFORMATION ON THE MOST HONORED BURROW-WARDEN'S GUEST.
I LIKE NOT THE PROSPECT OF DARK ELVES WANDERING ABOUT MY FRONT DOOR.
IT DOES SO DIMINISH THE NEIGHBORHOOD.

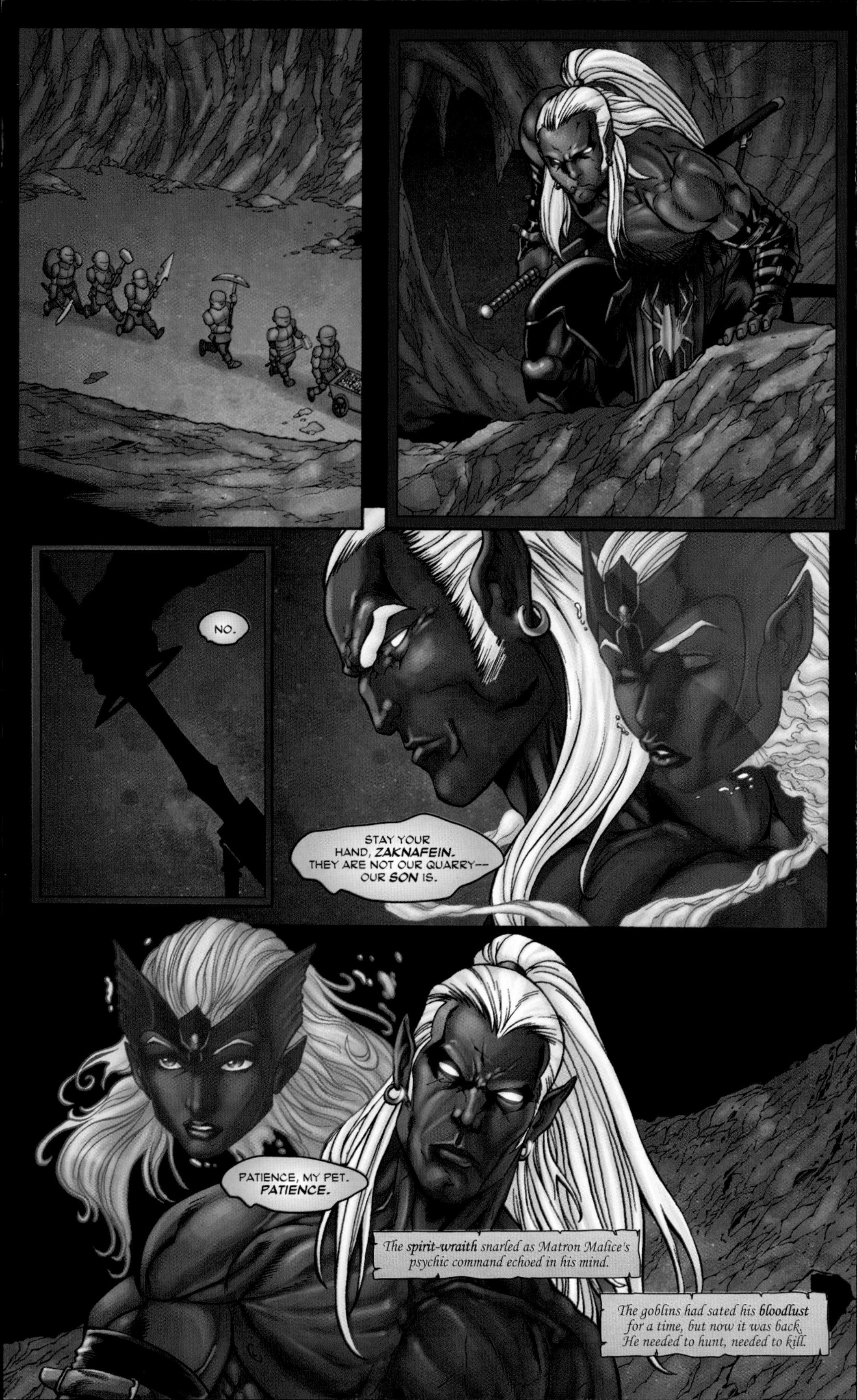
NO.
STAY YOUR HAND, ZAKNAFEIN. THEY ARE NOT OUR QUARRY-- OUR SON IS.
PATIENCE, MY PET. PATIENCE.
The spirit-wraith snarled as Matron Malice's psychic command echoed in his mind.
The goblins had sated his bloodlust for a time, but now it was back. He needed to hunt, needed to kill.

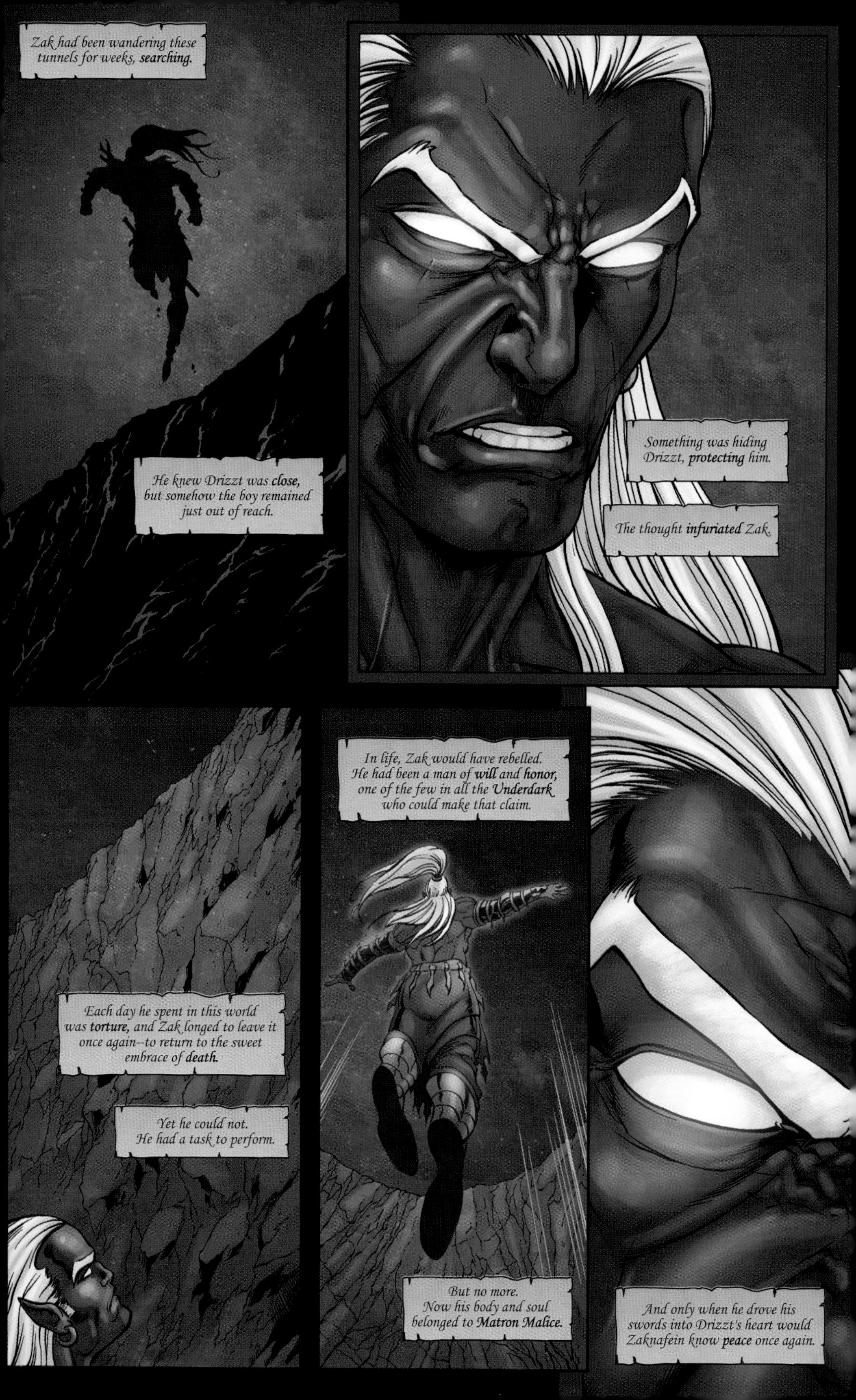
Zak had been wandering these tunnels for weeks, searching.
He knew Drizzt was close, but somehow the boy remained just out of reach.
Something was hiding Drizzt, protecting him.
The thought infuriated Zak.
Each day he spent in this world was torture, and Zak longed to leave it once again--to return to the sweet embrace of death.
Yet he could not. He had a task to perform.
In life, Zak would have rebelled. He had been a man of will and honor, one of the few in all the Underdark who could make that claim.
But no more. Now his body and soul belonged to Matron Malice.
And only when he drove his swords into Drizzt's heart would Zaknafein know peace once again.

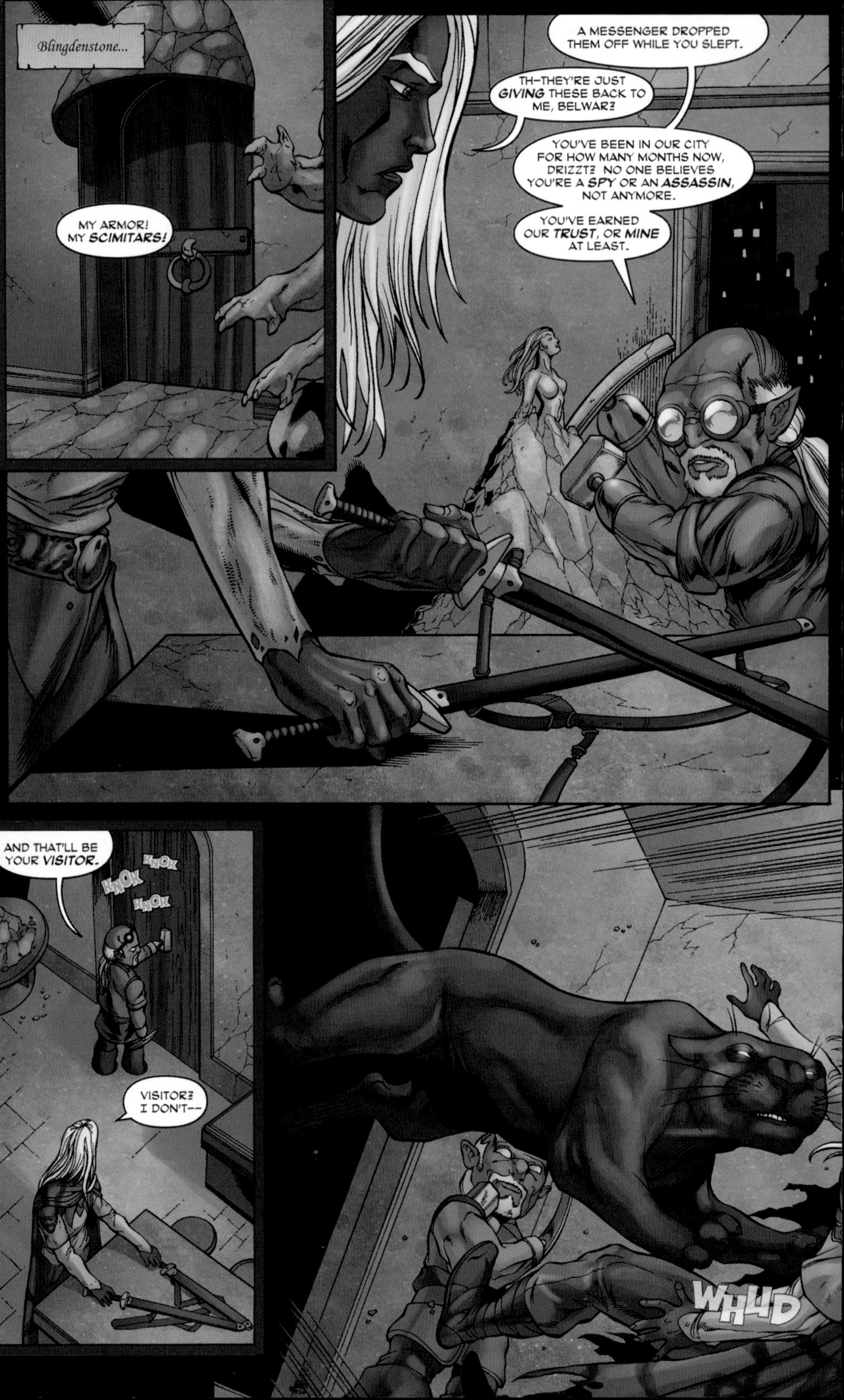

Blingdenstone...
MY ARMOR! MY SCIMITARS!
TH-THEY'RE JUST GIVING THESE BACK TO ME, BELWAR?
A MESSENGER DROPPED THEM OFF WHILE YOU SLEPT.
YOU'VE BEEN IN OUR CITY FOR HOW MANY MONTHS NOW, DRIZZT? NO ONE BELIEVES YOU'RE A SPY OR AN ASSASSIN, NOT ANYMORE.
YOU'VE EARNED OUR TRUST, OR MINE AT LEAST.
AND THAT'LL BE YOUR VISITOR.
KNOK KNOK KNOK
VISITOR? I DON'T--
WHUD

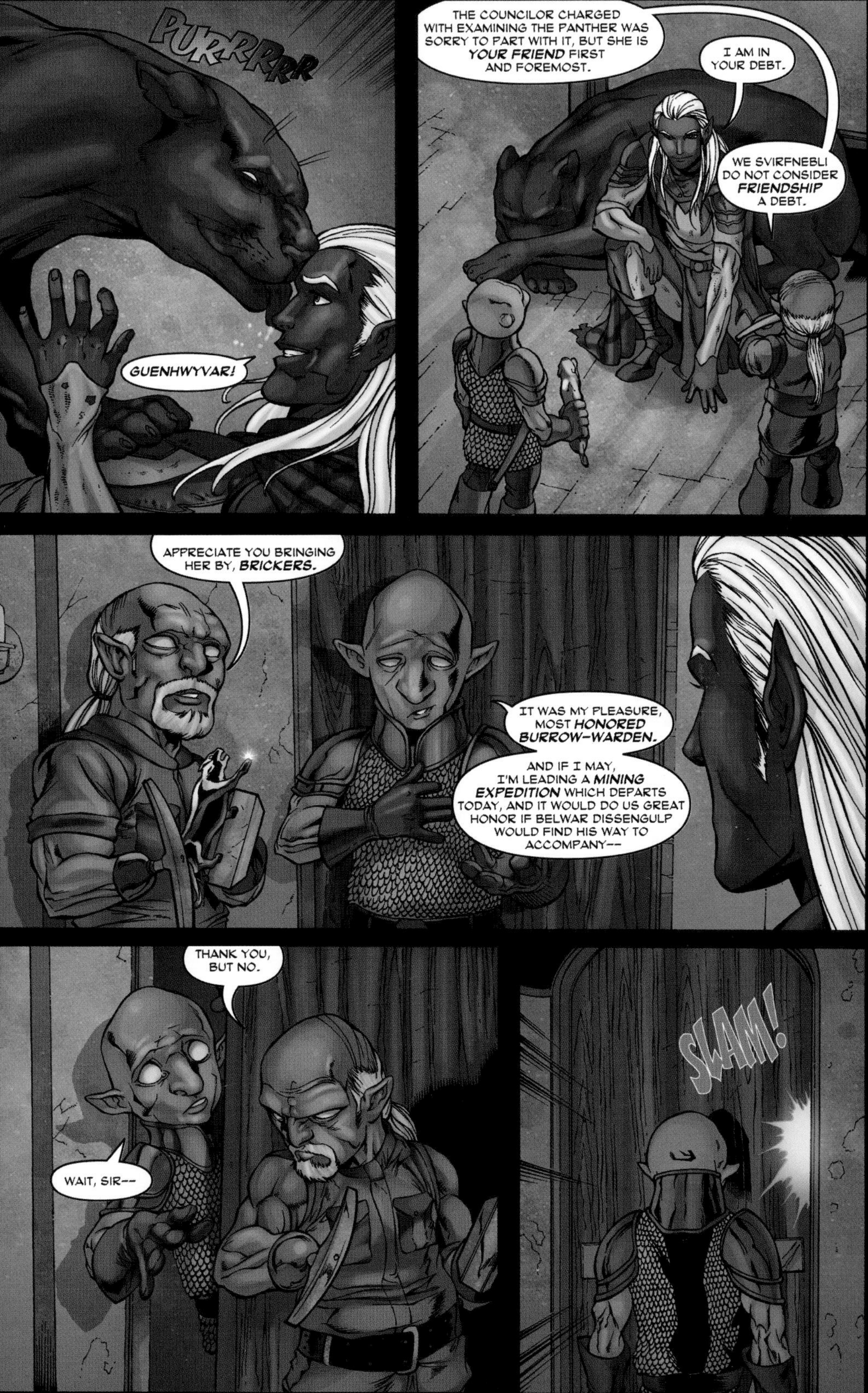
PURRRRRR
GUENHWYVAR!
THE COUNCILOR CHARGED WITH EXAMINING THE PANTHER WAS SORRY TO PART WITH IT, BUT SHE IS YOUR FRIEND FIRST AND FOREMOST.
I AM IN YOUR DEBT.
WE SVIRFNEBLI DO NOT CONSIDER FRIENDSHIP A DEBT.
APPRECIATE YOU BRINGING HER BY, BRICKERS.
IT WAS MY PLEASURE, MOST HONORED BURROW-WARDEN.
AND IF I MAY, I'M LEADING A MINING EXPEDITION WHICH DEPARTS TODAY, AND IT WOULD DO US GREAT HONOR IF BELWAR DISSENGULP WOULD FIND HIS WAY TO ACCOMPANY--
THANK YOU, BUT NO.
WAIT, SIR--
SLAM!

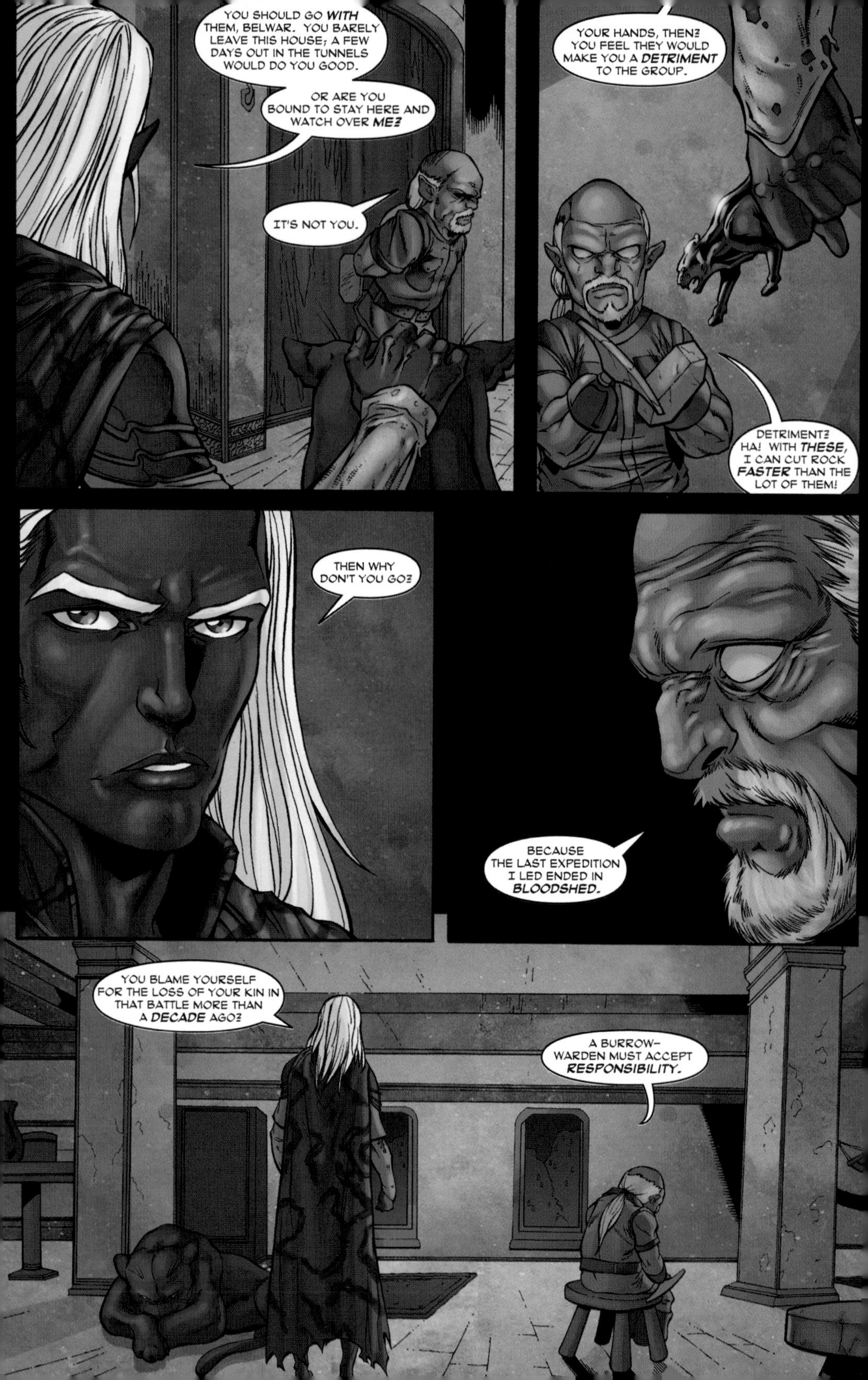
YOU SHOULD GO WITH THEM, BELWAR. YOU BARELY LEAVE THIS HOUSE; A FEW DAYS OUT IN THE TUNNELS WOULD DO YOU GOOD.
OR ARE YOU BOUND TO STAY HERE AND WATCH OVER ME?
IT'S NOT YOU.
YOUR HANDS, THEN? YOU FEEL THEY WOULD MAKE YOU A DETRIMENT TO THE GROUP.
DETRIMENT? HA! WITH THESE, I CAN CUT ROCK FASTER THAN THE LOT OF THEM!
THEN WHY DON'T YOU GO?
BECAUSE THE LAST EXPEDITION I LED ENDED IN BLOODSHED.
YOU BLAME YOURSELF FOR THE LOSS OF YOUR KIN IN THAT BATTLE MORE THAN A DECADE AGO?
A BURROW-WARDEN MUST ACCEPT RESPONSIBILITY.

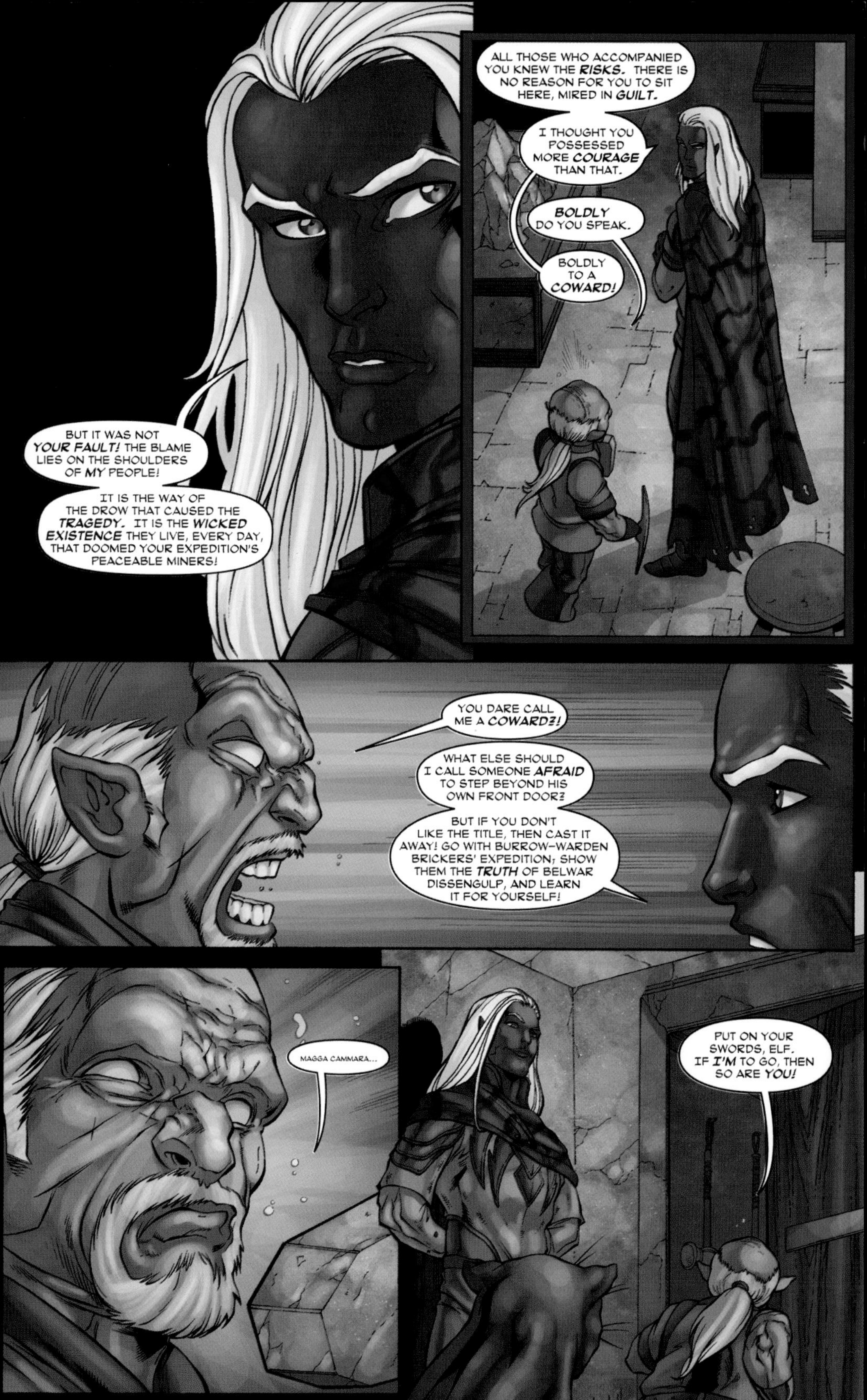
BUT IT WAS NOT YOUR FAULT! THE BLAME LIES ON THE SHOULDERS OF MY PEOPLE!
IT IS THE WAY OF THE DROW THAT CAUSED THE TRAGEDY. IT IS THE WICKED EXISTENCE THEY LIVE, EVERY DAY, THAT DOOMED YOUR EXPEDITION'S PEACEABLE MINERS!
ALL THOSE WHO ACCOMPANIED YOU KNEW THE RISKS. THERE IS NO REASON FOR YOU TO SIT HERE, MIRED IN GUILT.
I THOUGHT YOU POSSESSED MORE COURAGE THAN THAT.
BOLDLY DO YOU SPEAK.
BOLDLY TO A COWARD!
YOU DARE CALL ME A COWARD?!
WHAT ELSE SHOULD I CALL SOMEONE AFRAID TO STEP BEYOND HIS OWN FRONT DOOR?
BUT IF YOU DON'T LIKE THE TITLE, THEN CAST IT AWAY! GO WITH BURROW-WARDEN BRICKERS' EXPEDITION; SHOW THEM THE TRUTH OF BELWAR DISSENGULP, AND LEARN IT FOR YOURSELF!
MAGGA CAMMARA...
PUT ON YOUR SWORDS, ELF. IF I'M TO GO, THEN SO ARE YOU!

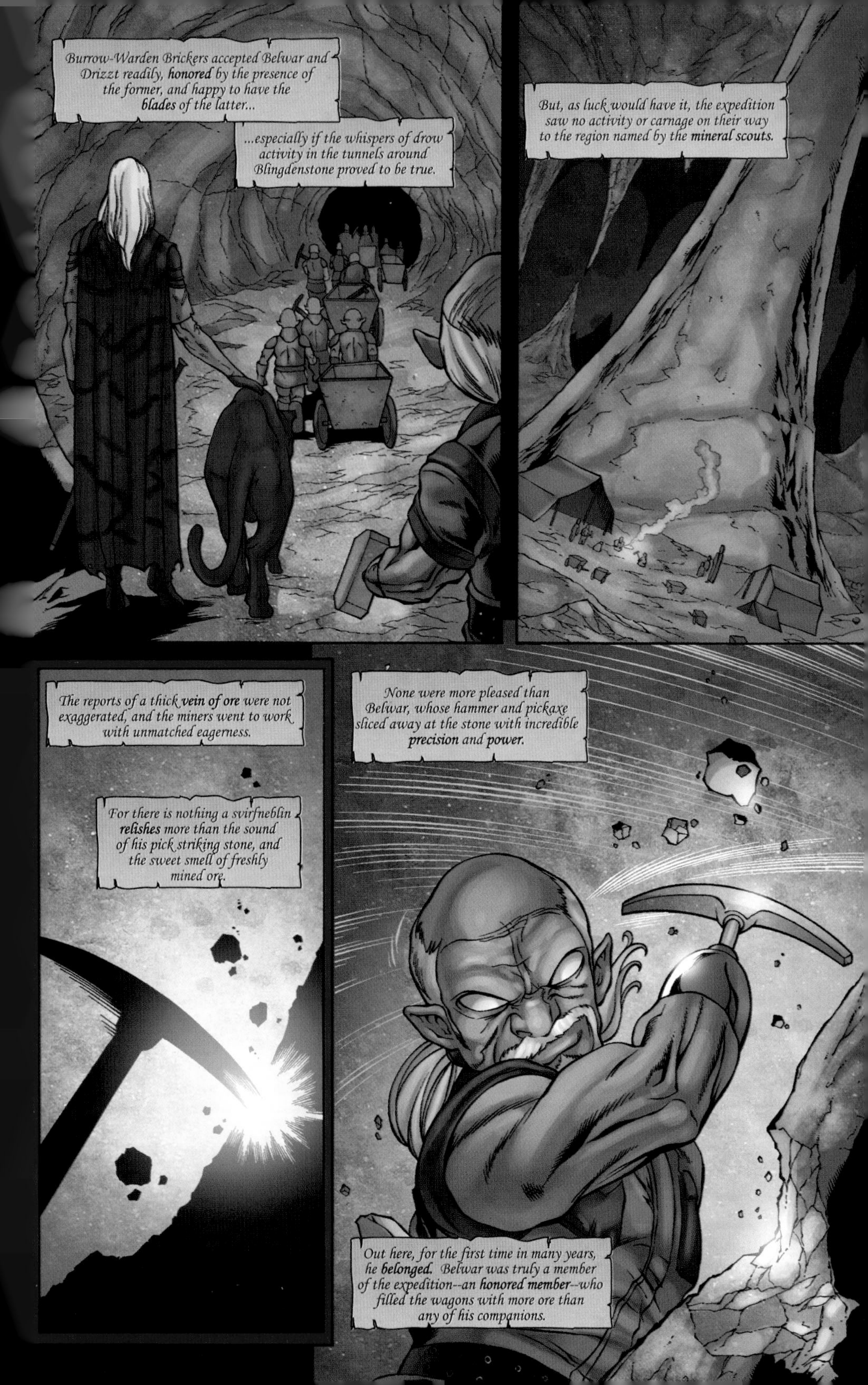
Burrow-Warden Brickers accepted Belwar and Drizzt readily, **honored** by the presence of the former, and happy to have the **blades** of the latter...
...especially if the whispers of drow activity in the tunnels around Blingdenstone proved to be true.
But, as luck would have it, the expedition saw no activity or carnage on their way to the region named by the **mineral scouts.**
The reports of a thick **vein of ore** were not exaggerated, and the miners went to work with unmatched eagerness.
For there is nothing a svirfneblin **relishes** more than the sound of his pick striking stone, and the sweet smell of freshly mined ore.
None were more pleased than Belwar, whose hammer and pickaxe sliced away at the stone with incredible **precision** and **power.**
Out here, for the first time in many years, he **belonged.** Belwar was truly a member of the expedition--an **honored member**--who filled the wagons with more ore than any of his companions.

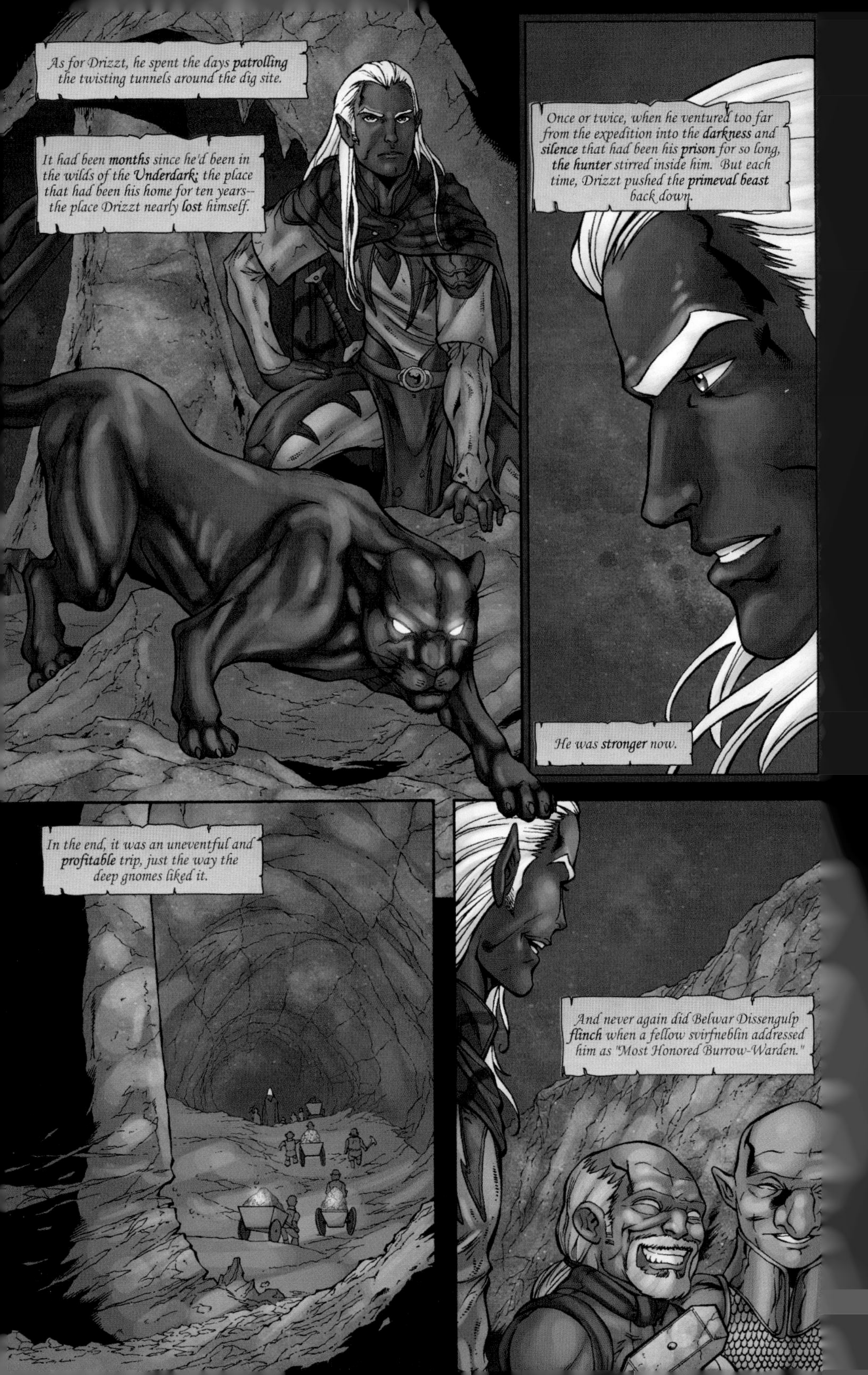
As for Drizzt, he spent the days **patrolling** the twisting tunnels around the dig site.
It had been **months** since he'd been in the wilds of the **Underdark**; the place that had been his home for ten years--the place Drizzt nearly **lost** himself.
Once or twice, when he ventured too far from the expedition into the **darkness** and **silence** that had been his **prison** for so long, **the hunter** stirred inside him. But each time, Drizzt pushed the **primeval beast** back down.
He was **stronger** now.
In the end, it was an uneventful and **profitable** trip, just the way the deep gnomes liked it.
And never again did Belwar Dissengulp **flinch** when a fellow svirfneblin addressed him as "Most Honored Burrow-Warden."

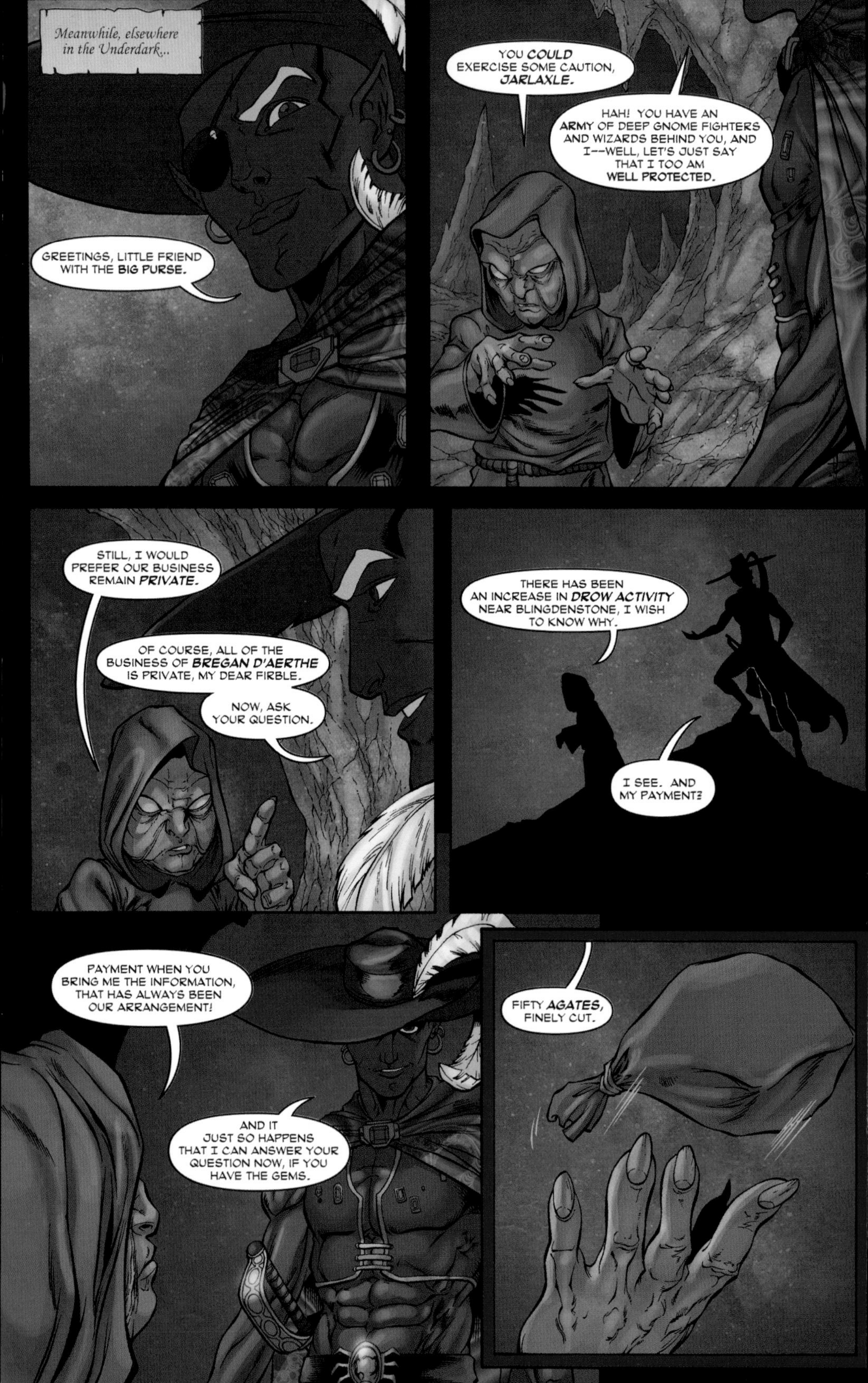
Meanwhile, elsewhere in the Underdark...
GREETINGS, LITTLE FRIEND WITH THE BIG PURSE.
YOU COULD EXERCISE SOME CAUTION, JARLAXLE.
HAH! YOU HAVE AN ARMY OF DEEP GNOME FIGHTERS AND WIZARDS BEHIND YOU, AND I--WELL, LET'S JUST SAY THAT I TOO AM WELL PROTECTED.
STILL, I WOULD PREFER OUR BUSINESS REMAIN PRIVATE.
OF COURSE, ALL OF THE BUSINESS OF BREGAN D'AERTHE IS PRIVATE, MY DEAR FIRBLE.
NOW, ASK YOUR QUESTION.
THERE HAS BEEN AN INCREASE IN DROW ACTIVITY NEAR BLINGDENSTONE, I WISH TO KNOW WHY.
I SEE. AND MY PAYMENT?
PAYMENT WHEN YOU BRING ME THE INFORMATION, THAT HAS ALWAYS BEEN OUR ARRANGEMENT!
AND IT JUST SO HAPPENS THAT I CAN ANSWER YOUR QUESTION NOW, IF YOU HAVE THE GEMS.
FIFTY AGATES, FINELY CUT.

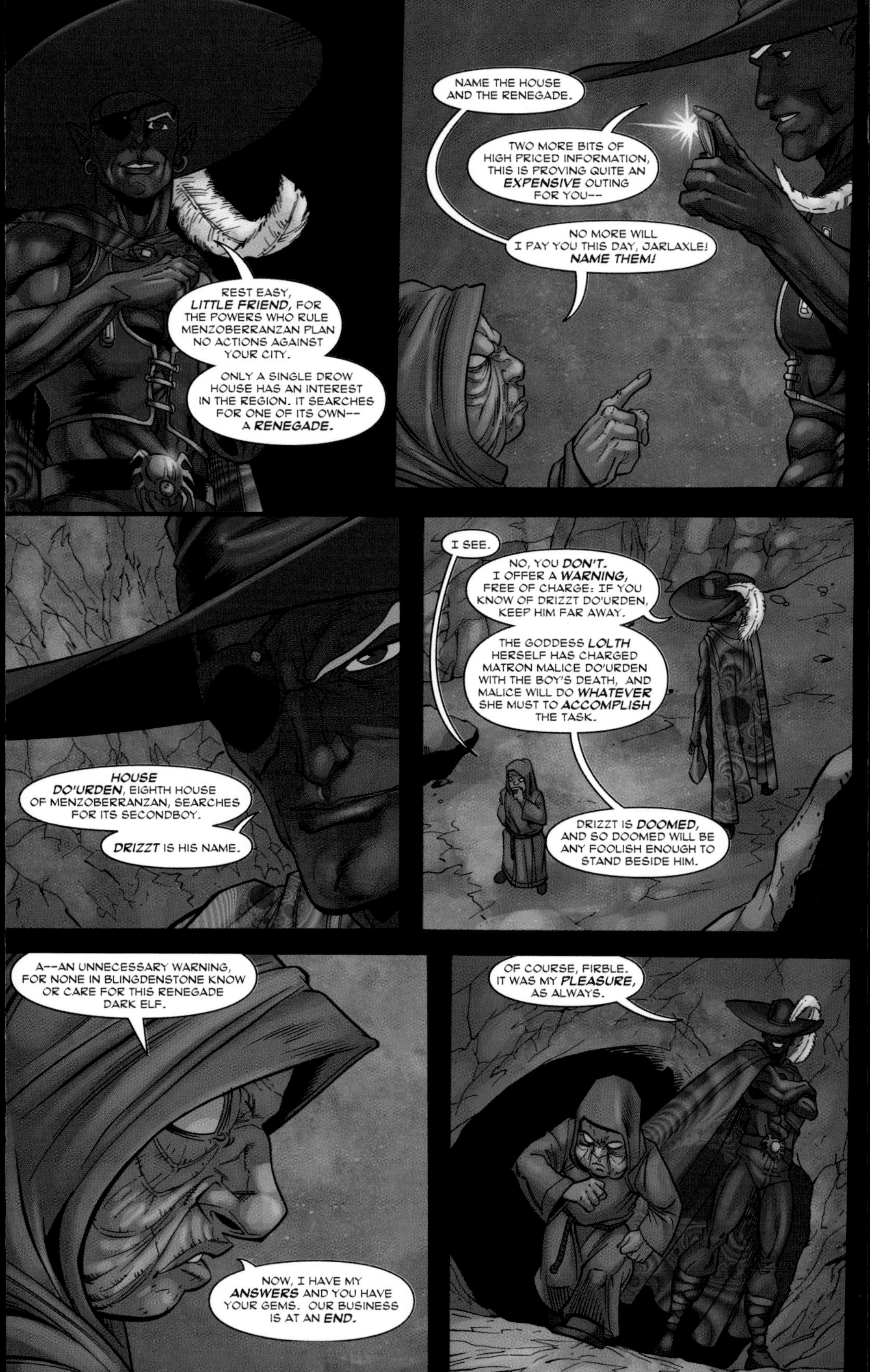
REST EASY, LITTLE FRIEND, FOR THE POWERS WHO RULE MENZOBERRANZAN PLAN NO ACTIONS AGAINST YOUR CITY.
ONLY A SINGLE DROW HOUSE HAS AN INTEREST IN THE REGION. IT SEARCHES FOR ONE OF ITS OWN-- A RENEGADE.
NAME THE HOUSE AND THE RENEGADE.
TWO MORE BITS OF HIGH PRICED INFORMATION, THIS IS PROVING QUITE AN EXPENSIVE OUTING FOR YOU--
NO MORE WILL I PAY YOU THIS DAY, JARLAXLE! NAME THEM!
HOUSE DO'URDEN, EIGHTH HOUSE OF MENZOBERRANZAN, SEARCHES FOR ITS SECONDBOY.
DRIZZT IS HIS NAME.
I SEE.
NO, YOU DON'T. I OFFER A WARNING, FREE OF CHARGE: IF YOU KNOW OF DRIZZT DO'URDEN, KEEP HIM FAR AWAY.
THE GODDESS LOLTH HERSELF HAS CHARGED MATRON MALICE DO'URDEN WITH THE BOY'S DEATH, AND MALICE WILL DO WHATEVER SHE MUST TO ACCOMPLISH THE TASK.
DRIZZT IS DOOMED, AND SO DOOMED WILL BE ANY FOOLISH ENOUGH TO STAND BESIDE HIM.
A--AN UNNECESSARY WARNING, FOR NONE IN BLINGDENSTONE KNOW OR CARE FOR THIS RENEGADE DARK ELF.
NOW, I HAVE MY ANSWERS AND YOU HAVE YOUR GEMS. OUR BUSINESS IS AT AN END.
OF COURSE, FIRBLE. IT WAS MY PLEASURE, AS ALWAYS.

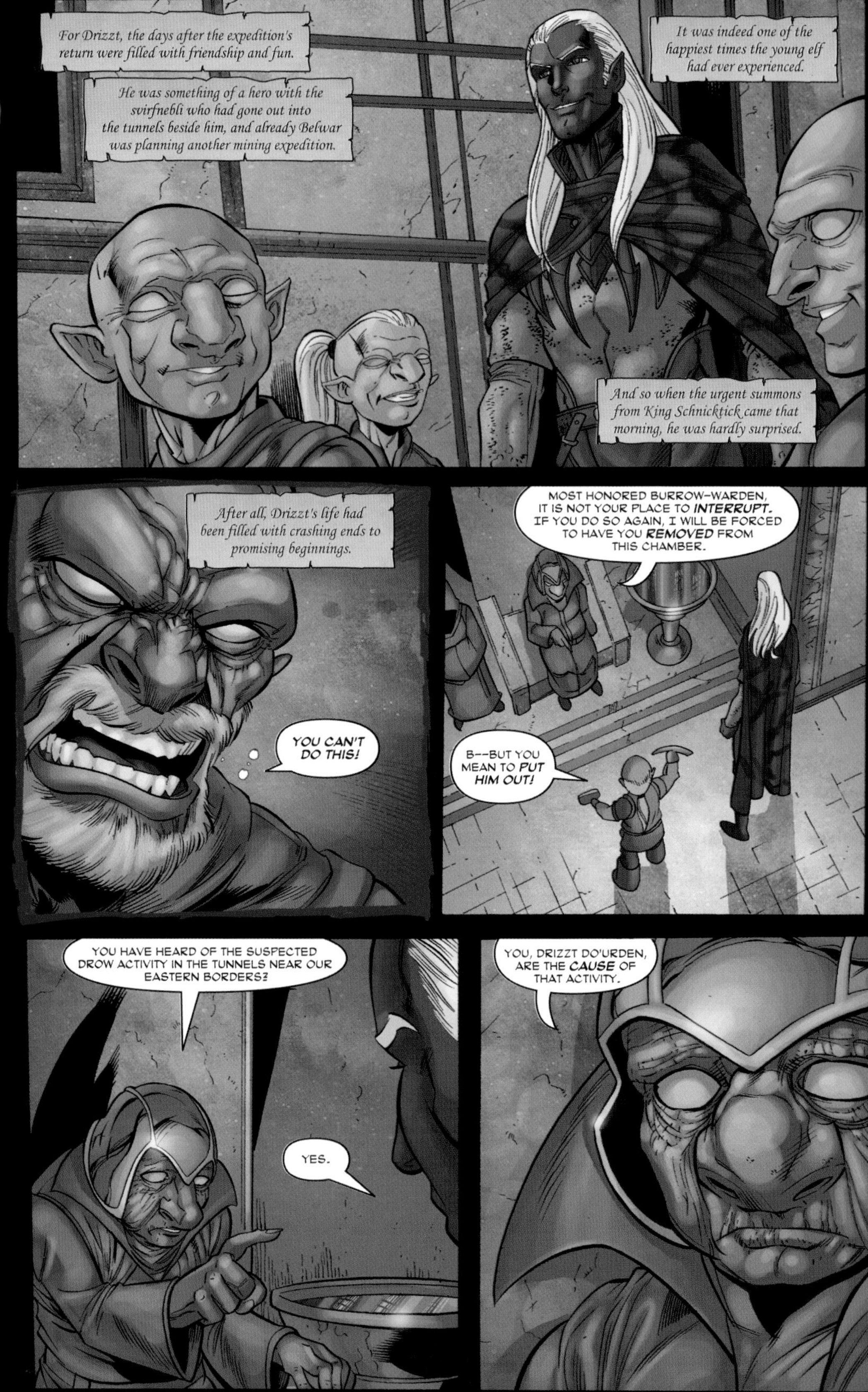
For Drizzt, the days after the expedition's return were filled with friendship and fun.
He was something of a hero with the svirfnebli who had gone out into the tunnels beside him, and already Belwar was planning another mining expedition.
It was indeed one of the happiest times the young elf had ever experienced.
And so when the urgent summons from King Schnicktick came that morning, he was hardly surprised.
After all, Drizzt's life had been filled with crashing ends to promising beginnings.
MOST HONORED BURROW-WARDEN, IT IS NOT YOUR PLACE TO INTERRUPT. IF YOU DO SO AGAIN, I WILL BE FORCED TO HAVE YOU REMOVED FROM THIS CHAMBER.
YOU CAN'T DO THIS!
B--BUT YOU MEAN TO PUT HIM OUT!
YOU HAVE HEARD OF THE SUSPECTED DROW ACTIVITY IN THE TUNNELS NEAR OUR EASTERN BORDERS?
YES.
YOU, DRIZZT DO'URDEN, ARE THE CAUSE OF THAT ACTIVITY.

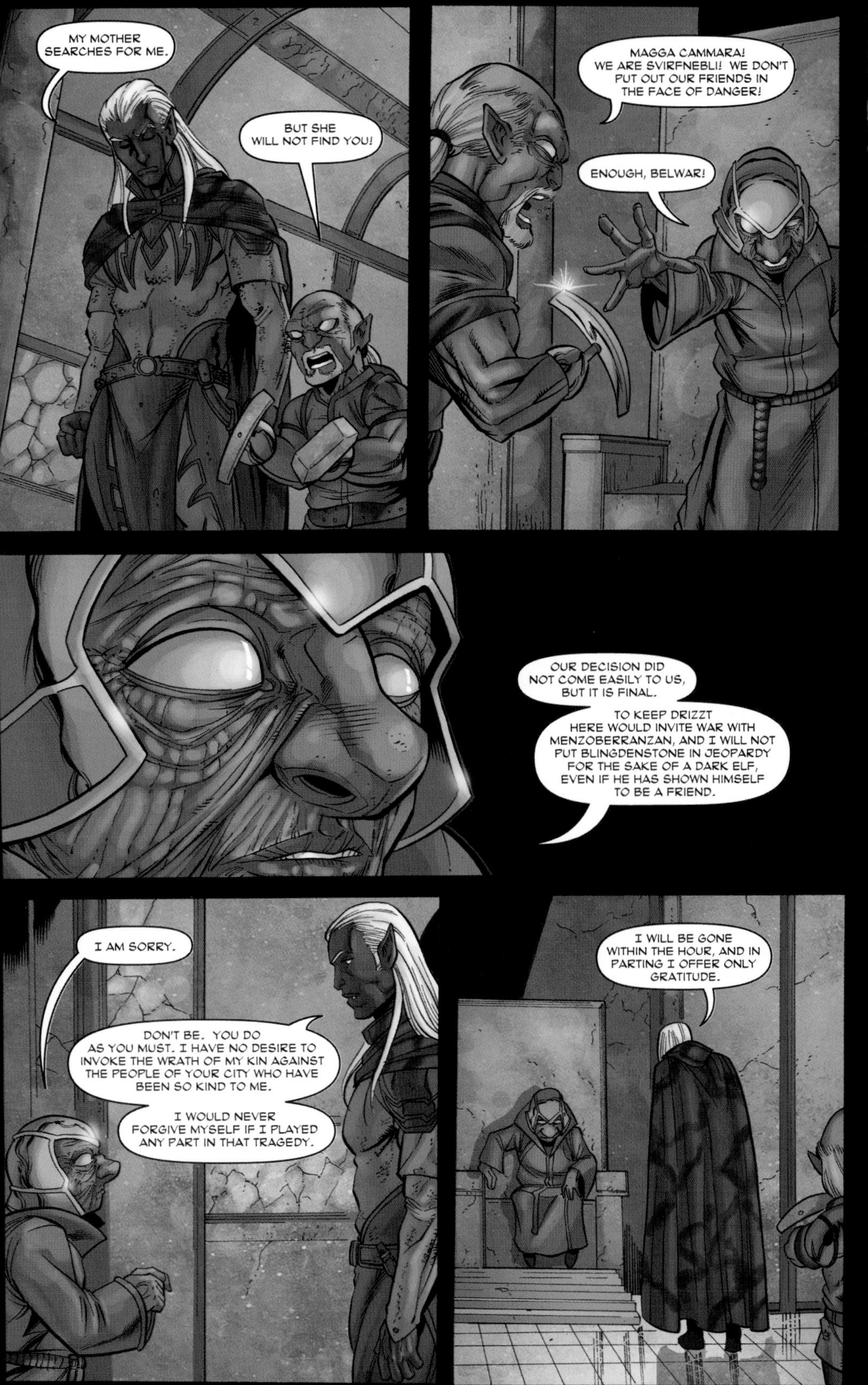
MY MOTHER SEARCHES FOR ME.
BUT SHE WILL NOT FIND YOU!
MAGGA CAMMARA! WE ARE SVIRFNEBLI! WE DON'T PUT OUT OUR FRIENDS IN THE FACE OF DANGER!
ENOUGH, BELWAR!
OUR DECISION DID NOT COME EASILY TO US, BUT IT IS FINAL.
TO KEEP DRIZZT HERE WOULD INVITE WAR WITH MENZOBERRANZAN, AND I WILL NOT PUT BLINGDENSTONE IN JEOPARDY FOR THE SAKE OF A DARK ELF, EVEN IF HE HAS SHOWN HIMSELF TO BE A FRIEND.
I AM SORRY.
DON'T BE. YOU DO AS YOU MUST. I HAVE NO DESIRE TO INVOKE THE WRATH OF MY KIN AGAINST THE PEOPLE OF YOUR CITY WHO HAVE BEEN SO KIND TO ME.
I WOULD NEVER FORGIVE MYSELF IF I PLAYED ANY PART IN THAT TRAGEDY.
I WILL BE GONE WITHIN THE HOUR, AND IN PARTING I OFFER ONLY GRATITUDE.

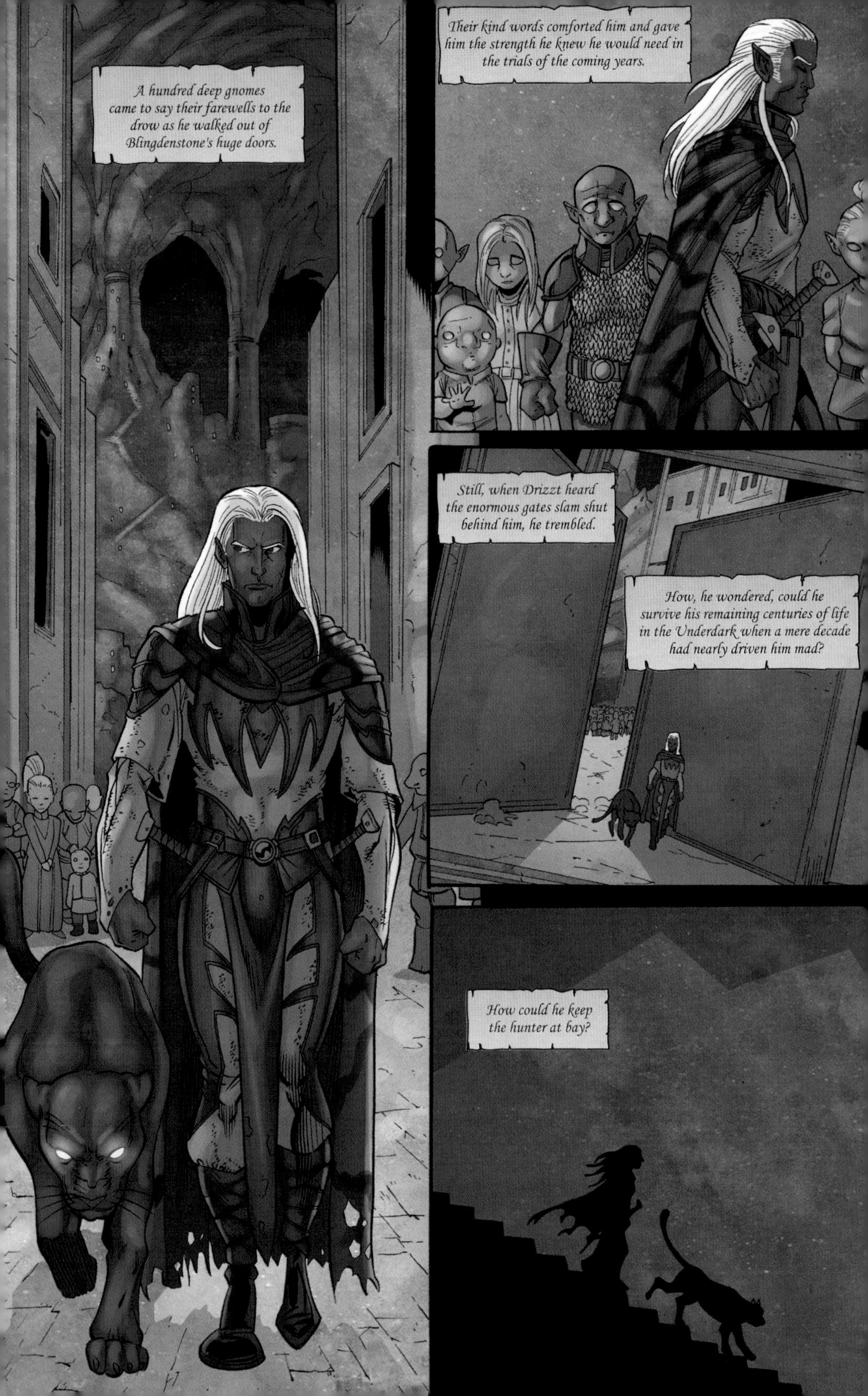
A hundred deep gnomes came to say their farewells to the drow as he walked out of Blingdenstone's huge doors.
Their kind words comforted him and gave him the strength he knew he would need in the trials of the coming years.
Still, when Drizzt heard the enormous gates slam shut behind him, he trembled.
How, he wondered, could he survive his remaining centuries of life in the Underdark when a mere decade had nearly driven him mad?
How could he keep the hunter at bay?

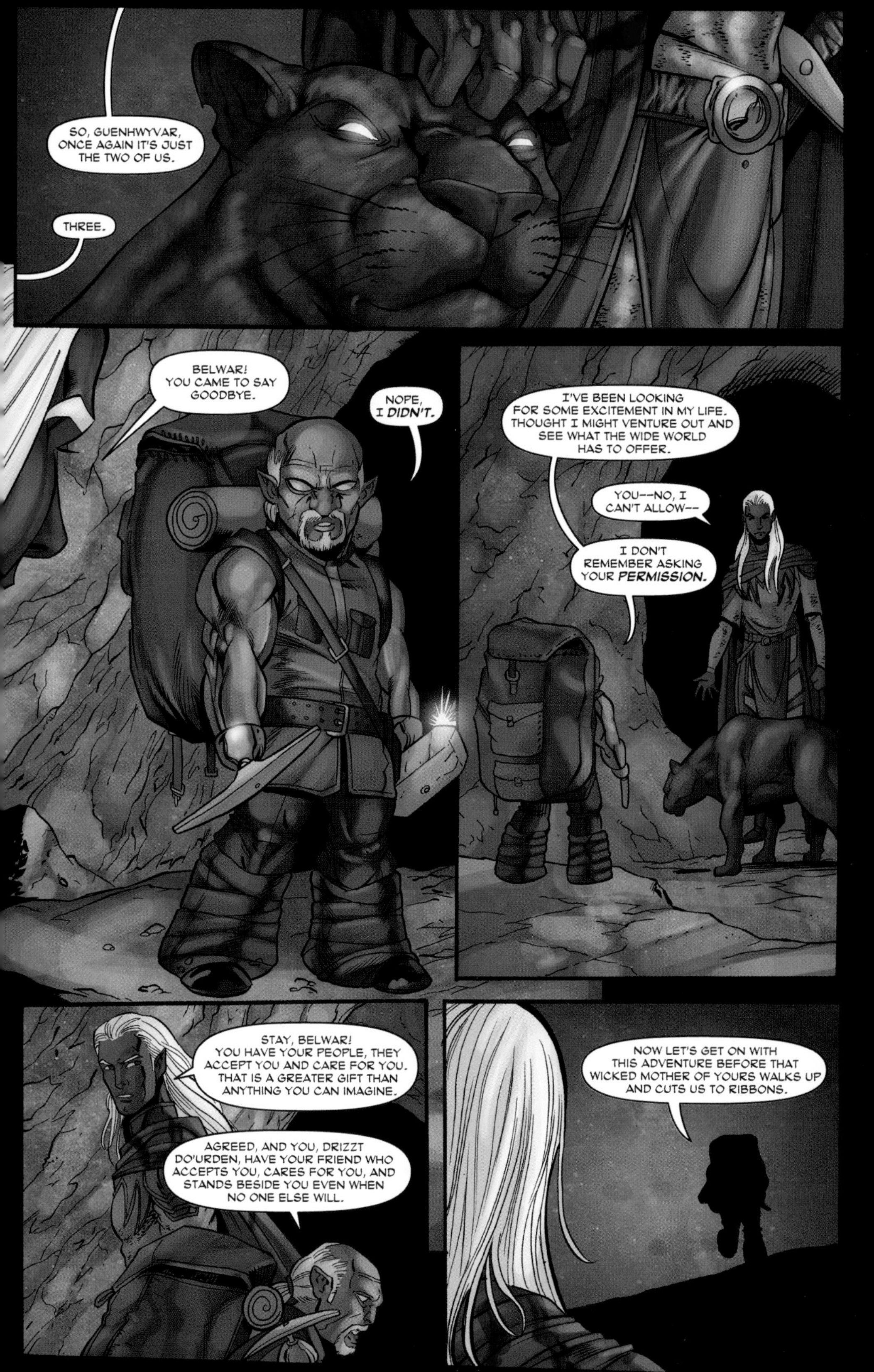
SO, GUENHWYVAR, ONCE AGAIN IT'S JUST THE TWO OF US.
THREE.
BELWAR! YOU CAME TO SAY GOODBYE.
NOPE, I *DIDN'T.*
I'VE BEEN LOOKING FOR SOME EXCITEMENT IN MY LIFE. THOUGHT I MIGHT VENTURE OUT AND SEE WHAT THE WIDE WORLD HAS TO OFFER.
YOU--NO, I CAN'T ALLOW--
I DON'T REMEMBER ASKING YOUR **PERMISSION.**
STAY, BELWAR! YOU HAVE YOUR PEOPLE, THEY ACCEPT YOU AND CARE FOR YOU. THAT IS A GREATER GIFT THAN ANYTHING YOU CAN IMAGINE.
AGREED, AND YOU, DRIZZT DO'URDEN, HAVE YOUR FRIEND WHO ACCEPTS YOU, CARES FOR YOU, AND STANDS BESIDE YOU EVEN WHEN NO ONE ELSE WILL.
NOW LET'S GET ON WITH THIS ADVENTURE BEFORE THAT WICKED MOTHER OF YOURS WALKS UP AND CUTS US TO RIBBONS.

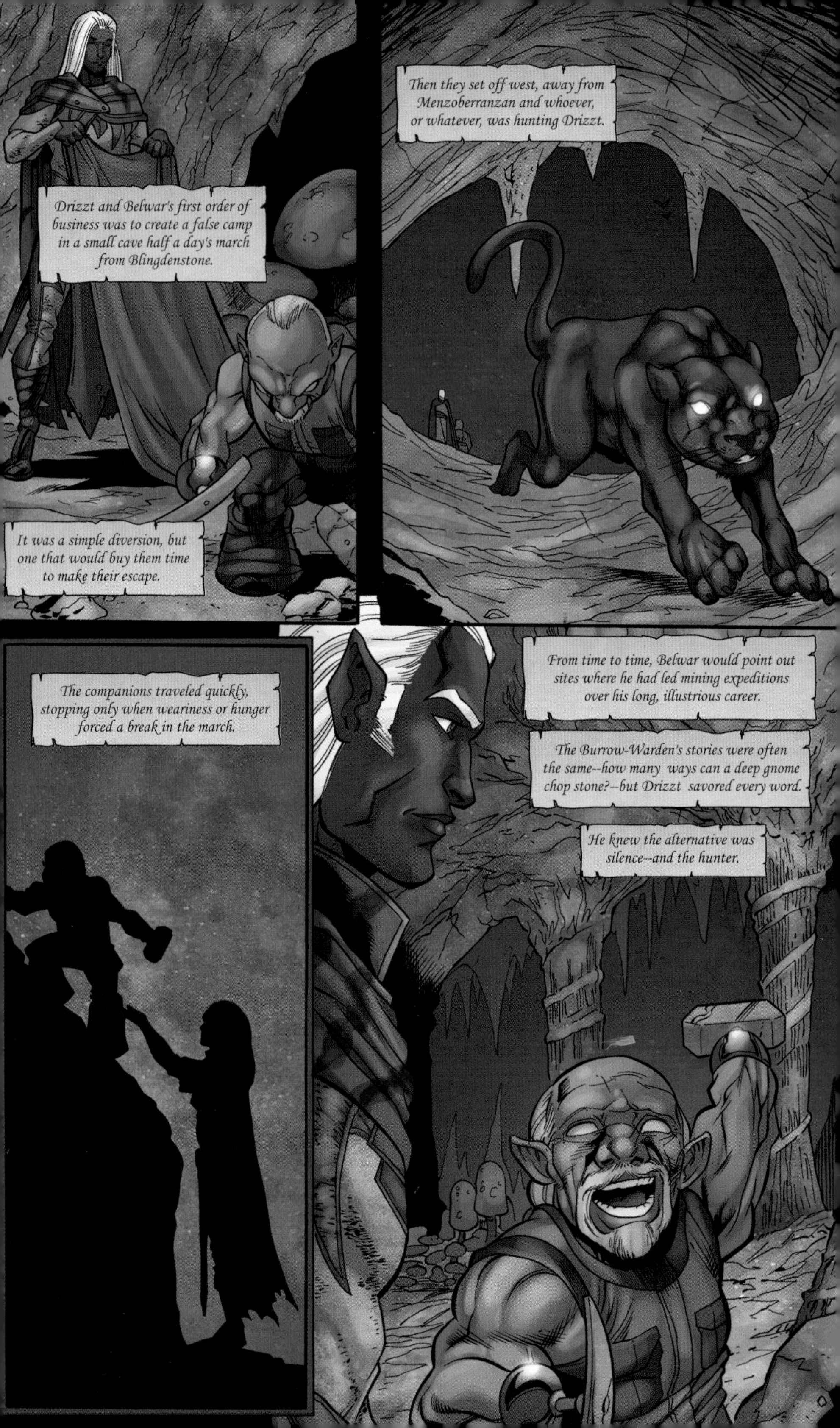
Drizzt and Belwar's first order of business was to create a false camp in a small cave half a day's march from Blingdenstone.
It was a simple diversion, but one that would buy them time to make their escape.
Then they set off west, away from Menzoberranzan and whoever, or whatever, was hunting Drizzt.
The companions traveled quickly, stopping only when weariness or hunger forced a break in the march.
From time to time, Belwar would point out sites where he had led mining expeditions over his long, illustrious career.
The Burrow-Warden's stories were often the same--how many ways can a deep gnome chop stone?--but Drizzt savored every word.
He knew the alternative was silence--and the hunter.

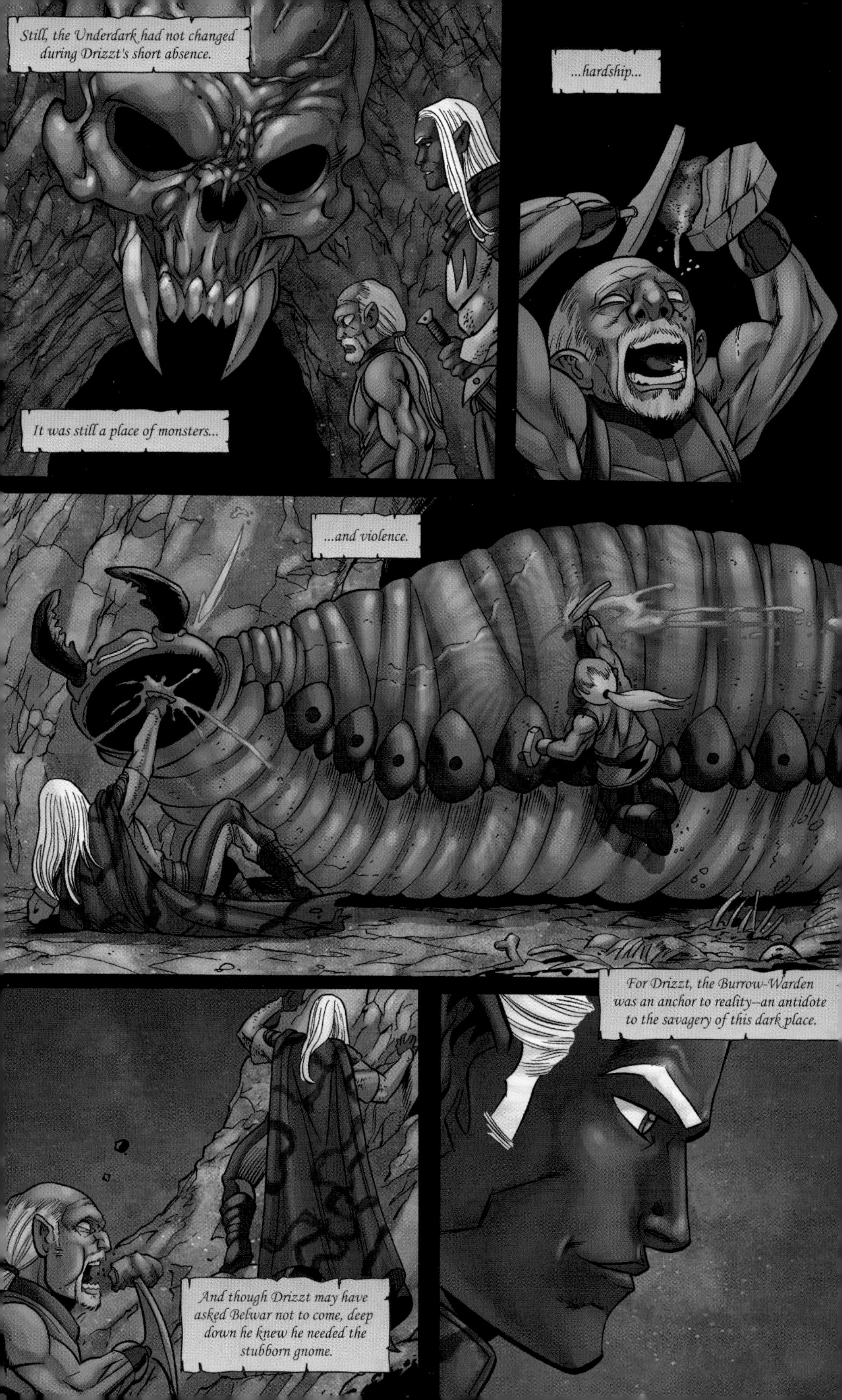
Still, the Underdark had not changed during Drizzt's short absence.
It was still a place of monsters...
...hardship...
...and violence.
And though Drizzt may have asked Belwar not to come, deep down he knew he needed the stubborn gnome.
For Drizzt, the Burrow-Warden was an anchor to reality--an antidote to the savagery of this dark place.

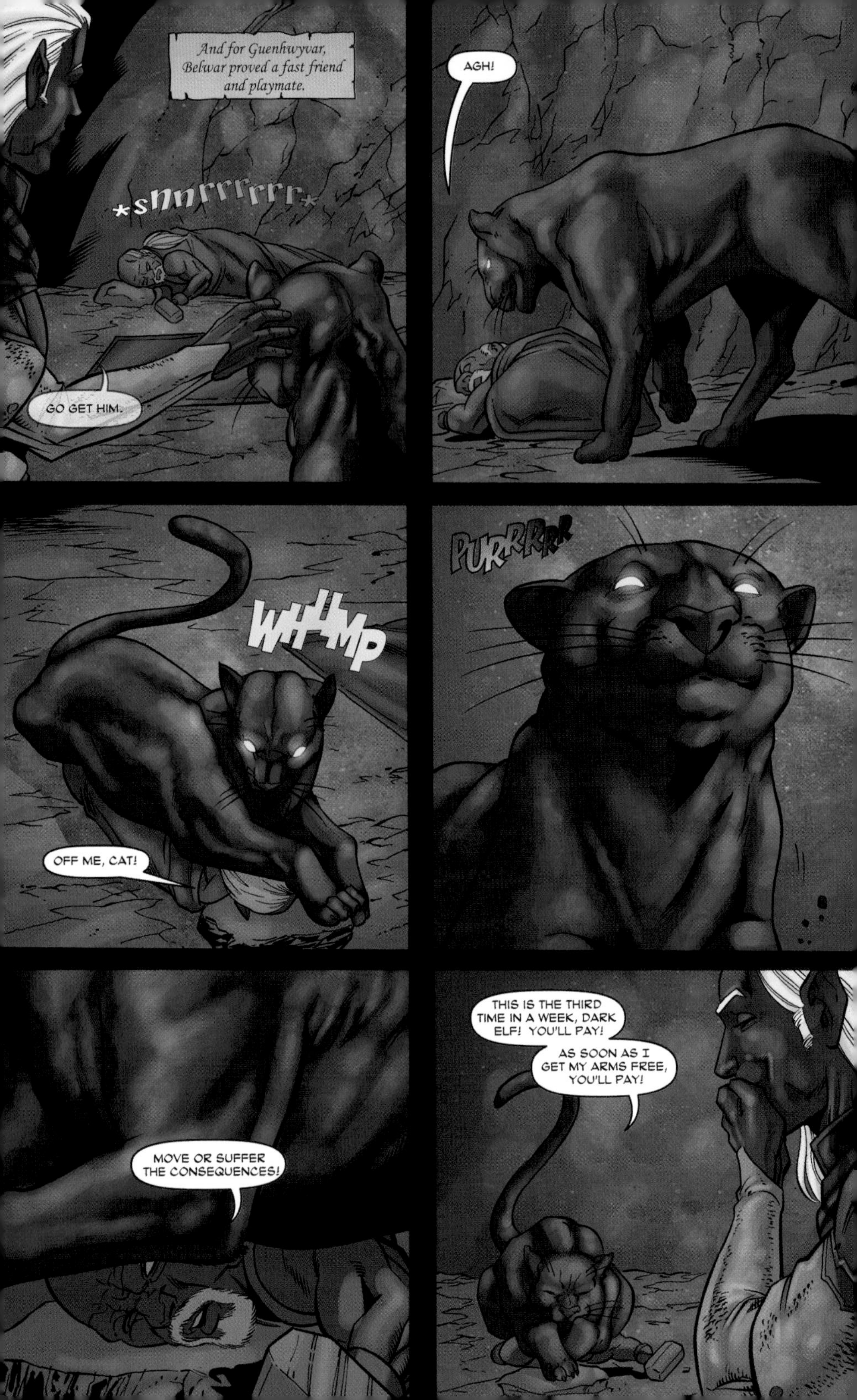
And for Guenhwyvar, Belwar proved a fast friend and playmate.
SNNRRRRRR
GO GET HIM.
AGH!
WHUMP
OFF ME, CAT!
PURRRRR
MOVE OR SUFFER THE CONSEQUENCES!
THIS IS THE THIRD TIME IN A WEEK, DARK ELF! YOU'LL PAY!
AS SOON AS I GET MY ARMS FREE, YOU'LL PAY!

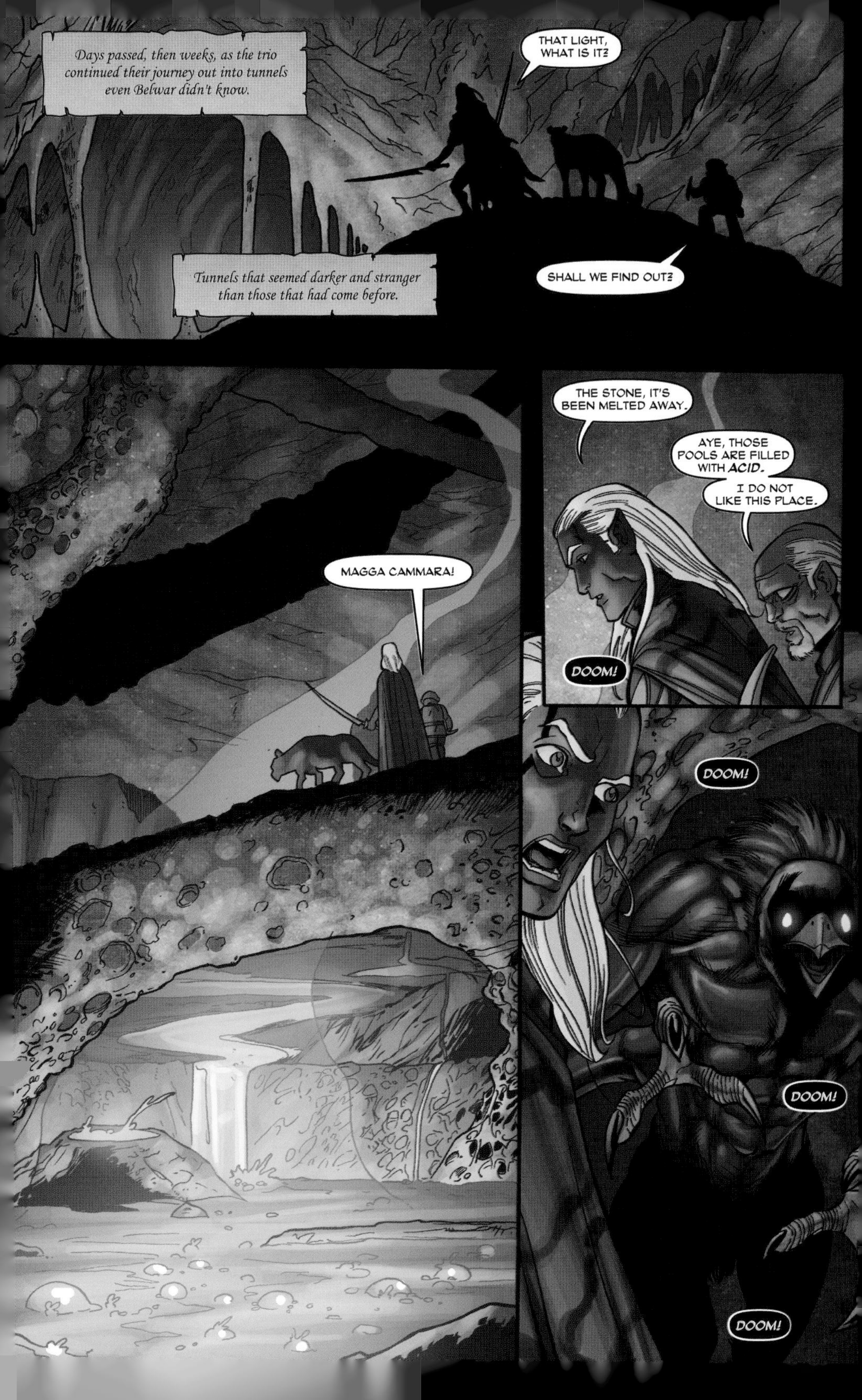
Days passed, then weeks, as the trio continued their journey out into tunnels even Belwar didn't know.
THAT LIGHT, WHAT IS IT?
Tunnels that seemed darker and stranger than those that had come before.
SHALL WE FIND OUT?
MAGGA CAMMARA!
THE STONE, IT'S BEEN MELTED AWAY.
AYE, THOSE POOLS ARE FILLED WITH ACID.
I DO NOT LIKE THIS PLACE.
DOOM!
DOOM!
DOOM!
DOOM!

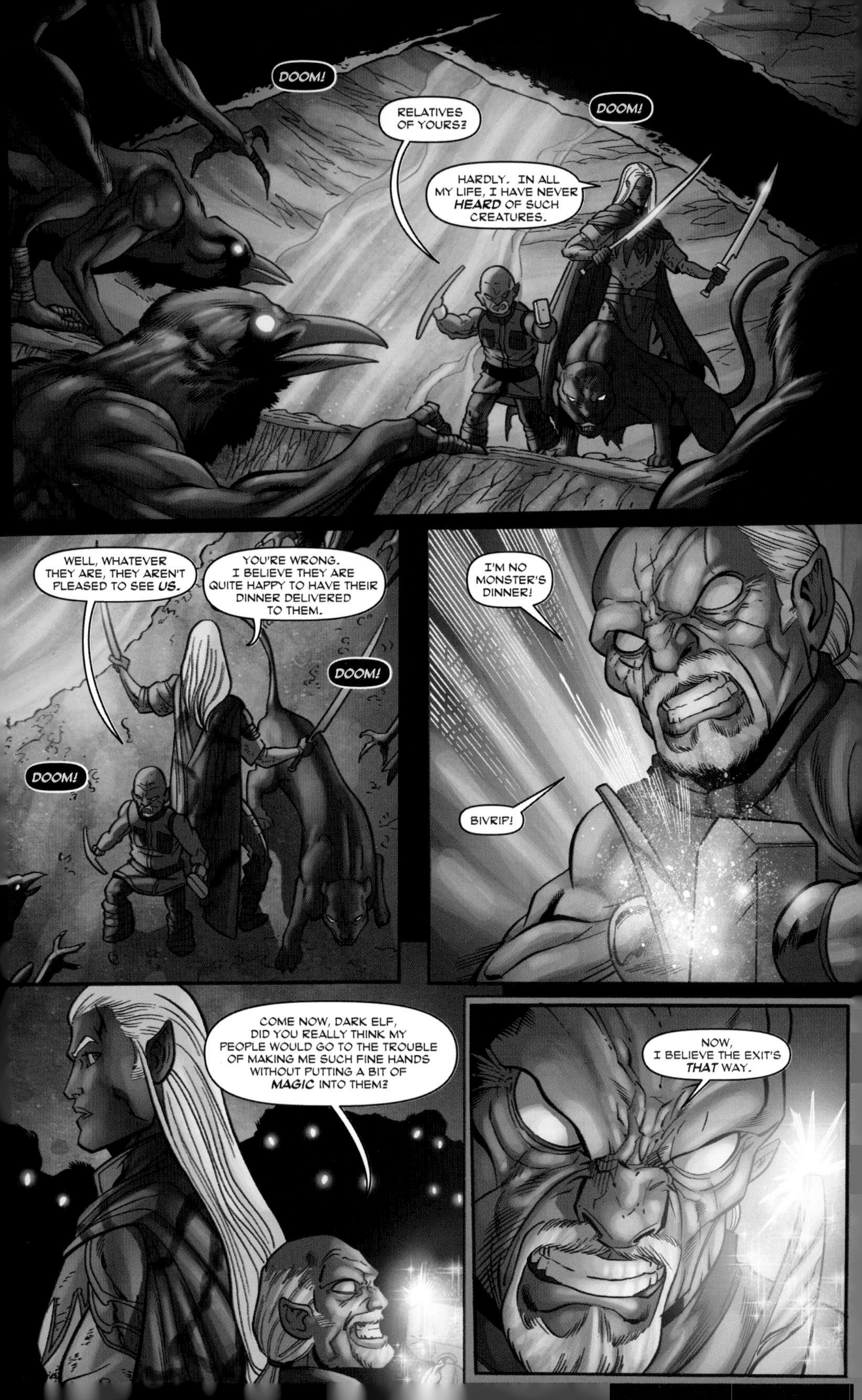

DOOM!
RELATIVES OF YOURS?
DOOM!
HARDLY. IN ALL MY LIFE, I HAVE NEVER HEARD OF SUCH CREATURES.
WELL, WHATEVER THEY ARE, THEY AREN'T PLEASED TO SEE US.
YOU'RE WRONG. I BELIEVE THEY ARE QUITE HAPPY TO HAVE THEIR DINNER DELIVERED TO THEM.
DOOM!
DOOM!
I'M NO MONSTER'S DINNER!
BIVRIP!
COME NOW, DARK ELF, DID YOU REALLY THINK MY PEOPLE WOULD GO TO THE TROUBLE OF MAKING ME SUCH FINE HANDS WITHOUT PUTTING A BIT OF MAGIC INTO THEM?
NOW, I BELIEVE THE EXIT'S THAT WAY.

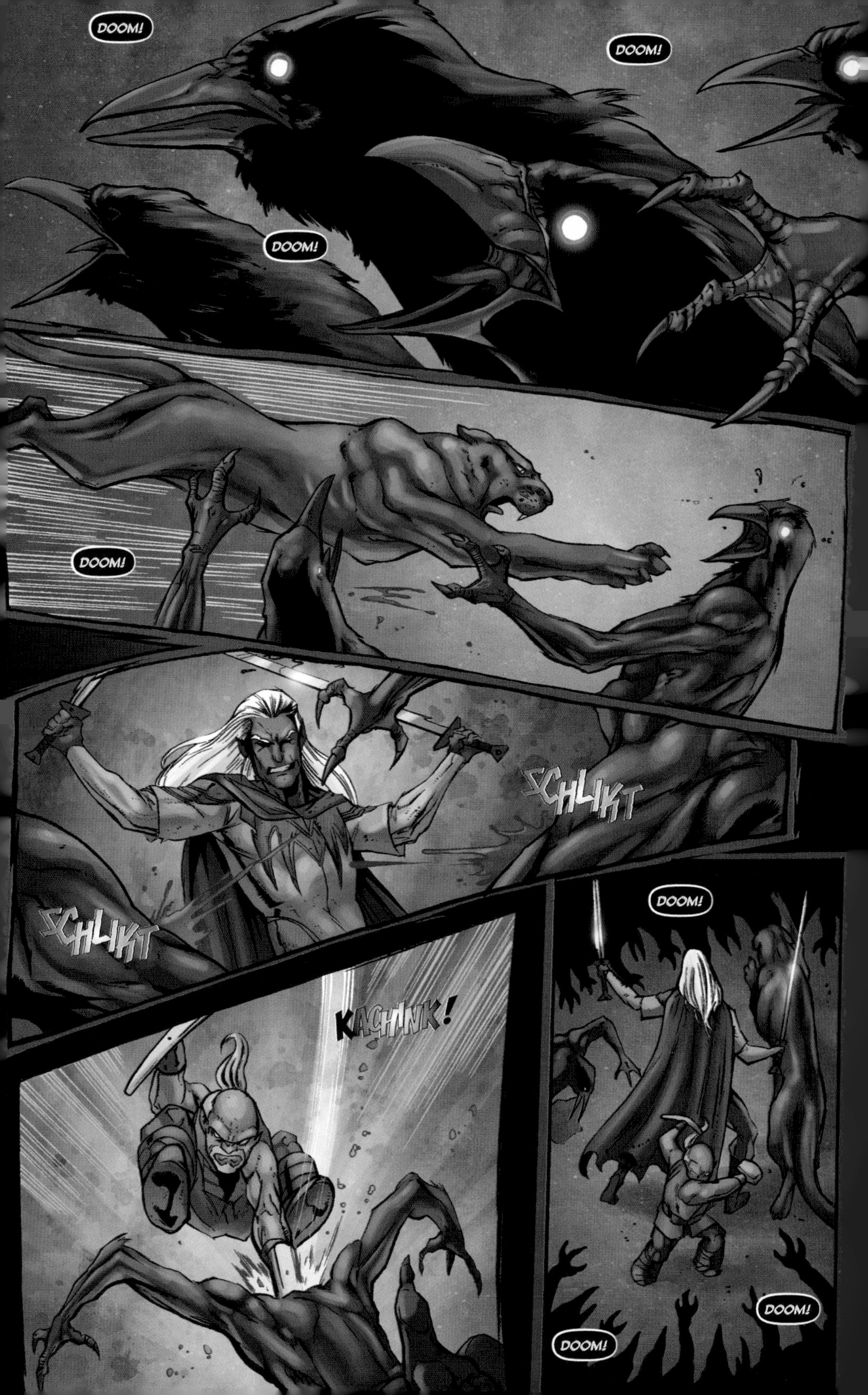
DOOM!
DOOM!
DOOM!
DOOM!
SCHLIKT
SCHLIKT
KACHINK!
DOOM!
DOOM!
DOOM!

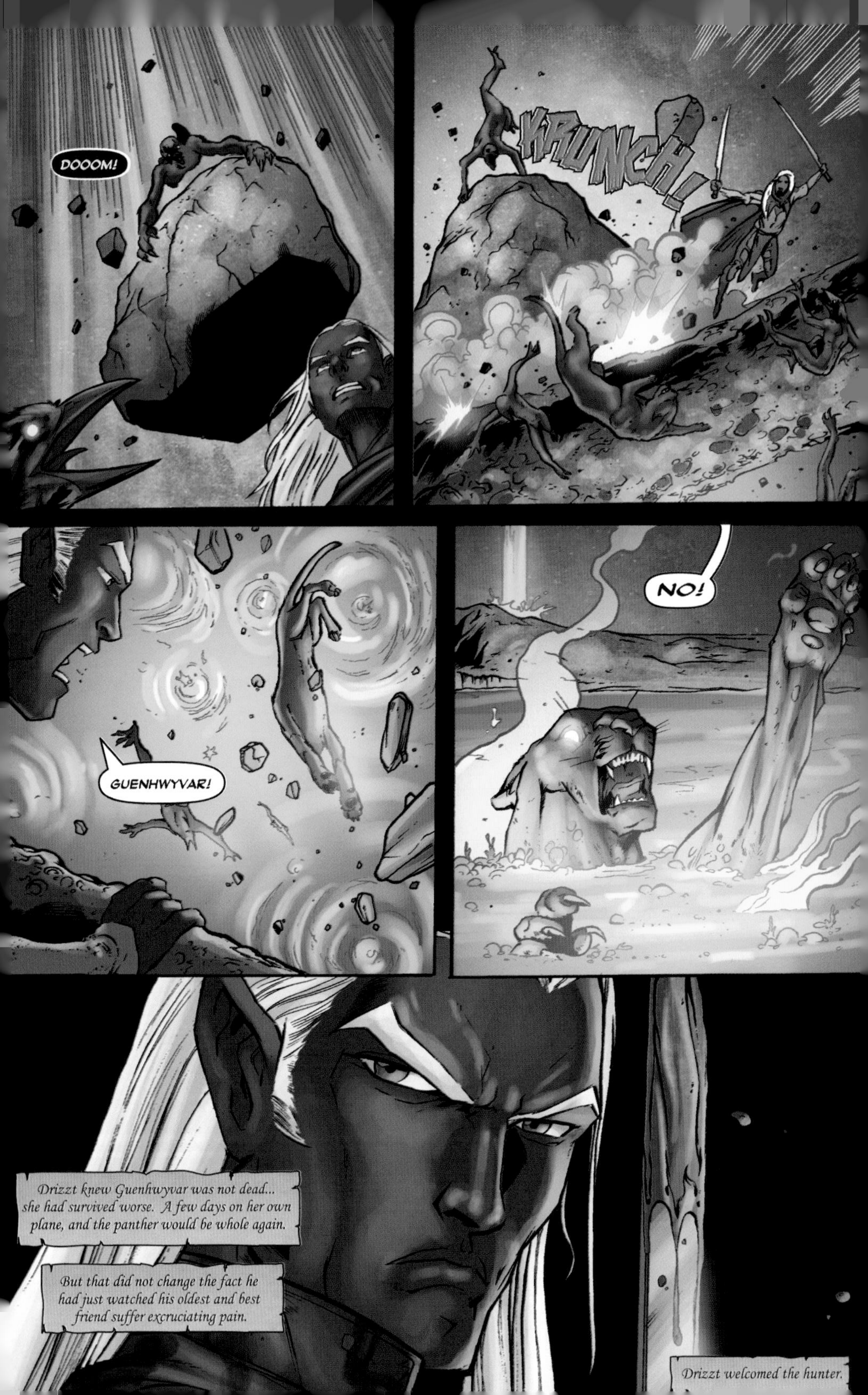
DOOOM!
KRUNCH!
GUENHWYVAR!
NO!
Drizzt knew Guenhwyvar was not dead... she had survived worse. A few days on her own plane, and the panther would be whole again.
But that did not change the fact he had just watched his oldest and best friend suffer excruciating pain.
Drizzt welcomed the hunter.

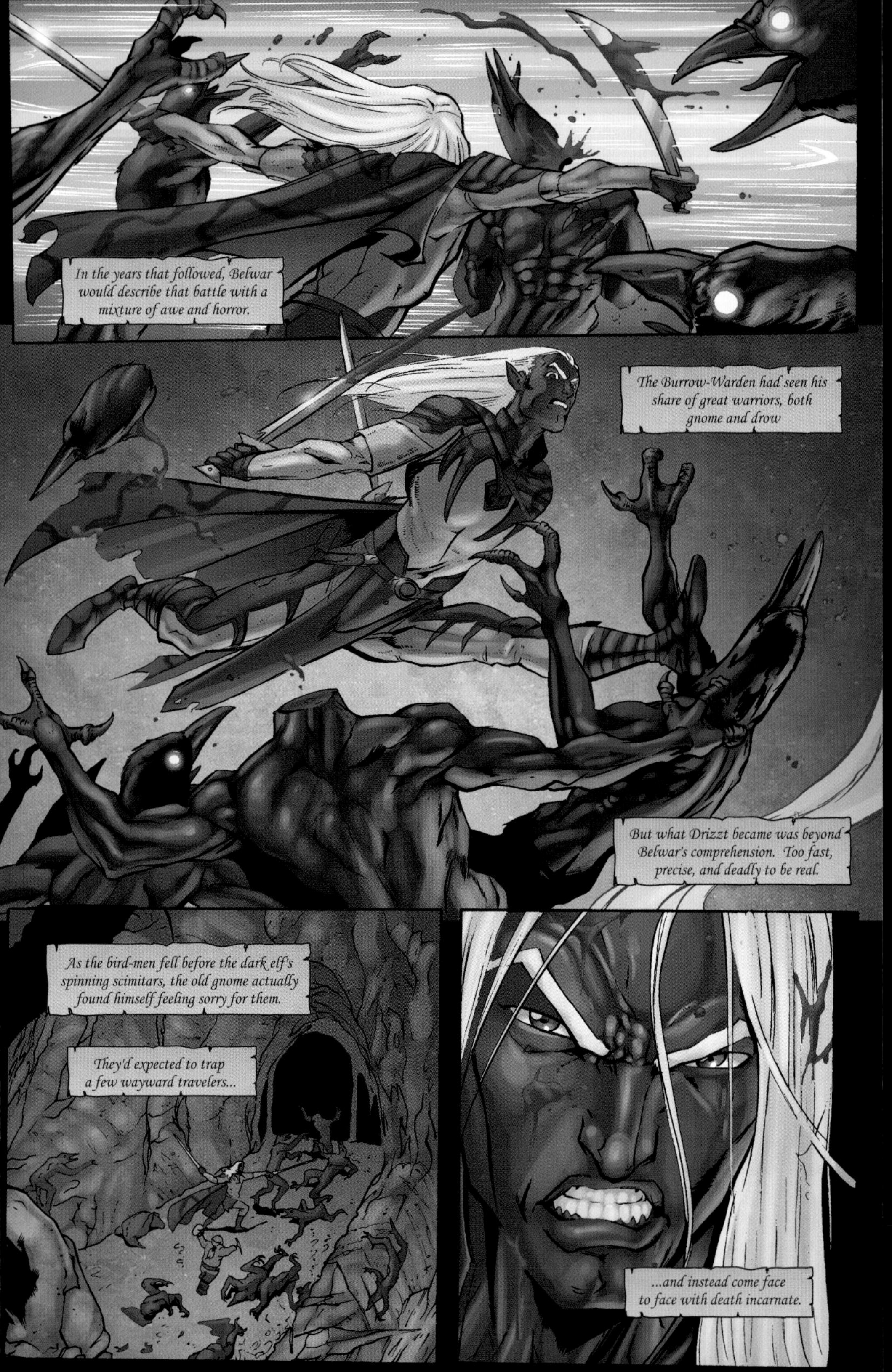
In the years that followed, Belwar would describe that battle with a mixture of awe and horror.
The Burrow-Warden had seen his share of great warriors, both gnome and drow
But what Drizzt became was beyond Belwar's comprehension. Too fast, precise, and deadly to be real.
As the bird-men fell before the dark elf's spinning scimitars, the old gnome actually found himself feeling sorry for them.
They'd expected to trap a few wayward travelers...
...and instead come face to face with death incarnate.

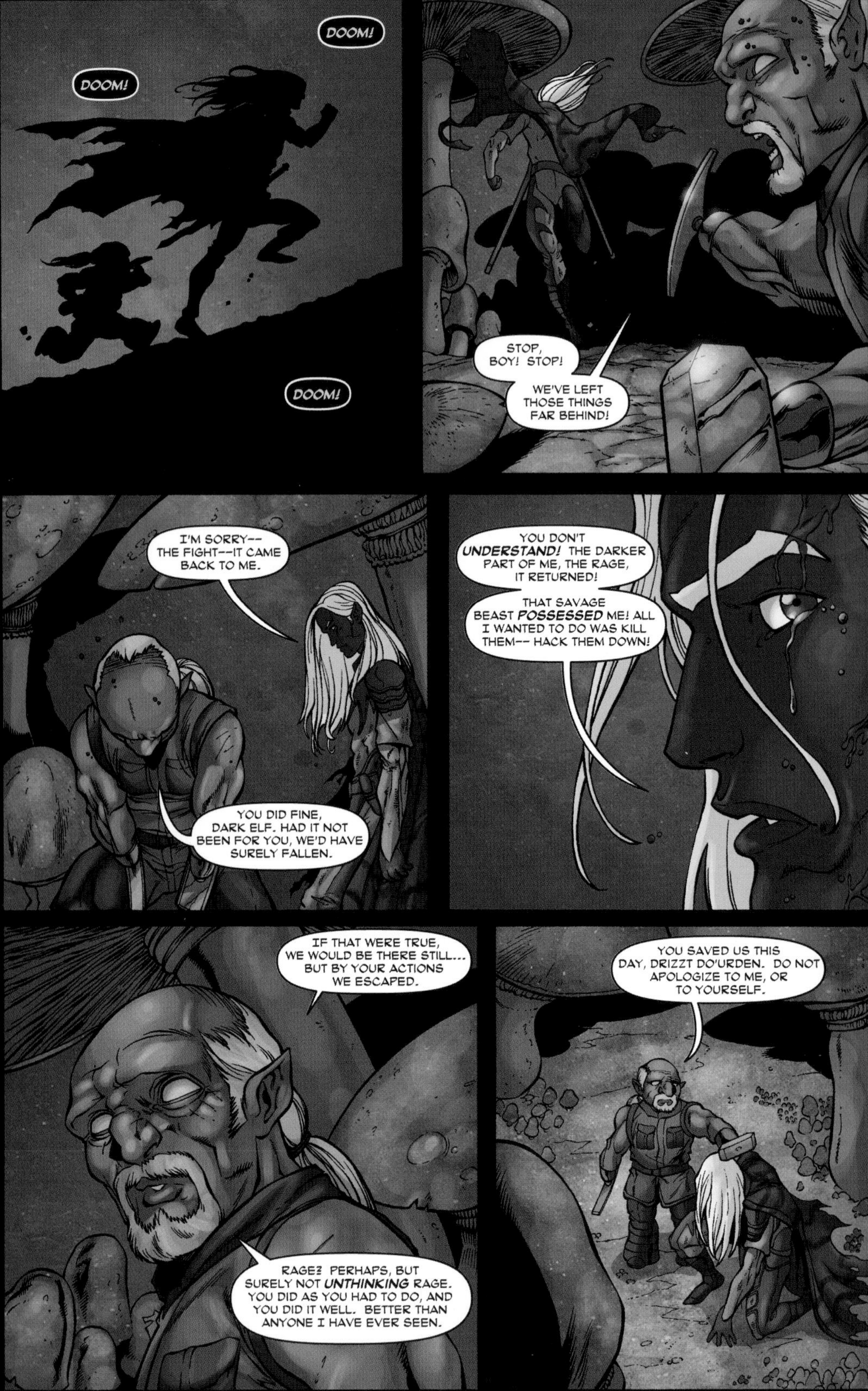
DOOM!
DOOM!
DOOM!
STOP, BOY! STOP!
WE'VE LEFT THOSE THINGS FAR BEHIND!
I'M SORRY-- THE FIGHT--IT CAME BACK TO ME.
YOU DID FINE, DARK ELF. HAD IT NOT BEEN FOR YOU, WE'D HAVE SURELY FALLEN.
YOU DON'T UNDERSTAND! THE DARKER PART OF ME, THE RAGE, IT RETURNED!
THAT SAVAGE BEAST POSSESSED ME! ALL I WANTED TO DO WAS KILL THEM-- HACK THEM DOWN!
IF THAT WERE TRUE, WE WOULD BE THERE STILL... BUT BY YOUR ACTIONS WE ESCAPED.
RAGE? PERHAPS, BUT SURELY NOT UNTHINKING RAGE. YOU DID AS YOU HAD TO DO, AND YOU DID IT WELL. BETTER THAN ANYONE I HAVE EVER SEEN.
YOU SAVED US THIS DAY, DRIZZT DO'URDEN. DO NOT APOLOGIZE TO ME, OR TO YOURSELF.

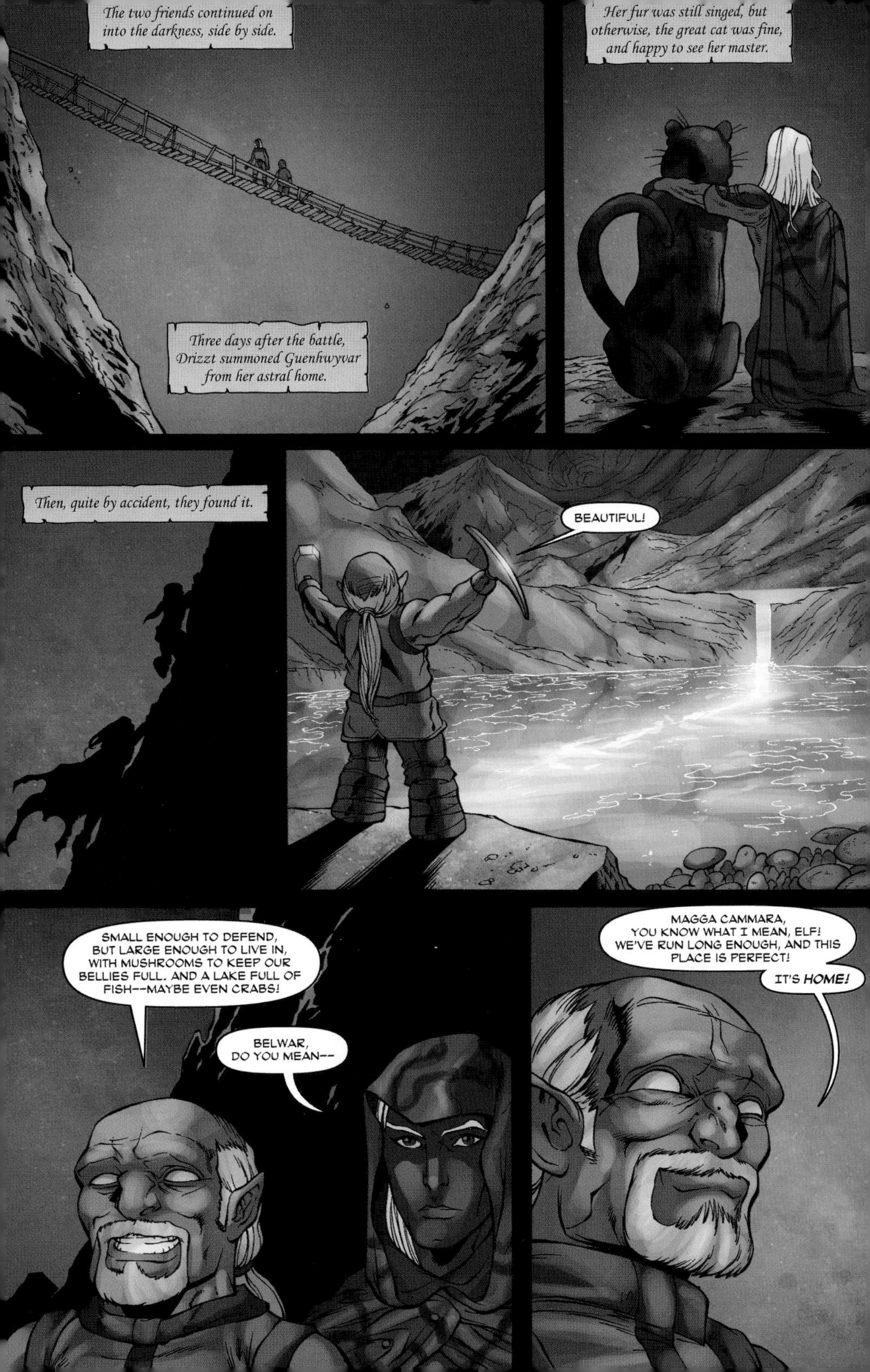
The two friends continued on into the darkness, side by side.
Three days after the battle, Drizzt summoned Guenhwyvar from her astral home.
Her fur was still singed, but otherwise, the great cat was fine, and happy to see her master.
Then, quite by accident, they found it.
BEAUTIFUL!
SMALL ENOUGH TO DEFEND, BUT LARGE ENOUGH TO LIVE IN, WITH MUSHROOMS TO KEEP OUR BELLIES FULL. AND A LAKE FULL OF FISH--MAYBE EVEN CRABS!
BELWAR, DO YOU MEAN--
MAGGA CAMMARA, YOU KNOW WHAT I MEAN, ELF! WE'VE RUN LONG ENOUGH, AND THIS PLACE IS PERFECT!
IT'S HOME!

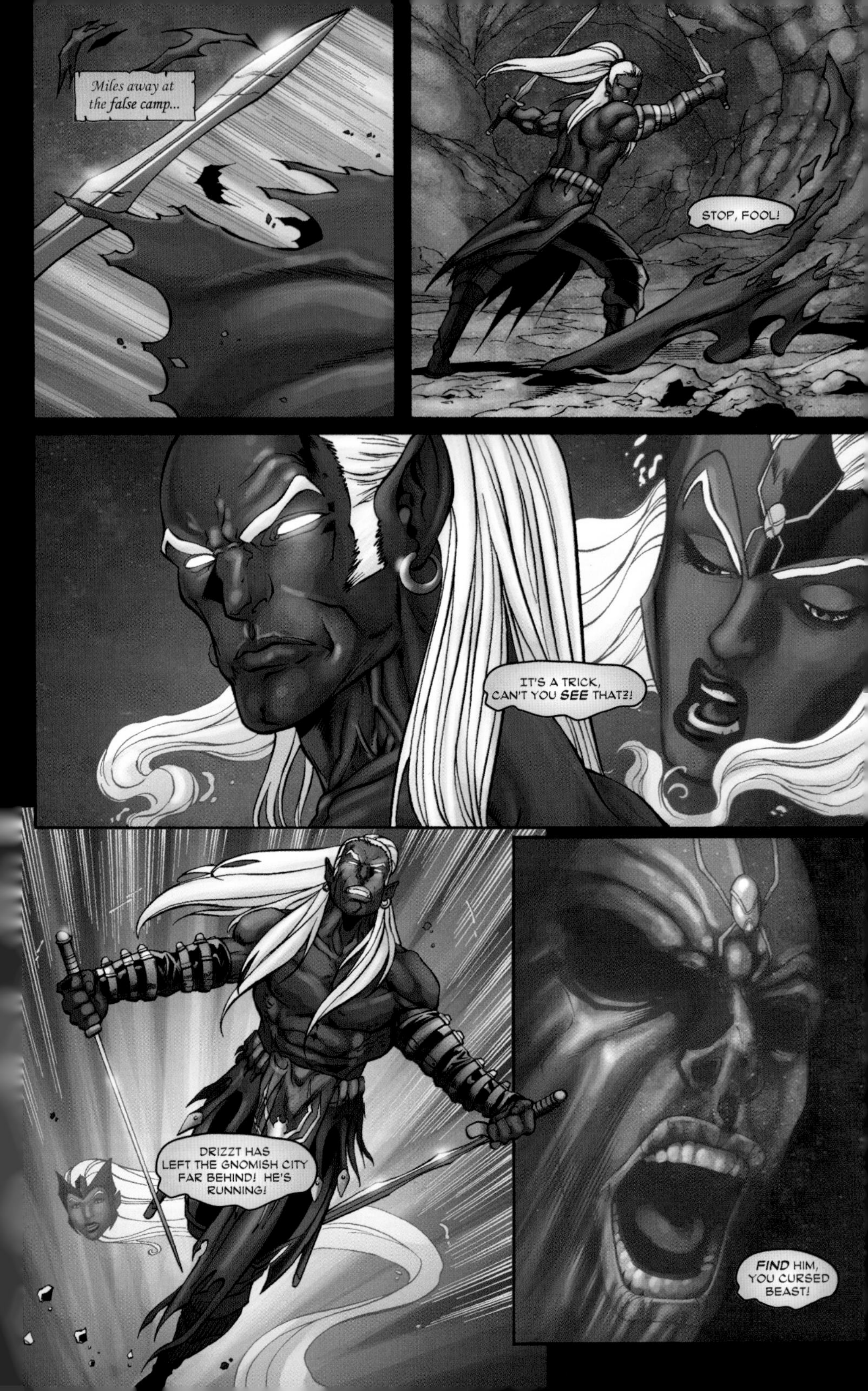
Miles away at the false camp...
STOP, FOOL!
IT'S A TRICK, CAN'T YOU SEE THAT?!
DRIZZT HAS LEFT THE GNOMISH CITY FAR BEHIND! HE'S RUNNING!
FIND HIM, YOU CURSED BEAST!

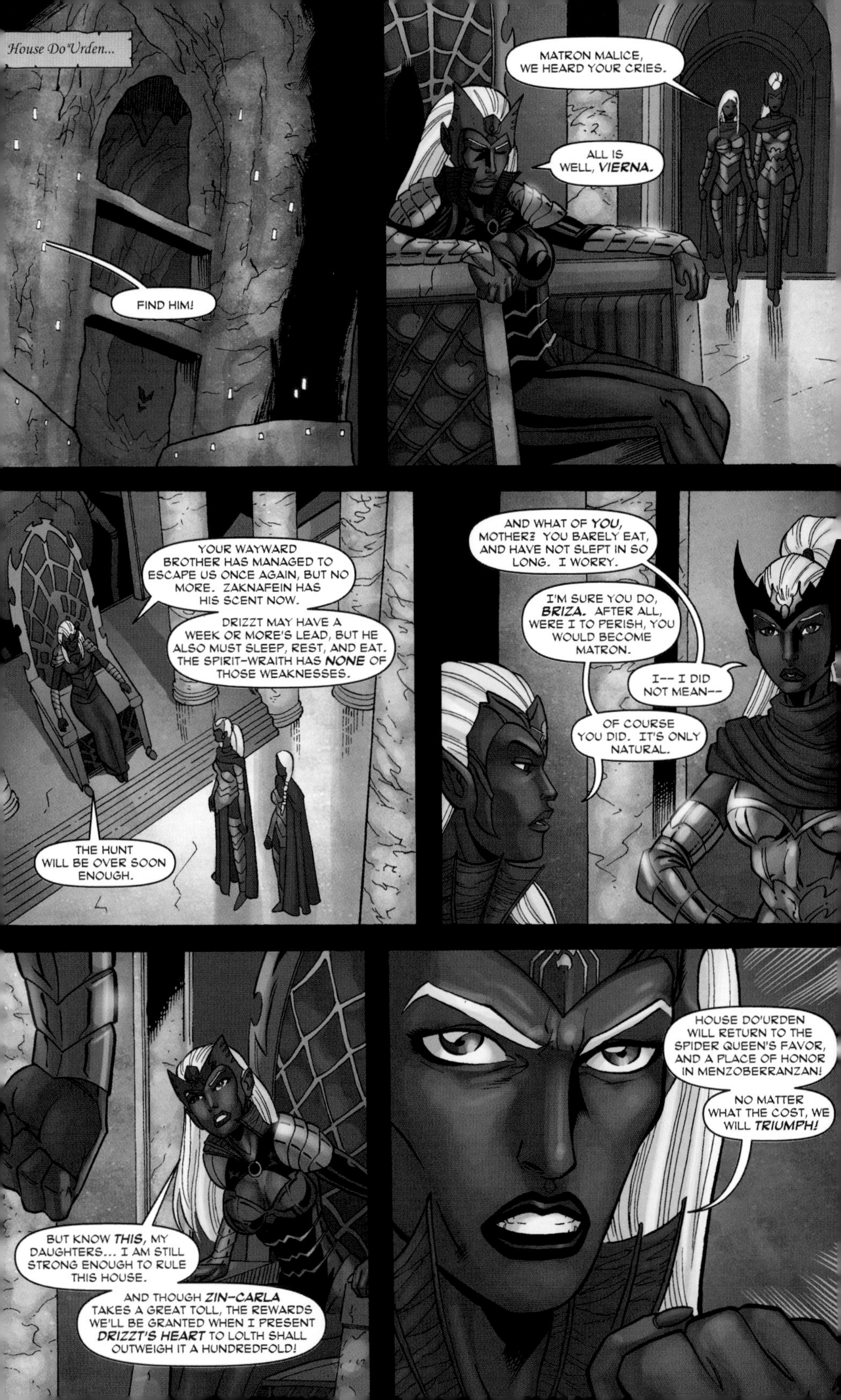
House Do'Urden...
FIND HIM!
MATRON MALICE, WE HEARD YOUR CRIES.
ALL IS WELL, VIERNA.
YOUR WAYWARD BROTHER HAS MANAGED TO ESCAPE US ONCE AGAIN, BUT NO MORE. ZAKNAFEIN HAS HIS SCENT NOW.
DRIZZT MAY HAVE A WEEK OR MORE'S LEAD, BUT HE ALSO MUST SLEEP, REST, AND EAT. THE SPIRIT-WRAITH HAS NONE OF THOSE WEAKNESSES.
THE HUNT WILL BE OVER SOON ENOUGH.
AND WHAT OF YOU, MOTHER? YOU BARELY EAT, AND HAVE NOT SLEPT IN SO LONG. I WORRY.
I'M SURE YOU DO, BRIZA. AFTER ALL, WERE I TO PERISH, YOU WOULD BECOME MATRON.
I-- I DID NOT MEAN--
OF COURSE YOU DID. IT'S ONLY NATURAL.
BUT KNOW THIS, MY DAUGHTERS... I AM STILL STRONG ENOUGH TO RULE THIS HOUSE.
AND THOUGH ZIN-CARLA TAKES A GREAT TOLL, THE REWARDS WE'LL BE GRANTED WHEN I PRESENT DRIZZT'S HEART TO LOLTH SHALL OUTWEIGH IT A HUNDREDFOLD!
HOUSE DO'URDEN WILL RETURN TO THE SPIDER QUEEN'S FAVOR, AND A PLACE OF HONOR IN MENZOBERRANZAN!
NO MATTER WHAT THE COST, WE WILL TRIUMPH!

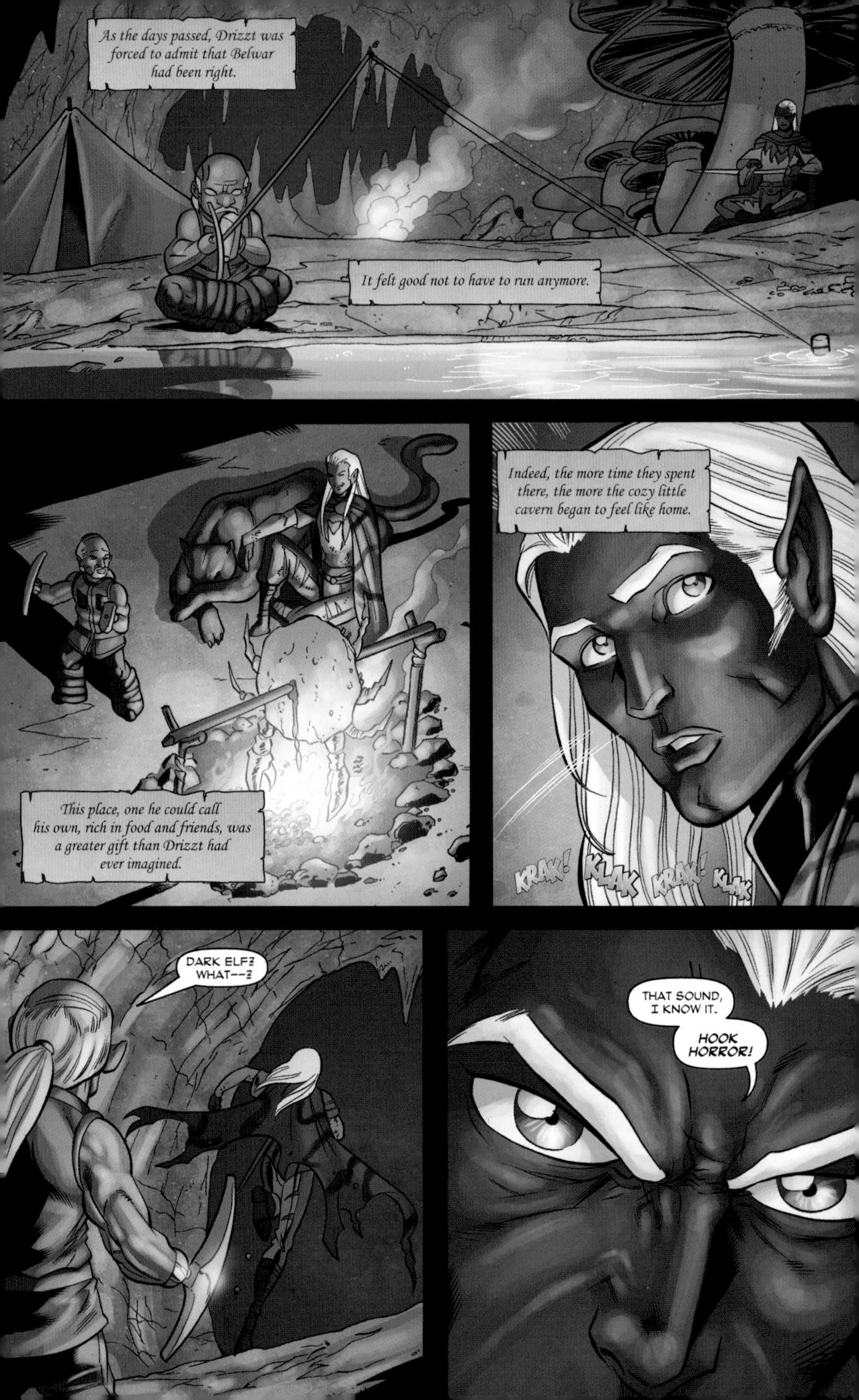
As the days passed, Drizzt was forced to admit that Belwar had been right.
It felt good not to have to run anymore.
This place, one he could call his own, rich in food and friends, was a greater gift than Drizzt had ever imagined.
Indeed, the more time they spent there, the more the cozy little cavern began to feel like home.
KRAK! KLAK KRAK! KLAK
DARK ELF? WHAT--?
THAT SOUND, I KNOW IT.
HOOK HORROR!

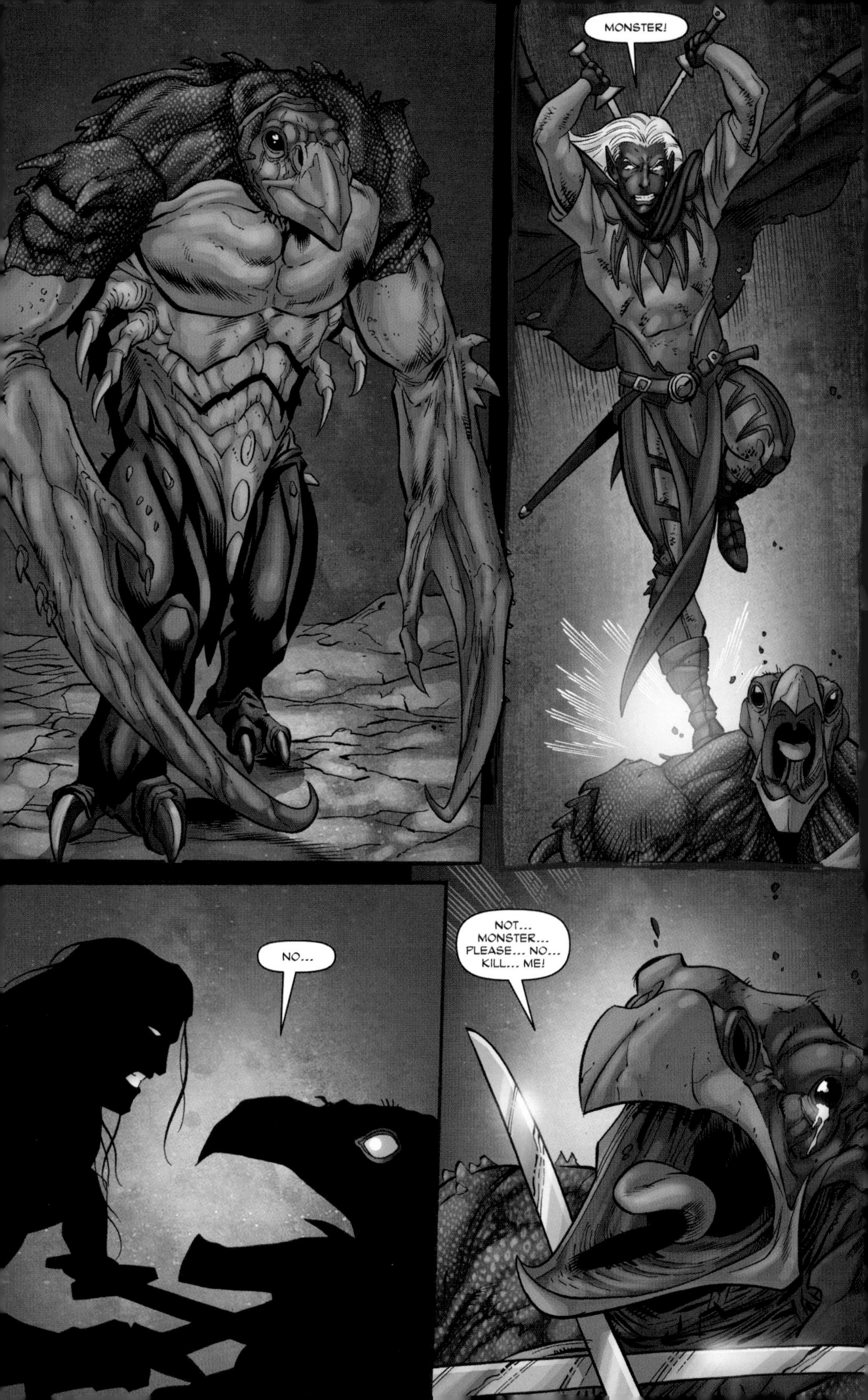
MONSTER!
NO...
NOT... MONSTER... PLEASE... NO... KILL... ME!

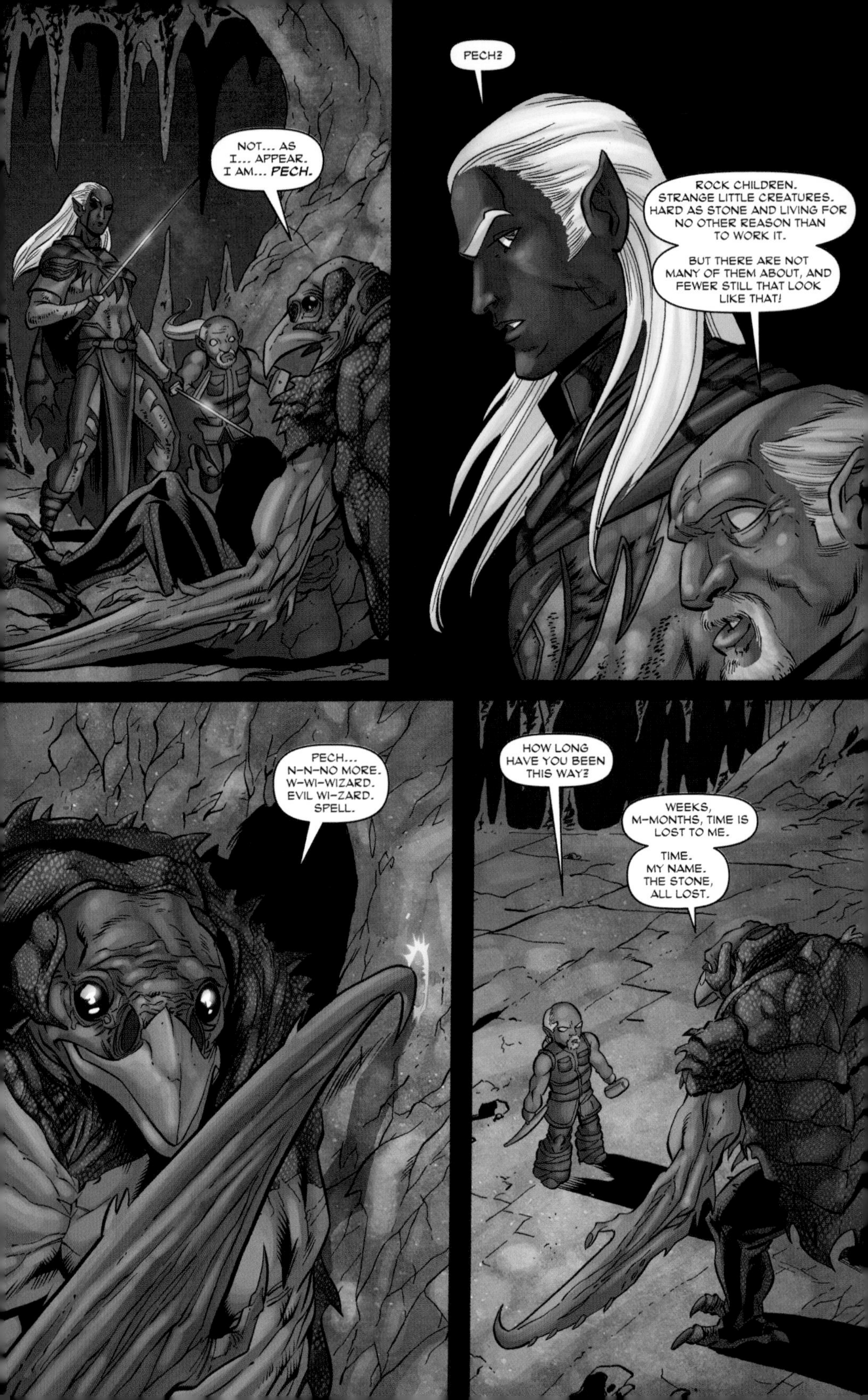
NOT... AS
I... APPEAR.
I AM... *PECH.*
PECH?
ROCK CHILDREN.
STRANGE LITTLE CREATURES.
HARD AS STONE AND LIVING FOR
NO OTHER REASON THAN
TO WORK IT.
BUT THERE ARE NOT
MANY OF THEM ABOUT, AND
FEWER STILL THAT LOOK
LIKE THAT!
PECH...
N-N-NO MORE.
W-WI-WIZARD.
EVIL WI-ZARD.
SPELL.
HOW LONG
HAVE YOU BEEN
THIS WAY?
WEEKS,
M-MONTHS, TIME IS
LOST TO ME.
TIME.
MY NAME.
THE STONE,
ALL LOST.

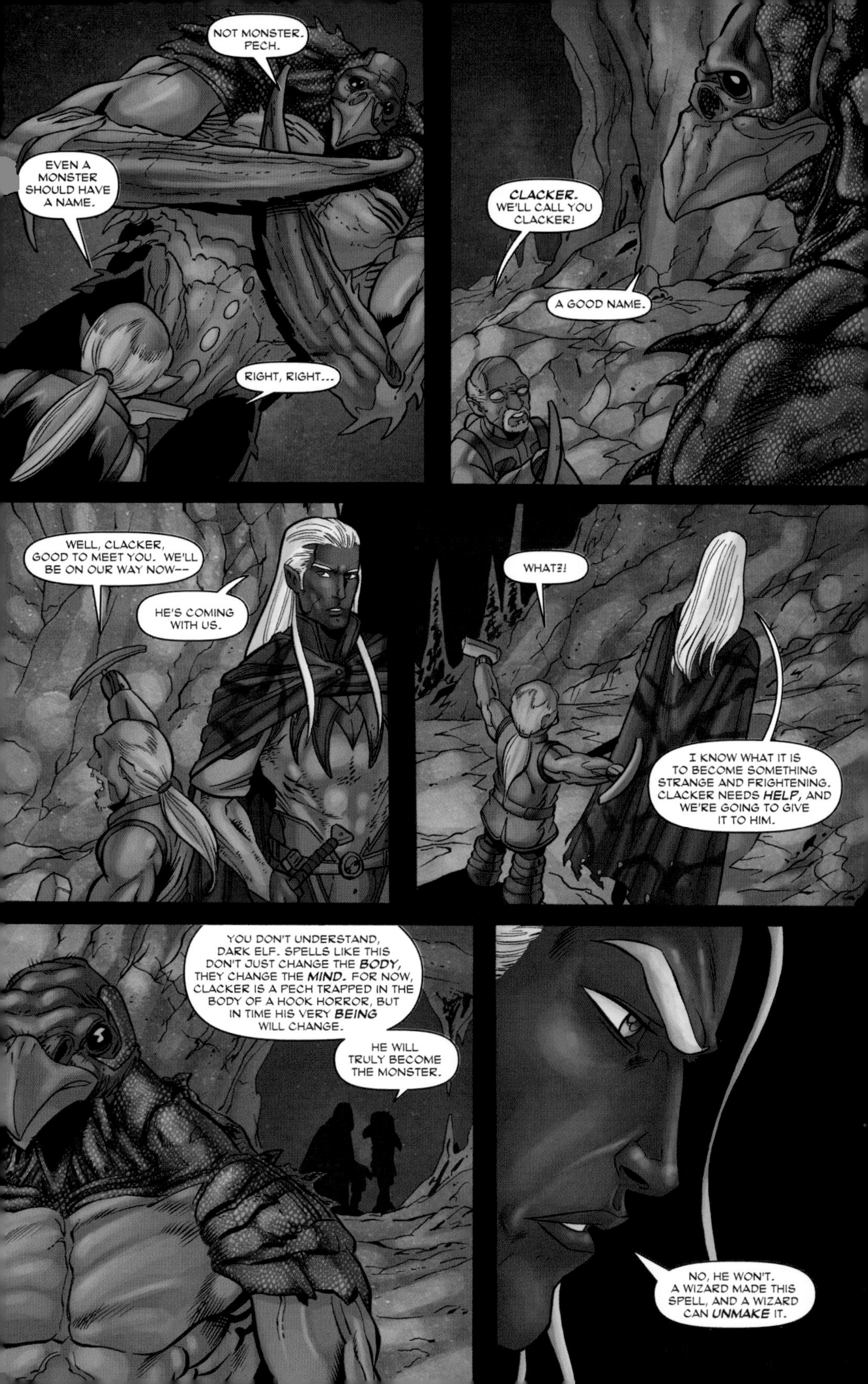
NOT MONSTER. PECH.
EVEN A MONSTER SHOULD HAVE A NAME.
RIGHT, RIGHT...
CLACKER. WE'LL CALL YOU CLACKER!
A GOOD NAME.
WELL, CLACKER, GOOD TO MEET YOU. WE'LL BE ON OUR WAY NOW--
HE'S COMING WITH US.
WHAT?!
I KNOW WHAT IT IS TO BECOME SOMETHING STRANGE AND FRIGHTENING. CLACKER NEEDS HELP, AND WE'RE GOING TO GIVE IT TO HIM.
YOU DON'T UNDERSTAND, DARK ELF. SPELLS LIKE THIS DON'T JUST CHANGE THE BODY, THEY CHANGE THE MIND. FOR NOW, CLACKER IS A PECH TRAPPED IN THE BODY OF A HOOK HORROR, BUT IN TIME HIS VERY BEING WILL CHANGE.
HE WILL TRULY BECOME THE MONSTER.
NO, HE WON'T. A WIZARD MADE THIS SPELL, AND A WIZARD CAN UNMAKE IT.

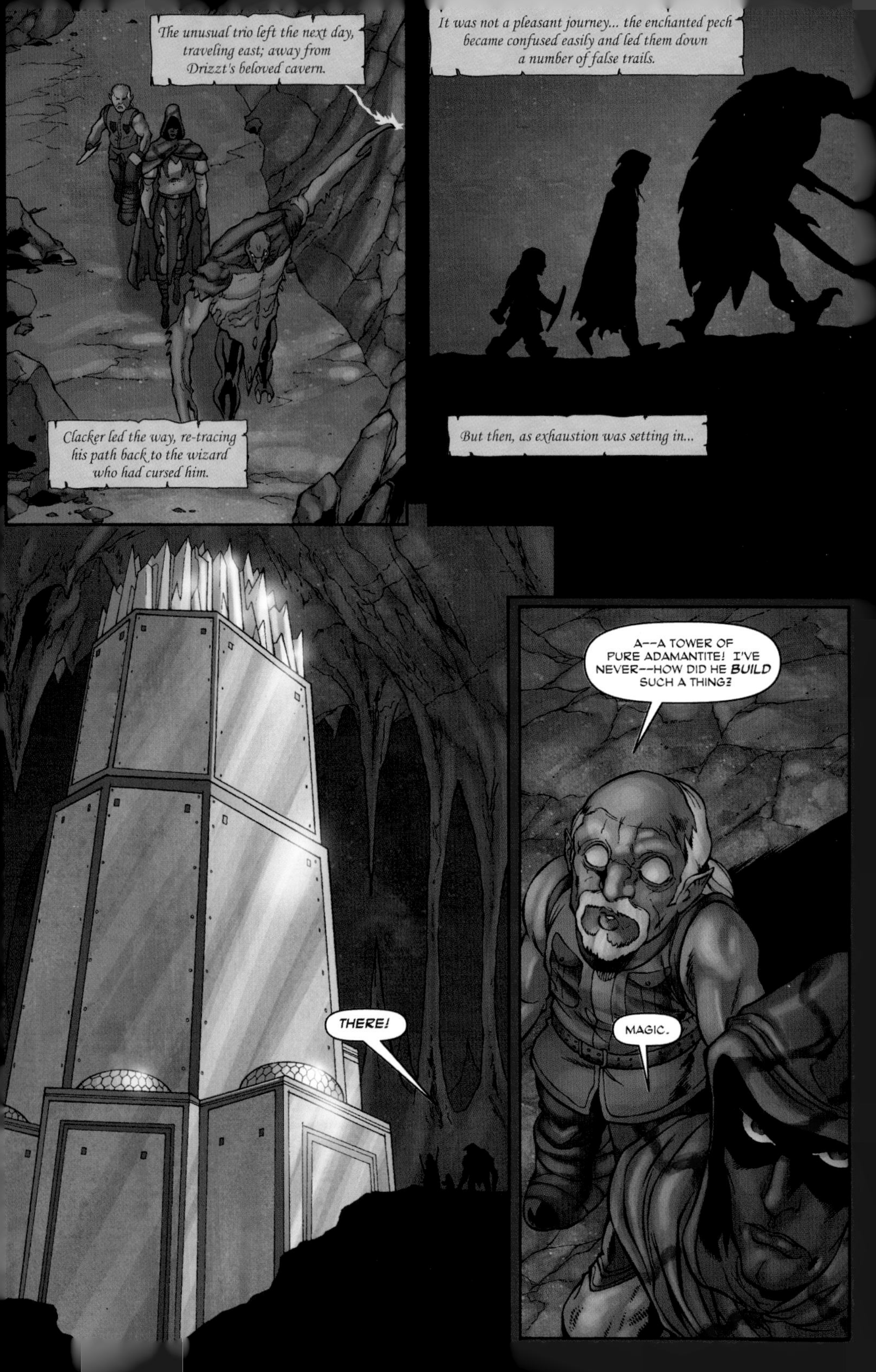

The unusual trio left the next day, traveling east; away from Drizzt's beloved cavern.
Clacker led the way, re-tracing his path back to the wizard who had cursed him.
It was not a pleasant journey... the enchanted pech became confused easily and led them down a number of false trails.
But then, as exhaustion was setting in...
THERE!
A--A TOWER OF PURE ADAMANTITE! I'VE NEVER--HOW DID HE BUILD SUCH A THING?
MAGIC.

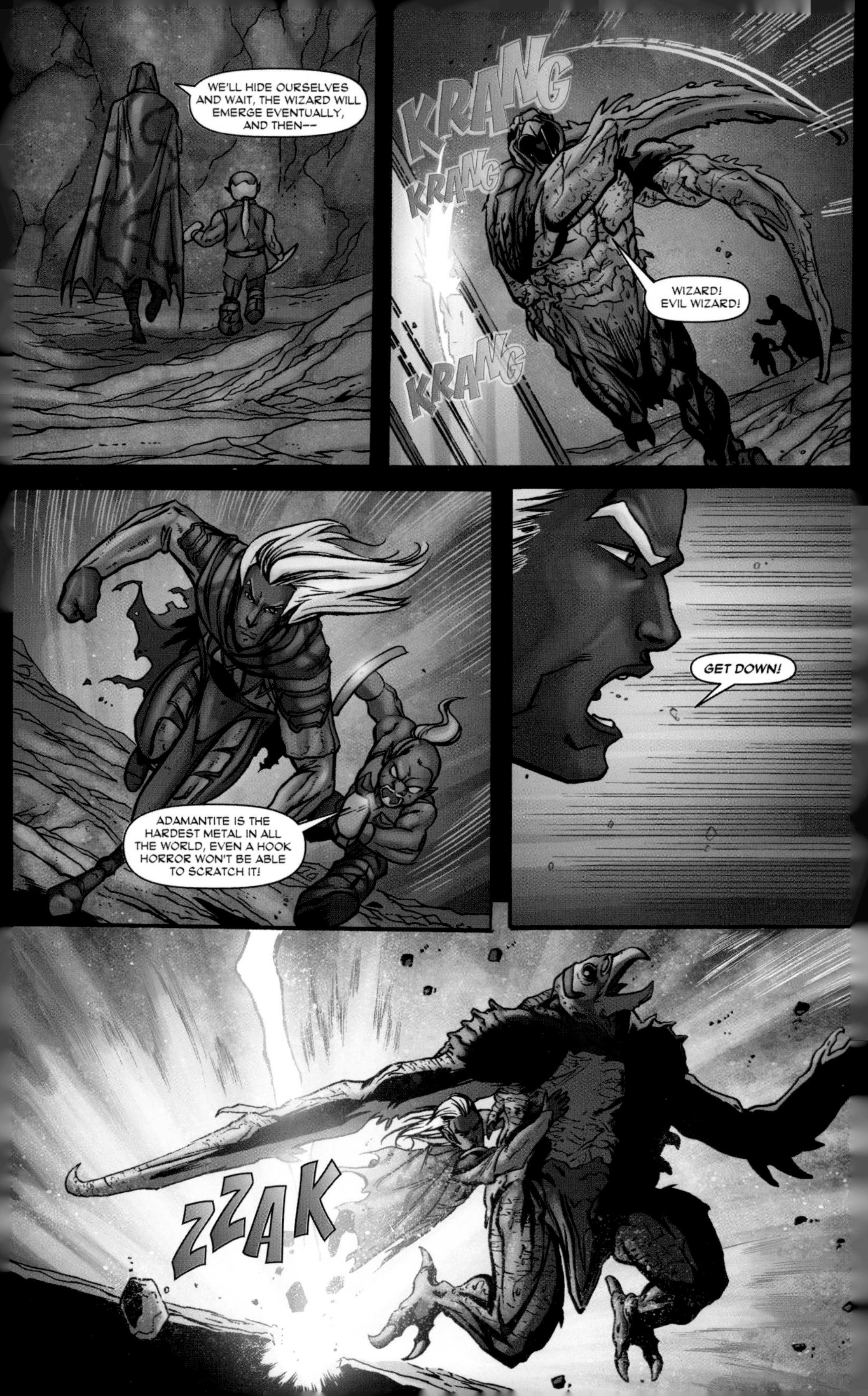
WE'LL HIDE OURSELVES AND WAIT, THE WIZARD WILL EMERGE EVENTUALLY, AND THEN--
KRANG
KRANG
WIZARD! EVIL WIZARD!
KRANG
ADAMANTITE IS THE HARDEST METAL IN ALL THE WORLD, EVEN A HOOK HORROR WON'T BE ABLE TO SCRATCH IT!
GET DOWN!
ZZAK

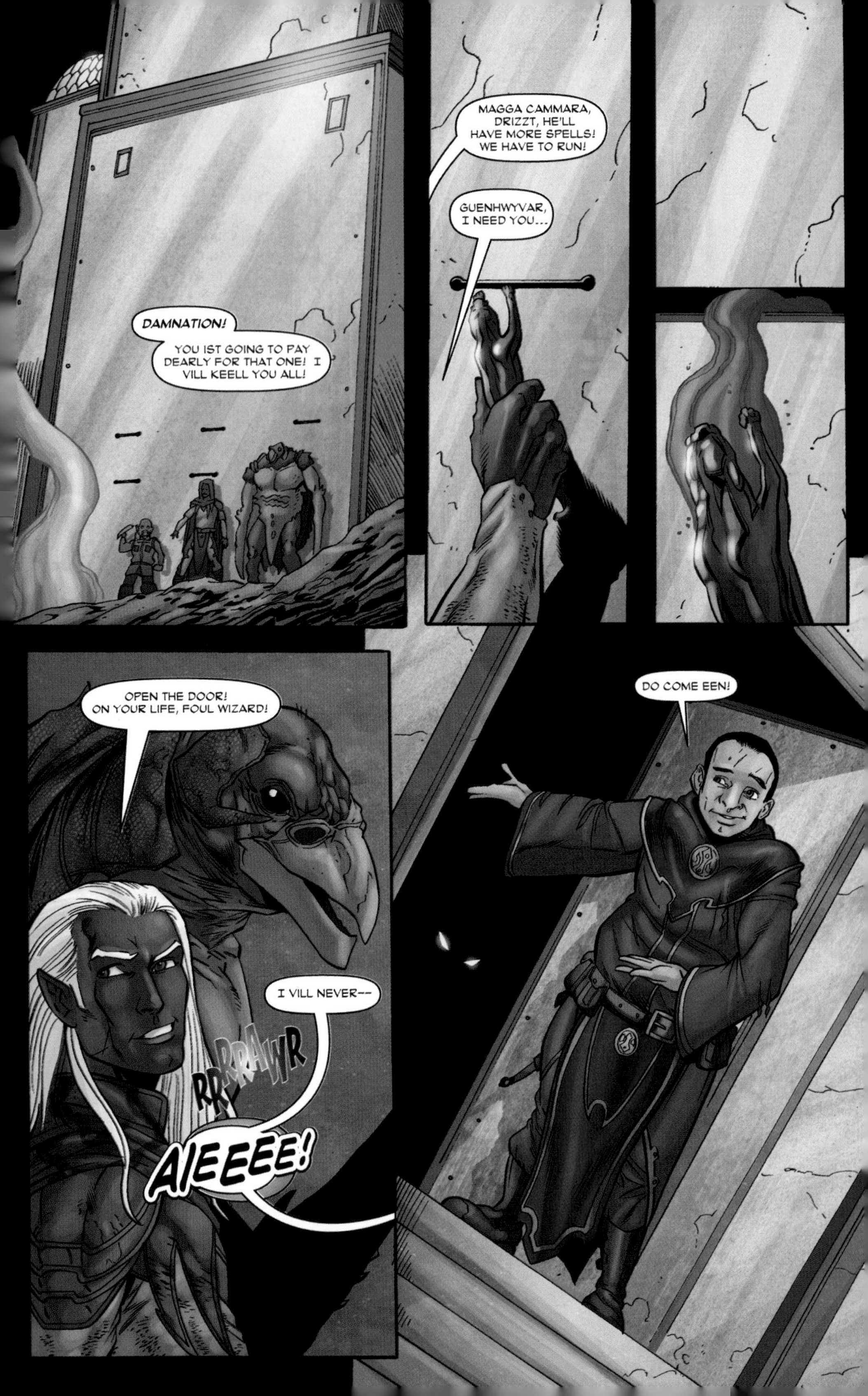
DAMNATION!
YOU IST GOING TO PAY DEARLY FOR THAT ONE! I VILL KEELL YOU ALL!
MAGGA CAMMARA, DRIZZT, HE'LL HAVE MORE SPELLS! WE HAVE TO RUN!
GUENHWYVAR, I NEED YOU...
OPEN THE DOOR! ON YOUR LIFE, FOUL WIZARD!
I VILL NEVER--
RRRRRAWR
AIEEEE!
DO COME EEN!

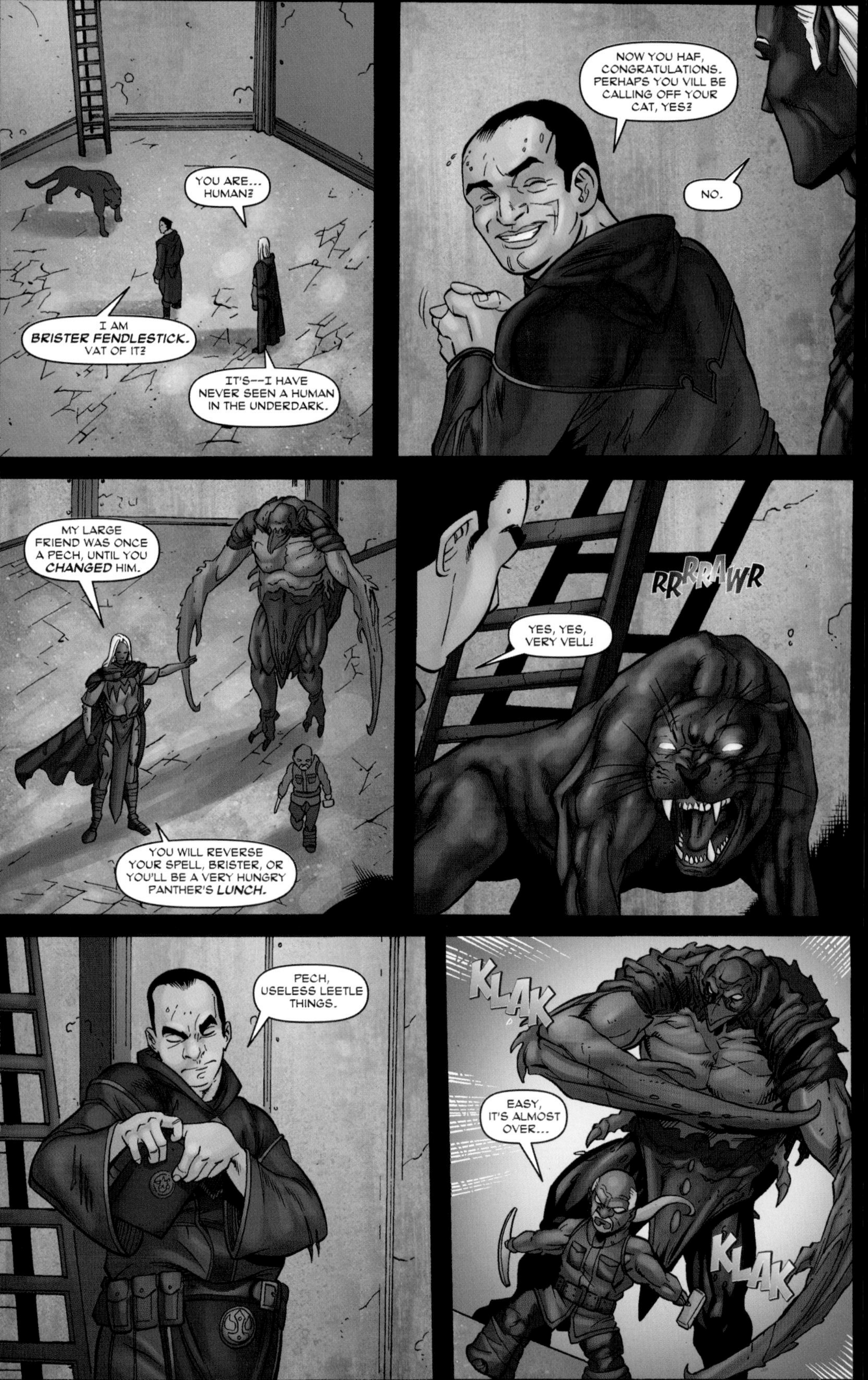
YOU ARE... HUMAN?
I AM BRISTER FENDLESTICK. VAT OF IT?
IT'S--I HAVE NEVER SEEN A HUMAN IN THE UNDERDARK.
NOW YOU HAF, CONGRATULATIONS. PERHAPS YOU VILL BE CALLING OFF YOUR CAT, YES?
NO.
MY LARGE FRIEND WAS ONCE A PECH, UNTIL YOU CHANGED HIM.
YOU WILL REVERSE YOUR SPELL, BRISTER, OR YOU'LL BE A VERY HUNGRY PANTHER'S LUNCH.
RRRRAWR
YES, YES, VERY VELL!
PECH, USELESS LEETLE THINGS.
KLAK
EASY, IT'S ALMOST OVER...
KLAK

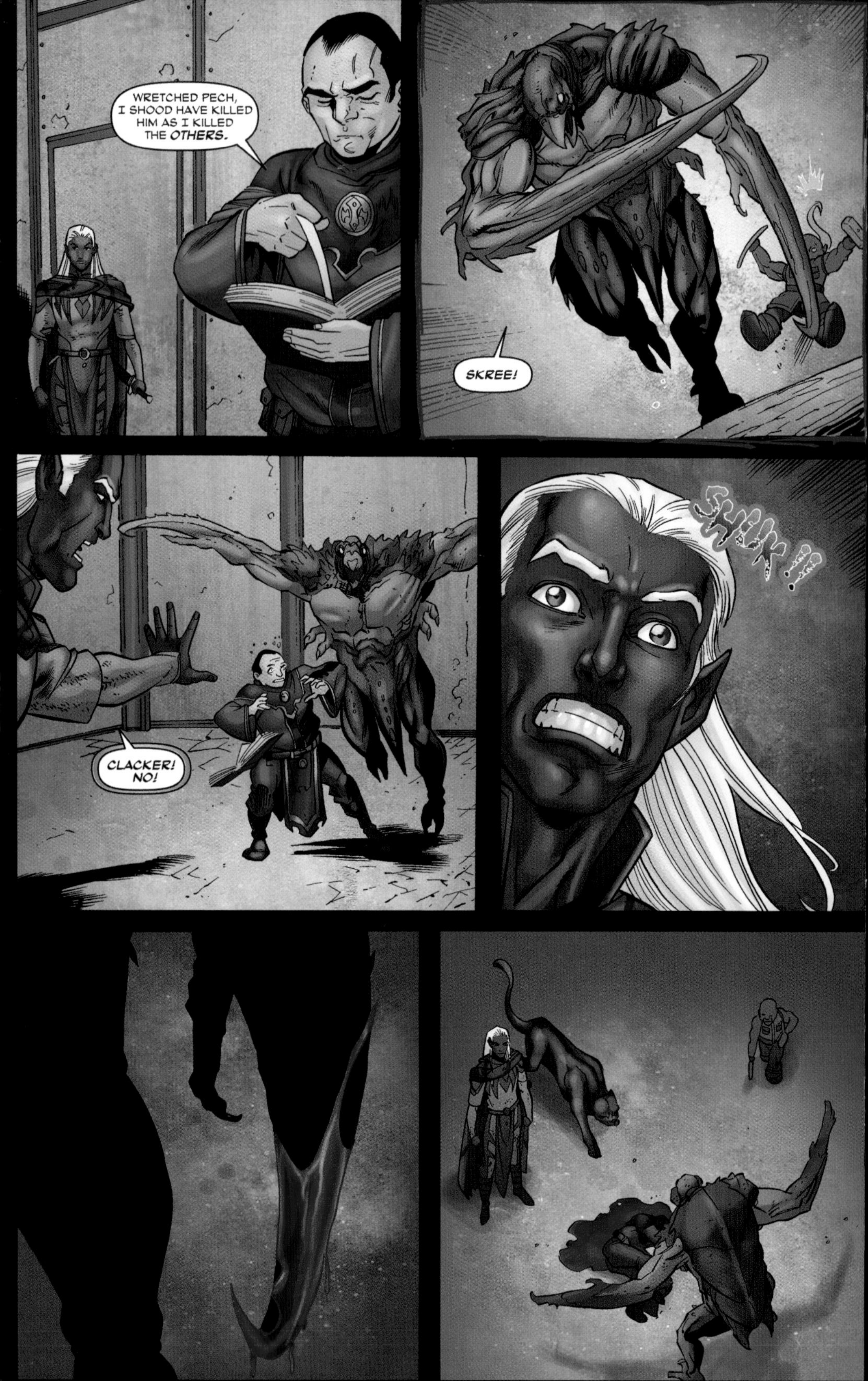
WRETCHED PECH, I SHOOD HAVE KILLED HIM AS I KILLED THE *OTHERS*.
SKREE!
CLACKER! NO!
SHUK!!

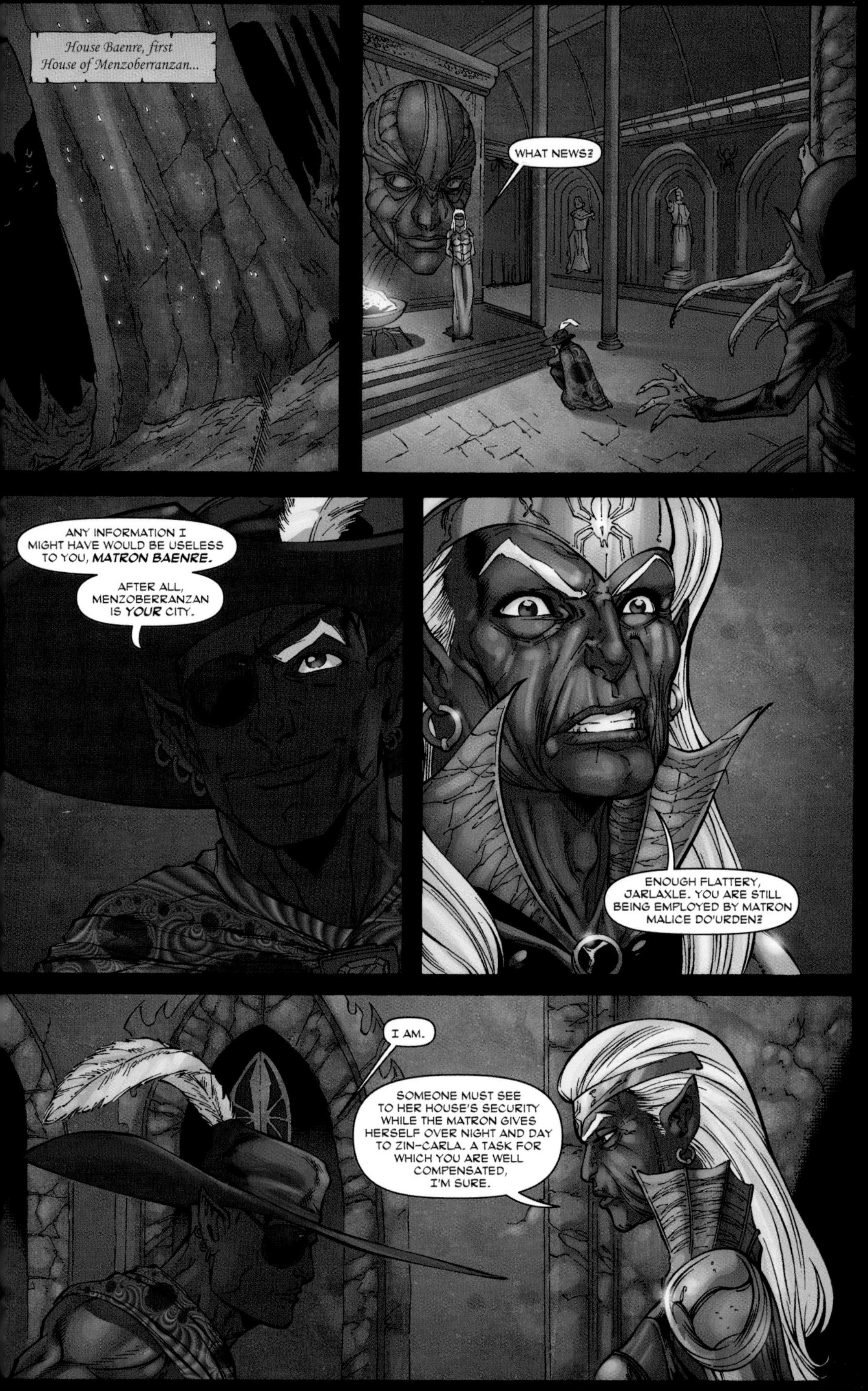

House Baenre, first House of Menzoberranzan...
WHAT NEWS?
ANY INFORMATION I MIGHT HAVE WOULD BE USELESS TO YOU, MATRON BAENRE.
AFTER ALL, MENZOBERRANZAN IS YOUR CITY.
ENOUGH FLATTERY, JARLAXLE. YOU ARE STILL BEING EMPLOYED BY MATRON MALICE DO'URDEN?
I AM.
SOMEONE MUST SEE TO HER HOUSE'S SECURITY WHILE THE MATRON GIVES HERSELF OVER NIGHT AND DAY TO ZIN-CARLA. A TASK FOR WHICH YOU ARE WELL COMPENSATED, I'M SURE.

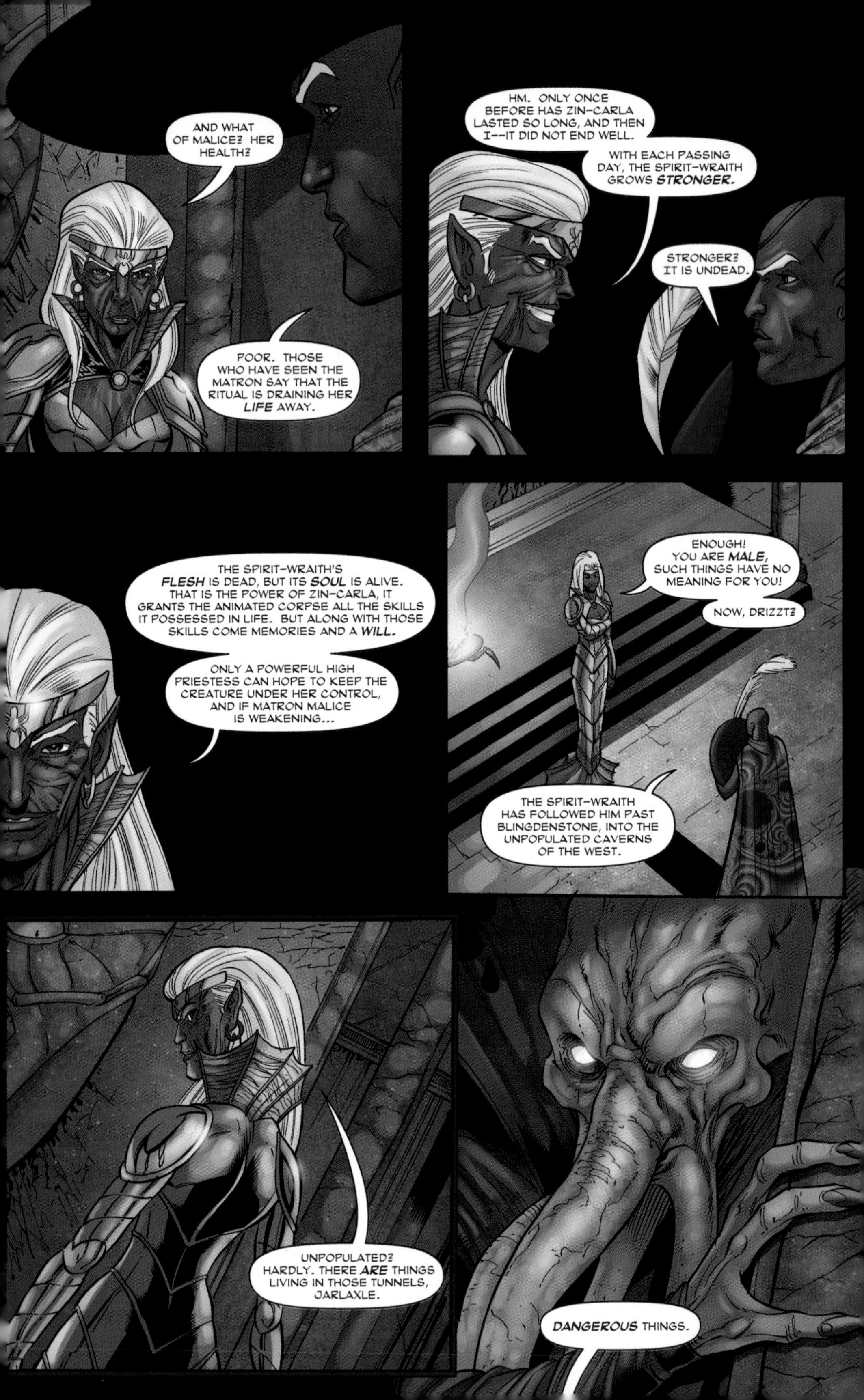
AND WHAT OF MALICE? HER HEALTH?
POOR. THOSE WHO HAVE SEEN THE MATRON SAY THAT THE RITUAL IS DRAINING HER LIFE AWAY.
HM. ONLY ONCE BEFORE HAS ZIN-CARLA LASTED SO LONG, AND THEN I--IT DID NOT END WELL.
WITH EACH PASSING DAY, THE SPIRIT-WRAITH GROWS STRONGER.
STRONGER? IT IS UNDEAD.
THE SPIRIT-WRAITH'S FLESH IS DEAD, BUT ITS SOUL IS ALIVE. THAT IS THE POWER OF ZIN-CARLA, IT GRANTS THE ANIMATED CORPSE ALL THE SKILLS IT POSSESSED IN LIFE. BUT ALONG WITH THOSE SKILLS COME MEMORIES AND A WILL.
ONLY A POWERFUL HIGH PRIESTESS CAN HOPE TO KEEP THE CREATURE UNDER HER CONTROL, AND IF MATRON MALICE IS WEAKENING...
ENOUGH! YOU ARE MALE, SUCH THINGS HAVE NO MEANING FOR YOU!
NOW, DRIZZT?
THE SPIRIT-WRAITH HAS FOLLOWED HIM PAST BLINGDENSTONE, INTO THE UNPOPULATED CAVERNS OF THE WEST.
UNPOPULATED? HARDLY. THERE ARE THINGS LIVING IN THOSE TUNNELS, JARLAXLE.
DANGEROUS THINGS.

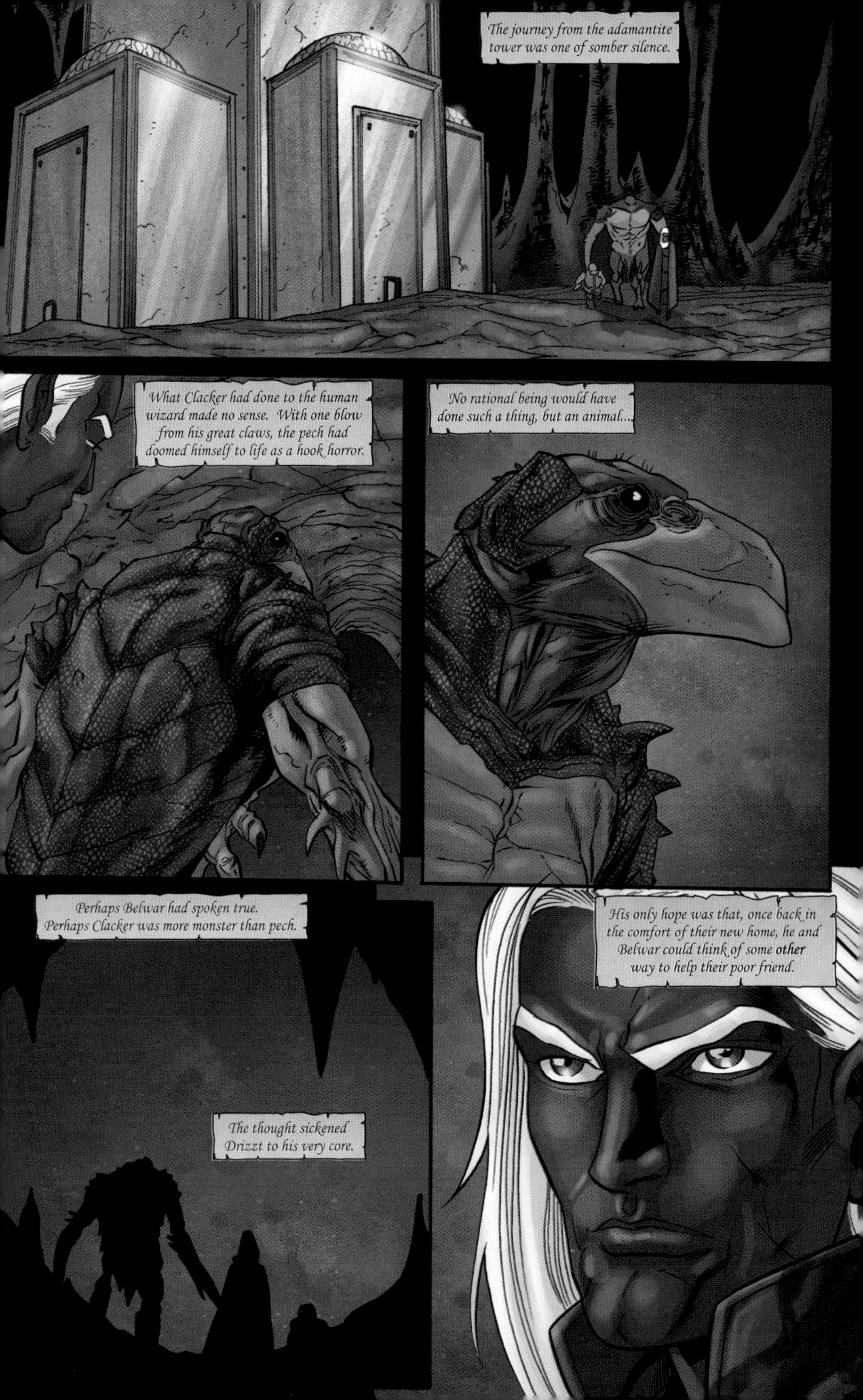
The journey from the adamantite tower was one of somber silence.
What Clacker had done to the human wizard made no sense. With one blow from his great claws, the pech had doomed himself to life as a hook horror.
No rational being would have done such a thing, but an animal...
Perhaps Belwar had spoken true. Perhaps Clacker was more monster than pech.
The thought sickened Drizzt to his very core.
His only hope was that, once back in the comfort of their new home, he and Belwar could think of some **other** way to help their poor friend.

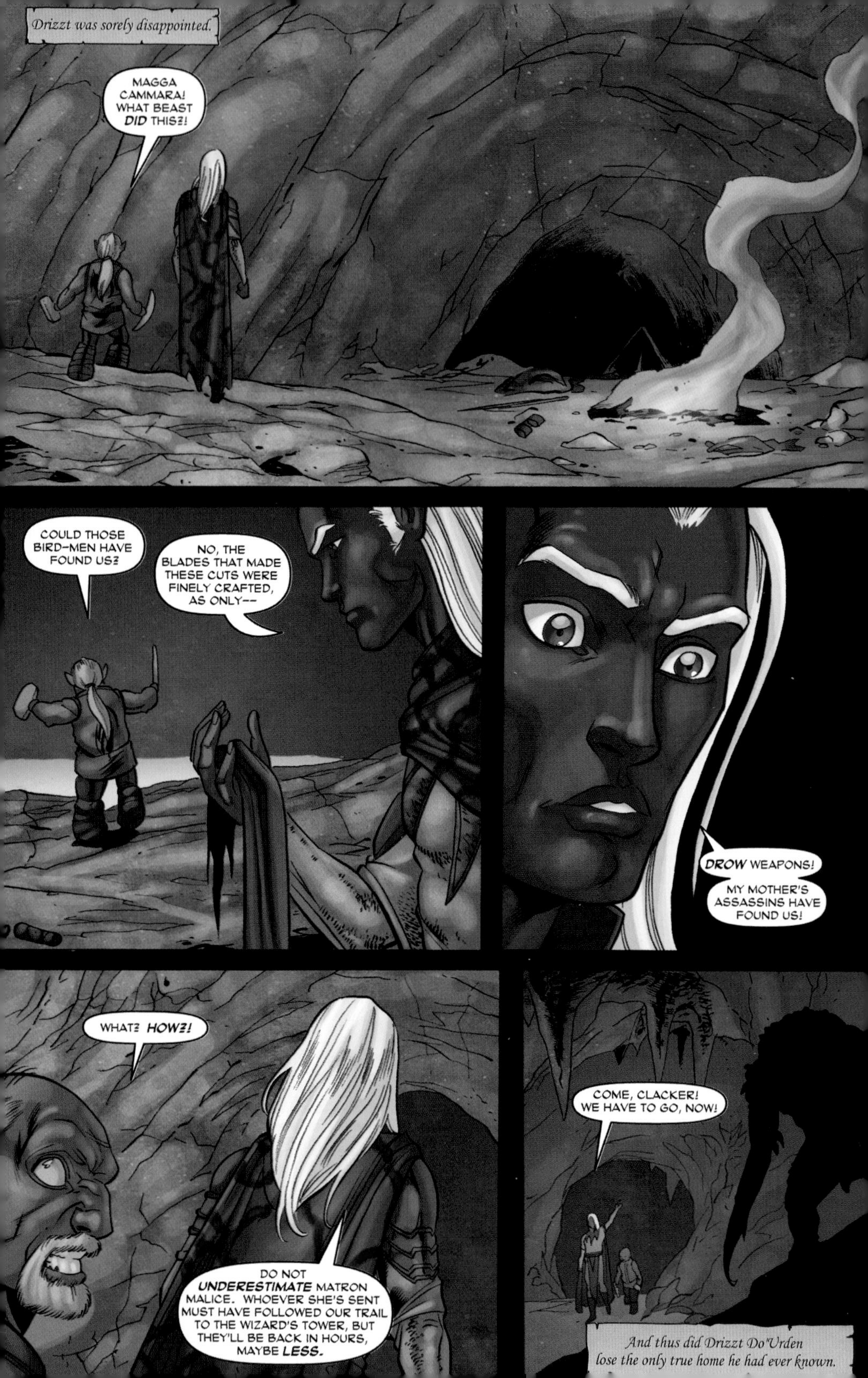
Drizzt was sorely disappointed.
MAGGA CAMMARA! WHAT BEAST DID THIS?!
COULD THOSE BIRD-MEN HAVE FOUND US?
NO, THE BLADES THAT MADE THESE CUTS WERE FINELY CRAFTED, AS ONLY--
DROW WEAPONS!
MY MOTHER'S ASSASSINS HAVE FOUND US!
WHAT? HOW?!
DO NOT UNDERESTIMATE MATRON MALICE. WHOEVER SHE'S SENT MUST HAVE FOLLOWED OUR TRAIL TO THE WIZARD'S TOWER, BUT THEY'LL BE BACK IN HOURS, MAYBE LESS.
COME, CLACKER! WE HAVE TO GO, NOW!
And thus did Drizzt Do'Urden lose the only true home he had ever known.

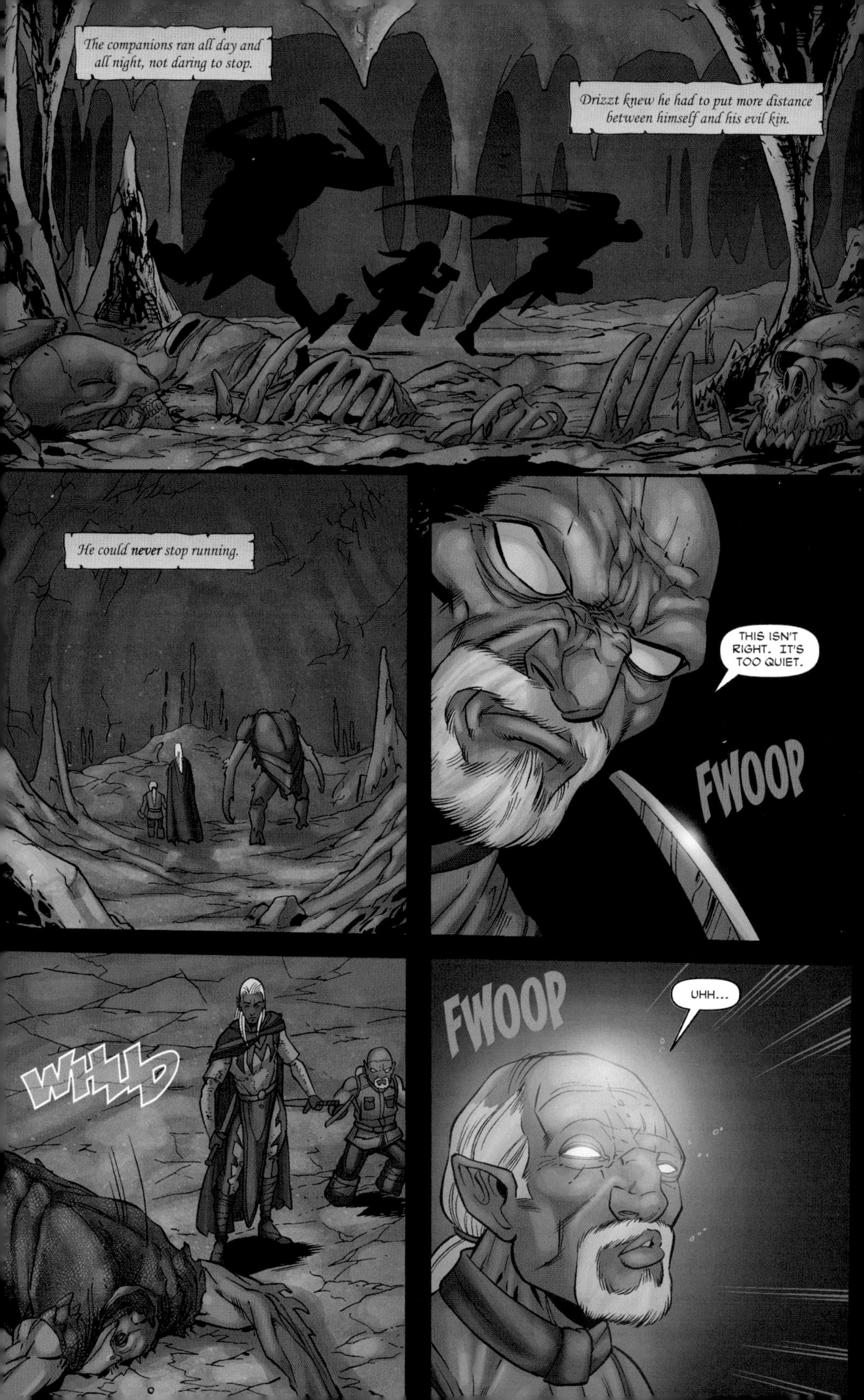
The companions ran all day and all night, not daring to stop.
Drizzt knew he had to put more distance between himself and his evil kin.
He could never stop running.
THIS ISN'T RIGHT. IT'S TOO QUIET.
FWOOP
WHUD
FWOOP
UHH...

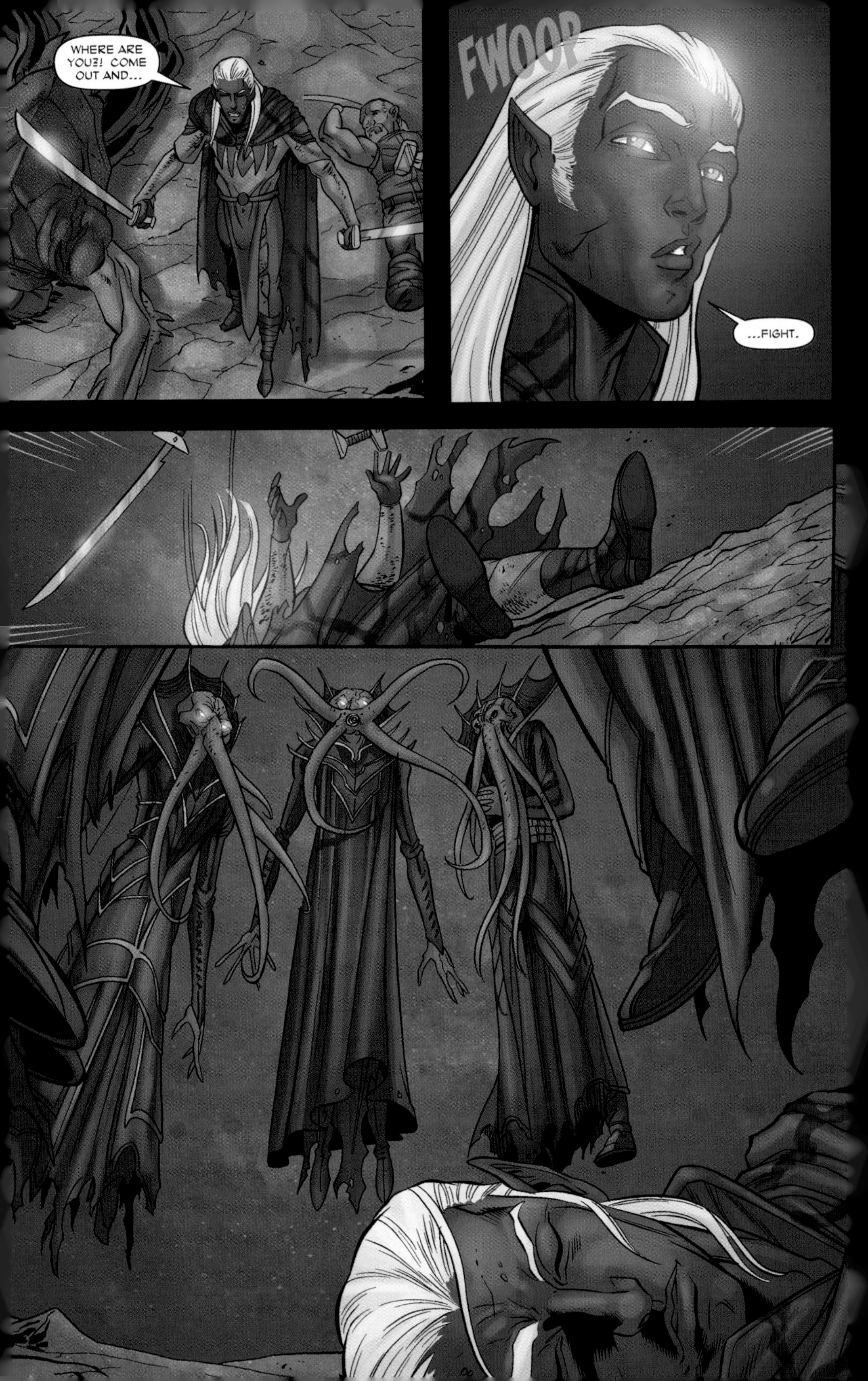
WHERE ARE YOU?! COME OUT AND...
FWOOP
...FIGHT.

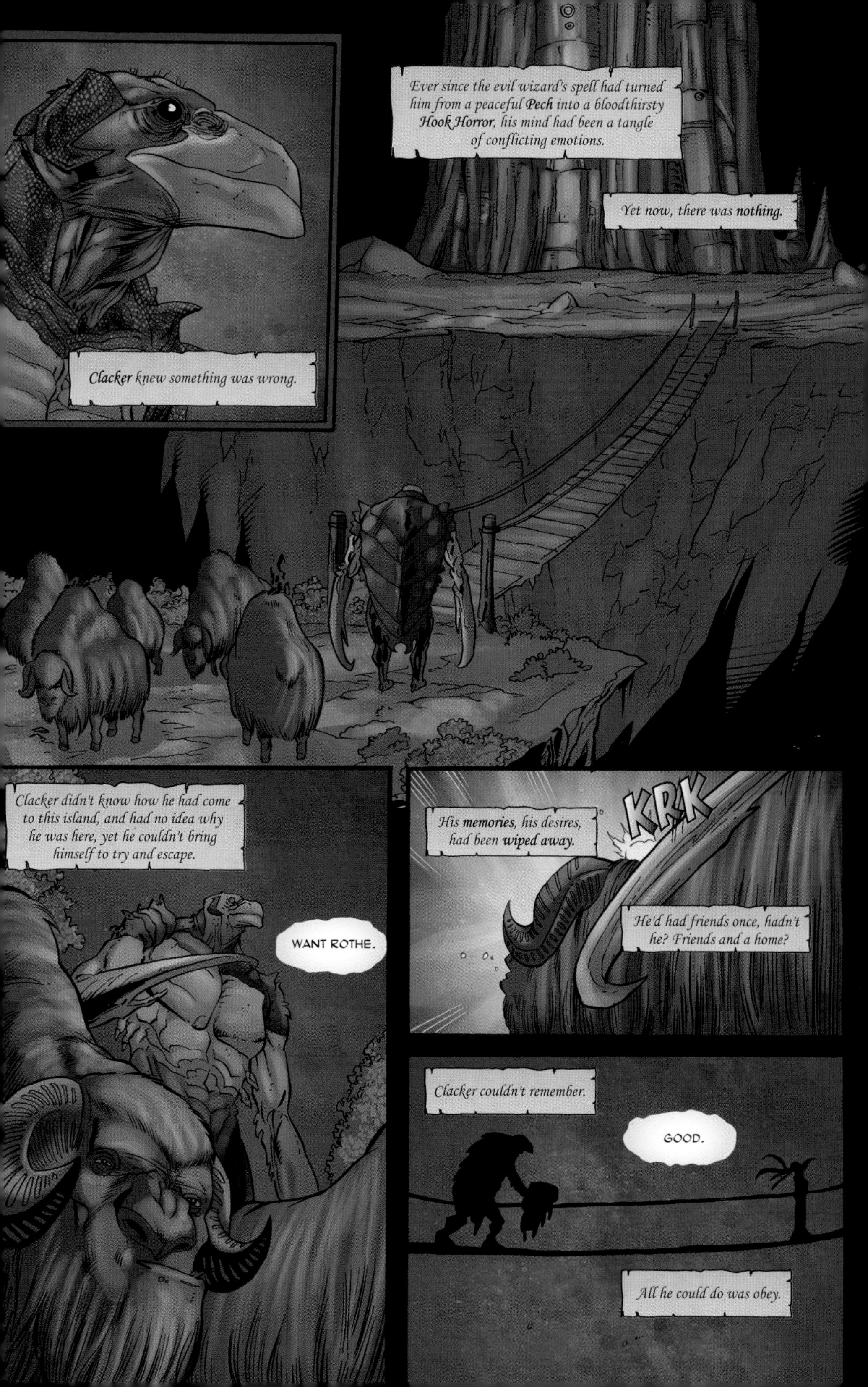
Clacker knew something was wrong.
Ever since the evil wizard's spell had turned him from a peaceful Pech into a bloodthirsty Hook Horror, his mind had been a tangle of conflicting emotions.
Yet now, there was nothing.
Clacker didn't know how he had come to this island, and had no idea why he was here, yet he couldn't bring himself to try and escape.
WANT ROTHE.
His memories, his desires, had been wiped away.
KRK
He'd had friends once, hadn't he? Friends and a home?
Clacker couldn't remember.
GOOD.
All he could do was obey.

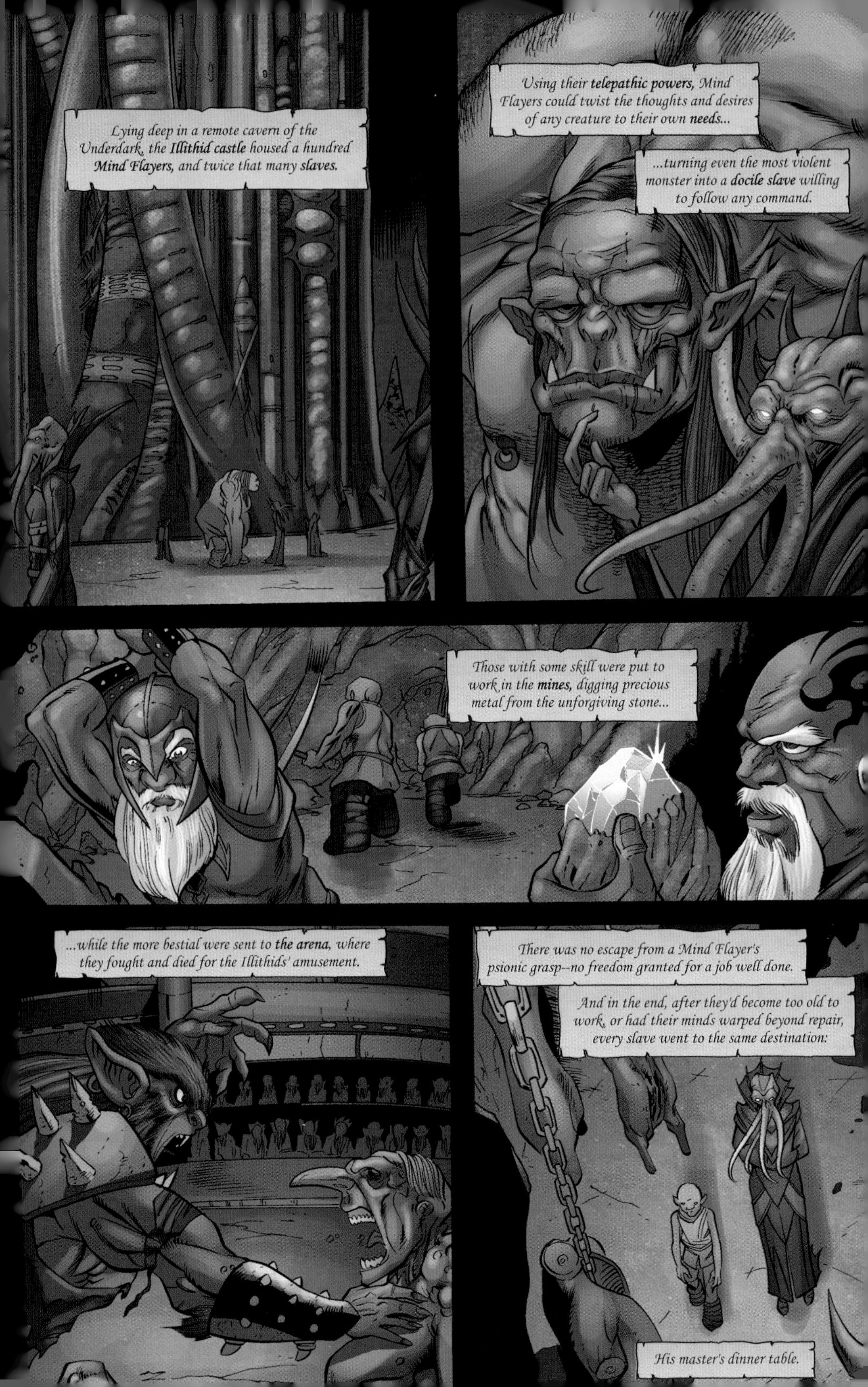
Lying deep in a remote cavern of the Underdark, the Illithid castle housed a hundred Mind Flayers, and twice that many slaves.
Using their telepathic powers, Mind Flayers could twist the thoughts and desires of any creature to their own needs...
...turning even the most violent monster into a docile slave willing to follow any command.
Those with some skill were put to work in the mines, digging precious metal from the unforgiving stone...
...while the more bestial were sent to the arena, where they fought and died for the Illithids' amusement.
There was no escape from a Mind Flayer's psionic grasp--no freedom granted for a job well done.
And in the end, after they'd become too old to work, or had their minds warped beyond repair, every slave went to the same destination:
His master's dinner table.

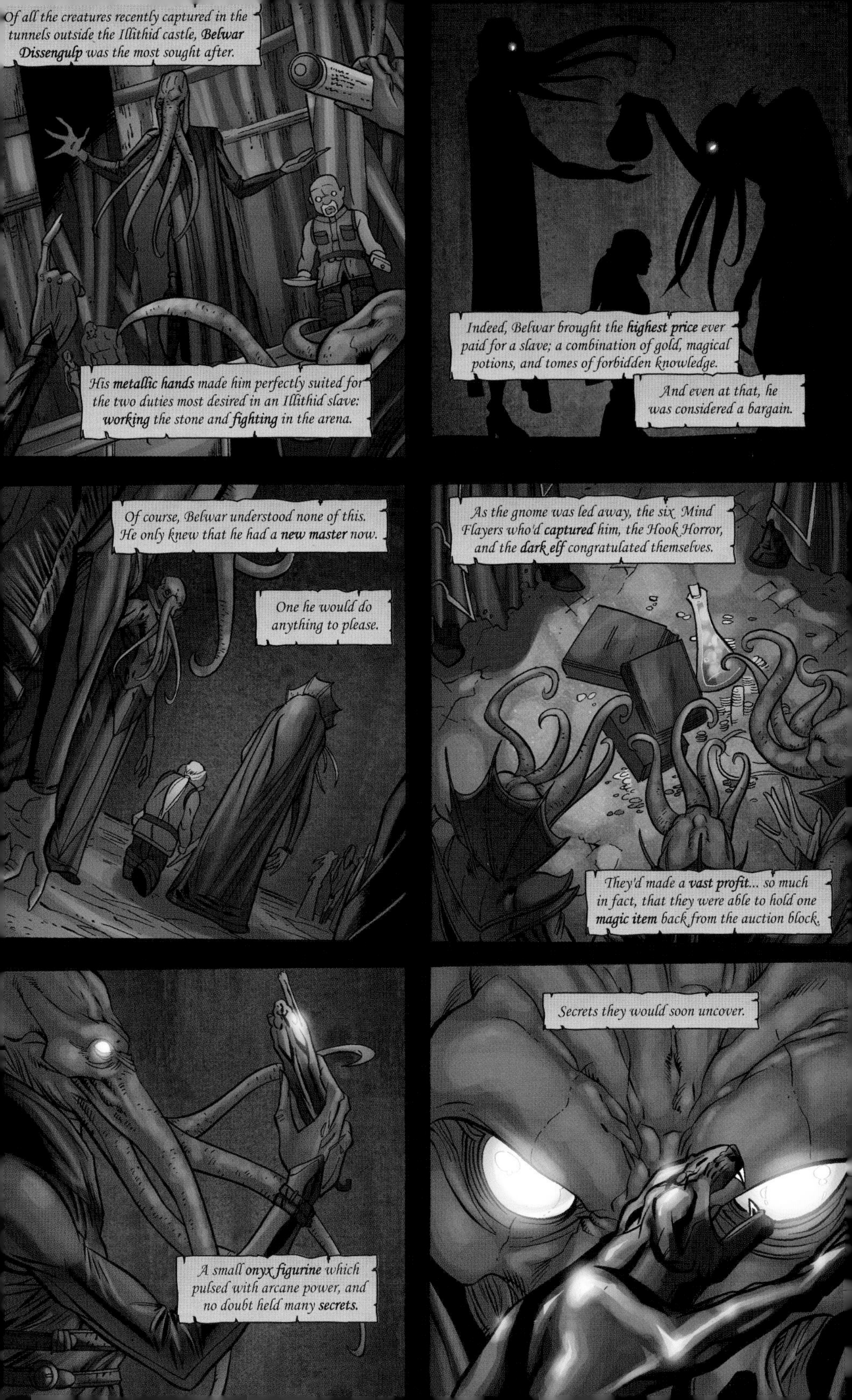
Of all the creatures recently captured in the tunnels outside the Illithid castle, Belwar Dissengulp was the most sought after.
His metallic hands made him perfectly suited for the two duties most desired in an Illithid slave: working the stone and fighting in the arena.
Indeed, Belwar brought the highest price ever paid for a slave; a combination of gold, magical potions, and tomes of forbidden knowledge.
And even at that, he was considered a bargain.
Of course, Belwar understood none of this. He only knew that he had a new master now.
One he would do anything to please.
As the gnome was led away, the six Mind Flayers who'd captured him, the Hook Horror, and the dark elf congratulated themselves.
They'd made a vast profit... so much in fact, that they were able to hold one magic item back from the auction block.
A small onyx figurine which pulsed with arcane power, and no doubt held many secrets.
Secrets they would soon uncover.

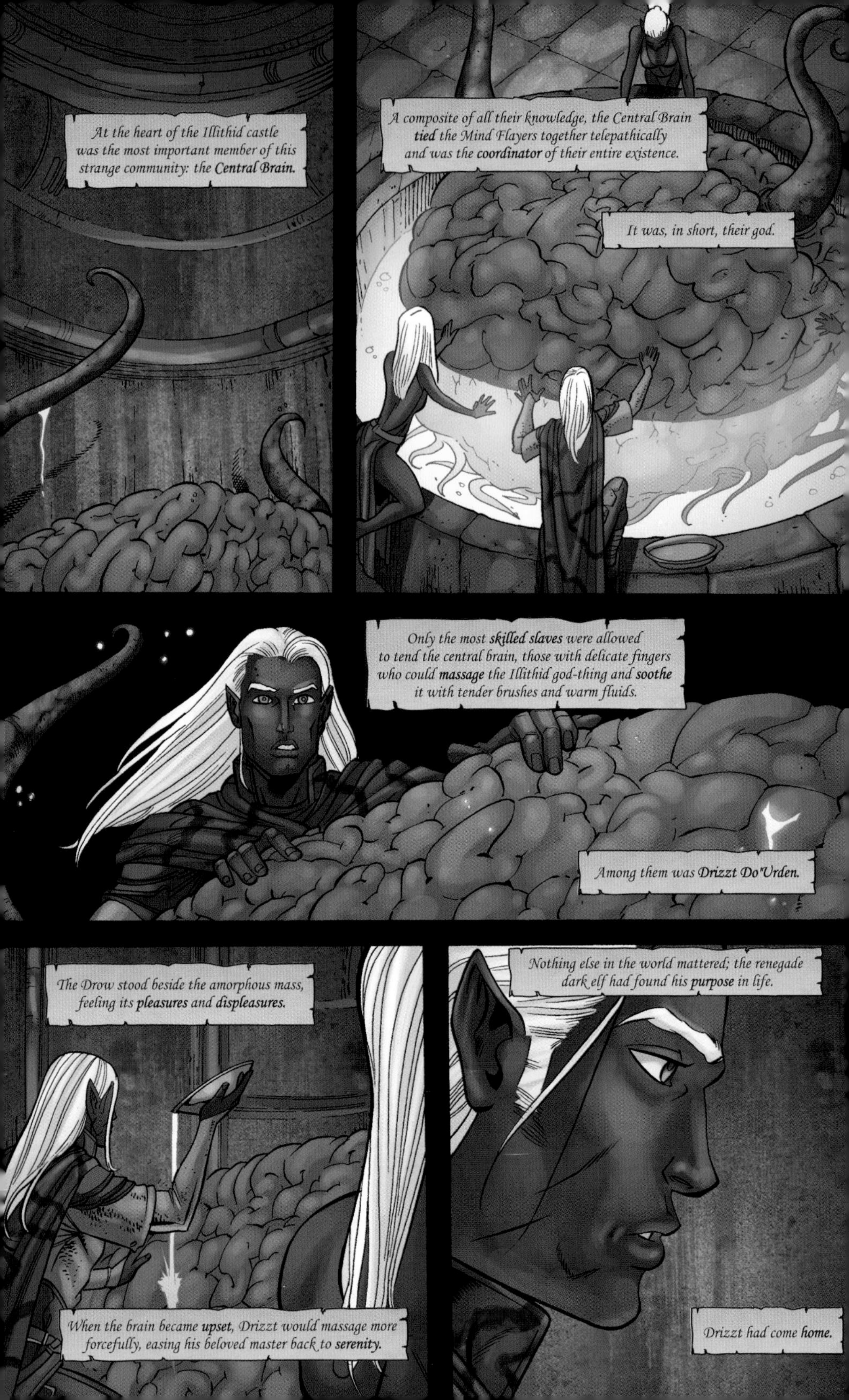
At the heart of the Illithid castle was the most important member of this strange community: the Central Brain.
A composite of all their knowledge, the Central Brain tied the Mind Flayers together telepathically and was the coordinator of their entire existence.
It was, in short, their god.
Only the most skilled slaves were allowed to tend the central brain, those with delicate fingers who could massage the Illithid god-thing and soothe it with tender brushes and warm fluids.
Among them was Drizzt Do'Urden.
The Drow stood beside the amorphous mass, feeling its pleasures and displeasures.
When the brain became upset, Drizzt would massage more forcefully, easing his beloved master back to serenity.
Nothing else in the world mattered; the renegade dark elf had found his purpose in life.
Drizzt had come home.

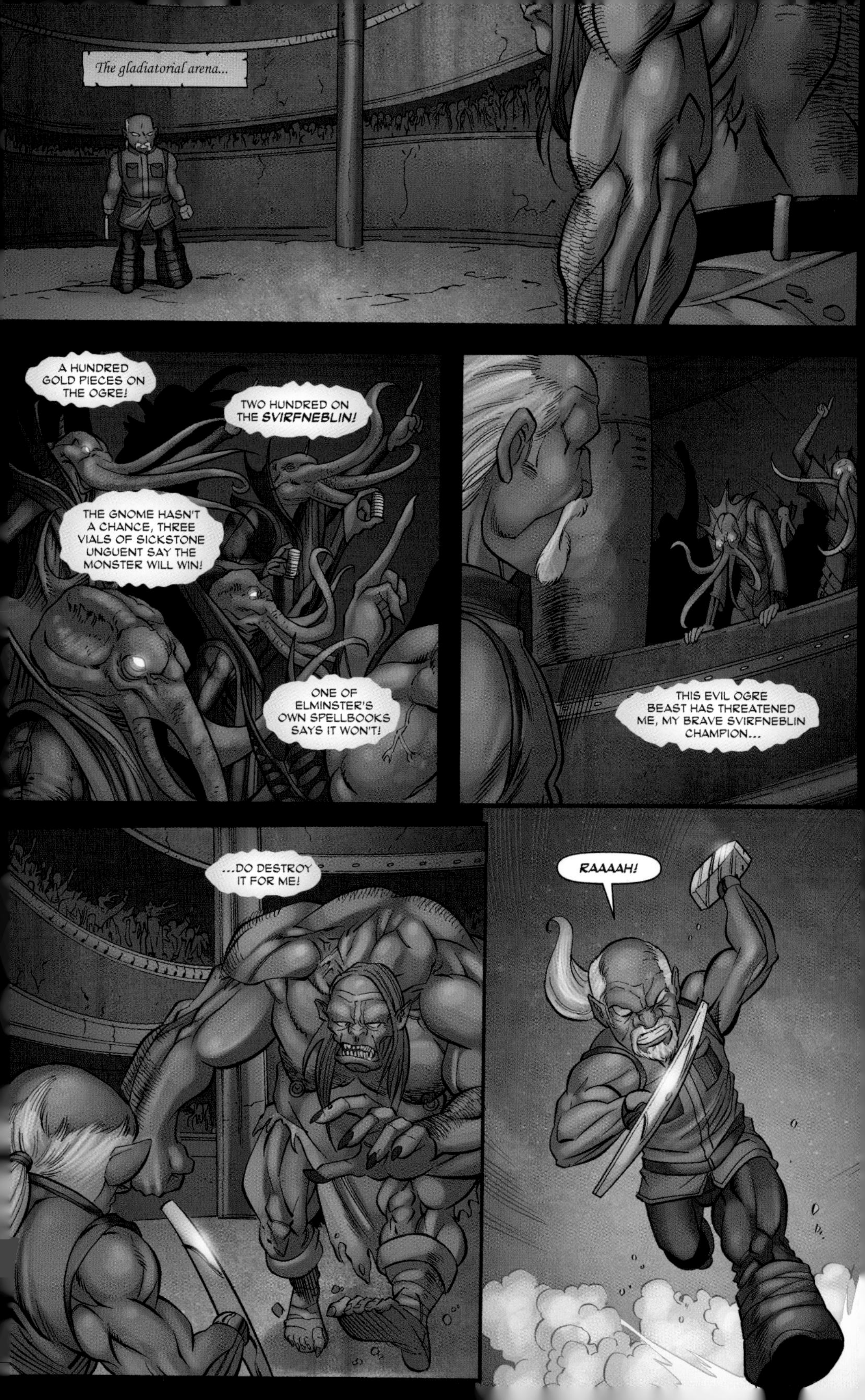

The gladiatorial arena...
A HUNDRED GOLD PIECES ON THE OGRE!
TWO HUNDRED ON THE SVIRFNEBLIN!
THE GNOME HASN'T A CHANCE, THREE VIALS OF SICKSTONE UNGUENT SAY THE MONSTER WILL WIN!
ONE OF ELMINSTER'S OWN SPELLBOOKS SAYS IT WON'T!
THIS EVIL OGRE BEAST HAS THREATENED ME, MY BRAVE SVIRFNEBLIN CHAMPION...
...DO DESTROY IT FOR ME!
RAAAAH!

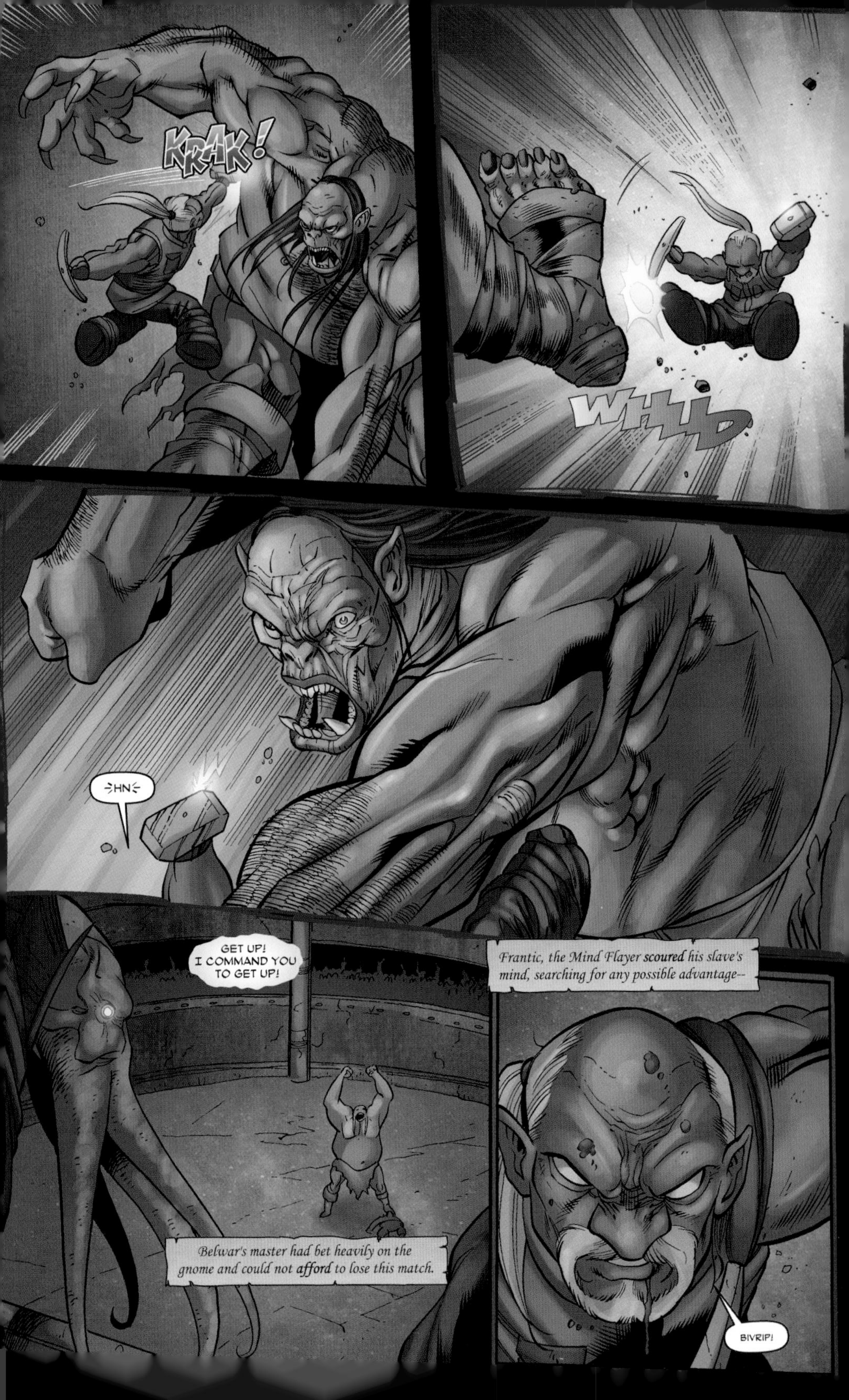
KRAK!
WHUD
HN
GET UP! I COMMAND YOU TO GET UP!
Frantic, the Mind Flayer *scoured* his slave's mind, searching for any possible advantage--
Belwar's master had bet heavily on the gnome and could not *afford* to lose this match.
BIVRIP!

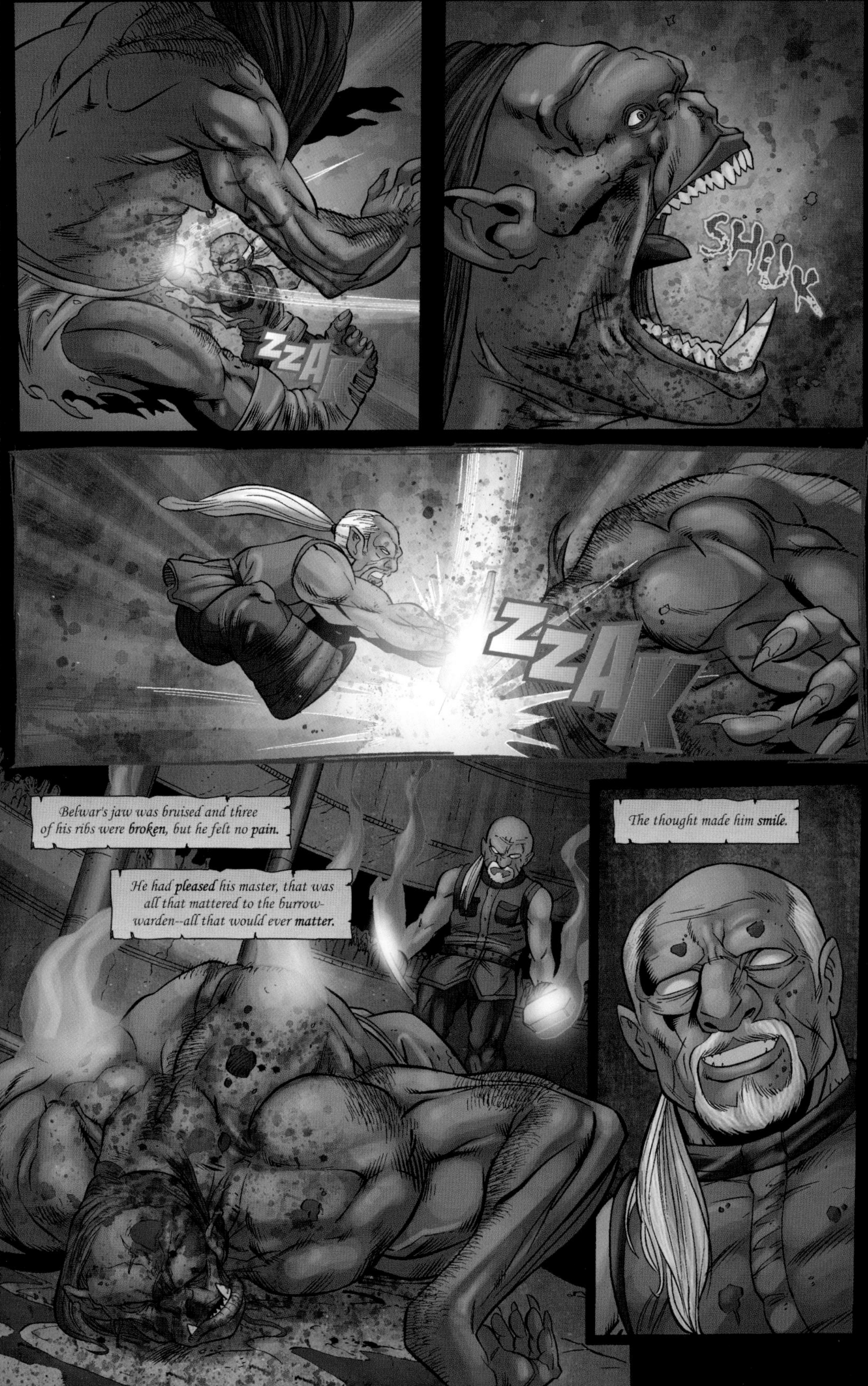
ZZAK
SHUK
ZZAK
Belwar's jaw was bruised and three of his ribs were broken, but he felt no pain.
He had pleased his master, that was all that mattered to the burrow-warden--all that would ever matter.
The thought made him smile.

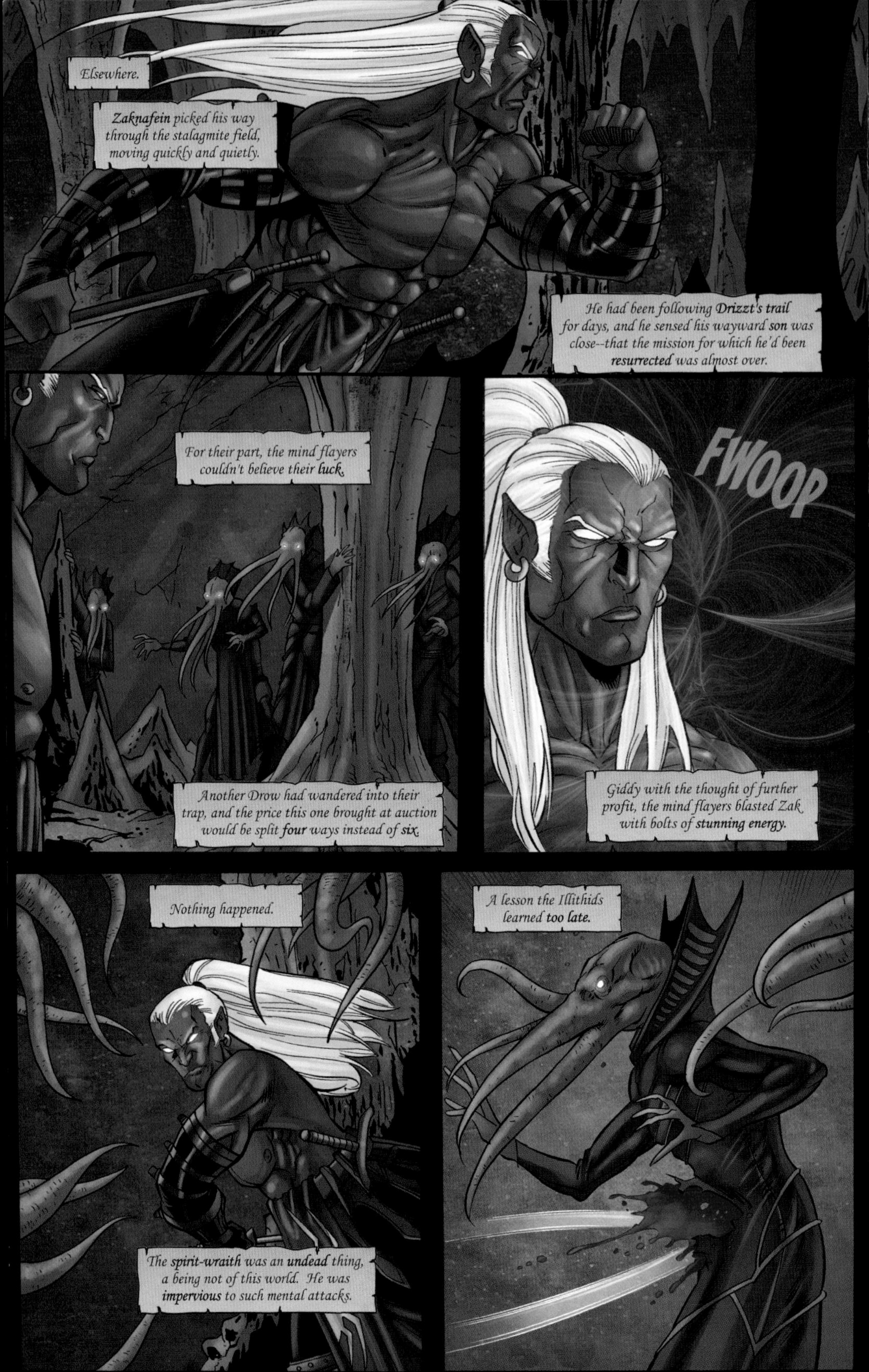
Elsewhere.
Zaknafein picked his way through the stalagmite field, moving quickly and quietly.
He had been following Drizzt's trail for days, and he sensed his wayward son was close--that the mission for which he'd been resurrected was almost over.
For their part, the mind flayers couldn't believe their luck.
Another Drow had wandered into their trap, and the price this one brought at auction would be split four ways instead of six.
FWOOP
Giddy with the thought of further profit, the mind flayers blasted Zak with bolts of stunning energy.
Nothing happened.
The spirit-wraith was an undead thing, a being not of this world. He was impervious to such mental attacks.
A lesson the Illithids learned too late.

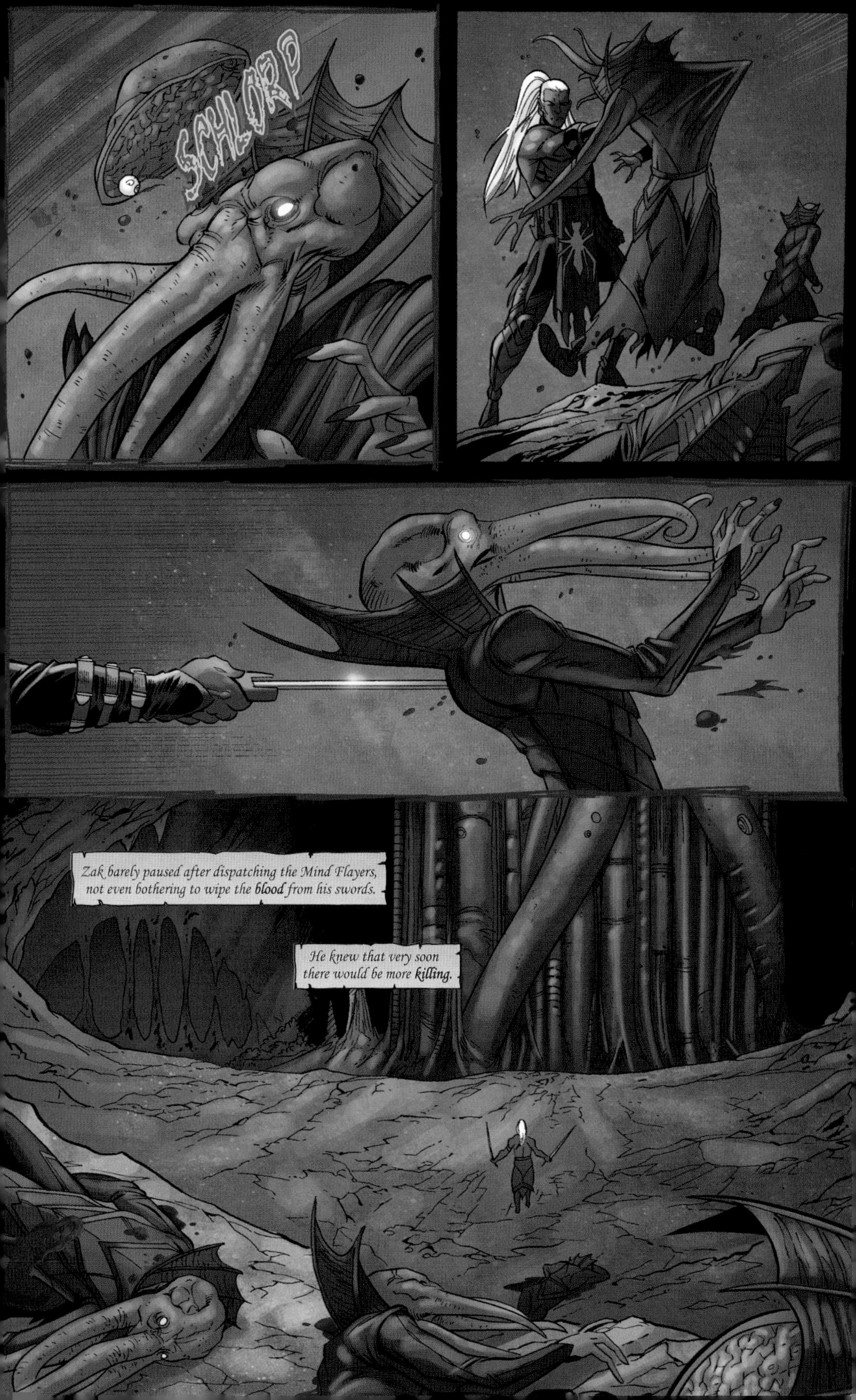
SCHLORP
Zak barely paused after dispatching the Mind Flayers, not even bothering to wipe the blood from his swords.
He knew that very soon there would be more killing.

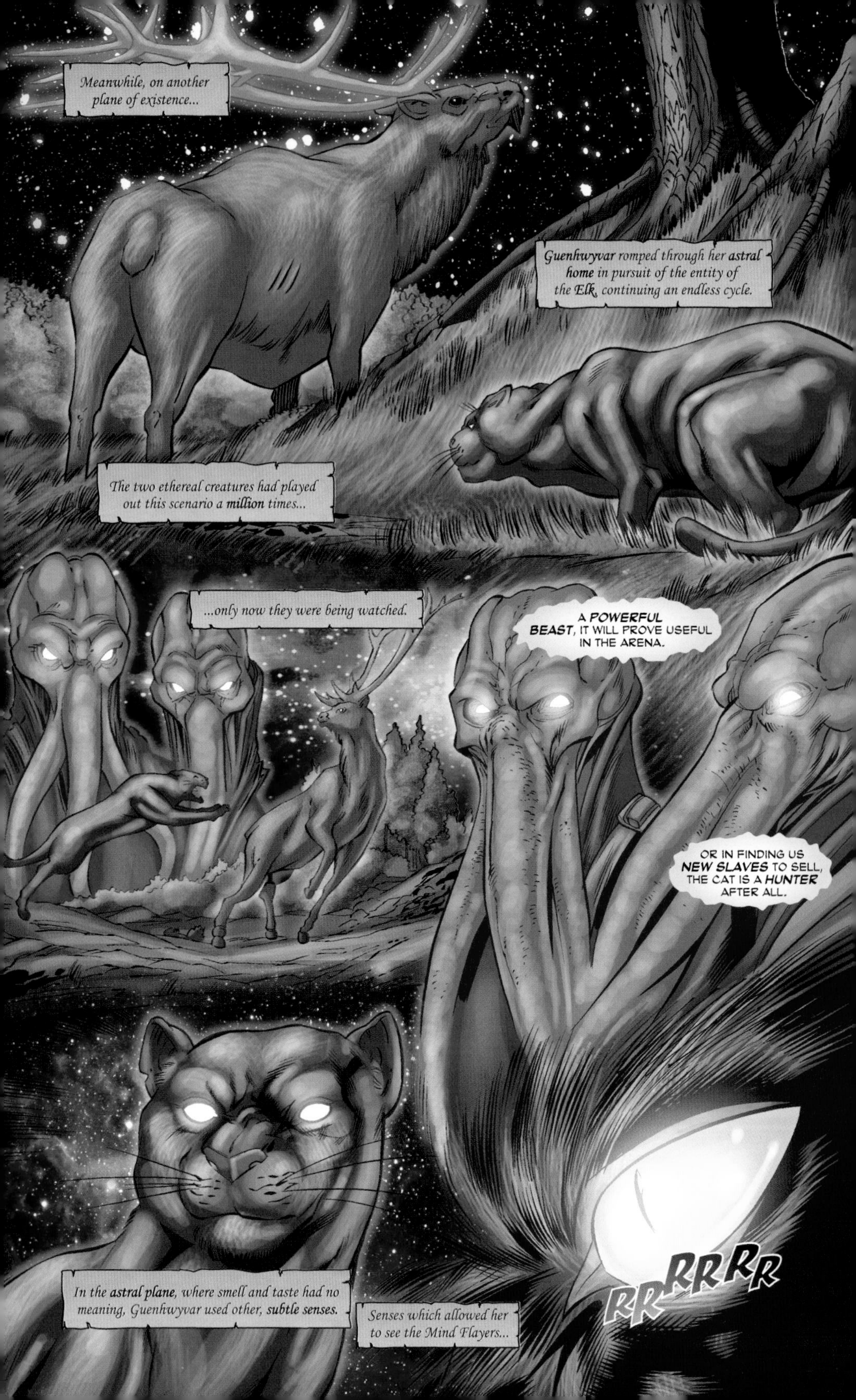
Meanwhile, on another plane of existence...
Guenhwyvar romped through her astral home in pursuit of the entity of the Elk, continuing an endless cycle.
The two ethereal creatures had played out this scenario a million times...
...only now they were being watched.
A POWERFUL BEAST, IT WILL PROVE USEFUL IN THE ARENA.
OR IN FINDING US NEW SLAVES TO SELL, THE CAT IS A HUNTER AFTER ALL.
In the astral plane, where smell and taste had no meaning, Guenhwyvar used other, subtle senses.
Senses which allowed her to see the Mind Flayers...
RRRRRRRR

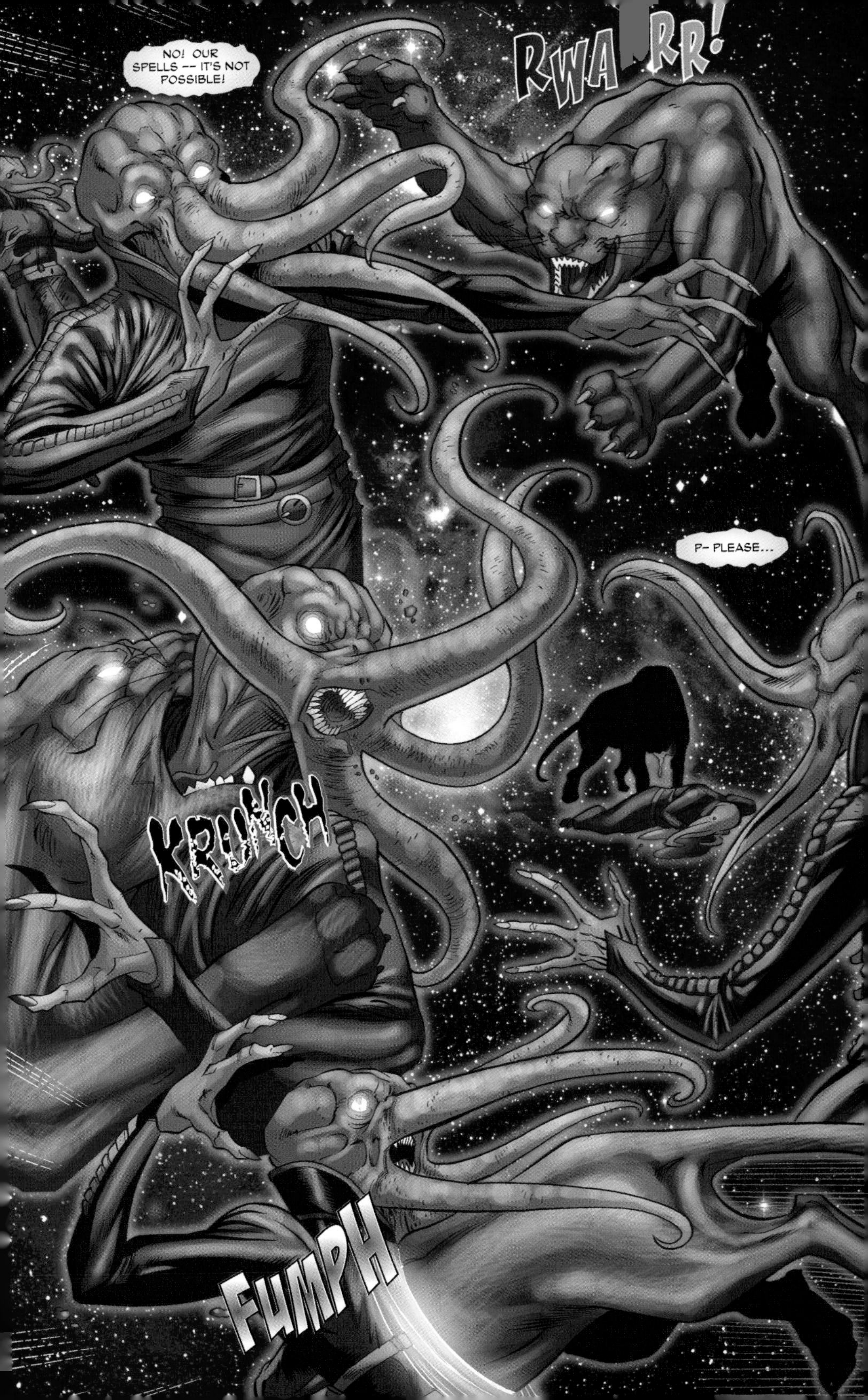
NO! OUR SPELLS -- IT'S NOT POSSIBLE!
RWA RR!
P- PLEASE...
KRUNCH
FUMPH

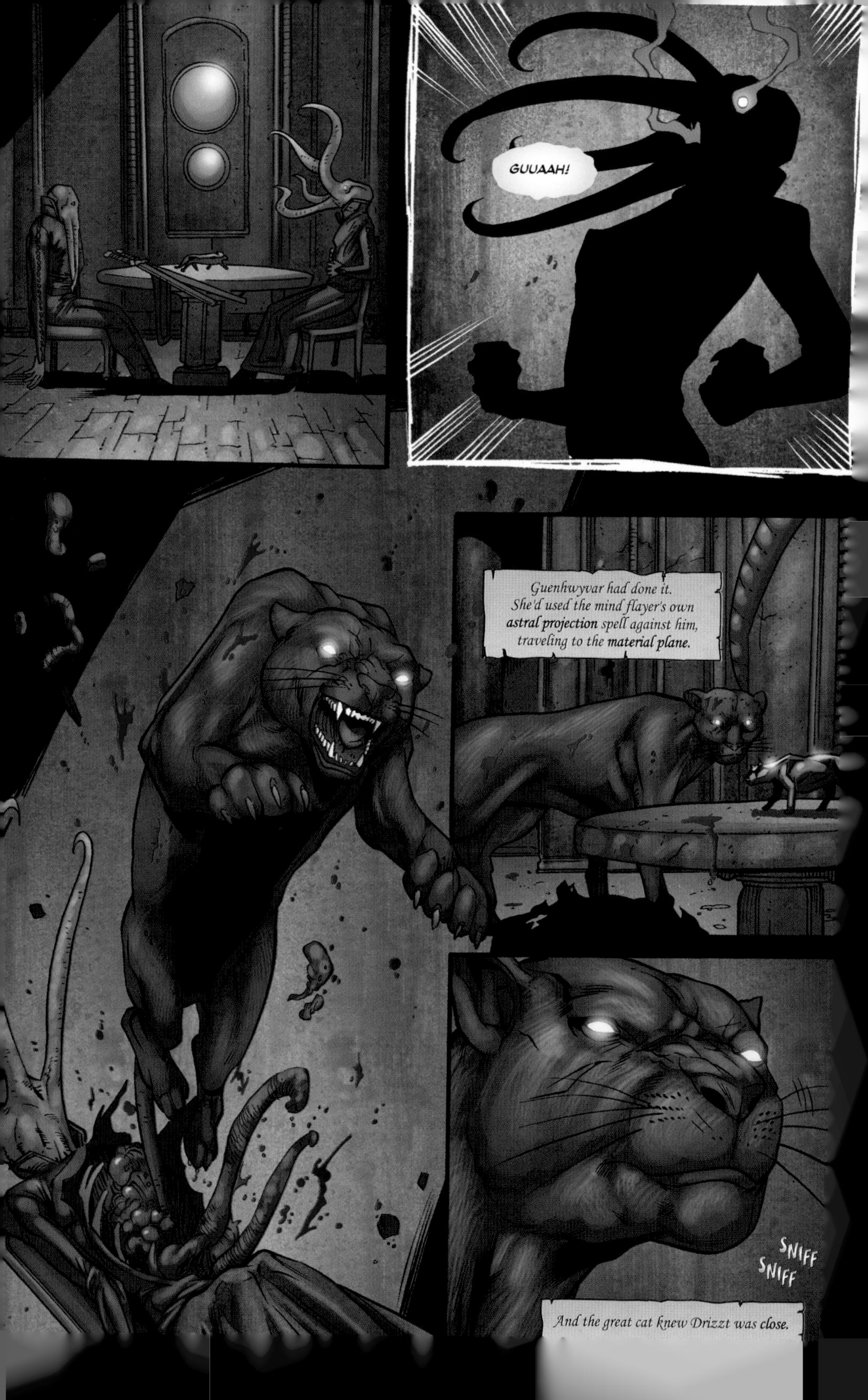
GUUAAH!
Guenhwyvar had done it. She'd used the mind flayer's own astral projection spell against him, traveling to the material plane.
SNIFF SNIFF
And the great cat knew Drizzt was close.

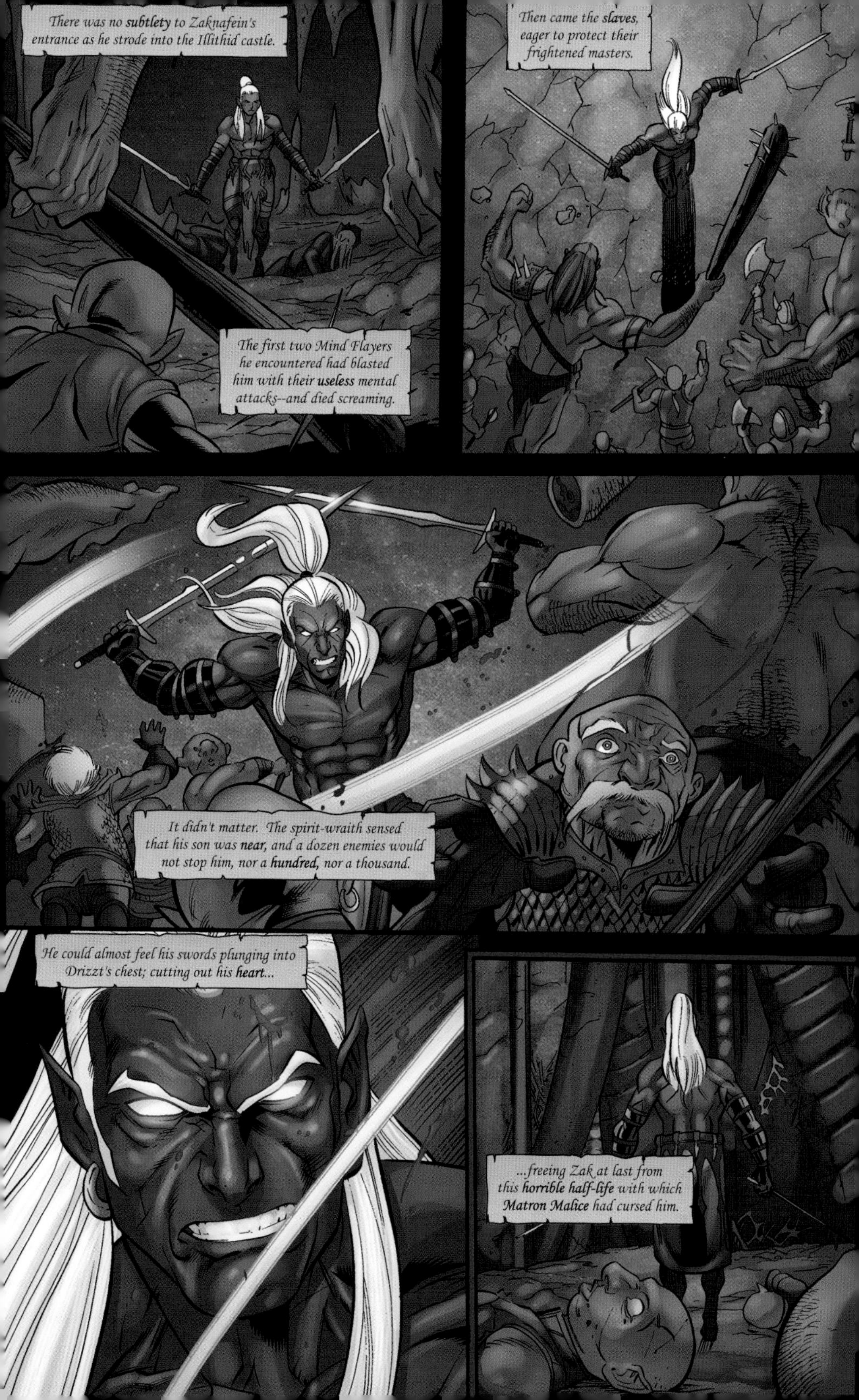
There was no subtlety to Zaknafein's entrance as he strode into the Illithid castle.
The first two Mind Flayers he encountered had blasted him with their useless mental attacks--and died screaming.
Then came the slaves, eager to protect their frightened masters.
It didn't matter. The spirit-wraith sensed that his son was near, and a dozen enemies would not stop him, nor a hundred, nor a thousand.
He could almost feel his swords plunging into Drizzt's chest; cutting out his heart...
...freeing Zak at last from this horrible half-life with which Matron Malice had cursed him.

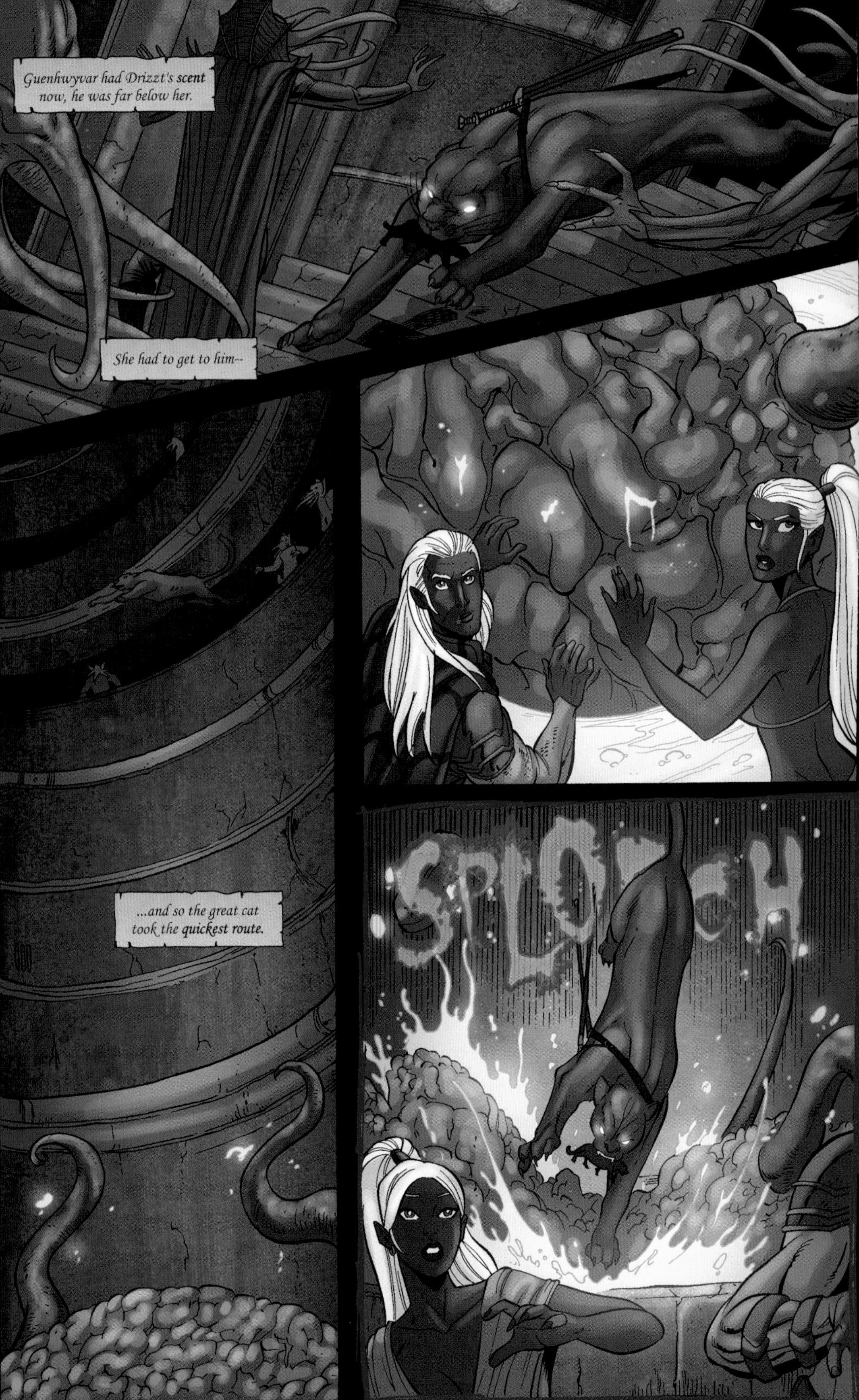

Guenhwyvar had Drizzt's **scent** now, he was far below her.
She had to get to him--
...and so the great cat took the **quickest route**.
SPLOOSH

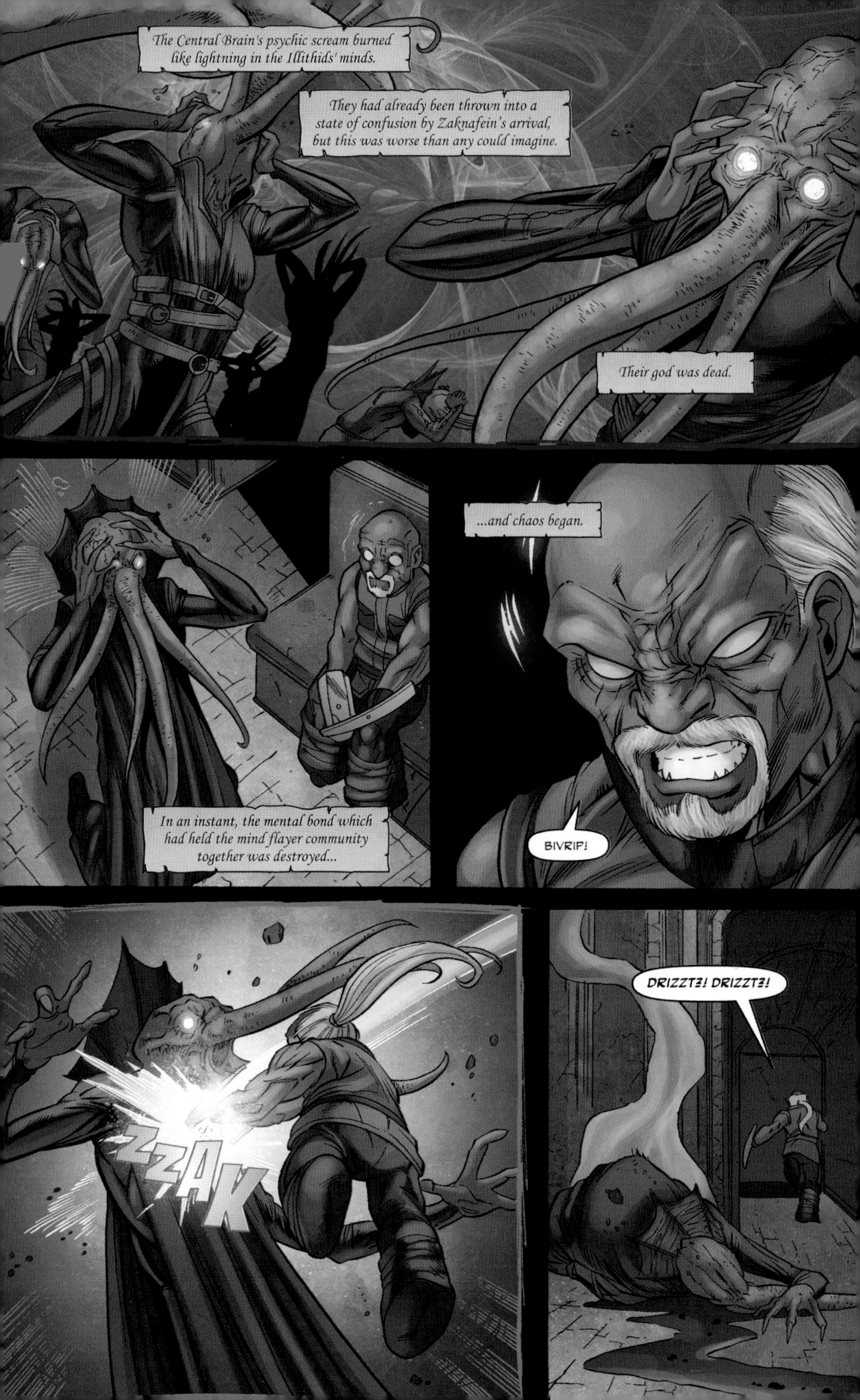
The Central Brain's psychic scream burned like lightning in the Illithids' minds.
They had already been thrown into a state of confusion by Zaknafein's arrival, but this was worse than any could imagine.
Their god was dead.
In an instant, the mental bond which had held the mind flayer community together was destroyed...
...and chaos began.
BIVRIP!
ZZAK
DRIZZT?! DRIZZT?!

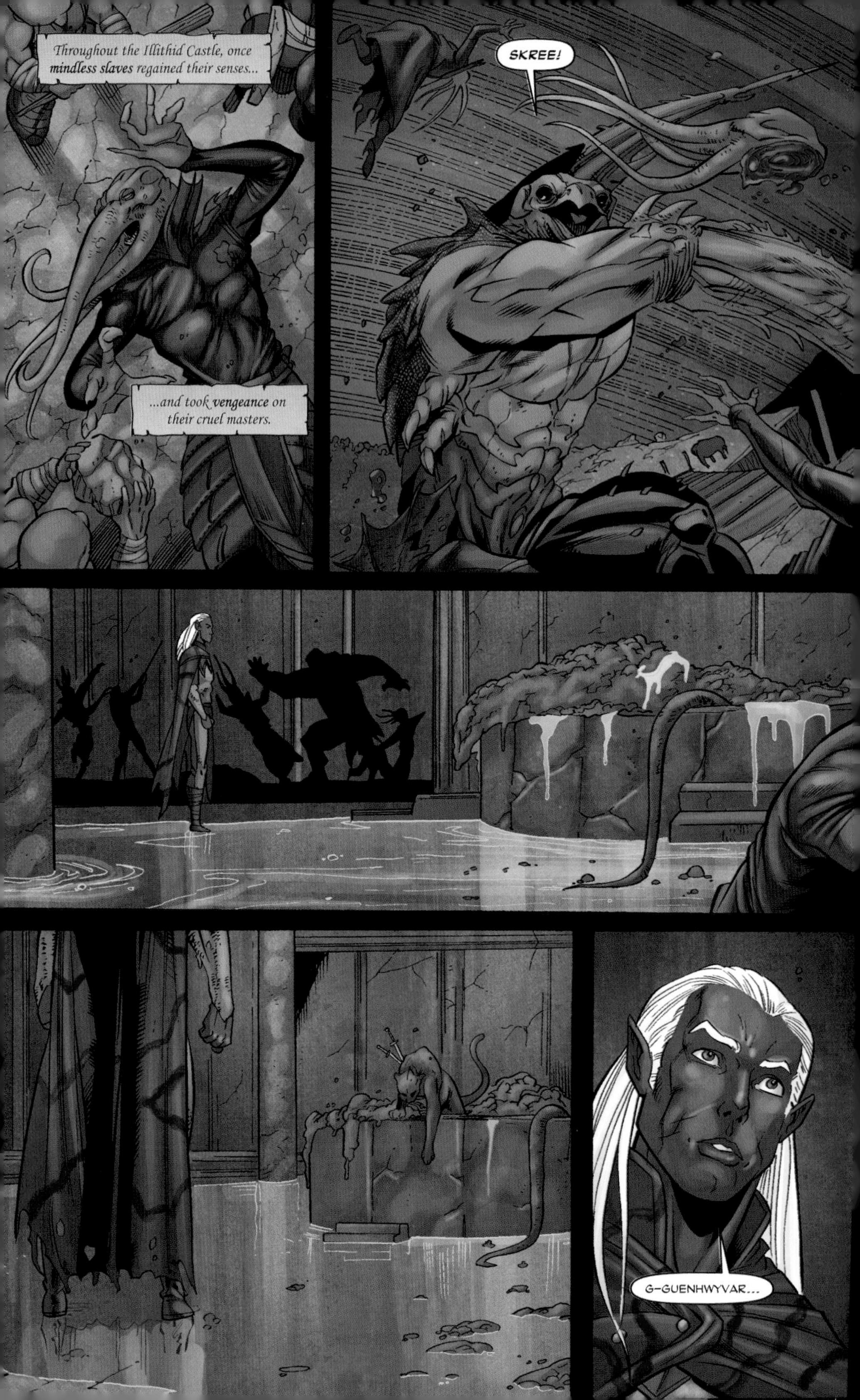
Throughout the Illithid Castle, once mindless slaves regained their senses...
...and took vengeance on their cruel masters.
SKREE!
G-GUENHWYVAR...

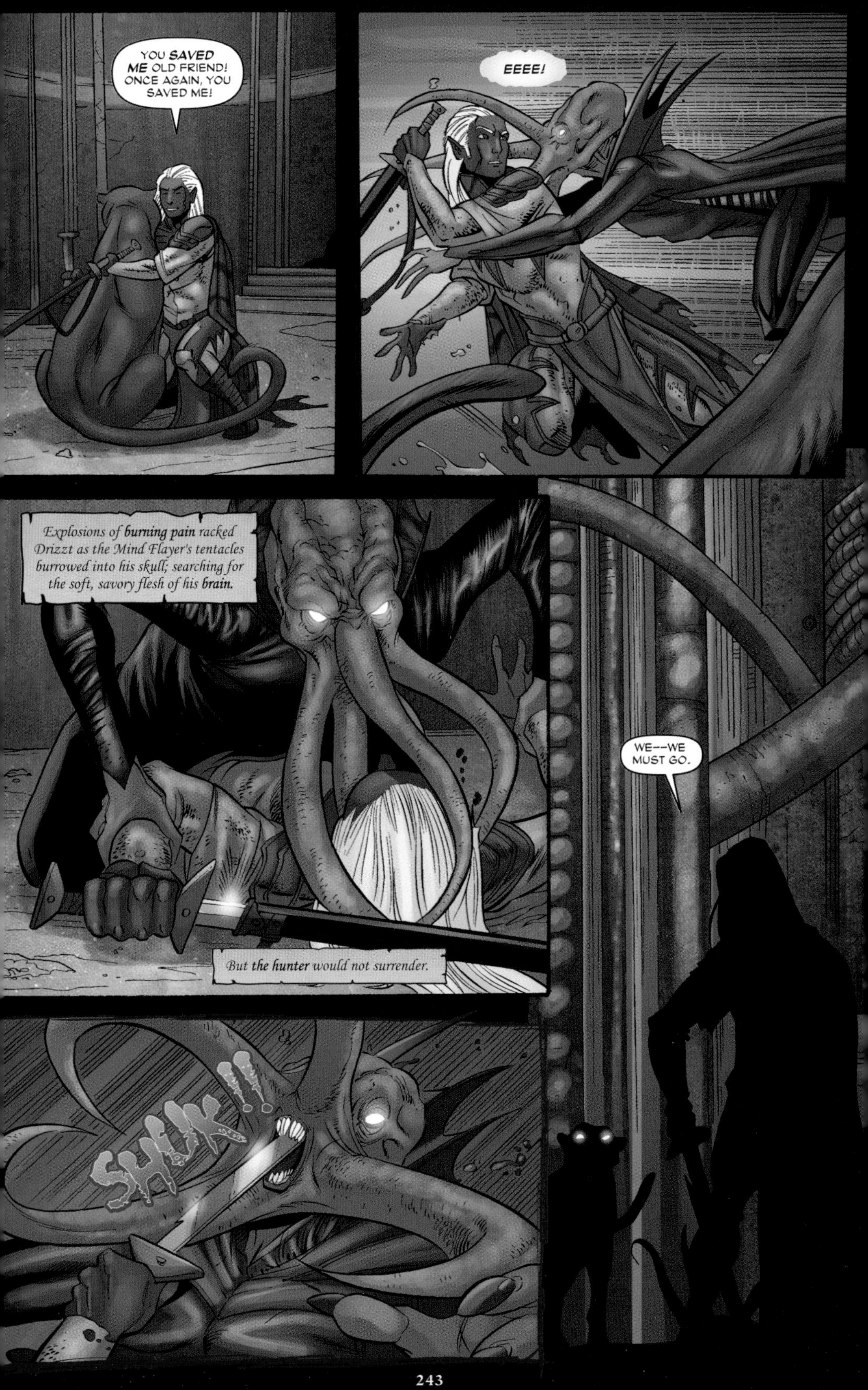
YOU SAVED ME OLD FRIEND! ONCE AGAIN, YOU SAVED ME!
EEEE!
Explosions of burning pain racked Drizzt as the Mind Flayer's tentacles burrowed into his skull; searching for the soft, savory flesh of his brain.
But the hunter would not surrender.
SHUK!!
WE--WE MUST GO.

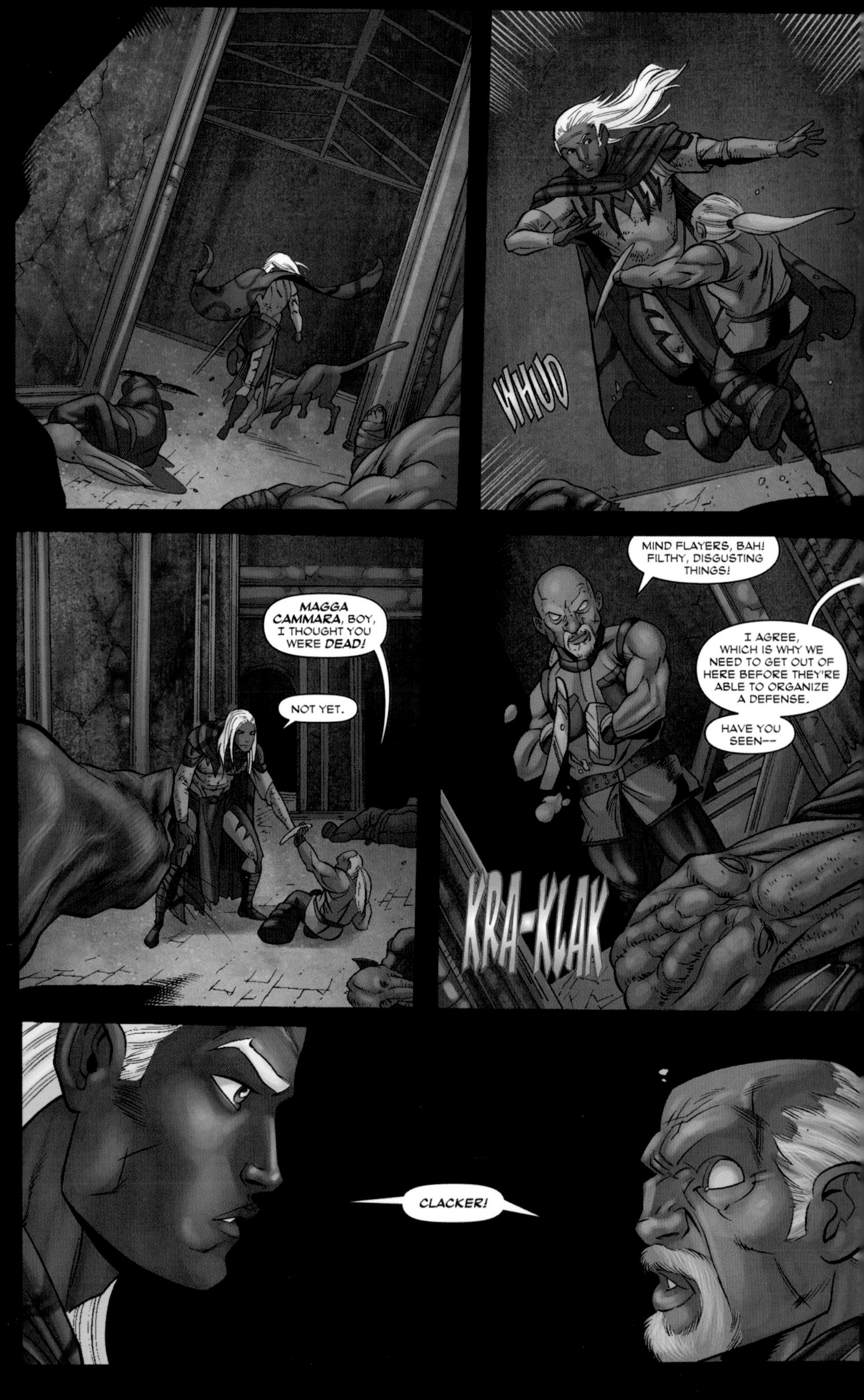
WHUD
MAGGA CAMMARA, BOY, I THOUGHT YOU WERE DEAD!
NOT YET.
MIND FLAYERS, BAH! FILTHY, DISGUSTING THINGS!
I AGREE, WHICH IS WHY WE NEED TO GET OUT OF HERE BEFORE THEY'RE ABLE TO ORGANIZE A DEFENSE.
HAVE YOU SEEN--
KRA-KLAK
CLACKER!

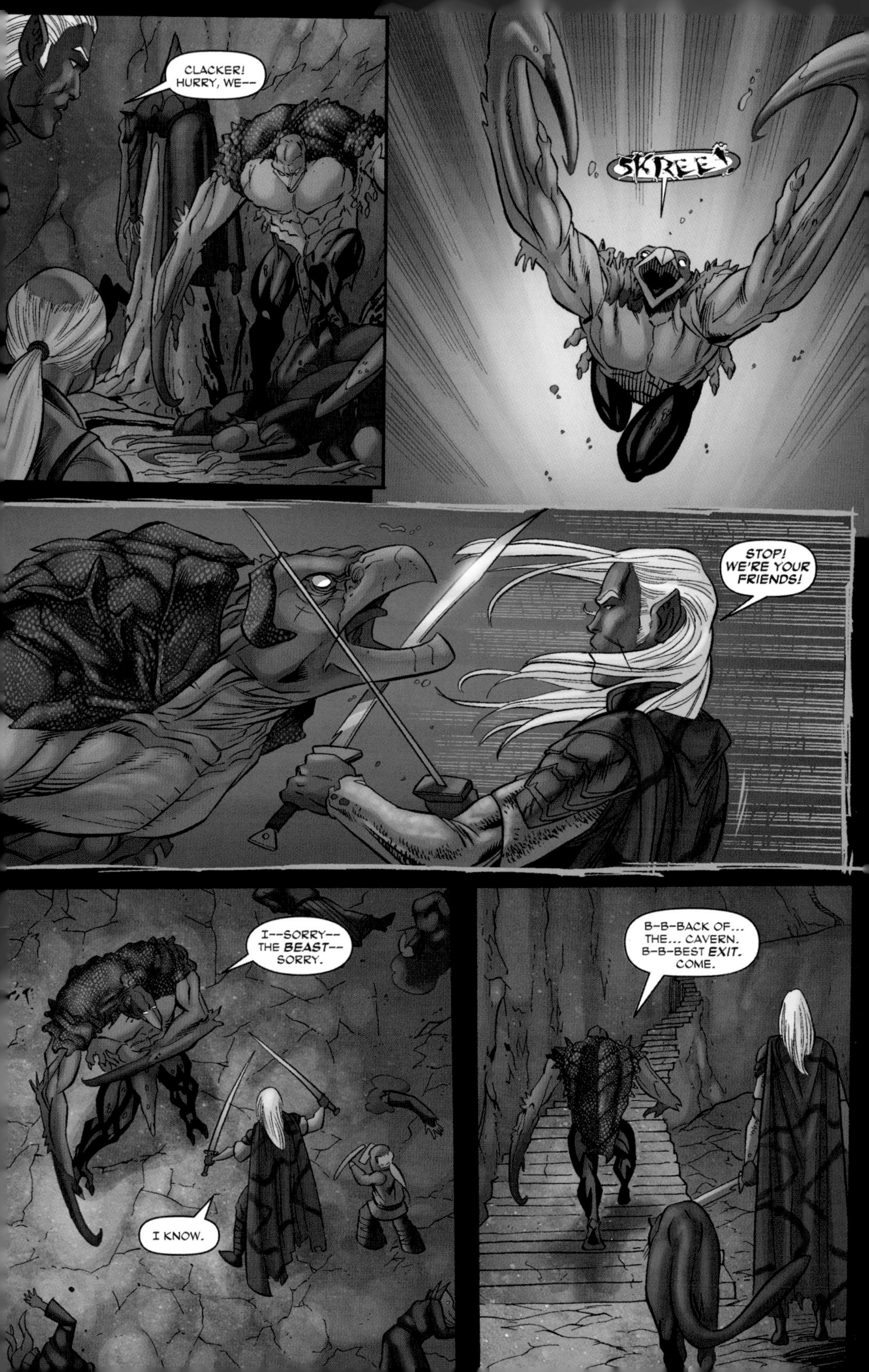

CLACKER! HURRY, WE--
SKREE!
STOP! WE'RE YOUR FRIENDS!
I--SORRY-- THE BEAST-- SORRY.
I KNOW.
B-B-BACK OF... THE... CAVERN. B-B-BEST EXIT. COME.

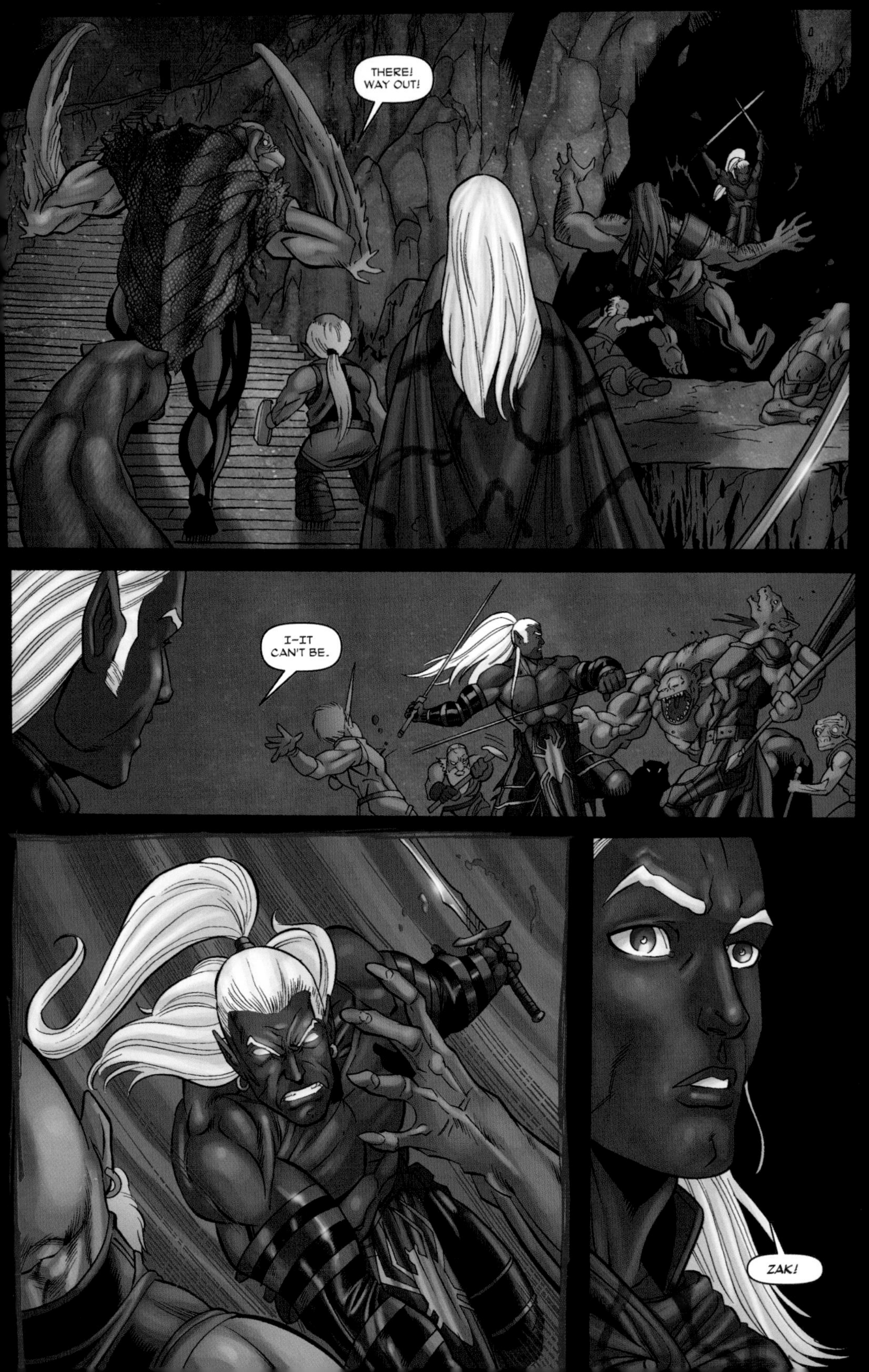
THERE! WAY OUT!
I-IT CAN'T BE.
ZAK!

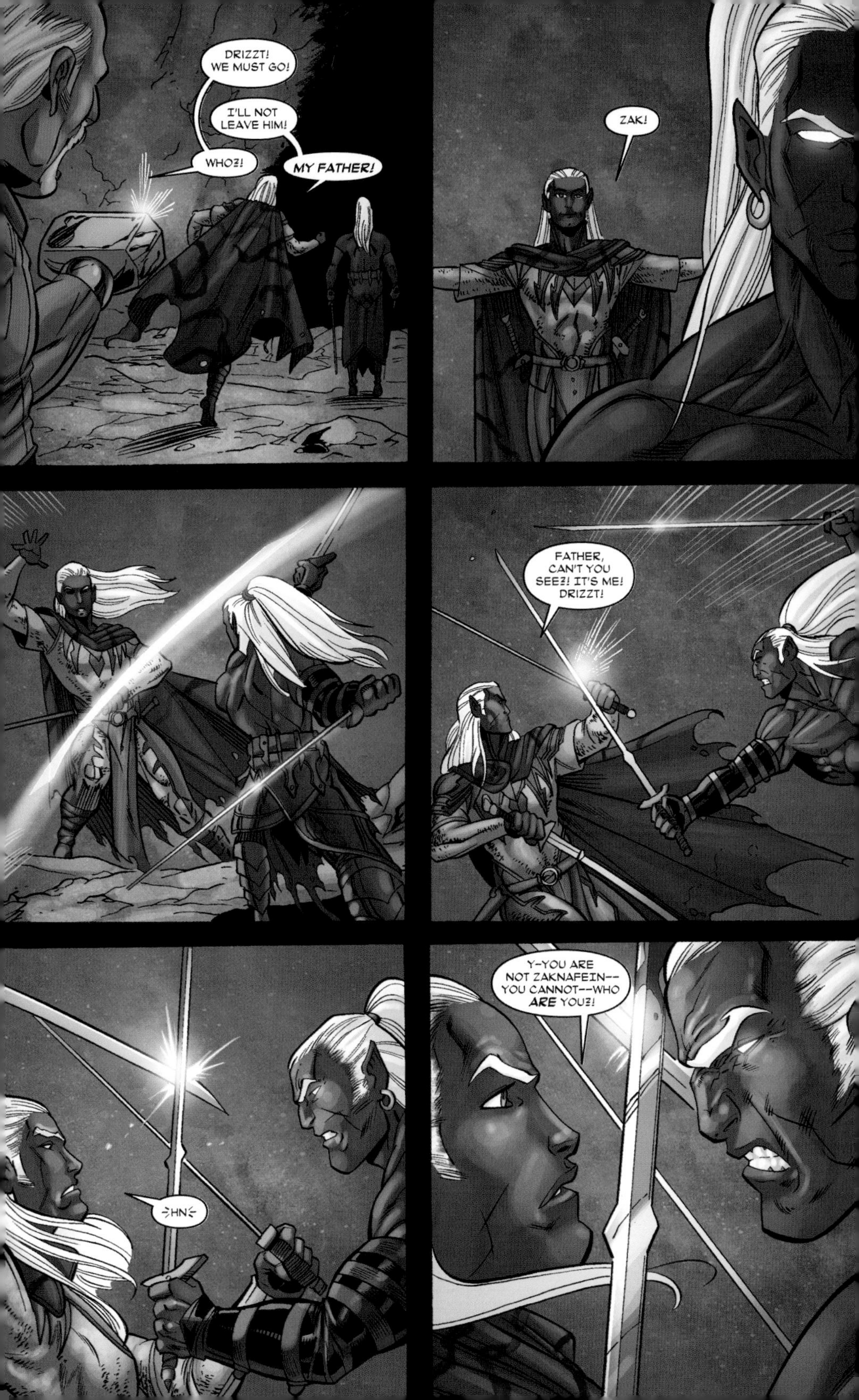
DRIZZT! WE MUST GO!
I'LL NOT LEAVE HIM!
WHO?!
MY FATHER!
ZAK!
FATHER, CAN'T YOU SEE?! IT'S ME! DRIZZT!
HN
Y-YOU ARE NOT ZAKNAFEIN-- YOU CANNOT--WHO ARE YOU?!

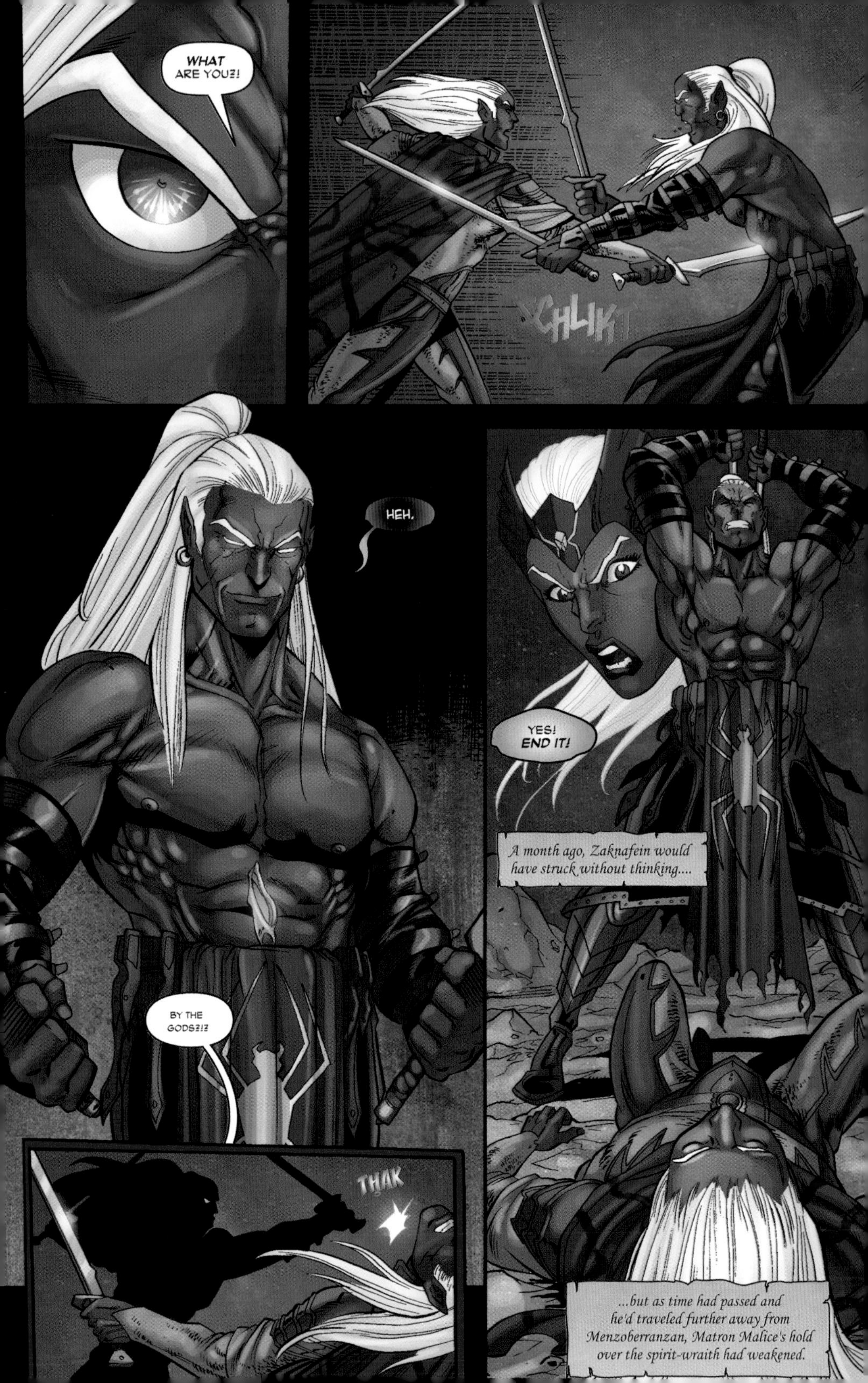

WHAT ARE YOU?!
CHLIK
HEH.
YES! END IT!
A month ago, Zaknafein would have struck without thinking....
BY THE GODS?!?
THAK
...but as time had passed and he'd traveled further away from Menzoberranzan, Matron Malice's hold over the spirit-wraith had weakened.

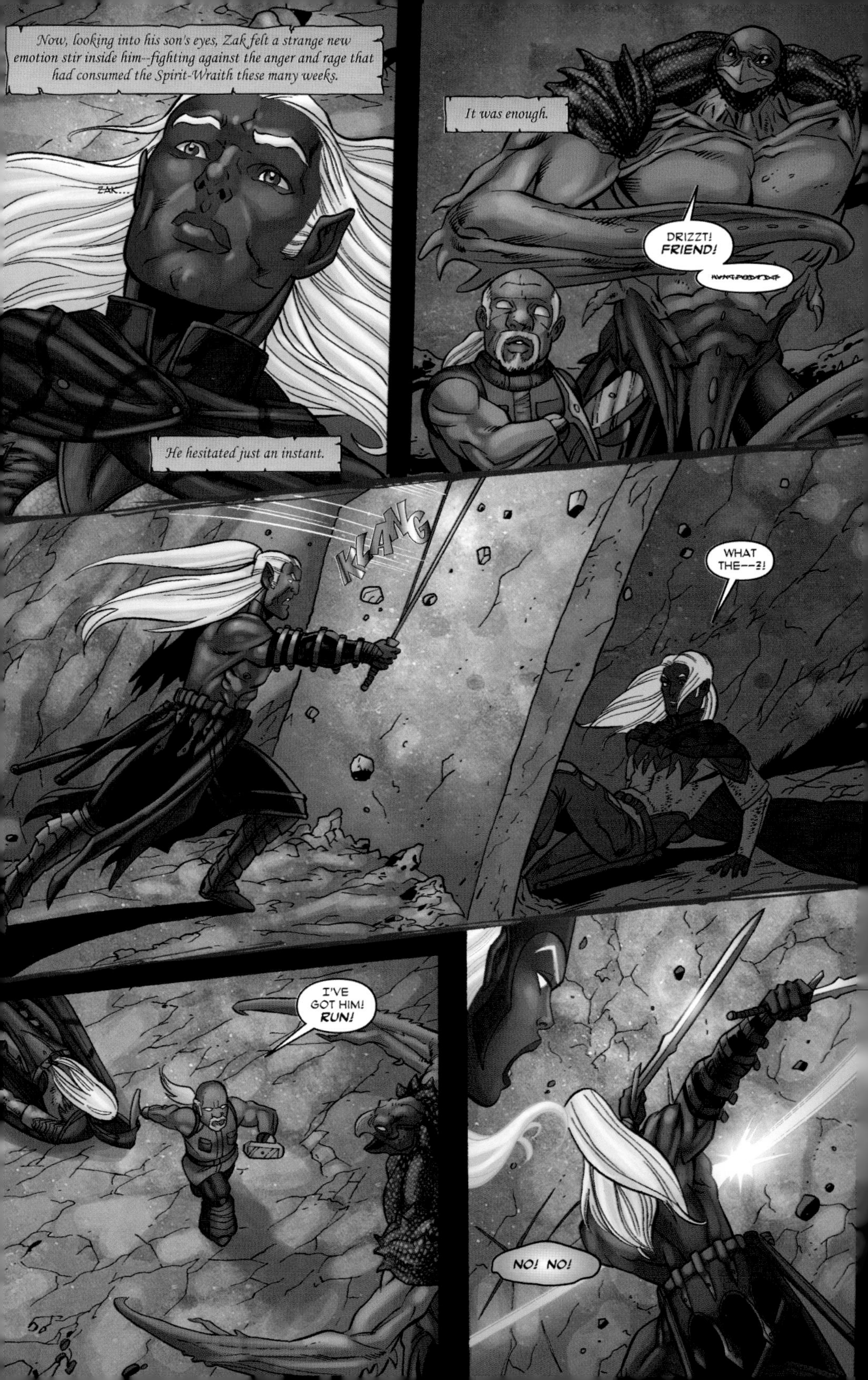
Now, looking into his son's eyes, Zak felt a strange new emotion stir inside him--fighting against the anger and rage that had consumed the Spirit-Wraith these many weeks.
ZAK...
He hesitated just an instant.
It was enough.
DRIZZT! FRIEND!
KLANG
WHAT THE--?!
I'VE GOT HIM! RUN!
NO! NO!

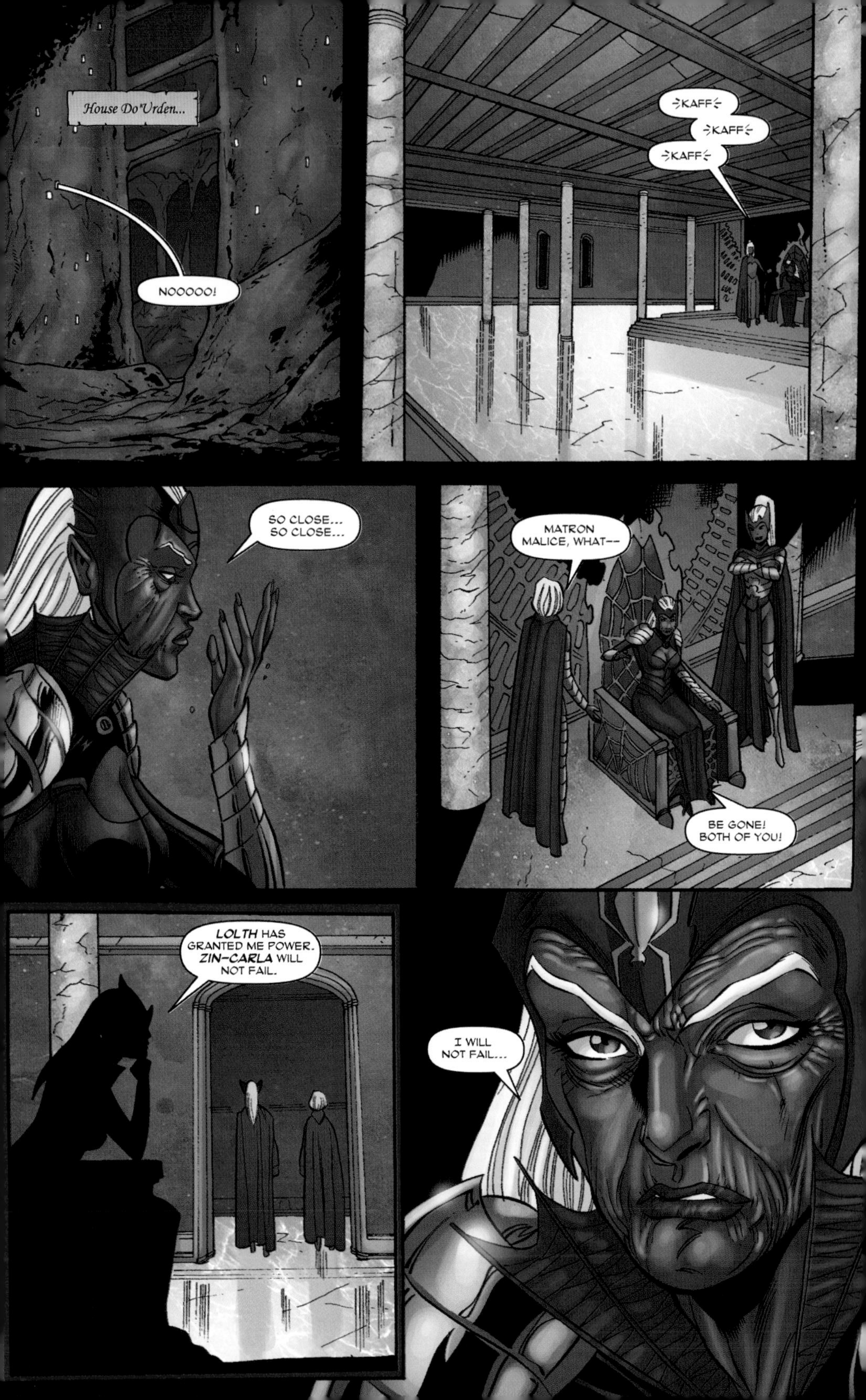

House Do'Urden...
NOOOOO!
KAFF
KAFF
KAFF
SO CLOSE... SO CLOSE...
MATRON MALICE, WHAT--
BE GONE! BOTH OF YOU!
LOLTH HAS GRANTED ME POWER. ZIN-CARLA WILL NOT FAIL.
I WILL NOT FAIL...

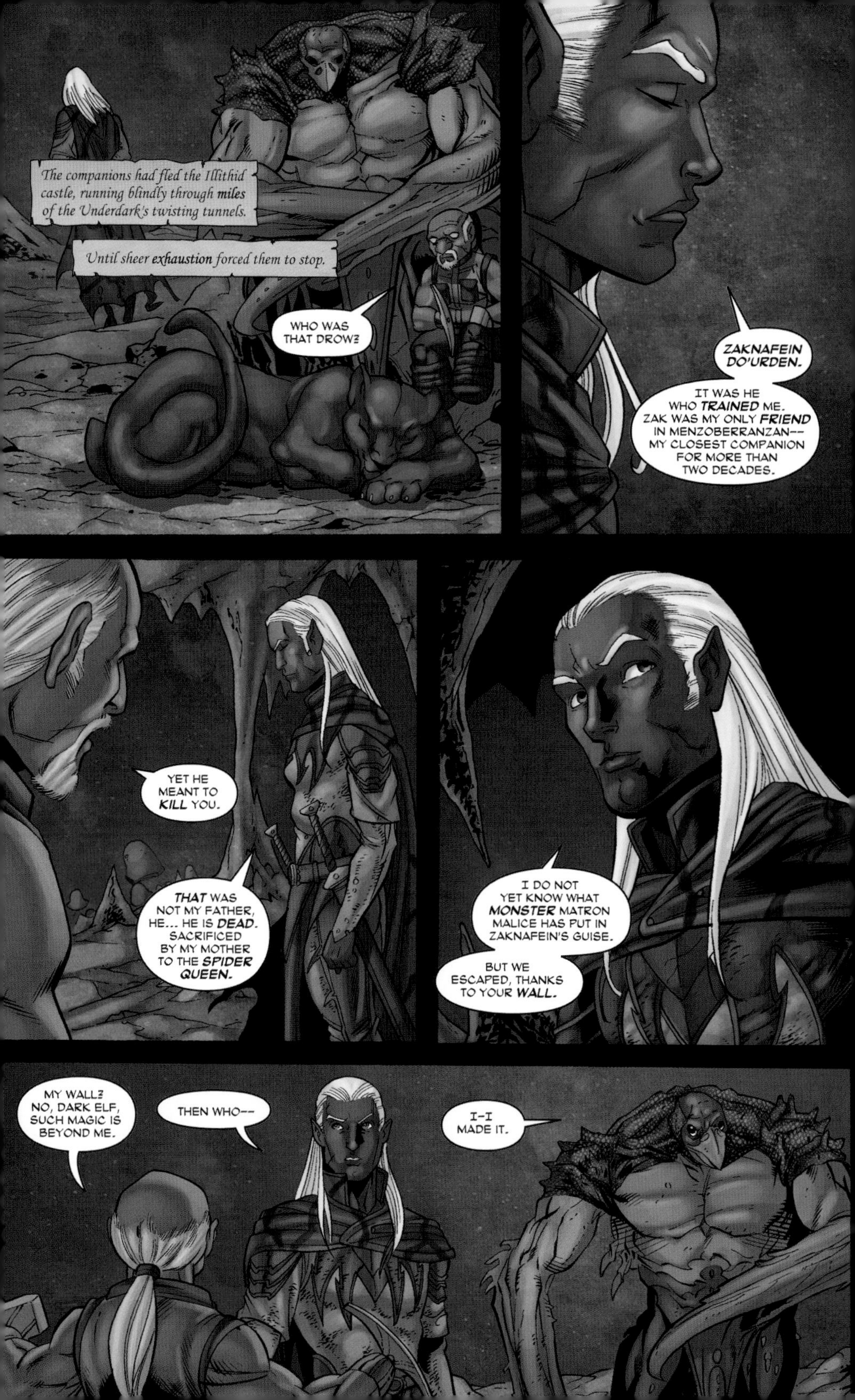
The companions had fled the Illithid castle, running blindly through miles of the Underdark's twisting tunnels.
Until sheer exhaustion forced them to stop.
WHO WAS THAT DROW?
ZAKNAFEIN DO'URDEN.
IT WAS HE WHO TRAINED ME. ZAK WAS MY ONLY FRIEND IN MENZOBERRANZAN-- MY CLOSEST COMPANION FOR MORE THAN TWO DECADES.
YET HE MEANT TO KILL YOU.
THAT WAS NOT MY FATHER, HE... HE IS DEAD. SACRIFICED BY MY MOTHER TO THE SPIDER QUEEN.
I DO NOT YET KNOW WHAT MONSTER MATRON MALICE HAS PUT IN ZAKNAFEIN'S GUISE.
BUT WE ESCAPED, THANKS TO YOUR WALL.
MY WALL? NO, DARK ELF, SUCH MAGIC IS BEYOND ME.
THEN WHO--
I-I MADE IT.

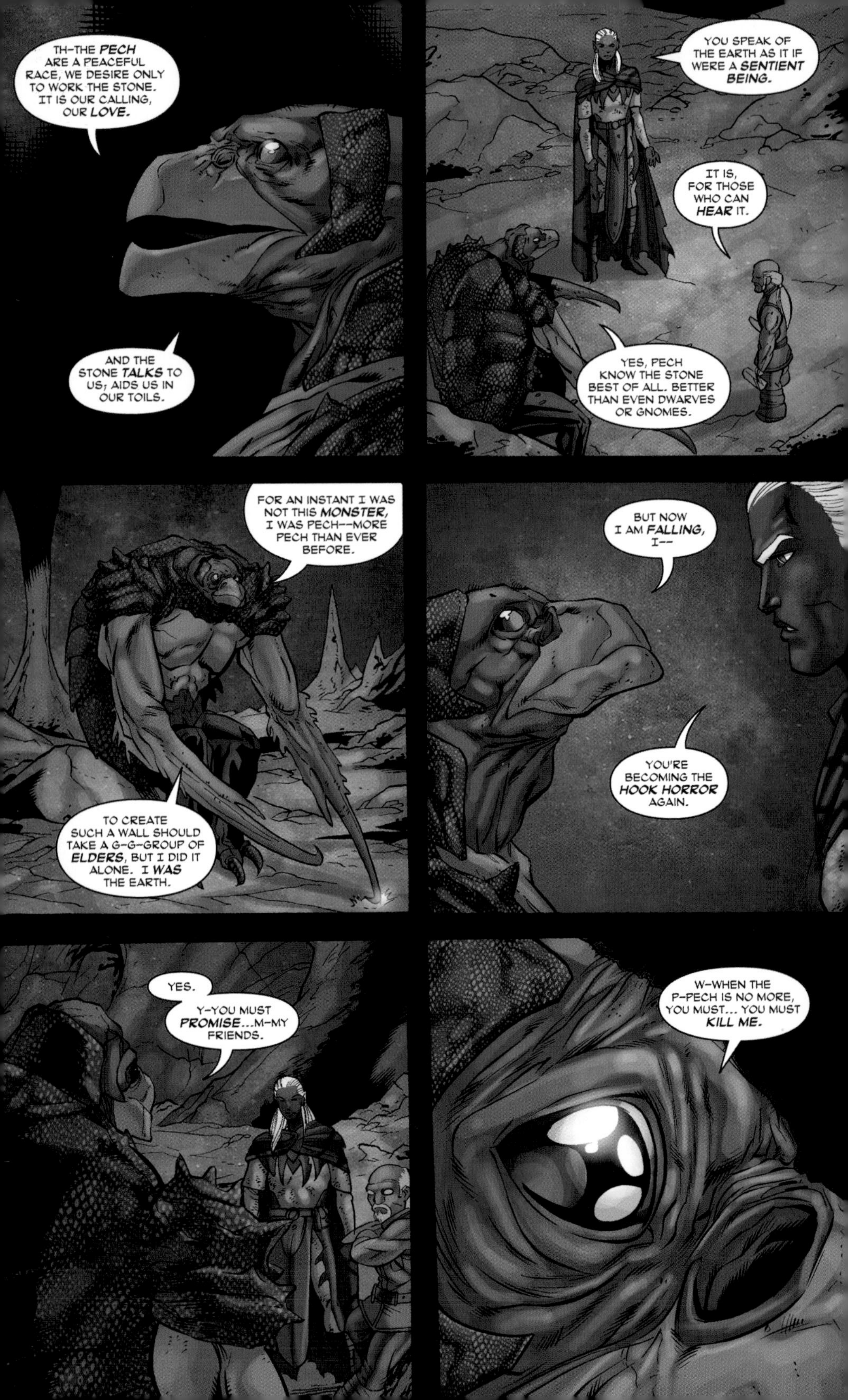
TH–THE PECH ARE A PEACEFUL RACE, WE DESIRE ONLY TO WORK THE STONE. IT IS OUR CALLING, OUR LOVE.
AND THE STONE TALKS TO US; AIDS US IN OUR TOILS.
YOU SPEAK OF THE EARTH AS IT IF WERE A SENTIENT BEING.
IT IS, FOR THOSE WHO CAN HEAR IT.
YES, PECH KNOW THE STONE BEST OF ALL. BETTER THAN EVEN DWARVES OR GNOMES.
FOR AN INSTANT I WAS NOT THIS MONSTER, I WAS PECH––MORE PECH THAN EVER BEFORE.
TO CREATE SUCH A WALL SHOULD TAKE A G–G–GROUP OF ELDERS, BUT I DID IT ALONE. I WAS THE EARTH.
BUT NOW I AM FALLING, I––
YOU'RE BECOMING THE HOOK HORROR AGAIN.
YES.
Y–YOU MUST PROMISE...M–MY FRIENDS.
W–WHEN THE P–PECH IS NO MORE, YOU MUST... YOU MUST KILL ME.

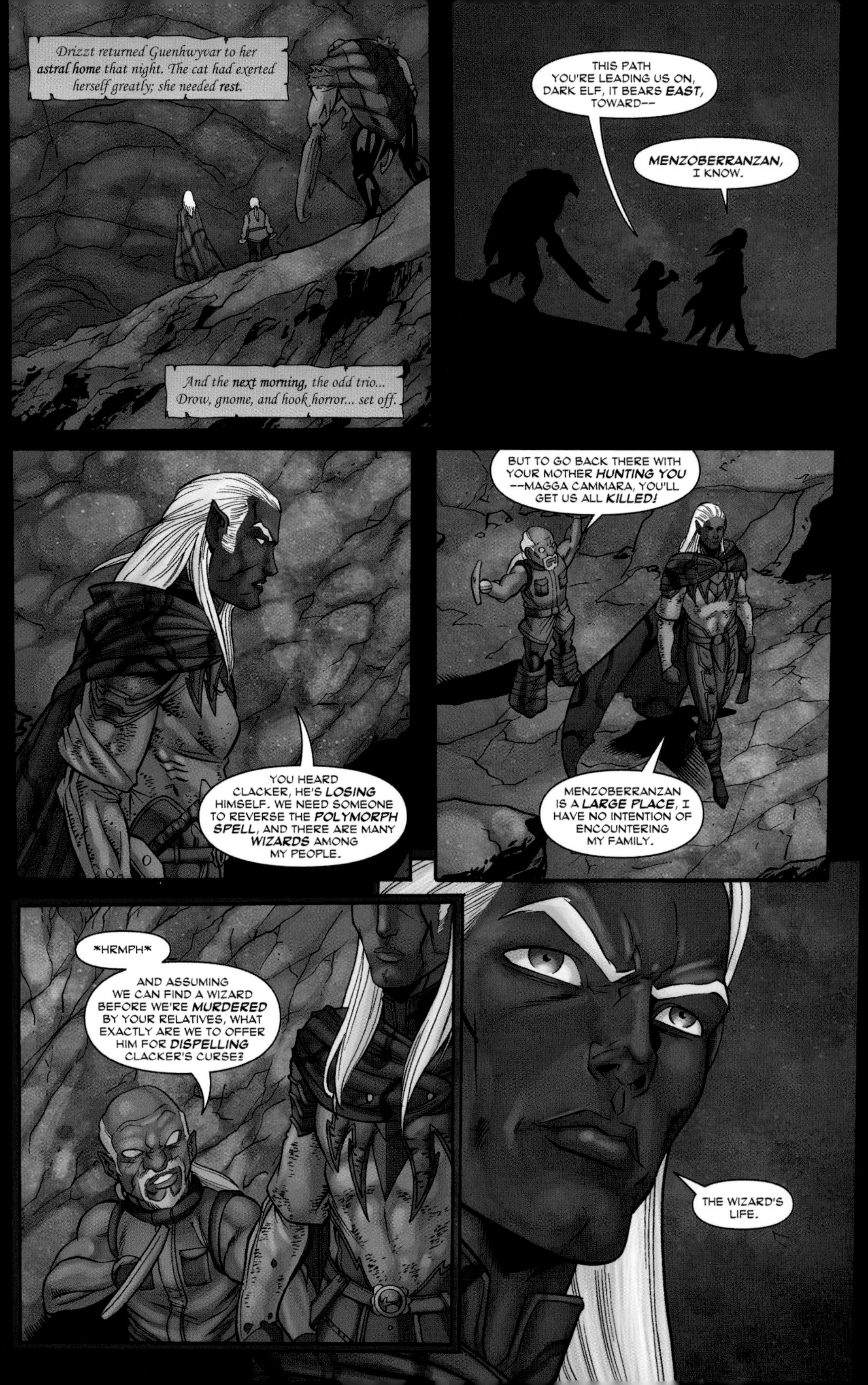
Drizzt returned Guenhwyvar to her astral home that night. The cat had exerted herself greatly; she needed rest.
And the next morning, the odd trio... Drow, gnome, and hook horror... set off.
THIS PATH YOU'RE LEADING US ON, DARK ELF, IT BEARS EAST, TOWARD--
MENZOBERRANZAN, I KNOW.
YOU HEARD CLACKER, HE'S LOSING HIMSELF. WE NEED SOMEONE TO REVERSE THE POLYMORPH SPELL, AND THERE ARE MANY WIZARDS AMONG MY PEOPLE.
BUT TO GO BACK THERE WITH YOUR MOTHER HUNTING YOU --MAGGA CAMMARA, YOU'LL GET US ALL KILLED!
MENZOBERRANZAN IS A LARGE PLACE, I HAVE NO INTENTION OF ENCOUNTERING MY FAMILY.
HRMPH
AND ASSUMING WE CAN FIND A WIZARD BEFORE WE'RE MURDERED BY YOUR RELATIVES, WHAT EXACTLY ARE WE TO OFFER HIM FOR DISPELLING CLACKER'S CURSE?
THE WIZARD'S LIFE.

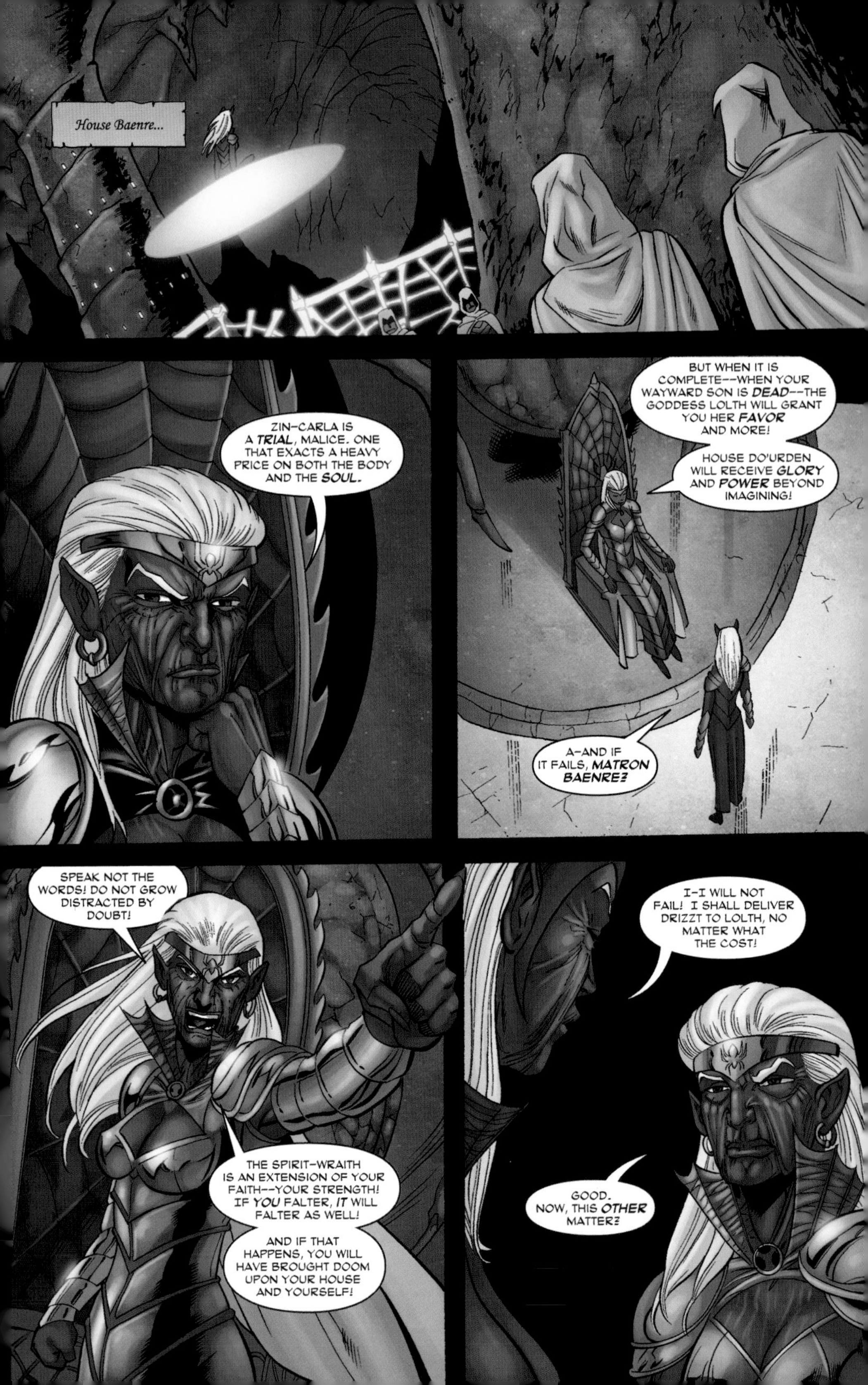
House Baenre...
ZIN-CARLA IS A TRIAL, MALICE. ONE THAT EXACTS A HEAVY PRICE ON BOTH THE BODY AND THE SOUL.
BUT WHEN IT IS COMPLETE--WHEN YOUR WAYWARD SON IS DEAD--THE GODDESS LOLTH WILL GRANT YOU HER FAVOR AND MORE!
HOUSE DO'URDEN WILL RECEIVE GLORY AND POWER BEYOND IMAGINING!
A-AND IF IT FAILS, MATRON BAENRE?
SPEAK NOT THE WORDS! DO NOT GROW DISTRACTED BY DOUBT!
THE SPIRIT-WRAITH IS AN EXTENSION OF YOUR FAITH--YOUR STRENGTH! IF YOU FALTER, IT WILL FALTER AS WELL!
AND IF THAT HAPPENS, YOU WILL HAVE BROUGHT DOOM UPON YOUR HOUSE AND YOURSELF!
I-I WILL NOT FAIL! I SHALL DELIVER DRIZZT TO LOLTH, NO MATTER WHAT THE COST!
GOOD. NOW, THIS OTHER MATTER?

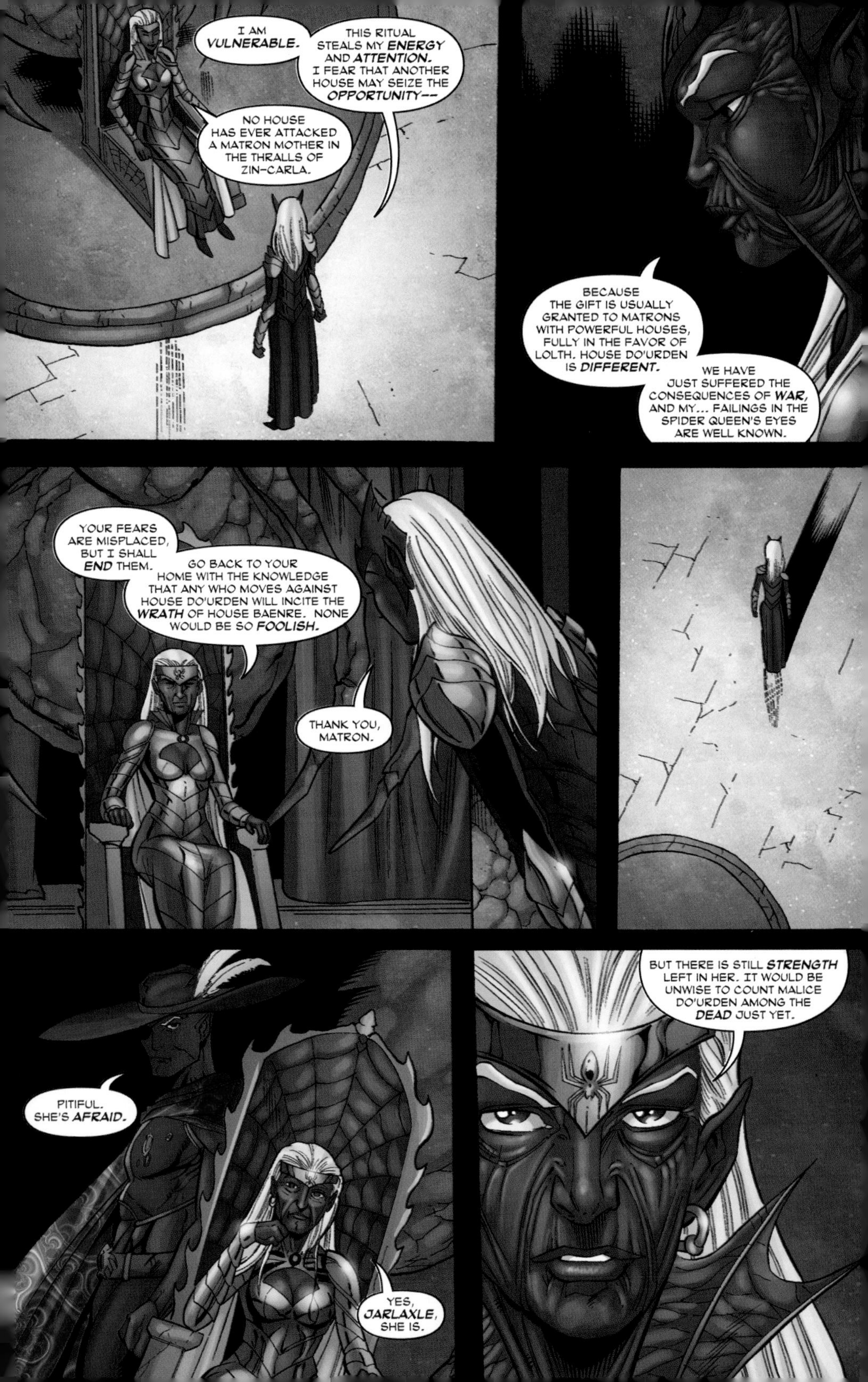
I AM VULNERABLE.
THIS RITUAL STEALS MY ENERGY AND ATTENTION. I FEAR THAT ANOTHER HOUSE MAY SEIZE THE OPPORTUNITY--
NO HOUSE HAS EVER ATTACKED A MATRON MOTHER IN THE THRALLS OF ZIN-CARLA.
BECAUSE THE GIFT IS USUALLY GRANTED TO MATRONS WITH POWERFUL HOUSES, FULLY IN THE FAVOR OF LOLTH. HOUSE DO'URDEN IS DIFFERENT.
WE HAVE JUST SUFFERED THE CONSEQUENCES OF WAR, AND MY... FAILINGS IN THE SPIDER QUEEN'S EYES ARE WELL KNOWN.
YOUR FEARS ARE MISPLACED, BUT I SHALL END THEM.
GO BACK TO YOUR HOME WITH THE KNOWLEDGE THAT ANY WHO MOVES AGAINST HOUSE DO'URDEN WILL INCITE THE WRATH OF HOUSE BAENRE. NONE WOULD BE SO FOOLISH.
THANK YOU, MATRON.
PITIFUL. SHE'S AFRAID.
YES, JARLAXLE, SHE IS.
BUT THERE IS STILL STRENGTH LEFT IN HER. IT WOULD BE UNWISE TO COUNT MALICE DO'URDEN AMONG THE DEAD JUST YET.

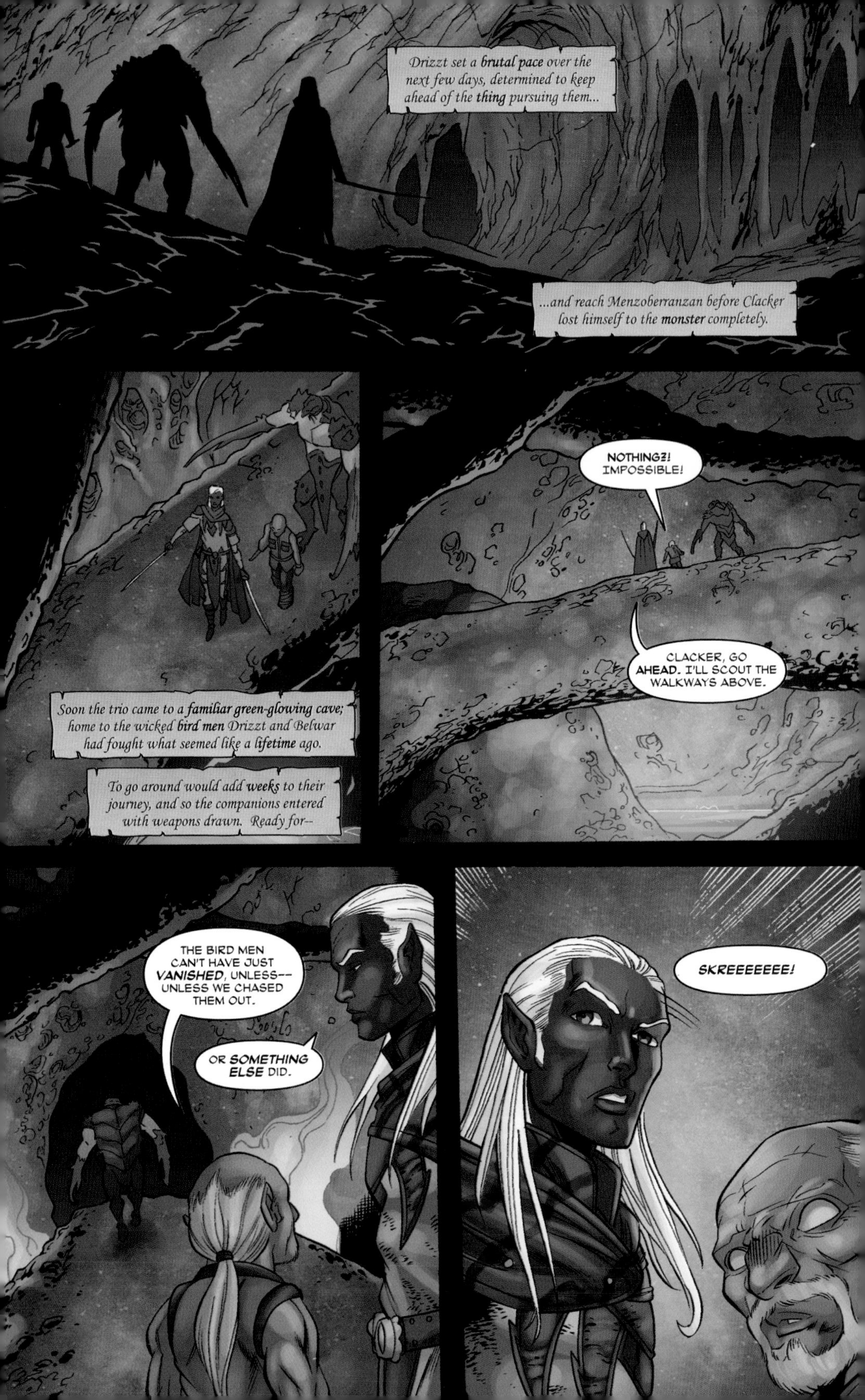
Drizzt set a brutal pace over the next few days, determined to keep ahead of the thing pursuing them...
...and reach Menzoberranzan before Clacker lost himself to the monster completely.
Soon the trio came to a familiar green-glowing cave; home to the wicked bird men Drizzt and Belwar had fought what seemed like a lifetime ago.
To go around would add weeks to their journey, and so the companions entered with weapons drawn. Ready for--
NOTHINGZ! IMPOSSIBLE!
CLACKER, GO AHEAD. I'LL SCOUT THE WALKWAYS ABOVE.
THE BIRD MEN CAN'T HAVE JUST VANISHED, UNLESS-- UNLESS WE CHASED THEM OUT.
OR SOMETHING ELSE DID.
SKREEEEEEE!

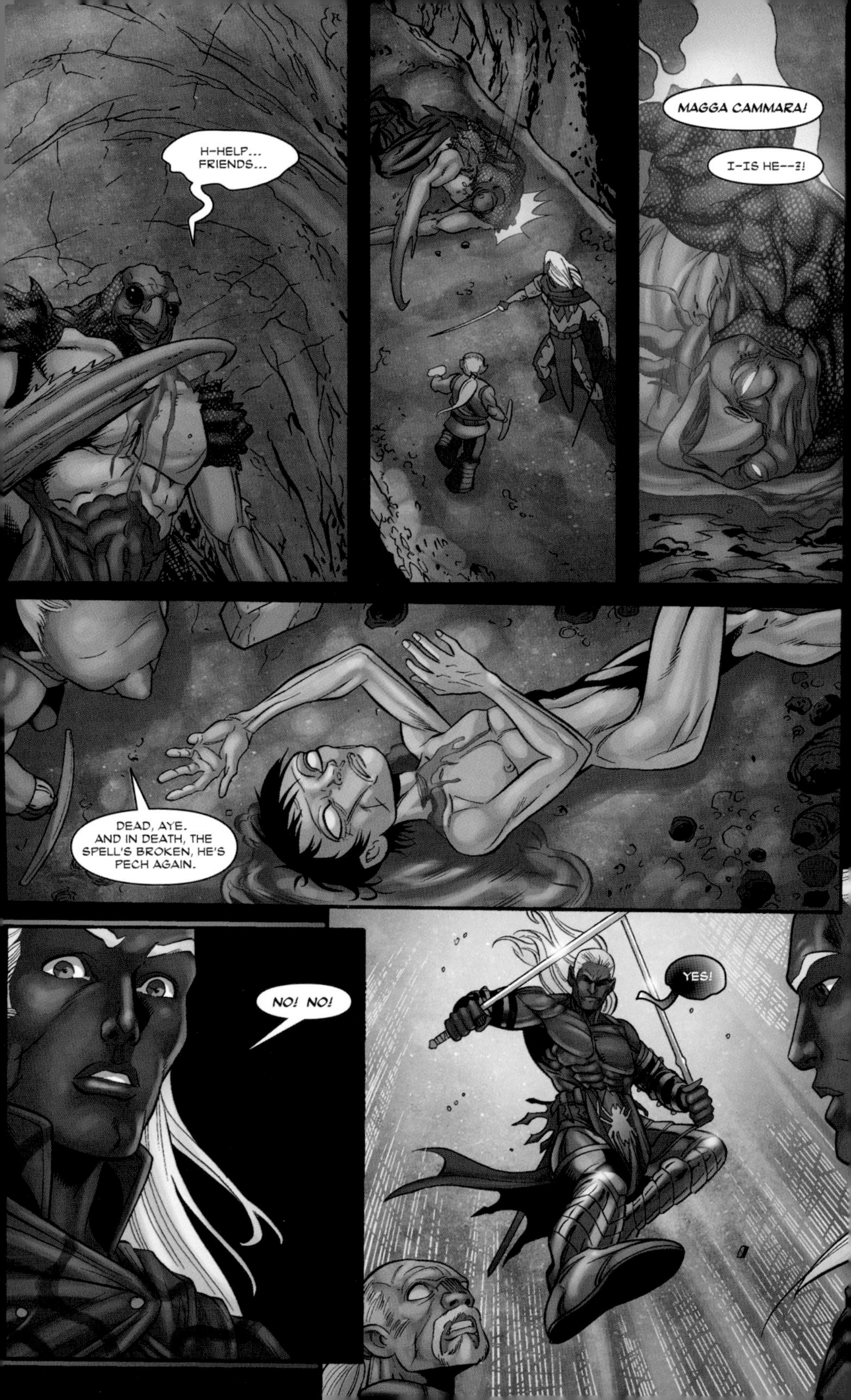
H-HELP...
FRIENDS...
MAGGA CAMMARA!
I-IS HE--?!
DEAD, AYE.
AND IN DEATH, THE
SPELL'S BROKEN, HE'S
PECH AGAIN.
NO! NO!
YES!

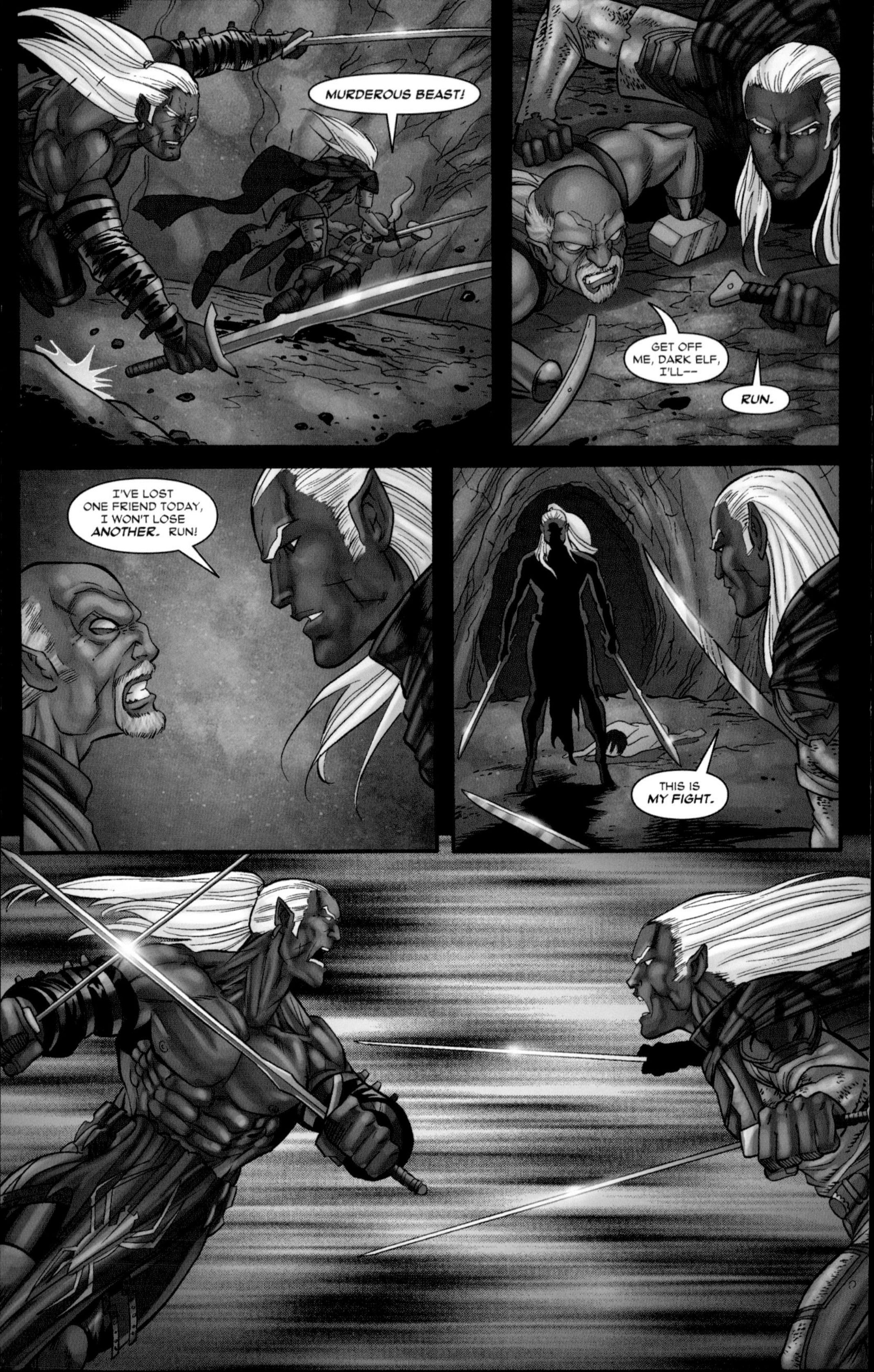
MURDEROUS BEAST!
GET OFF ME, DARK ELF, I'LL--
RUN.
I'VE LOST ONE FRIEND TODAY, I WON'T LOSE ANOTHER. RUN!
THIS IS MY FIGHT.

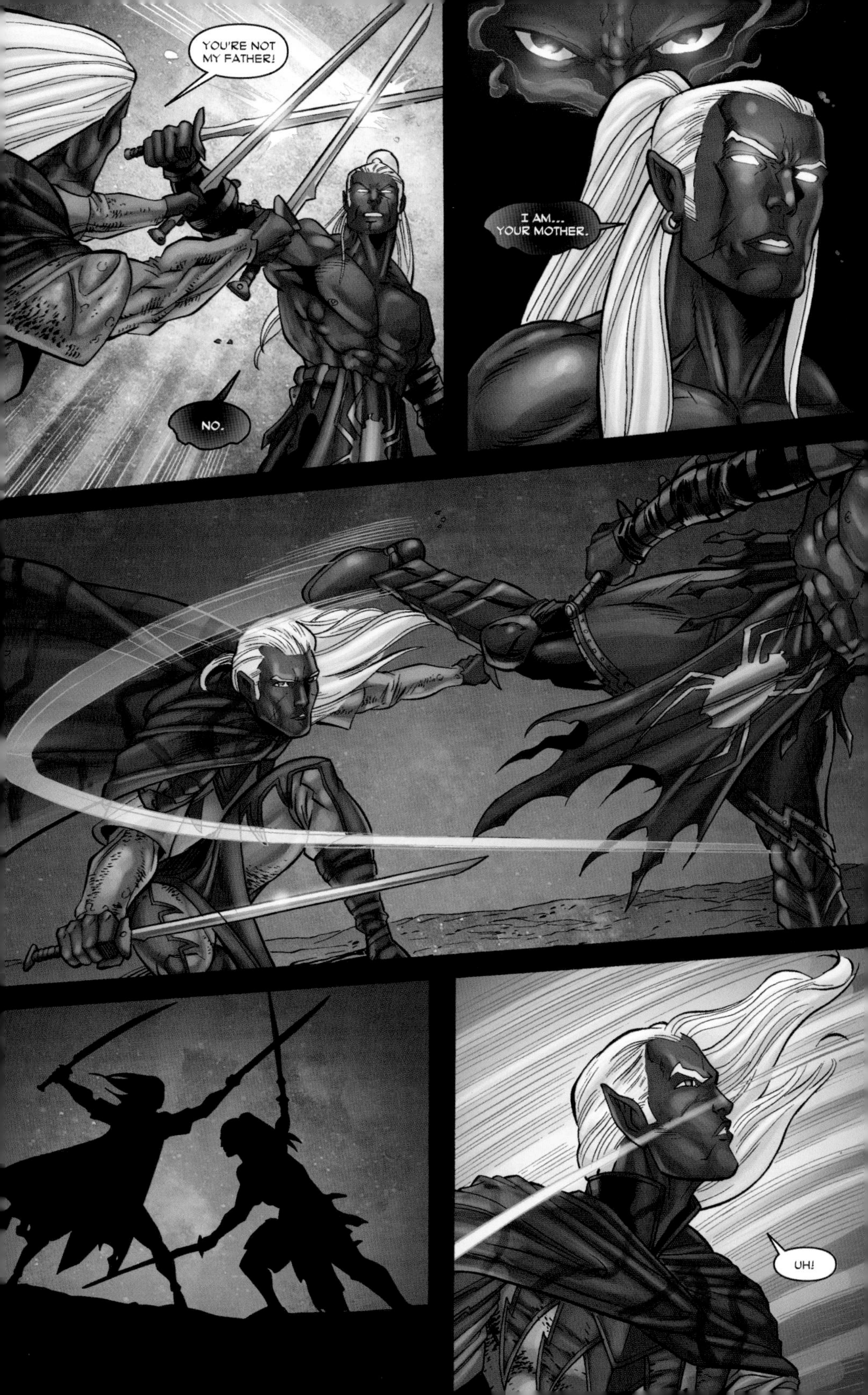
YOU'RE NOT MY FATHER!
NO.
I AM... YOUR MOTHER.
UH!

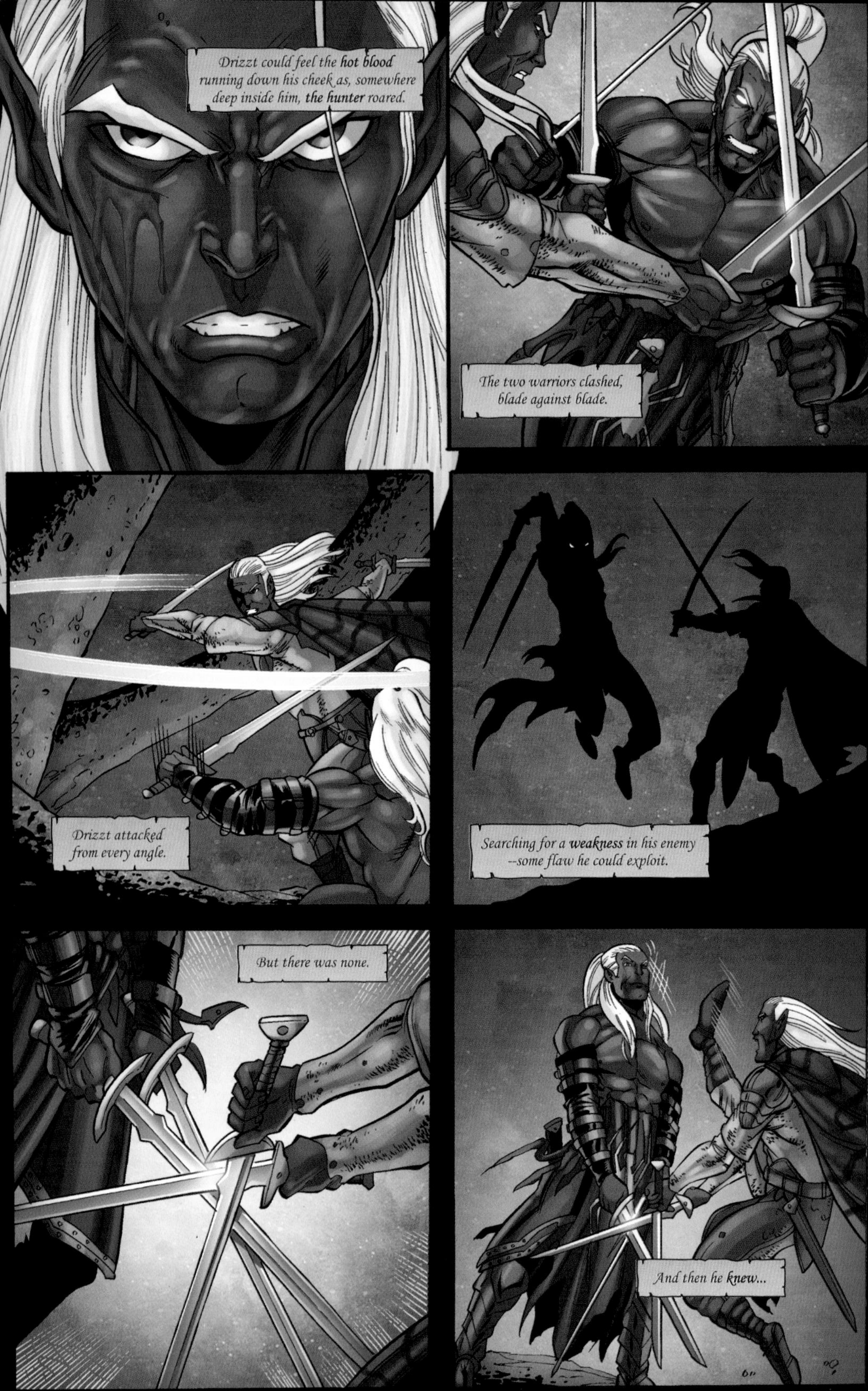
Drizzt could feel the hot blood running down his cheek as, somewhere deep inside him, the hunter roared.
The two warriors clashed, blade against blade.
Drizzt attacked from every angle.
Searching for a weakness in his enemy --some flaw he could exploit.
But there was none.
And then he knew...

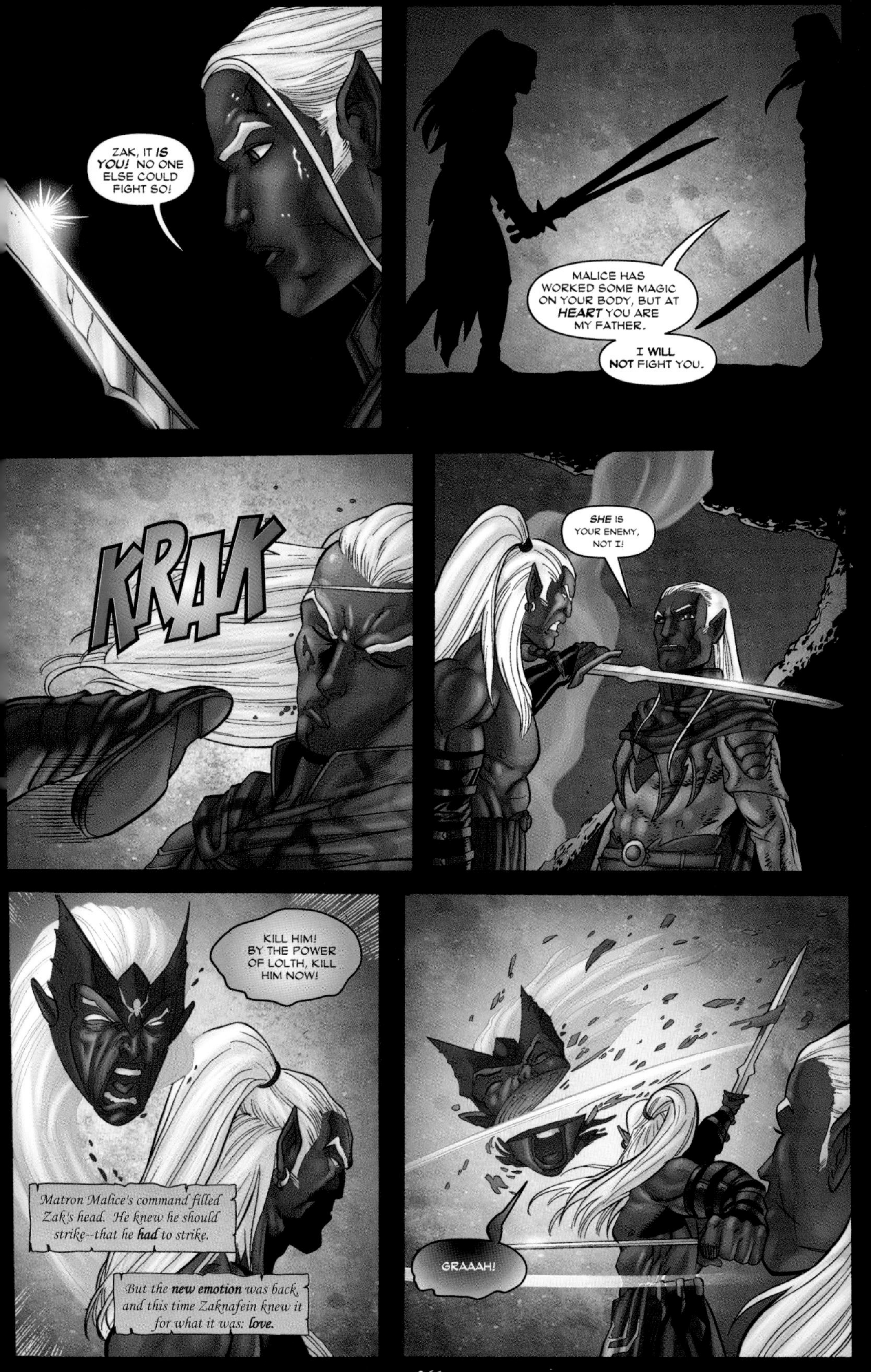
ZAK, IT IS YOU! NO ONE ELSE COULD FIGHT SO!
MALICE HAS WORKED SOME MAGIC ON YOUR BODY, BUT AT HEART YOU ARE MY FATHER.
I WILL NOT FIGHT YOU.
KRAK
SHE IS YOUR ENEMY, NOT I!
KILL HIM! BY THE POWER OF LOLTH, KILL HIM NOW!
Matron Malice's command filled Zak's head. He knew he should strike--that he had to strike.
But the new emotion was back, and this time Zaknafein knew it for what it was: love.
GRAAAH!

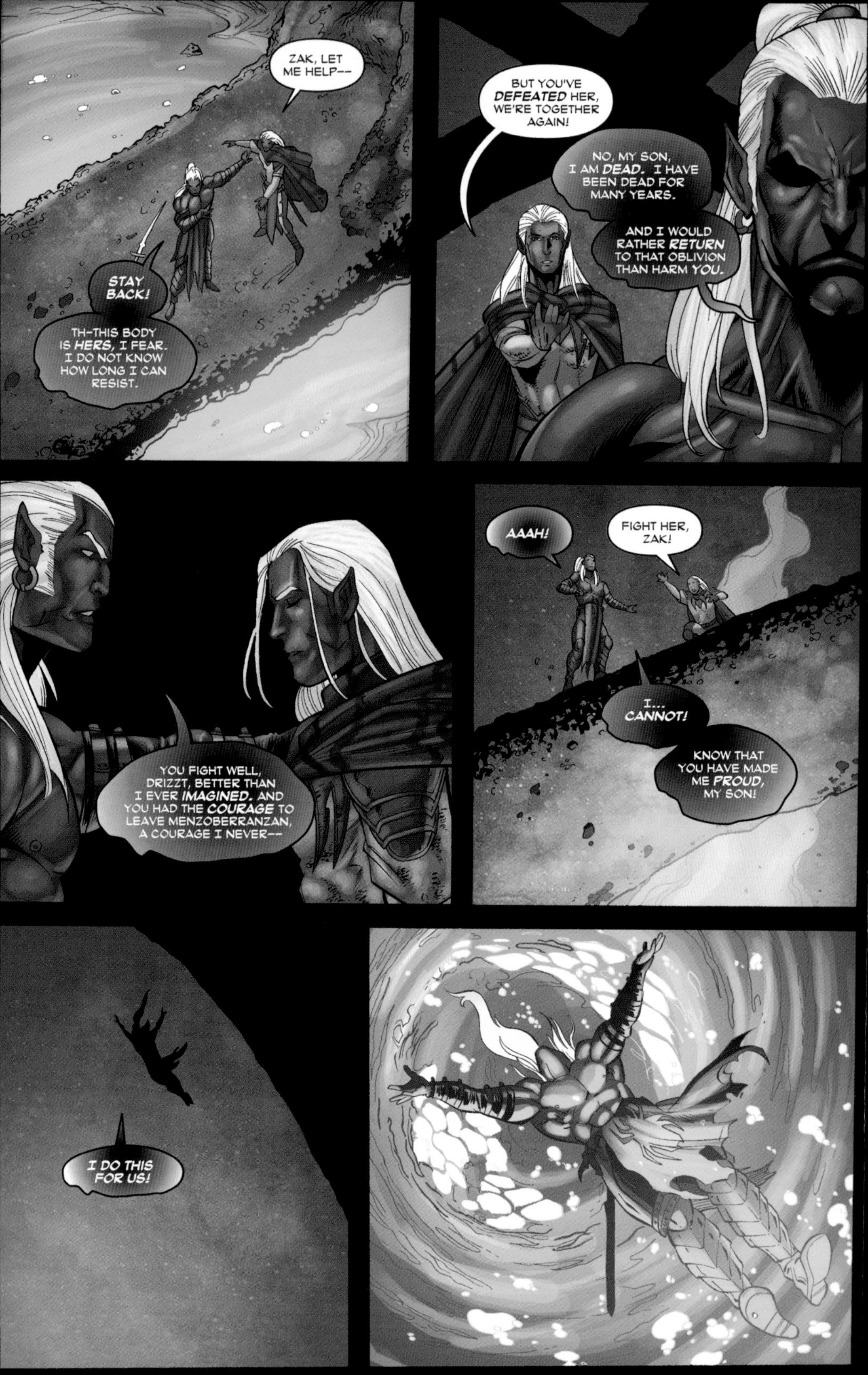
ZAK, LET ME HELP--
STAY BACK!
TH-THIS BODY IS HERS, I FEAR. I DO NOT KNOW HOW LONG I CAN RESIST.
BUT YOU'VE DEFEATED HER, WE'RE TOGETHER AGAIN!
NO, MY SON, I AM DEAD. I HAVE BEEN DEAD FOR MANY YEARS.
AND I WOULD RATHER RETURN TO THAT OBLIVION THAN HARM YOU.
YOU FIGHT WELL, DRIZZT, BETTER THAN I EVER IMAGINED. AND YOU HAD THE COURAGE TO LEAVE MENZOBERRANZAN, A COURAGE I NEVER--
AAAH!
FIGHT HER, ZAK!
I... CANNOT!
KNOW THAT YOU HAVE MADE ME PROUD, MY SON!
I DO THIS FOR US!

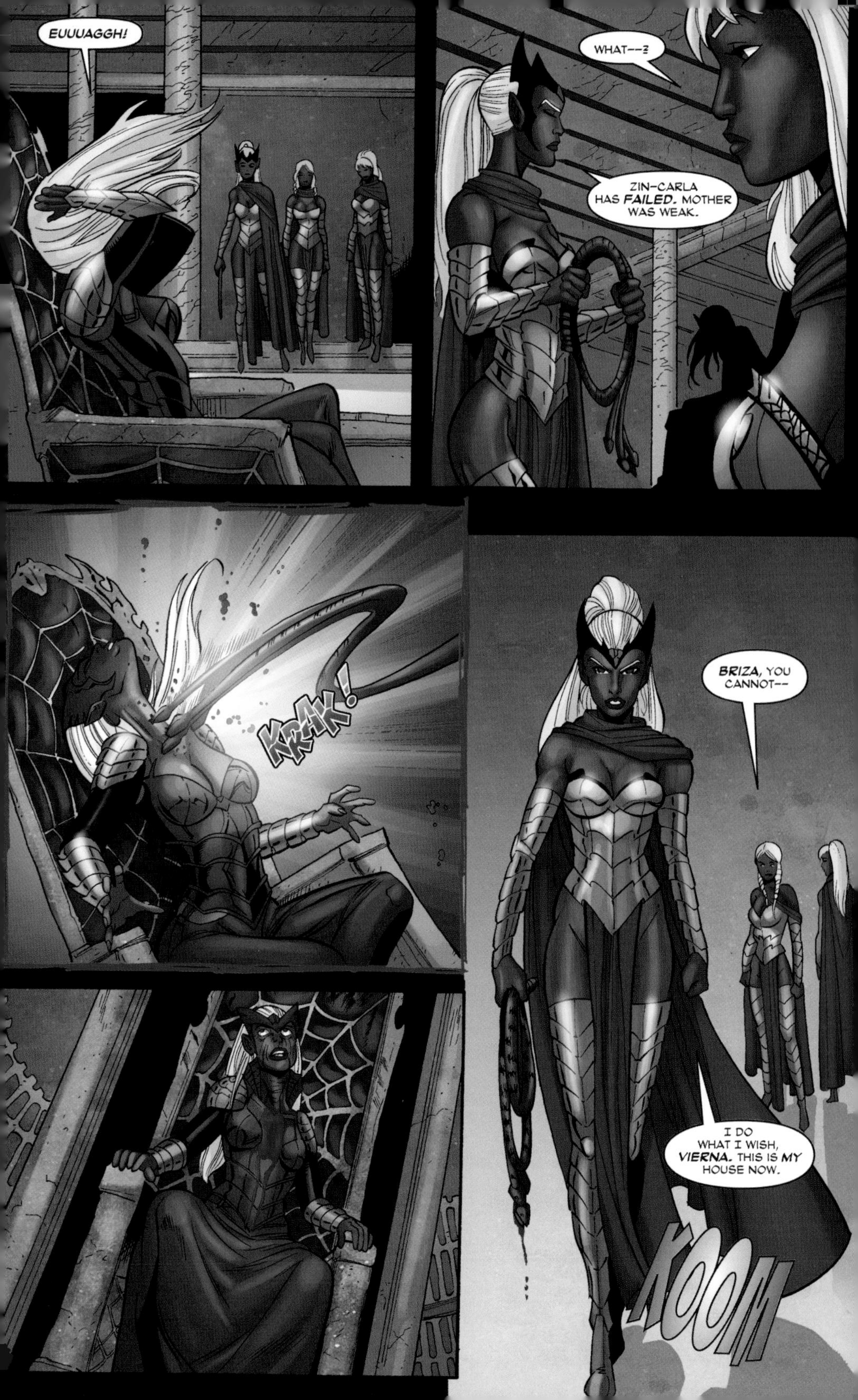
EUUUAGGH!
WHAT--?
ZIN-CARLA HAS FAILED. MOTHER WAS WEAK.
KRAK!
BRIZA, YOU CANNOT--
I DO WHAT I WISH, VIERNA. THIS IS MY HOUSE NOW.
KOOM

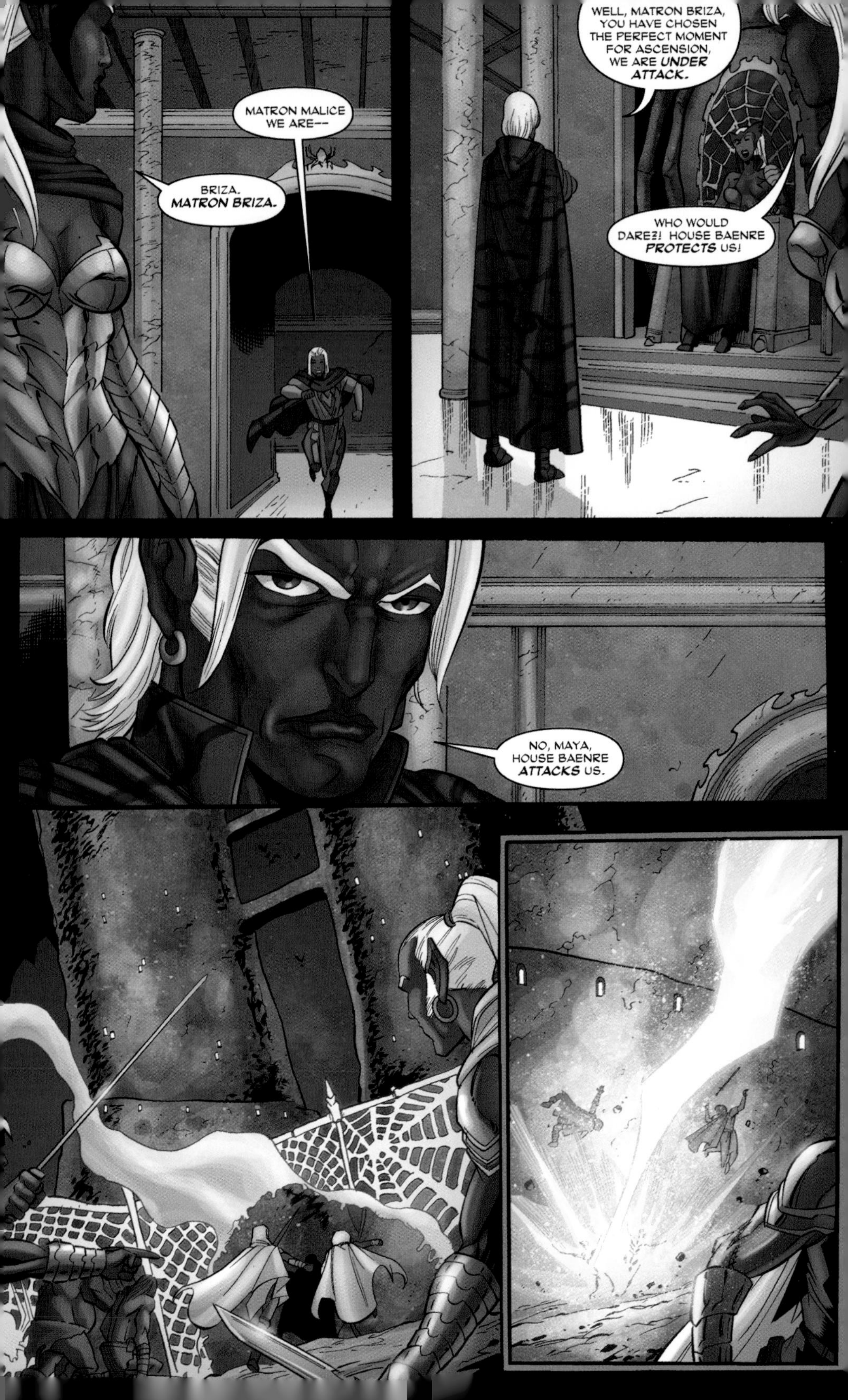

MATRON MALICE WE ARE--
BRIZA. MATRON BRIZA.
WELL, MATRON BRIZA, YOU HAVE CHOSEN THE PERFECT MOMENT FOR ASCENSION, WE ARE UNDER ATTACK.
WHO WOULD DARE?! HOUSE BAENRE PROTECTS US!
NO, MAYA, HOUSE BAENRE ATTACKS US.

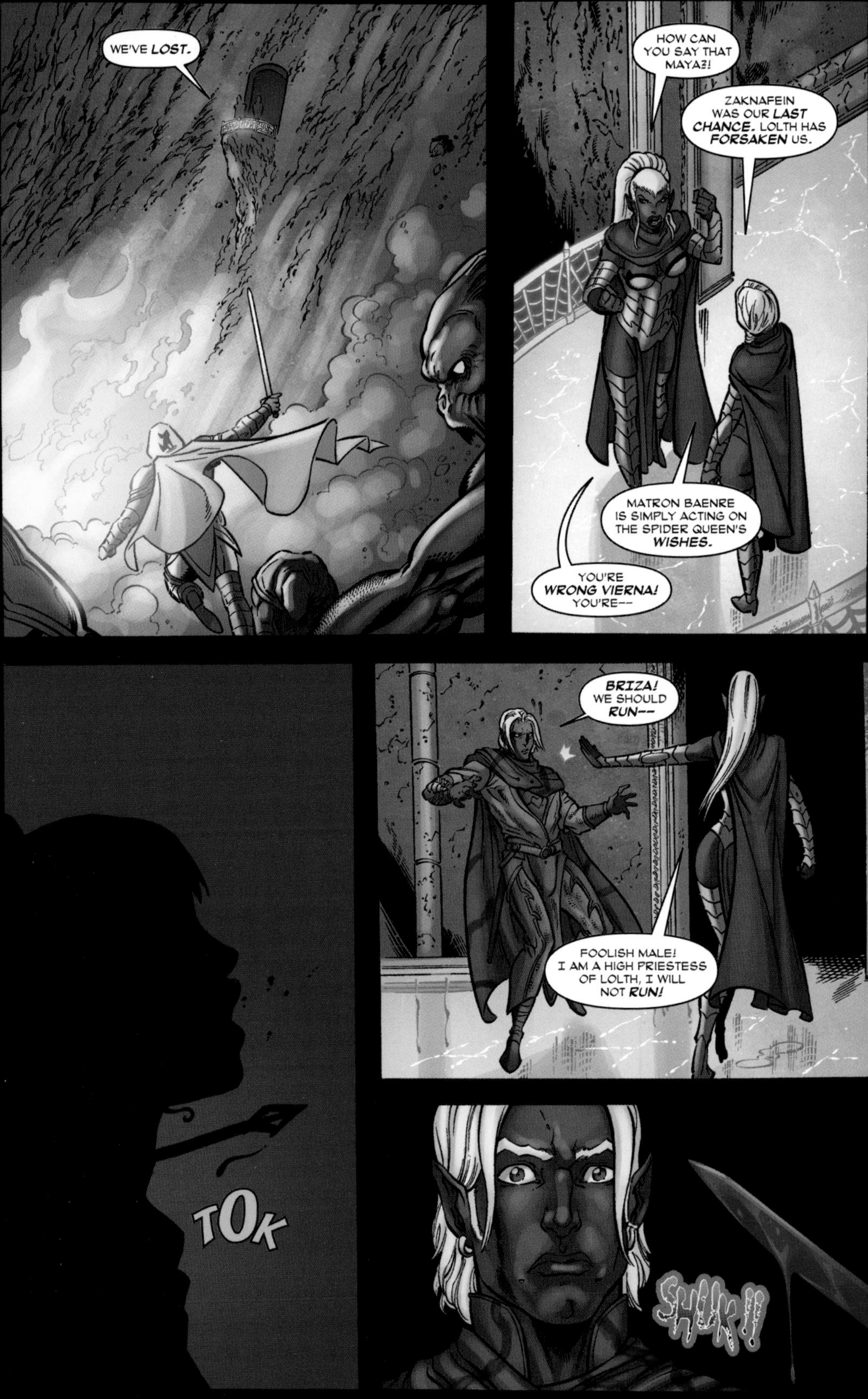
WE'VE LOST.
HOW CAN YOU SAY THAT MAYA?!
ZAKNAFEIN WAS OUR LAST CHANCE. LOLTH HAS FORSAKEN US.
MATRON BAENRE IS SIMPLY ACTING ON THE SPIDER QUEEN'S WISHES.
YOU'RE WRONG VIERNA! YOU'RE--
BRIZA! WE SHOULD RUN--
FOOLISH MALE! I AM A HIGH PRIESTESS OF LOLTH, I WILL NOT RUN!
TOK
SHUK!!

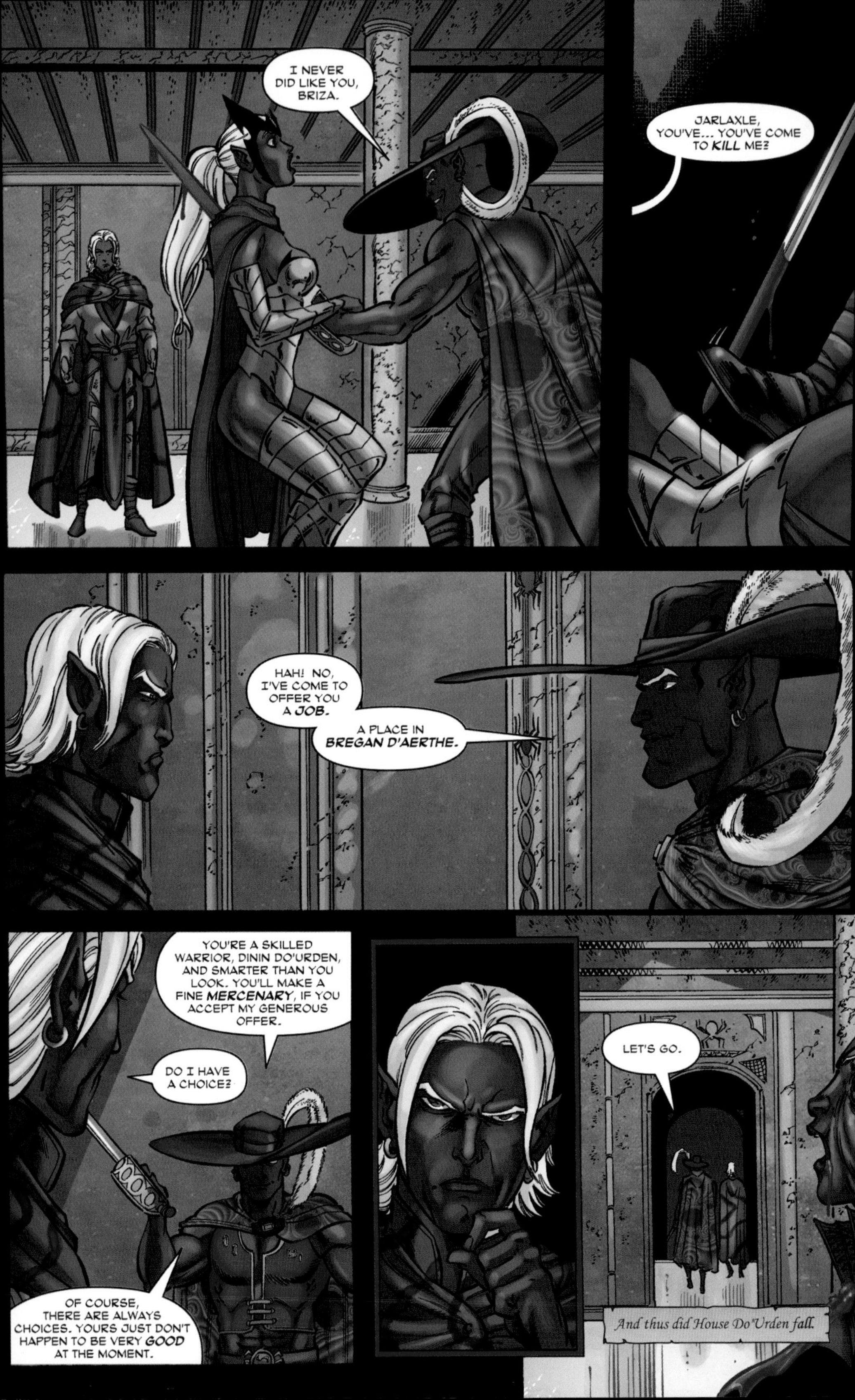
I NEVER DID LIKE YOU, BRIZA.
JARLAXLE, YOU'VE... YOU'VE COME TO KILL ME?
HAH! NO, I'VE COME TO OFFER YOU A JOB.
A PLACE IN BREGAN D'AERTHE.
YOU'RE A SKILLED WARRIOR, DININ DO'URDEN, AND SMARTER THAN YOU LOOK. YOU'LL MAKE A FINE MERCENARY, IF YOU ACCEPT MY GENEROUS OFFER.
DO I HAVE A CHOICE?
OF COURSE, THERE ARE ALWAYS CHOICES. YOURS JUST DON'T HAPPEN TO BE VERY GOOD AT THE MOMENT.
LET'S GO.
And thus did House Do'Urden fall.

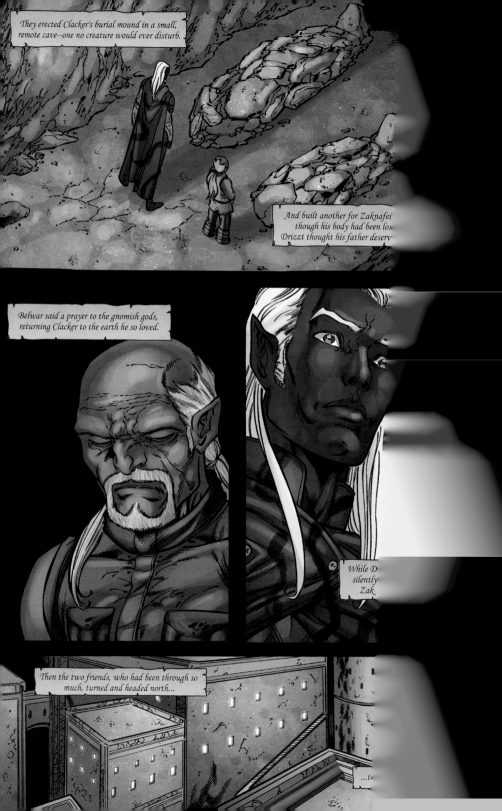

They erected Clacker's burial mound in a small, remote cave--one no creature would ever disturb.

And built another for Zaknafei though his body had been los Drizzt thought his father deserv

Belwar said a prayer to the gnomish gods, returning Clacker to the earth he so loved.

While D silently Zak

Then the two friends, who had been through so much, turned and headed north...

...t

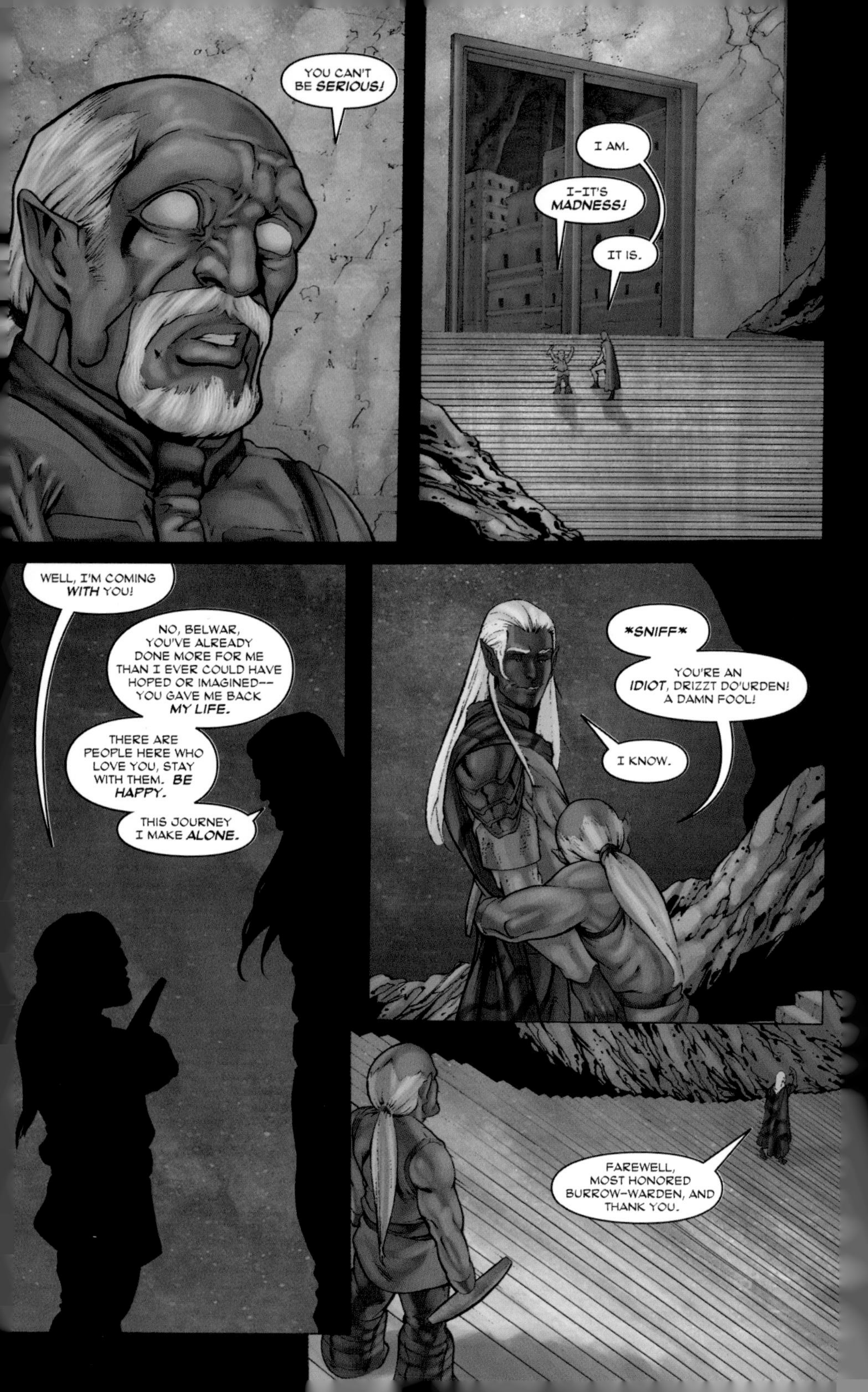
YOU CAN'T BE SERIOUS!
I AM.
I-IT'S MADNESS!
IT IS.
WELL, I'M COMING WITH YOU!
NO, BELWAR, YOU'VE ALREADY DONE MORE FOR ME THAN I EVER COULD HAVE HOPED OR IMAGINED-- YOU GAVE ME BACK MY LIFE.
THERE ARE PEOPLE HERE WHO LOVE YOU, STAY WITH THEM. BE HAPPY.
THIS JOURNEY I MAKE ALONE.
SNIFF
YOU'RE AN IDIOT, DRIZZT DO'URDEN! A DAMN FOOL!
I KNOW.
FAREWELL, MOST HONORED BURROW-WARDEN, AND THANK YOU.

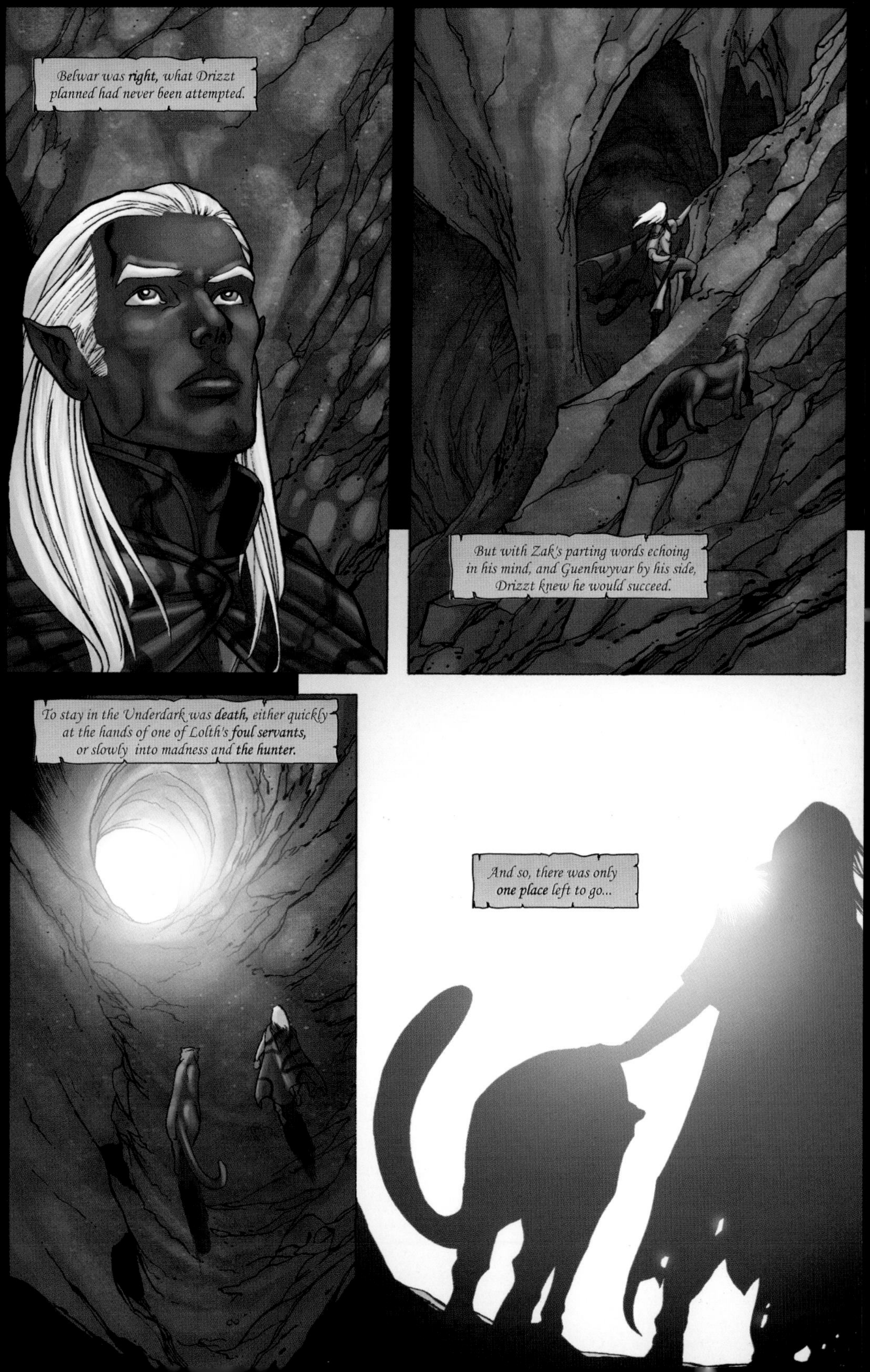
Belwar was right, what Drizzt planned had never been attempted.
But with Zak's parting words echoing in his mind, and Guenhwyvar by his side, Drizzt knew he would succeed.
To stay in the Underdark was death, either quickly at the hands of one of Lolth's foul servants, or slowly into madness and the hunter.
And so, there was only one place left to go...

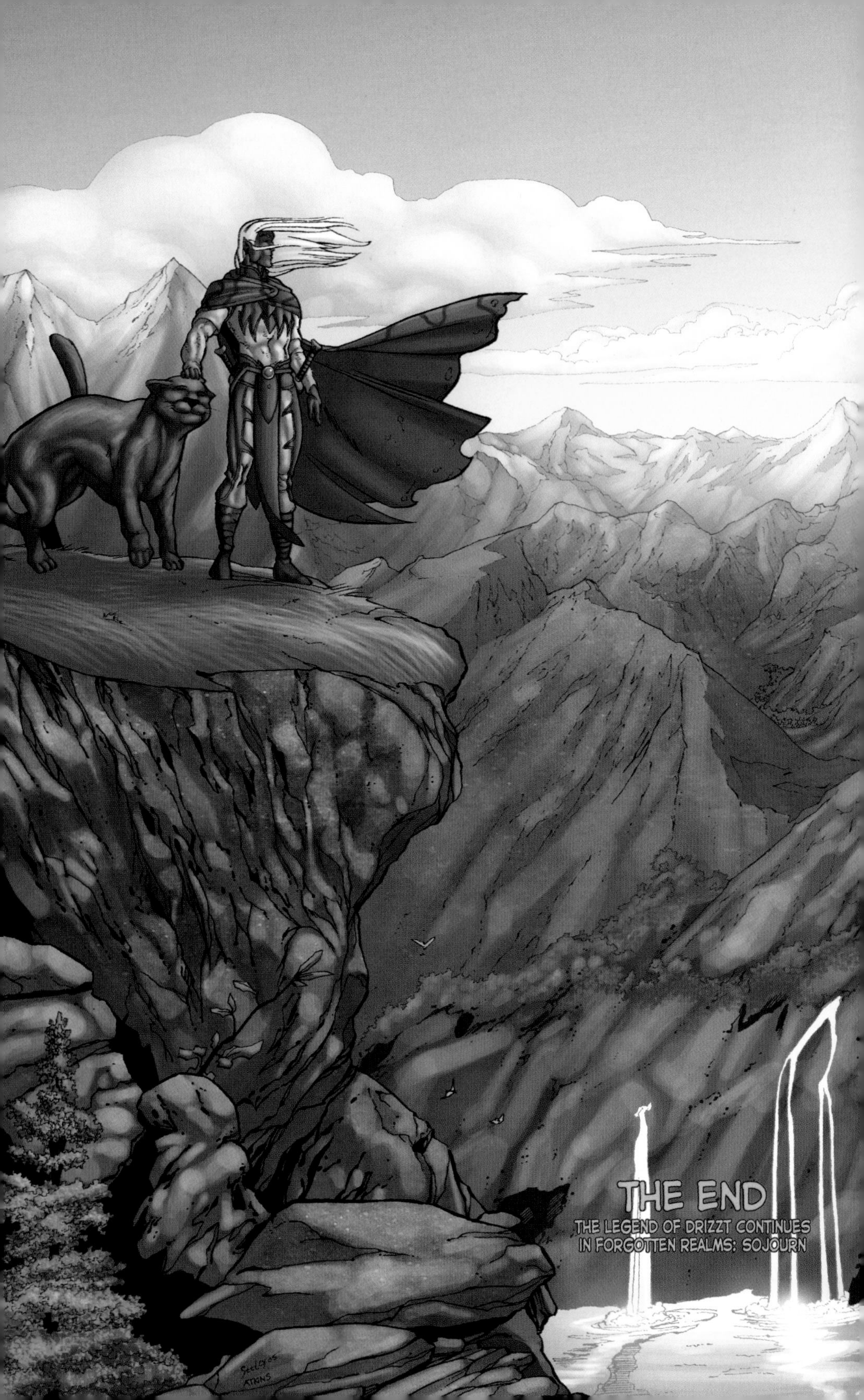
THE END
THE LEGEND OF DRIZZT CONTINUES
IN FORGOTTEN REALMS: SOJOURN
Seeley 05
ATKINS

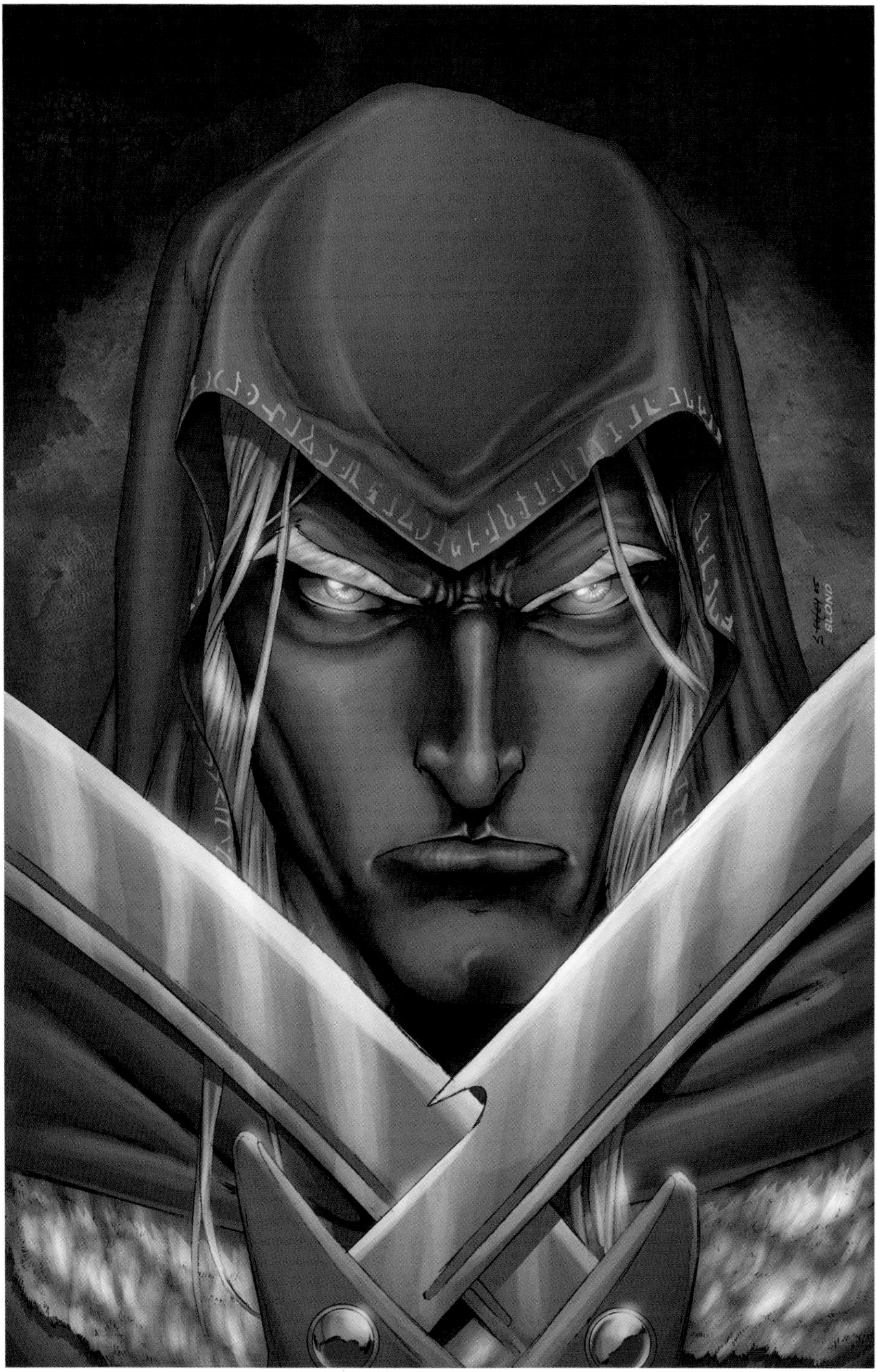
BLOND

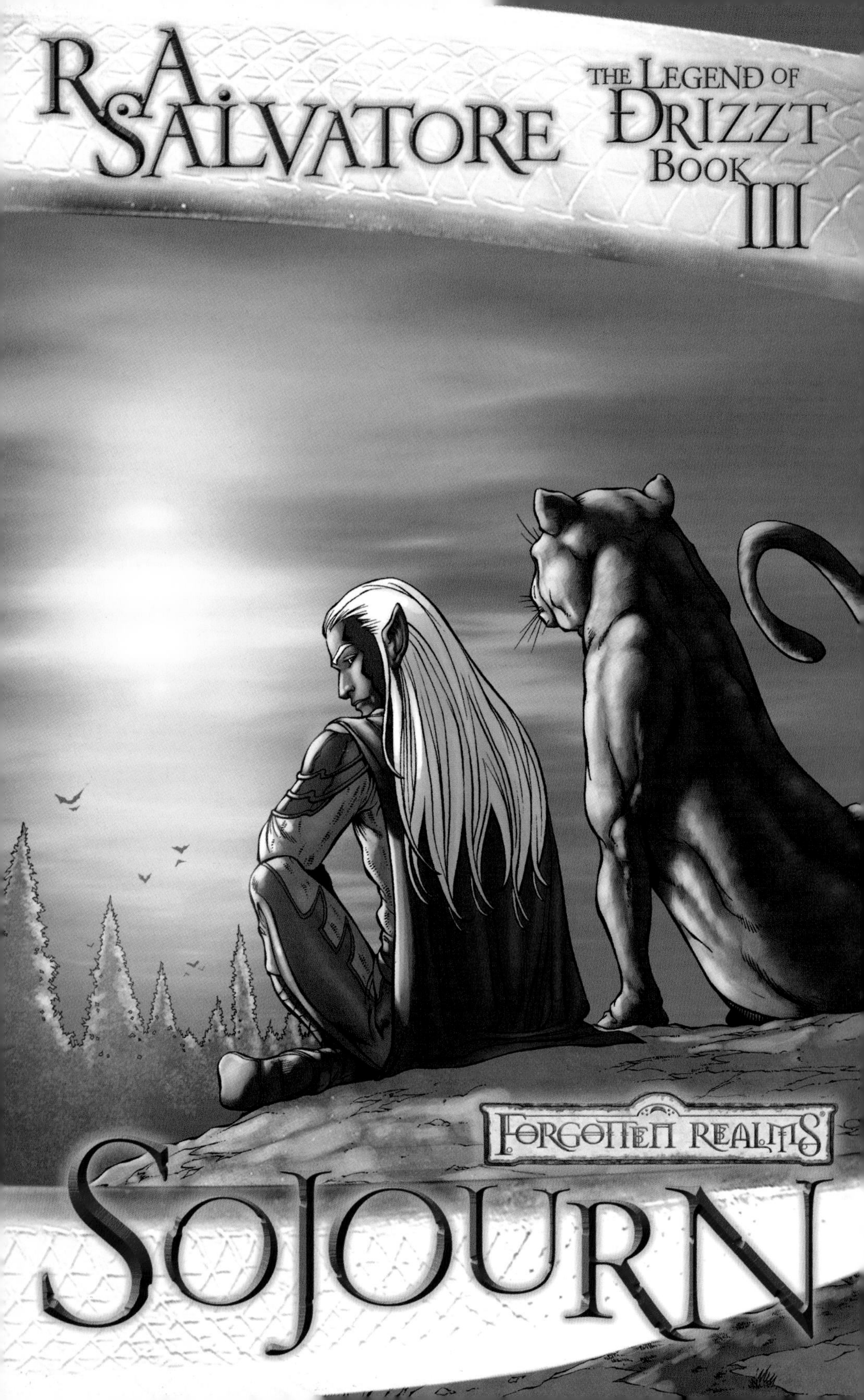
R.A. SALVATORE
THE LEGEND OF DRIZZT
BOOK III
FORGOTTEN REALMS
SOJOURN

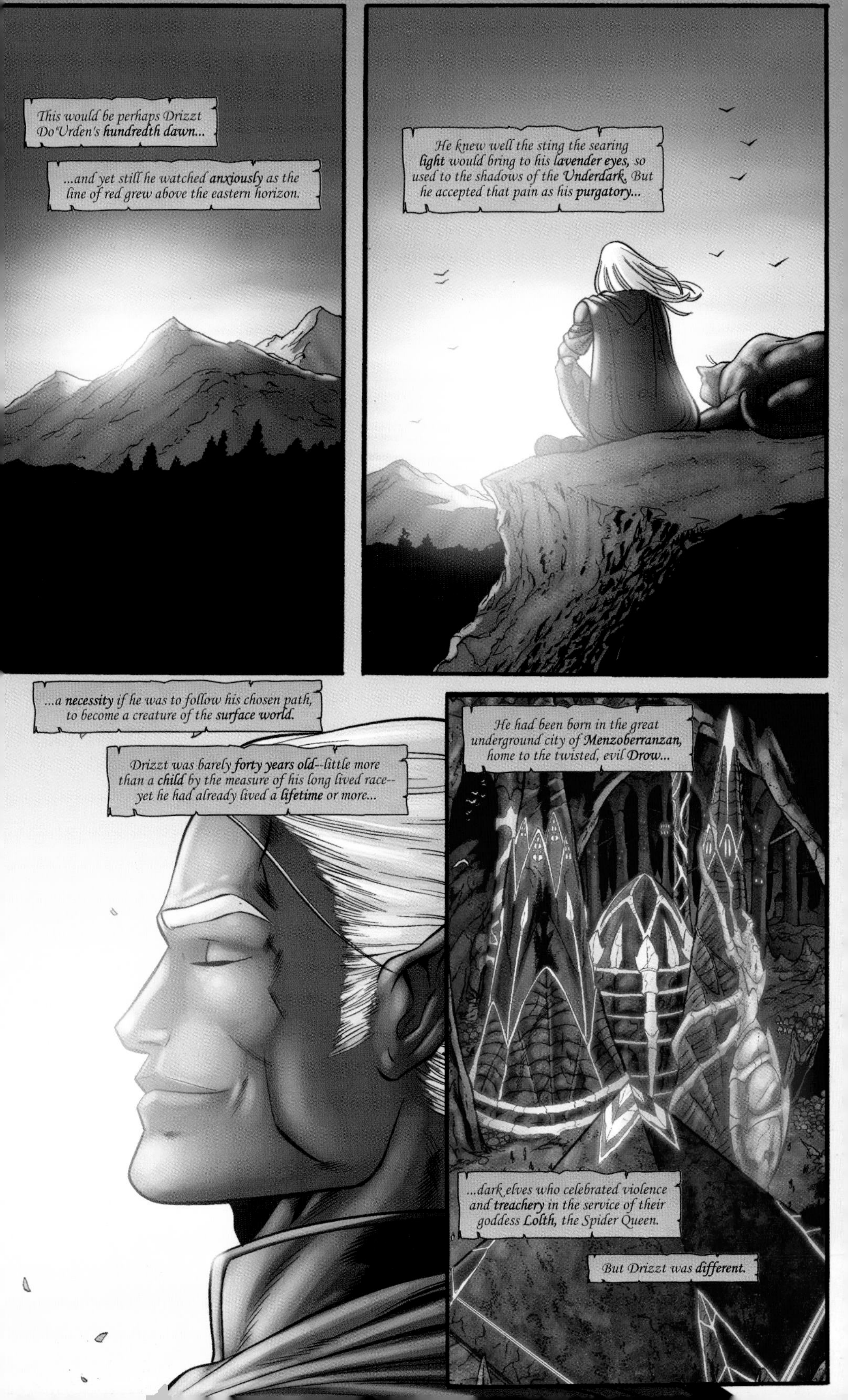
This would be perhaps Drizzt Do'Urden's **hundredth dawn**...
...and yet still he watched **anxiously** as the line of red grew above the eastern horizon.
He knew well the sting the searing **light** would bring to his **lavender eyes**, so used to the shadows of the **Underdark**. But he accepted that pain as his **purgatory**...
...a **necessity** if he was to follow his chosen path, to become a creature of the **surface world**.
Drizzt was barely **forty years old**--little more than a **child** by the measure of his long lived race--yet he had already lived a **lifetime** or more...
He had been born in the great underground city of **Menzoberranzan**, home to the twisted, evil **Drow**...
...dark elves who celebrated violence and **treachery** in the service of their goddess **Lolth**, the Spider Queen.
But Drizzt was **different**.

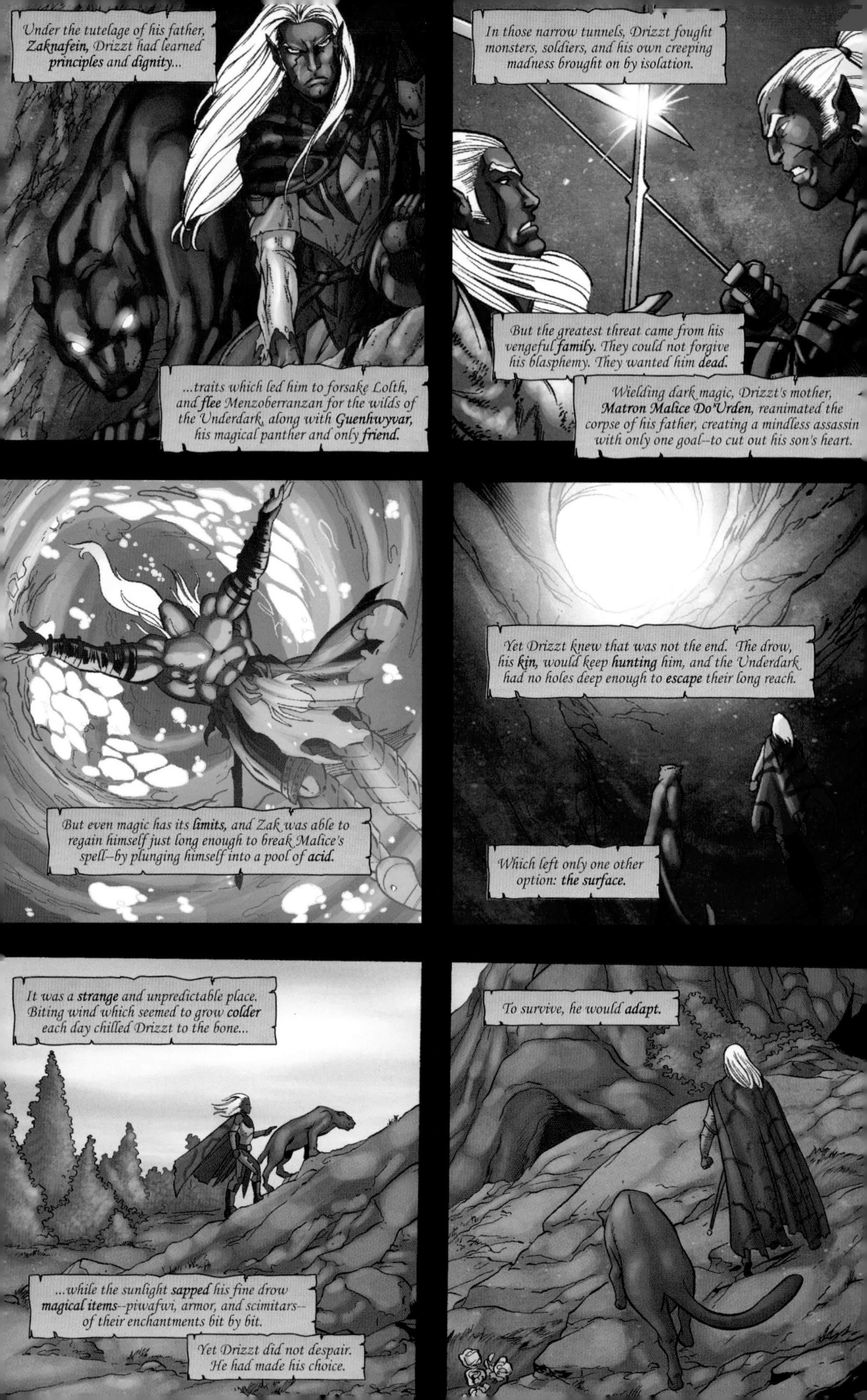
Under the tutelage of his father, Zaknafein, Drizzt had learned principles and dignity...
...traits which led him to forsake Lolth, and flee Menzoberranzan for the wilds of the Underdark, along with Guenhwyvar, his magical panther and only friend.
In those narrow tunnels, Drizzt fought monsters, soldiers, and his own creeping madness brought on by isolation.
But the greatest threat came from his vengeful family. They could not forgive his blasphemy. They wanted him dead.
Wielding dark magic, Drizzt's mother, Matron Malice Do'Urden, reanimated the corpse of his father, creating a mindless assassin with only one goal--to cut out his son's heart.
But even magic has its limits, and Zak was able to regain himself just long enough to break Malice's spell--by plunging himself into a pool of acid.
Yet Drizzt knew that was not the end. The drow, his kin, would keep hunting him, and the Underdark had no holes deep enough to escape their long reach.
Which left only one other option: the surface.
It was a strange and unpredictable place. Biting wind which seemed to grow colder each day chilled Drizzt to the bone...
...while the sunlight sapped his fine drow magical items--piwafwi, armor, and scimitars--of their enchantments bit by bit.
Yet Drizzt did not despair. He had made his choice.
To survive, he would adapt.

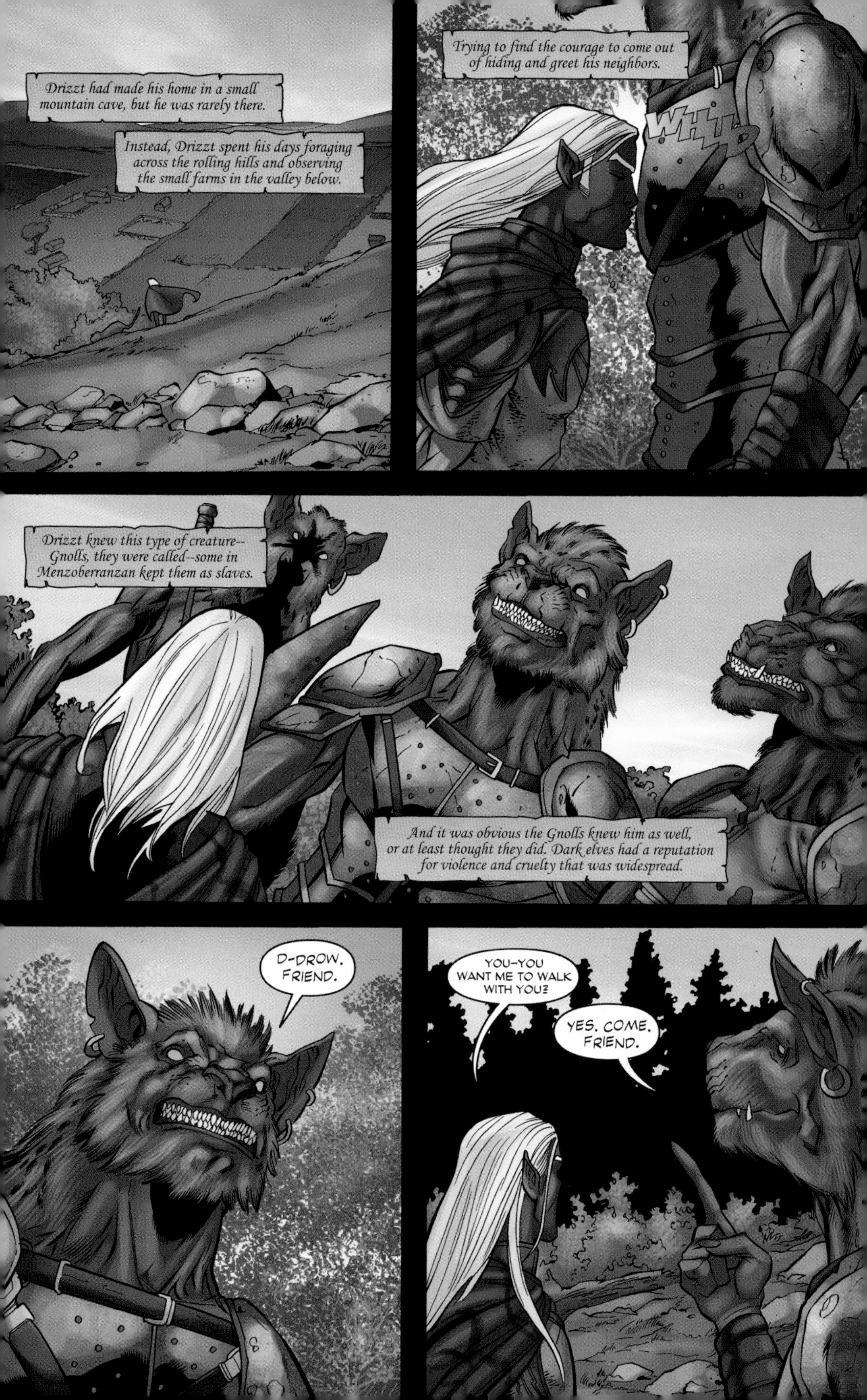

Drizzt had made his home in a small mountain cave, but he was rarely there.
Instead, Drizzt spent his days foraging across the rolling hills and observing the small farms in the valley below.
Trying to find the courage to come out of hiding and greet his neighbors.
WHUD
Drizzt knew this type of creature--Gnolls, they were called--some in Menzoberranzan kept them as slaves.
And it was obvious the Gnolls knew him as well, or at least thought they did. Dark elves had a reputation for violence and cruelty that was widespread.
D-DROW. FRIEND.
YOU-YOU WANT ME TO WALK WITH YOU?
YES. COME. FRIEND.

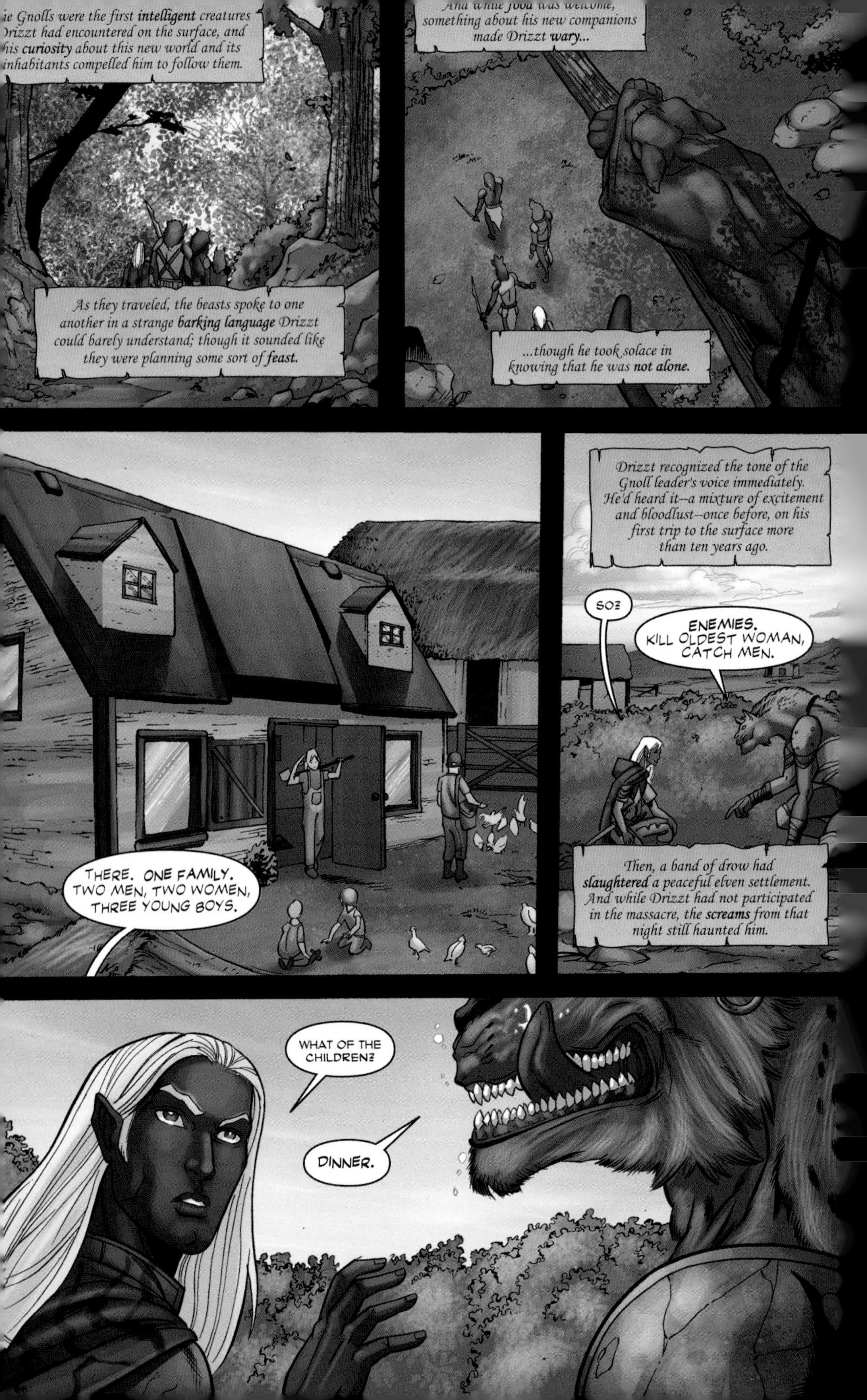

ie Gnolls were the first intelligent creatures
)rizzt had encountered on the surface, and
his curiosity about this new world and its
inhabitants compelled him to follow them.
As they traveled, the beasts spoke to one another in a strange barking language Drizzt could barely understand; though it sounded like they were planning some sort of feast.
something about his new companions made Drizzt wary...
...though he took solace in knowing that he was not alone.
THERE. ONE FAMILY. TWO MEN, TWO WOMEN, THREE YOUNG BOYS.
Drizzt recognized the tone of the Gnoll leader's voice immediately. He'd heard it--a mixture of excitement and bloodlust--once before, on his first trip to the surface more than ten years ago.
SO?
ENEMIES. KILL OLDEST WOMAN, CATCH MEN.
Then, a band of drow had slaughtered a peaceful elven settlement. And while Drizzt had not participated in the massacre, the screams from that night still haunted him.
WHAT OF THE CHILDREN?
DINNER.

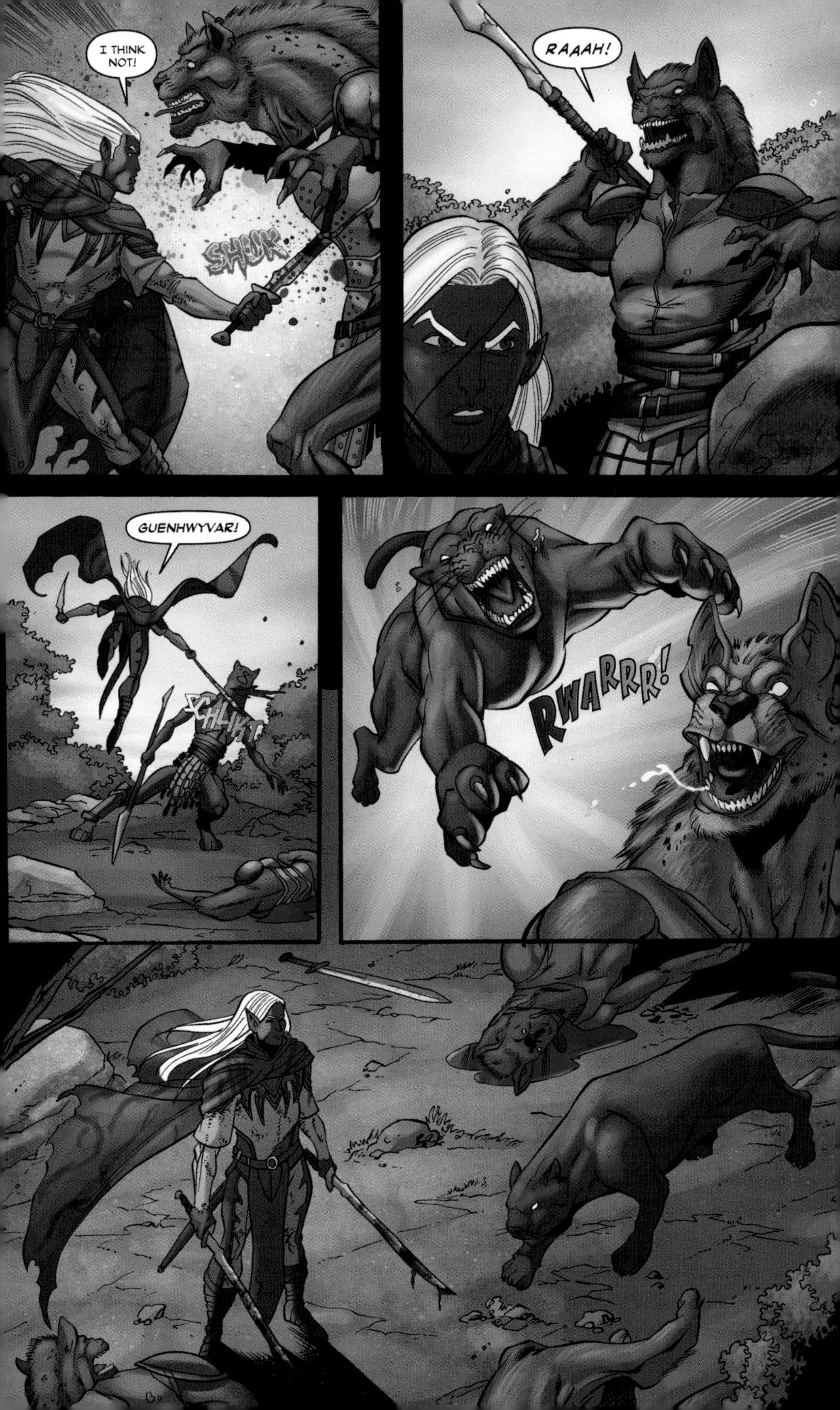
I THINK NOT!
SHUK
RAAAH!
GUENHWYVAR!
SCHLIKT
RWARRR!

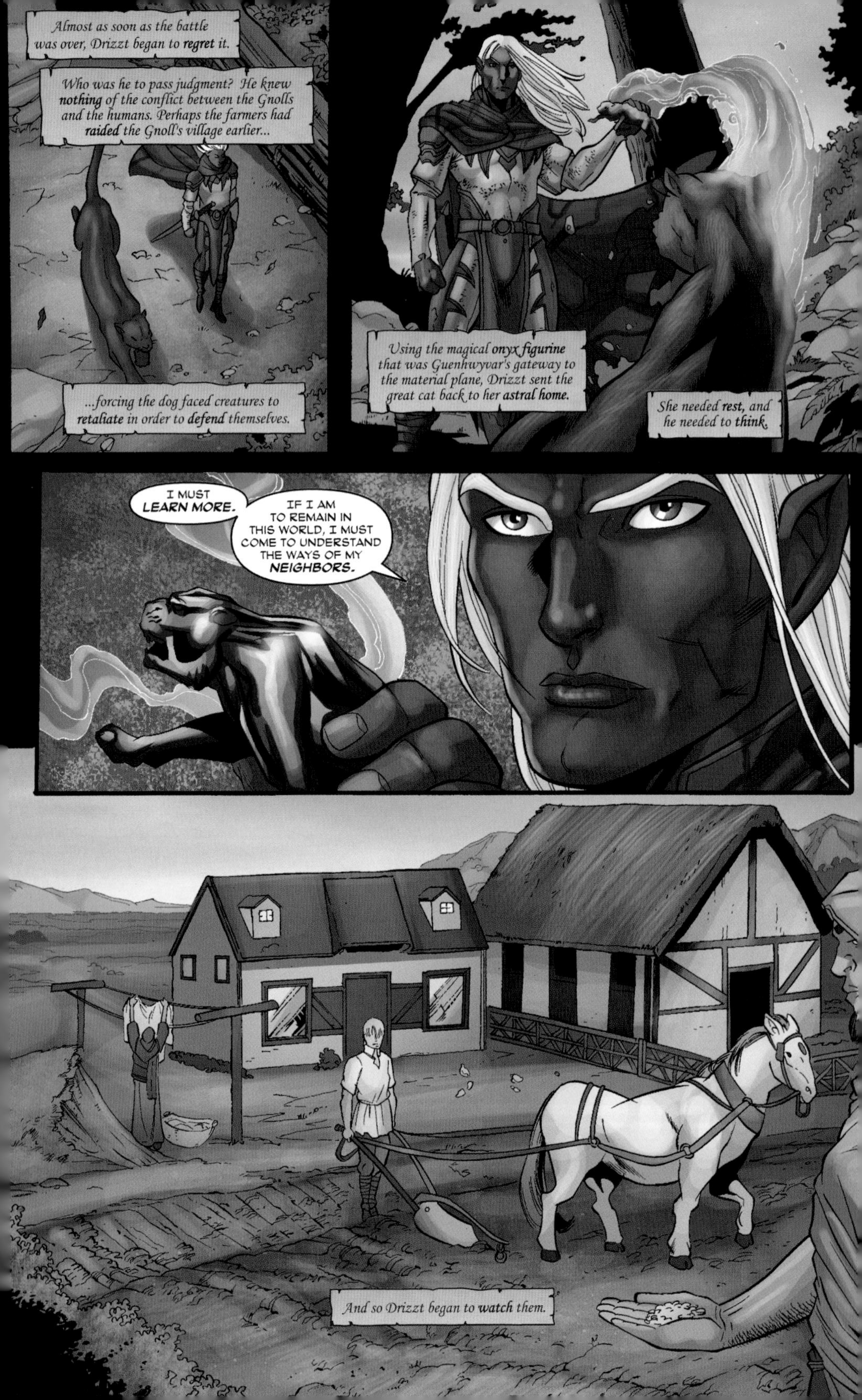
Almost as soon as the battle was over, Drizzt began to regret it.
Who was he to pass judgment? He knew nothing of the conflict between the Gnolls and the humans. Perhaps the farmers had raided the Gnoll's village earlier...
...forcing the dog faced creatures to retaliate in order to defend themselves.
Using the magical onyx figurine that was Guenhwyvar's gateway to the material plane, Drizzt sent the great cat back to her astral home.
She needed rest, and he needed to think.
I MUST LEARN MORE.
IF I AM TO REMAIN IN THIS WORLD, I MUST COME TO UNDERSTAND THE WAYS OF MY NEIGHBORS.
And so Drizzt began to watch them.

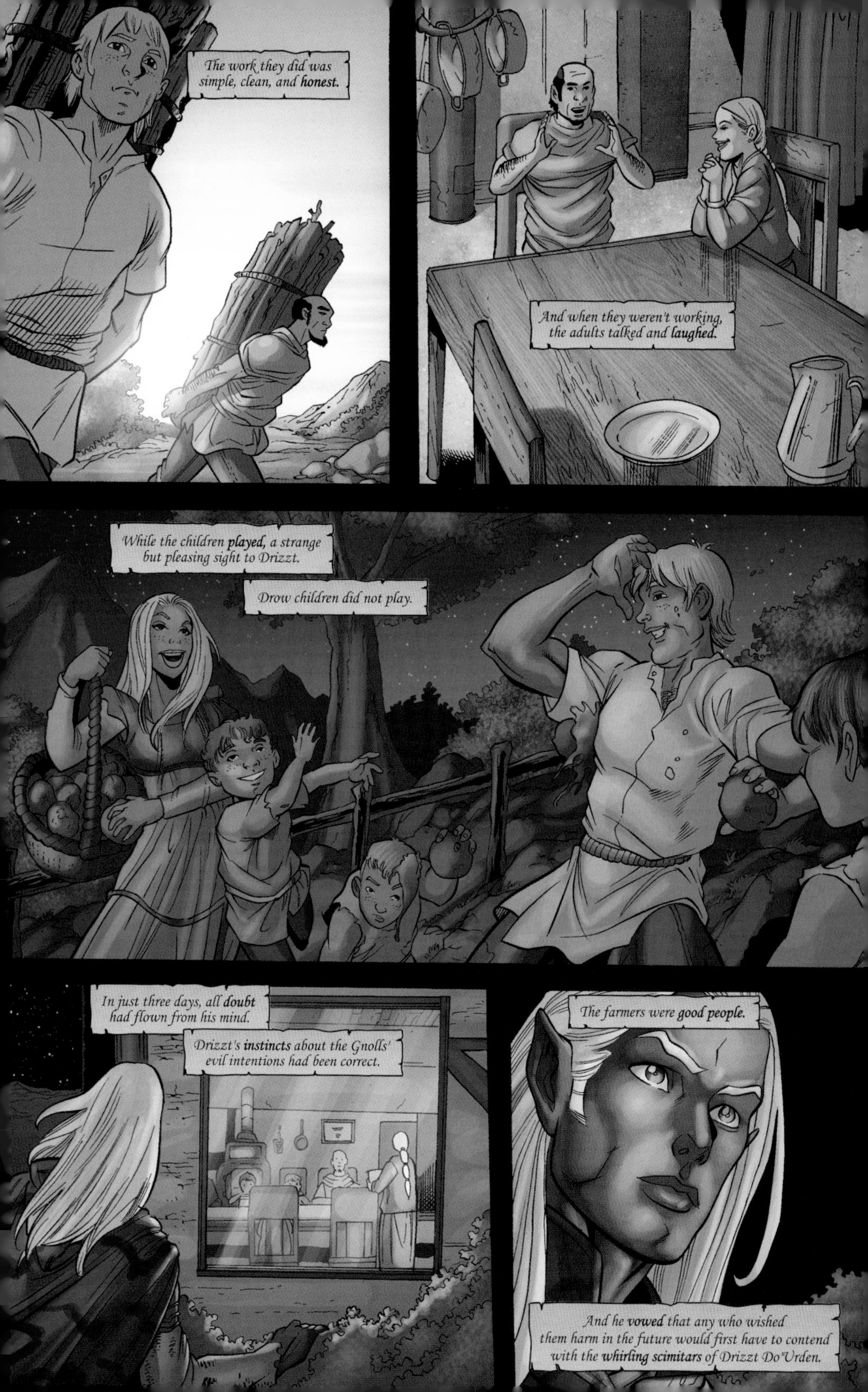
The work they did was simple, clean, and honest.
And when they weren't working, the adults talked and laughed.
While the children played, a strange but pleasing sight to Drizzt.
Drow children did not play.
In just three days, all doubt had flown from his mind.
Drizzt's instincts about the Gnolls' evil intentions had been correct.
The farmers were good people.
And he vowed that any who wished them harm in the future would first have to contend with the whirling scimitars of Drizzt Do'Urden.

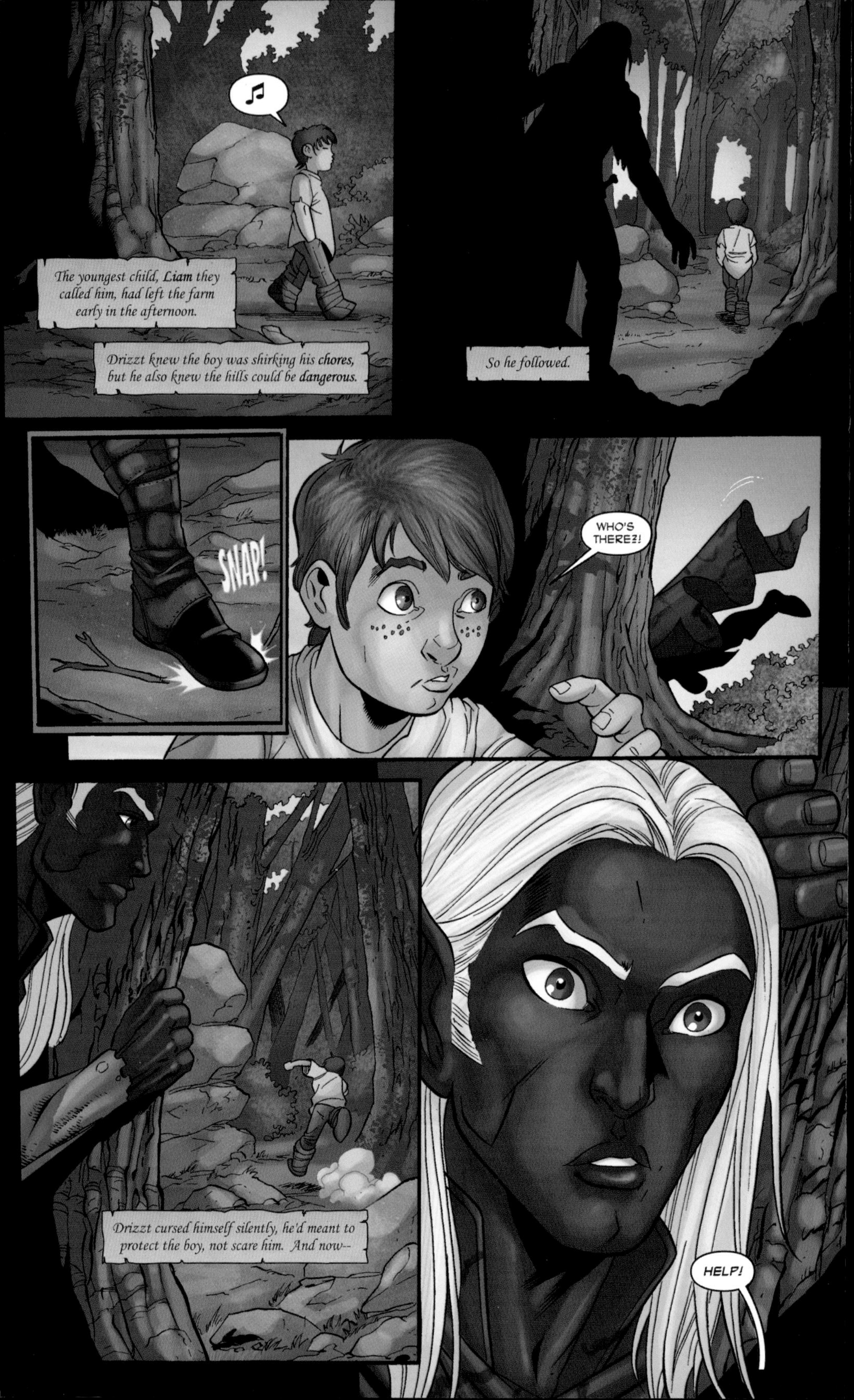

♫
The youngest child, Liam they called him, had left the farm early in the afternoon.
Drizzt knew the boy was shirking his chores, but he also knew the hills could be dangerous.
So he followed.
SNAP!
WHO'S THERE?!
Drizzt cursed himself silently, he'd meant to protect the boy, not scare him. And now--
HELP!

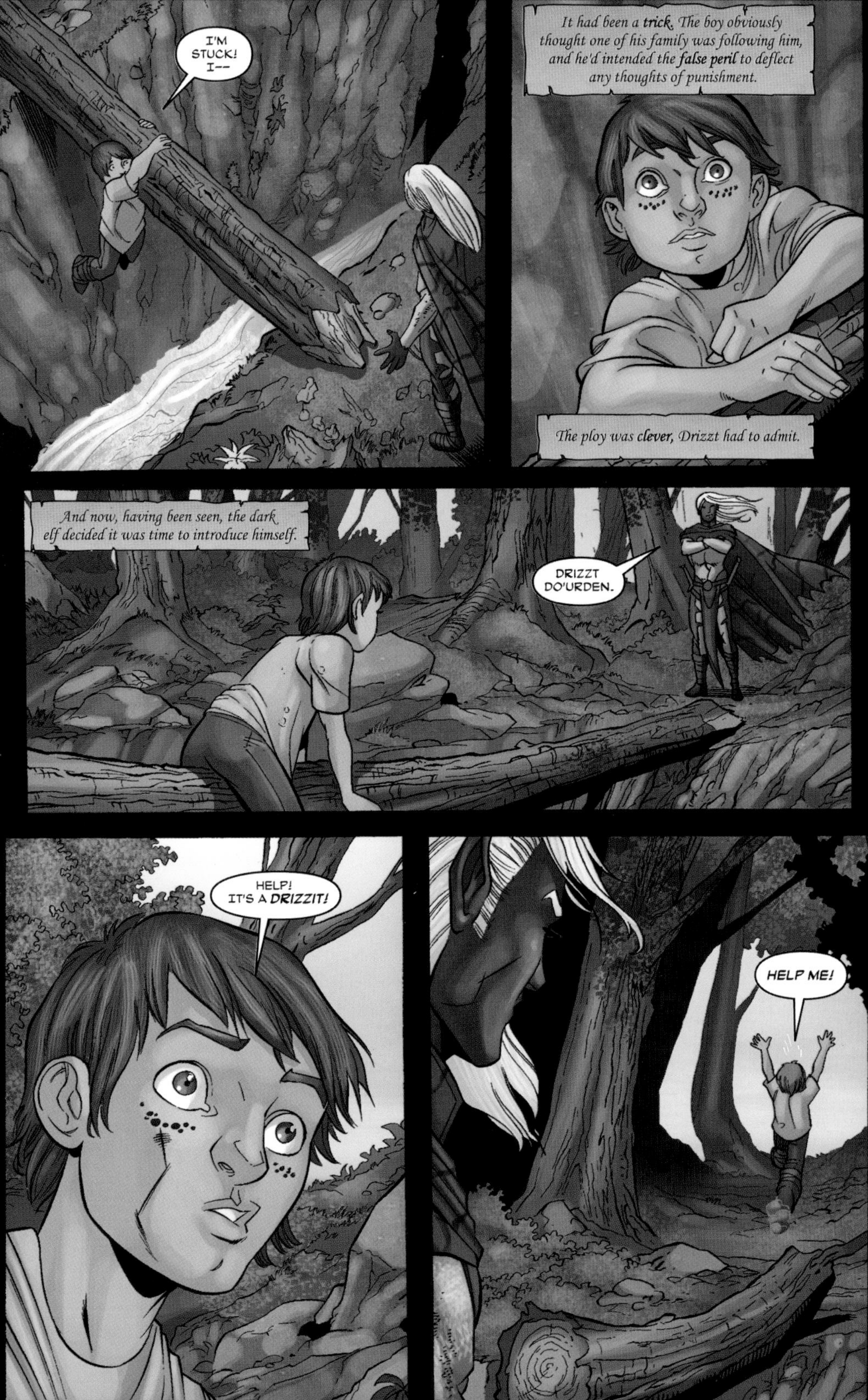
I'M STUCK! I--
It had been a trick. The boy obviously thought one of his family was following him, and he'd intended the false peril to deflect any thoughts of punishment.
The ploy was clever, Drizzt had to admit.
And now, having been seen, the dark elf decided it was time to introduce himself.
DRIZZT DO'URDEN.
HELP! IT'S A DRIZZIT!
HELP ME!

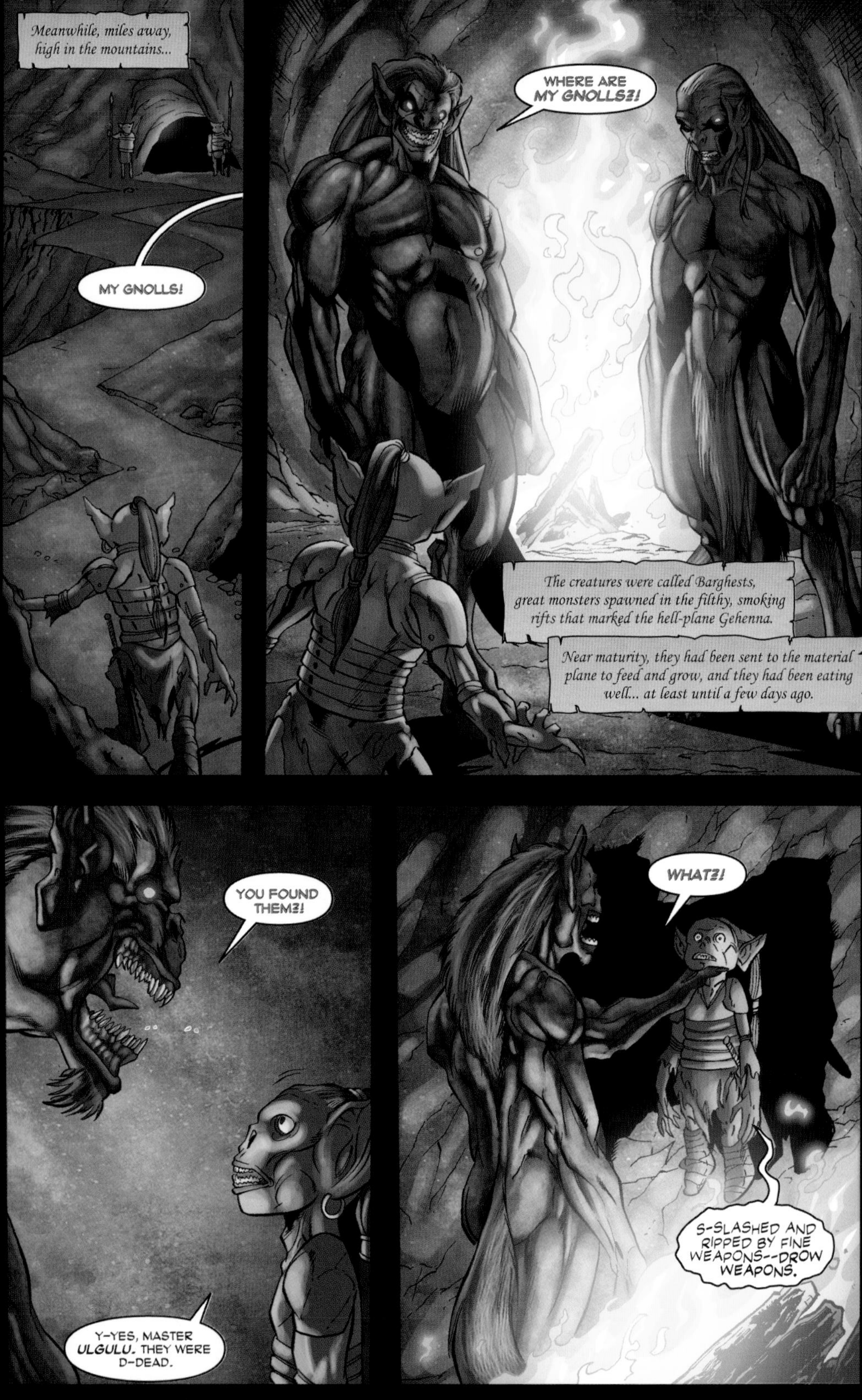
Meanwhile, miles away, high in the mountains...
MY GNOLLS!
WHERE ARE MY GNOLLS?!
The creatures were called Barghests, great monsters spawned in the filthy, smoking rifts that marked the hell-plane Gehenna.
Near maturity, they had been sent to the material plane to feed and grow, and they had been eating well... at least until a few days ago.
YOU FOUND THEM?!
Y-YES, MASTER ULGULU. THEY WERE D-DEAD.
WHAT?!
S-SLASHED AND RIPPED BY FINE WEAPONS--DROW WEAPONS.

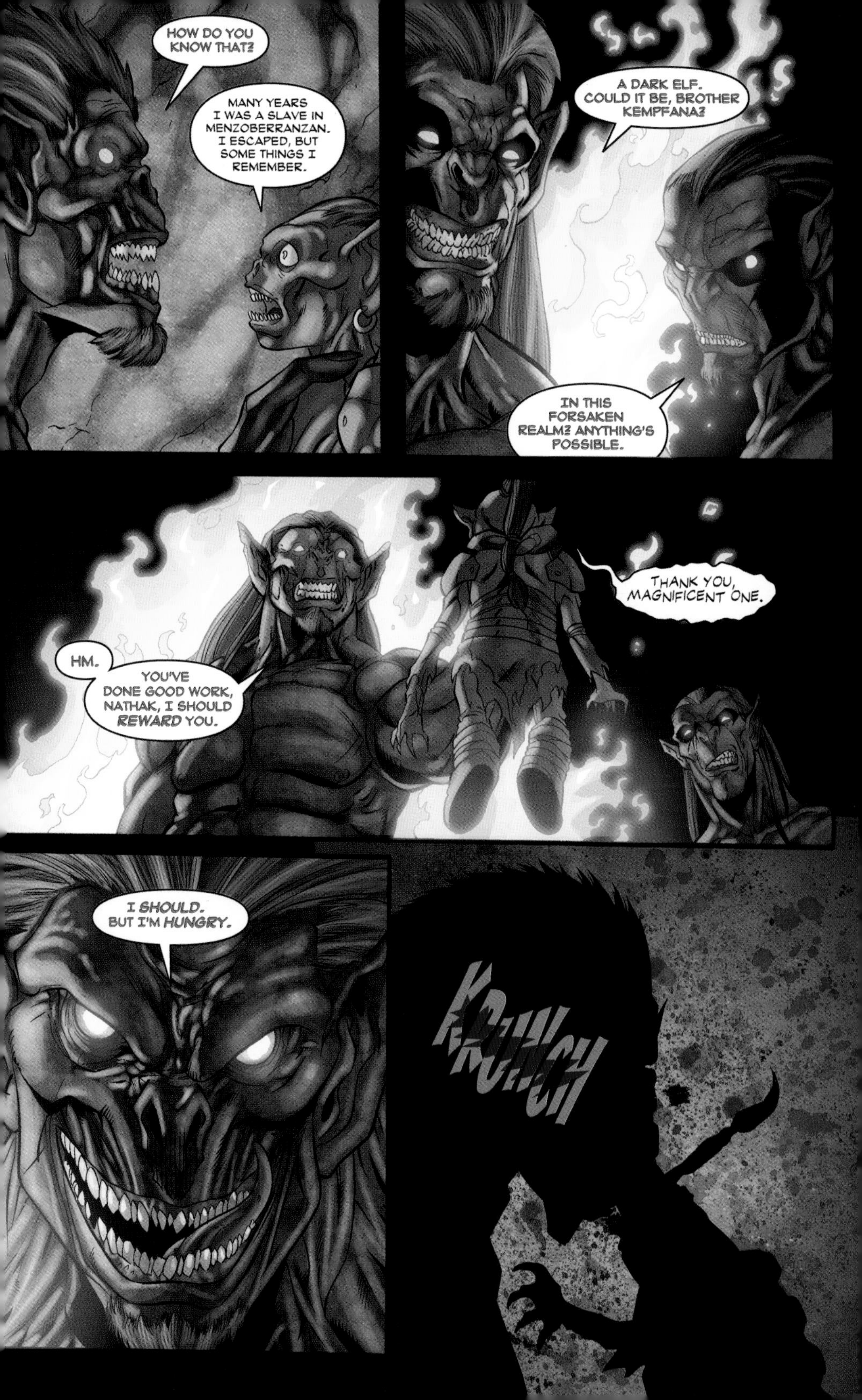
HOW DO YOU KNOW THAT?
MANY YEARS I WAS A SLAVE IN MENZOBERRANZAN. I ESCAPED, BUT SOME THINGS I REMEMBER.
A DARK ELF. COULD IT BE, BROTHER KEMPFANA?
IN THIS FORSAKEN REALM? ANYTHING'S POSSIBLE.
THANK YOU, MAGNIFICENT ONE.
HM.
YOU'VE DONE GOOD WORK, NATHAK, I SHOULD REWARD YOU.
I SHOULD. BUT I'M HUNGRY.
KRUNCH

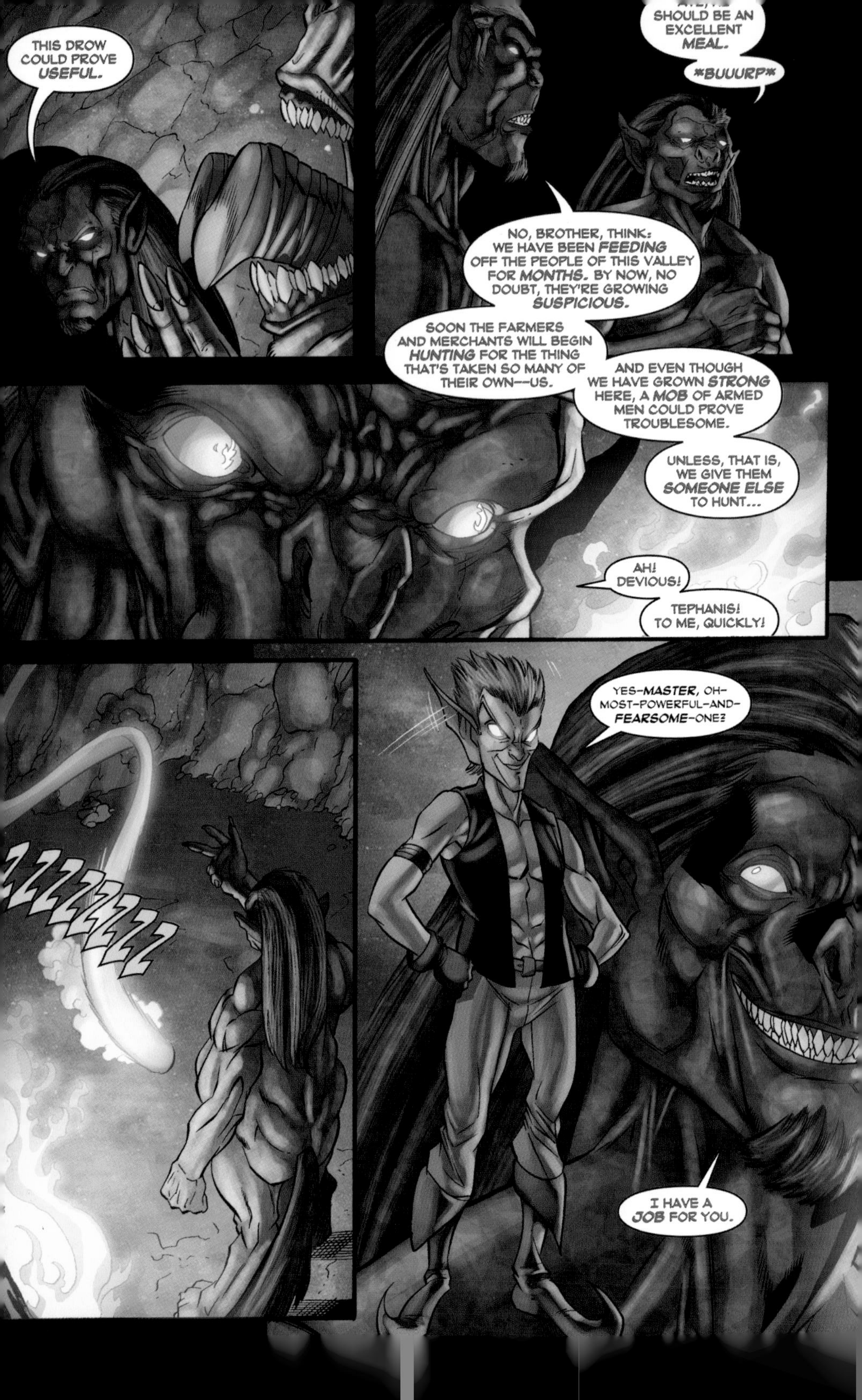
THIS DROW COULD PROVE *USEFUL.*
SHOULD BE AN EXCELLENT *MEAL.*
BUUURP
NO, BROTHER, THINK: WE HAVE BEEN *FEEDING* OFF THE PEOPLE OF THIS VALLEY FOR *MONTHS.* BY NOW, NO DOUBT, THEY'RE GROWING *SUSPICIOUS.*
SOON THE FARMERS AND MERCHANTS WILL BEGIN *HUNTING* FOR THE THING THAT'S TAKEN SO MANY OF THEIR OWN--US.
AND EVEN THOUGH WE HAVE GROWN *STRONG* HERE, A *MOB* OF ARMED MEN COULD PROVE TROUBLESOME.
UNLESS, THAT IS, WE GIVE THEM *SOMEONE ELSE* TO HUNT...
AH! DEVIOUS!
TEPHANIS! TO ME, QUICKLY!
YES-*MASTER,* OH-MOST-POWERFUL-AND-*FEARSOME*-ONE?
I HAVE A *JOB* FOR YOU.

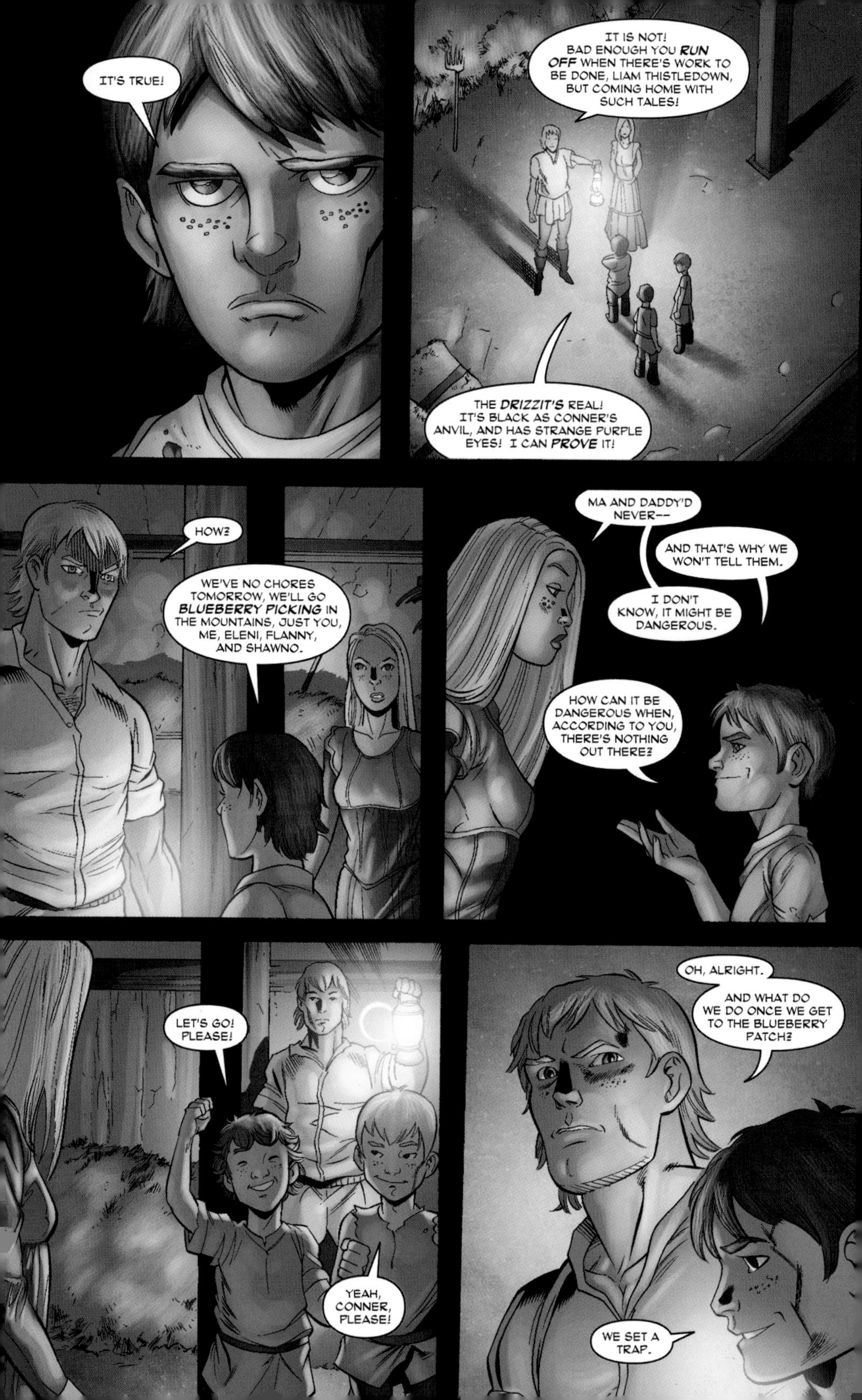
IT'S TRUE!
IT IS NOT! BAD ENOUGH YOU RUN OFF WHEN THERE'S WORK TO BE DONE, LIAM THISTLEDOWN, BUT COMING HOME WITH SUCH TALES!
THE DRIZZIT'S REAL! IT'S BLACK AS CONNER'S ANVIL, AND HAS STRANGE PURPLE EYES! I CAN PROVE IT!
HOW?
WE'VE NO CHORES TOMORROW, WE'LL GO BLUEBERRY PICKING IN THE MOUNTAINS, JUST YOU, ME, ELENI, FLANNY, AND SHAWNO.
MA AND DADDY'D NEVER--
AND THAT'S WHY WE WON'T TELL THEM.
I DON'T KNOW, IT MIGHT BE DANGEROUS.
HOW CAN IT BE DANGEROUS WHEN, ACCORDING TO YOU, THERE'S NOTHING OUT THERE?
LET'S GO! PLEASE!
YEAH, CONNER, PLEASE!
OH, ALRIGHT.
AND WHAT DO WE DO ONCE WE GET TO THE BLUEBERRY PATCH?
WE SET A TRAP.

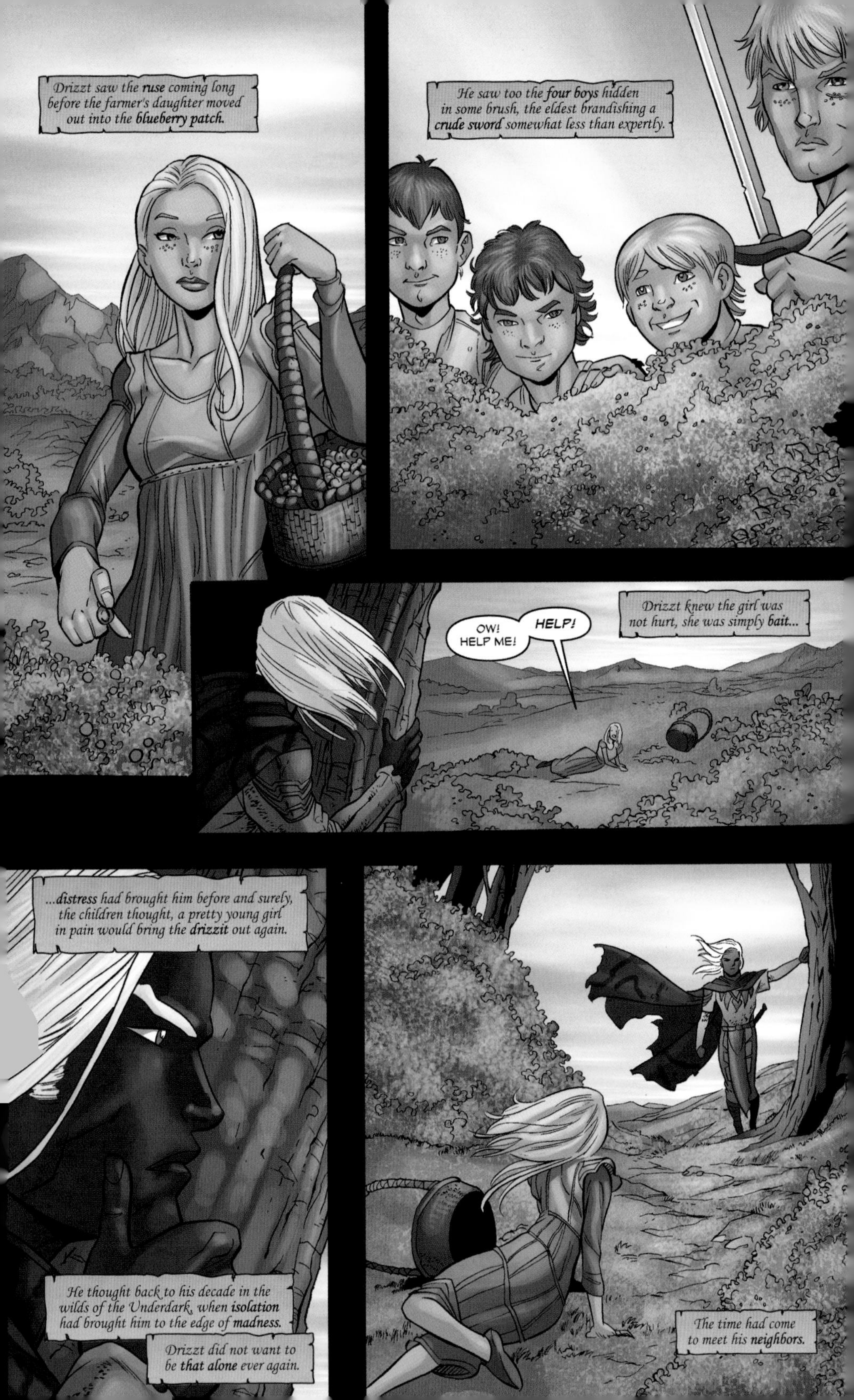
Drizzt saw the ruse coming long before the farmer's daughter moved out into the blueberry patch.
He saw too the four boys hidden in some brush, the eldest brandishing a crude sword somewhat less than expertly.
OW! HELP ME!
HELP!
Drizzt knew the girl was not hurt, she was simply bait...
...distress had brought him before and surely, the children thought, a pretty young girl in pain would bring the drizzit out again.
He thought back to his decade in the wilds of the Underdark, when isolation had brought him to the edge of madness.
Drizzt did not want to be that alone ever again.
The time had come to meet his neighbors.

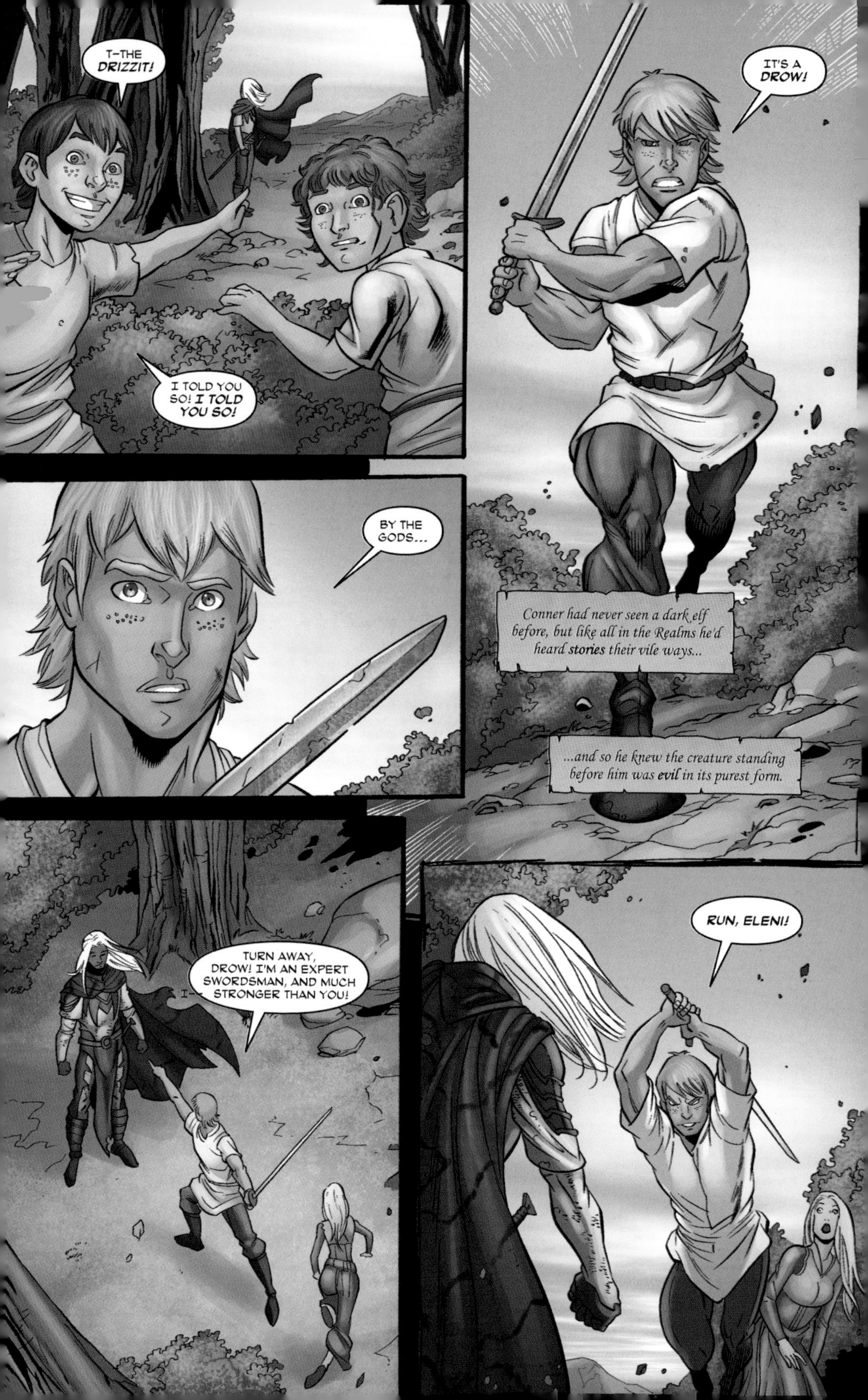
T-THE DRIZZIT!
I TOLD YOU SO! I TOLD YOU SO!
BY THE GODS...
IT'S A DROW!
Conner had never seen a dark elf before, but like all in the Realms he'd heard stories their vile ways...
...and so he knew the creature standing before him was evil in its purest form.
I--
TURN AWAY, DROW! I'M AN EXPERT SWORDSMAN, AND MUCH STRONGER THAN YOU!
RUN, ELENI!

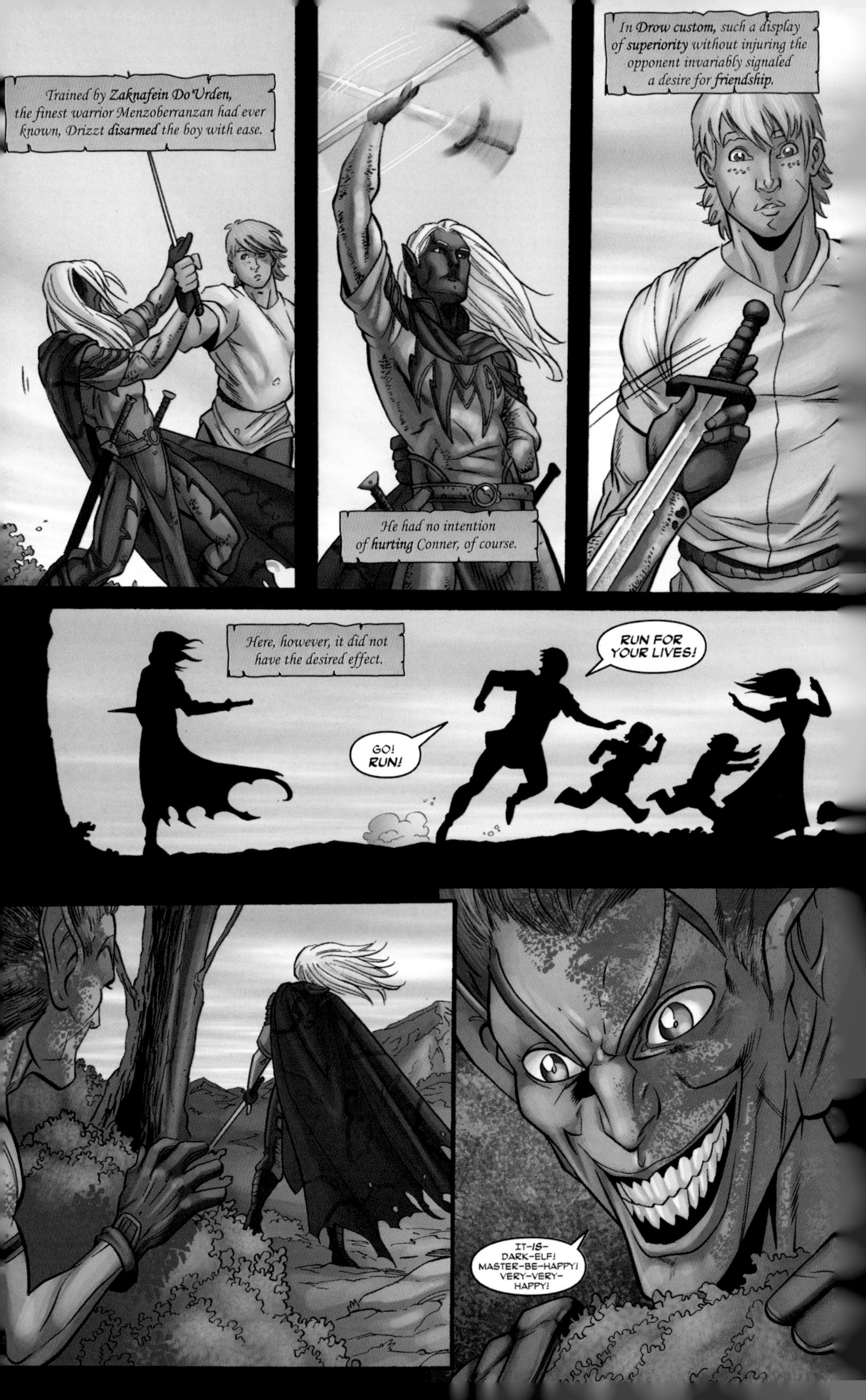
Trained by Zaknafein Do'Urden, the finest warrior Menzoberranzan had ever known, Drizzt disarmed the boy with ease.
He had no intention of hurting Conner, of course.
In Drow custom, such a display of superiority without injuring the opponent invariably signaled a desire for friendship.
Here, however, it did not have the desired effect.
RUN FOR YOUR LIVES!
GO! RUN!
IT-IS-DARK-ELF! MASTER-BE-HAPPY! VERY-VERY-HAPPY!

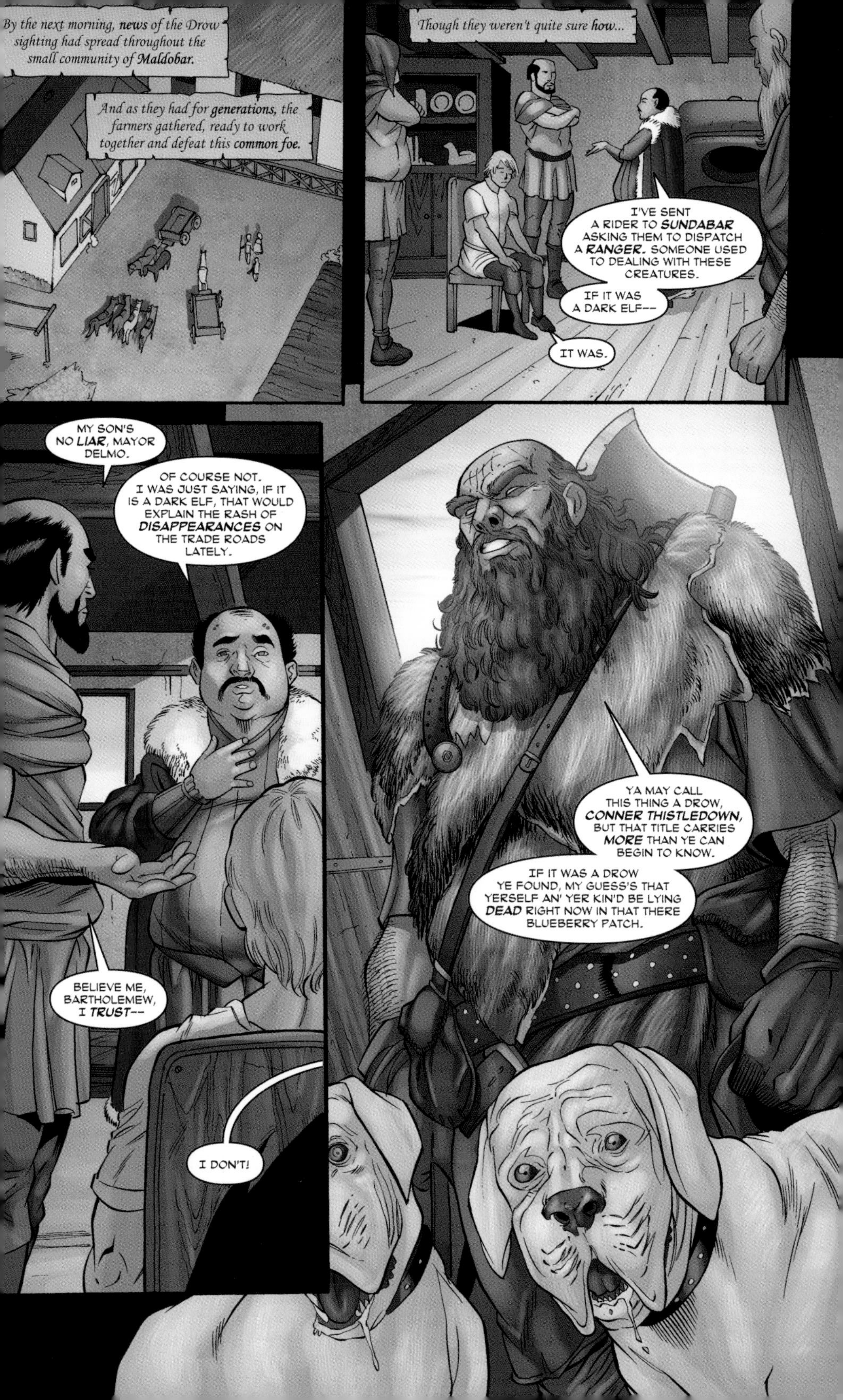

By the next morning, news of the Drow sighting had spread throughout the small community of Maldobar.
And as they had for generations, the farmers gathered, ready to work together and defeat this common foe.
Though they weren't quite sure how...
I'VE SENT A RIDER TO SUNDABAR ASKING THEM TO DISPATCH A RANGER. SOMEONE USED TO DEALING WITH THESE CREATURES.
IF IT WAS A DARK ELF--
IT WAS.
MY SON'S NO LIAR, MAYOR DELMO.
OF COURSE NOT. I WAS JUST SAYING, IF IT IS A DARK ELF, THAT WOULD EXPLAIN THE RASH OF DISAPPEARANCES ON THE TRADE ROADS LATELY.
BELIEVE ME, BARTHOLEMEW, I TRUST--
I DON'T!
YA MAY CALL THIS THING A DROW, CONNER THISTLEDOWN, BUT THAT TITLE CARRIES MORE THAN YE CAN BEGIN TO KNOW.
IF IT WAS A DROW YE FOUND, MY GUESS'S THAT YERSELF AN' YER KIN'D BE LYING DEAD RIGHT NOW IN THAT THERE BLUEBERRY PATCH.

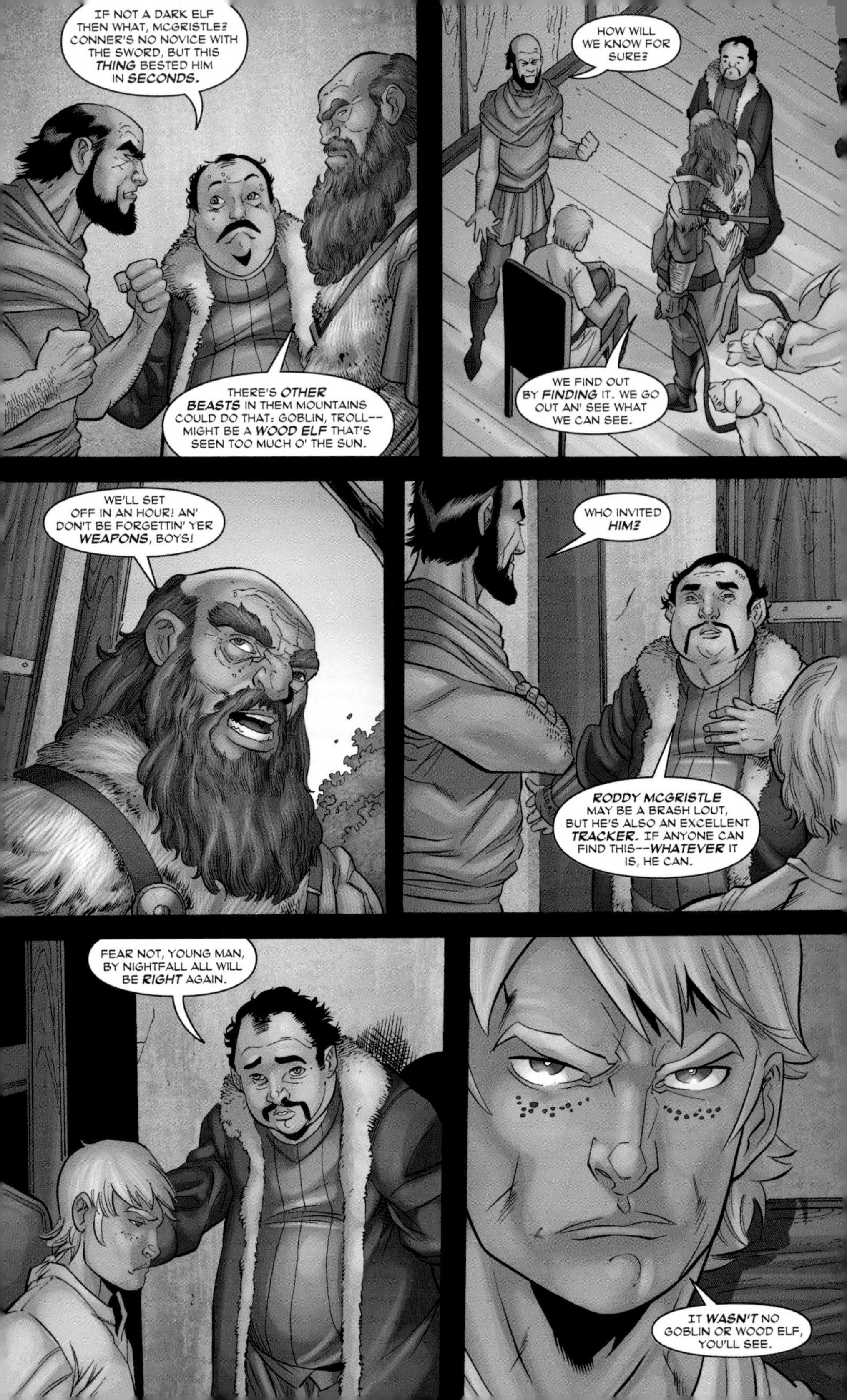
IF NOT A DARK ELF THEN WHAT, MCGRISTLE? CONNER'S NO NOVICE WITH THE SWORD, BUT THIS THING BESTED HIM IN SECONDS.
THERE'S OTHER BEASTS IN THEM MOUNTAINS COULD DO THAT: GOBLIN, TROLL-- MIGHT BE A WOOD ELF THAT'S SEEN TOO MUCH O' THE SUN.
HOW WILL WE KNOW FOR SURE?
WE FIND OUT BY FINDING IT. WE GO OUT AN' SEE WHAT WE CAN SEE.
WE'LL SET OFF IN AN HOUR! AN' DON'T BE FORGETTIN' YER WEAPONS, BOYS!
WHO INVITED HIM?
RODDY MCGRISTLE MAY BE A BRASH LOUT, BUT HE'S ALSO AN EXCELLENT TRACKER. IF ANYONE CAN FIND THIS--WHATEVER IT IS, HE CAN.
FEAR NOT, YOUNG MAN, BY NIGHTFALL ALL WILL BE RIGHT AGAIN.
IT WASN'T NO GOBLIN OR WOOD ELF, YOU'LL SEE.

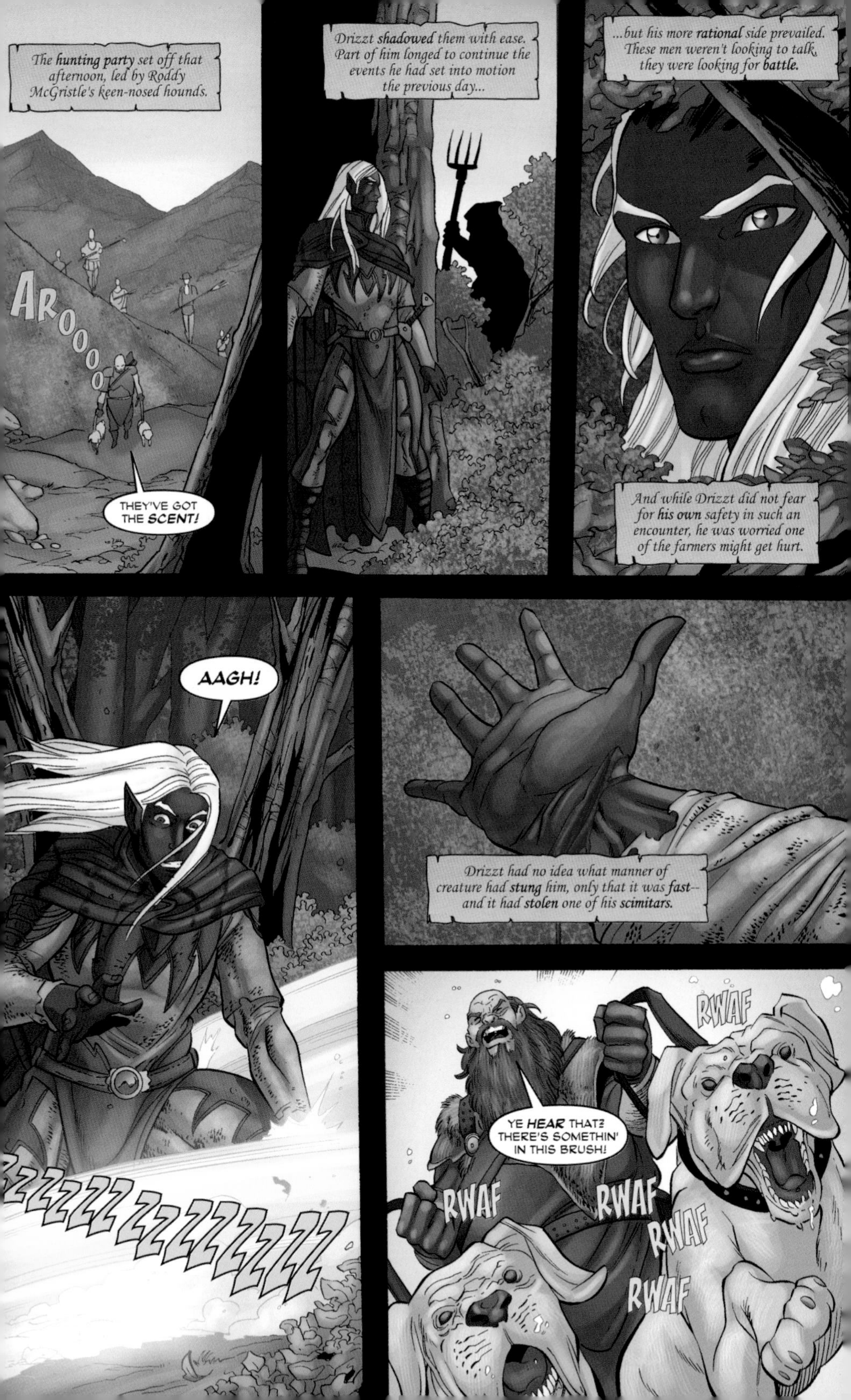
The hunting party set off that afternoon, led by Roddy McGristle's keen-nosed hounds.
AROOOOO
THEY'VE GOT THE SCENT!
Drizzt shadowed them with ease. Part of him longed to continue the events he had set into motion the previous day...
...but his more rational side prevailed. These men weren't looking to talk, they were looking for battle.
And while Drizzt did not fear for his own safety in such an encounter, he was worried one of the farmers might get hurt.
AAGH!
ZZZZZZZZZZZZZZZZZZ
Drizzt had no idea what manner of creature had stung him, only that it was fast--and it had stolen one of his scimitars.
RWAF
YE HEAR THAT? THERE'S SOMETHIN' IN THIS BRUSH!
RWAF
RWAF
RWAF
RWAF

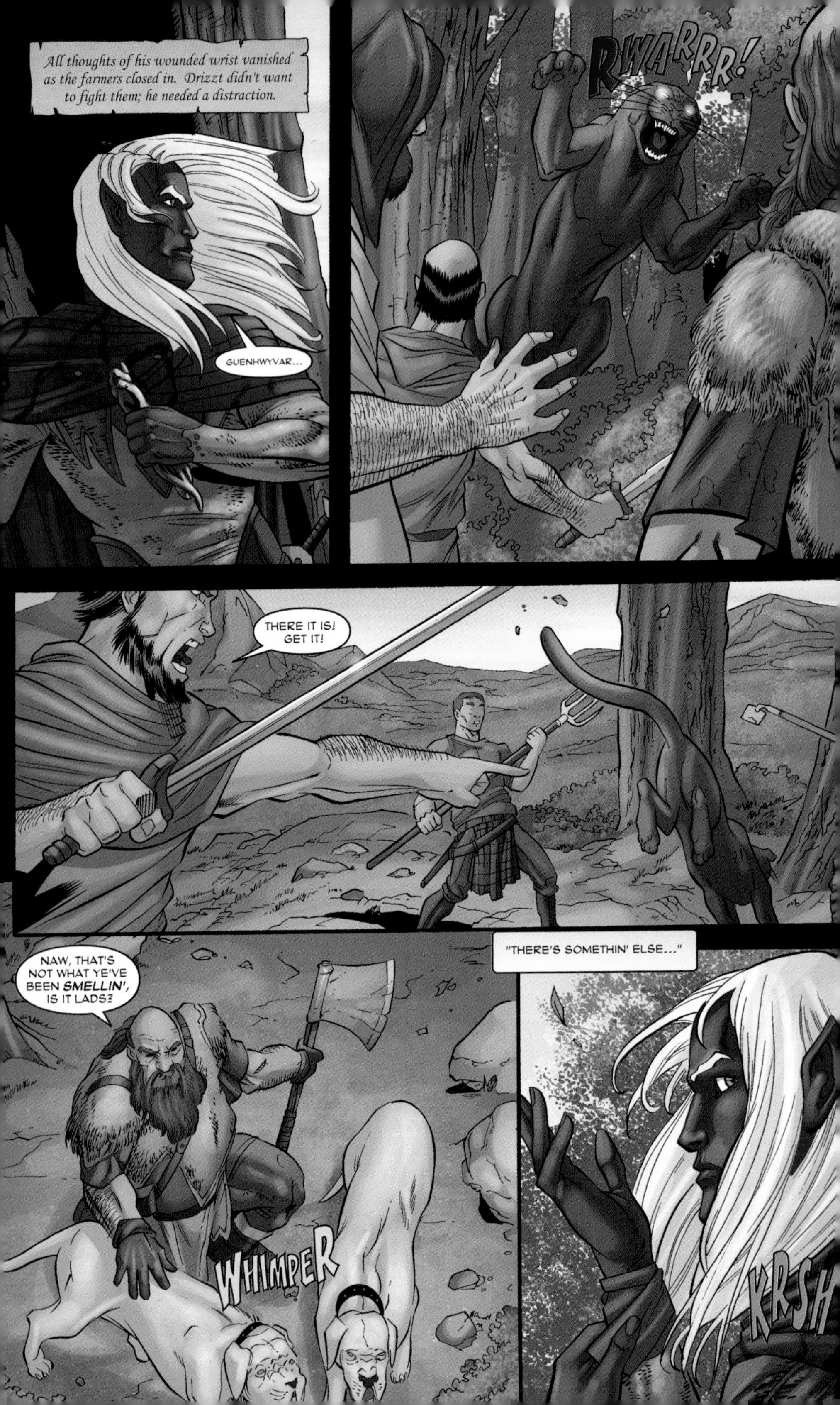

All thoughts of his wounded wrist vanished as the farmers closed in. Drizzt didn't want to fight them; he needed a distraction.
GUENHWYVAR...
RWARRR!
THERE IT IS! GET IT!
NAW, THAT'S NOT WHAT YE'VE BEEN SMELLIN', IS IT LADS?
WHIMPER
"THERE'S SOMETHIN' ELSE..."
KRSH

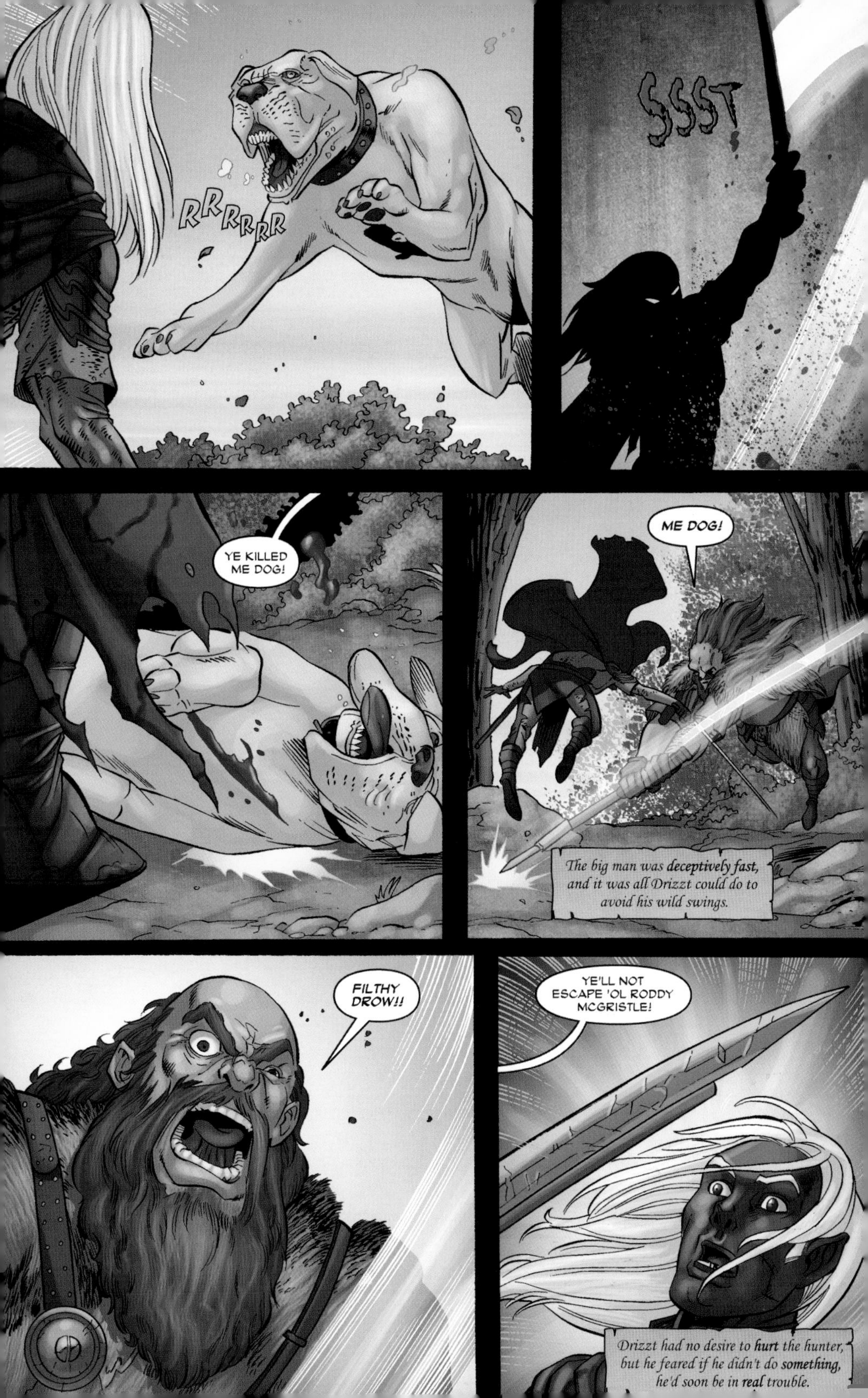
RRRRRRR
SSST
YE KILLED ME DOG!
ME DOG!
The big man was deceptively fast, and it was all Drizzt could do to avoid his wild swings.
FILTHY DROW!!
YE'LL NOT ESCAPE 'OL RODDY MCGRISTLE!
Drizzt had no desire to hurt the hunter, but he feared if he didn't do something, he'd soon be in real trouble.

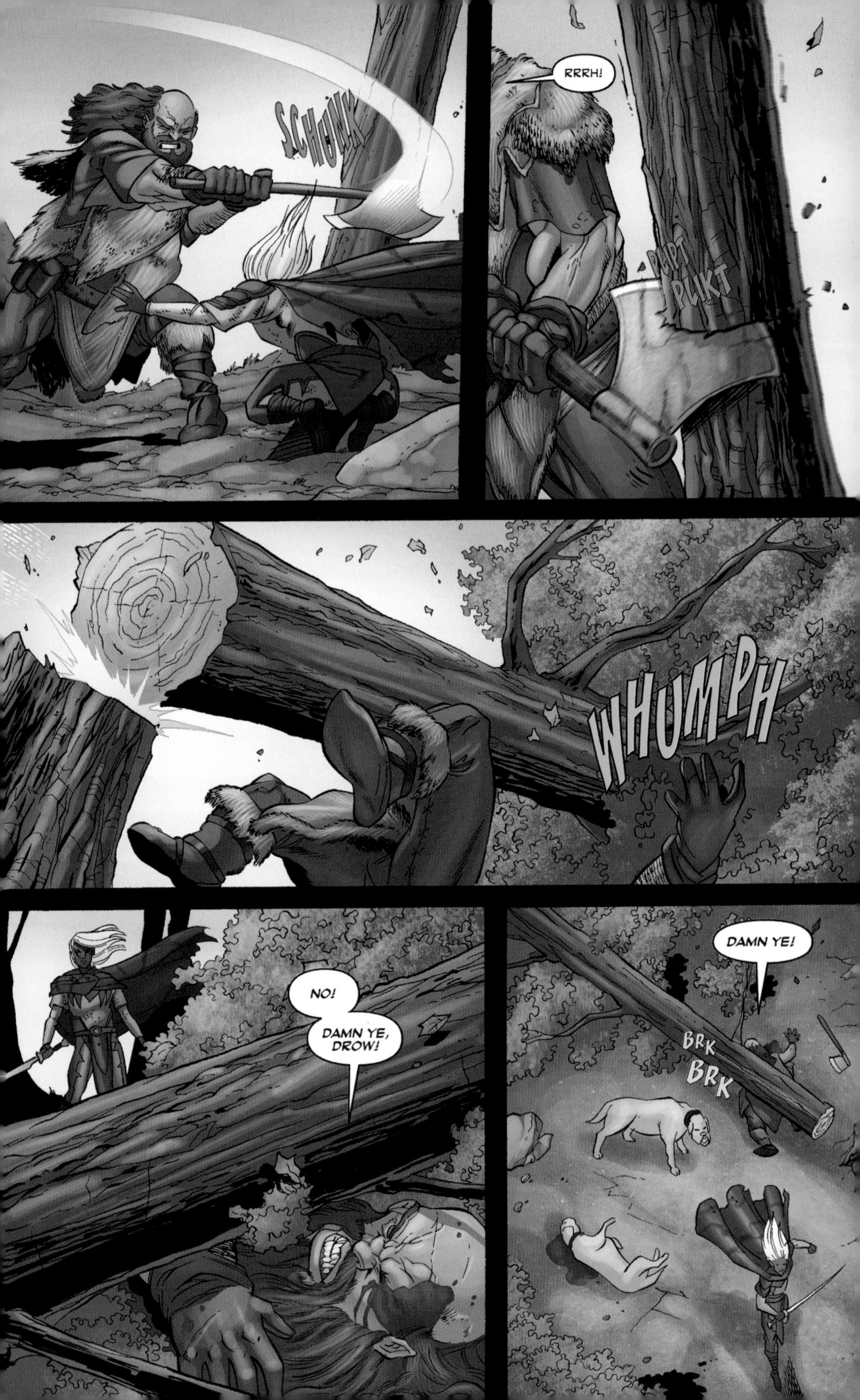
SCHUNK
RRRH!
PLIPT
PLIKT
WHUMPH
NO!
DAMN YE, DROW!
DAMN YE!
BRK
BRK

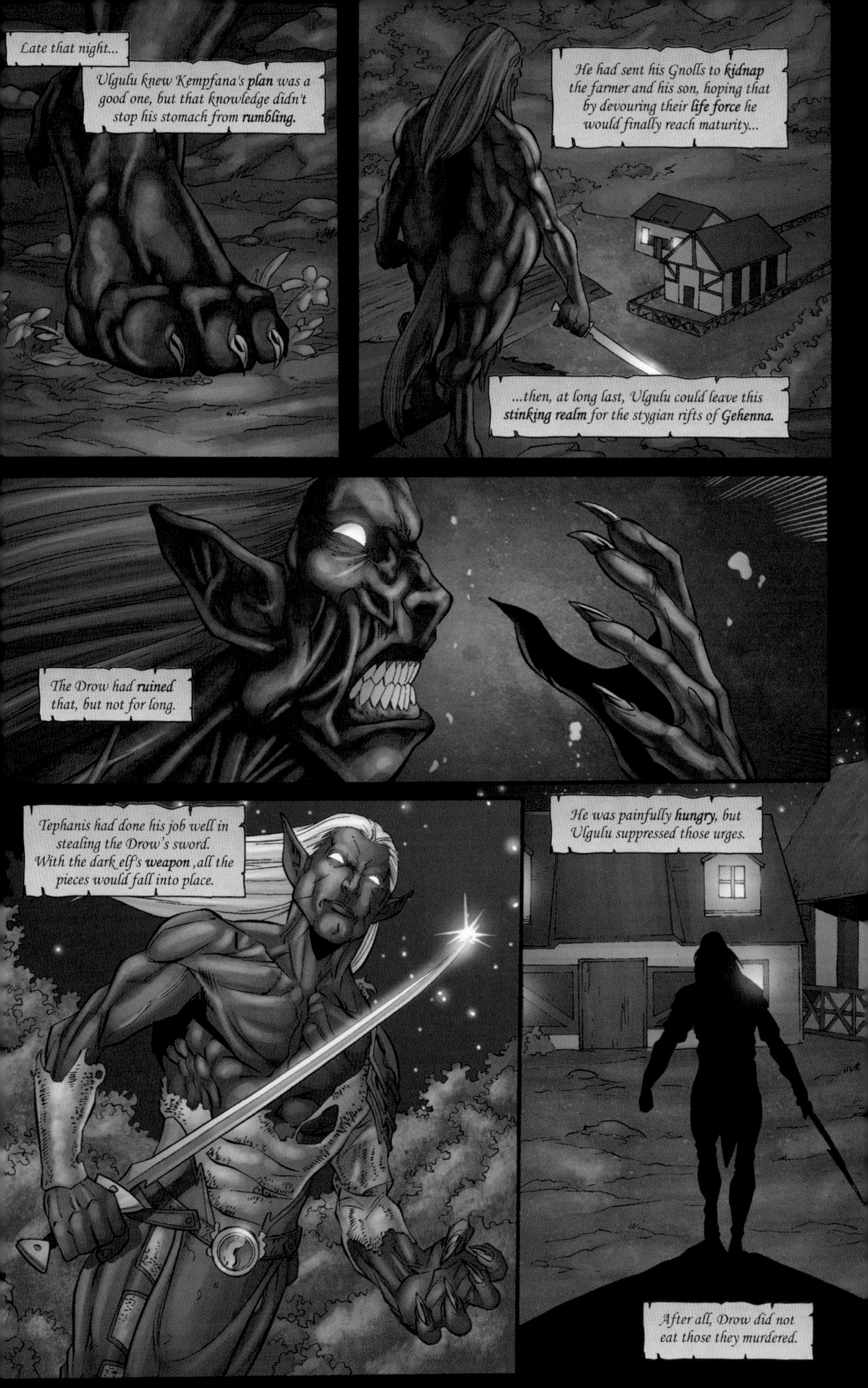
Late that night...
Ulgulu knew Kempfana's plan was a good one, but that knowledge didn't stop his stomach from rumbling.
He had sent his Gnolls to kidnap the farmer and his son, hoping that by devouring their life force he would finally reach maturity...
...then, at long last, Ulgulu could leave this stinking realm for the stygian rifts of Gehenna.
The Drow had ruined that, but not for long.
Tephanis had done his job well in stealing the Drow's sword. With the dark elf's weapon ,all the pieces would fall into place.
He was painfully hungry, but Ulgulu suppressed those urges.
After all, Drow did not eat those they murdered.

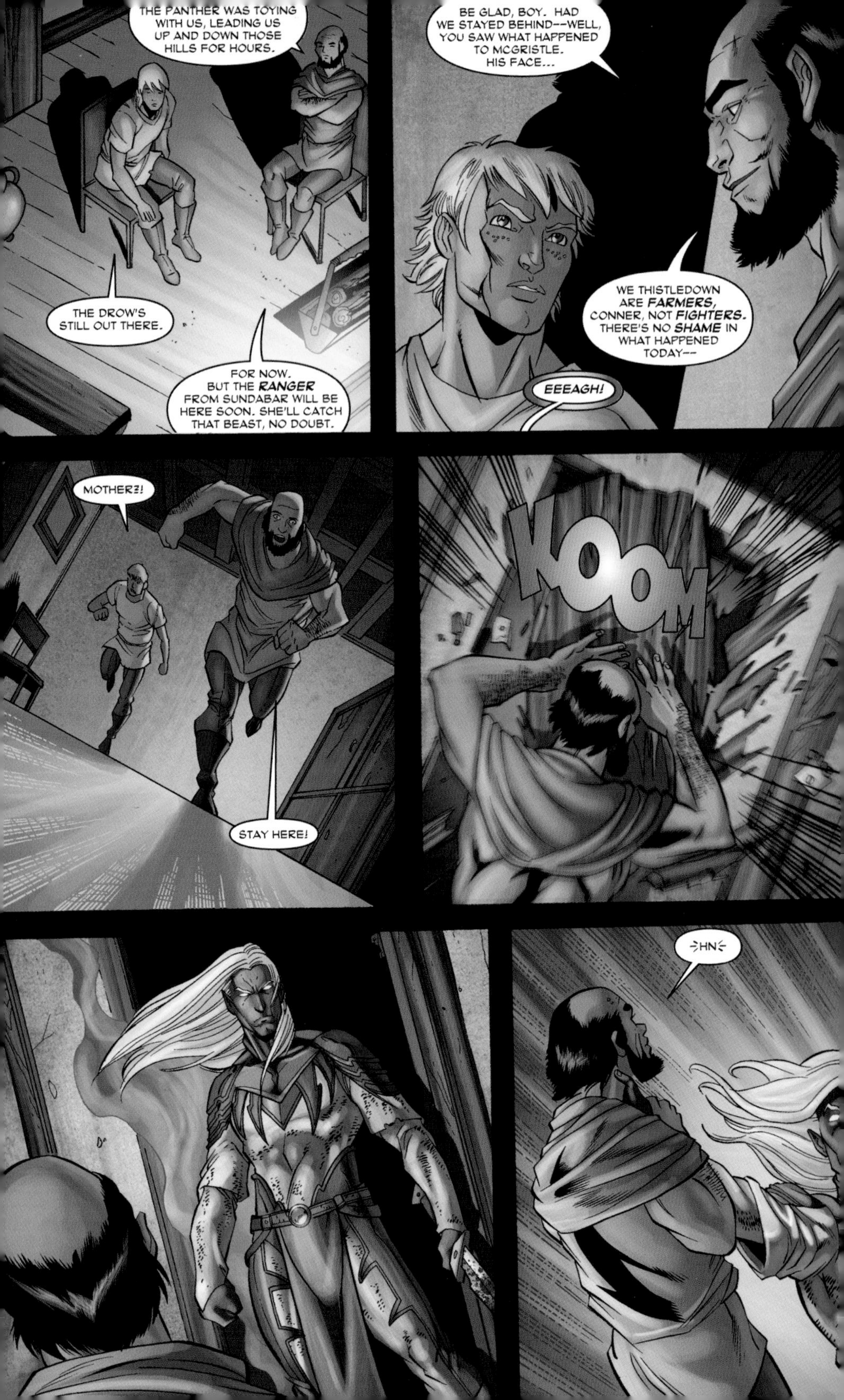
THE PANTHER WAS TOYING WITH US, LEADING US UP AND DOWN THOSE HILLS FOR HOURS.
THE DROW'S STILL OUT THERE.
FOR NOW. BUT THE RANGER FROM SUNDABAR WILL BE HERE SOON. SHE'LL CATCH THAT BEAST, NO DOUBT.
BE GLAD, BOY. HAD WE STAYED BEHIND--WELL, YOU SAW WHAT HAPPENED TO MCGRISTLE. HIS FACE...
WE THISTLEDOWN ARE FARMERS, CONNER, NOT FIGHTERS. THERE'S NO SHAME IN WHAT HAPPENED TODAY--
EEEAGH!
MOTHER?!
STAY HERE!
KOOM
HN

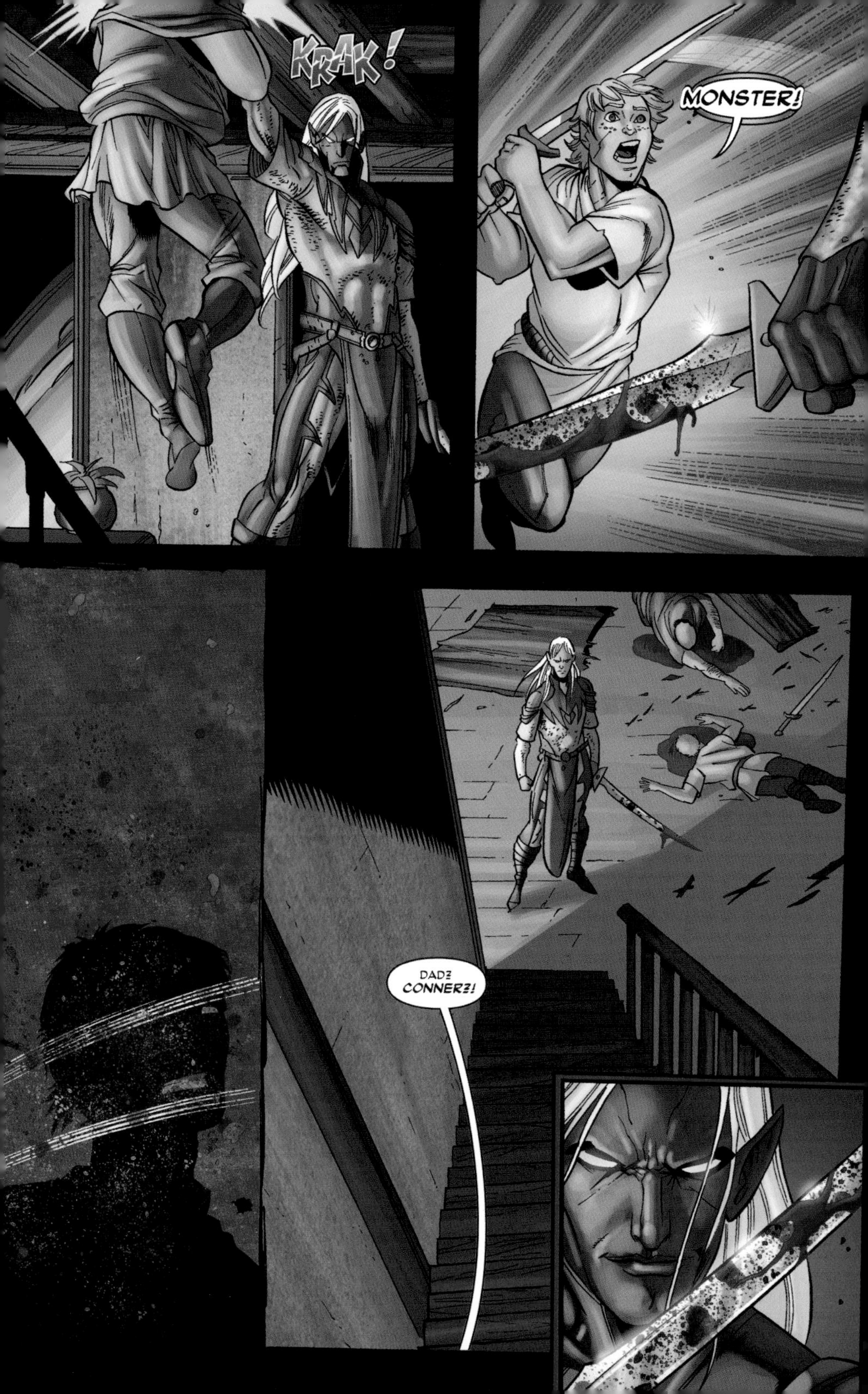
KRAK!
MONSTER!
DAD? CONNER?!

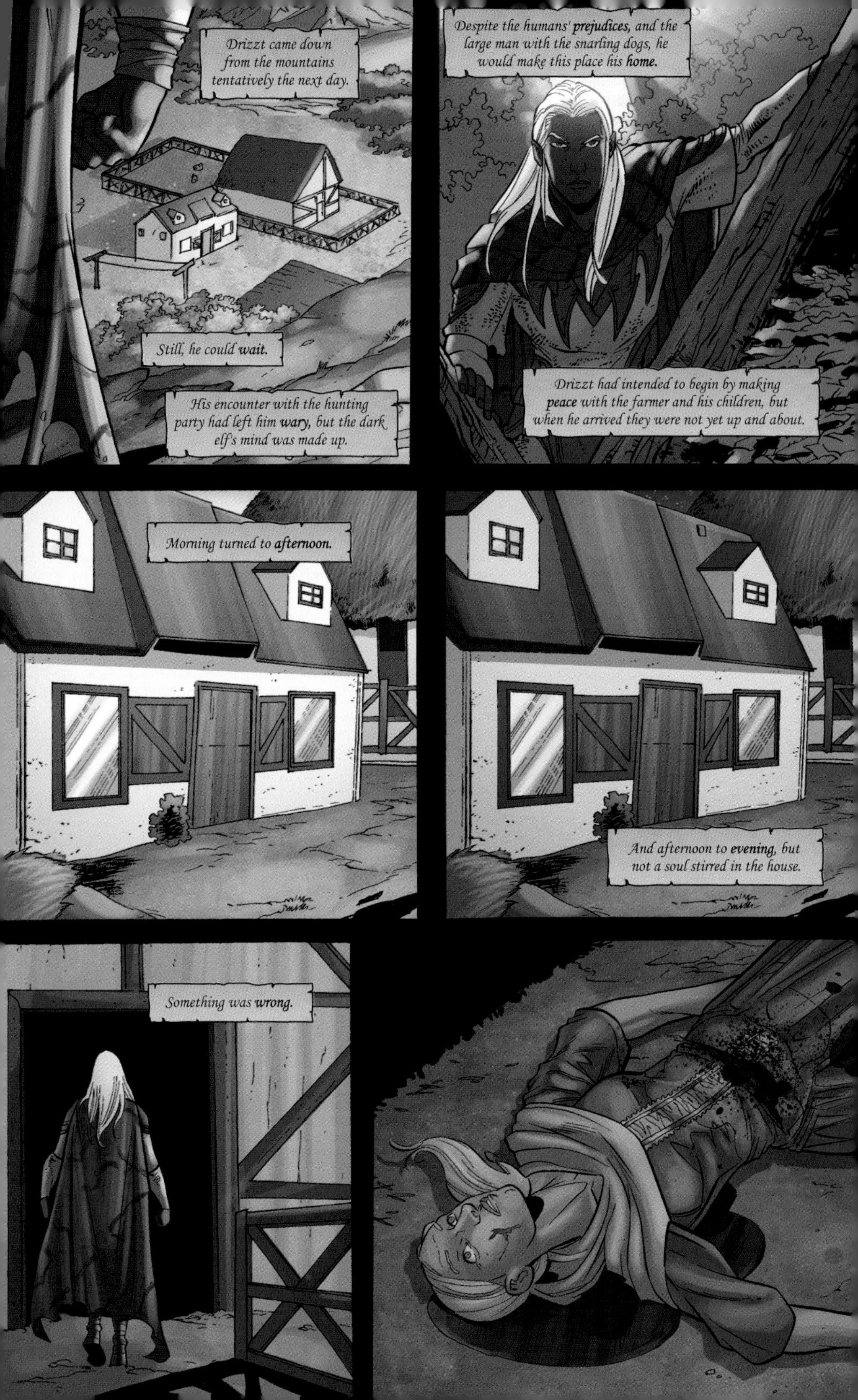
Drizzt came down from the mountains tentatively the next day.
Still, he could **wait.**
His encounter with the hunting party had left him **wary,** but the dark elf's mind was made up.
Despite the humans' **prejudices,** and the large man with the snarling dogs, he would make this place his **home.**
Drizzt had intended to begin by making **peace** with the farmer and his children, but when he arrived they were not yet up and about.
Morning turned to **afternoon.**
And afternoon to **evening,** but not a soul stirred in the house.
Something was **wrong.**

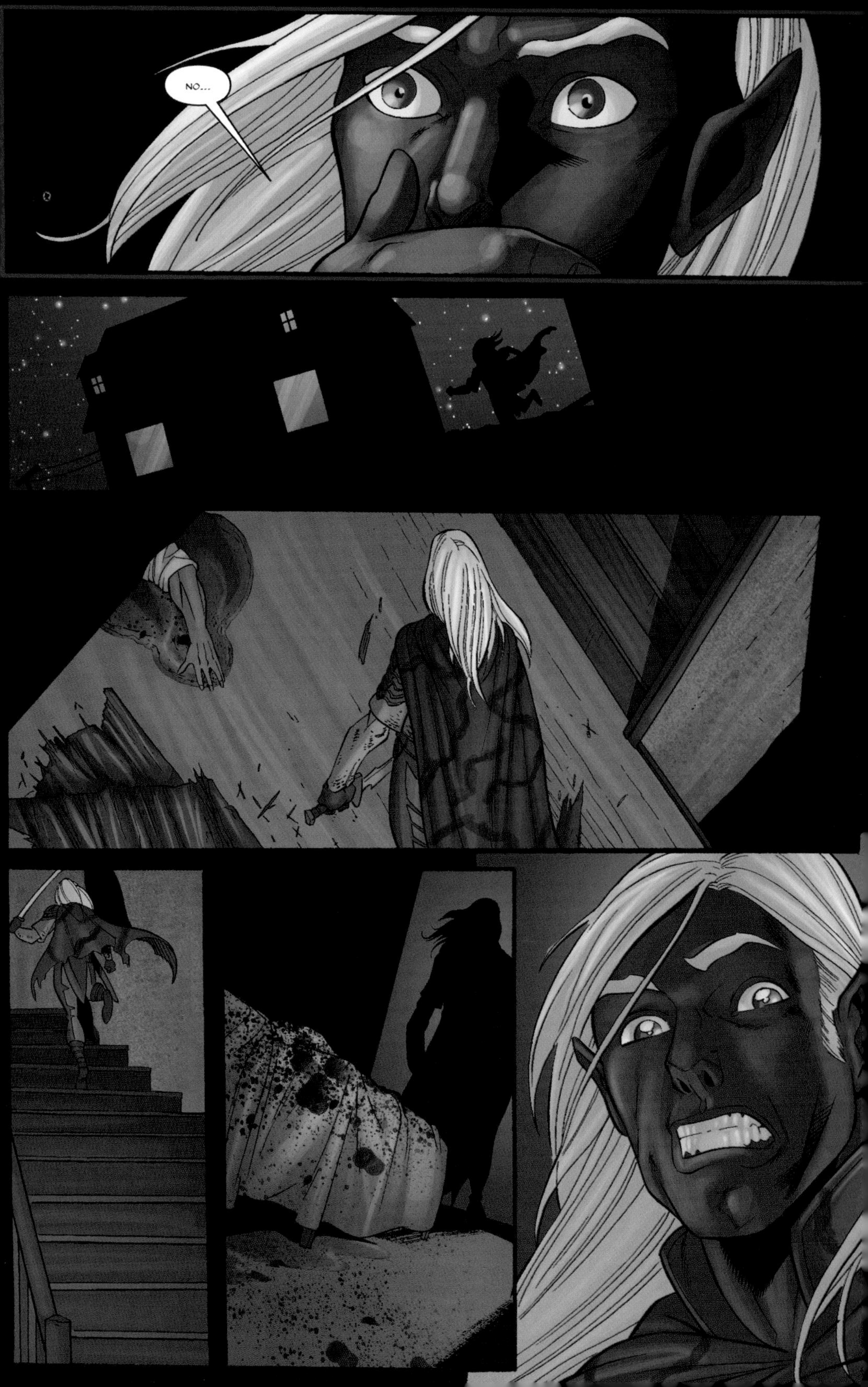
NO...

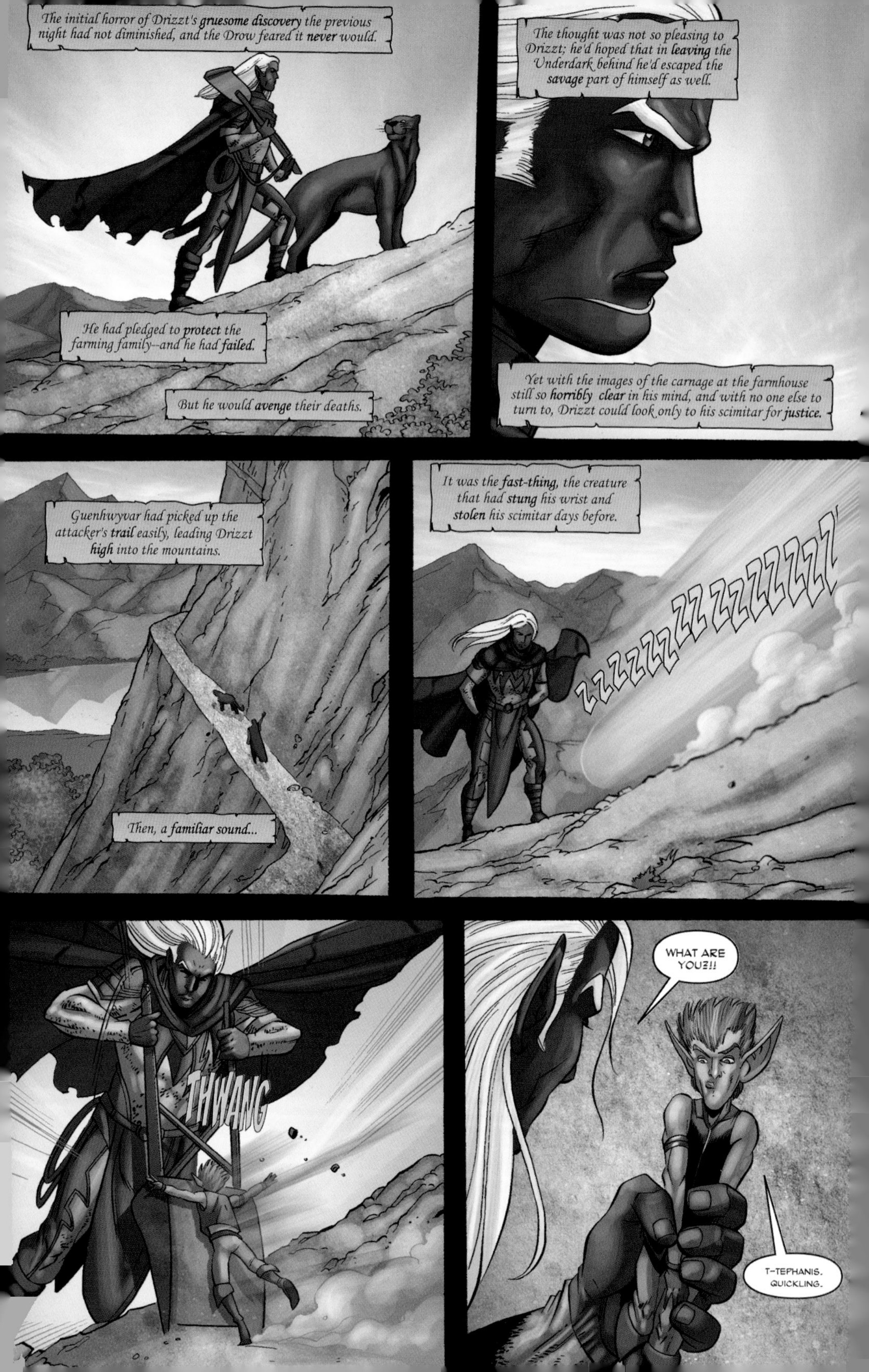
The initial horror of Drizzt's gruesome discovery the previous night had not diminished, and the Drow feared it never would.
He had pledged to protect the farming family--and he had failed.
But he would avenge their deaths.
The thought was not so pleasing to Drizzt; he'd hoped that in leaving the Underdark behind he'd escaped the savage part of himself as well.
Yet with the images of the carnage at the farmhouse still so horribly clear in his mind, and with no one else to turn to, Drizzt could look only to his scimitar for justice.
Guenhwyvar had picked up the attacker's trail easily, leading Drizzt high into the mountains.
Then, a familiar sound...
It was the fast-thing, the creature that had stung his wrist and stolen his scimitar days before.
ZZZZZZZZZ ZZZZZZZZZ
THWANG
WHAT ARE YOU?!!
T-TEPHANIS. QUICKLING.

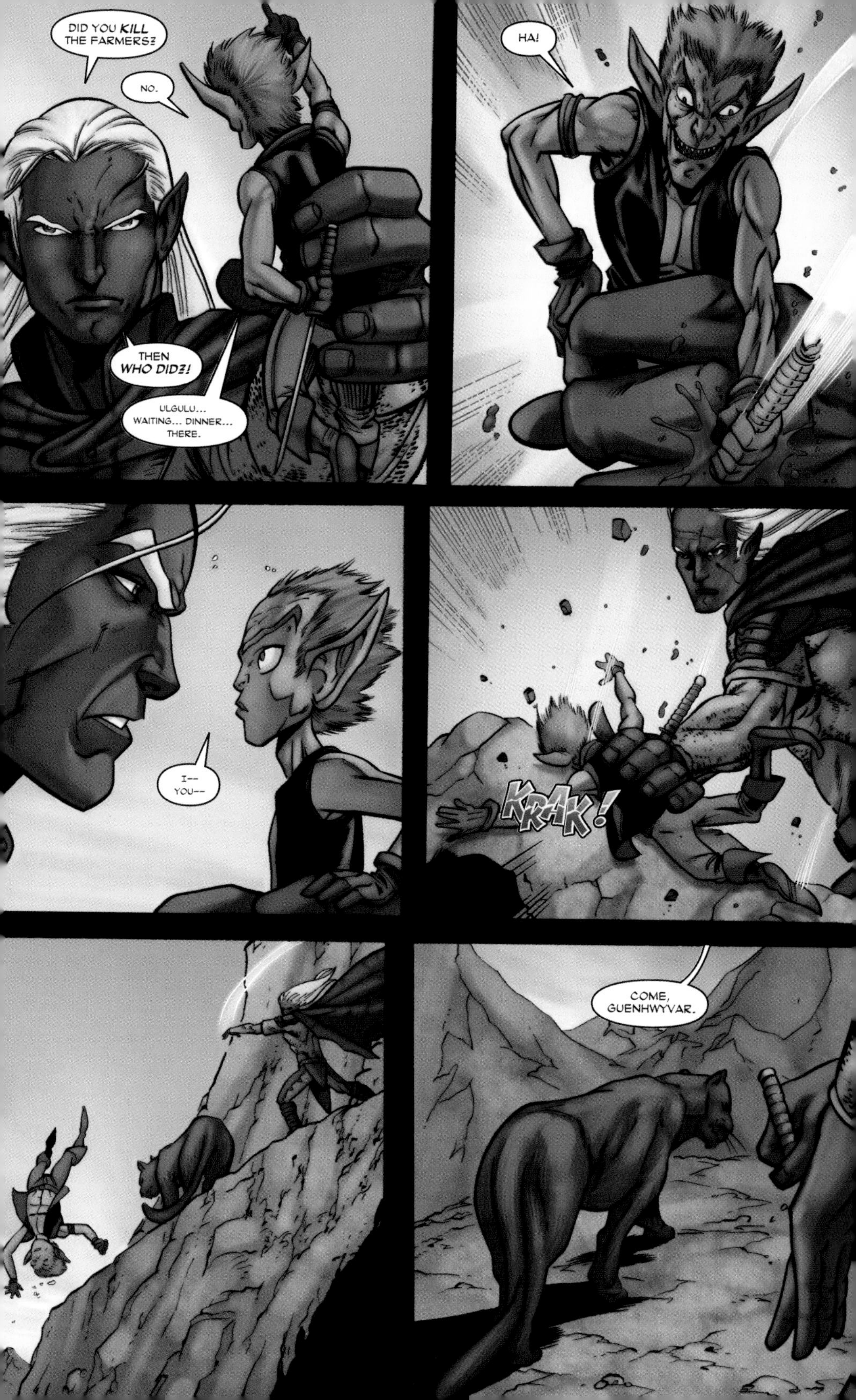
DID YOU KILL THE FARMERS?
NO.
THEN WHO DID?!
ULGULU... WAITING... DINNER... THERE.
HA!
I-- YOU--
KRAK!
COME, GUENHWYVAR.

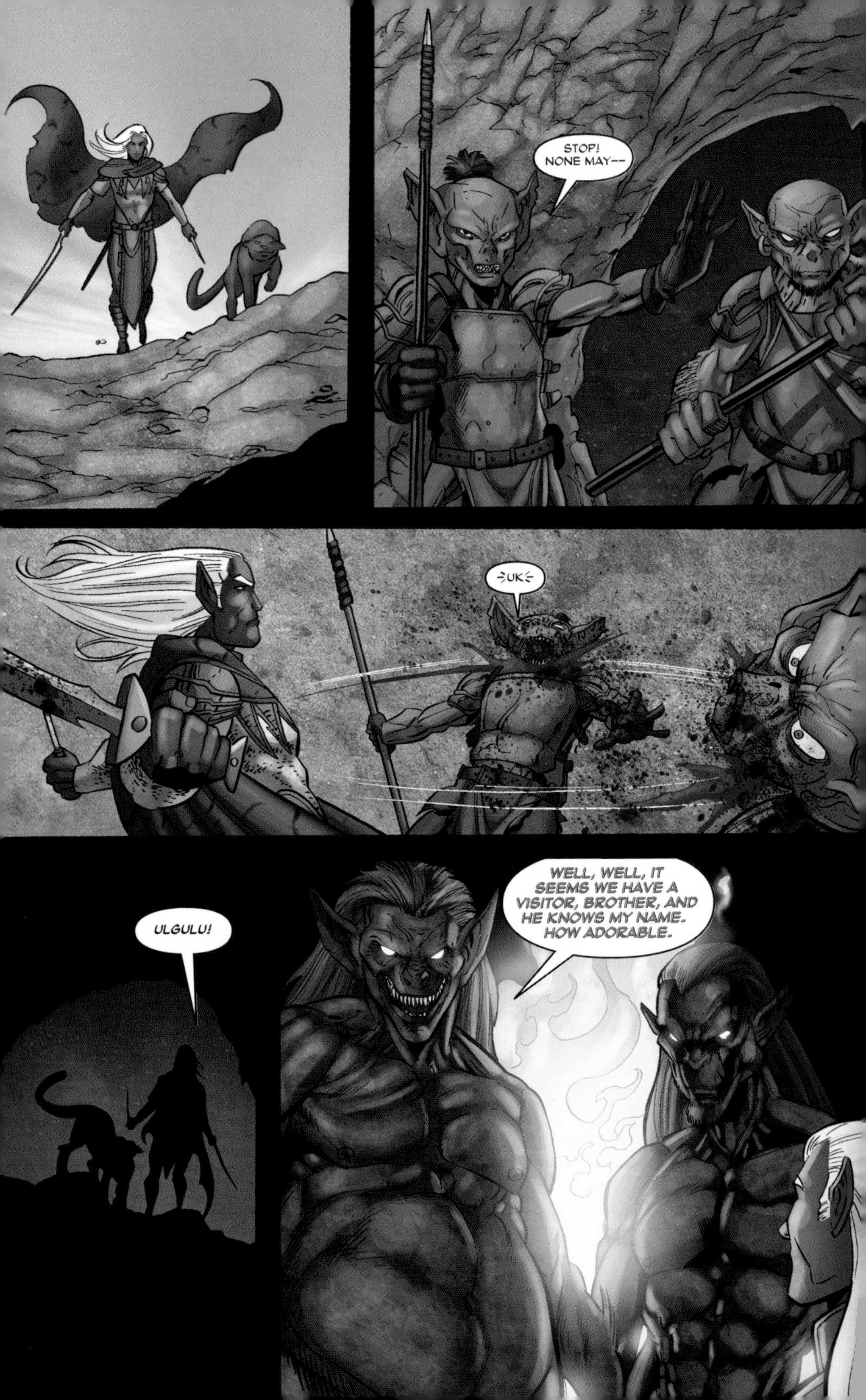
STOP! NONE MAY--
UK
ULGULU!
WELL, WELL, IT SEEMS WE HAVE A VISITOR, BROTHER, AND HE KNOWS MY NAME. HOW ADORABLE.

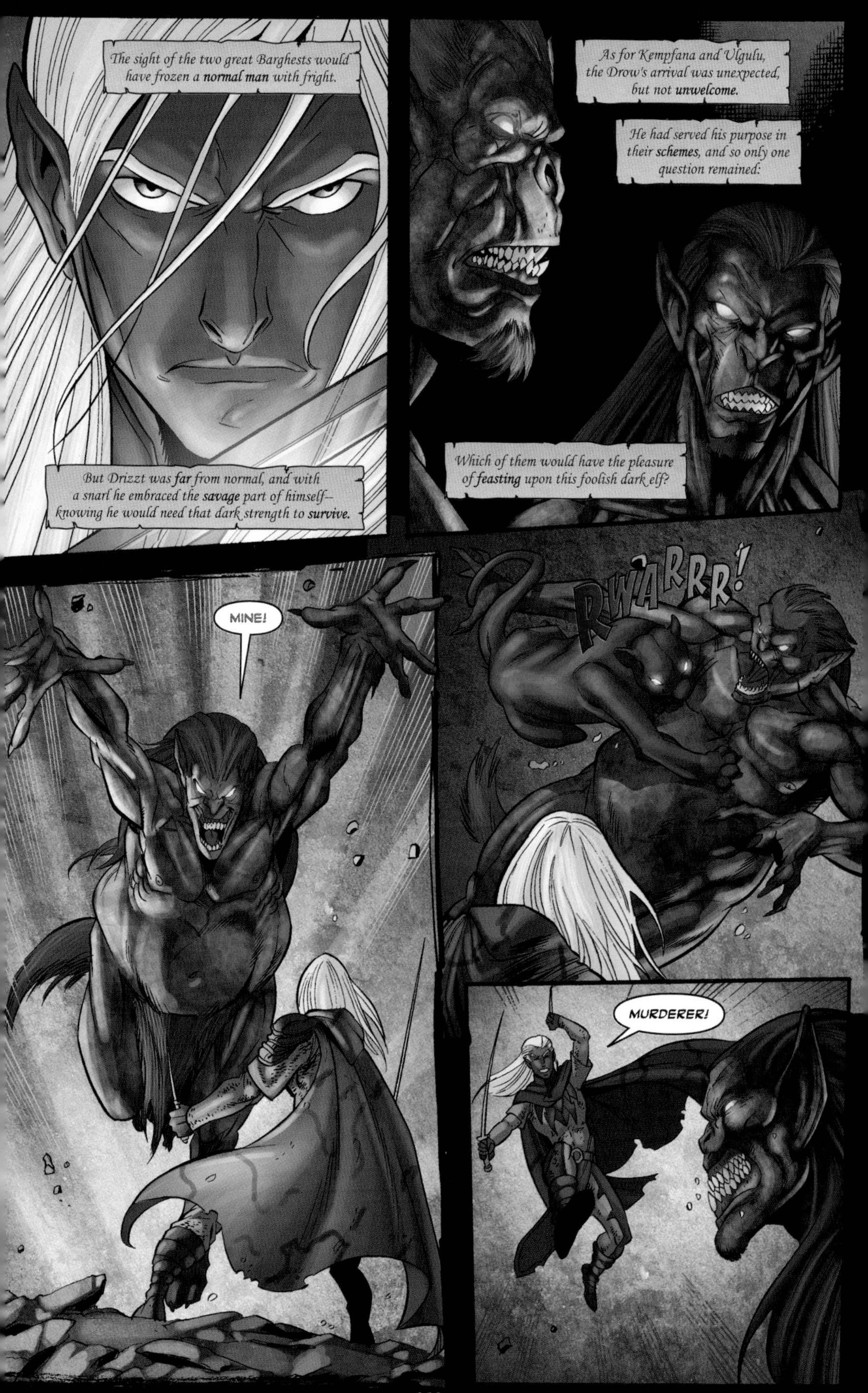

The sight of the two great Barghests would have frozen a normal man with fright.
But Drizzt was far from normal, and with a snarl he embraced the savage part of himself--knowing he would need that dark strength to survive.
As for Kempfana and Ulgulu, the Drow's arrival was unexpected, but not unwelcome.
He had served his purpose in their schemes, and so only one question remained:
Which of them would have the pleasure of feasting upon this foolish dark elf?
MINE!
RWARRR!
MURDERER!

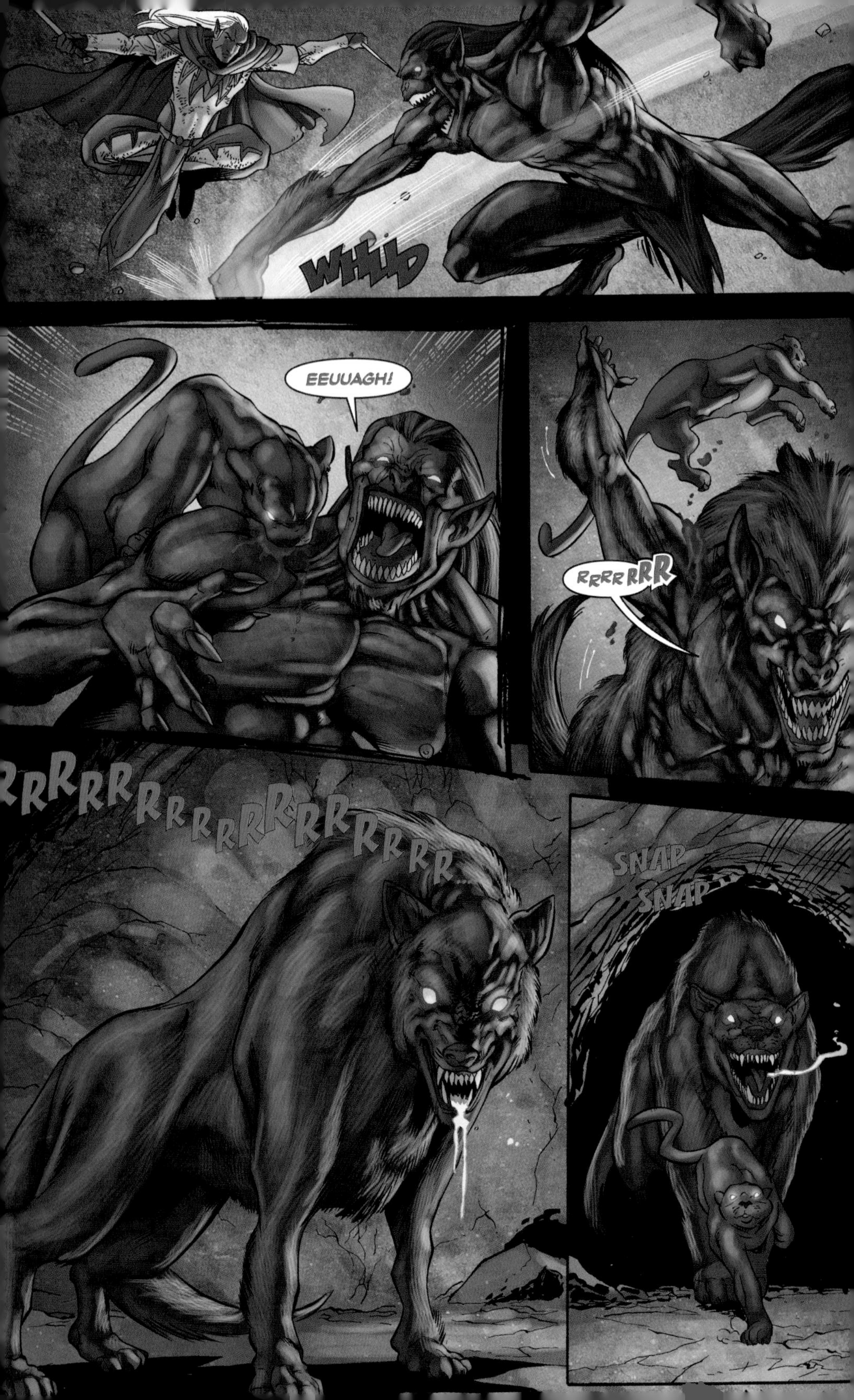
WHUD
EEUUAGH!
RRRRRRR
RRRRRRRRRRRRRRRRRRR
SNAP
SNAP

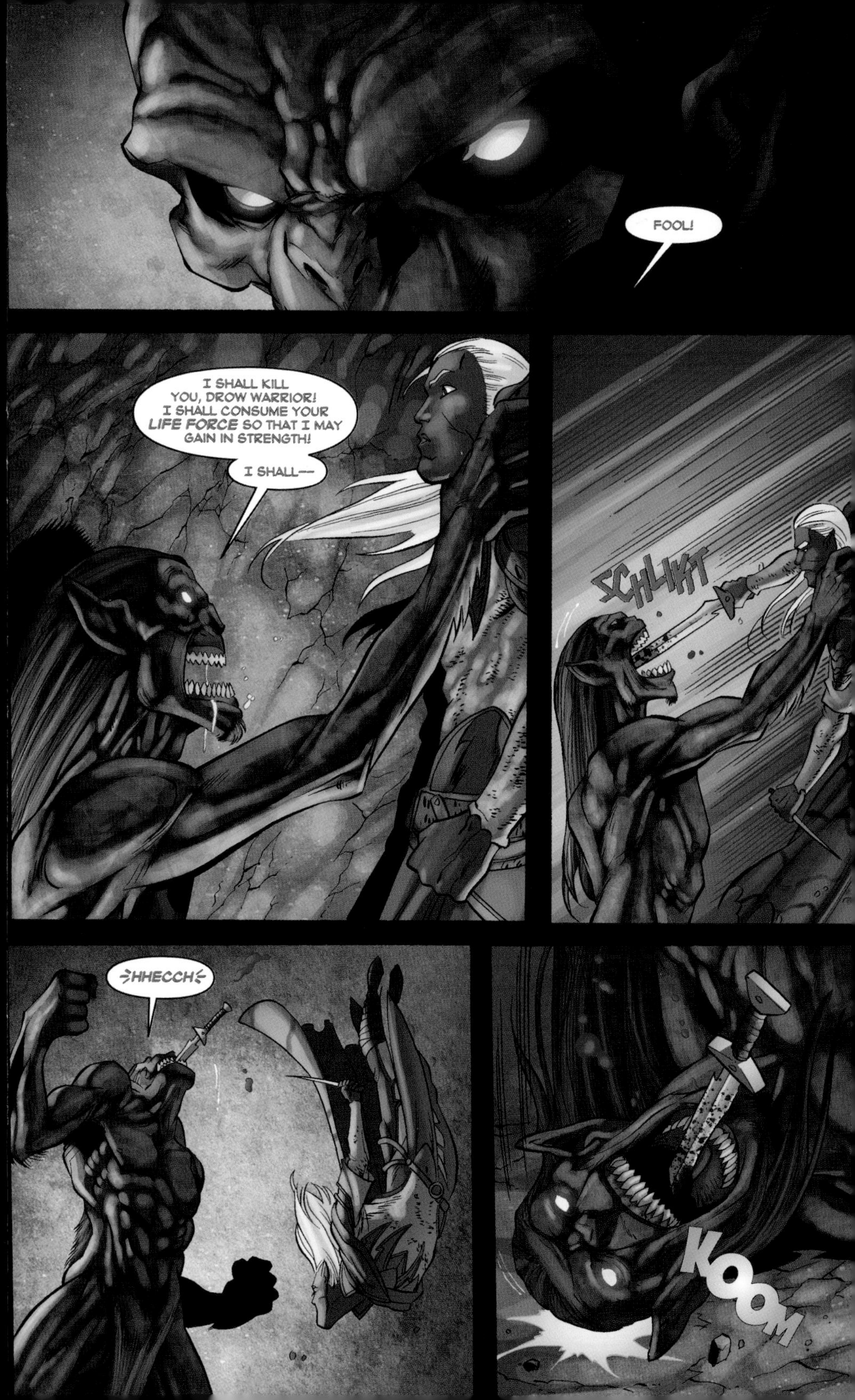
FOOL!
I SHALL KILL YOU, DROW WARRIOR! I SHALL CONSUME YOUR LIFE FORCE SO THAT I MAY GAIN IN STRENGTH!
I SHALL--
SCHLIKT
HHECCH
KOOM

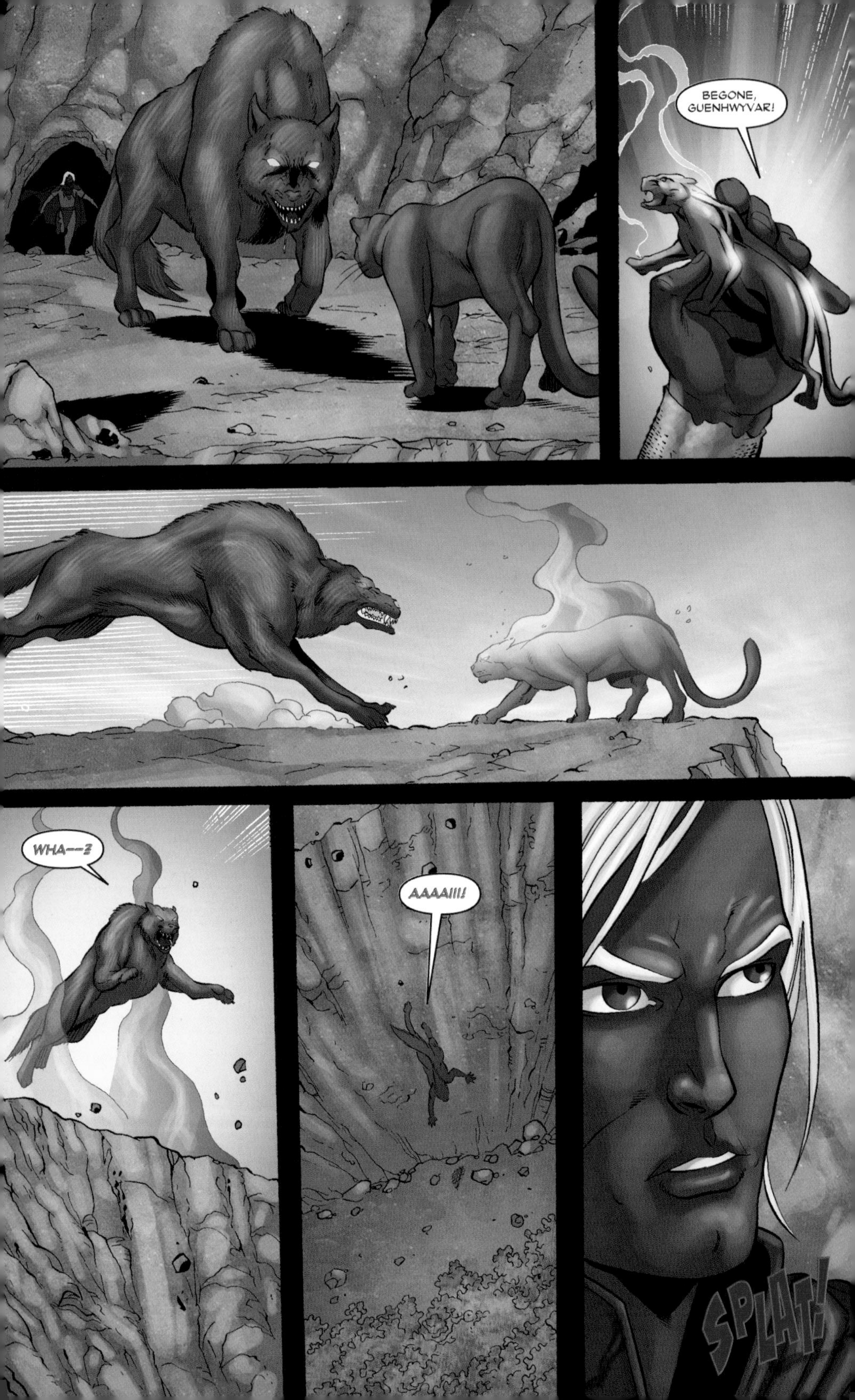
BEGONE, GUENHWYVAR!
WHA--?
AAAAIII!
SPLAT!

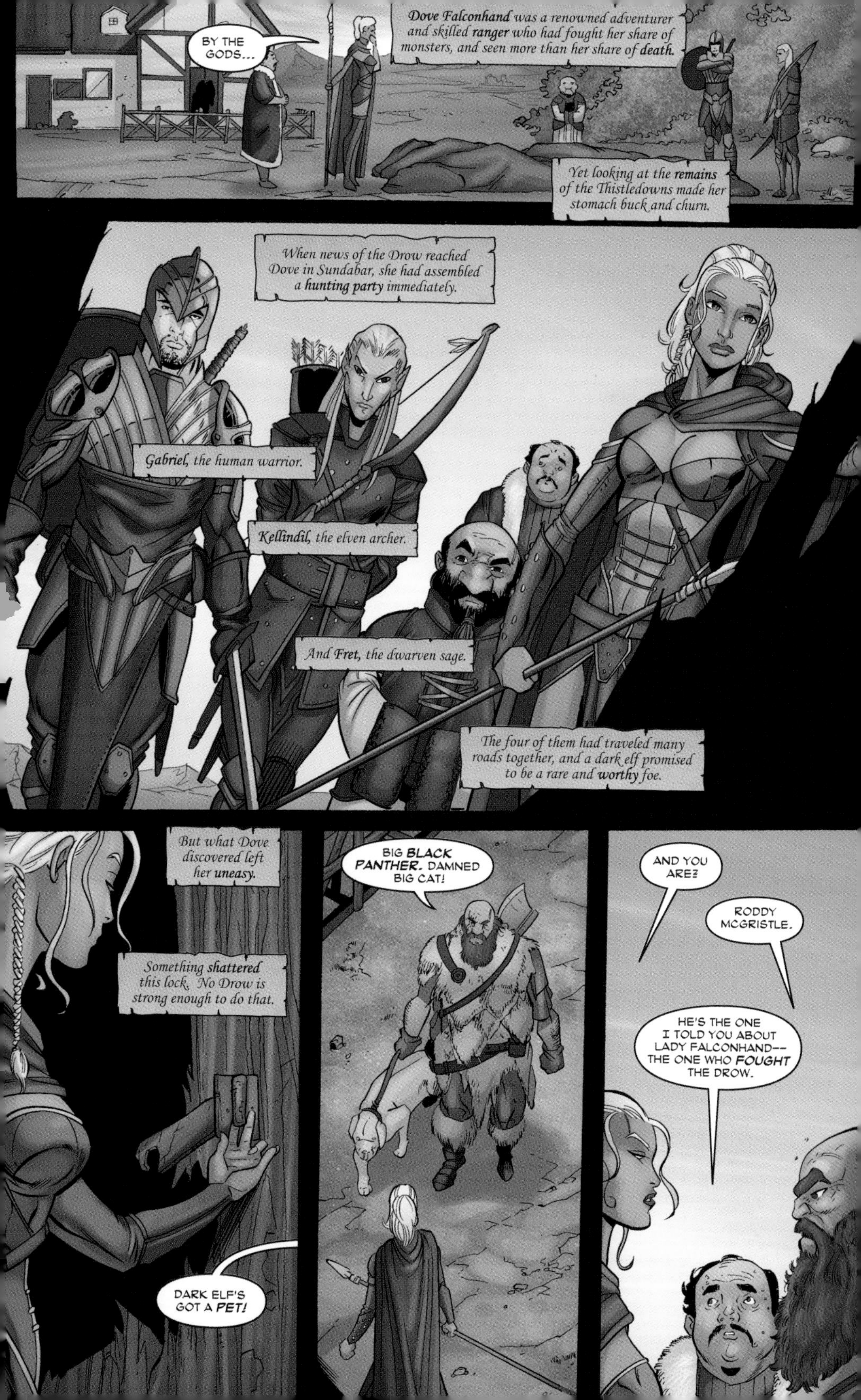

Dove Falconhand was a renowned adventurer and skilled ranger who had fought her share of monsters, and seen more than her share of death.
BY THE GODS...
Yet looking at the remains of the Thistledowns made her stomach buck and churn.
When news of the Drow reached Dove in Sundabar, she had assembled a hunting party immediately.
Gabriel, the human warrior.
Kellindil, the elven archer.
And Fret, the dwarven sage.
The four of them had traveled many roads together, and a dark elf promised to be a rare and worthy foe.
But what Dove discovered left her uneasy.
Something shattered this lock. No Drow is strong enough to do that.
DARK ELF'S GOT A PET!
BIG BLACK PANTHER. DAMNED BIG CAT!
AND YOU ARE?
RODDY MCGRISTLE.
HE'S THE ONE I TOLD YOU ABOUT LADY FALCONHAND-- THE ONE WHO FOUGHT THE DROW.

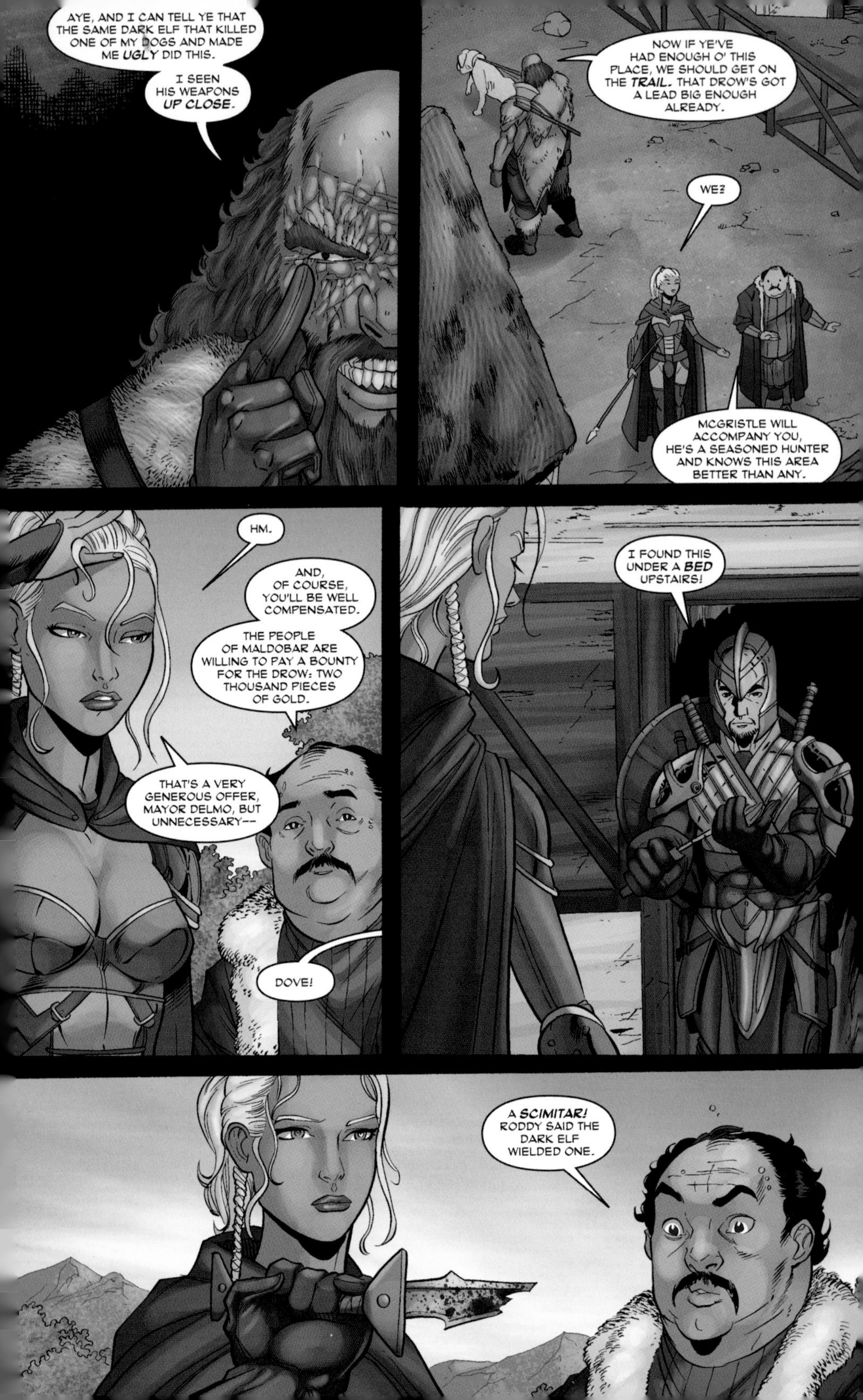

AYE, AND I CAN TELL YE THAT THE SAME DARK ELF THAT KILLED ONE OF MY DOGS AND MADE ME *UGLY* DID THIS.
I SEEN HIS WEAPONS *UP CLOSE*.
NOW IF YE'VE HAD ENOUGH O' THIS PLACE, WE SHOULD GET ON THE *TRAIL*. THAT DROW'S GOT A LEAD BIG ENOUGH ALREADY.
WE?
MCGRISTLE WILL ACCOMPANY YOU, HE'S A SEASONED HUNTER AND KNOWS THIS AREA BETTER THAN ANY.
HM.
AND, OF COURSE, YOU'LL BE WELL COMPENSATED.
THE PEOPLE OF MALDOBAR ARE WILLING TO PAY A BOUNTY FOR THE DROW: TWO THOUSAND PIECES OF GOLD.
THAT'S A VERY GENEROUS OFFER, MAYOR DELMO, BUT UNNECESSARY--
DOVE!
I FOUND THIS UNDER A *BED* UPSTAIRS!
A *SCIMITAR!* RODDY SAID THE DARK ELF WIELDED ONE.

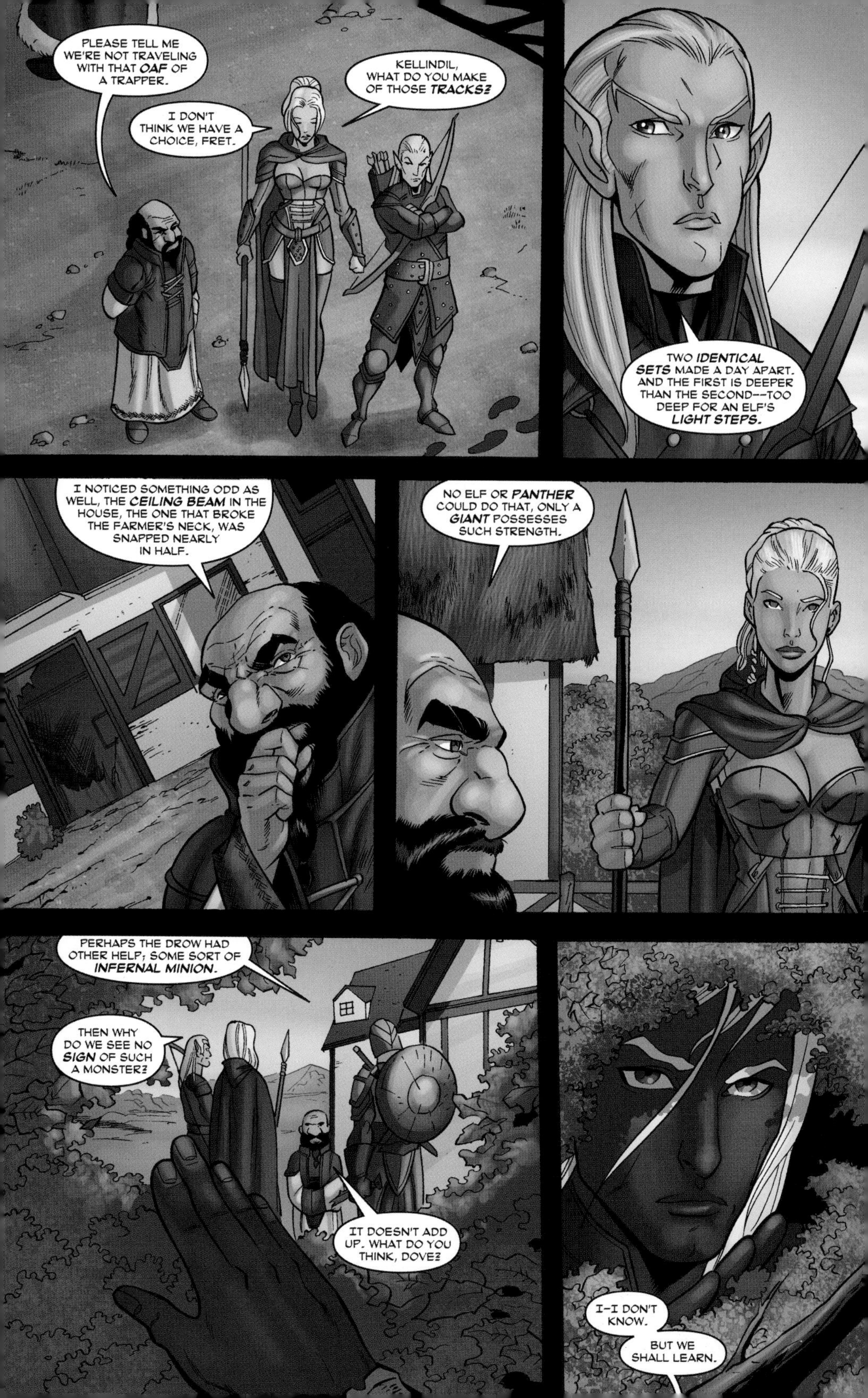
PLEASE TELL ME WE'RE NOT TRAVELING WITH THAT OAF OF A TRAPPER.
I DON'T THINK WE HAVE A CHOICE, FRET.
KELLINDIL, WHAT DO YOU MAKE OF THOSE TRACKS?
TWO IDENTICAL SETS MADE A DAY APART. AND THE FIRST IS DEEPER THAN THE SECOND--TOO DEEP FOR AN ELF'S LIGHT STEPS.
I NOTICED SOMETHING ODD AS WELL, THE CEILING BEAM IN THE HOUSE, THE ONE THAT BROKE THE FARMER'S NECK, WAS SNAPPED NEARLY IN HALF.
NO ELF OR PANTHER COULD DO THAT, ONLY A GIANT POSSESSES SUCH STRENGTH.
PERHAPS THE DROW HAD OTHER HELP; SOME SORT OF INFERNAL MINION.
THEN WHY DO WE SEE NO SIGN OF SUCH A MONSTER?
IT DOESN'T ADD UP. WHAT DO YOU THINK, DOVE?
I-I DON'T KNOW.
BUT WE SHALL LEARN.

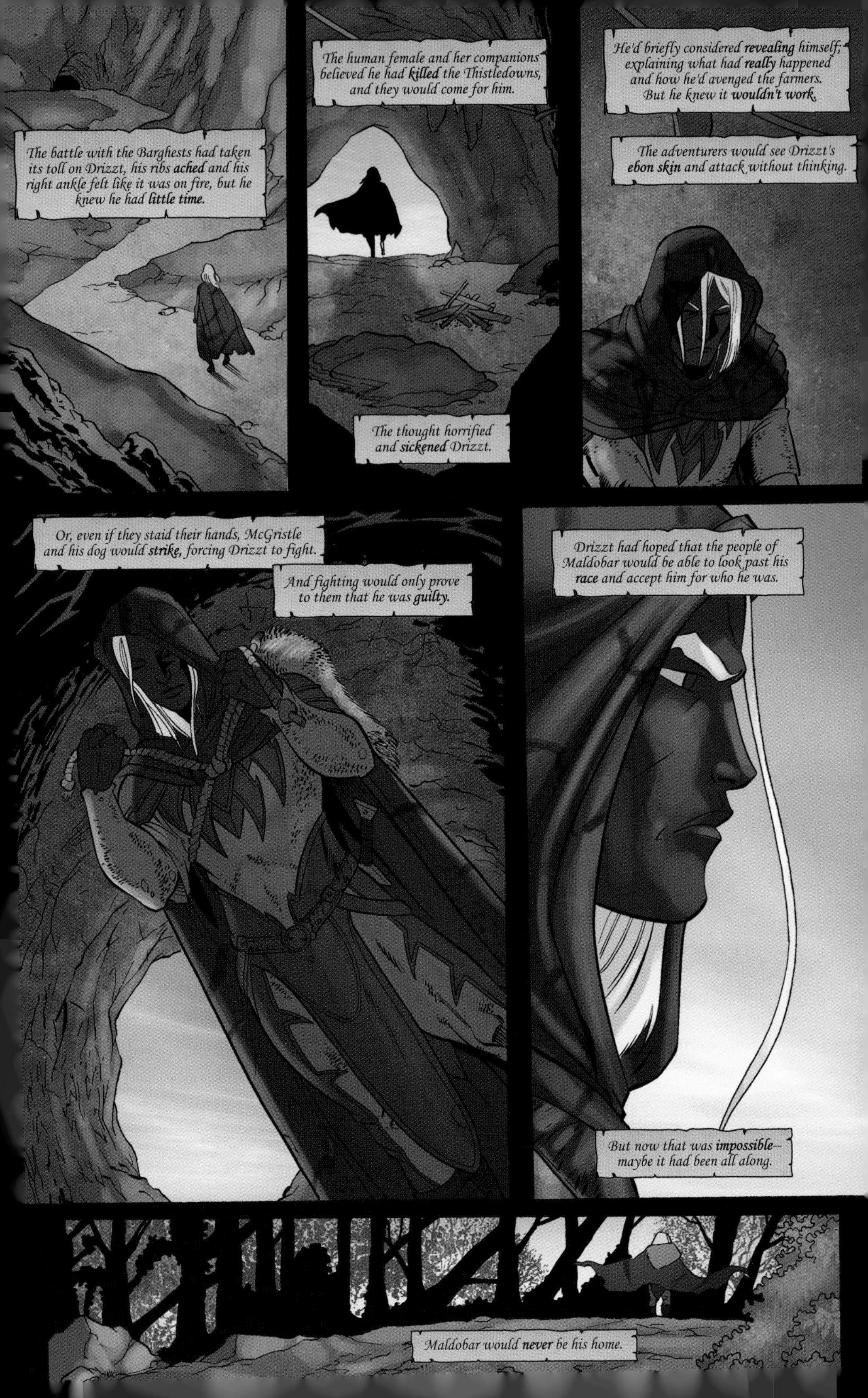
The battle with the Barghests had taken its toll on Drizzt, his ribs ached and his right ankle felt like it was on fire, but he knew he had little time.
The human female and her companions believed he had killed the Thistledowns, and they would come for him.
The thought horrified and sickened Drizzt.
He'd briefly considered revealing himself; explaining what had really happened and how he'd avenged the farmers. But he knew it wouldn't work.
The adventurers would see Drizzt's ebon skin and attack without thinking.
Or, even if they staid their hands, McGristle and his dog would strike, forcing Drizzt to fight.
And fighting would only prove to them that he was guilty.
Drizzt had hoped that the people of Maldobar would be able to look past his race and accept him for who he was.
But now that was impossible--maybe it had been all along.
Maldobar would never be his home.

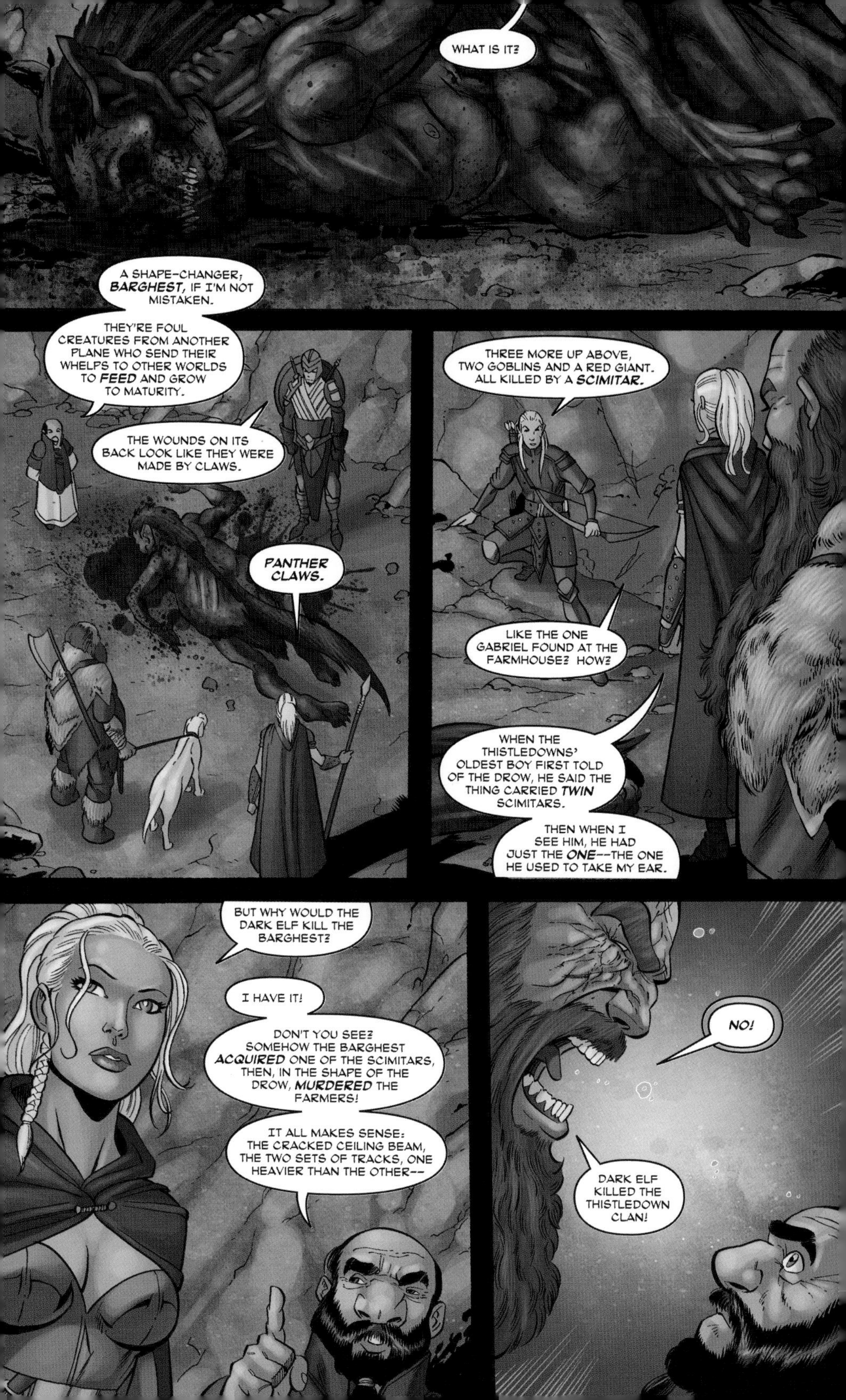
WHAT IS IT?
A SHAPE-CHANGER; BARGHEST, IF I'M NOT MISTAKEN.
THEY'RE FOUL CREATURES FROM ANOTHER PLANE WHO SEND THEIR WHELPS TO OTHER WORLDS TO FEED AND GROW TO MATURITY.
THE WOUNDS ON ITS BACK LOOK LIKE THEY WERE MADE BY CLAWS.
PANTHER CLAWS.
THREE MORE UP ABOVE, TWO GOBLINS AND A RED GIANT. ALL KILLED BY A SCIMITAR.
LIKE THE ONE GABRIEL FOUND AT THE FARMHOUSE? HOW?
WHEN THE THISTLEDOWNS' OLDEST BOY FIRST TOLD OF THE DROW, HE SAID THE THING CARRIED TWIN SCIMITARS.
THEN WHEN I SEE HIM, HE HAD JUST THE ONE--THE ONE HE USED TO TAKE MY EAR.
BUT WHY WOULD THE DARK ELF KILL THE BARGHEST?
I HAVE IT!
DON'T YOU SEE? SOMEHOW THE BARGHEST ACQUIRED ONE OF THE SCIMITARS, THEN, IN THE SHAPE OF THE DROW, MURDERED THE FARMERS!
IT ALL MAKES SENSE: THE CRACKED CEILING BEAM, THE TWO SETS OF TRACKS, ONE HEAVIER THAN THE OTHER--
NO!
DARK ELF KILLED THE THISTLEDOWN CLAN!

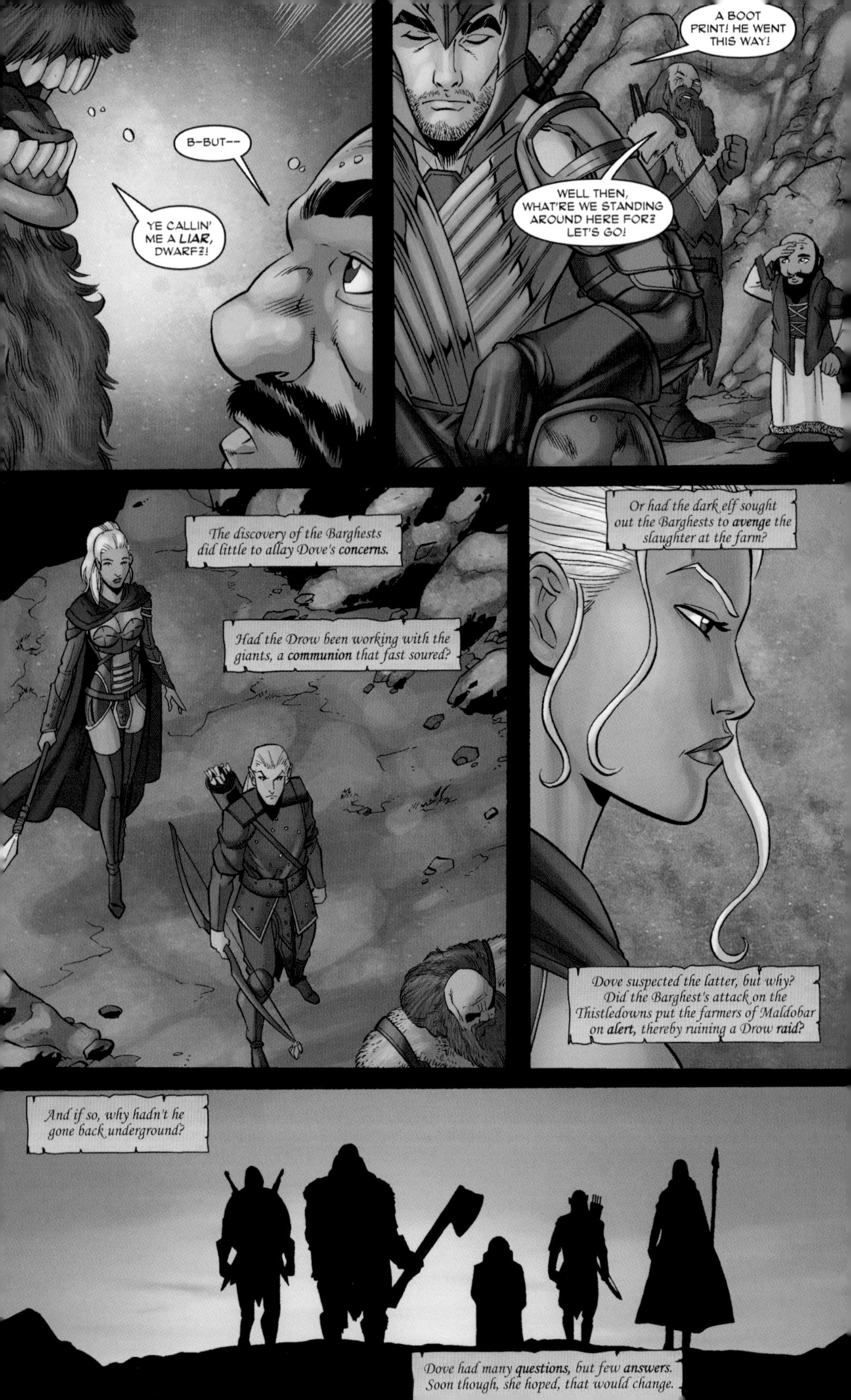
B-BUT--
YE CALLIN' ME A LIAR, DWARF?!
A BOOT PRINT! HE WENT THIS WAY!
WELL THEN, WHAT'RE WE STANDING AROUND HERE FOR? LET'S GO!
The discovery of the Barghests did little to allay Dove's concerns.
Had the Drow been working with the giants, a communion that fast soured?
Or had the dark elf sought out the Barghests to avenge the slaughter at the farm?
Dove suspected the latter, but why? Did the Barghest's attack on the Thistledowns put the farmers of Maldobar on alert, thereby ruining a Drow raid?
And if so, why hadn't he gone back underground?
Dove had many questions, but few answers. Soon though, she hoped, that would change.

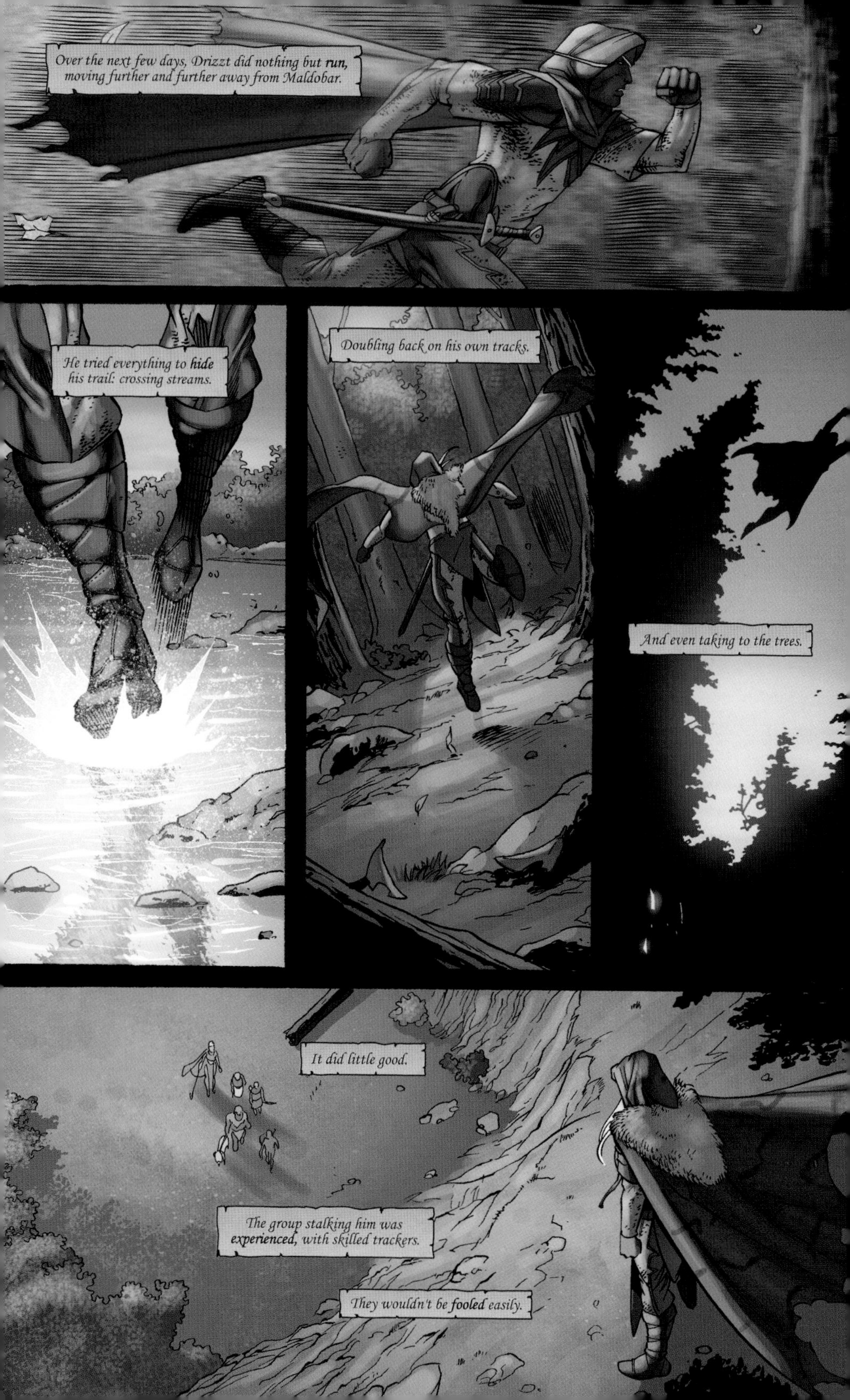
Over the next few days, Drizzt did nothing but **run**, moving further and further away from Maldobar.
He tried everything to **hide** his trail: crossing streams.
Doubling back on his own tracks.
And even taking to the trees.
It did little good.
The group stalking him was **experienced**, with skilled trackers.
They wouldn't be **fooled** easily.

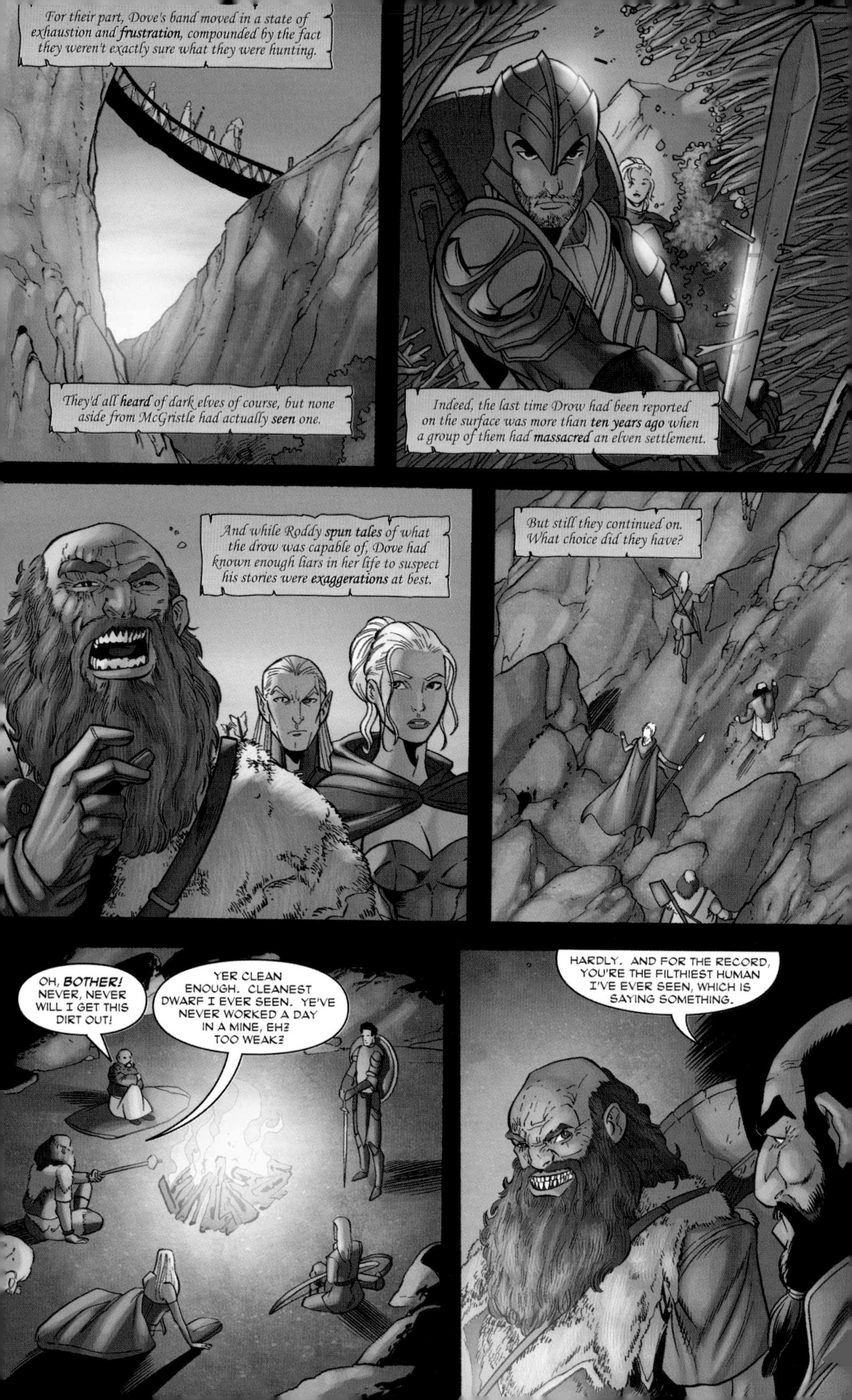
For their part, Dove's band moved in a state of exhaustion and frustration, compounded by the fact they weren't exactly sure what they were hunting.
They'd all heard of dark elves of course, but none aside from McGristle had actually seen one.
Indeed, the last time Drow had been reported on the surface was more than ten years ago when a group of them had massacred an elven settlement.
And while Roddy spun tales of what the drow was capable of, Dove had known enough liars in her life to suspect his stories were exaggerations at best.
But still they continued on. What choice did they have?
OH, BOTHER! NEVER, NEVER WILL I GET THIS DIRT OUT!
YER CLEAN ENOUGH. CLEANEST DWARF I EVER SEEN. YE'VE NEVER WORKED A DAY IN A MINE, EH? TOO WEAK?
HARDLY. AND FOR THE RECORD, YOU'RE THE FILTHIEST HUMAN I'VE EVER SEEN, WHICH IS SAYING SOMETHING.

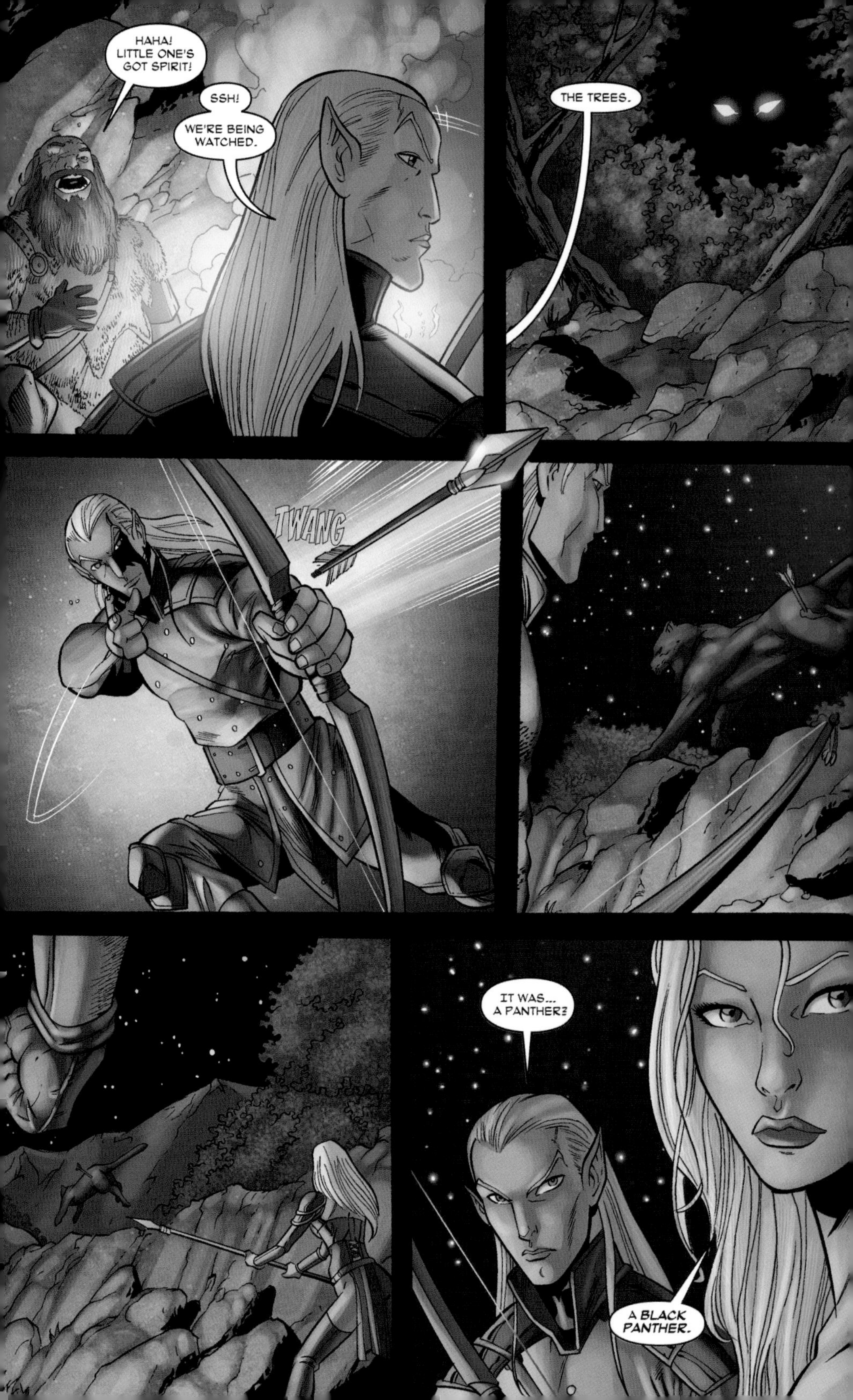
HAHA! LITTLE ONE'S GOT SPIRIT!
SSH!
WE'RE BEING WATCHED.
THE TREES.
TWANG
IT WAS... A PANTHER?
A BLACK PANTHER.

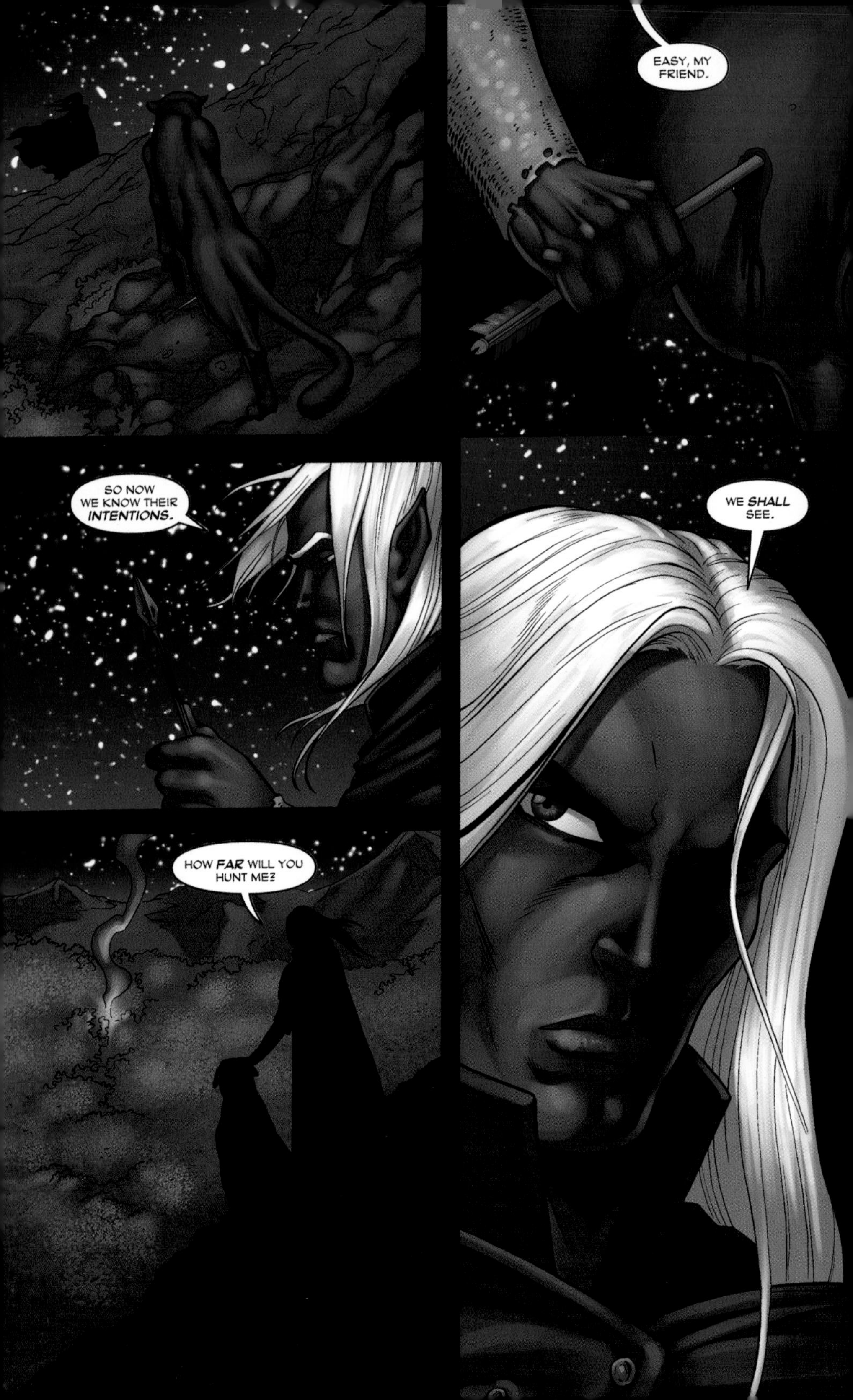
EASY, MY FRIEND.
SO NOW WE KNOW THEIR INTENTIONS.
WE SHALL SEE.
HOW FAR WILL YOU HUNT ME?

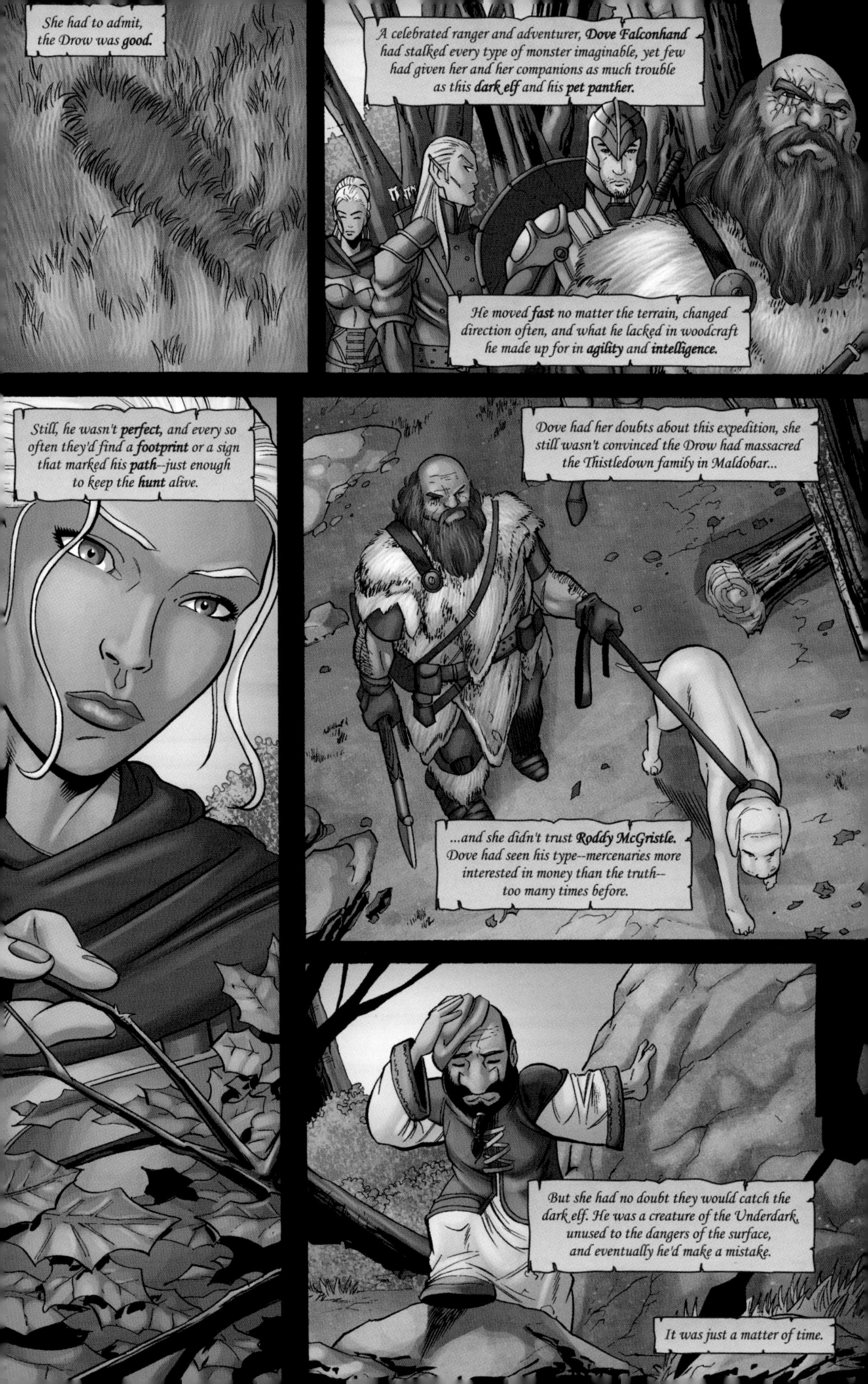
She had to admit, the Drow was good.
A celebrated ranger and adventurer, Dove Falconhand had stalked every type of monster imaginable, yet few had given her and her companions as much trouble as this dark elf and his pet panther.
He moved fast no matter the terrain, changed direction often, and what he lacked in woodcraft he made up for in agility and intelligence.
Still, he wasn't perfect, and every so often they'd find a footprint or a sign that marked his path--just enough to keep the hunt alive.
Dove had her doubts about this expedition, she still wasn't convinced the Drow had massacred the Thistledown family in Maldobar...
...and she didn't trust Roddy McGristle. Dove had seen his type--mercenaries more interested in money than the truth--too many times before.
But she had no doubt they would catch the dark elf. He was a creature of the Underdark, unused to the dangers of the surface, and eventually he'd make a mistake.
It was just a matter of time.

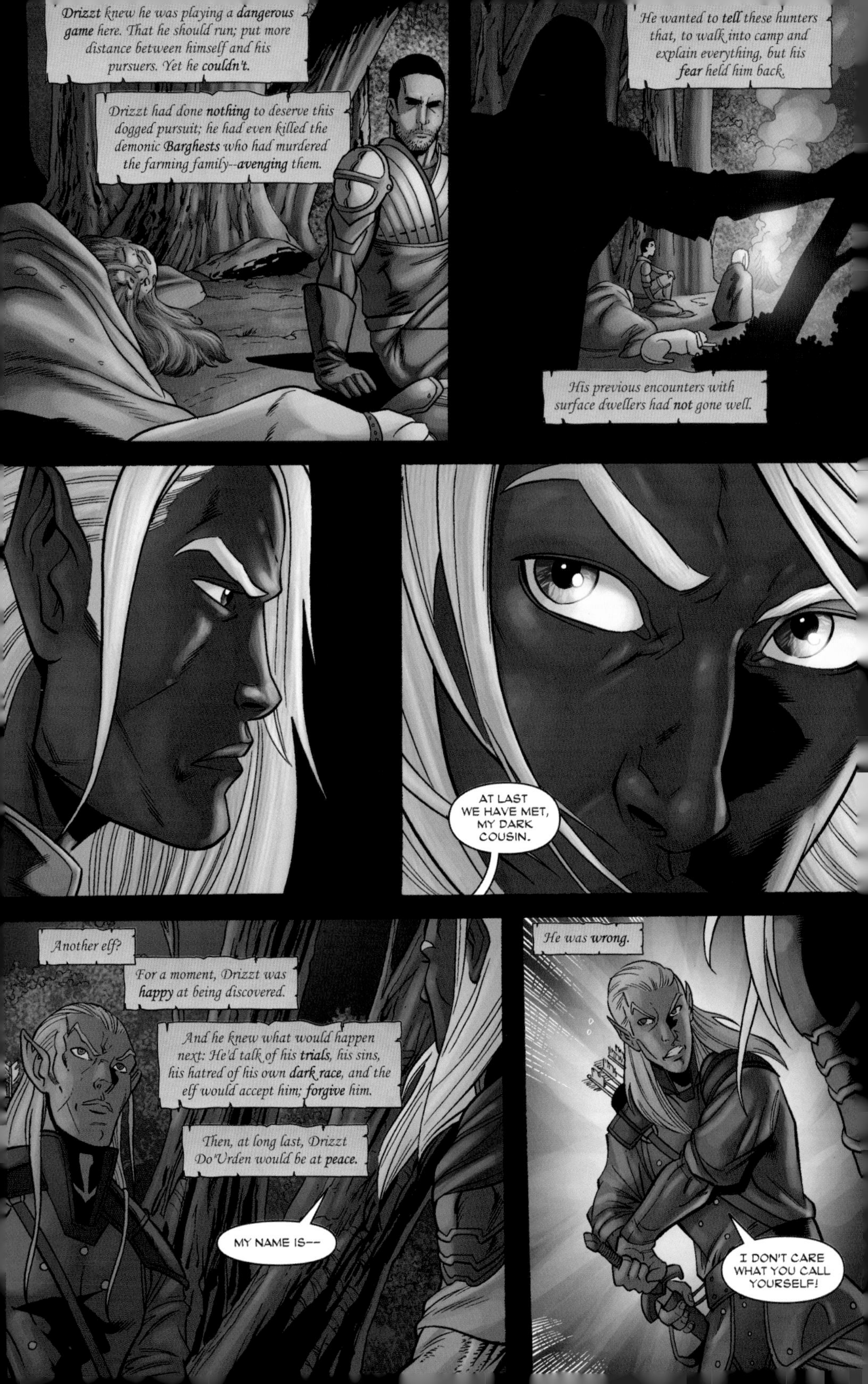
Drizzt knew he was playing a dangerous game here. That he should run; put more distance between himself and his pursuers. Yet he couldn't.
Drizzt had done nothing to deserve this dogged pursuit; he had even killed the demonic Barghests who had murdered the farming family--avenging them.
He wanted to tell these hunters that, to walk into camp and explain everything, but his fear held him back.
His previous encounters with surface dwellers had not gone well.
AT LAST WE HAVE MET, MY DARK COUSIN.
Another elf?
For a moment, Drizzt was happy at being discovered.
And he knew what would happen next: He'd talk of his trials, his sins, his hatred of his own dark race, and the elf would accept him; forgive him.
Then, at long last, Drizzt Do'Urden would be at peace.
MY NAME IS--
He was wrong.
I DON'T CARE WHAT YOU CALL YOURSELF!

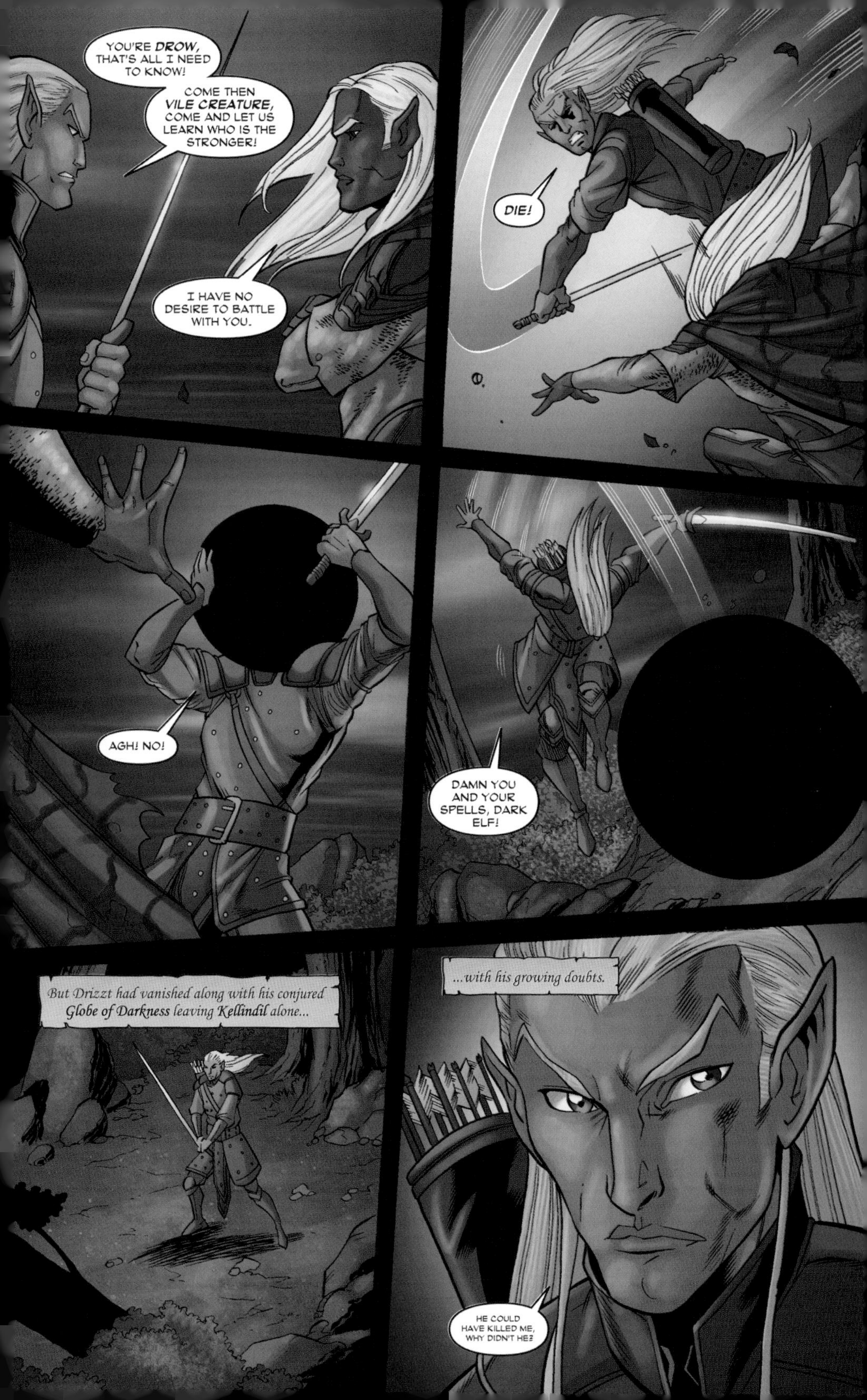
YOU'RE DROW, THAT'S ALL I NEED TO KNOW!
COME THEN VILE CREATURE, COME AND LET US LEARN WHO IS THE STRONGER!
I HAVE NO DESIRE TO BATTLE WITH YOU.
DIE!
AGH! NO!
DAMN YOU AND YOUR SPELLS, DARK ELF!
But Drizzt had vanished along with his conjured Globe of Darkness leaving Kellindil alone...
...with his growing doubts.
HE COULD HAVE KILLED ME, WHY DIDN'T HE?

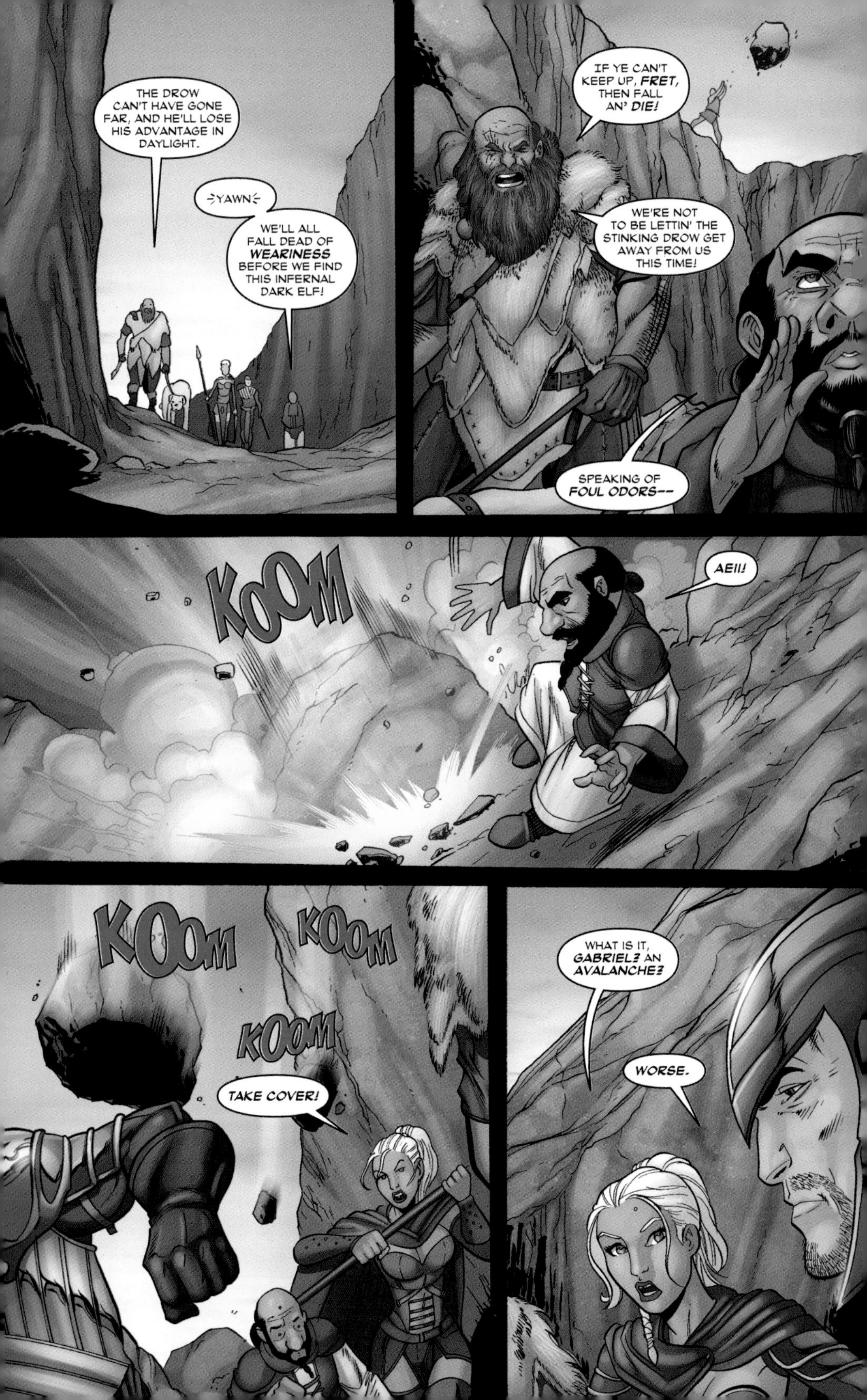
THE DROW CAN'T HAVE GONE FAR, AND HE'LL LOSE HIS ADVANTAGE IN DAYLIGHT.
YAWN
WE'LL ALL FALL DEAD OF WEARINESS BEFORE WE FIND THIS INFERNAL DARK ELF!
IF YE CAN'T KEEP UP, FRET, THEN FALL AN' DIE!
WE'RE NOT TO BE LETTIN' THE STINKING DROW GET AWAY FROM US THIS TIME!
SPEAKING OF FOUL ODORS--
KOOM
AEII!
KOOM
KOOM
KOOM
TAKE COVER!
WHAT IS IT, GABRIEL? AN AVALANCHE?
WORSE.

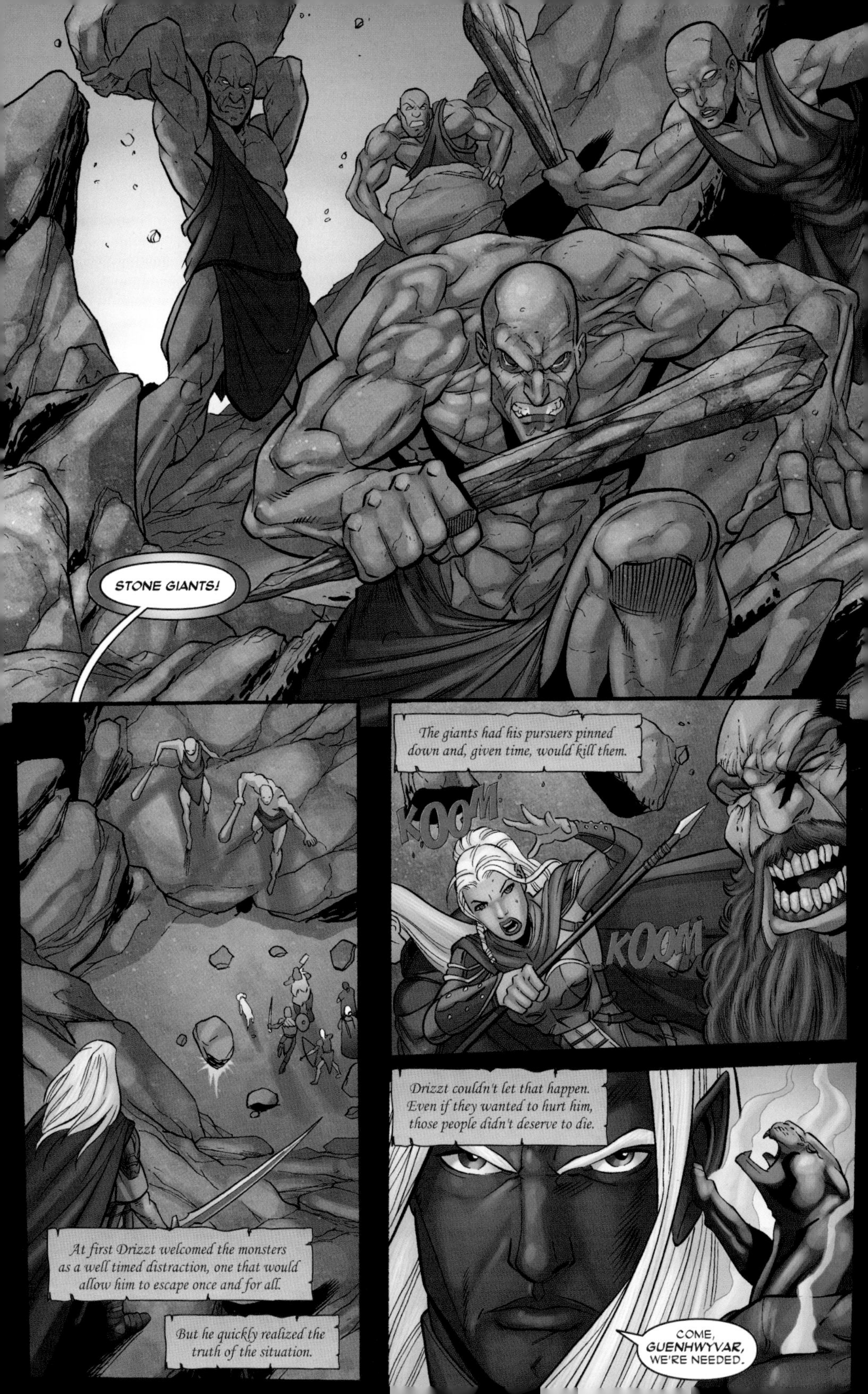
STONE GIANTS!
At first Drizzt welcomed the monsters as a well timed distraction, one that would allow him to escape once and for all.
But he quickly realized the truth of the situation.
The giants had his pursuers pinned down and, given time, would kill them.
KOOM
KOOM
Drizzt couldn't let that happen. Even if they wanted to hurt him, those people didn't deserve to die.
COME, GUENHWYVAR, WE'RE NEEDED.

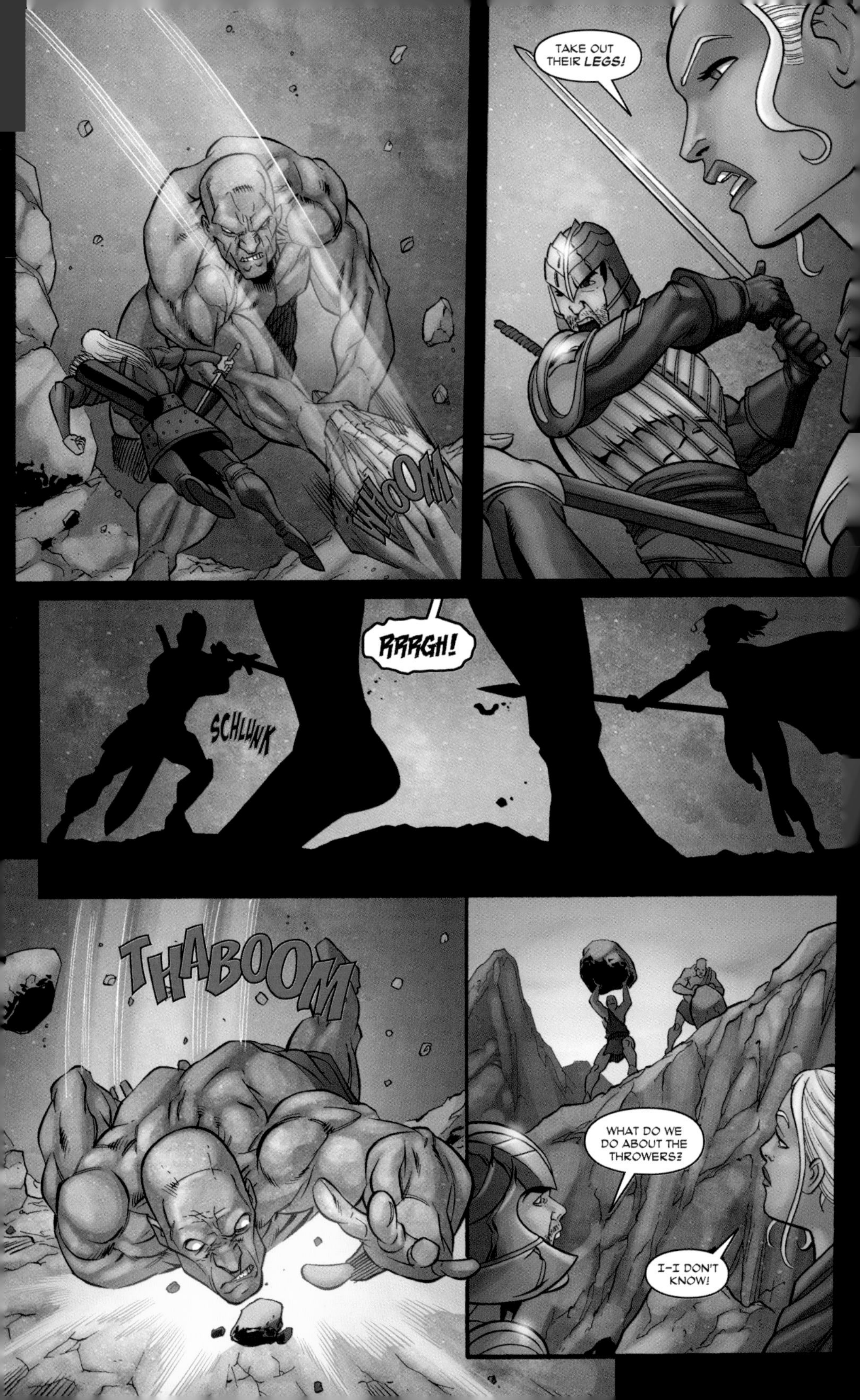
WHOOM
TAKE OUT THEIR LEGS!
RRRGH!
SCHLUNK
THABOOM
WHAT DO WE DO ABOUT THE THROWERS?
I-I DON'T KNOW!

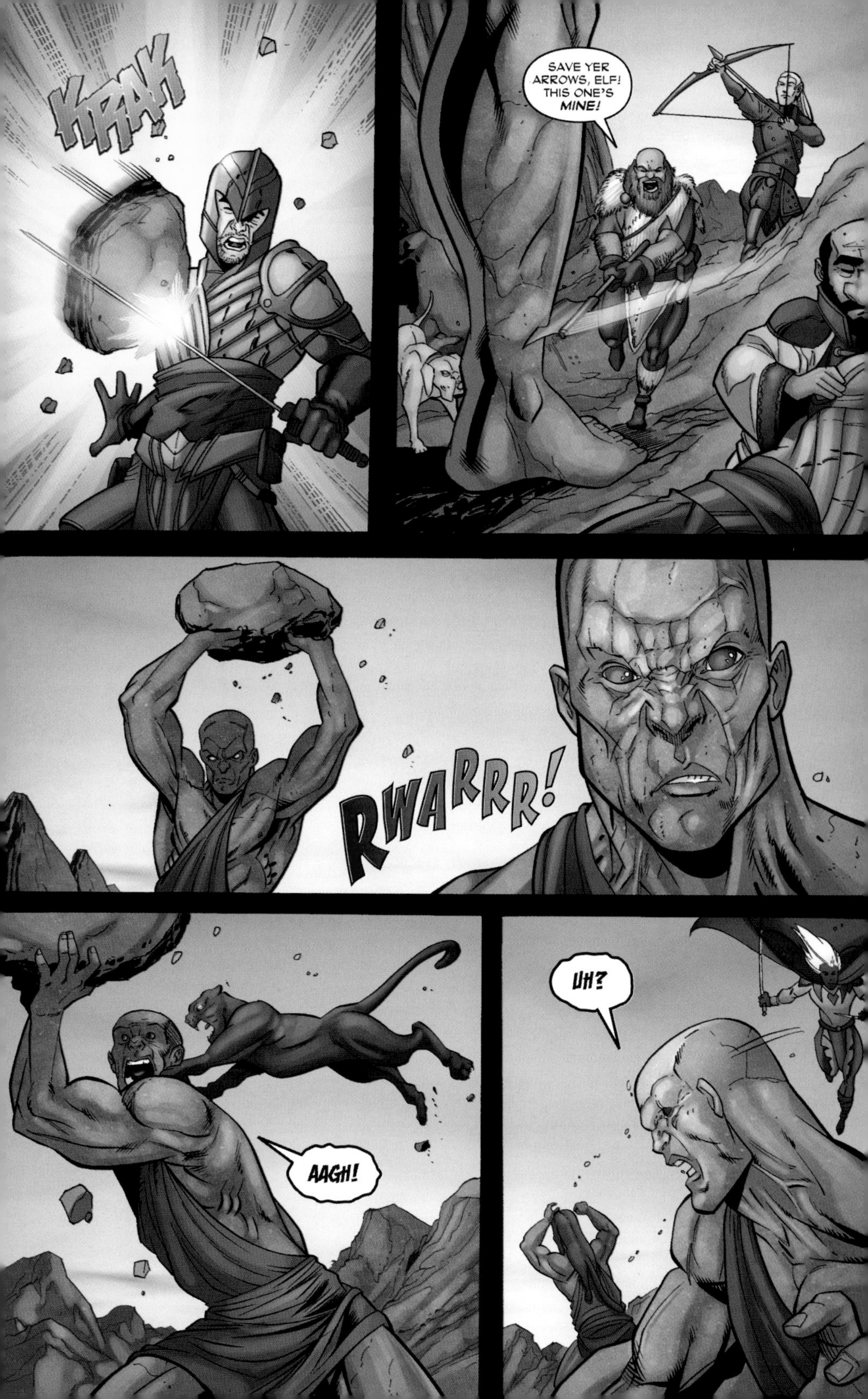
KRAK
SAVE YER ARROWS, ELF! THIS ONE'S MINE!
RWARRR!
AAGH!
UH?

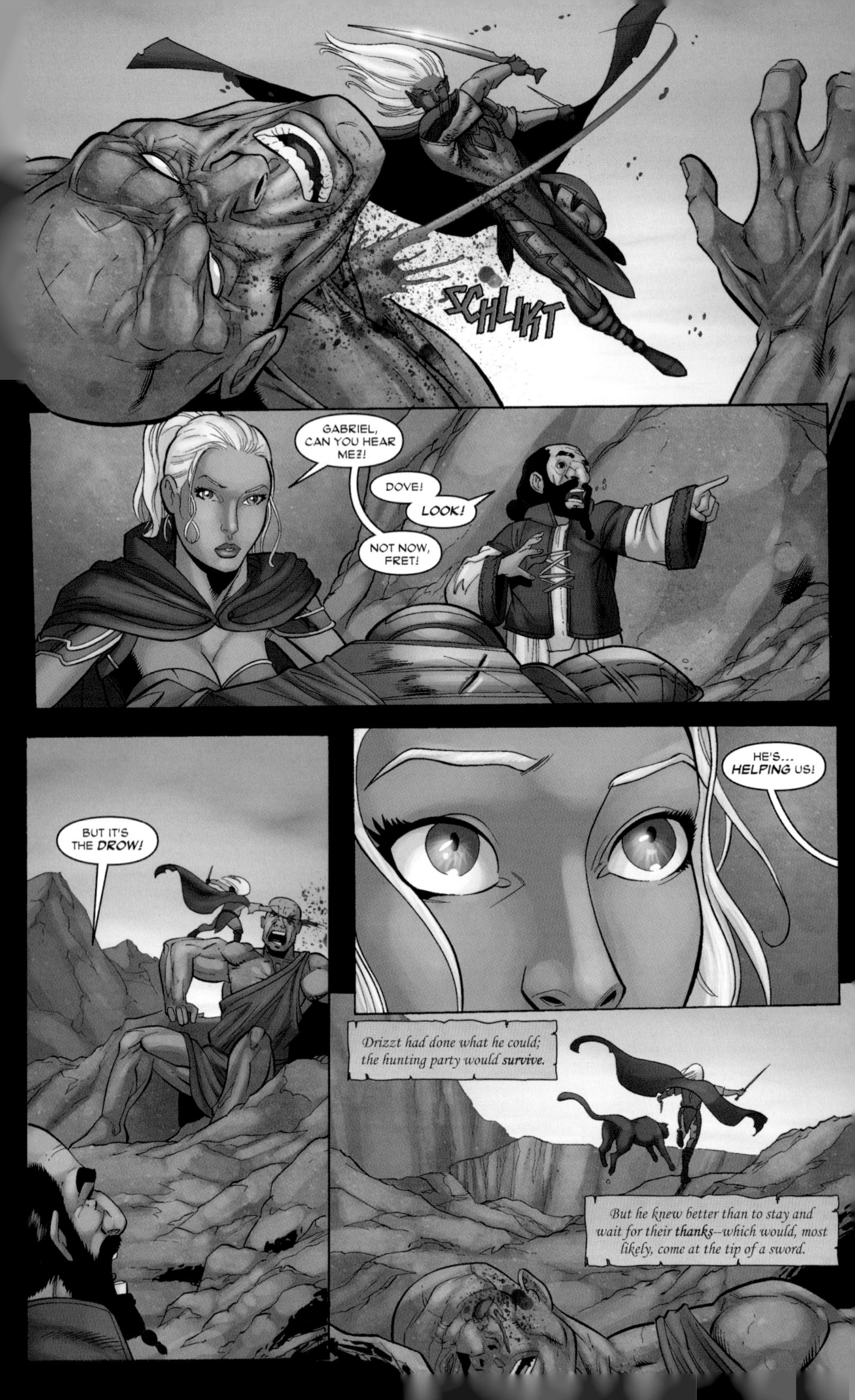
SCHLIKT
GABRIEL, CAN YOU HEAR ME?!
DOVE!
LOOK!
NOT NOW, FRET!
BUT IT'S THE *DROW!*
HE'S... *HELPING* US!
Drizzt had done what he could; the hunting party would survive.
But he knew better than to stay and wait for their thanks--which would, most likely, come at the tip of a sword.

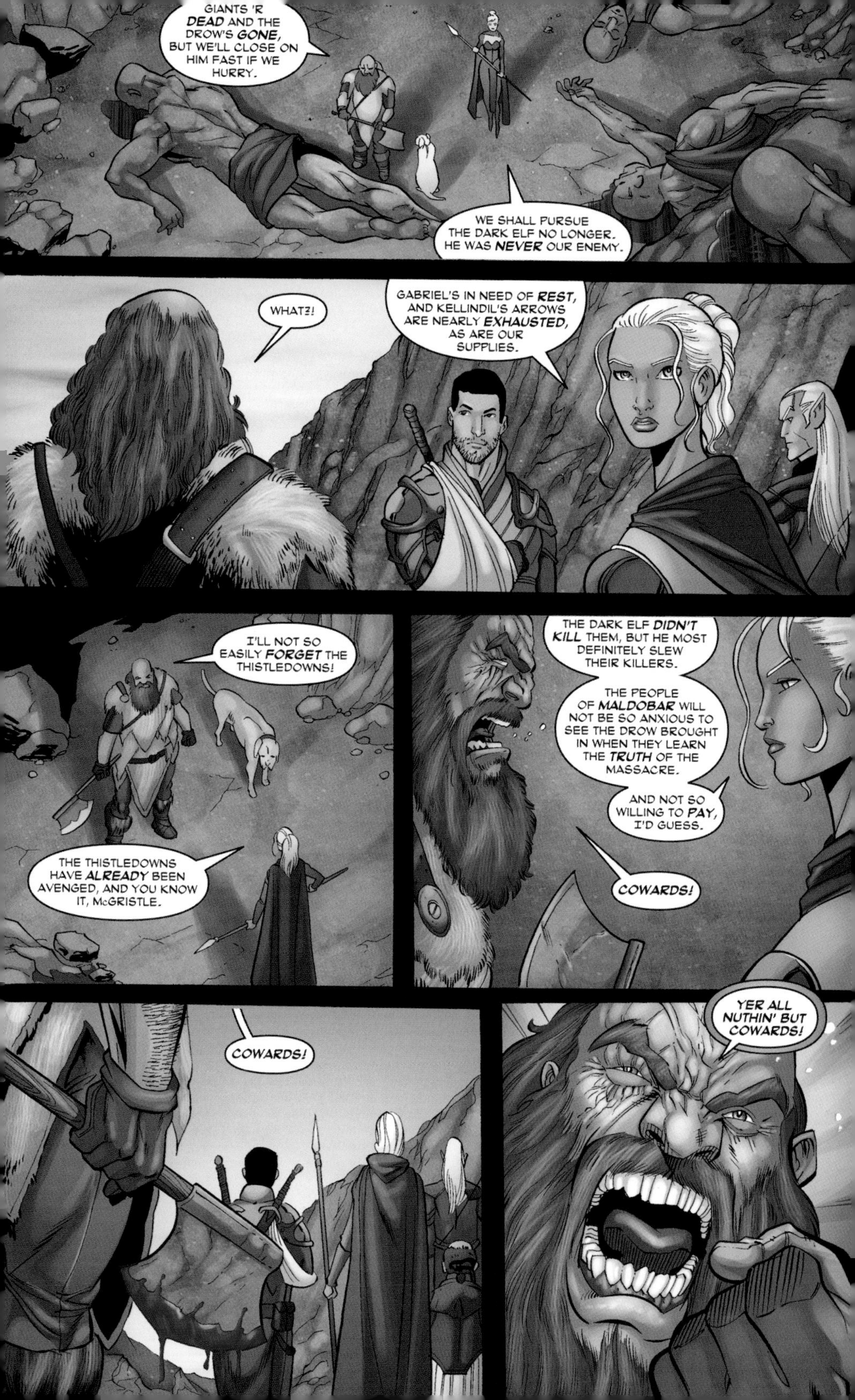
GIANTS 'R DEAD AND THE DROW'S GONE, BUT WE'LL CLOSE ON HIM FAST IF WE HURRY.
WE SHALL PURSUE THE DARK ELF NO LONGER. HE WAS NEVER OUR ENEMY.
WHAT?!
GABRIEL'S IN NEED OF REST, AND KELLINDIL'S ARROWS ARE NEARLY EXHAUSTED, AS ARE OUR SUPPLIES.
I'LL NOT SO EASILY FORGET THE THISTLEDOWNS!
THE THISTLEDOWNS HAVE ALREADY BEEN AVENGED, AND YOU KNOW IT, McGRISTLE.
THE DARK ELF DIDN'T KILL THEM, BUT HE MOST DEFINITELY SLEW THEIR KILLERS.
THE PEOPLE OF MALDOBAR WILL NOT BE SO ANXIOUS TO SEE THE DROW BROUGHT IN WHEN THEY LEARN THE TRUTH OF THE MASSACRE.
AND NOT SO WILLING TO PAY, I'D GUESS.
COWARDS!
COWARDS!
YER ALL NUTHIN' BUT COWARDS!

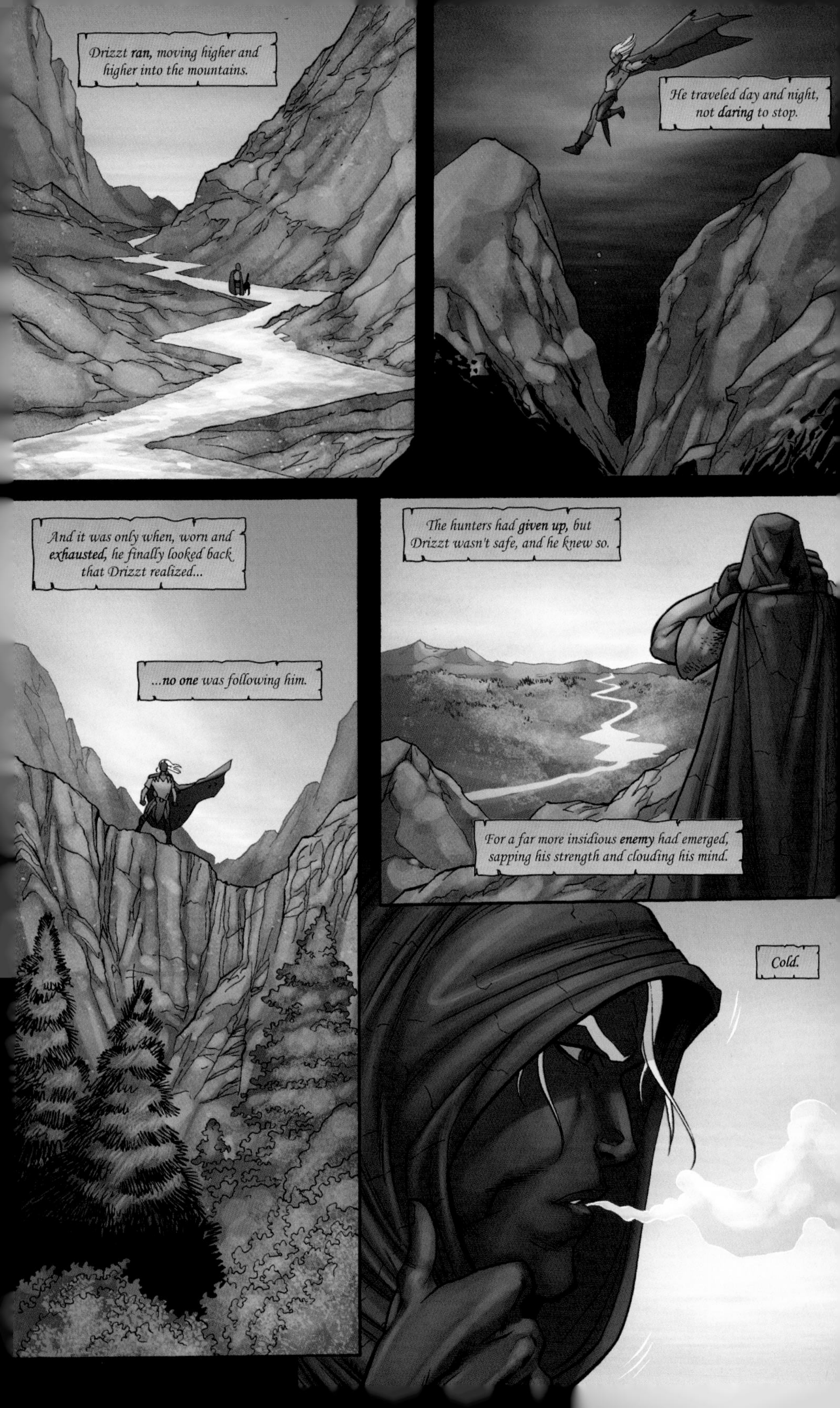
Drizzt ran, moving higher and higher into the mountains.
He traveled day and night, not daring to stop.
And it was only when, worn and exhausted, he finally looked back that Drizzt realized...
...no one was following him.
The hunters had given up, but Drizzt wasn't safe, and he knew so.
For a far more insidious enemy had emerged, sapping his strength and clouding his mind.
Cold.

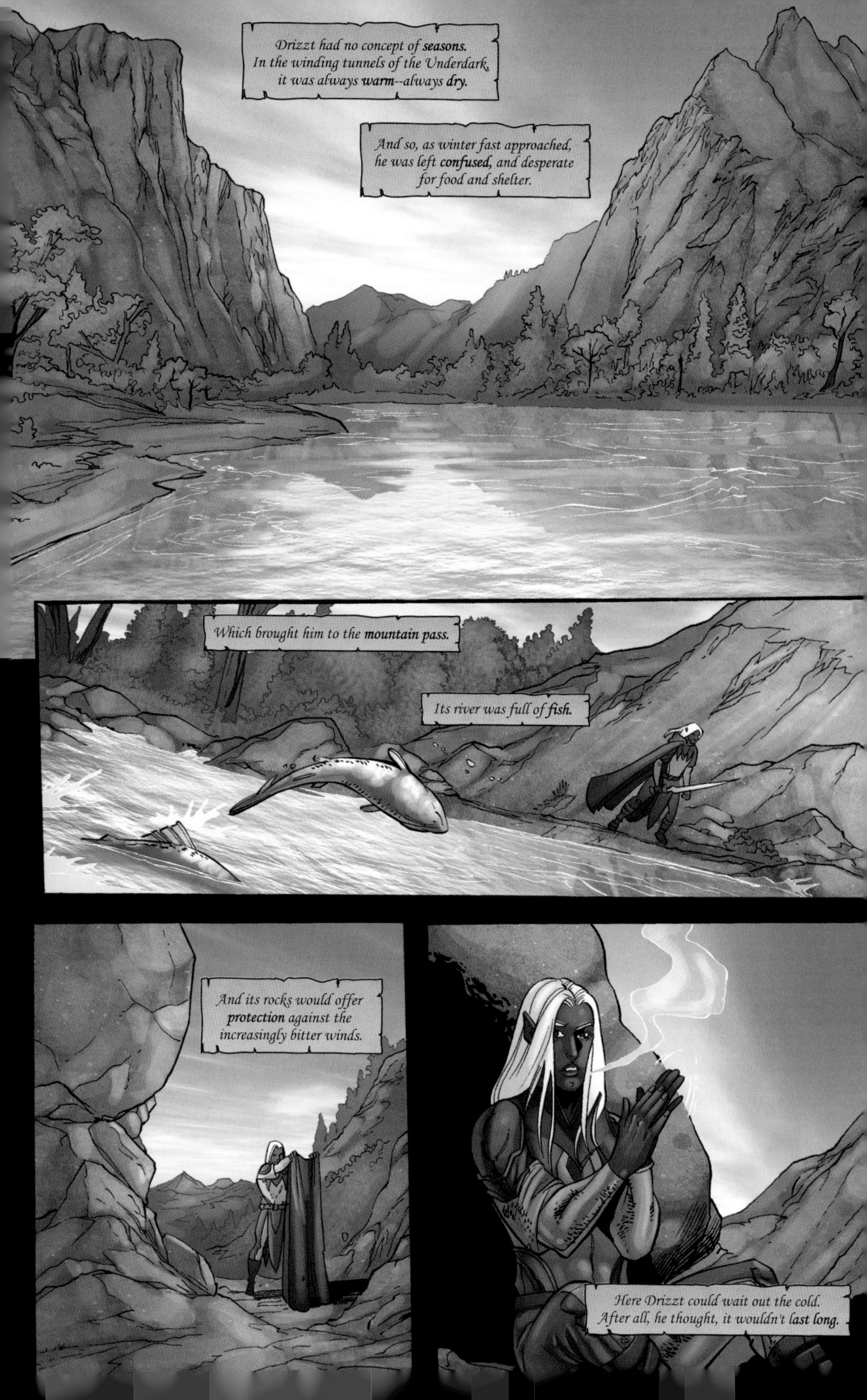
Drizzt had no concept of seasons. In the winding tunnels of the Underdark, it was always warm--always dry.
And so, as winter fast approached, he was left confused, and desperate for food and shelter.
Which brought him to the mountain pass.
Its river was full of fish.
And its rocks would offer protection against the increasingly bitter winds.
Here Drizzt could wait out the cold. After all, he thought, it wouldn't last long.

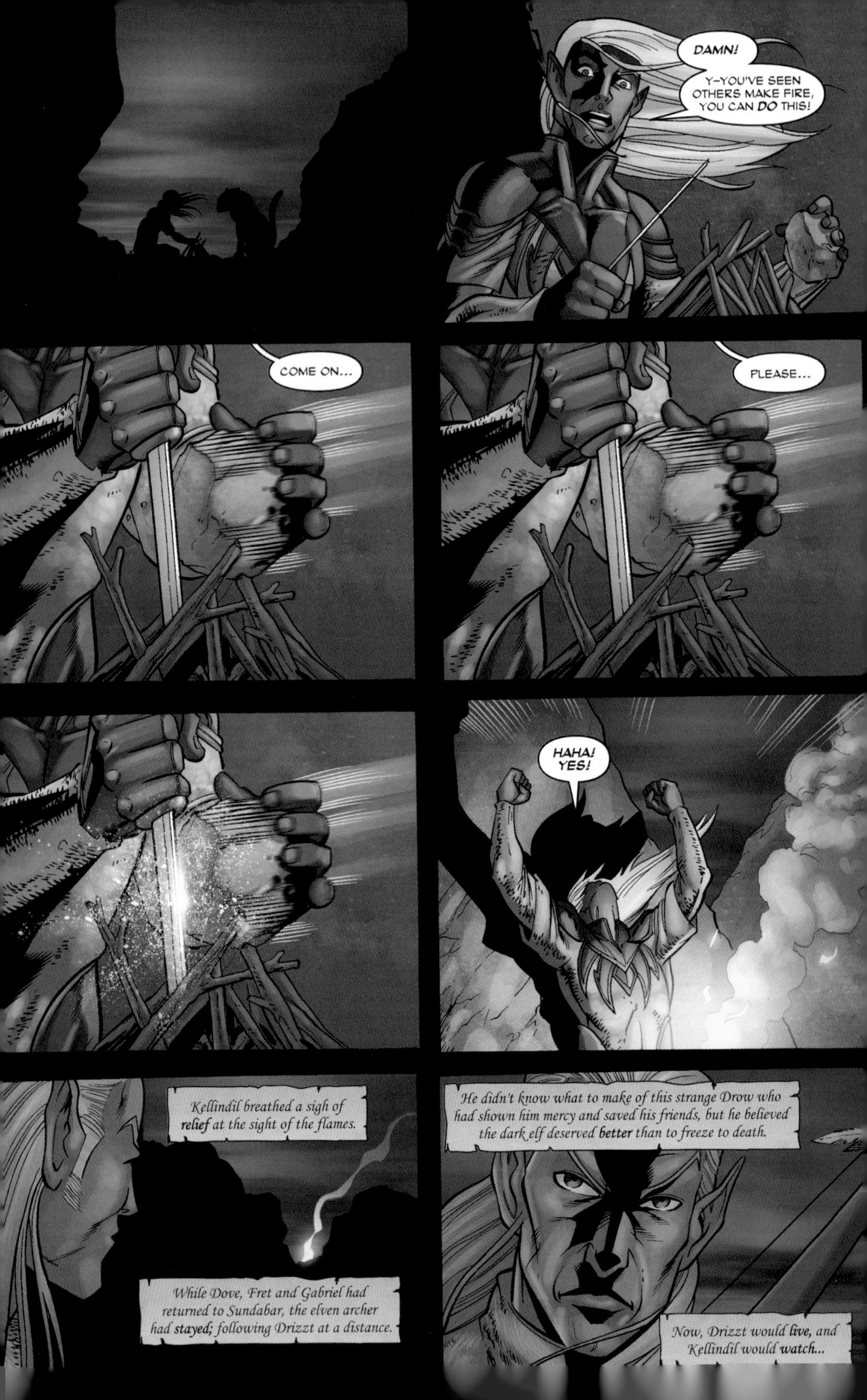
DAMN!
Y-YOU'VE SEEN OTHERS MAKE FIRE, YOU CAN DO THIS!
COME ON...
PLEASE...
HAHA! YES!
Kellindil breathed a sigh of relief at the sight of the flames.
While Dove, Fret and Gabriel had returned to Sundabar, the elven archer had stayed; following Drizzt at a distance.
He didn't know what to make of this strange Drow who had shown him mercy and saved his friends, but he believed the dark elf deserved better than to freeze to death.
Now, Drizzt would live, and Kellindil would watch...

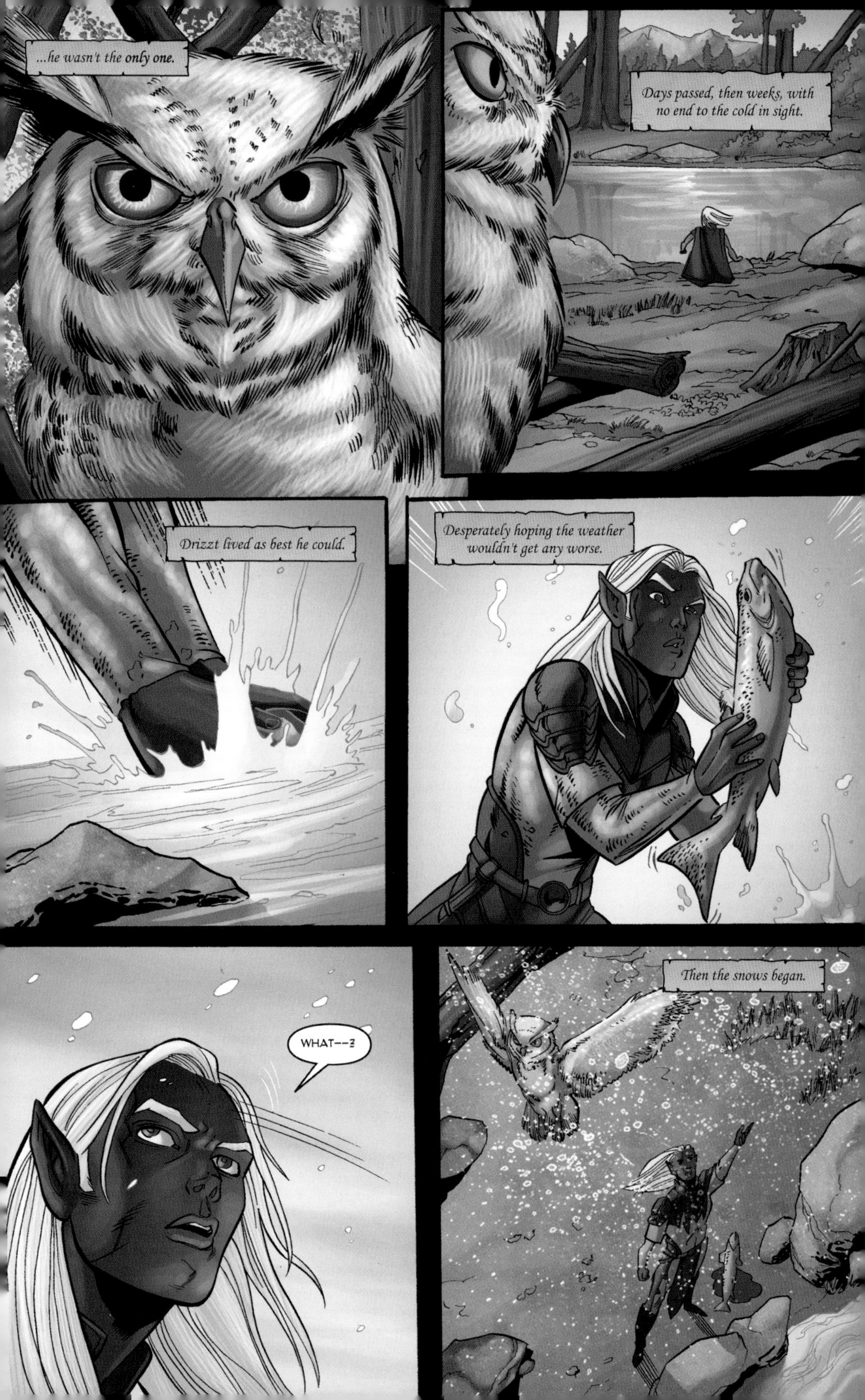
...he wasn't the only one.
Days passed, then weeks, with no end to the cold in sight.
Drizzt lived as best he could.
Desperately hoping the weather wouldn't get any worse.
WHAT--?
Then the snows began.

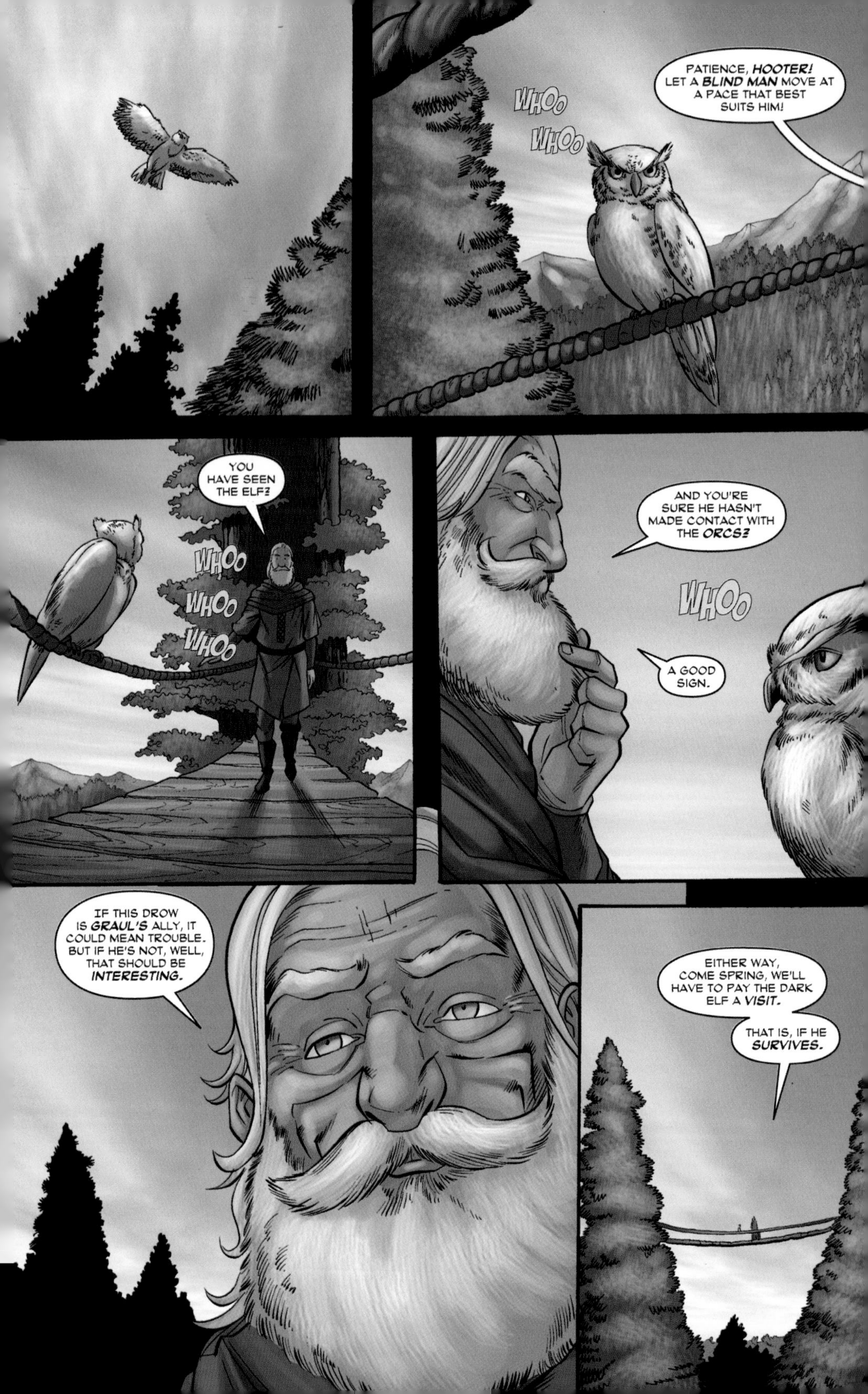

WHOO
WHOO
PATIENCE, HOOTER! LET A BLIND MAN MOVE AT A PACE THAT BEST SUITS HIM!
YOU HAVE SEEN THE ELF?
WHOO
WHOO
WHOO
AND YOU'RE SURE HE HASN'T MADE CONTACT WITH THE ORCS?
WHOO
A GOOD SIGN.
IF THIS DROW IS GRAUL'S ALLY, IT COULD MEAN TROUBLE. BUT IF HE'S NOT, WELL, THAT SHOULD BE INTERESTING.
EITHER WAY, COME SPRING, WE'LL HAVE TO PAY THE DARK ELF A VISIT.
THAT IS, IF HE SURVIVES.

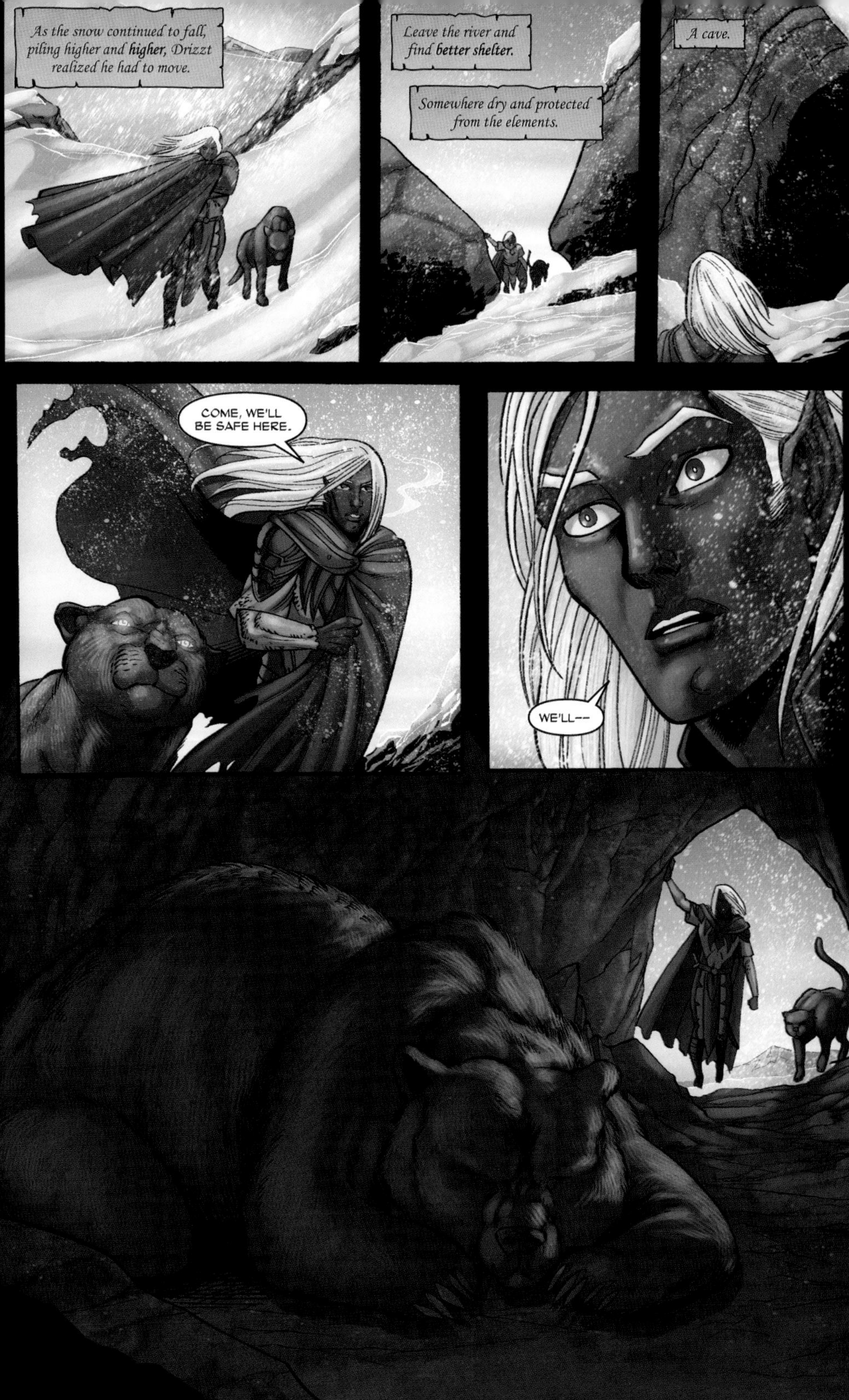
As the snow continued to fall, piling higher and higher, Drizzt realized he had to move.
Leave the river and find better shelter.
Somewhere dry and protected from the elements.
A cave.
COME, WE'LL BE SAFE HERE.
WE'LL--

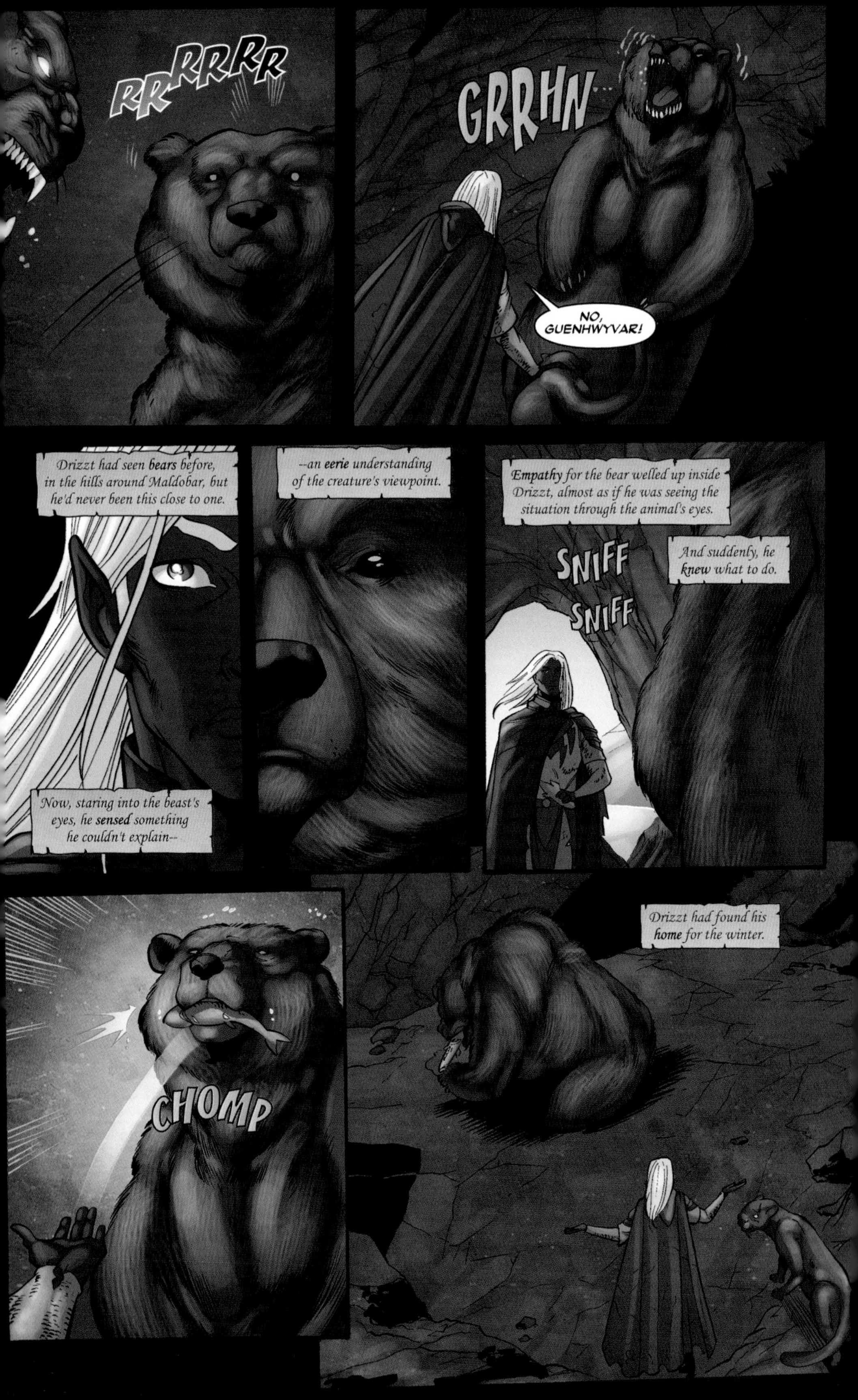
RRRRRRR
GRRHN...
NO, GUENHWYVAR!
Drizzt had seen bears before, in the hills around Maldobar, but he'd never been this close to one.
Now, staring into the beast's eyes, he sensed something he couldn't explain--
--an eerie understanding of the creature's viewpoint.
Empathy for the bear welled up inside Drizzt, almost as if he was seeing the situation through the animal's eyes.
SNIFF
SNIFF
And suddenly, he knew what to do.
CHOMP
Drizzt had found his home for the winter.

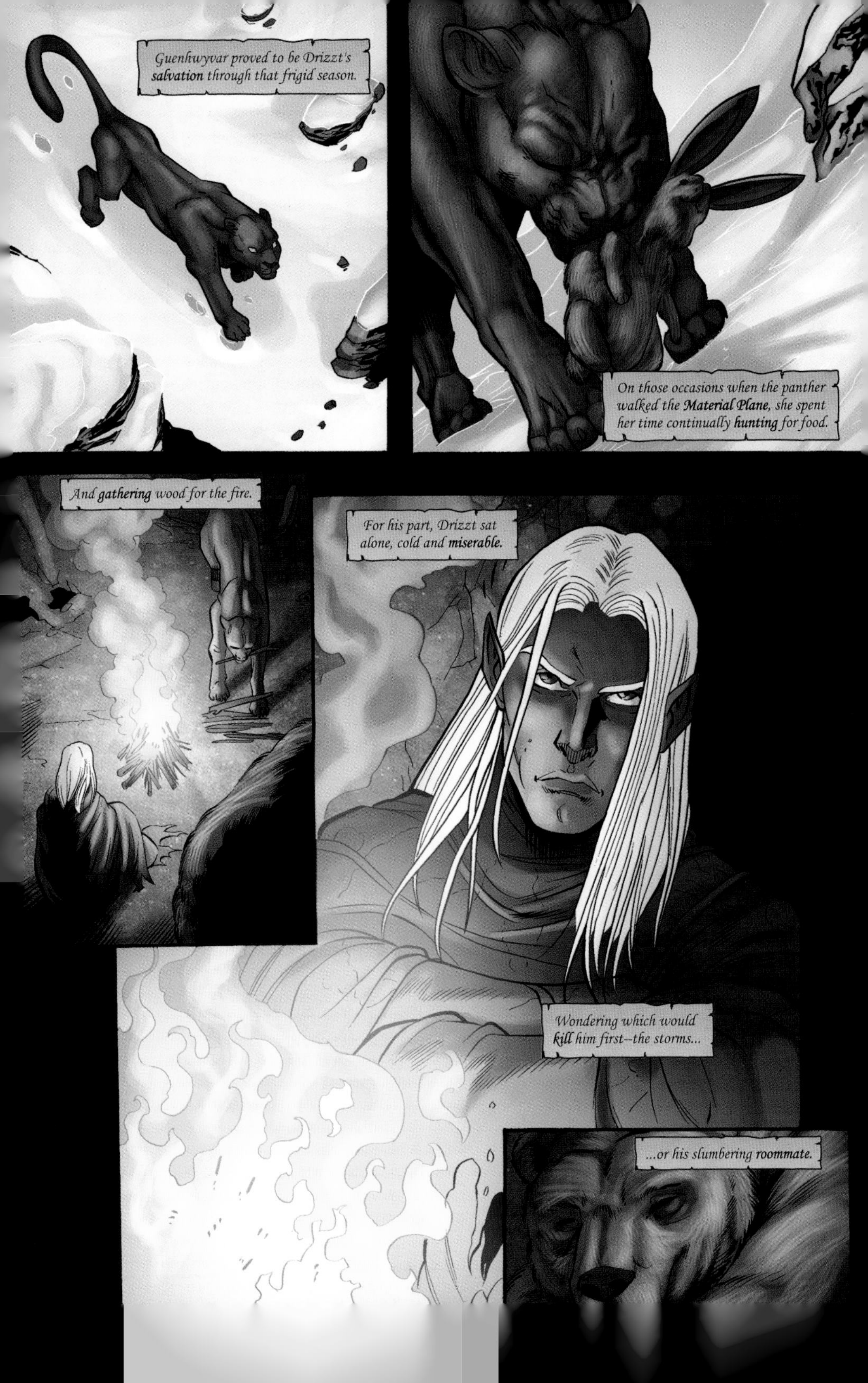
Guenhwyvar proved to be Drizzt's salvation through that frigid season.
On those occasions when the panther walked the Material Plane, she spent her time continually hunting for food.
And gathering wood for the fire.
For his part, Drizzt sat alone, cold and miserable.
Wondering which would kill him first--the storms...
...or his slumbering roommate.

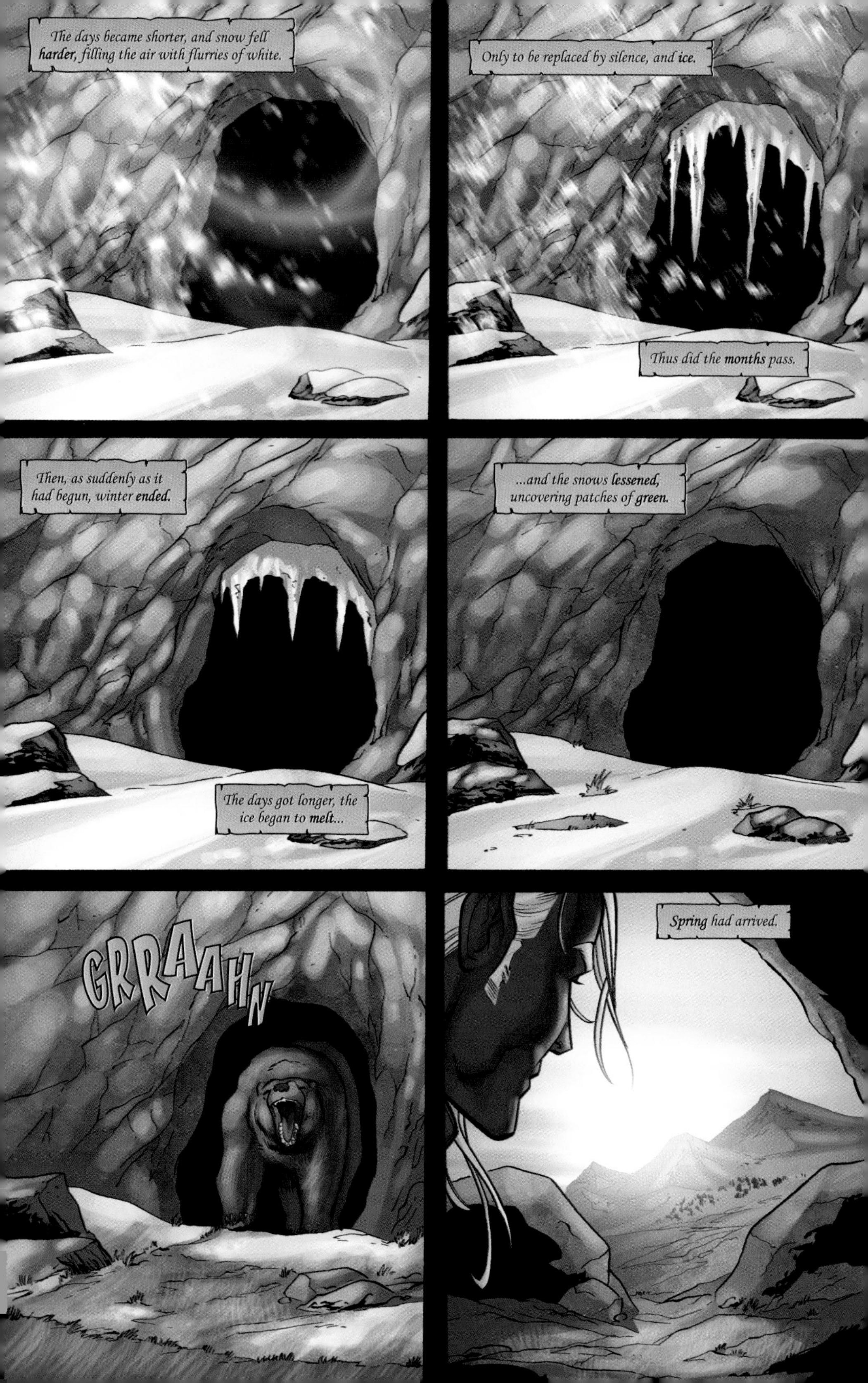
The days became shorter, and snow fell harder, filling the air with flurries of white.
Only to be replaced by silence, and ice.
Thus did the months pass.
Then, as suddenly as it had begun, winter ended.
The days got longer, the ice began to melt...
...and the snows lessened, uncovering patches of green.
GRRAAHN
Spring had arrived.

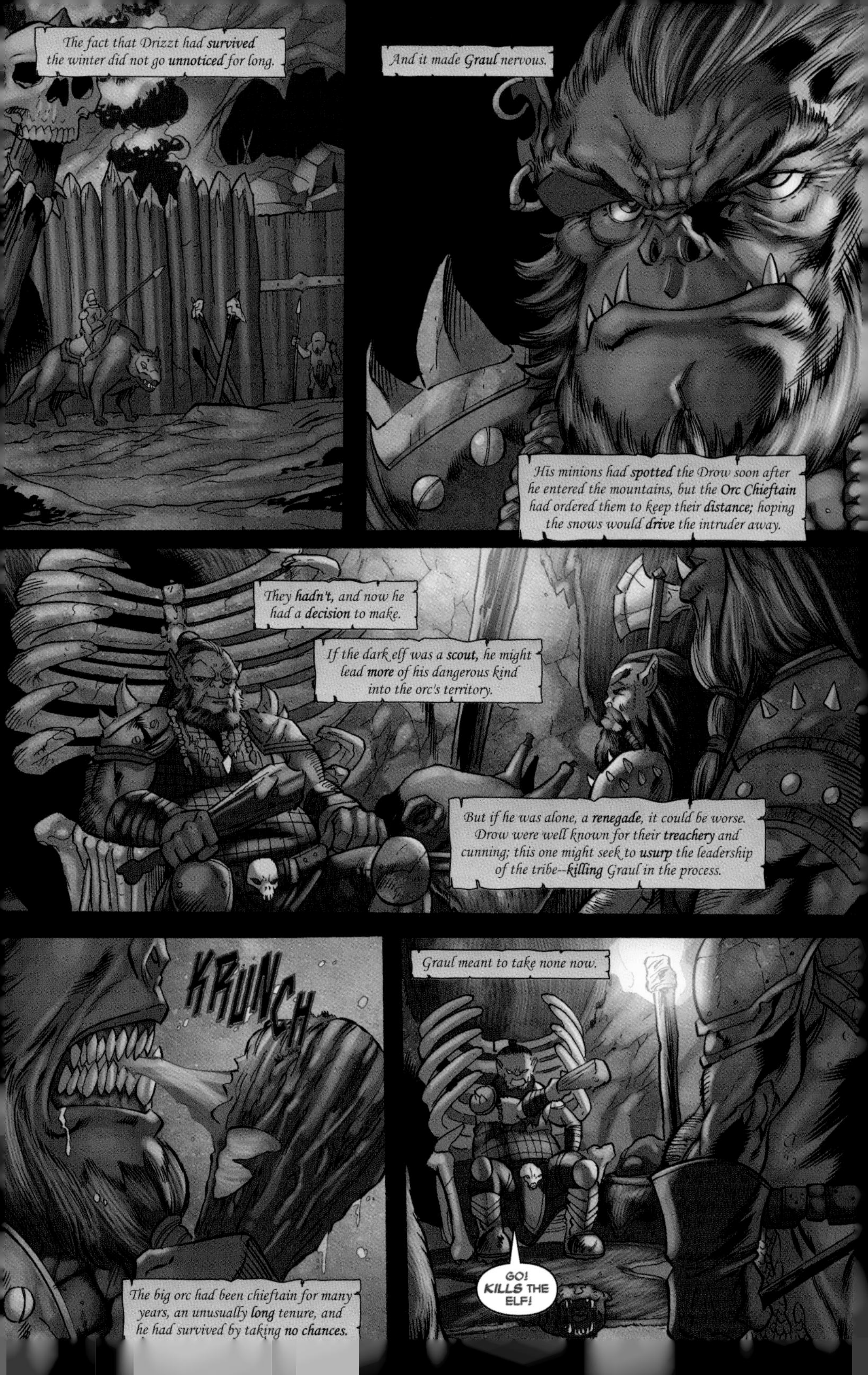
The fact that Drizzt had survived the winter did not go unnoticed for long.
And it made Graul nervous.
His minions had spotted the Drow soon after he entered the mountains, but the Orc Chieftain had ordered them to keep their distance; hoping the snows would drive the intruder away.
They hadn't, and now he had a decision to make.
If the dark elf was a scout, he might lead more of his dangerous kind into the orc's territory.
But if he was alone, a renegade, it could be worse. Drow were well known for their treachery and cunning; this one might seek to usurp the leadership of the tribe--killing Graul in the process.
KRUNCH
The big orc had been chieftain for many years, an unusually long tenure, and he had survived by taking no chances.
Graul meant to take none now.
GO! KILLS THE ELF!

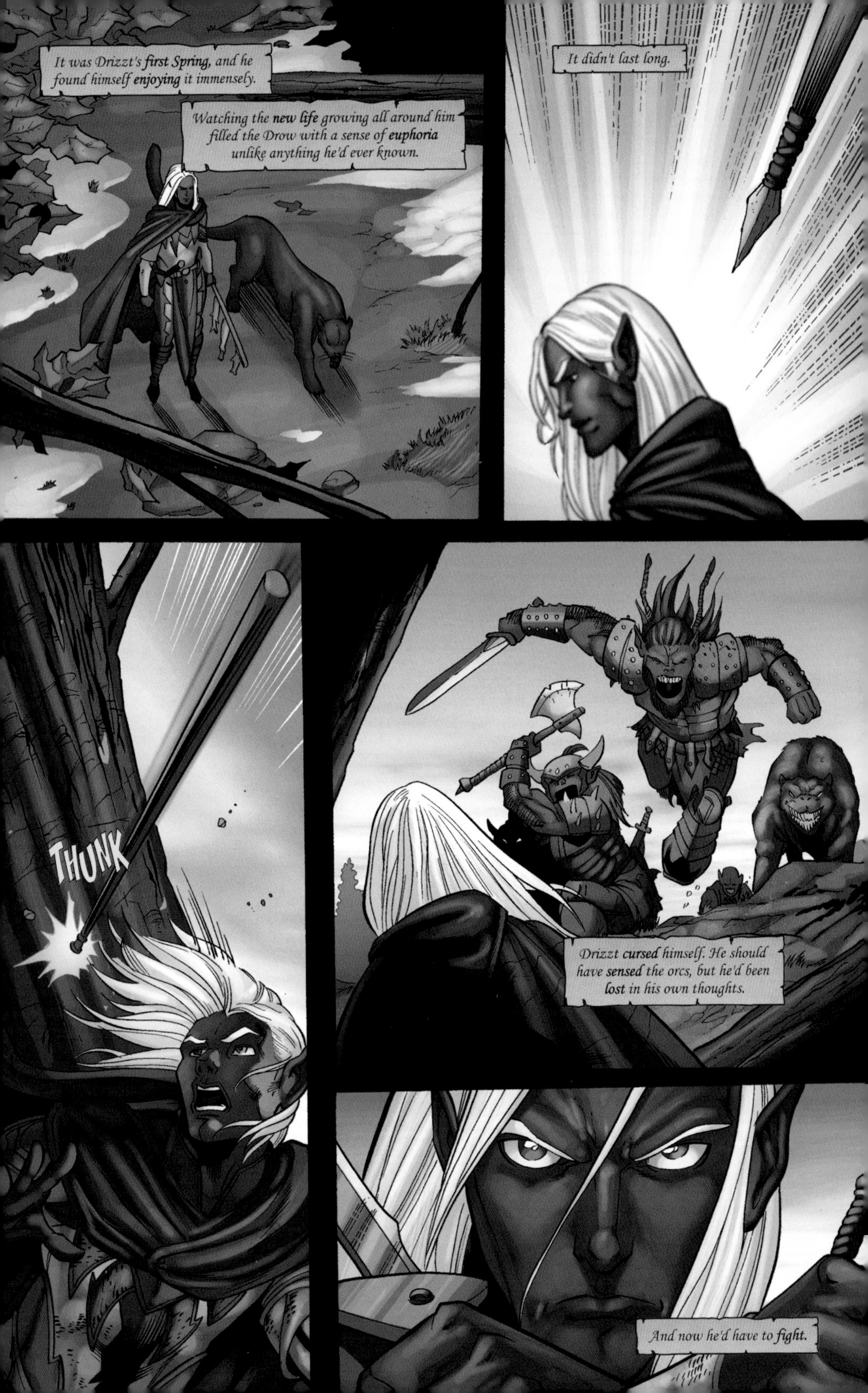

It was Drizzt's first Spring, and he found himself enjoying it immensely.
Watching the new life growing all around him filled the Drow with a sense of euphoria unlike anything he'd ever known.
It didn't last long.
THUNK
Drizzt cursed himself. He should have sensed the orcs, but he'd been lost in his own thoughts.
And now he'd have to fight.

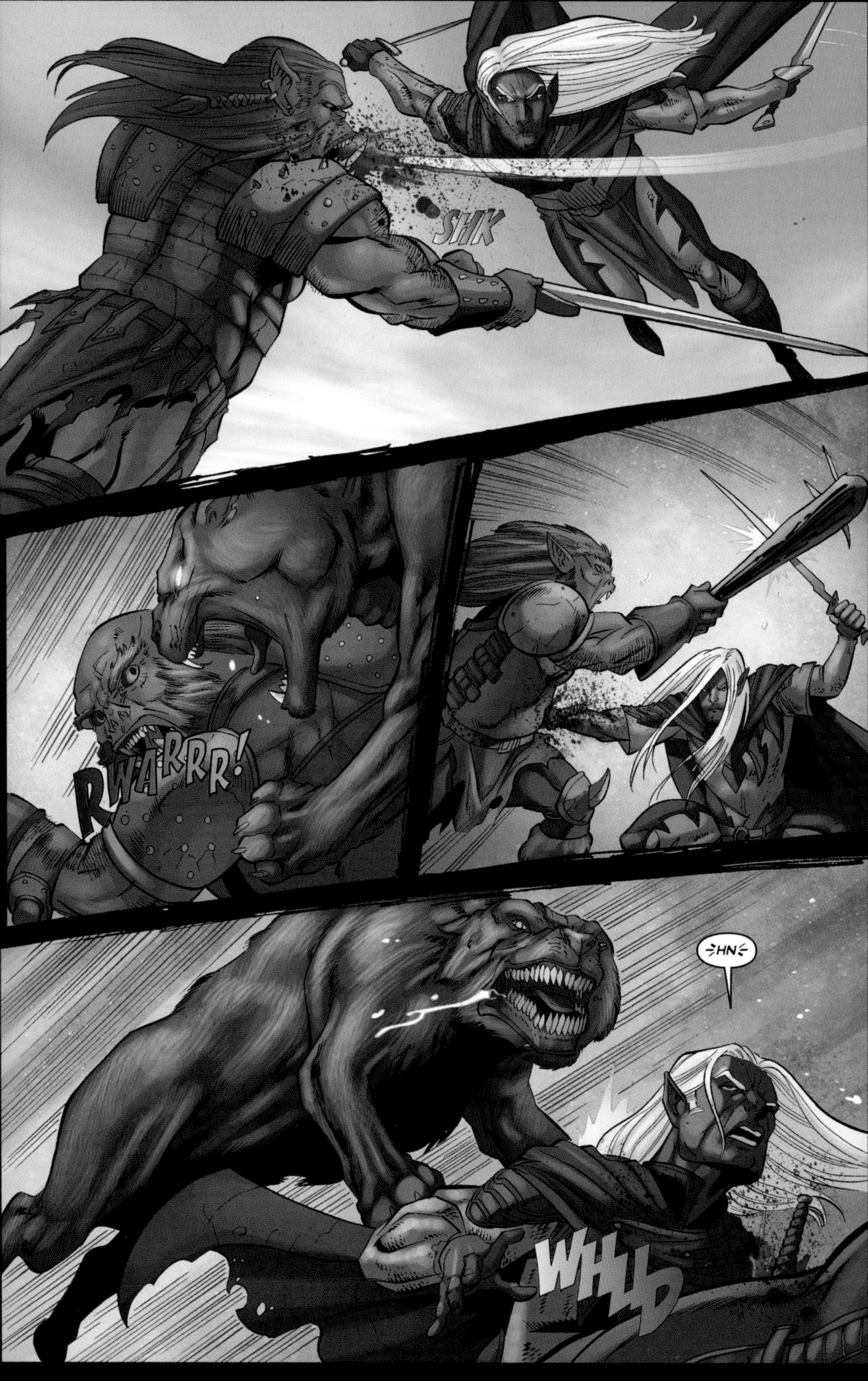
SHK
RWARRR!
HN
WHUD

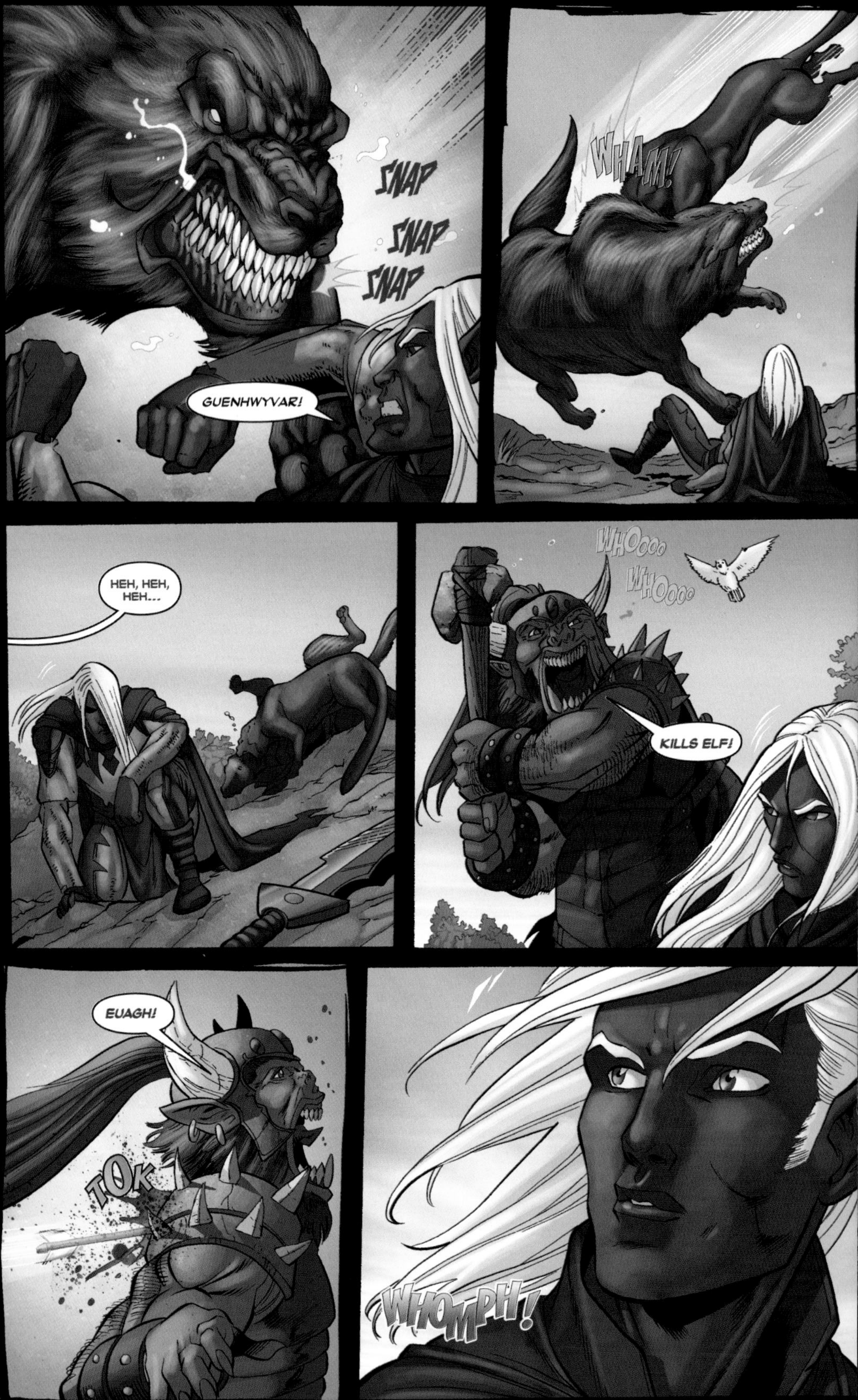
SNAP
SNAP
SNAP
GUENHWYVAR!
WHAM!
HEH, HEH, HEH...
WHOOOO
WHOOOO
KILLS ELF!
EUAGH!
TOK
WHOMPH!

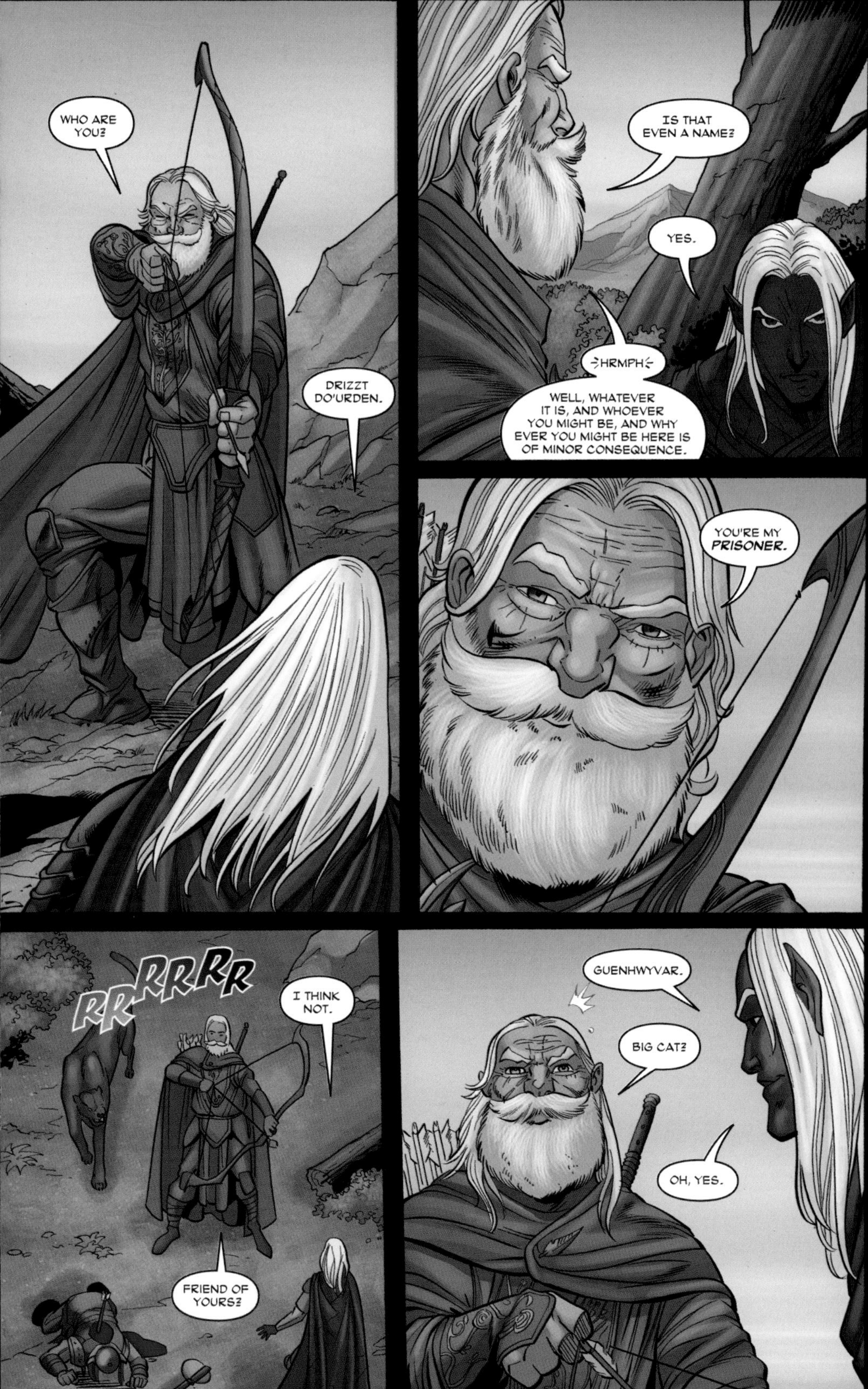
WHO ARE YOU?
DRIZZT DO'URDEN.
IS THAT EVEN A NAME?
YES.
HRMPH
WELL, WHATEVER IT IS, AND WHOEVER YOU MIGHT BE, AND WHY EVER YOU MIGHT BE HERE IS OF MINOR CONSEQUENCE.
YOU'RE MY PRISONER.
RRRRRRR
I THINK NOT.
FRIEND OF YOURS?
GUENHWYVAR.
BIG CAT?
OH, YES.

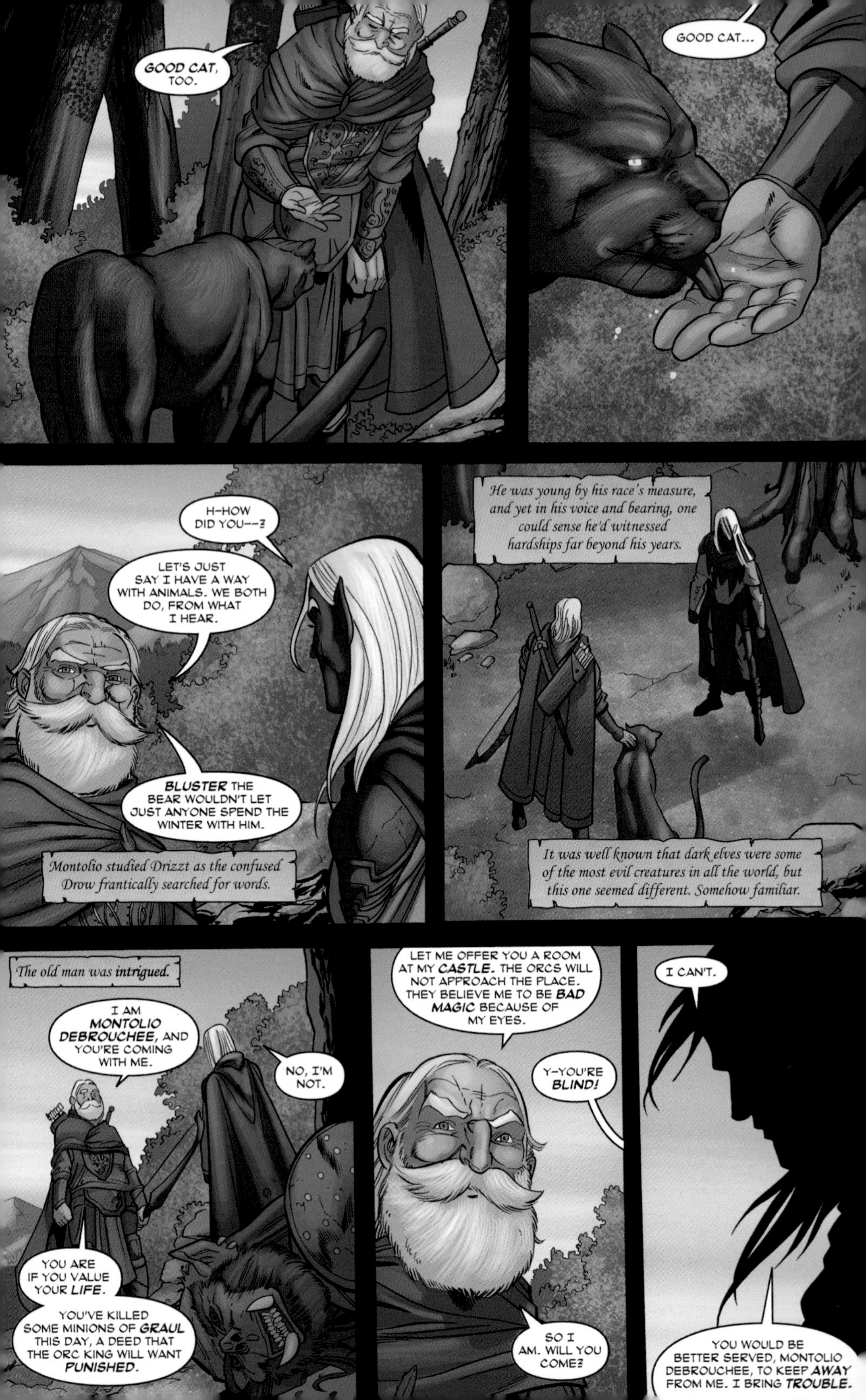
GOOD CAT, TOO.
GOOD CAT...
H-HOW DID YOU--?
LET'S JUST SAY I HAVE A WAY WITH ANIMALS. WE BOTH DO, FROM WHAT I HEAR.
BLUSTER THE BEAR WOULDN'T LET JUST ANYONE SPEND THE WINTER WITH HIM.
Montolio studied Drizzt as the confused Drow frantically searched for words.
He was young by his race's measure, and yet in his voice and bearing, one could sense he'd witnessed hardships far beyond his years.
It was well known that dark elves were some of the most evil creatures in all the world, but this one seemed different. Somehow familiar.
The old man was intrigued.
I AM MONTOLIO DEBROUCHEE, AND YOU'RE COMING WITH ME.
NO, I'M NOT.
YOU ARE IF YOU VALUE YOUR LIFE.
YOU'VE KILLED SOME MINIONS OF GRAUL THIS DAY, A DEED THAT THE ORC KING WILL WANT PUNISHED.
LET ME OFFER YOU A ROOM AT MY CASTLE. THE ORCS WILL NOT APPROACH THE PLACE. THEY BELIEVE ME TO BE BAD MAGIC BECAUSE OF MY EYES.
Y-YOU'RE BLIND!
SO I AM. WILL YOU COME?
I CAN'T.
YOU WOULD BE BETTER SERVED, MONTOLIO DEBROUCHEE, TO KEEP AWAY FROM ME. I BRING TROUBLE.

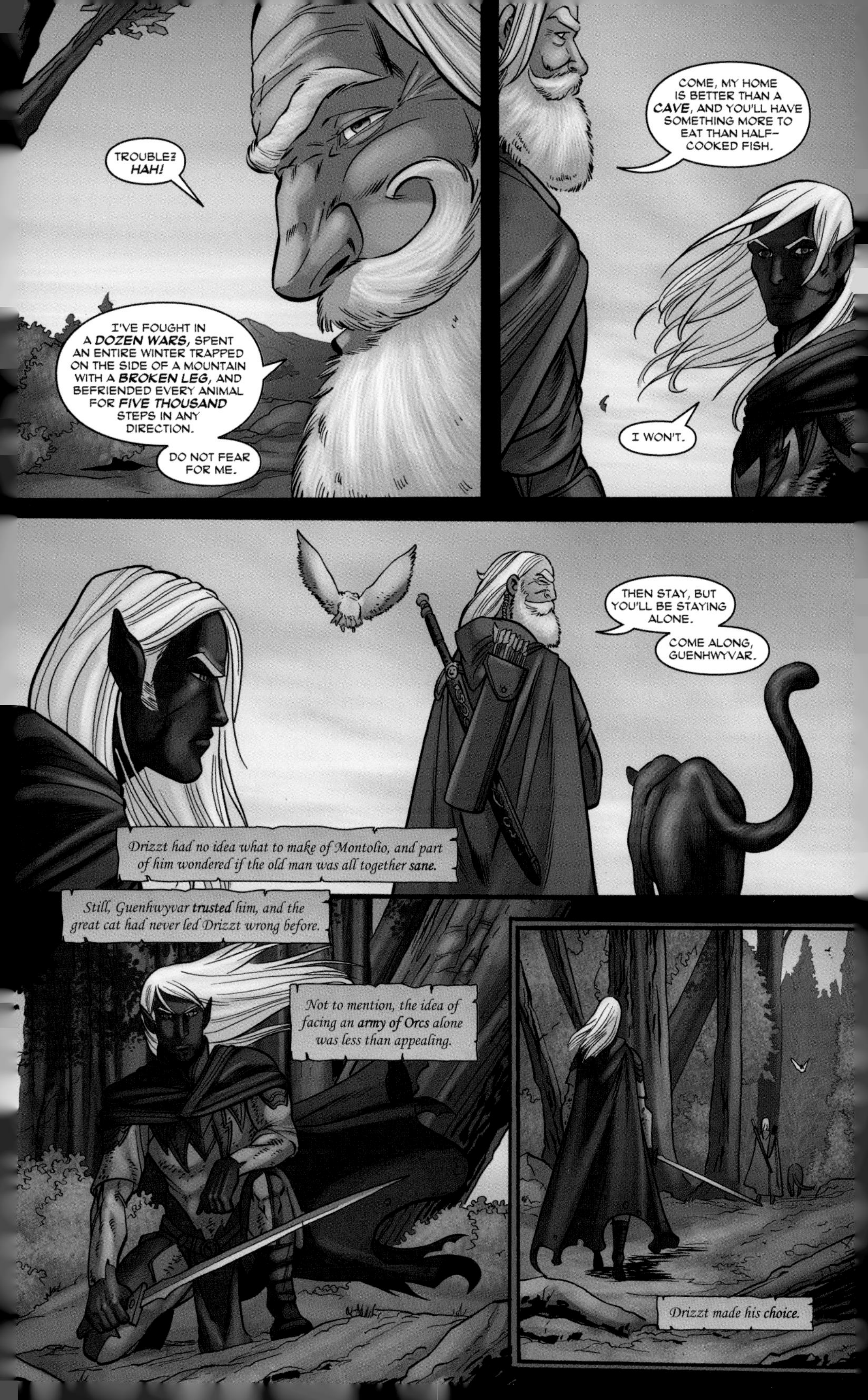
TROUBLE? HAH!
I'VE FOUGHT IN A DOZEN WARS, SPENT AN ENTIRE WINTER TRAPPED ON THE SIDE OF A MOUNTAIN WITH A BROKEN LEG, AND BEFRIENDED EVERY ANIMAL FOR FIVE THOUSAND STEPS IN ANY DIRECTION.
DO NOT FEAR FOR ME.
COME, MY HOME IS BETTER THAN A CAVE, AND YOU'LL HAVE SOMETHING MORE TO EAT THAN HALF-COOKED FISH.
I WON'T.
THEN STAY, BUT YOU'LL BE STAYING ALONE.
COME ALONG, GUENHWYVAR.
Drizzt had no idea what to make of Montolio, and part of him wondered if the old man was all together sane.
Still, Guenhwyvar trusted him, and the great cat had never led Drizzt wrong before.
Not to mention, the idea of facing an army of Orcs alone was less than appealing.
Drizzt made his choice.

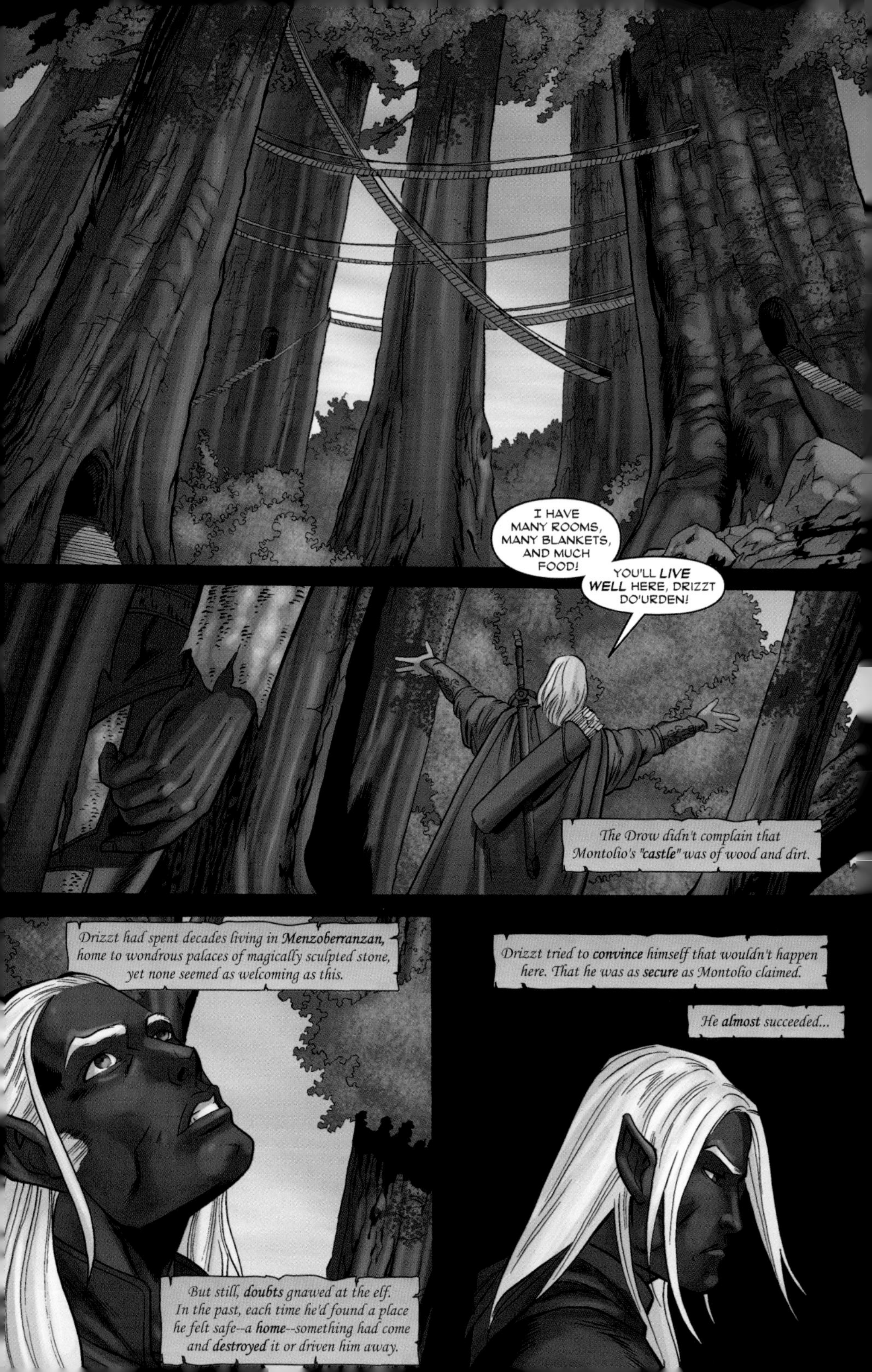
I HAVE MANY ROOMS, MANY BLANKETS, AND MUCH FOOD!
YOU'LL LIVE WELL HERE, DRIZZT DO'URDEN!
The Drow didn't complain that Montolio's "castle" was of wood and dirt.
Drizzt had spent decades living in Menzoberranzan, home to wondrous palaces of magically sculpted stone, yet none seemed as welcoming as this.
But still, doubts gnawed at the elf. In the past, each time he'd found a place he felt safe--a home--something had come and destroyed it or driven him away.
Drizzt tried to convince himself that wouldn't happen here. That he was as secure as Montolio claimed.
He almost succeeded...

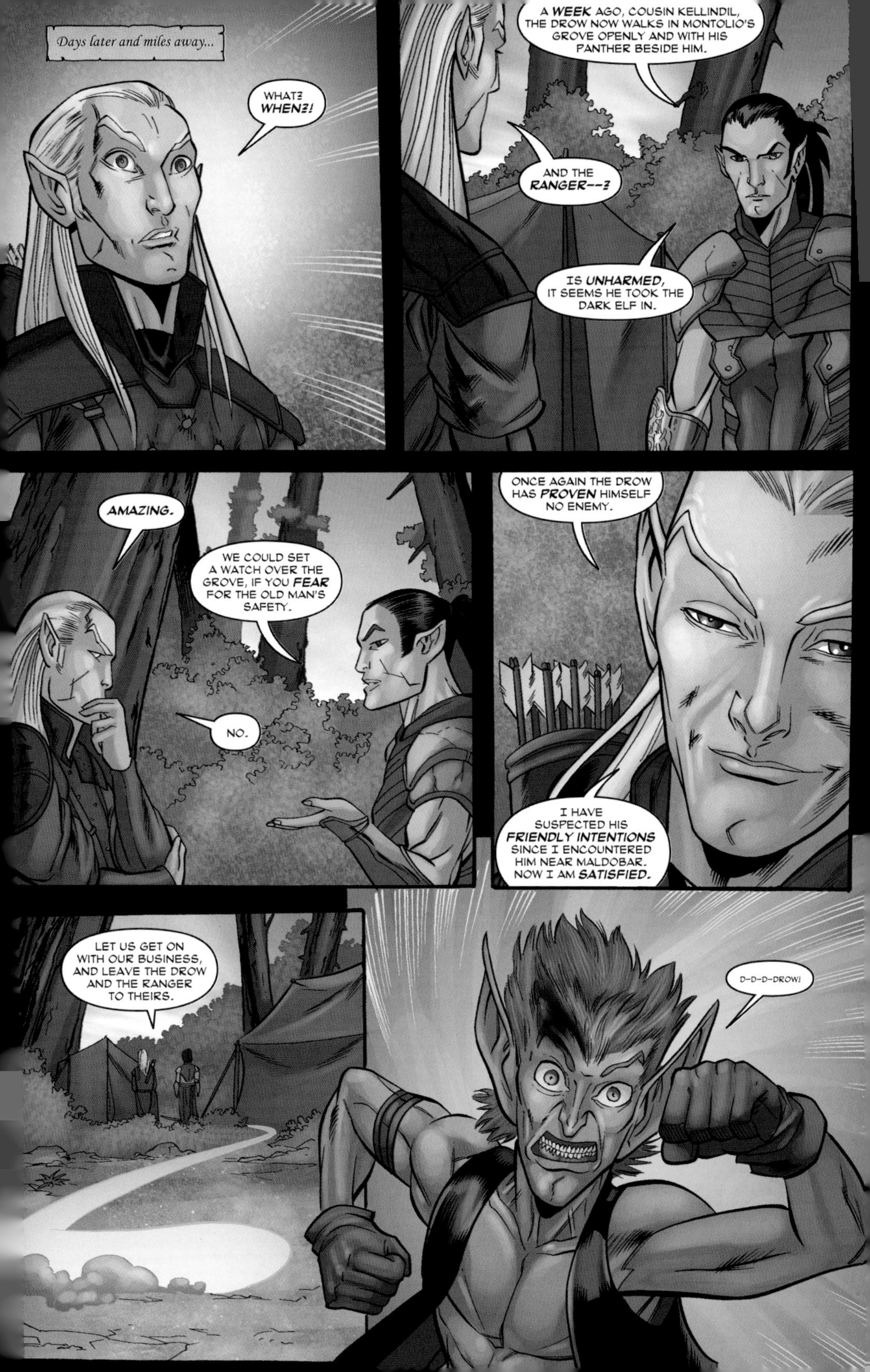
Days later and miles away...
WHAT? WHEN?!
A WEEK AGO, COUSIN KELLINDIL, THE DROW NOW WALKS IN MONTOLIO'S GROVE OPENLY AND WITH HIS PANTHER BESIDE HIM.
AND THE RANGER--?
IS UNHARMED, IT SEEMS HE TOOK THE DARK ELF IN.
AMAZING.
WE COULD SET A WATCH OVER THE GROVE, IF YOU FEAR FOR THE OLD MAN'S SAFETY.
NO.
ONCE AGAIN THE DROW HAS PROVEN HIMSELF NO ENEMY.
I HAVE SUSPECTED HIS FRIENDLY INTENTIONS SINCE I ENCOUNTERED HIM NEAR MALDOBAR. NOW I AM SATISFIED.
LET US GET ON WITH OUR BUSINESS, AND LEAVE THE DROW AND THE RANGER TO THEIRS.
D-D-D-DROW!

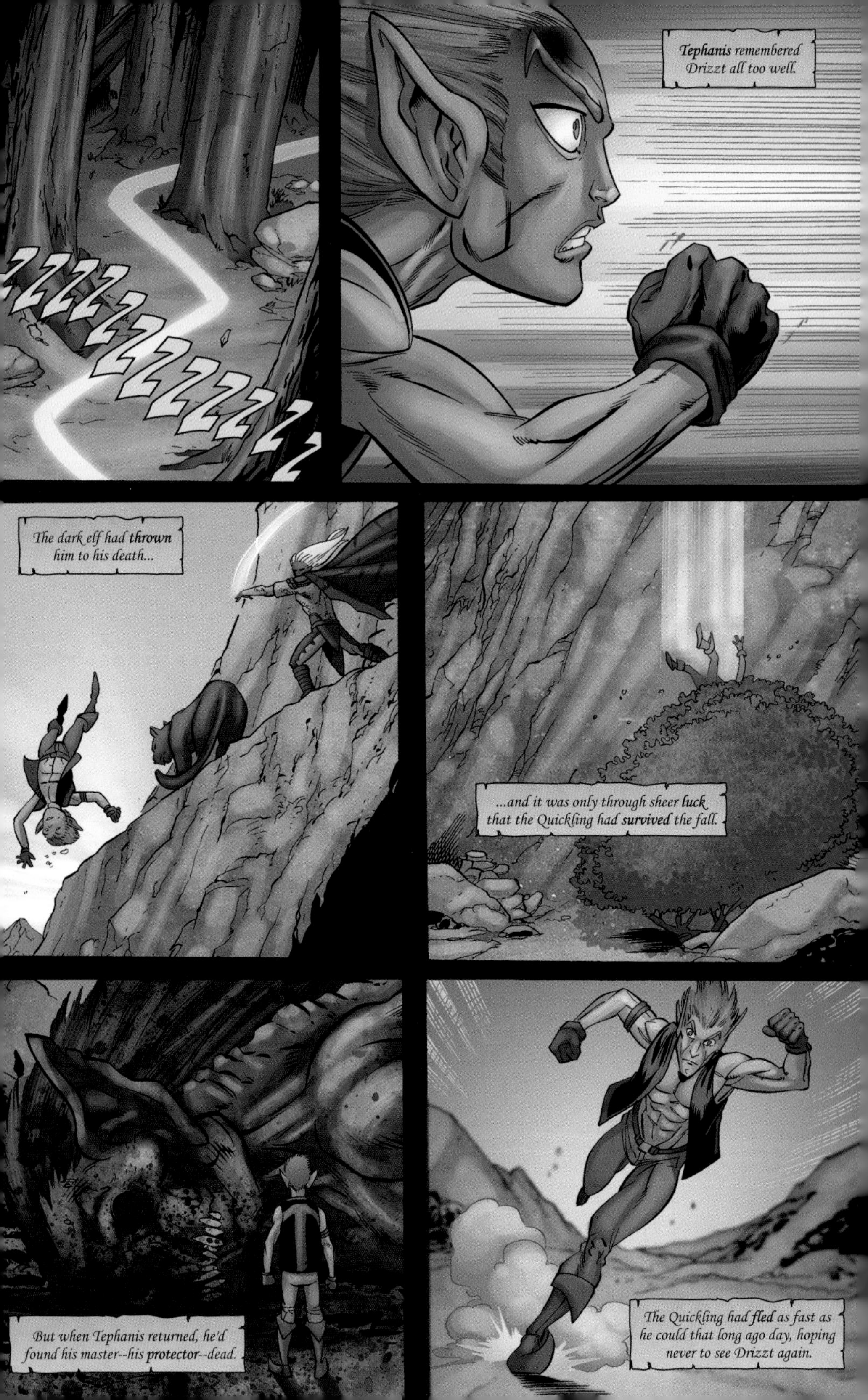
Tephanis remembered Drizzt all too well.
The dark elf had thrown him to his death...
...and it was only through sheer luck that the Quickling had survived the fall.
But when Tephanis returned, he'd found his master--his protector--dead.
The Quickling had fled as fast as he could that long ago day, hoping never to see Drizzt again.

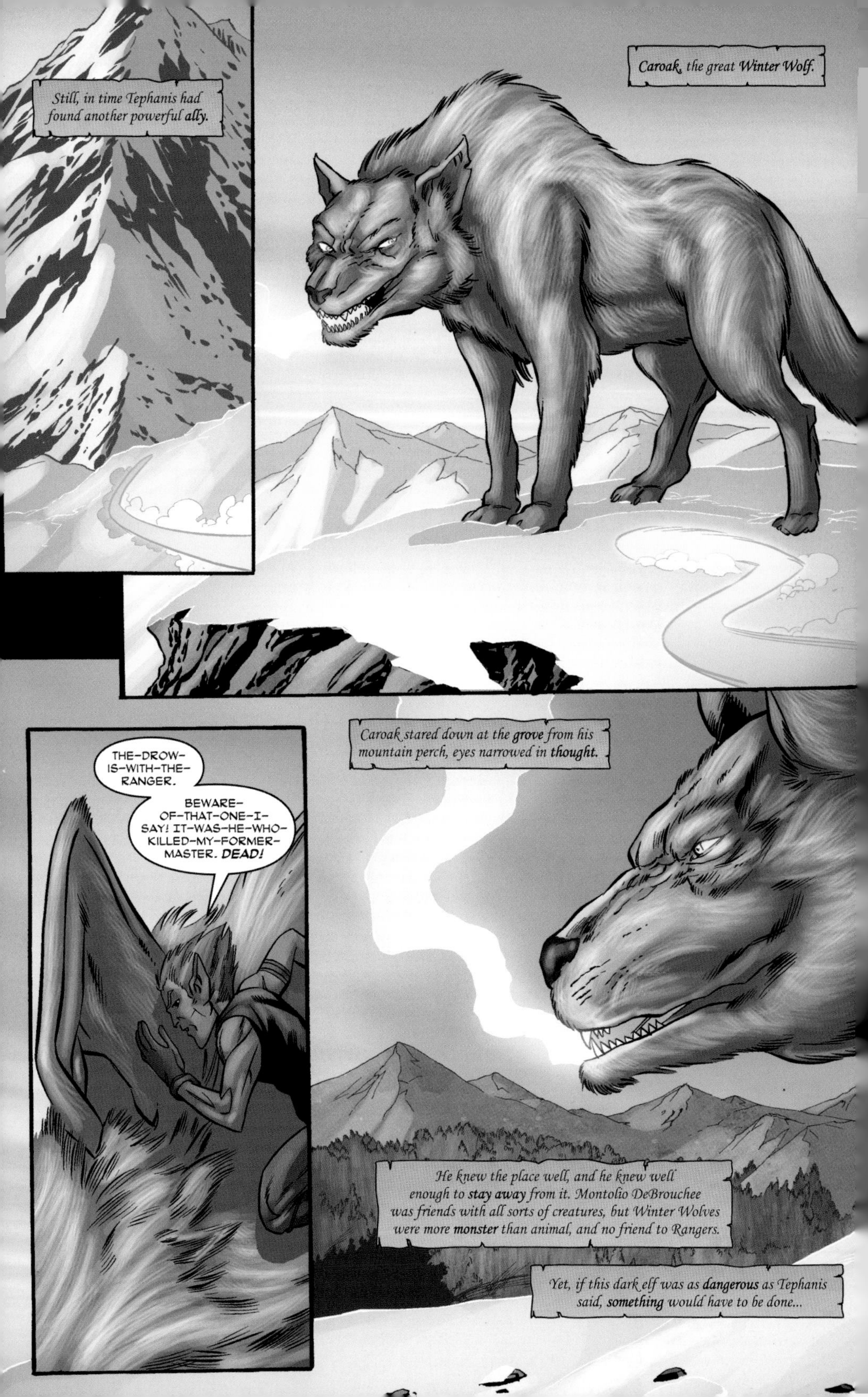
Still, in time Tephanis had found another powerful ally.
Caroak, the great Winter Wolf.
Caroak stared down at the grove from his mountain perch, eyes narrowed in thought.
THE-DROW-IS-WITH-THE-RANGER.
BEWARE-OF-THAT-ONE-I-SAY! IT-WAS-HE-WHO-KILLED-MY-FORMER-MASTER. DEAD!
He knew the place well, and he knew well enough to stay away from it. Montolio DeBrouchee was friends with all sorts of creatures, but Winter Wolves were more monster than animal, and no friend to Rangers.
Yet, if this dark elf was as dangerous as Tephanis said, something would have to be done...

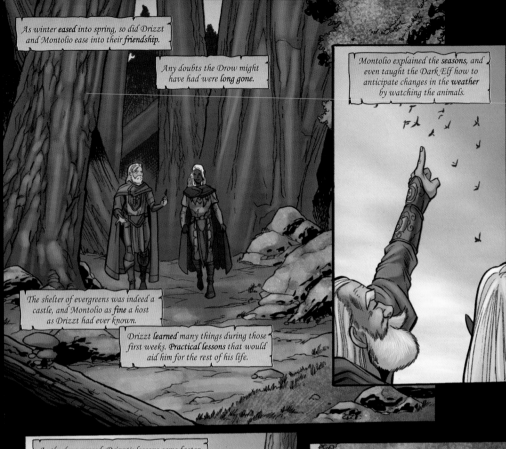

As winter **eased** into spring, so did Drizzt and Montolio ease into their **friendship**.

Any doubts the Drow might have had were long **gone**.

Montolio explained the **seasons**, and even taught the Dark Elf how to anticipate changes in the **weather** by watching the animals.

The shelter of evergreens was indeed a castle, and Montolio as **fine** a host as Drizzt had ever known.

Drizzt **learned** many things during those first weeks. **Practical lessons** that would aid him for the rest of his life.

As the days passed, Drizzt's lessons came faster.

Montolio concentrated on the life around them, the **animals**...

...and the **plants**.

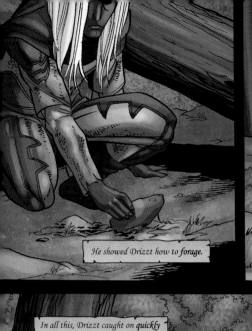

He showed Drizzt how to forage.

And how to understand the *emotions* of an animal simply by observing its movements.

In all this, Drizzt caught on *quickly* as Montolio had suspected he would.

He never would have believed it until he had **witnessed** it personally, but this **unusual Drow** possessed the demeanor of a surface elf.

WHOOOO

Perhaps even...

THE *HEART* OF A RANGER.

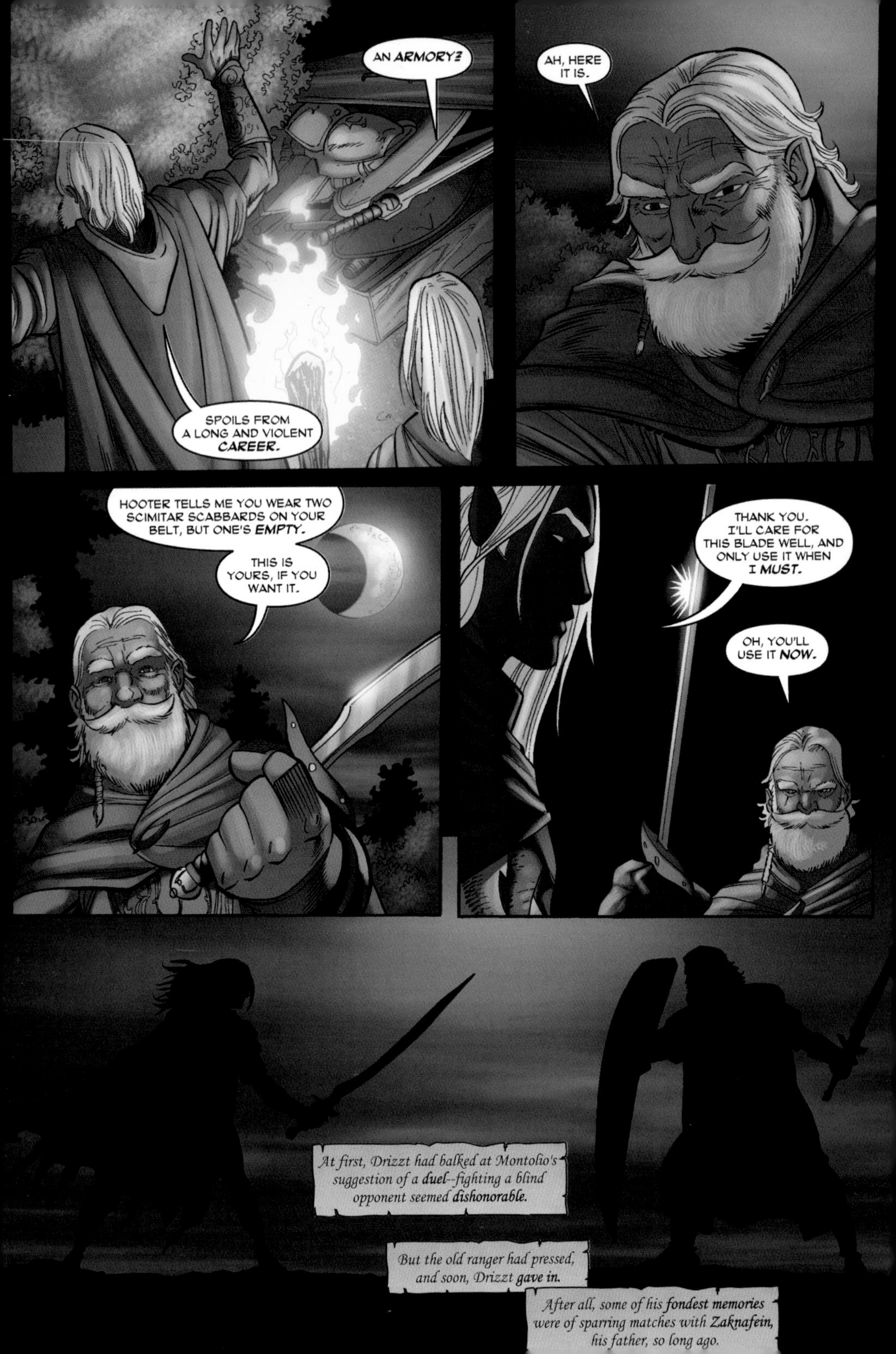
AN ARMORY?
SPOILS FROM A LONG AND VIOLENT CAREER.
AH, HERE IT IS.
HOOTER TELLS ME YOU WEAR TWO SCIMITAR SCABBARDS ON YOUR BELT, BUT ONE'S EMPTY.
THIS IS YOURS, IF YOU WANT IT.
THANK YOU. I'LL CARE FOR THIS BLADE WELL, AND ONLY USE IT WHEN I MUST.
OH, YOU'LL USE IT NOW.
At first, Drizzt had balked at Montolio's suggestion of a duel--fighting a blind opponent seemed dishonorable.
But the old ranger had pressed, and soon, Drizzt gave in.
After all, some of his fondest memories were of sparring matches with Zaknafein, his father, so long ago.

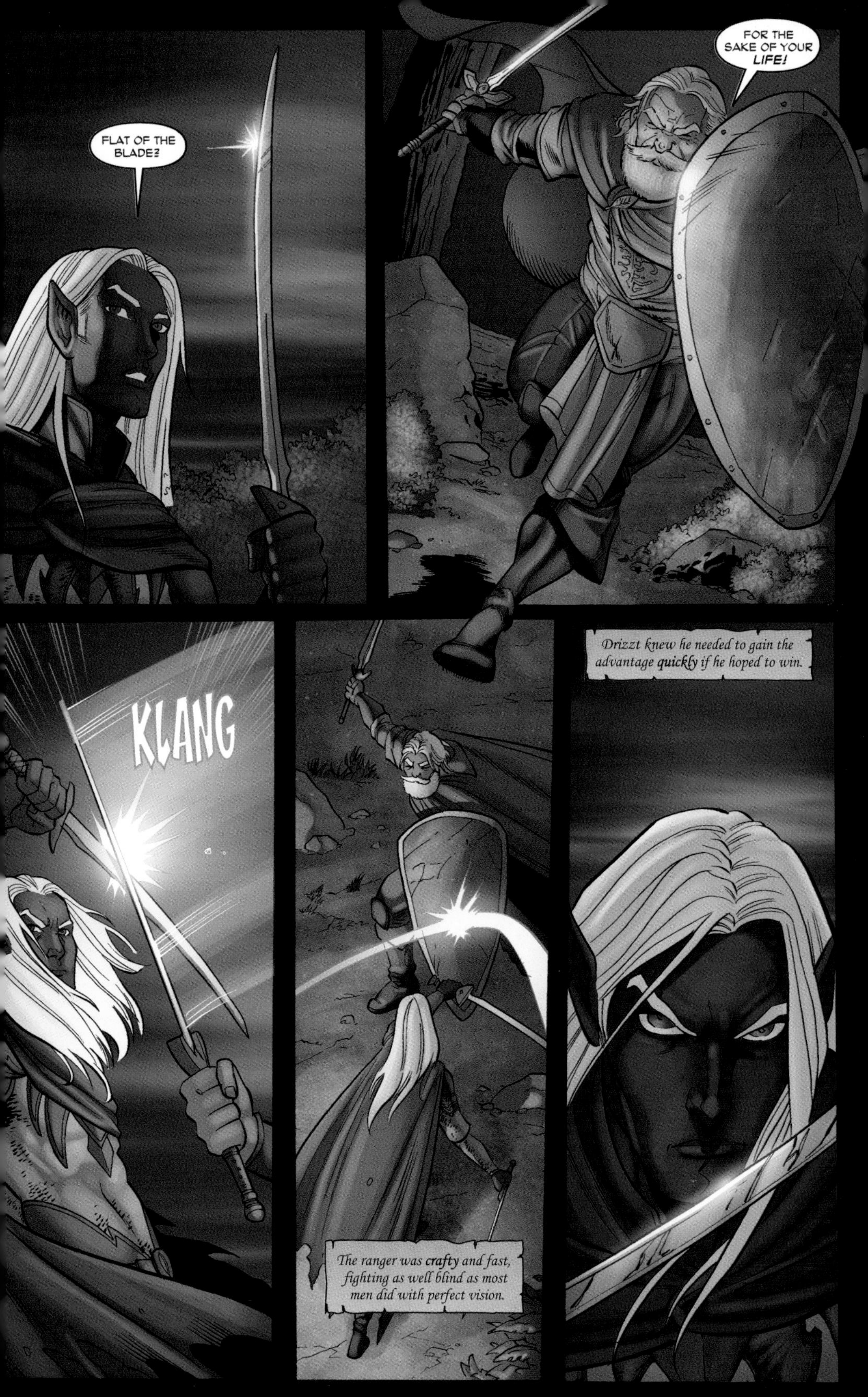
FLAT OF THE BLADE?
FOR THE SAKE OF YOUR LIFE!
KLANG
The ranger was crafty and fast, fighting as well blind as most men did with perfect vision.
Drizzt knew he needed to gain the advantage quickly if he hoped to win.

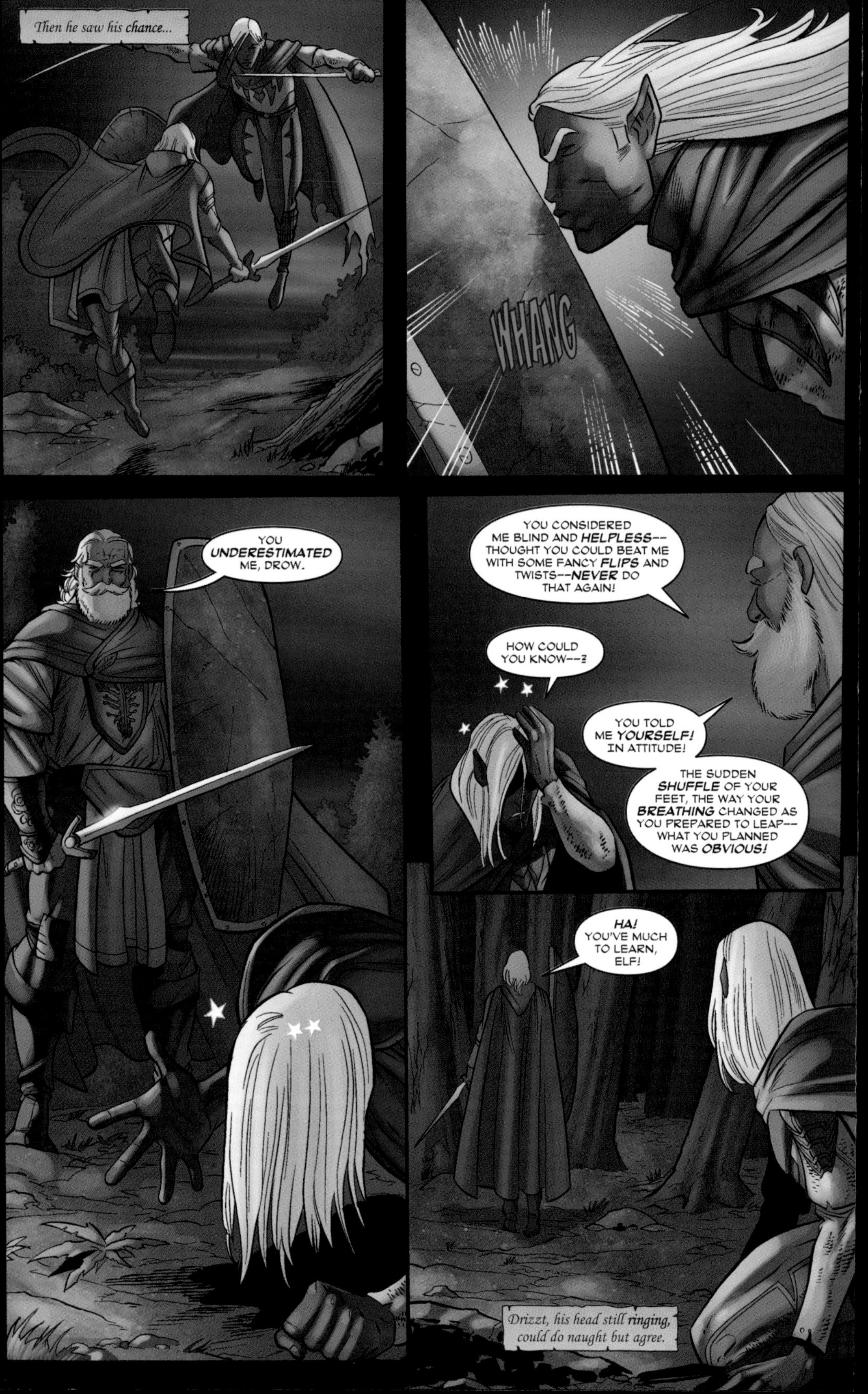
Then he saw his chance...
WHANG
YOU UNDERESTIMATED ME, DROW.
YOU CONSIDERED ME BLIND AND HELPLESS-- THOUGHT YOU COULD BEAT ME WITH SOME FANCY FLIPS AND TWISTS--NEVER DO THAT AGAIN!
HOW COULD YOU KNOW--?
YOU TOLD ME YOURSELF! IN ATTITUDE!
THE SUDDEN SHUFFLE OF YOUR FEET, THE WAY YOUR BREATHING CHANGED AS YOU PREPARED TO LEAP-- WHAT YOU PLANNED WAS OBVIOUS!
HA! YOU'VE MUCH TO LEARN, ELF!
Drizzt, his head still ringing, could do naught but agree.

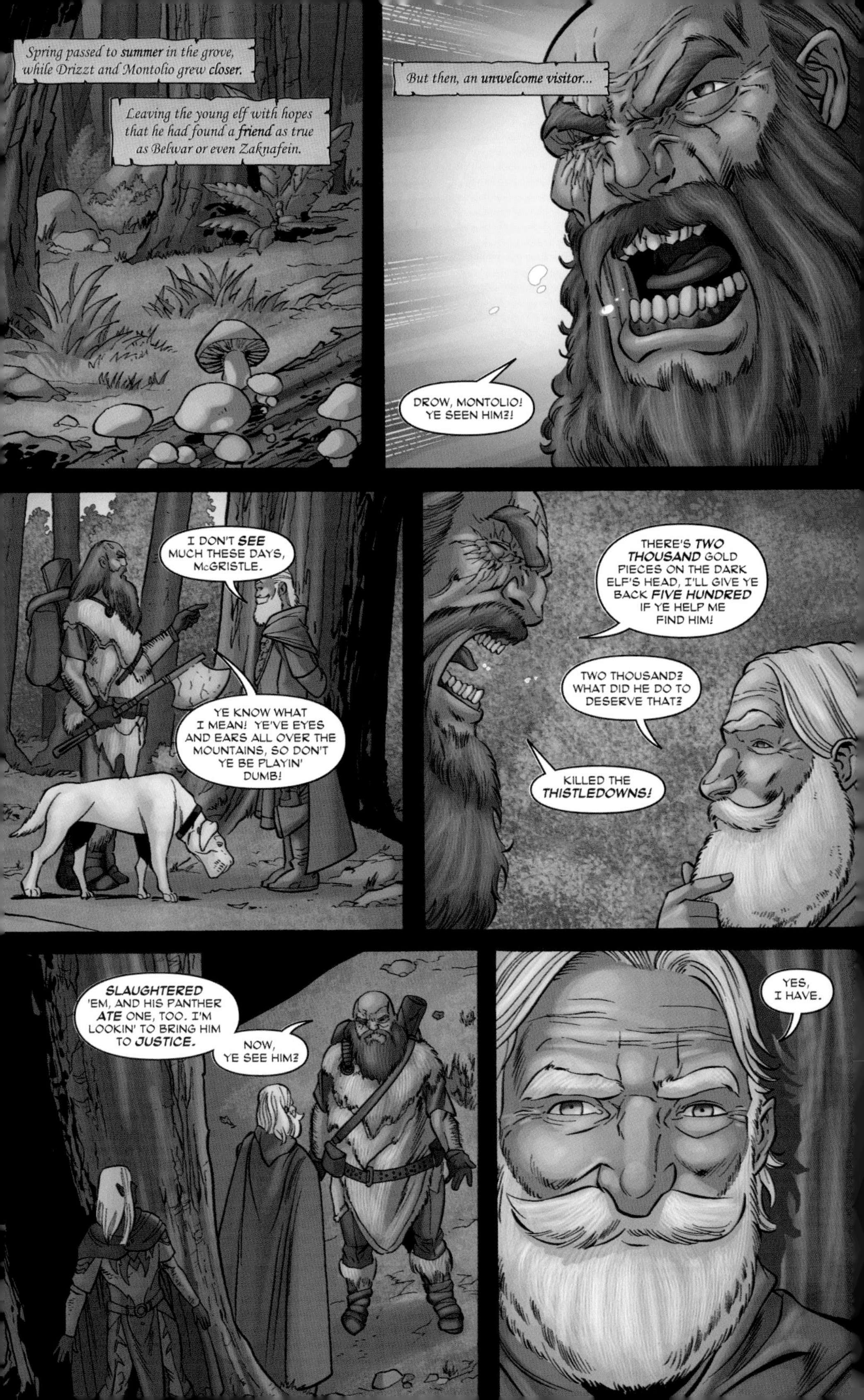
Spring passed to summer in the grove, while Drizzt and Montolio grew closer.
Leaving the young elf with hopes that he had found a friend as true as Belwar or even Zaknafein.
But then, an unwelcome visitor...
DROW, MONTOLIO! YE SEEN HIM?!
I DON'T SEE MUCH THESE DAYS, McGRISTLE.
YE KNOW WHAT I MEAN! YE'VE EYES AND EARS ALL OVER THE MOUNTAINS, SO DON'T YE BE PLAYIN' DUMB!
THERE'S TWO THOUSAND GOLD PIECES ON THE DARK ELF'S HEAD, I'LL GIVE YE BACK FIVE HUNDRED IF YE HELP ME FIND HIM!
TWO THOUSAND? WHAT DID HE DO TO DESERVE THAT?
KILLED THE THISTLEDOWNS!
SLAUGHTERED 'EM, AND HIS PANTHER ATE ONE, TOO. I'M LOOKIN' TO BRING HIM TO JUSTICE.
NOW, YE SEE HIM?
YES, I HAVE.

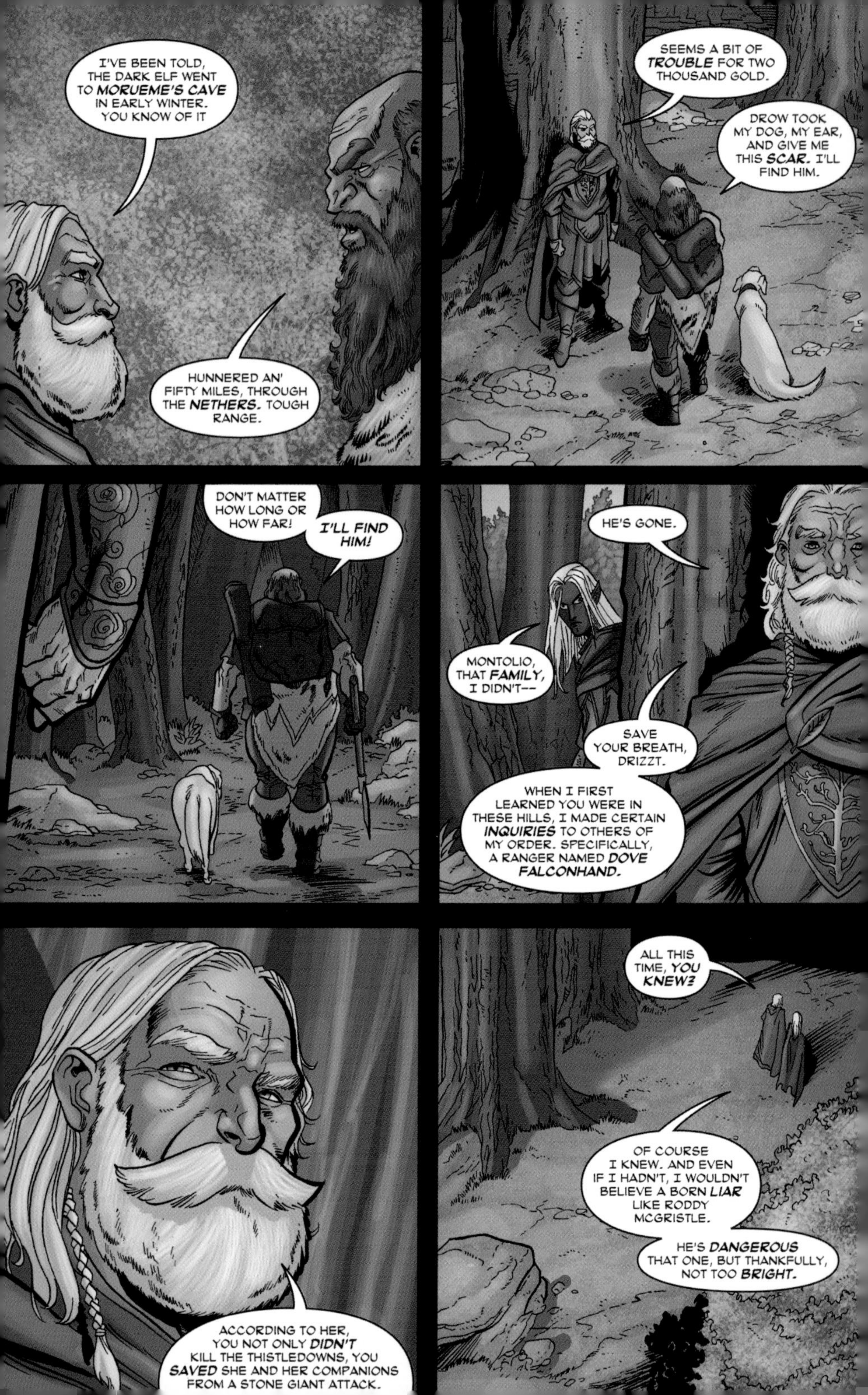
I'VE BEEN TOLD, THE DARK ELF WENT TO MORUEME'S CAVE IN EARLY WINTER. YOU KNOW OF IT
HUNNERED AN' FIFTY MILES, THROUGH THE NETHERS. TOUGH RANGE.
SEEMS A BIT OF TROUBLE FOR TWO THOUSAND GOLD.
DROW TOOK MY DOG, MY EAR, AND GIVE ME THIS SCAR. I'LL FIND HIM.
DON'T MATTER HOW LONG OR HOW FAR!
I'LL FIND HIM!
HE'S GONE.
MONTOLIO, THAT FAMILY, I DIDN'T--
SAVE YOUR BREATH, DRIZZT.
WHEN I FIRST LEARNED YOU WERE IN THESE HILLS, I MADE CERTAIN INQUIRIES TO OTHERS OF MY ORDER. SPECIFICALLY, A RANGER NAMED DOVE FALCONHAND.
ACCORDING TO HER, YOU NOT ONLY DIDN'T KILL THE THISTLEDOWNS, YOU SAVED SHE AND HER COMPANIONS FROM A STONE GIANT ATTACK.
ALL THIS TIME, YOU KNEW?
OF COURSE I KNEW. AND EVEN IF I HADN'T, I WOULDN'T BELIEVE A BORN LIAR LIKE RODDY MCGRISTLE.
HE'S DANGEROUS THAT ONE, BUT THANKFULLY, NOT TOO BRIGHT.

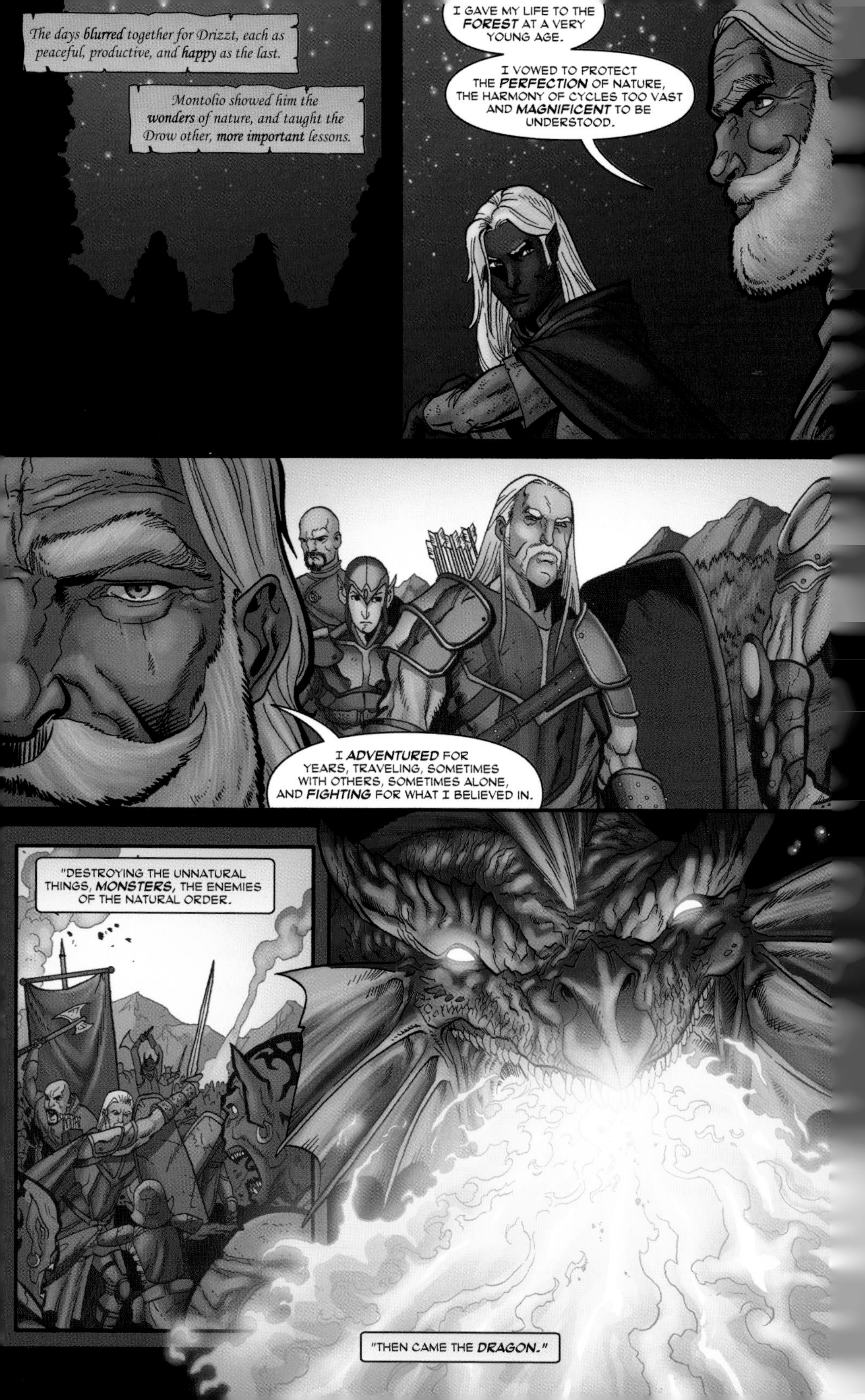
The days blurred together for Drizzt, each as peaceful, productive, and happy as the last.
Montolio showed him the wonders of nature, and taught the Drow other, more important lessons.
I GAVE MY LIFE TO THE FOREST AT A VERY YOUNG AGE.
I VOWED TO PROTECT THE PERFECTION OF NATURE, THE HARMONY OF CYCLES TOO VAST AND MAGNIFICENT TO BE UNDERSTOOD.
I ADVENTURED FOR YEARS, TRAVELING, SOMETIMES WITH OTHERS, SOMETIMES ALONE, AND FIGHTING FOR WHAT I BELIEVED IN.
"DESTROYING THE UNNATURAL THINGS, MONSTERS, THE ENEMIES OF THE NATURAL ORDER.
"THEN CAME THE DRAGON."

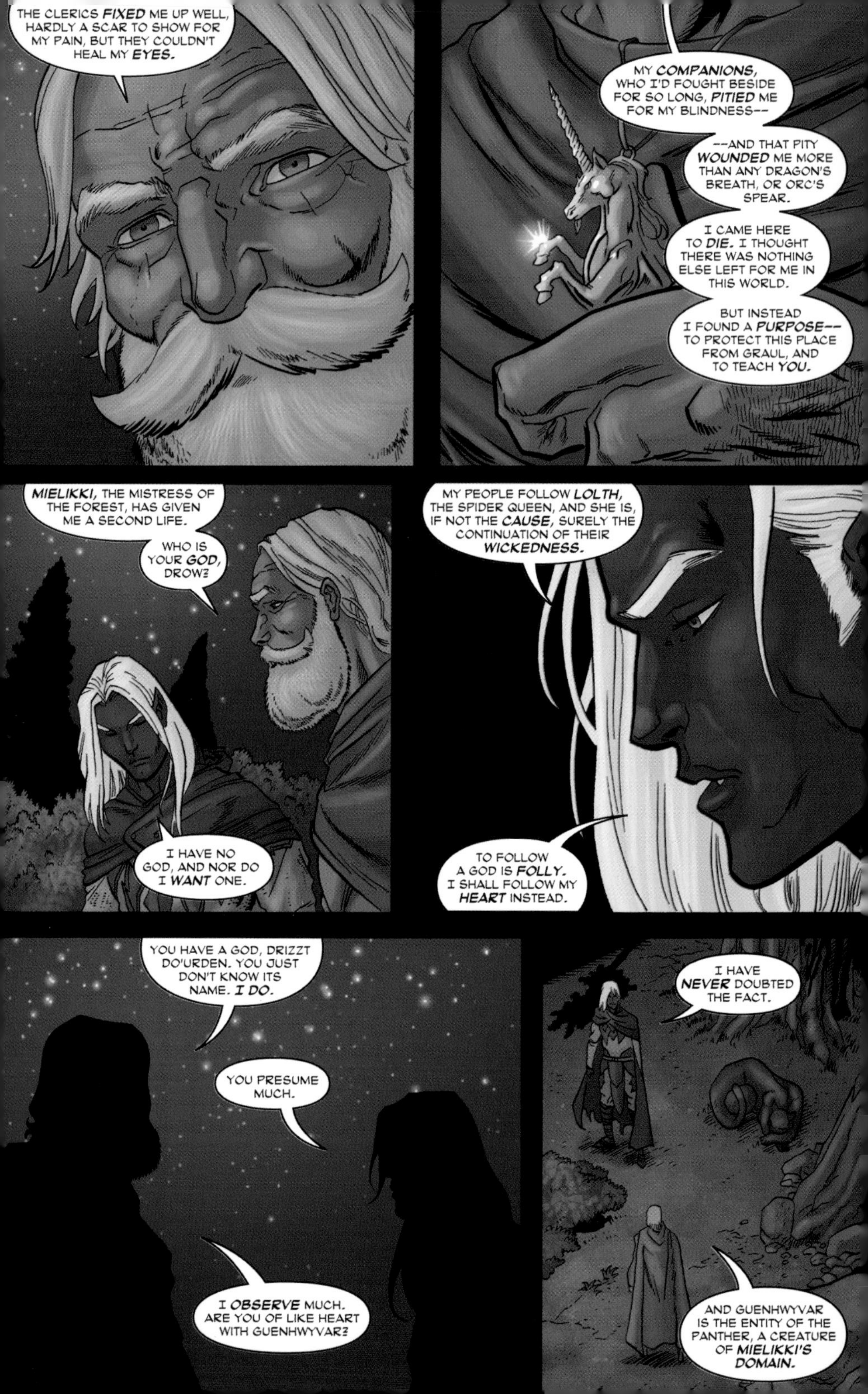
THE CLERICS FIXED ME UP WELL, HARDLY A SCAR TO SHOW FOR MY PAIN, BUT THEY COULDN'T HEAL MY EYES.
MY COMPANIONS, WHO I'D FOUGHT BESIDE FOR SO LONG, PITIED ME FOR MY BLINDNESS--
--AND THAT PITY WOUNDED ME MORE THAN ANY DRAGON'S BREATH, OR ORC'S SPEAR.
I CAME HERE TO DIE. I THOUGHT THERE WAS NOTHING ELSE LEFT FOR ME IN THIS WORLD.
BUT INSTEAD I FOUND A PURPOSE-- TO PROTECT THIS PLACE FROM GRAUL, AND TO TEACH YOU.
MIELIKKI, THE MISTRESS OF THE FOREST, HAS GIVEN ME A SECOND LIFE.
WHO IS YOUR GOD, DROW?
I HAVE NO GOD, AND NOR DO I WANT ONE.
MY PEOPLE FOLLOW LOLTH, THE SPIDER QUEEN, AND SHE IS, IF NOT THE CAUSE, SURELY THE CONTINUATION OF THEIR WICKEDNESS.
TO FOLLOW A GOD IS FOLLY. I SHALL FOLLOW MY HEART INSTEAD.
YOU HAVE A GOD, DRIZZT DO'URDEN. YOU JUST DON'T KNOW ITS NAME. I DO.
YOU PRESUME MUCH.
I OBSERVE MUCH. ARE YOU OF LIKE HEART WITH GUENHWYVAR?
I HAVE NEVER DOUBTED THE FACT.
AND GUENHWYVAR IS THE ENTITY OF THE PANTHER, A CREATURE OF MIELIKKI'S DOMAIN.

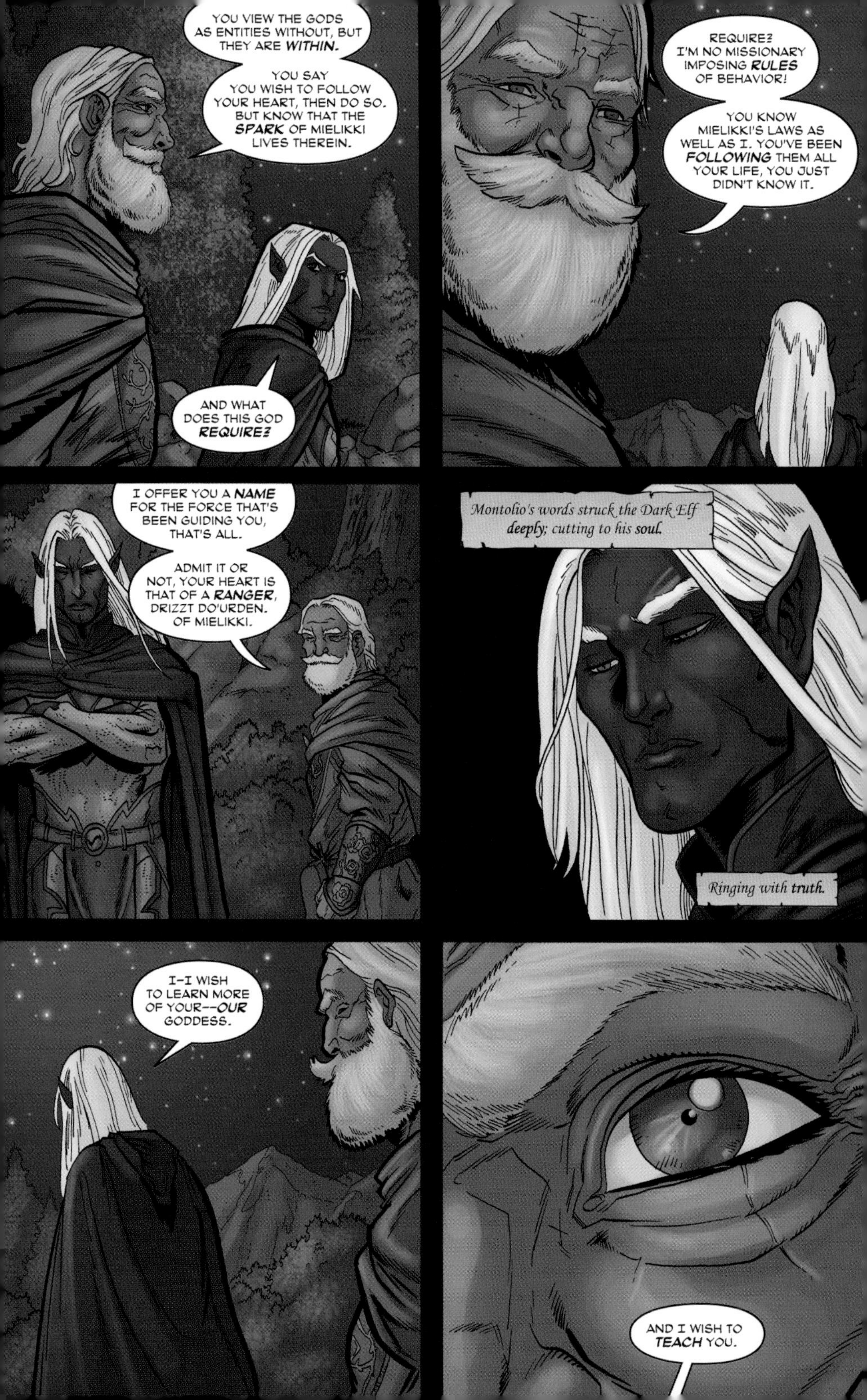
YOU VIEW THE GODS AS ENTITIES WITHOUT, BUT THEY ARE WITHIN.
YOU SAY YOU WISH TO FOLLOW YOUR HEART, THEN DO SO. BUT KNOW THAT THE SPARK OF MIELIKKI LIVES THEREIN.
AND WHAT DOES THIS GOD REQUIRE?
REQUIRE? I'M NO MISSIONARY IMPOSING RULES OF BEHAVIOR!
YOU KNOW MIELIKKI'S LAWS AS WELL AS I. YOU'VE BEEN FOLLOWING THEM ALL YOUR LIFE, YOU JUST DIDN'T KNOW IT.
I OFFER YOU A NAME FOR THE FORCE THAT'S BEEN GUIDING YOU, THAT'S ALL.
ADMIT IT OR NOT, YOUR HEART IS THAT OF A RANGER, DRIZZT DO'URDEN. OF MIELIKKI.
Montolio's words struck the Dark Elf deeply; cutting to his soul.
Ringing with truth.
I-I WISH TO LEARN MORE OF YOUR--OUR GODDESS.
AND I WISH TO TEACH YOU.

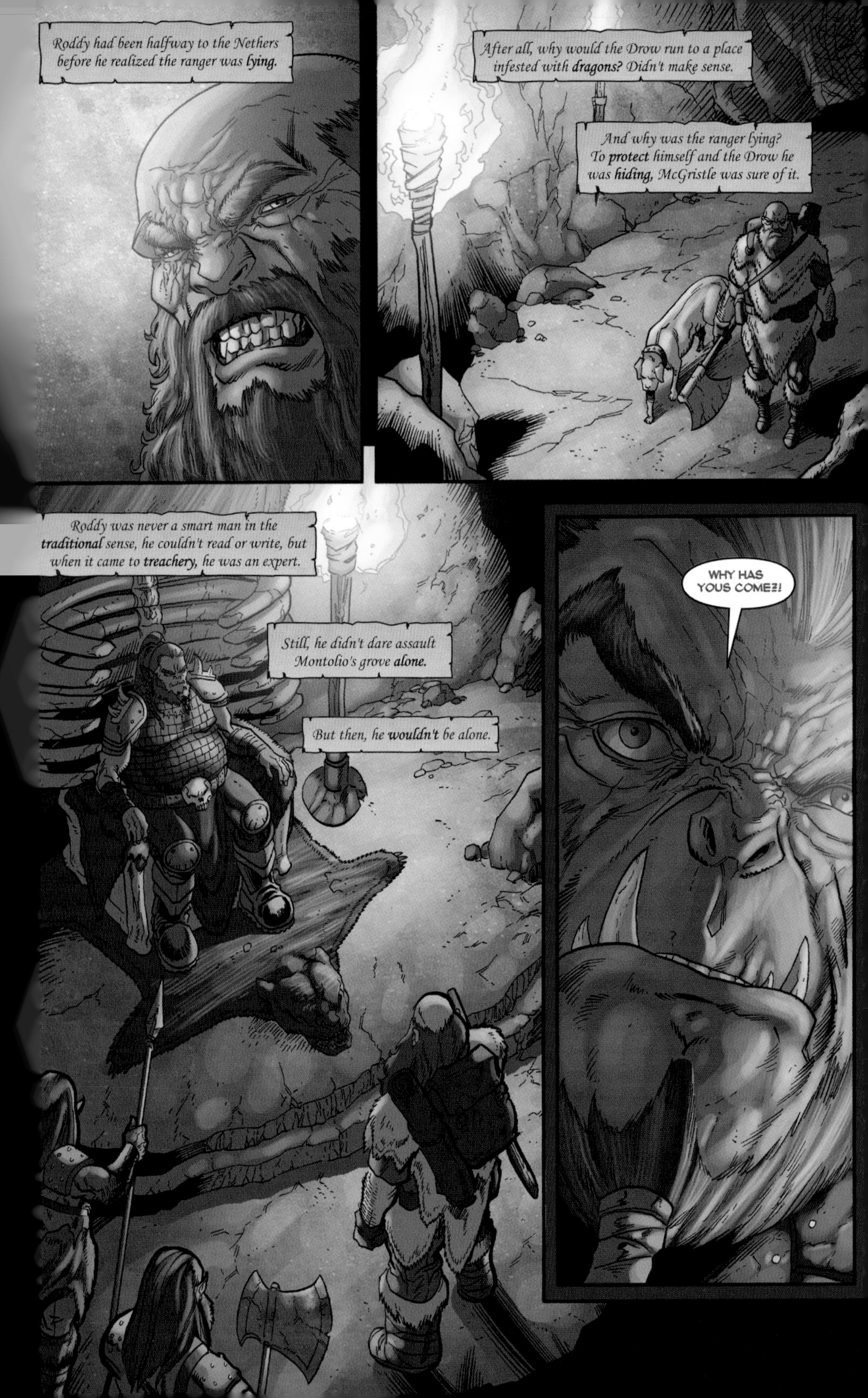
Roddy had been halfway to the Nethers before he realized the ranger was lying.
After all, why would the Drow run to a place infested with dragons? Didn't make sense.
And why was the ranger lying? To protect himself and the Drow he was hiding, McGristle was sure of it.
Roddy was never a smart man in the traditional sense, he couldn't read or write, but when it came to treachery, he was an expert.
Still, he didn't dare assault Montolio's grove alone.
But then, he wouldn't be alone.
WHY HAS YOUS COMEZ!

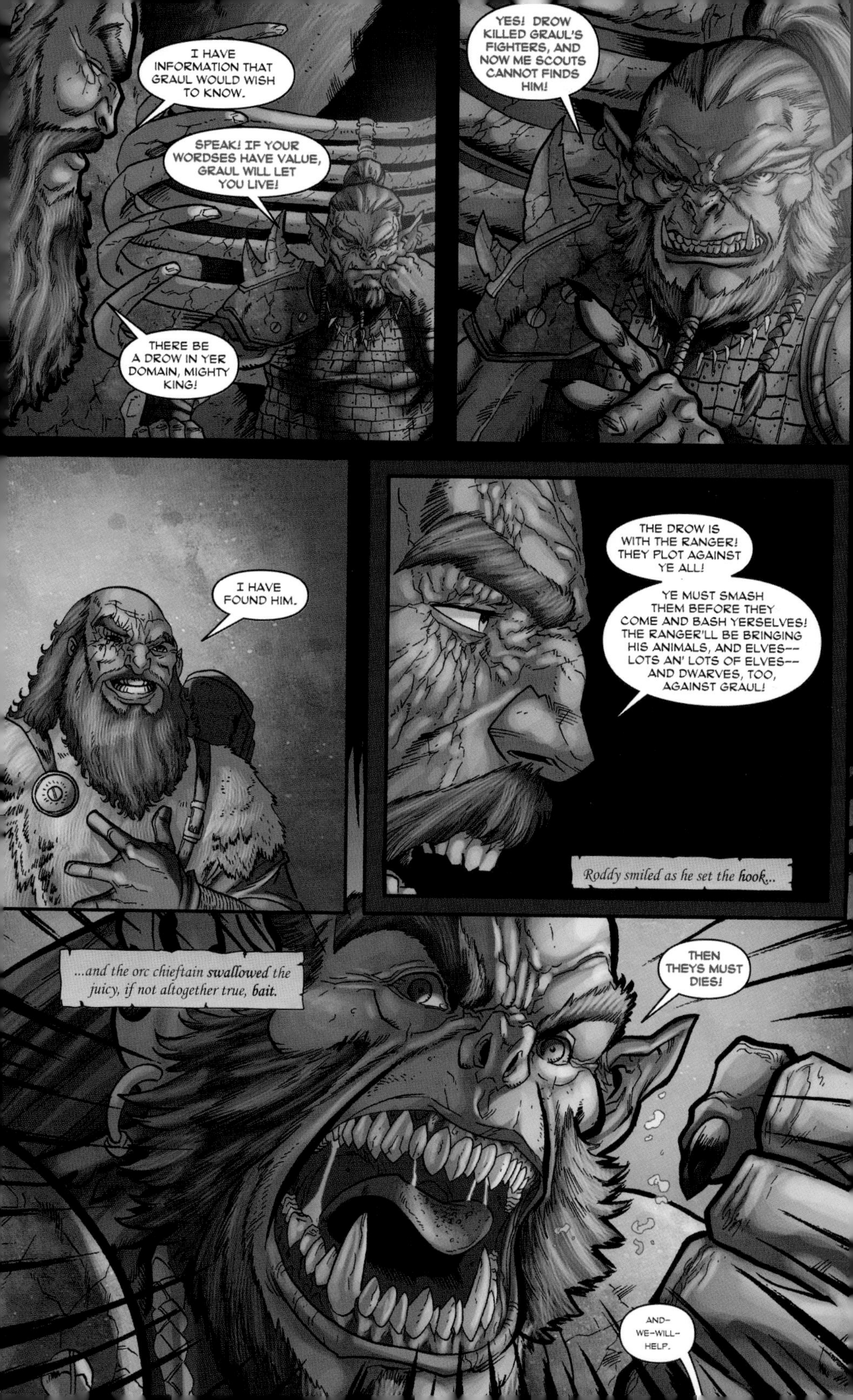

I HAVE INFORMATION THAT GRAUL WOULD WISH TO KNOW.
SPEAK! IF YOUR WORDSES HAVE VALUE, GRAUL WILL LET YOU LIVE!
THERE BE A DROW IN YER DOMAIN, MIGHTY KING!
YES! DROW KILLED GRAUL'S FIGHTERS, AND NOW ME SCOUTS CANNOT FINDS HIM!
I HAVE FOUND HIM.
THE DROW IS WITH THE RANGER! THEY PLOT AGAINST YE ALL!
YE MUST SMASH THEM BEFORE THEY COME AND BASH YERSELVES! THE RANGER'LL BE BRINGING HIS ANIMALS, AND ELVES-- LOTS AN' LOTS OF ELVES-- AND DWARVES, TOO, AGAINST GRAUL!
Roddy smiled as he set the hook...
...and the orc chieftain swallowed the juicy, if not altogether true, bait.
THEN THEYS MUST DIES!
AND-WE-WILL-HELP.

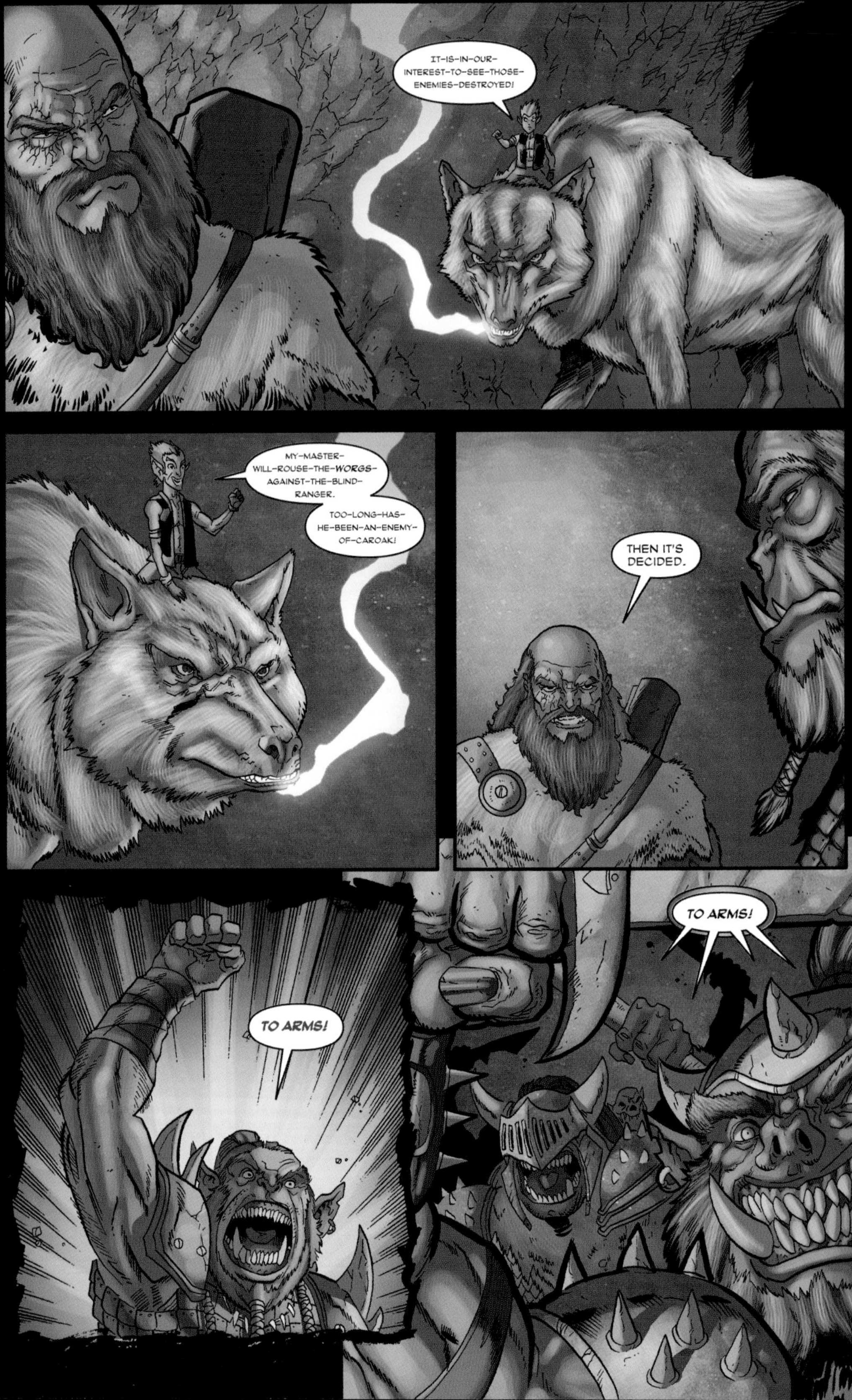
IT-IS-IN-OUR-INTEREST-TO-SEE-THOSE-ENEMIES-DESTROYED!
MY-MASTER-WILL-ROUSE-THE-**WORGS**-AGAINST-THE-BLIND-RANGER.
TOO-LONG-HAS-HE-BEEN-AN-ENEMY-OF-CAROAK!
THEN IT'S DECIDED.
TO ARMS!
TO ARMS!

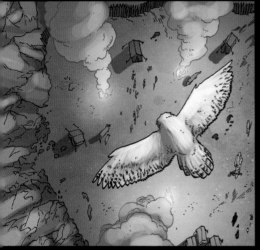

WHOOOO

WHOOOO WHOOOO WHOOOO
WHOOOO

SO THE TIME HAS *FINALLY* COME.

WHAT ARE YOU TALKING ABOUT, MONTOLIO?

WAR, DRIZZT DO'URDEN.

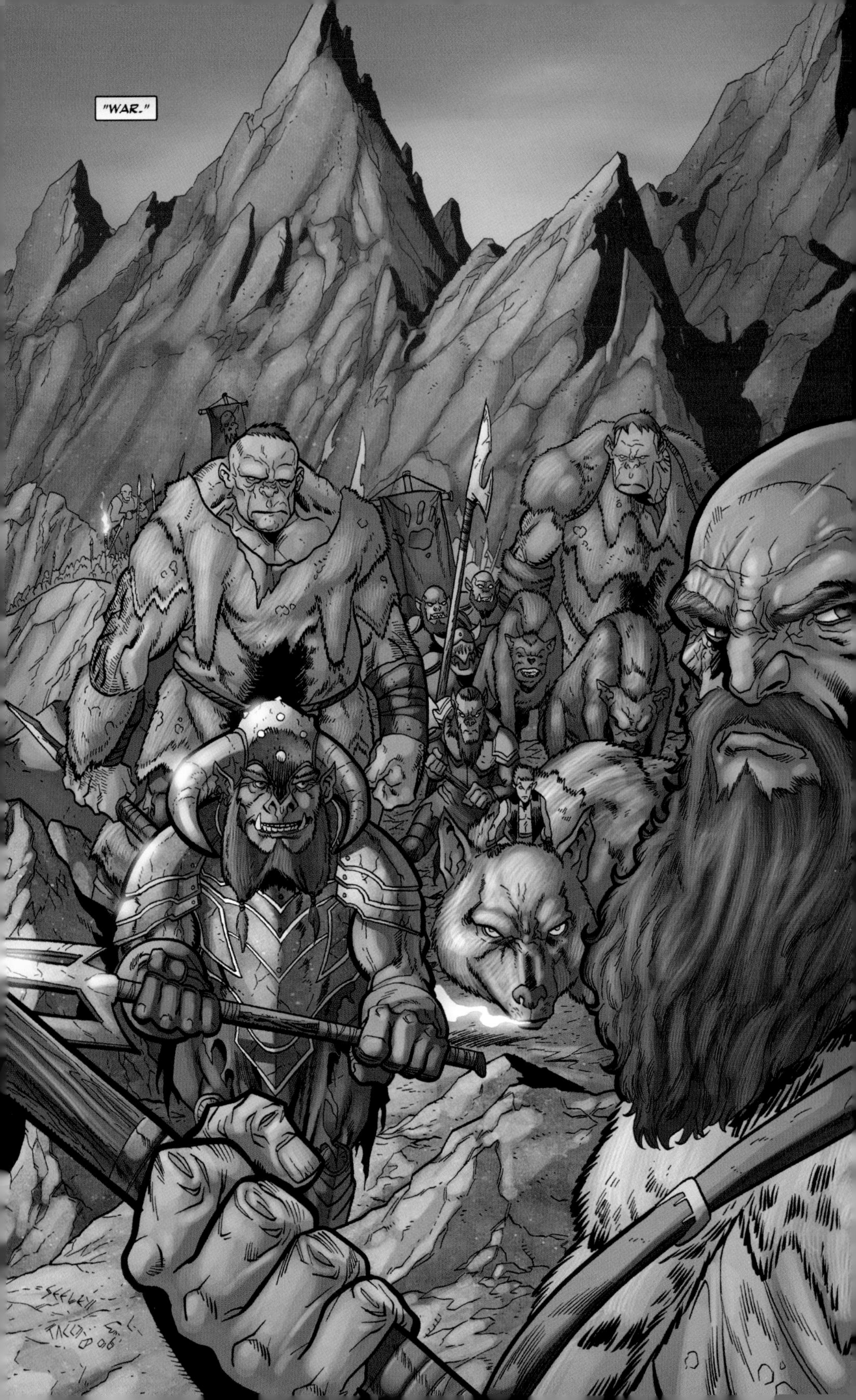
"WAR."

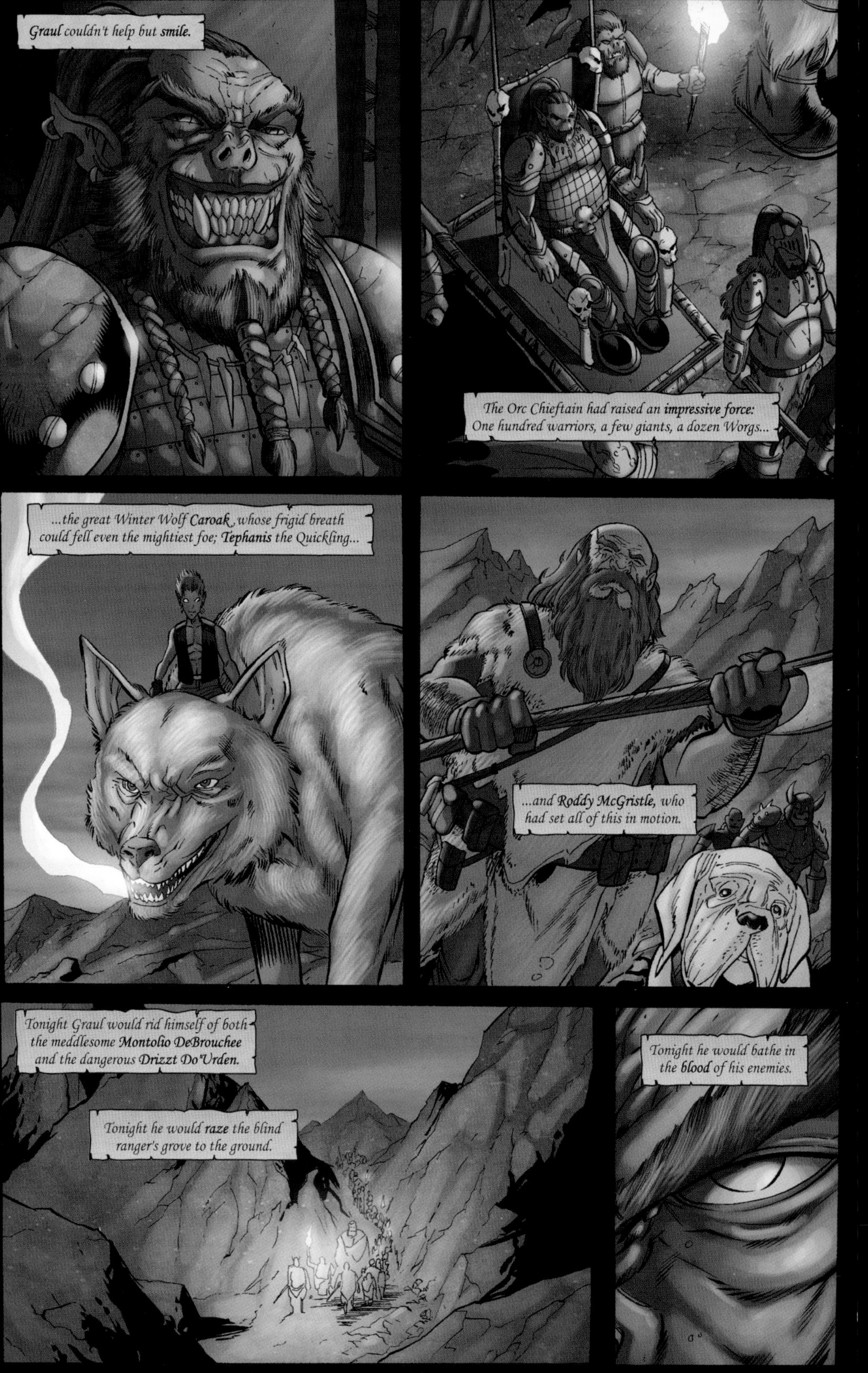
Graul couldn't help but smile.
The Orc Chieftain had raised an impressive force: One hundred warriors, a few giants, a dozen Worgs...
...the great Winter Wolf Caroak, whose frigid breath could fell even the mightiest foe; Tephanis the Quickling...
...and Roddy McGristle, who had set all of this in motion.
Tonight Graul would rid himself of both the meddlesome Montolio DeBrouchee and the dangerous Drizzt Do'Urden.
Tonight he would raze the blind ranger's grove to the ground.
Tonight he would bathe in the blood of his enemies.

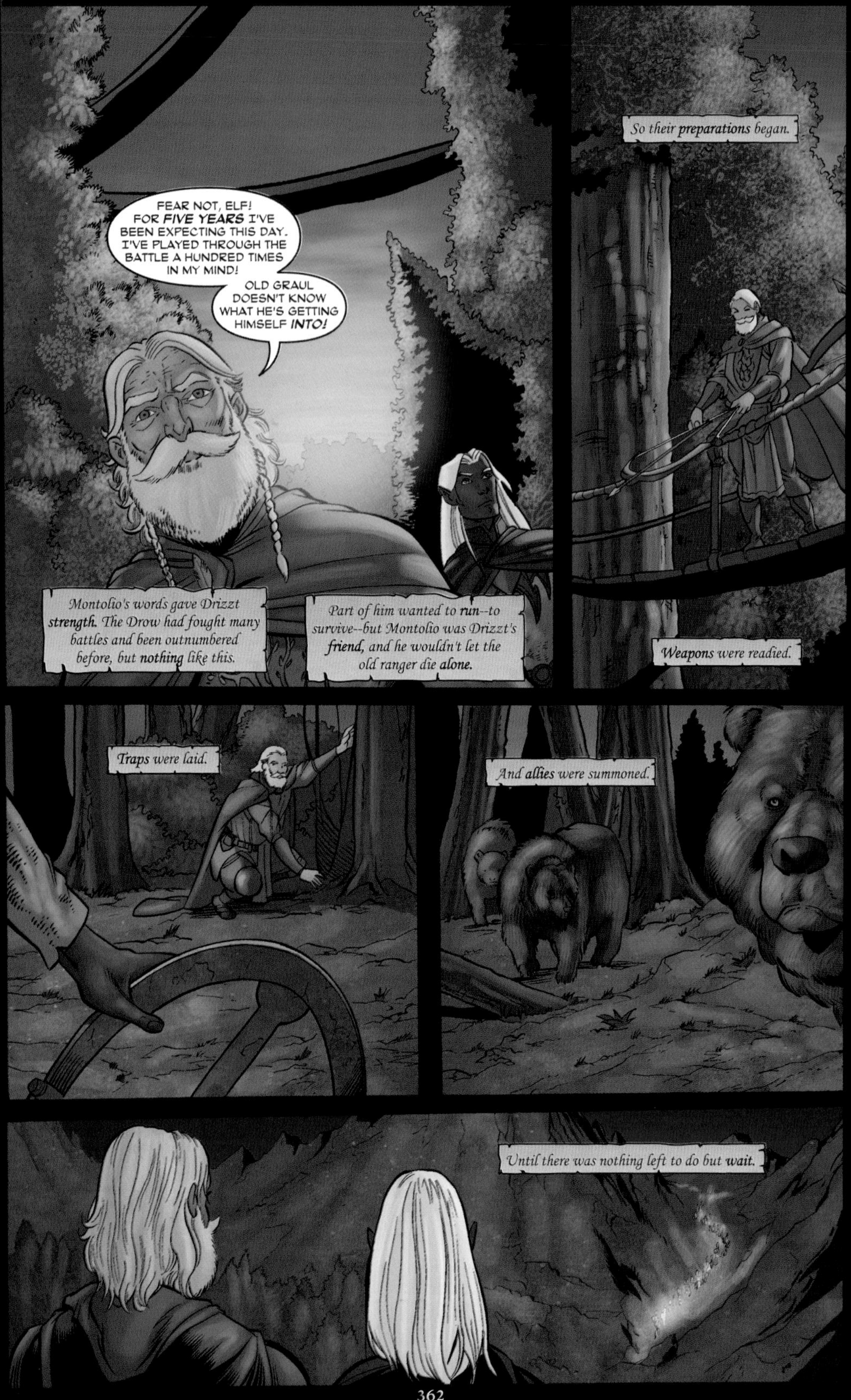
FEAR NOT, ELF! FOR FIVE YEARS I'VE BEEN EXPECTING THIS DAY. I'VE PLAYED THROUGH THE BATTLE A HUNDRED TIMES IN MY MIND!
OLD GRAUL DOESN'T KNOW WHAT HE'S GETTING HIMSELF INTO!
Montolio's words gave Drizzt strength. The Drow had fought many battles and been outnumbered before, but nothing like this.
Part of him wanted to run--to survive--but Montolio was Drizzt's friend, and he wouldn't let the old ranger die alone.
So their preparations began.
Weapons were readied.
Traps were laid.
And allies were summoned.
Until there was nothing left to do but wait.

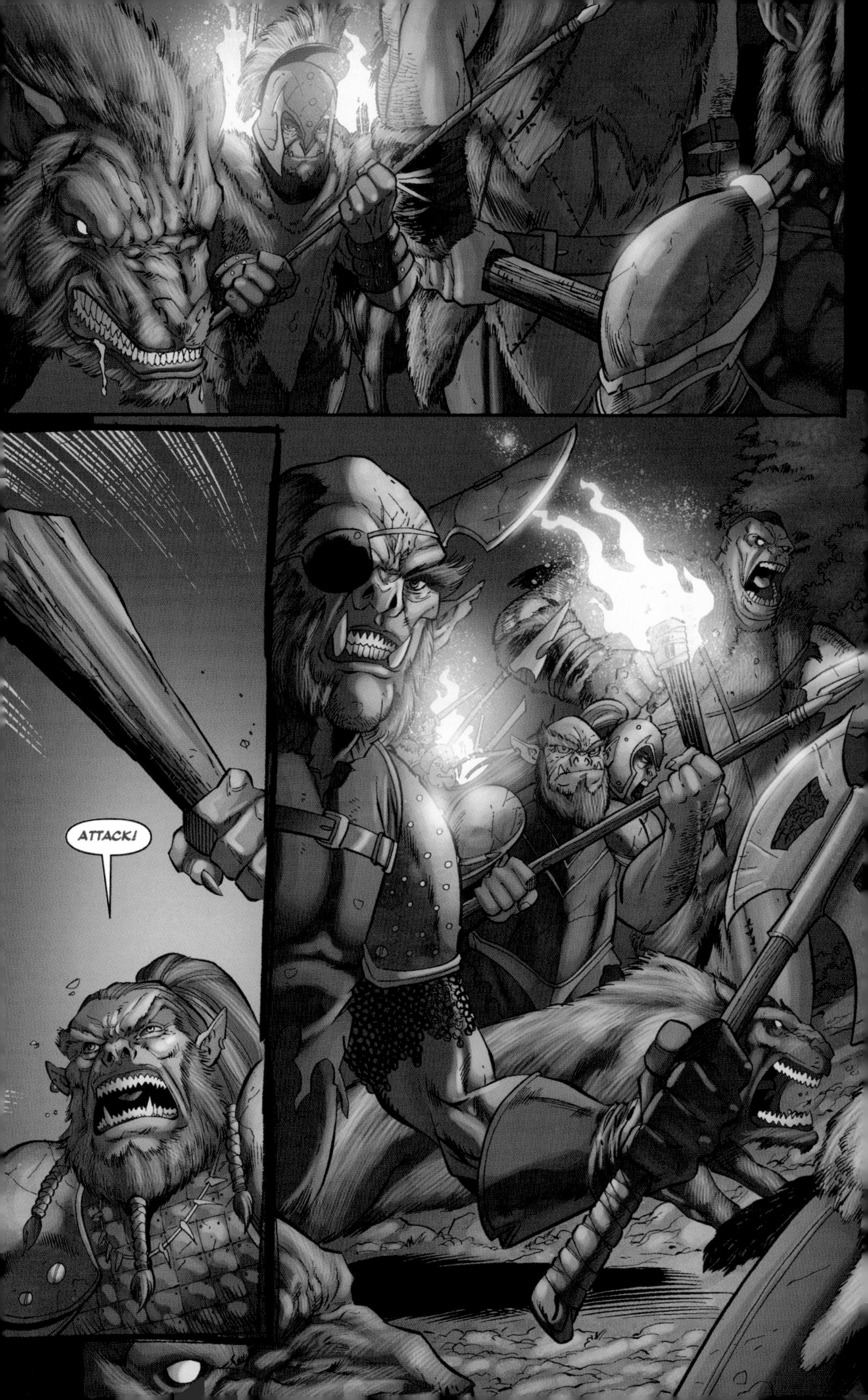
ATTACK!

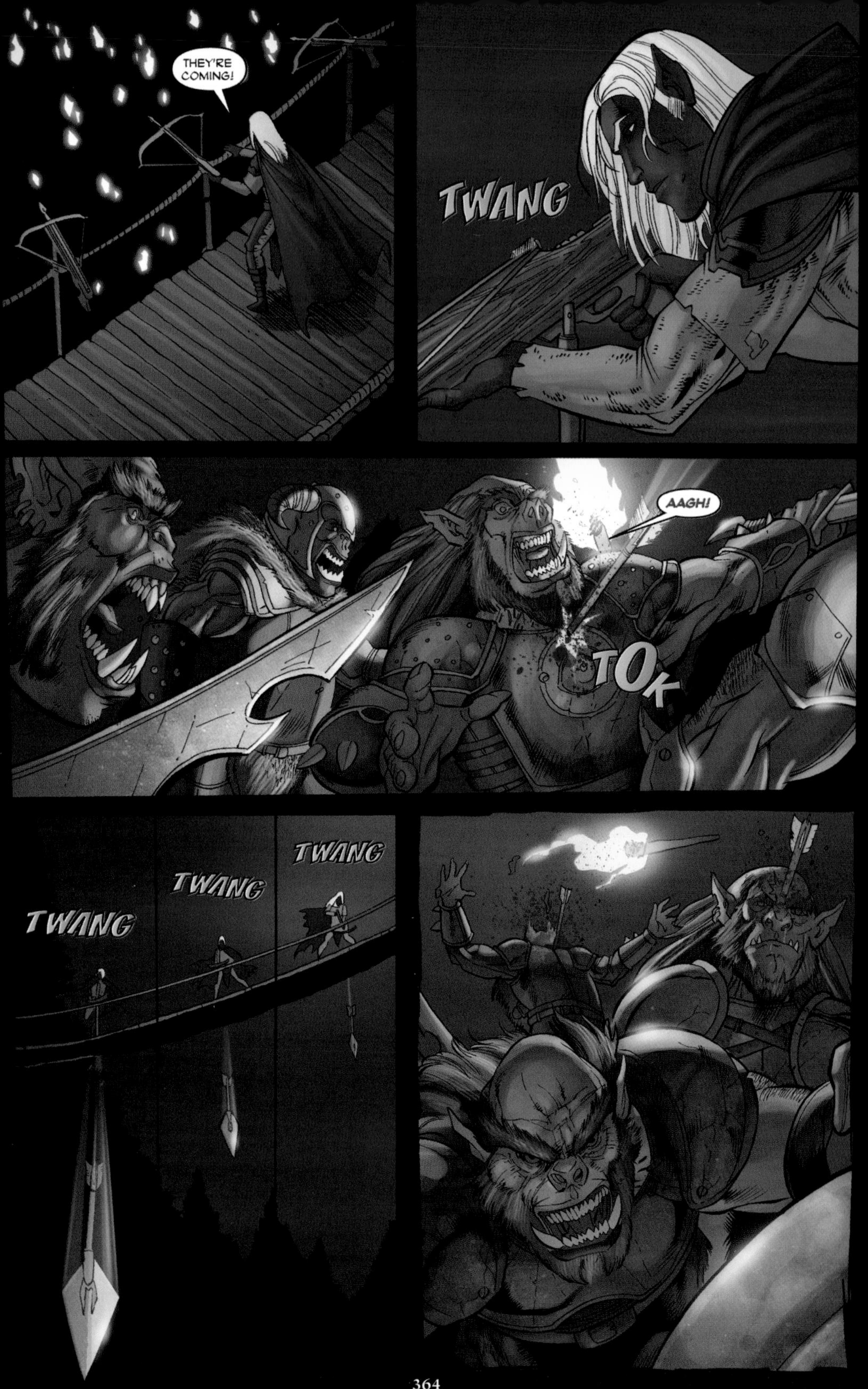
THEY'RE COMING!
TWANG
AAGH!
TOK
TWANG
TWANG
TWANG

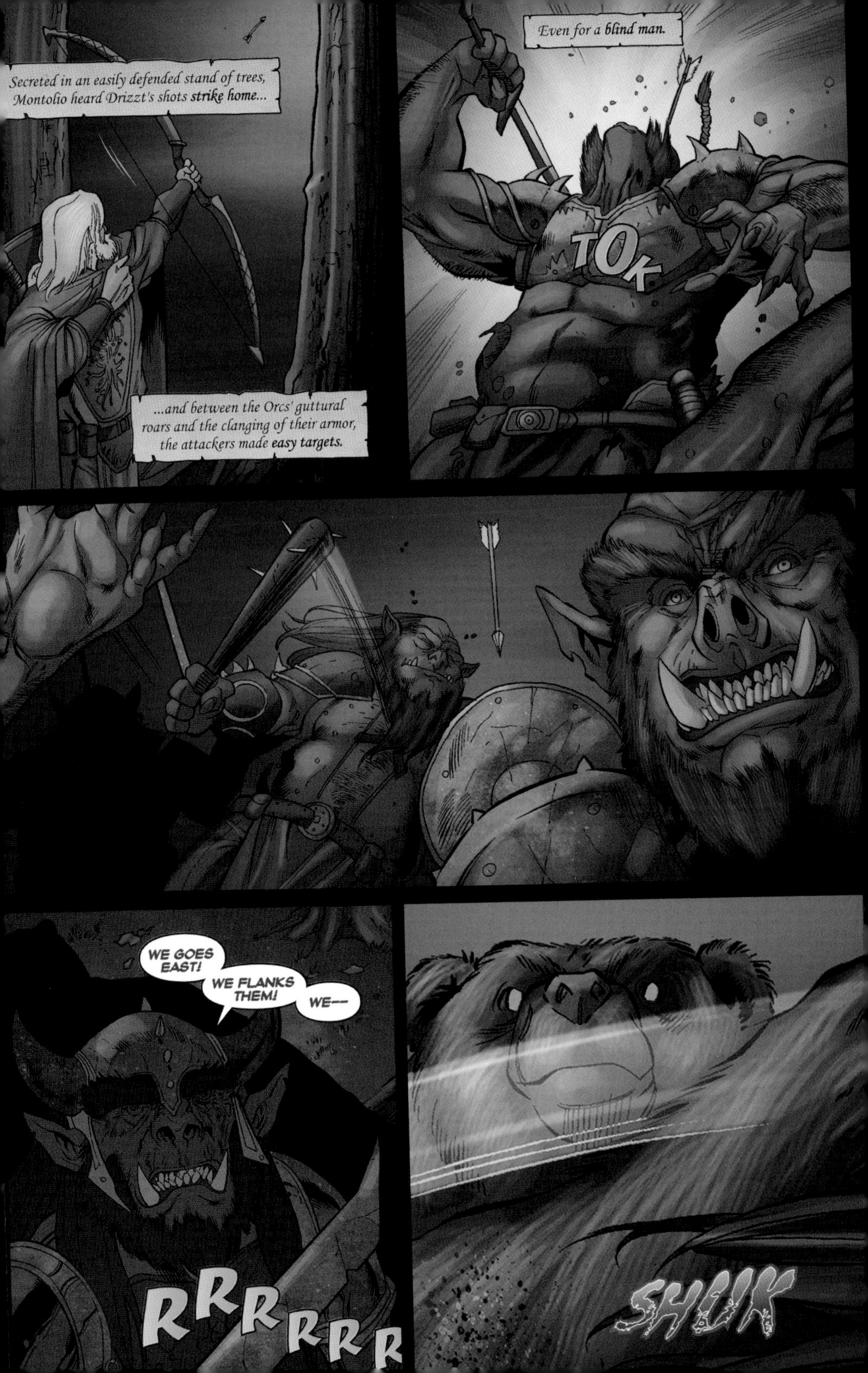
Secreted in an easily defended stand of trees, Montolio heard Drizzt's shots strike home...
...and between the Orcs' guttural roars and the clanging of their armor, the attackers made easy targets.
Even for a blind man.
TOK
WE GOES EAST!
WE FLANKS THEM!
WE--
RRRRRRR
SHUK

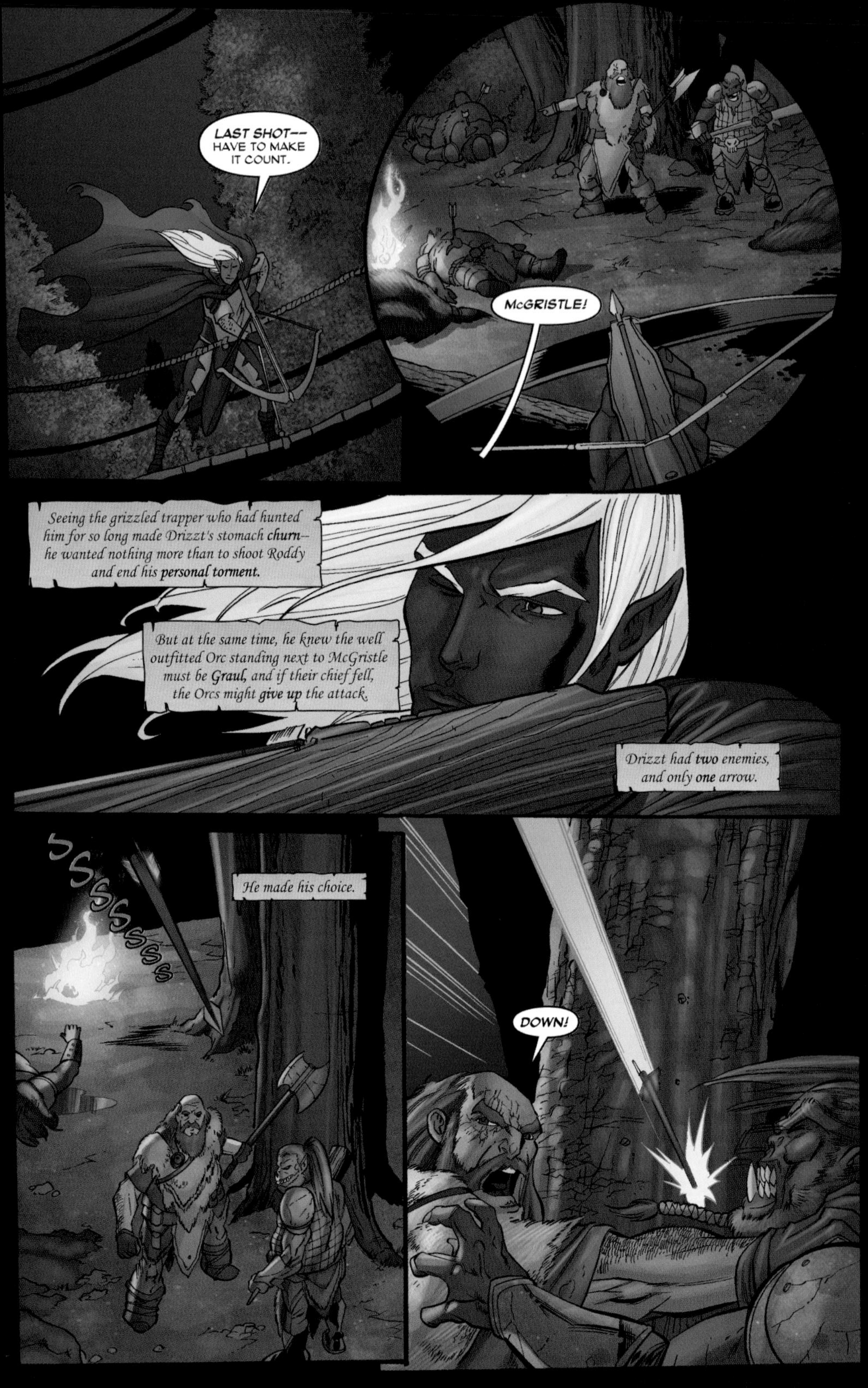
LAST SHOT-- HAVE TO MAKE IT COUNT.
McGRISTLE!
Seeing the grizzled trapper who had hunted him for so long made Drizzt's stomach churn--he wanted nothing more than to shoot Roddy and end his personal torment.
But at the same time, he knew the well outfitted Orc standing next to McGristle must be Graul, and if their chief fell, the Orcs might give up the attack.
Drizzt had two enemies, and only one arrow.
SSSSSSSS
He made his choice.
DOWN!

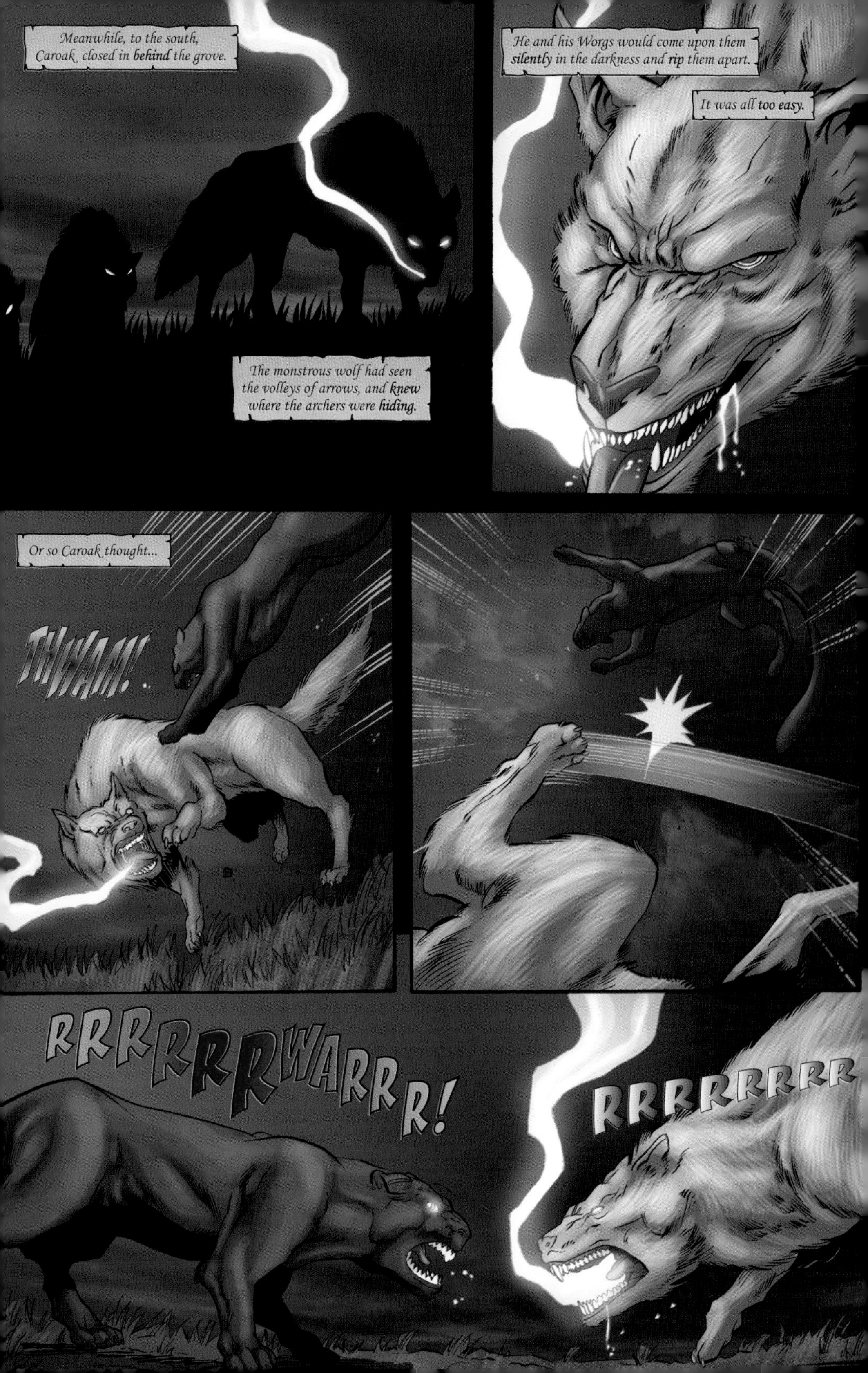

Meanwhile, to the south, Caroak closed in behind the grove.
The monstrous wolf had seen the volleys of arrows, and knew where the archers were hiding.
He and his Worgs would come upon them silently in the darkness and rip them apart.
It was all too easy.
Or so Caroak thought...
THWAM!
RRRRRRWARRRR!
RRRRRRRRR

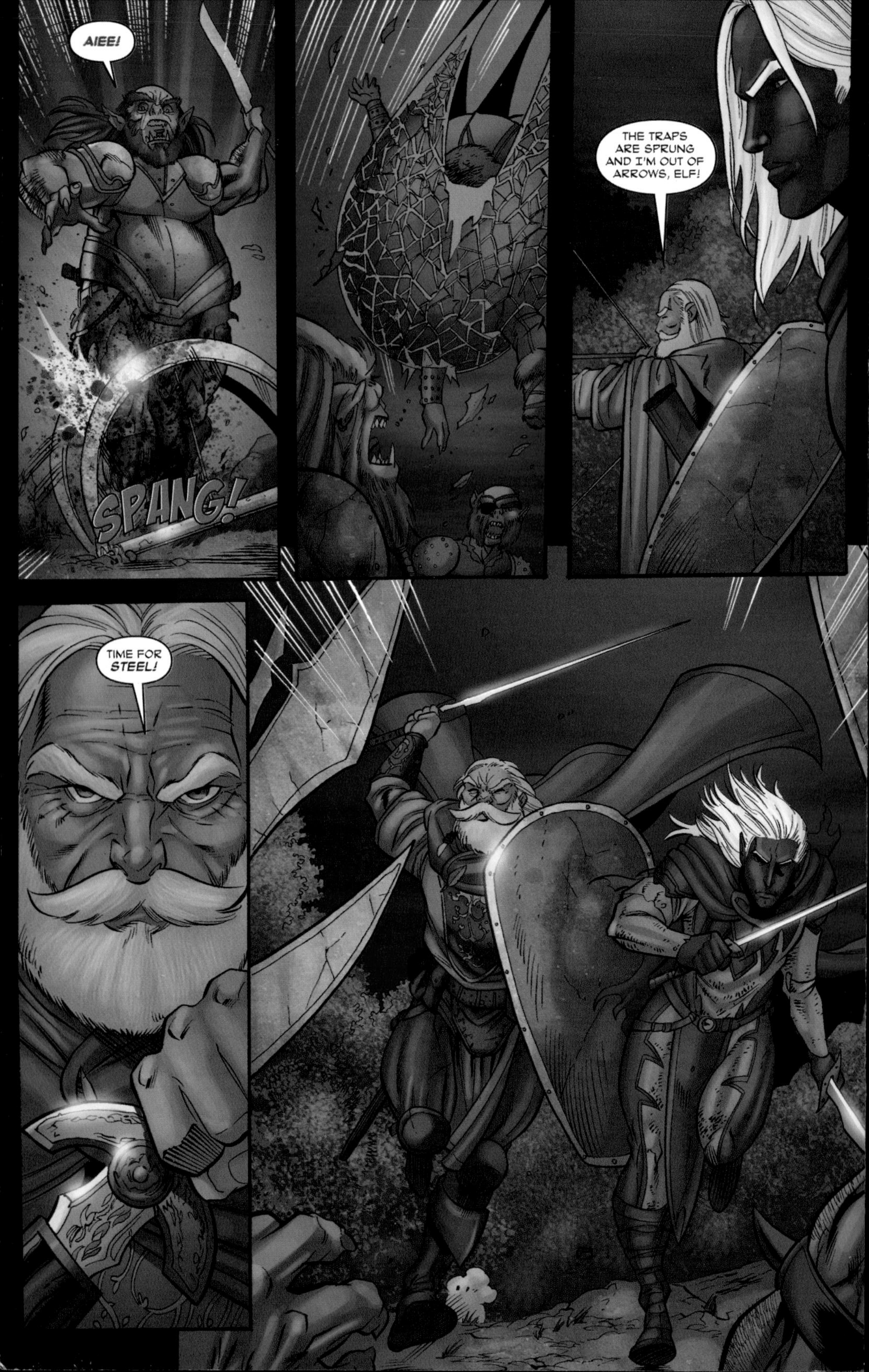
AIEE!
SPANG!
THE TRAPS ARE SPRUNG AND I'M OUT OF ARROWS, ELF!
TIME FOR STEEL!

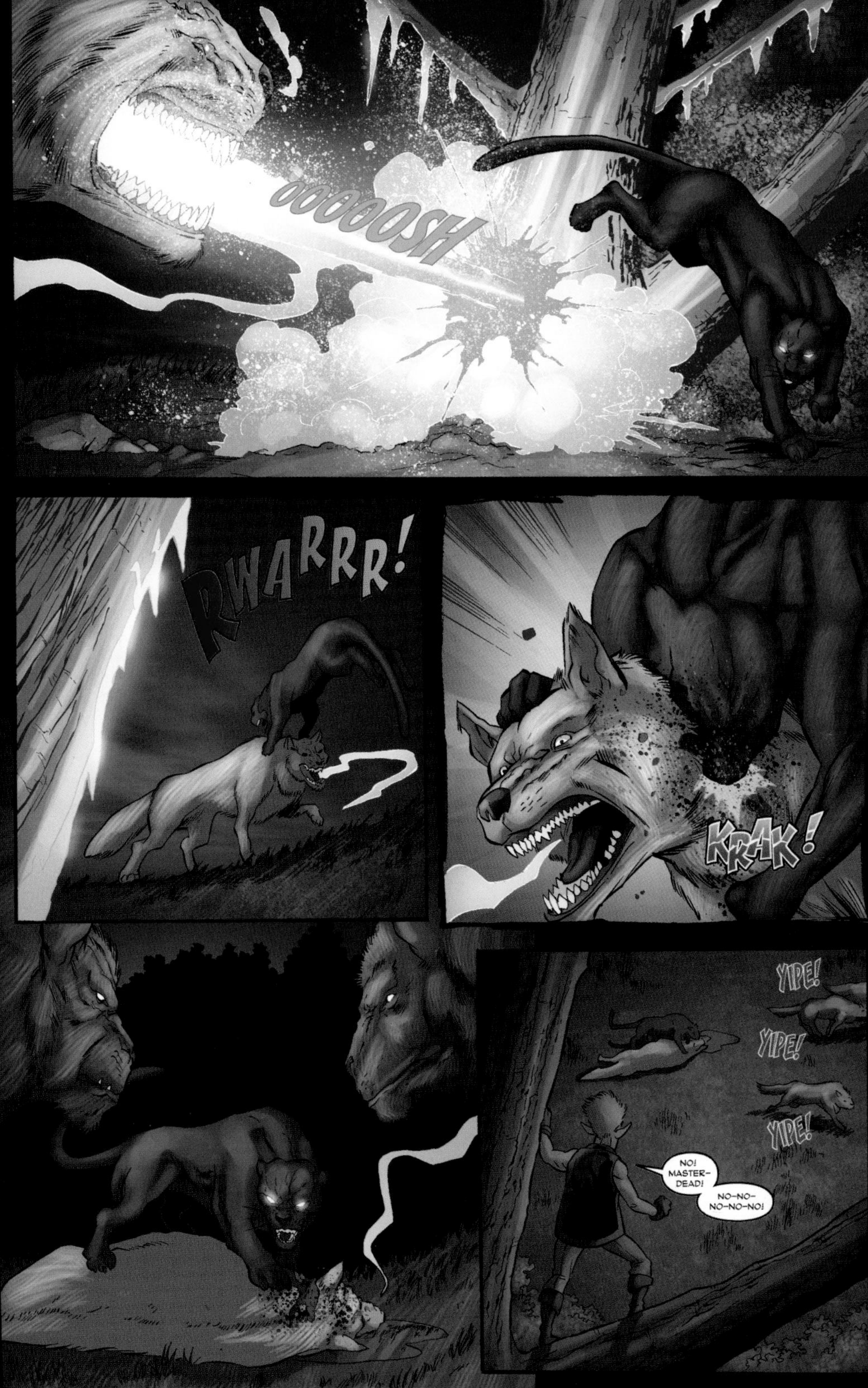
OOOOOOSH
RWARRR!
KRAK!
YIPE!
YIPE!
YIPE!
NO! MASTER-DEAD!
NO-NO-NO-NO-NO!

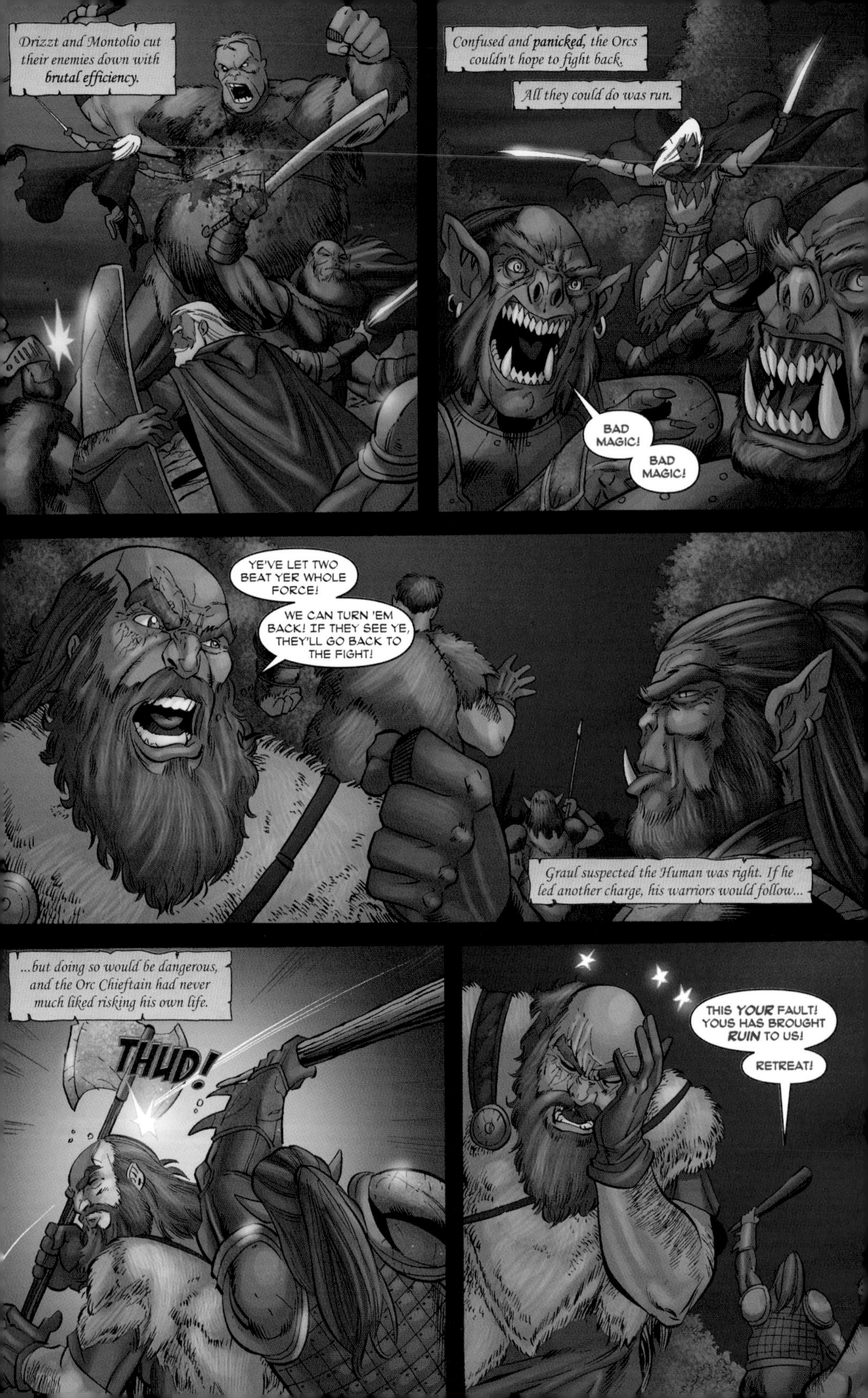
Drizzt and Montolio cut their enemies down with brutal efficiency.
Confused and panicked, the Orcs couldn't hope to fight back.
All they could do was run.
BAD MAGIC!
BAD MAGIC!
YE'VE LET TWO BEAT YER WHOLE FORCE!
WE CAN TURN 'EM BACK! IF THEY SEE YE, THEY'LL GO BACK TO THE FIGHT!
Graul suspected the Human was right. If he led another charge, his warriors would follow...
...but doing so would be dangerous, and the Orc Chieftain had never much liked risking his own life.
THUD!
THIS YOUR FAULT! YOUS HAS BROUGHT RUIN TO US!
RETREAT!

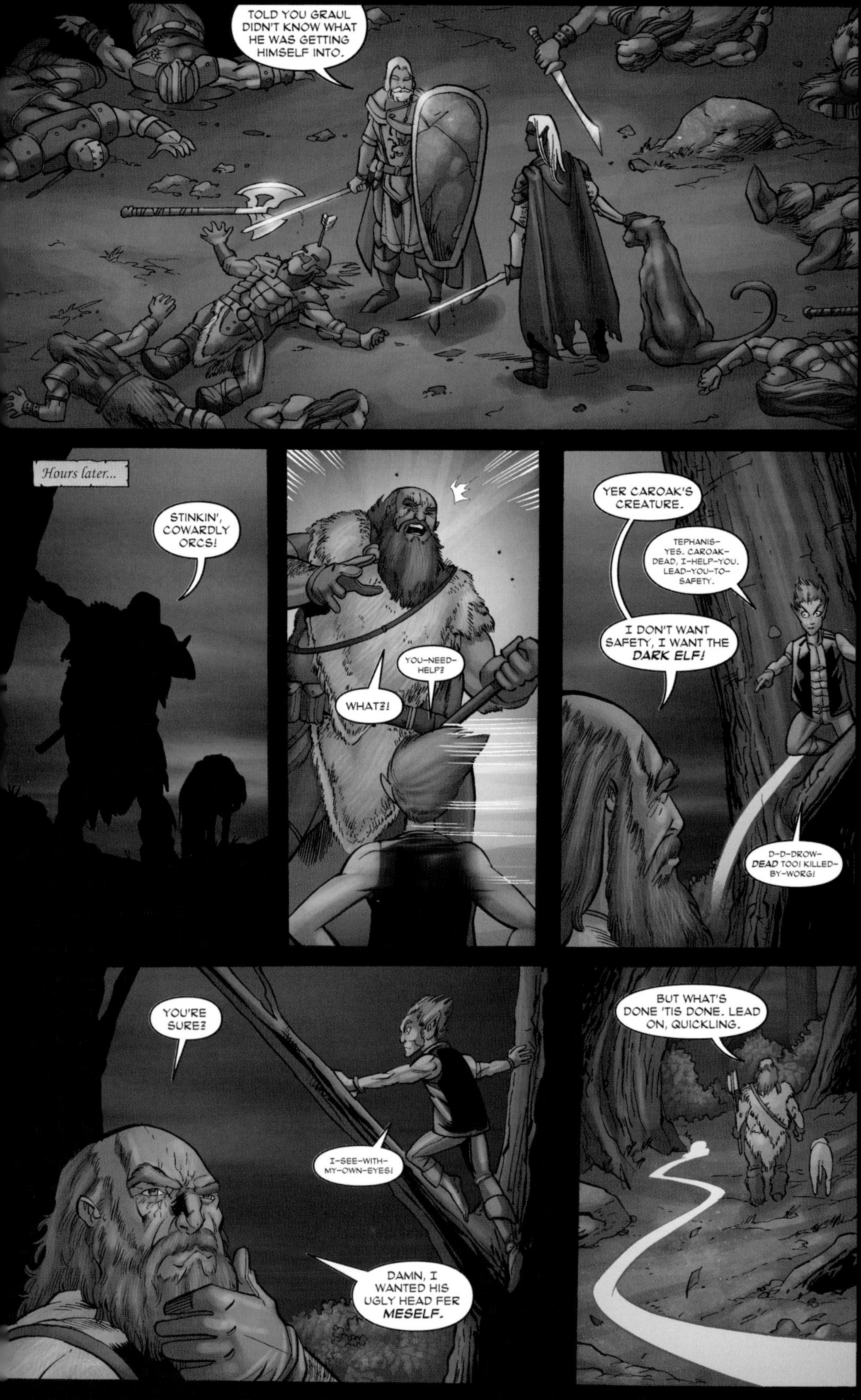
TOLD YOU GRAUL DIDN'T KNOW WHAT HE WAS GETTING HIMSELF INTO.
Hours later...
STINKIN', COWARDLY ORCS!
WHAT?!
YOU-NEED-HELP?
YER CAROAK'S CREATURE.
TEPHANIS-YES. CAROAK-DEAD, I-HELP-YOU. LEAD-YOU-TO-SAFETY.
I DON'T WANT SAFETY, I WANT THE DARK ELF!
D-D-DROW-DEAD TOO! KILLED-BY-WORG!
YOU'RE SURE?
I-SEE-WITH-MY-OWN-EYES!
DAMN, I WANTED HIS UGLY HEAD FER MESELF.
BUT WHAT'S DONE 'TIS DONE. LEAD ON, QUICKLING.

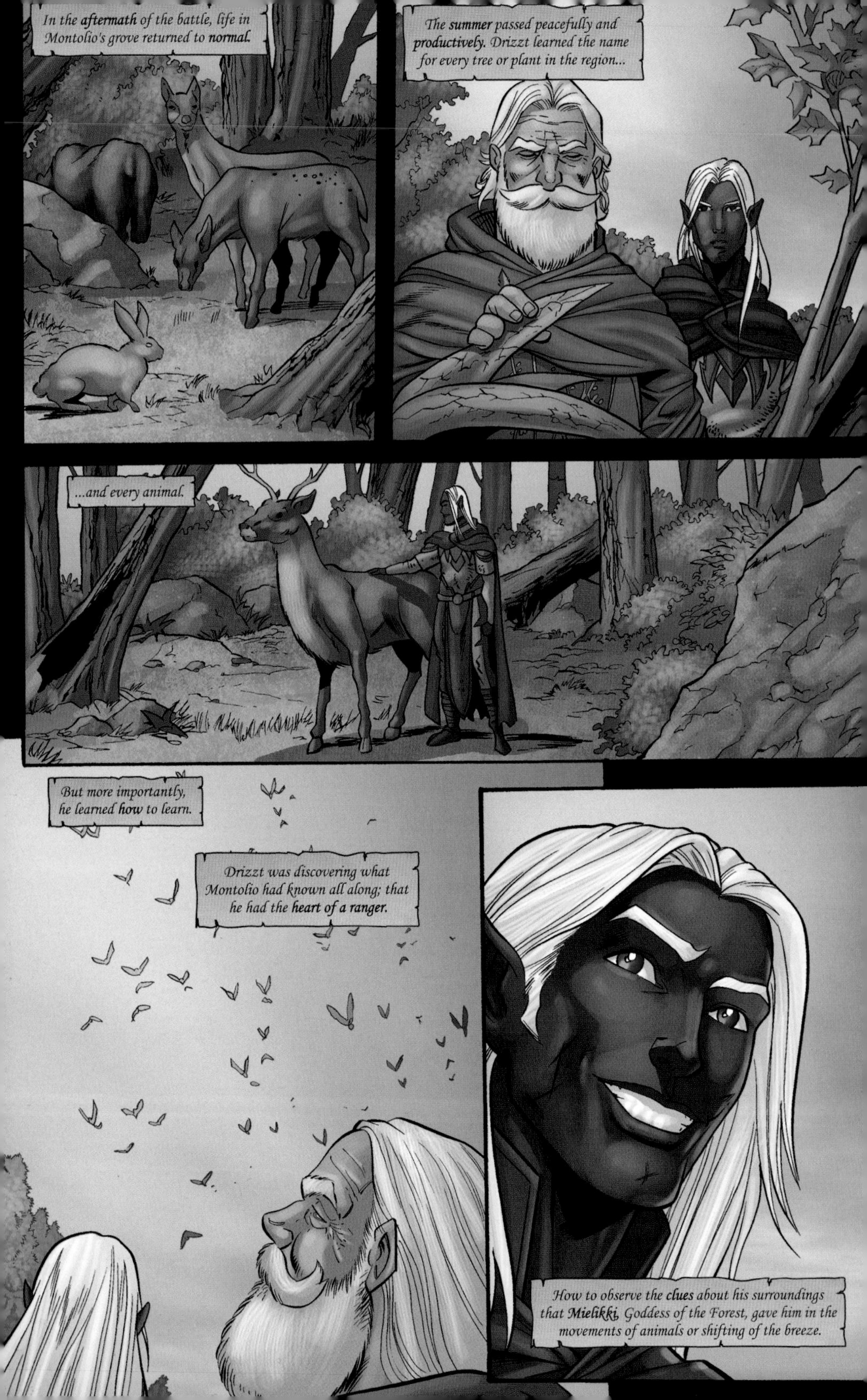
In the aftermath of the battle, life in Montolio's grove returned to normal.
The summer passed peacefully and productively. Drizzt learned the name for every tree or plant in the region...
...and every animal.
But more importantly, he learned how to learn.
Drizzt was discovering what Montolio had known all along; that he had the heart of a ranger.
How to observe the clues about his surroundings that Mielikki, Goddess of the Forest, gave him in the movements of animals or shifting of the breeze.

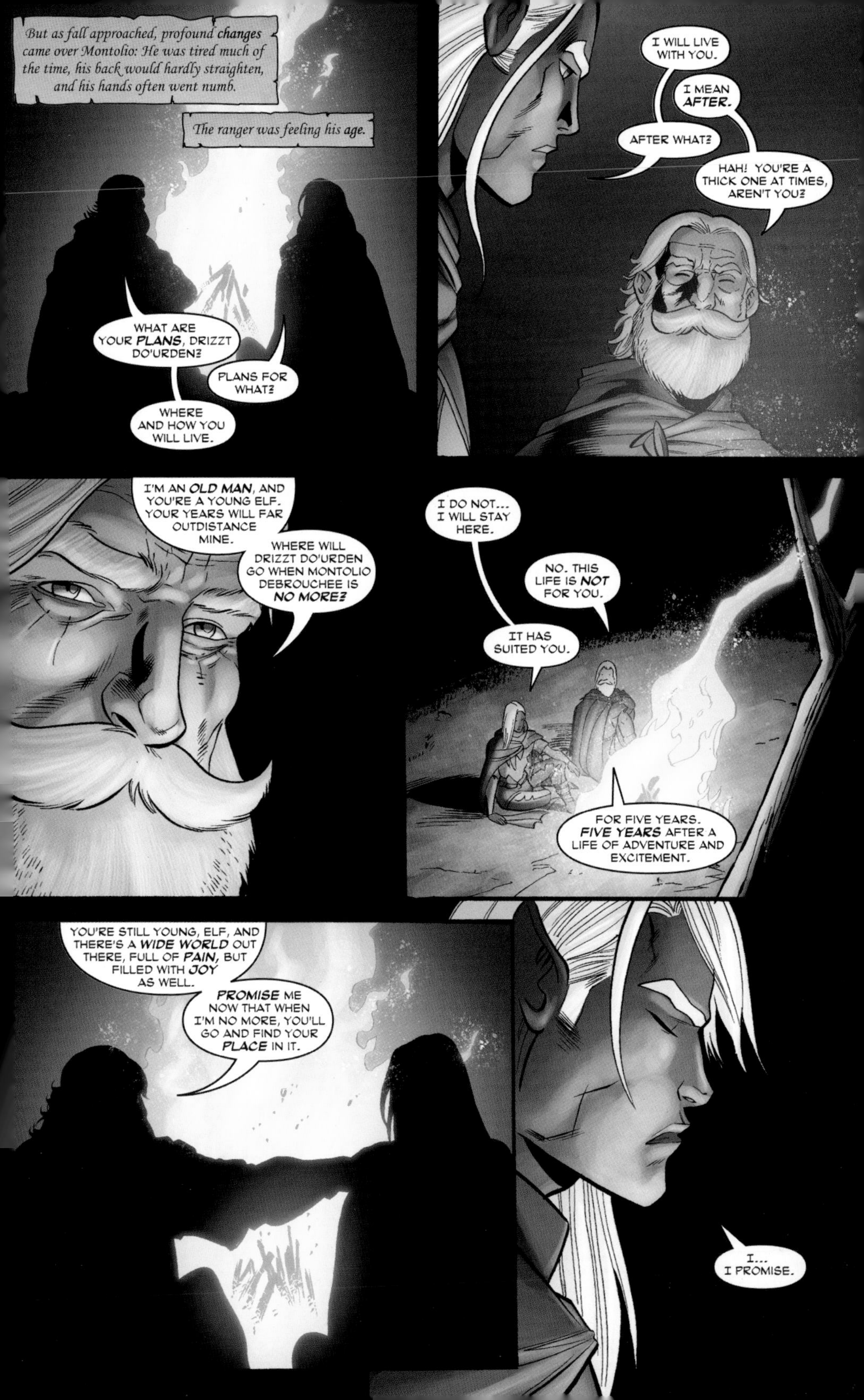

But as fall approached, profound changes came over Montolio: He was tired much of the time, his back would hardly straighten, and his hands often went numb.
The ranger was feeling his age.
WHAT ARE YOUR PLANS, DRIZZT DO'URDEN?
PLANS FOR WHAT?
WHERE AND HOW YOU WILL LIVE.
I WILL LIVE WITH YOU.
I MEAN AFTER.
AFTER WHAT?
HAH! YOU'RE A THICK ONE AT TIMES, AREN'T YOU?
I'M AN OLD MAN, AND YOU'RE A YOUNG ELF. YOUR YEARS WILL FAR OUTDISTANCE MINE.
WHERE WILL DRIZZT DO'URDEN GO WHEN MONTOLIO DEBROUCHEE IS NO MORE?
I DO NOT... I WILL STAY HERE.
NO. THIS LIFE IS NOT FOR YOU.
IT HAS SUITED YOU.
FOR FIVE YEARS. FIVE YEARS AFTER A LIFE OF ADVENTURE AND EXCITEMENT.
YOU'RE STILL YOUNG, ELF, AND THERE'S A WIDE WORLD OUT THERE, FULL OF PAIN, BUT FILLED WITH JOY AS WELL.
PROMISE ME NOW THAT WHEN I'M NO MORE, YOU'LL GO AND FIND YOUR PLACE IN IT.
I... I PROMISE.

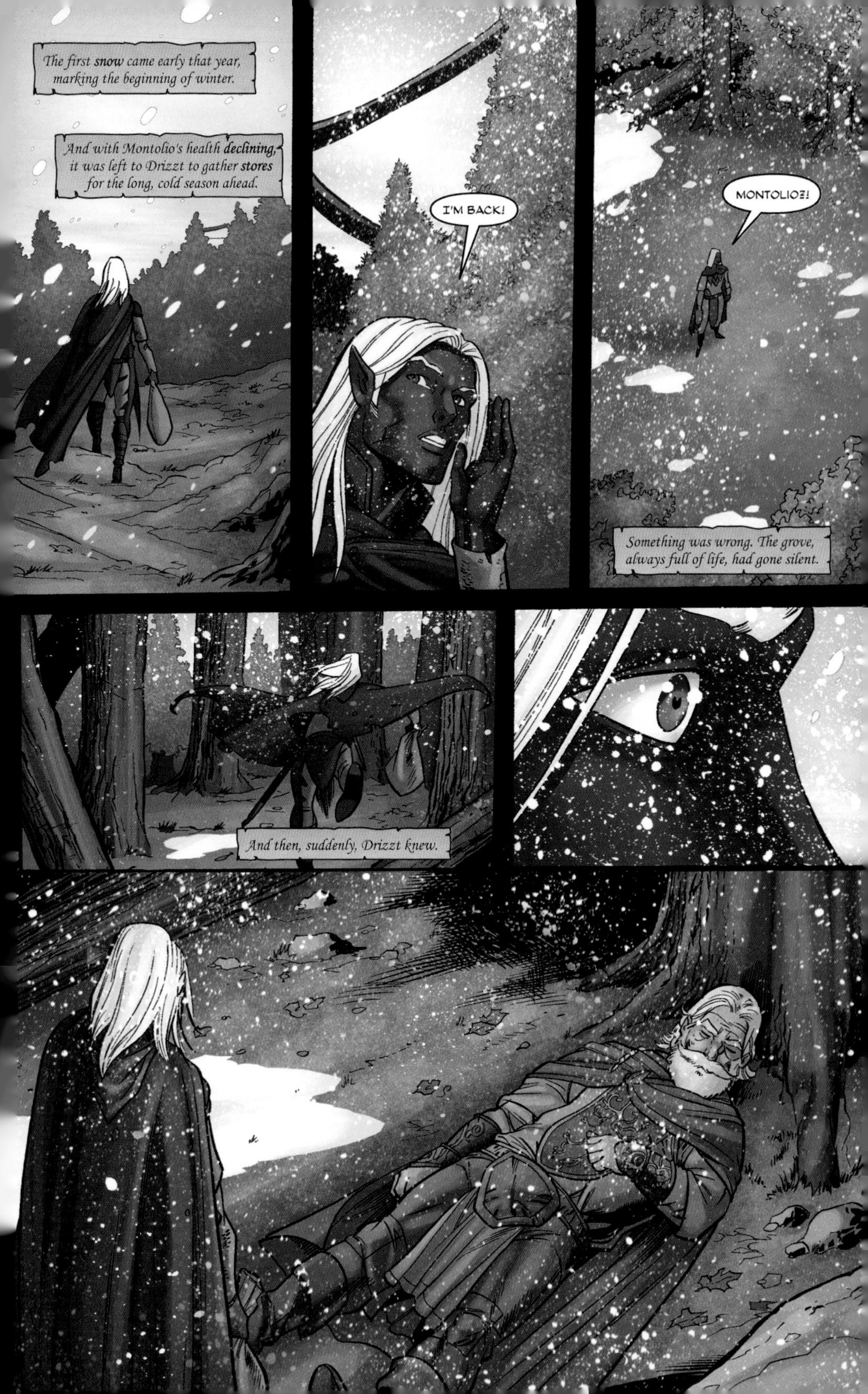
The first snow came early that year, marking the beginning of winter.
And with Montolio's health declining, it was left to Drizzt to gather stores for the long, cold season ahead.
I'M BACK!
MONTOLIO?!
Something was wrong. The grove, always full of life, had gone silent.
And then, suddenly, Drizzt knew.

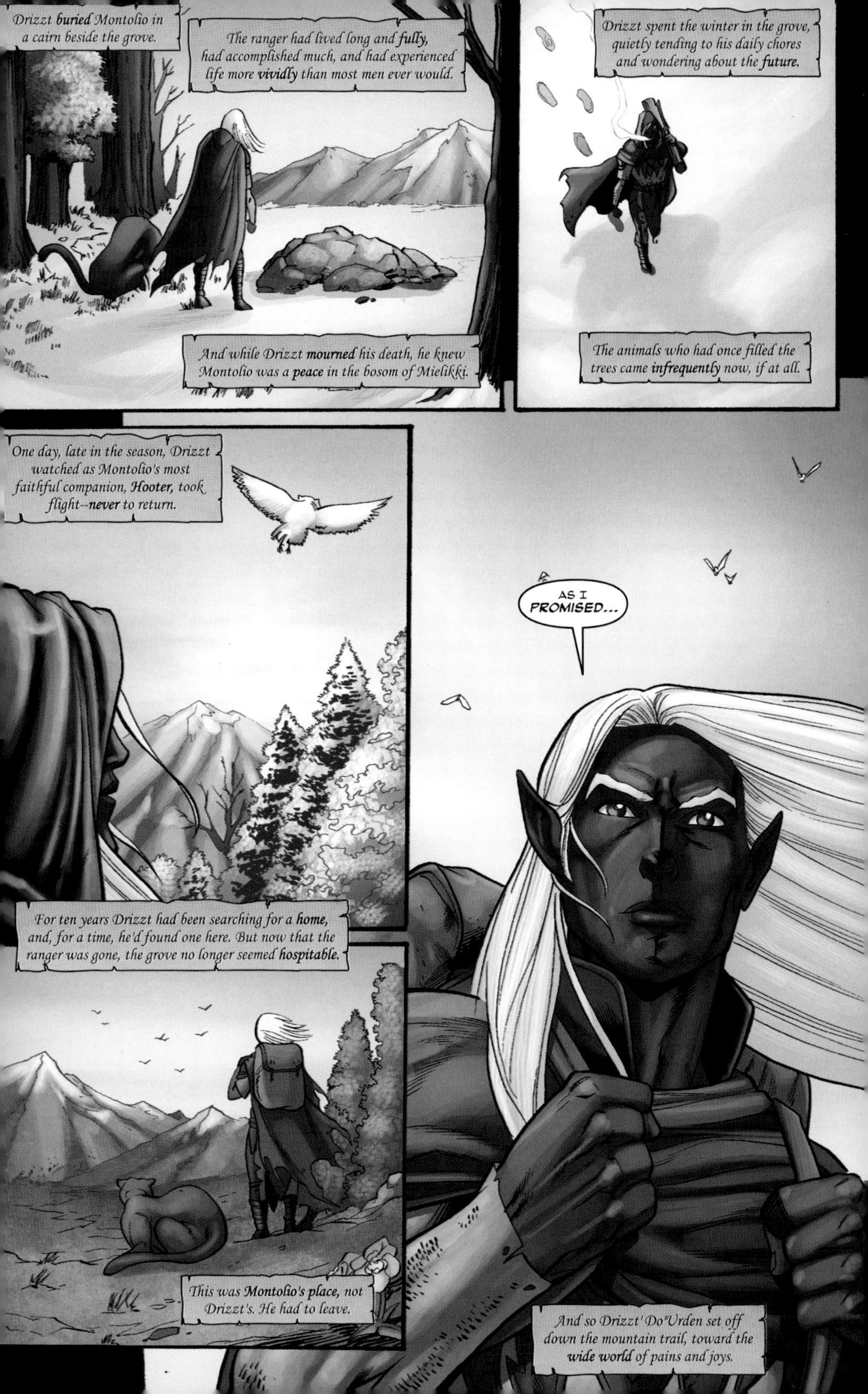
Drizzt buried Montolio in a cairn beside the grove.
The ranger had lived long and fully, had accomplished much, and had experienced life more vividly than most men ever would.
And while Drizzt mourned his death, he knew Montolio was a peace in the bosom of Mielikki.
Drizzt spent the winter in the grove, quietly tending to his daily chores and wondering about the future.
The animals who had once filled the trees came infrequently now, if at all.
One day, late in the season, Drizzt watched as Montolio's most faithful companion, Hooter, took flight--never to return.
For ten years Drizzt had been searching for a home, and, for a time, he'd found one here. But now that the ranger was gone, the grove no longer seemed hospitable.
This was Montolio's place, not Drizzt's. He had to leave.
AS I PROMISED...
And so Drizzt' Do'Urden set off down the mountain trail, toward the wide world of pains and joys.

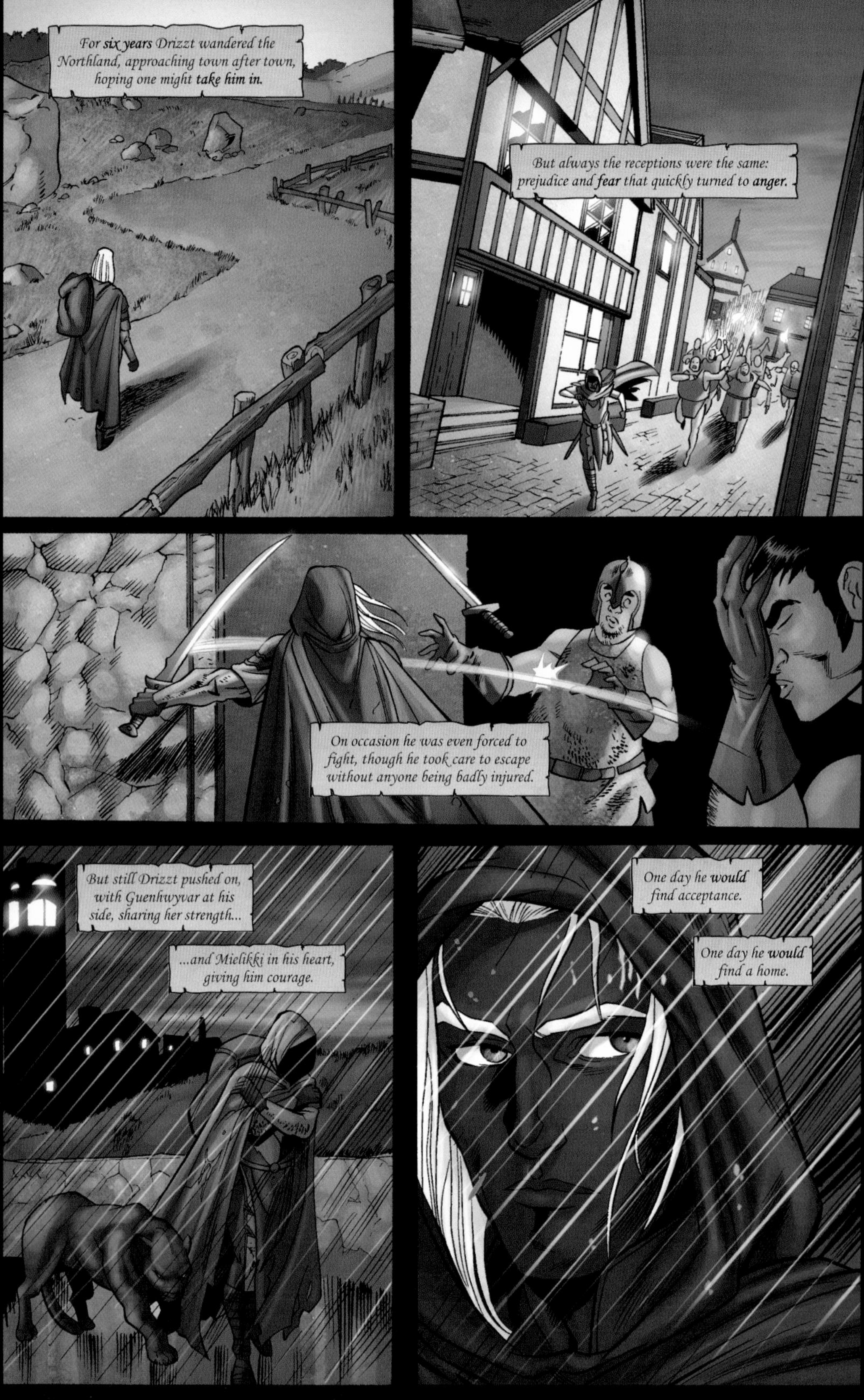
For six years Drizzt wandered the Northland, approaching town after town, hoping one might take him in.
But always the receptions were the same: prejudice and fear that quickly turned to anger.
On occasion he was even forced to fight, though he took care to escape without anyone being badly injured.
But still Drizzt pushed on, with Guenhwyvar at his side, sharing her strength...
...and Mielikki in his heart, giving him courage.
One day he would find acceptance.
One day he would find a home.

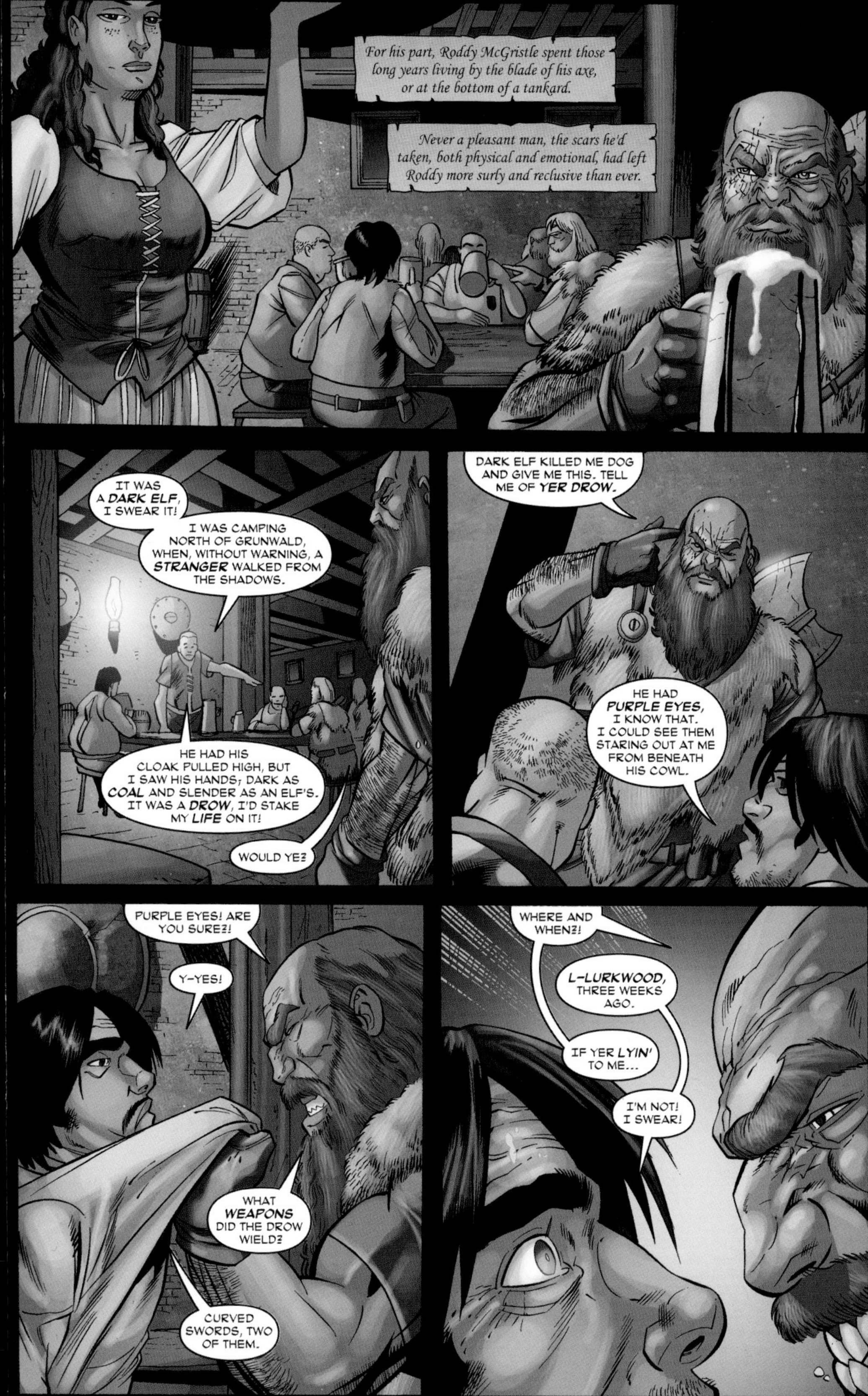
For his part, Roddy McGristle spent those long years living by the blade of his axe, or at the bottom of a tankard.
Never a pleasant man, the scars he'd taken, both physical and emotional, had left Roddy more surly and reclusive than ever.
IT WAS A DARK ELF, I SWEAR IT!
I WAS CAMPING NORTH OF GRUNWALD, WHEN, WITHOUT WARNING, A STRANGER WALKED FROM THE SHADOWS.
HE HAD HIS CLOAK PULLED HIGH, BUT I SAW HIS HANDS; DARK AS COAL AND SLENDER AS AN ELF'S. IT WAS A DROW, I'D STAKE MY LIFE ON IT!
WOULD YE?
DARK ELF KILLED ME DOG AND GIVE ME THIS. TELL ME OF YER DROW.
HE HAD PURPLE EYES, I KNOW THAT. I COULD SEE THEM STARING OUT AT ME FROM BENEATH HIS COWL.
PURPLE EYES! ARE YOU SURE?!
Y-YES!
WHAT WEAPONS DID THE DROW WIELD?
CURVED SWORDS, TWO OF THEM.
WHERE AND WHEN?!
L-LURKWOOD, THREE WEEKS AGO.
IF YER LYIN' TO ME...
I'M NOT! I SWEAR!

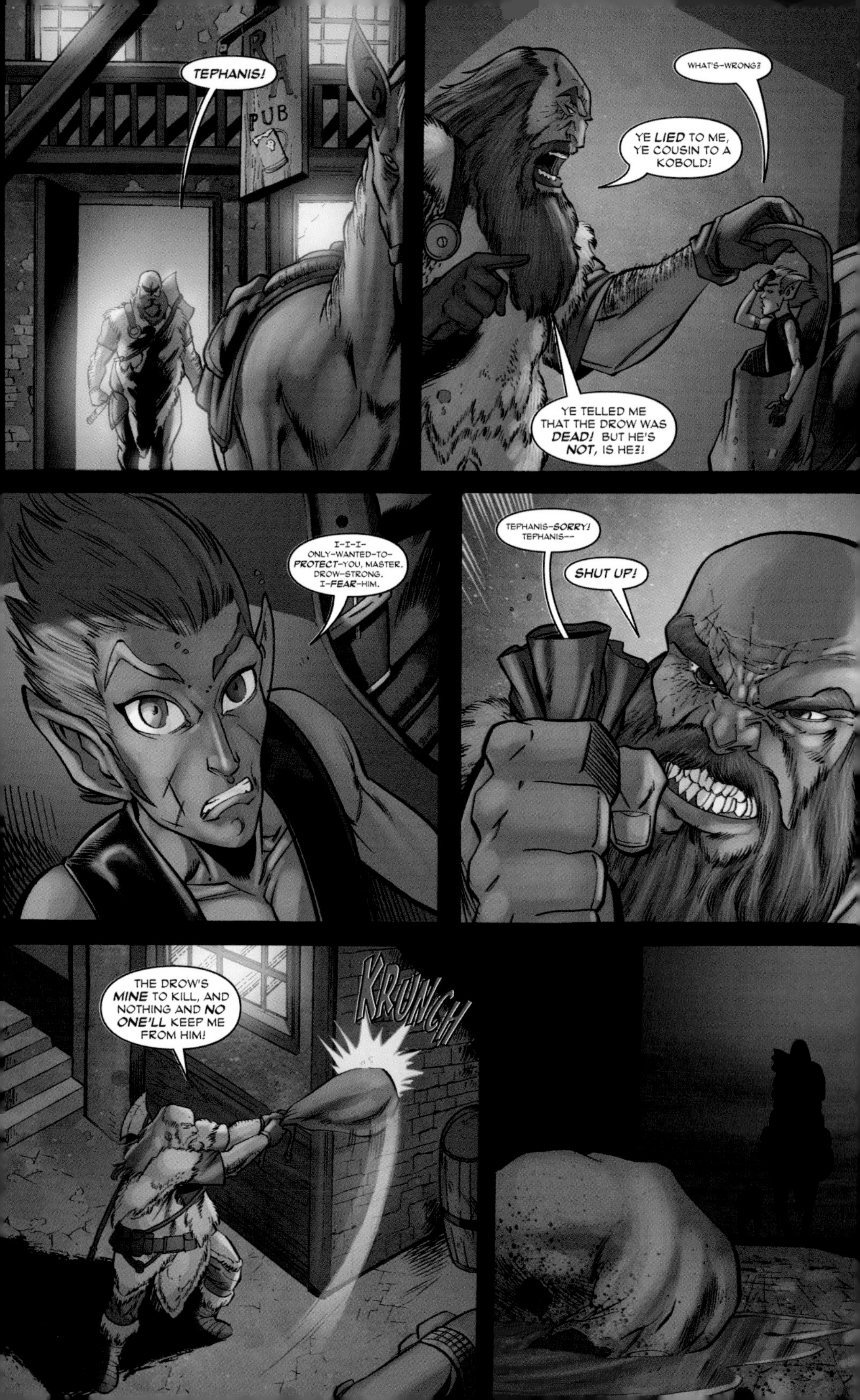
TEPHANIS!
PUB
WHAT'S-WRONG?
YE LIED TO ME, YE COUSIN TO A KOBOLD!
YE TELLED ME THAT THE DROW WAS DEAD! BUT HE'S NOT, IS HE?!
I-I-I-ONLY-WANTED-TO-PROTECT-YOU, MASTER. DROW-STRONG. I-FEAR-HIM.
TEPHANIS-SORRY! TEPHANIS--
SHUT UP!
THE DROW'S MINE TO KILL, AND NOTHING AND NO ONE'LL KEEP ME FROM HIM!
KRUNCH

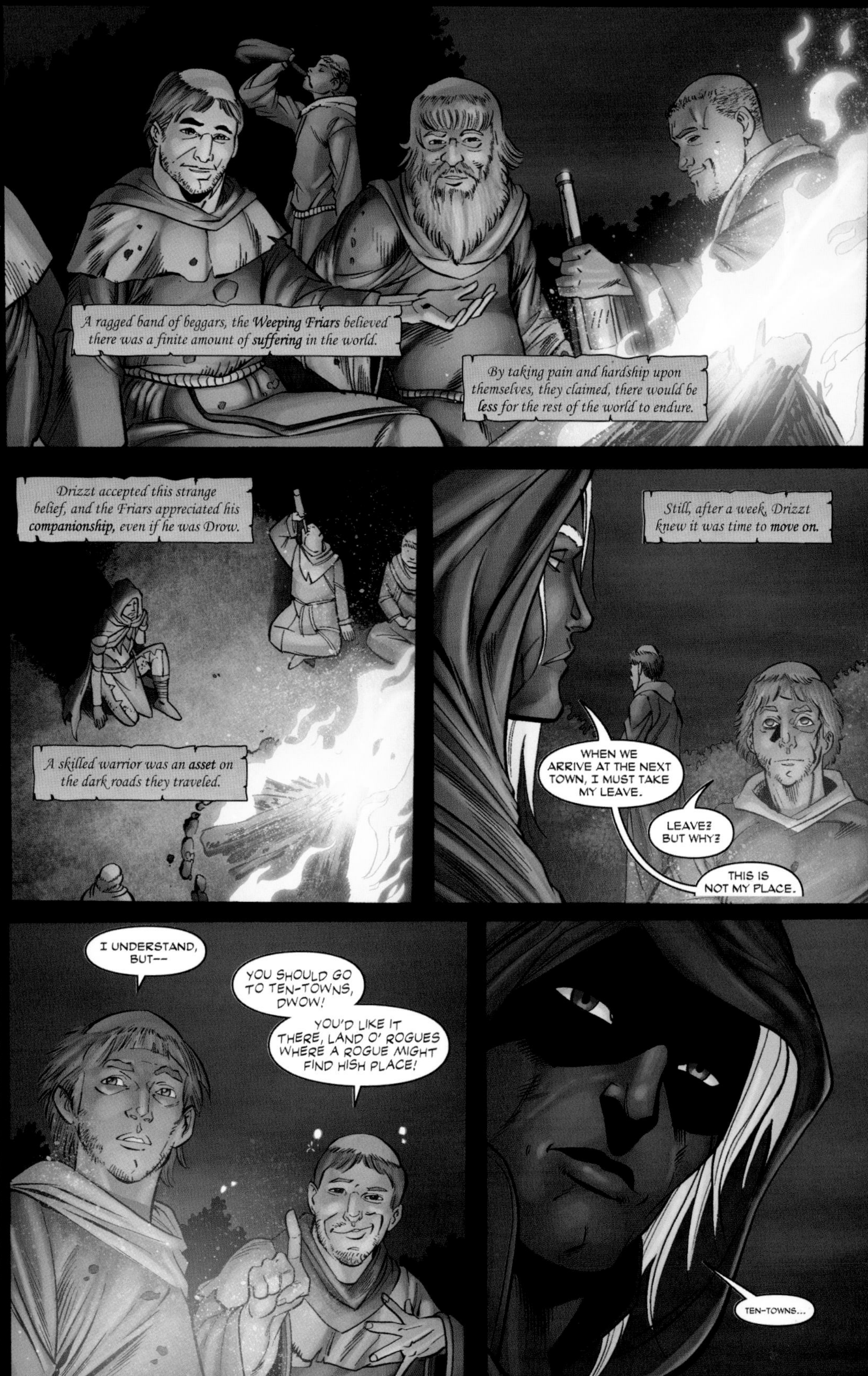
A ragged band of beggars, the Weeping Friars believed there was a finite amount of suffering in the world.
By taking pain and hardship upon themselves, they claimed, there would be less for the rest of the world to endure.
Drizzt accepted this strange belief, and the Friars appreciated his companionship, even if he was Drow.
A skilled warrior was an asset on the dark roads they traveled.
Still, after a week, Drizzt knew it was time to move on.
WHEN WE ARRIVE AT THE NEXT TOWN, I MUST TAKE MY LEAVE.
LEAVE? BUT WHY?
THIS IS NOT MY PLACE.
I UNDERSTAND, BUT--
YOU SHOULD GO TO TEN-TOWNS, DWOW!
YOU'D LIKE IT THERE, LAND O' ROGUES WHERE A ROGUE MIGHT FIND HISH PLACE!
TEN-TOWNS...

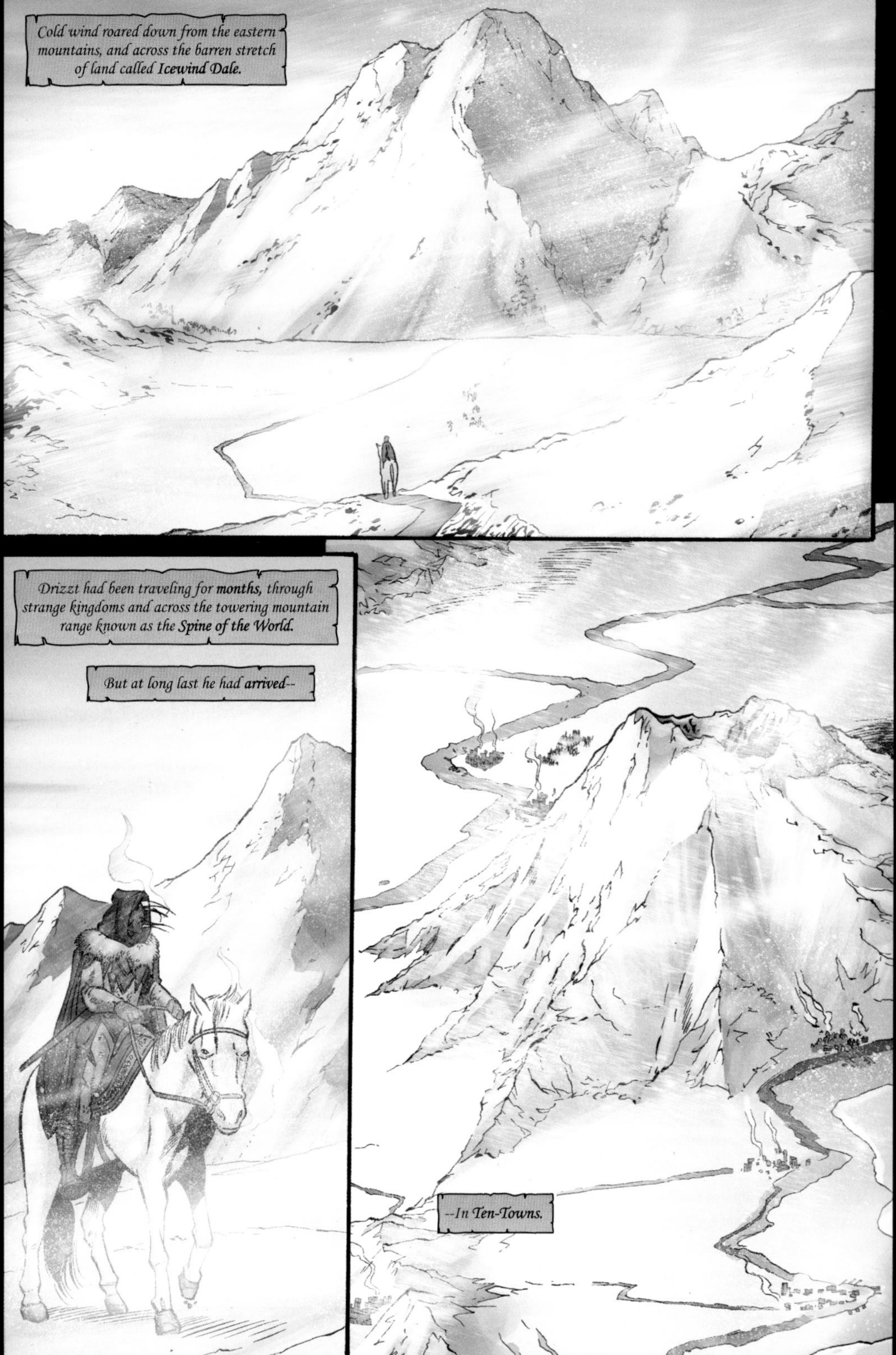
Cold wind roared down from the eastern mountains, and across the barren stretch of land called Icewind Dale.
Drizzt had been traveling for months, through strange kingdoms and across the towering mountain range known as the Spine of the World.
But at long last he had arrived--
--In Ten-Towns.

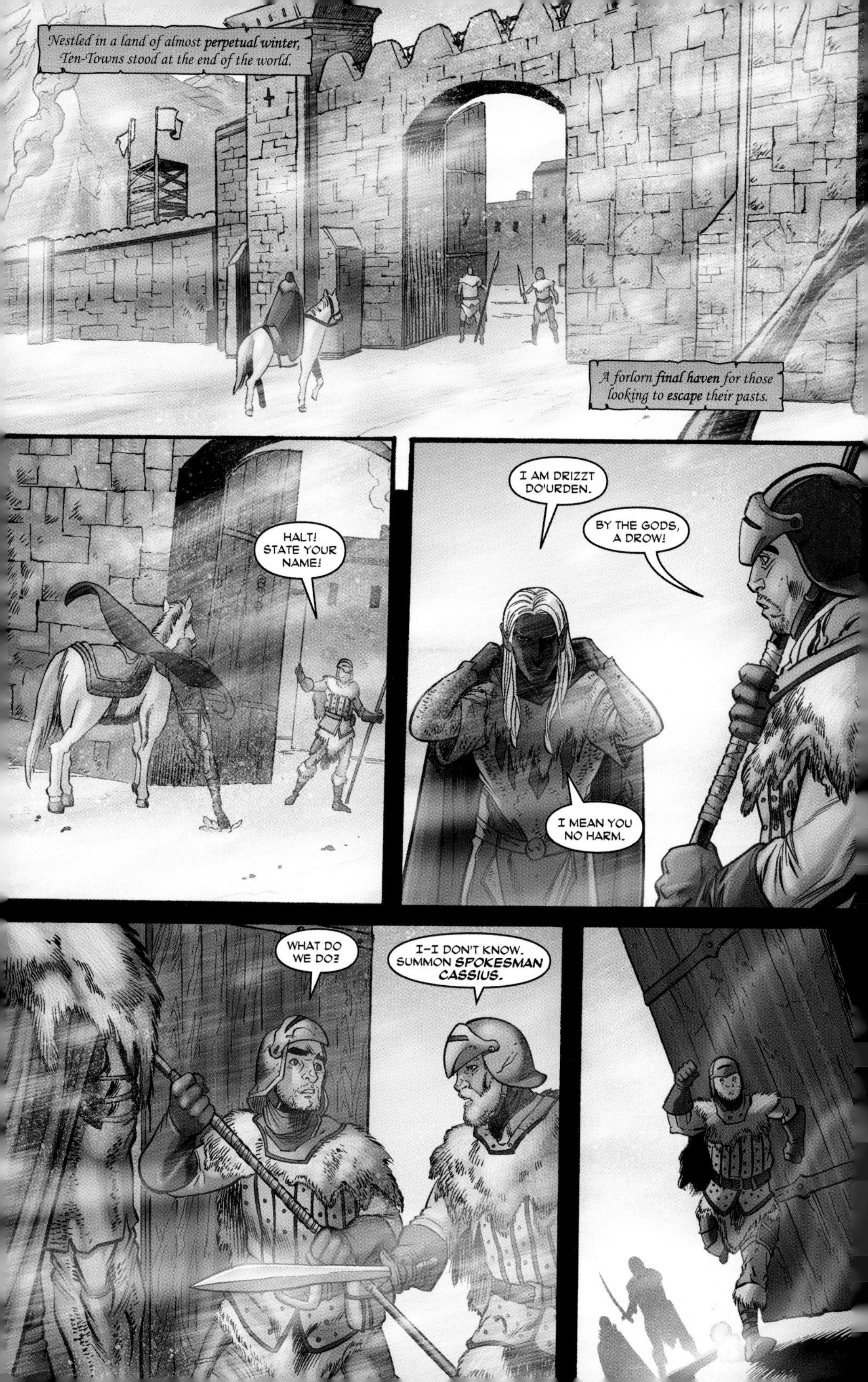

Nestled in a land of almost perpetual winter, Ten-Towns stood at the end of the world.
A forlorn final haven for those looking to escape their pasts.
HALT! STATE YOUR NAME!
I AM DRIZZT DO'URDEN.
BY THE GODS, A DROW!
I MEAN YOU NO HARM.
WHAT DO WE DO?
I-I DON'T KNOW. SUMMON SPOKESMAN CASSIUS.

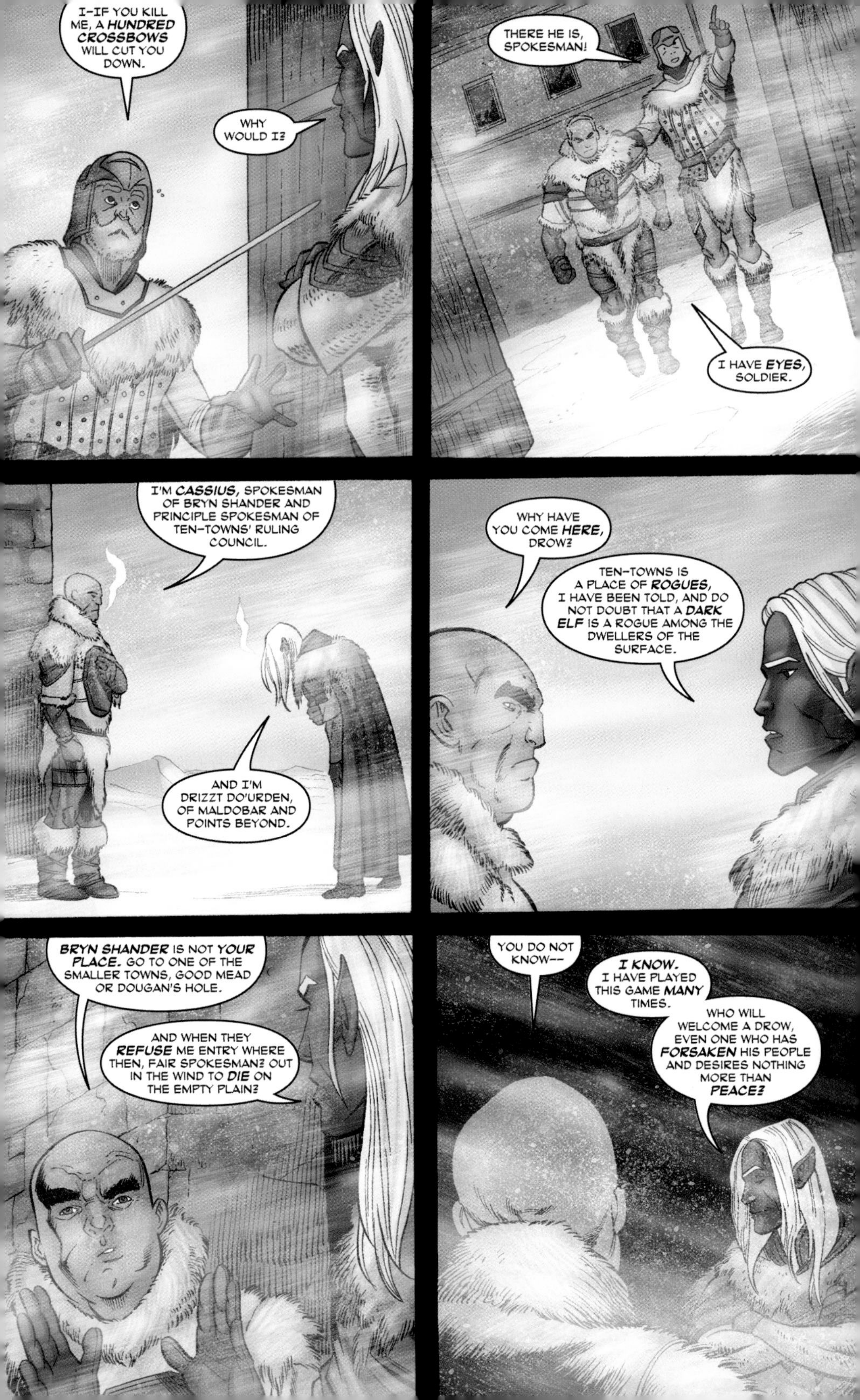

I-IF YOU KILL ME, A HUNDRED CROSSBOWS WILL CUT YOU DOWN.
WHY WOULD I?
THERE HE IS, SPOKESMAN!
I HAVE EYES, SOLDIER.
I'M CASSIUS, SPOKESMAN OF BRYN SHANDER AND PRINCIPLE SPOKESMAN OF TEN-TOWNS' RULING COUNCIL.
AND I'M DRIZZT DO'URDEN, OF MALDOBAR AND POINTS BEYOND.
WHY HAVE YOU COME HERE, DROW?
TEN-TOWNS IS A PLACE OF ROGUES, I HAVE BEEN TOLD, AND DO NOT DOUBT THAT A DARK ELF IS A ROGUE AMONG THE DWELLERS OF THE SURFACE.
BRYN SHANDER IS NOT YOUR PLACE. GO TO ONE OF THE SMALLER TOWNS, GOOD MEAD OR DOUGAN'S HOLE.
AND WHEN THEY REFUSE ME ENTRY WHERE THEN, FAIR SPOKESMAN? OUT IN THE WIND TO DIE ON THE EMPTY PLAIN?
YOU DO NOT KNOW--
I KNOW. I HAVE PLAYED THIS GAME MANY TIMES.
WHO WILL WELCOME A DROW, EVEN ONE WHO HAS FORSAKEN HIS PEOPLE AND DESIRES NOTHING MORE THAN PEACE?

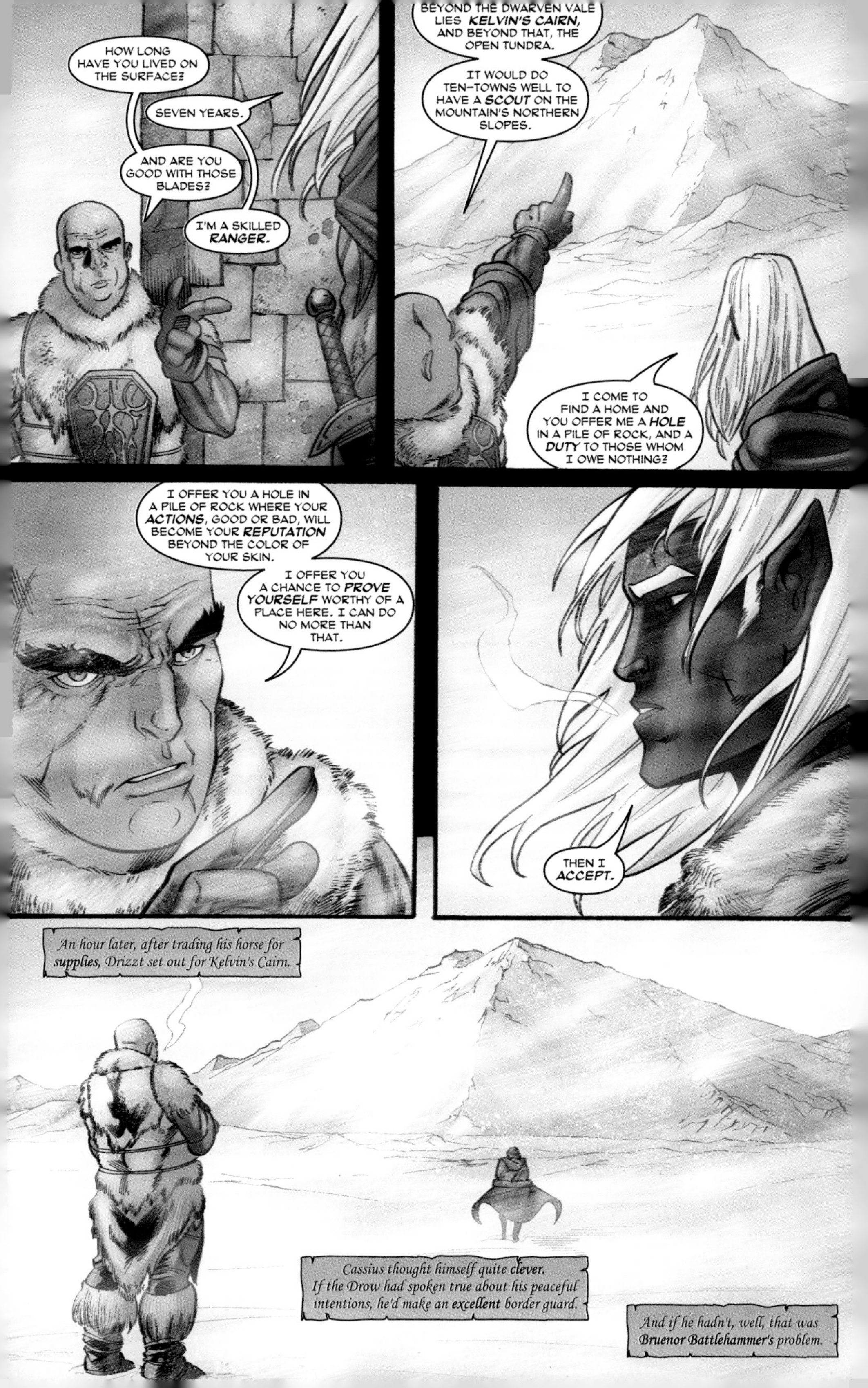
HOW LONG HAVE YOU LIVED ON THE SURFACE?
SEVEN YEARS.
AND ARE YOU GOOD WITH THOSE BLADES?
I'M A SKILLED RANGER.
BEYOND THE DWARVEN VALE LIES KELVIN'S CAIRN, AND BEYOND THAT, THE OPEN TUNDRA.
IT WOULD DO TEN-TOWNS WELL TO HAVE A SCOUT ON THE MOUNTAIN'S NORTHERN SLOPES.
I COME TO FIND A HOME AND YOU OFFER ME A HOLE IN A PILE OF ROCK, AND A DUTY TO THOSE WHOM I OWE NOTHING?
I OFFER YOU A HOLE IN A PILE OF ROCK WHERE YOUR ACTIONS, GOOD OR BAD, WILL BECOME YOUR REPUTATION BEYOND THE COLOR OF YOUR SKIN.
I OFFER YOU A CHANCE TO PROVE YOURSELF WORTHY OF A PLACE HERE. I CAN DO NO MORE THAN THAT.
THEN I ACCEPT.
An hour later, after trading his horse for supplies, Drizzt set out for Kelvin's Cairn.
Cassius thought himself quite clever. If the Drow had spoken true about his peaceful intentions, he'd make an excellent border guard.
And if he hadn't, well, that was Bruenor Battlehammer's problem.

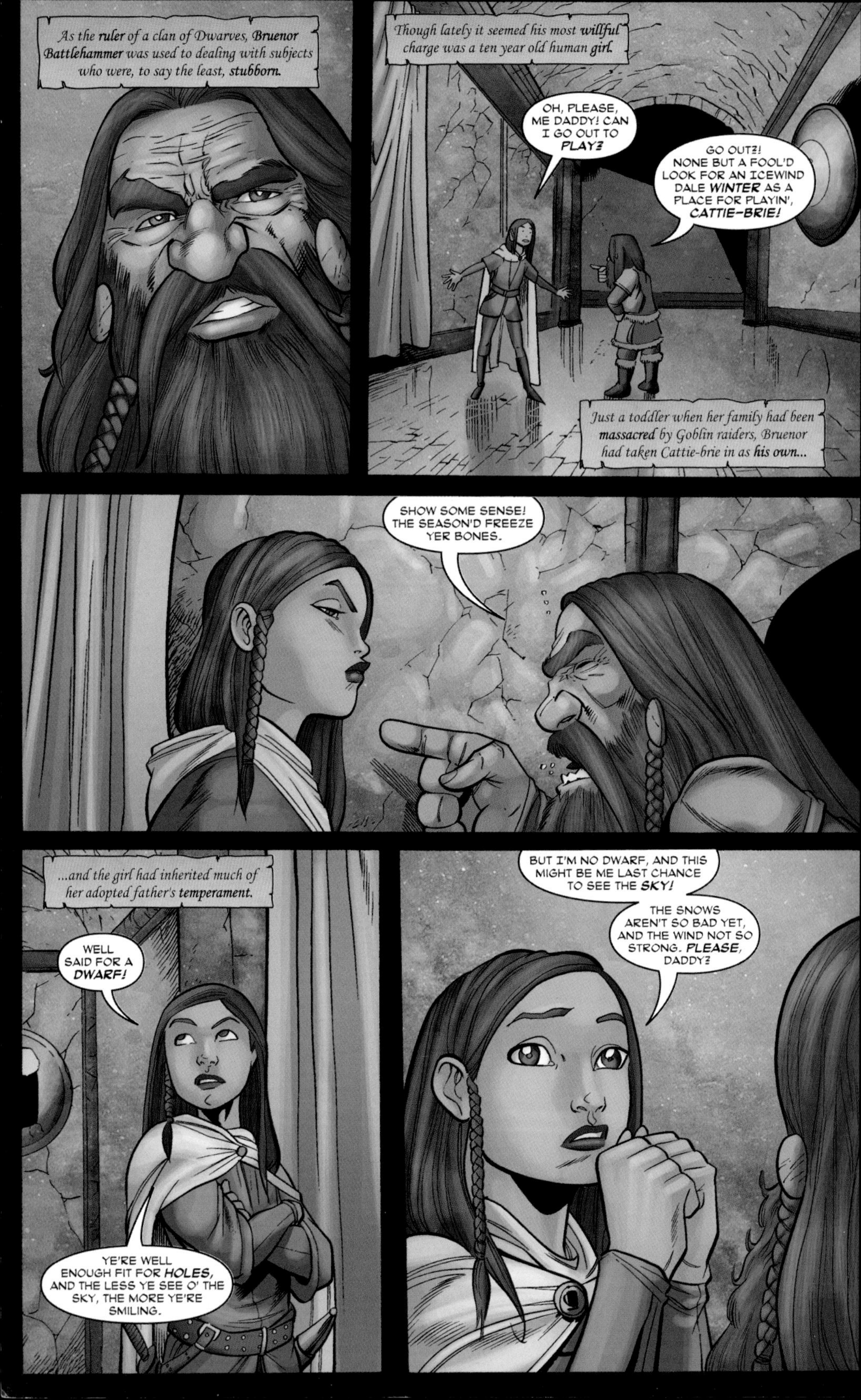
As the ruler of a clan of Dwarves, Bruenor Battlehammer was used to dealing with subjects who were, to say the least, stubborn.
Though lately it seemed his most willful charge was a ten year old human girl.
OH, PLEASE, ME DADDY! CAN I GO OUT TO PLAY?
GO OUT?! NONE BUT A FOOL'D LOOK FOR AN ICEWIND DALE WINTER AS A PLACE FOR PLAYIN', CATTIE-BRIE!
Just a toddler when her family had been massacred by Goblin raiders, Bruenor had taken Cattie-brie in as his own...
SHOW SOME SENSE! THE SEASON'D FREEZE YER BONES.
...and the girl had inherited much of her adopted father's temperament.
WELL SAID FOR A DWARF!
YE'RE WELL ENOUGH FIT FOR HOLES, AND THE LESS YE SEE O' THE SKY, THE MORE YE'RE SMILING.
BUT I'M NO DWARF, AND THIS MIGHT BE ME LAST CHANCE TO SEE THE SKY!
THE SNOWS AREN'T SO BAD YET, AND THE WIND NOT SO STRONG. PLEASE, DADDY?

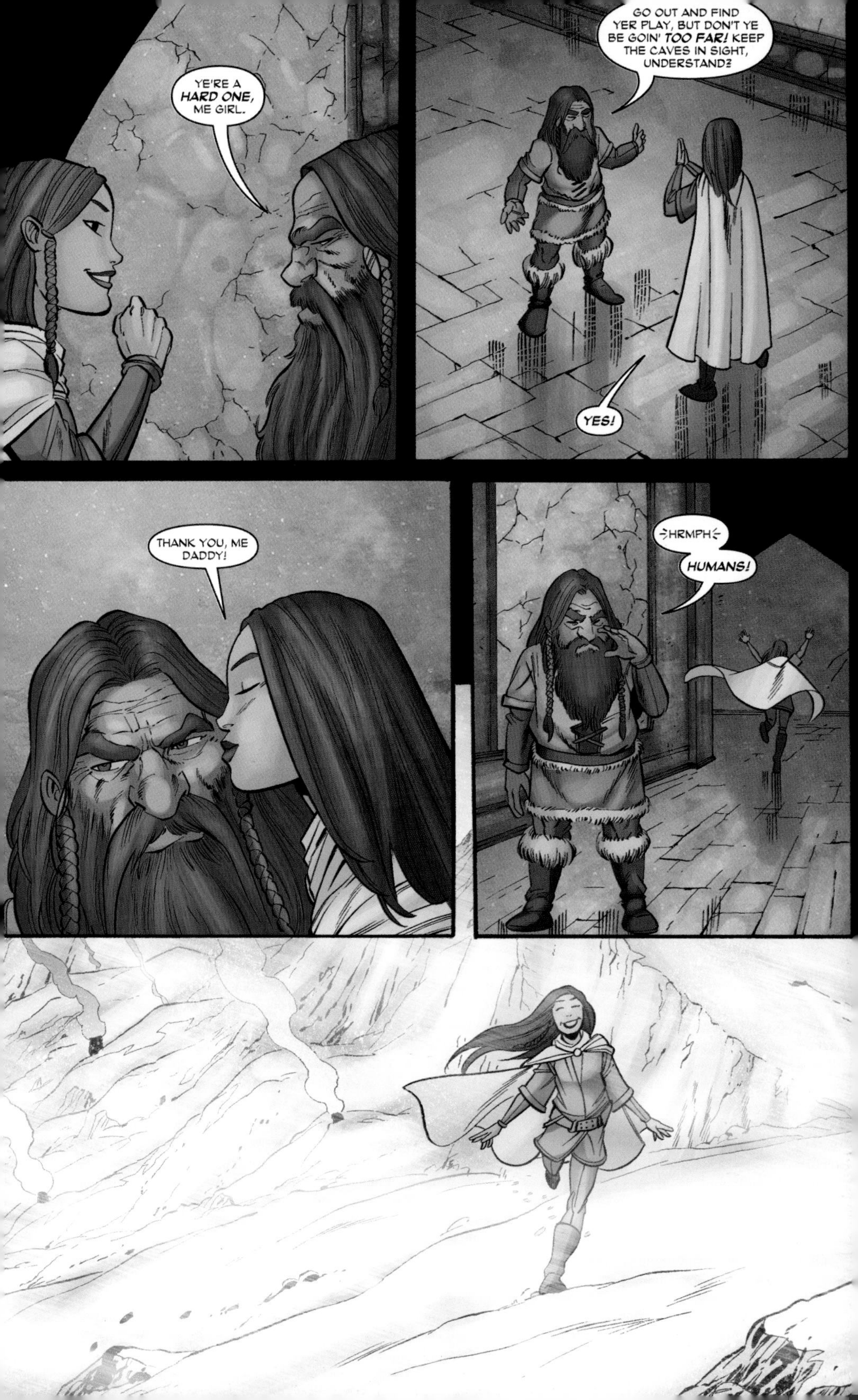
YE'RE A HARD ONE, ME GIRL.
GO OUT AND FIND YER PLAY, BUT DON'T YE BE GOIN' TOO FAR! KEEP THE CAVES IN SIGHT, UNDERSTAND?
YES!
THANK YOU, ME DADDY!
HRMPH
HUMANS!

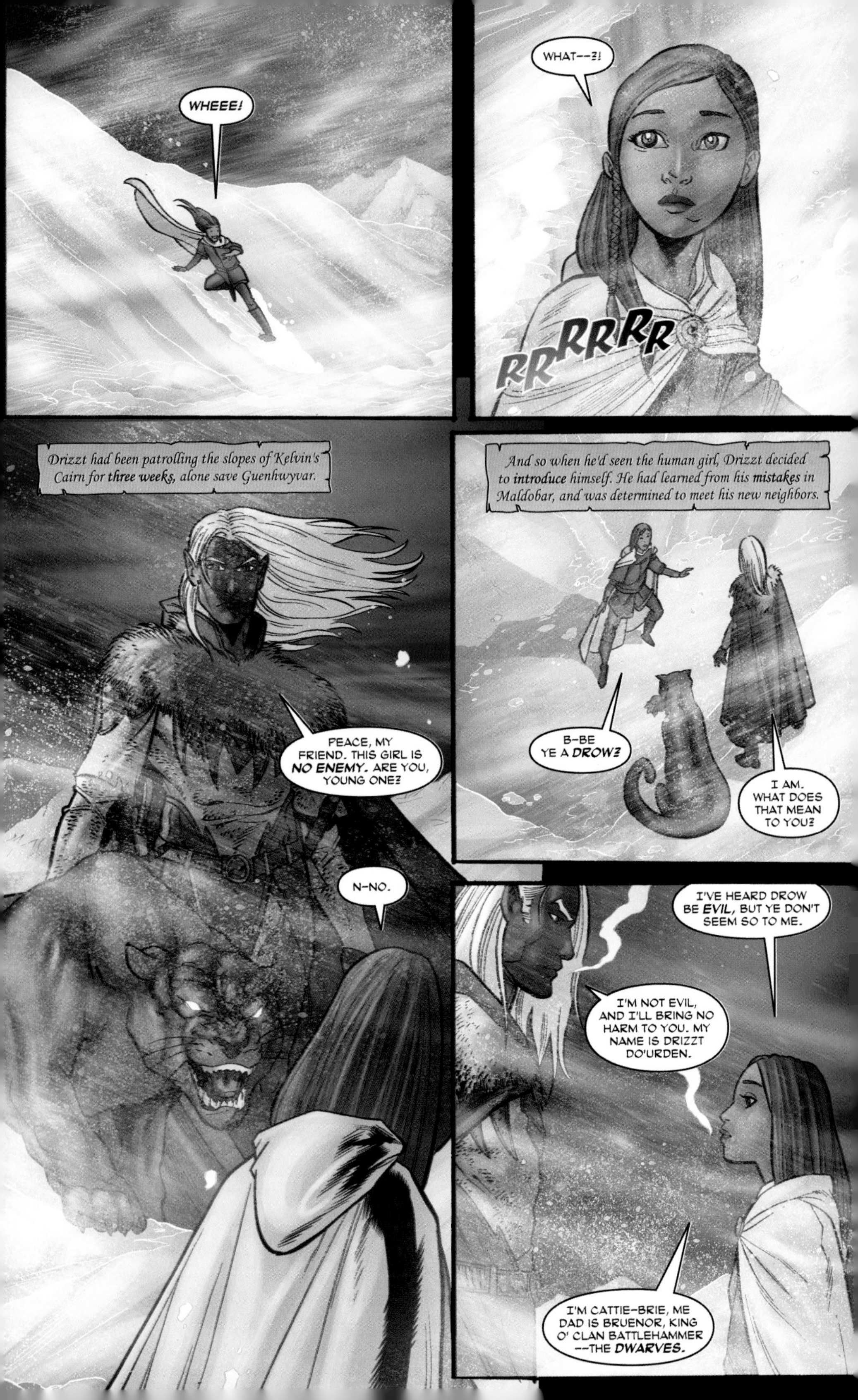
WHEEE!
WHAT--?!
RRRRRRR
Drizzt had been patrolling the slopes of Kelvin's Cairn for three weeks, alone save Guenhwyvar.
PEACE, MY FRIEND. THIS GIRL IS NO ENEMY. ARE YOU, YOUNG ONE?
N-NO.
And so when he'd seen the human girl, Drizzt decided to introduce himself. He had learned from his mistakes in Maldobar, and was determined to meet his new neighbors.
B-BE YE A DROW?
I AM. WHAT DOES THAT MEAN TO YOU?
I'VE HEARD DROW BE EVIL, BUT YE DON'T SEEM SO TO ME.
I'M NOT EVIL, AND I'LL BRING NO HARM TO YOU. MY NAME IS DRIZZT DO'URDEN.
I'M CATTIE-BRIE, ME DAD IS BRUENOR, KING O' CLAN BATTLEHAMMER --THE DWARVES.

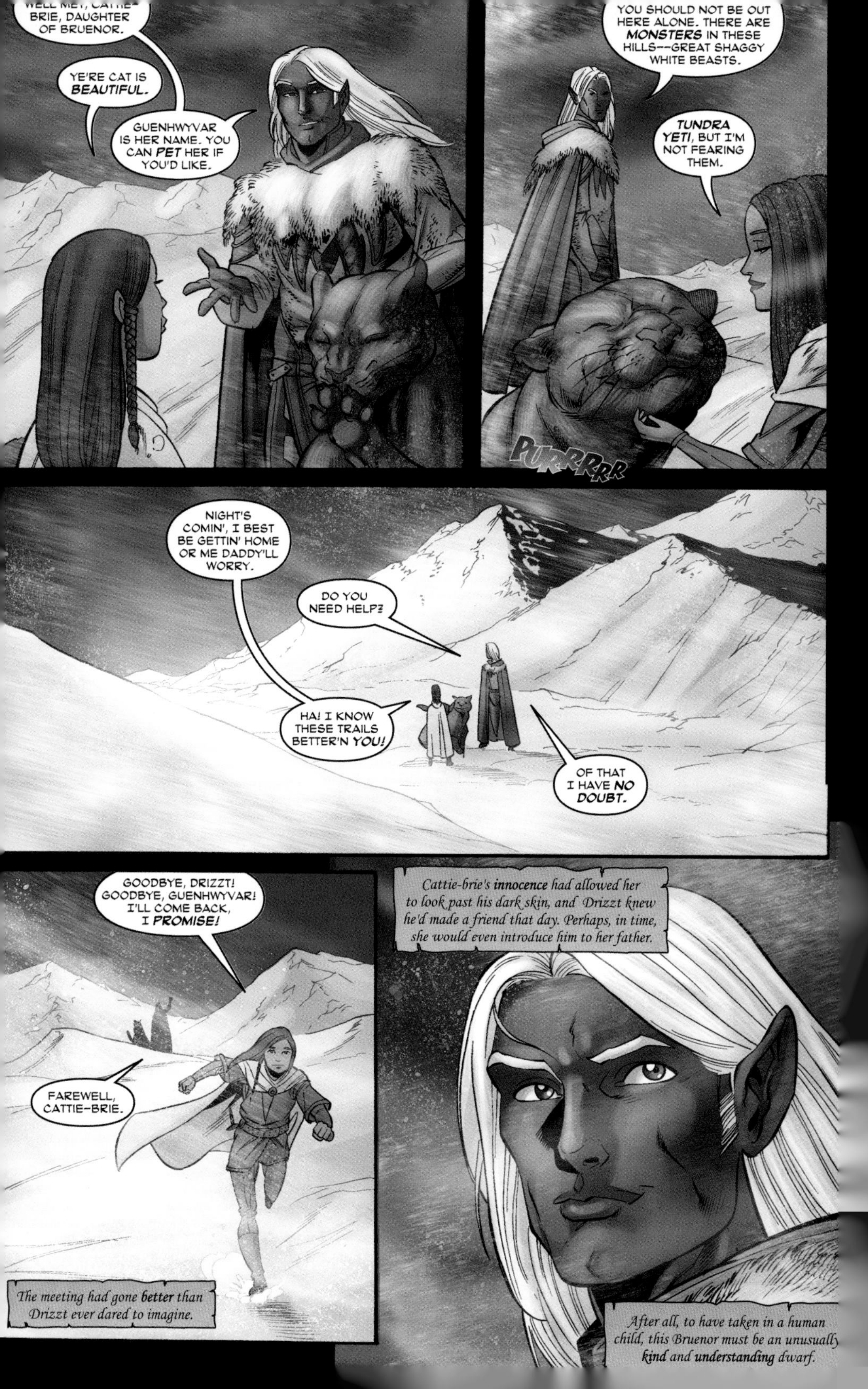
BRIE, DAUGHTER OF BRUENOR.
YE'RE CAT IS BEAUTIFUL.
GUENHWYVAR IS HER NAME. YOU CAN PET HER IF YOU'D LIKE.
YOU SHOULD NOT BE OUT HERE ALONE. THERE ARE MONSTERS IN THESE HILLS--GREAT SHAGGY WHITE BEASTS.
TUNDRA YETI, BUT I'M NOT FEARING THEM.
PURRRRR
NIGHT'S COMIN', I BEST BE GETTIN' HOME OR ME DADDY'LL WORRY.
DO YOU NEED HELP?
HA! I KNOW THESE TRAILS BETTER'N YOU!
OF THAT I HAVE NO DOUBT.
GOODBYE, DRIZZT! GOODBYE, GUENHWYVAR! I'LL COME BACK, I PROMISE!
FAREWELL, CATTIE-BRIE.
The meeting had gone better than Drizzt ever dared to imagine.
Cattie-brie's innocence had allowed her to look past his dark skin, and Drizzt knew he'd made a friend that day. Perhaps, in time, she would even introduce him to her father.
After all, to have taken in a human child, this Bruenor must be an unusuall kind and understanding dwarf.

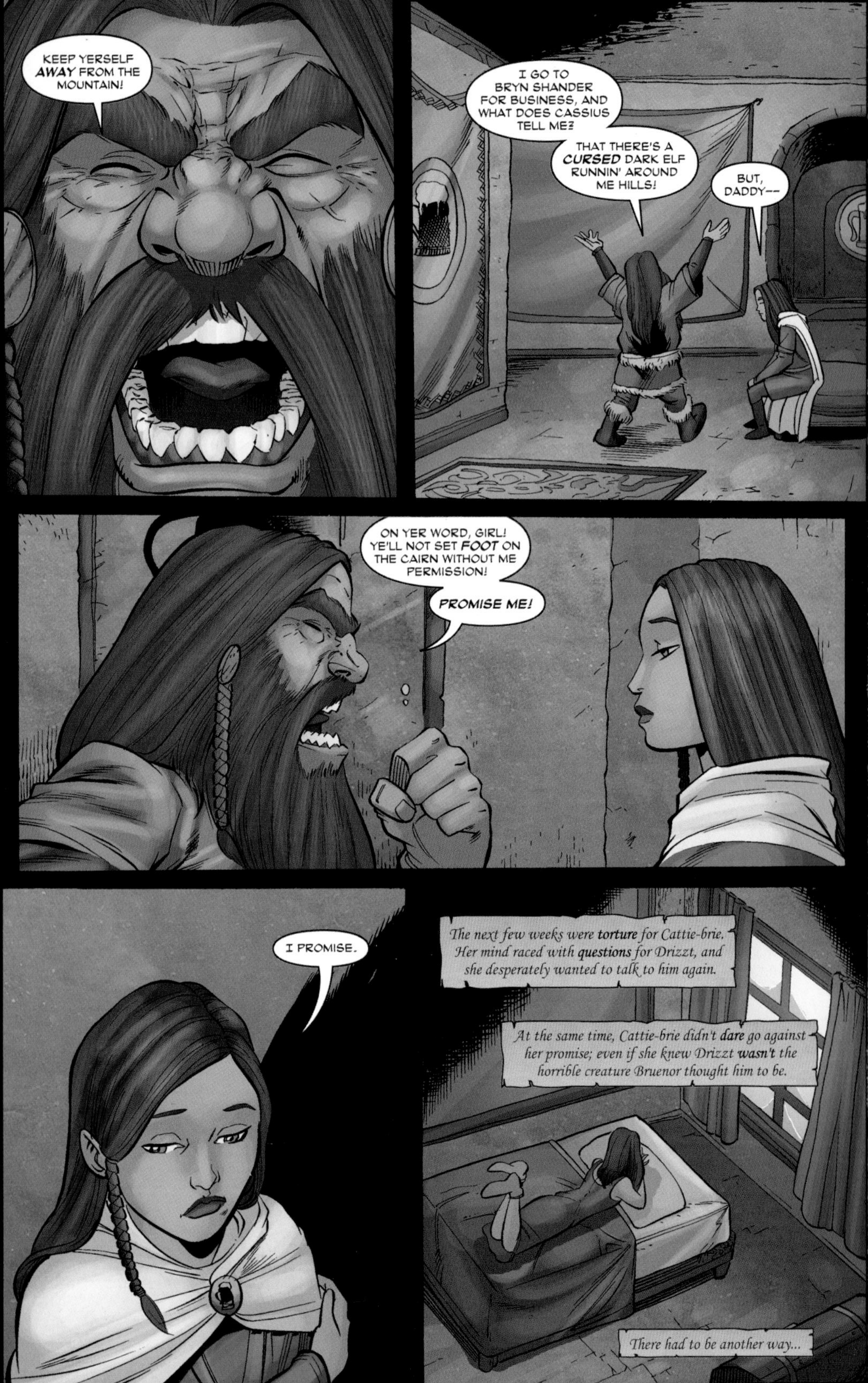
KEEP YERSELF AWAY FROM THE MOUNTAIN!
I GO TO BRYN SHANDER FOR BUSINESS, AND WHAT DOES CASSIUS TELL ME?
THAT THERE'S A CURSED DARK ELF RUNNIN' AROUND ME HILLS!
BUT, DADDY--
ON YER WORD, GIRL! YE'LL NOT SET FOOT ON THE CAIRN WITHOUT ME PERMISSION!
PROMISE ME!
I PROMISE.
The next few weeks were torture for Cattie-brie. Her mind raced with questions for Drizzt, and she desperately wanted to talk to him again.
At the same time, Cattie-brie didn't dare go against her promise; even if she knew Drizzt wasn't the horrible creature Bruenor thought him to be.
There had to be another way...

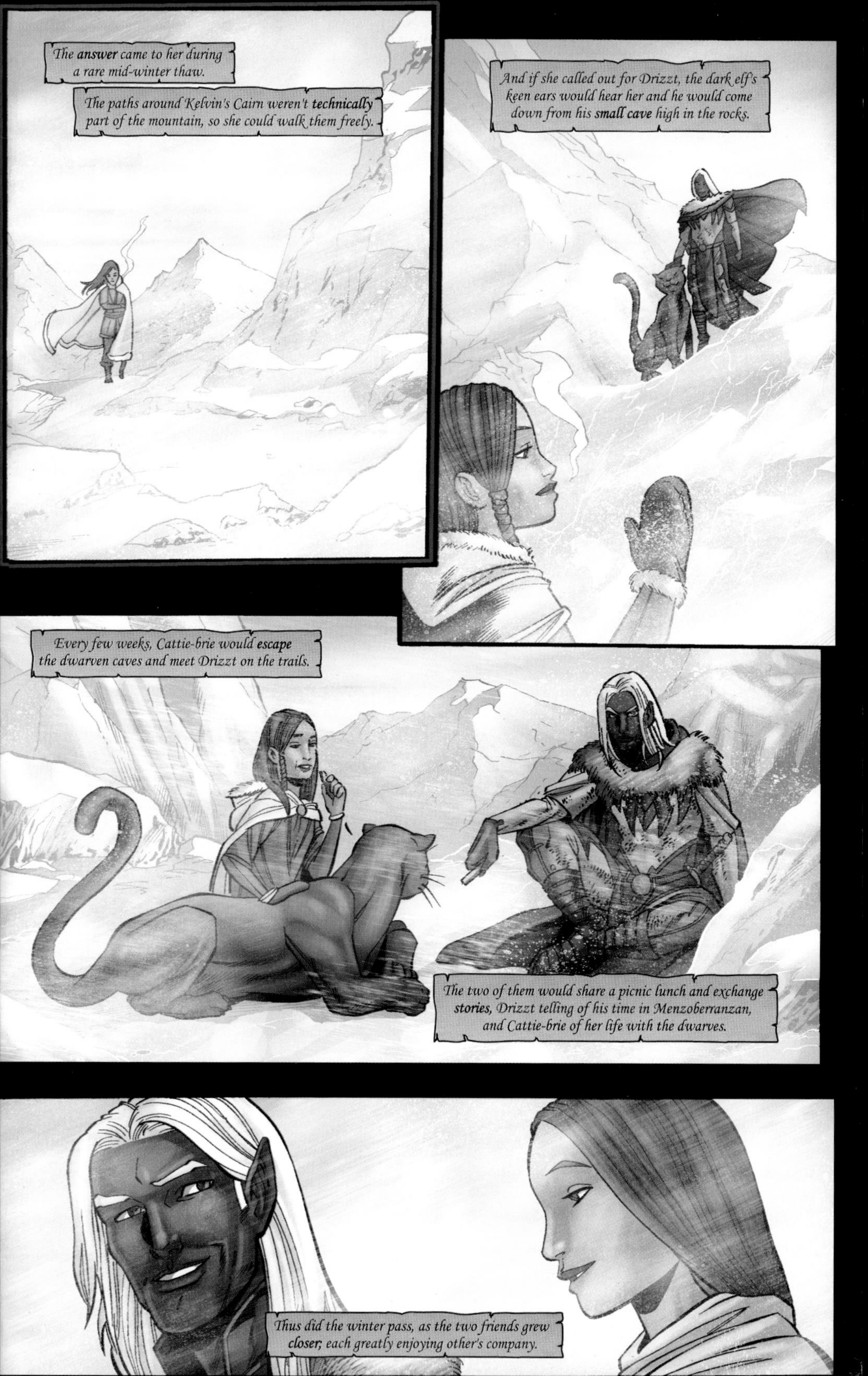

The **answer** came to her during a rare mid-winter thaw.
The paths around Kelvin's Cairn weren't **technically** part of the mountain, so she could walk them freely.
And if she called out for Drizzt, the dark elf's keen ears would hear her and he would come down from his **small cave** high in the rocks.
Every few weeks, Cattie-brie would **escape** the dwarven caves and meet Drizzt on the trails.
The two of them would share a picnic lunch and exchange **stories**, Drizzt telling of his time in Menzoberranzan, and Cattie-brie of her life with the dwarves.
Thus did the winter pass, as the two friends grew **closer**, each greatly enjoying other's company.

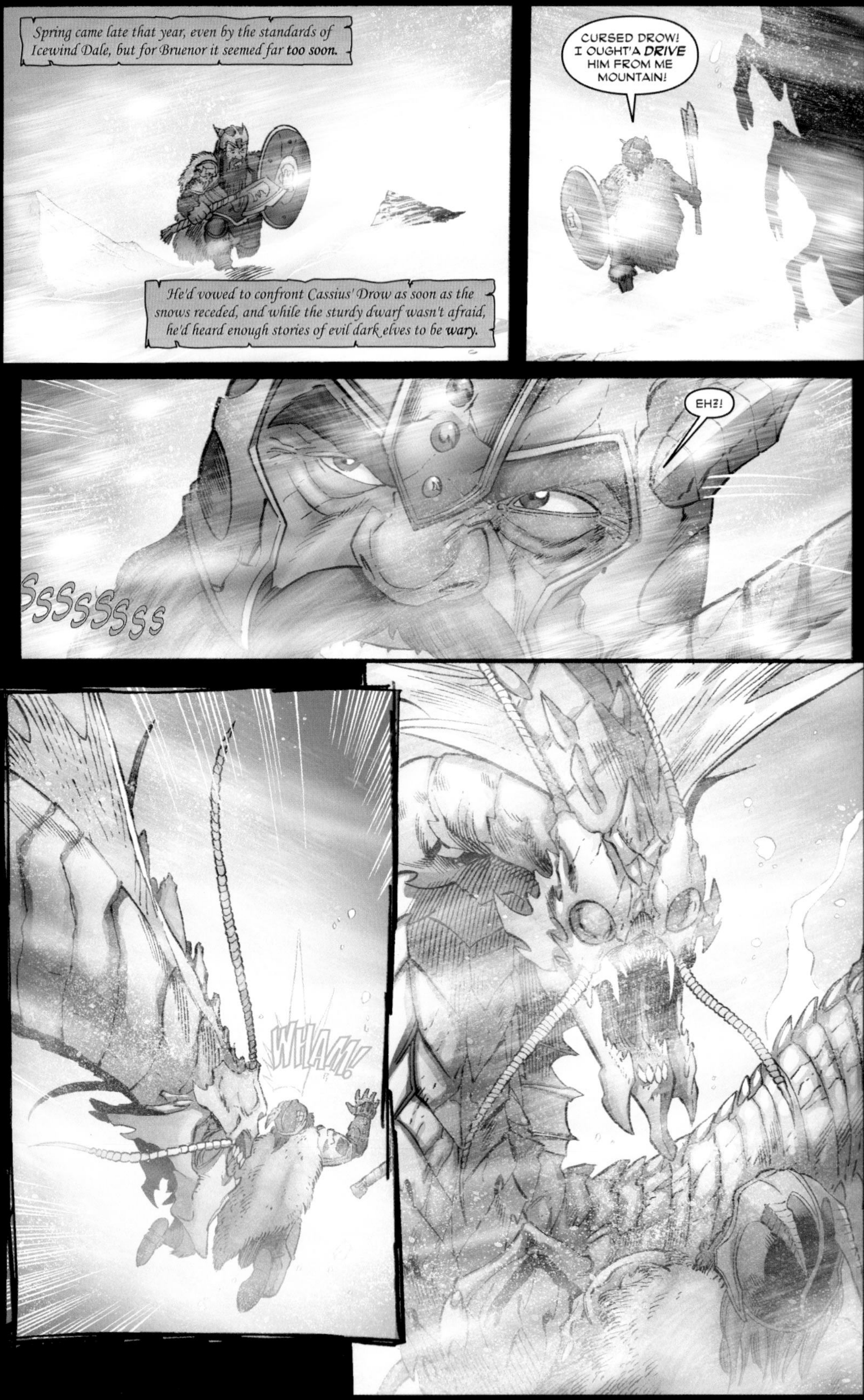
Spring came late that year, even by the standards of Icewind Dale, but for Bruenor it seemed far too soon.
He'd vowed to confront Cassius' Drow as soon as the snows receded, and while the sturdy dwarf wasn't afraid, he'd heard enough stories of evil dark elves to be wary.
CURSED DROW! I OUGHT'A DRIVE HIM FROM ME MOUNTAIN!
EH?!
SSSSSSSS
WHAM!

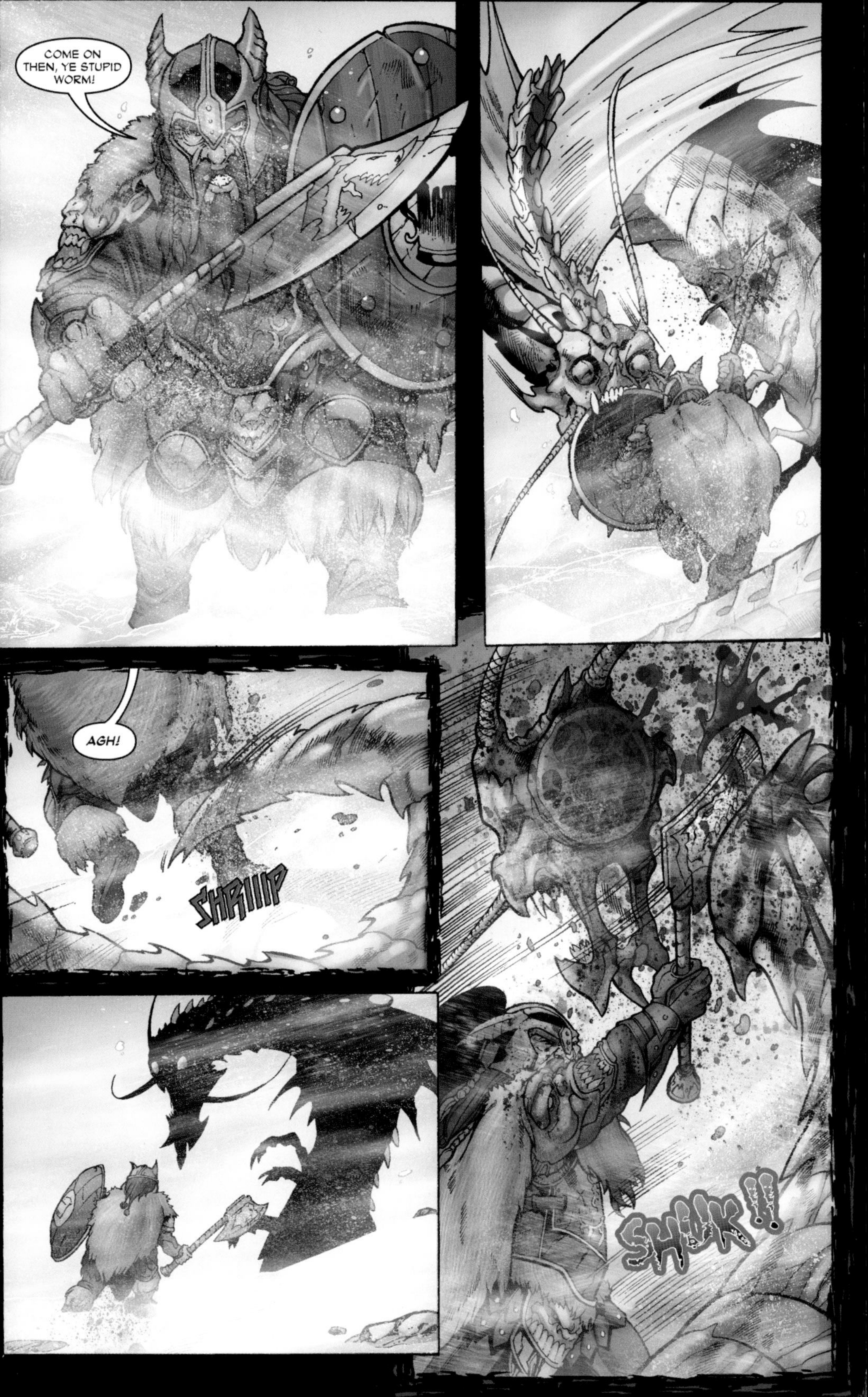
COME ON THEN, YE STUPID WORM!
AGH!
SHRIIIP
SHUK!!

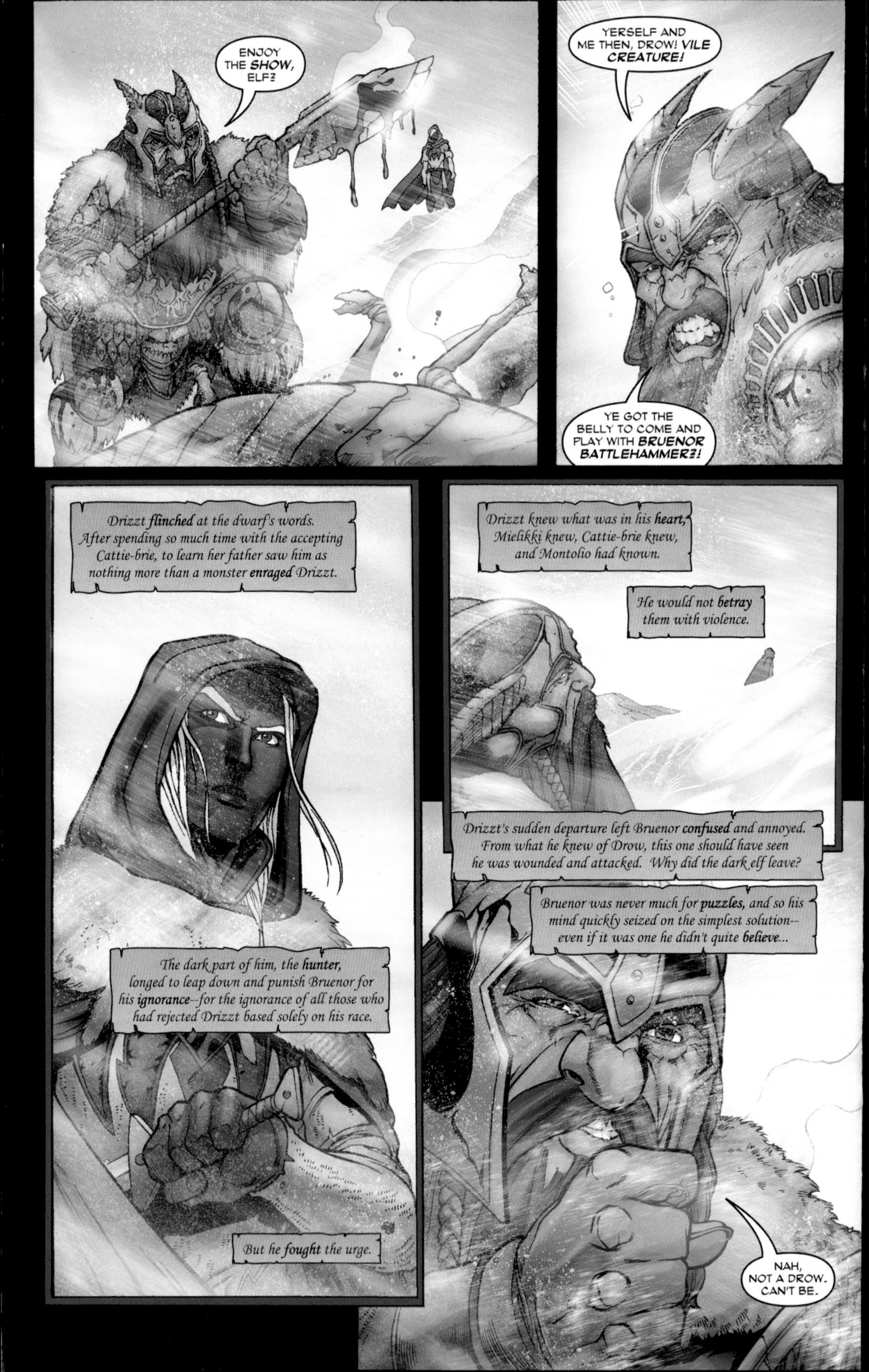

ENJOY THE SHOW, ELF?
YERSELF AND ME THEN, DROW! VILE CREATURE!
YE GOT THE BELLY TO COME AND PLAY WITH BRUENOR BATTLEHAMMER?!
Drizzt flinched at the dwarf's words. After spending so much time with the accepting Cattie-brie, to learn her father saw him as nothing more than a monster enraged Drizzt.
The dark part of him, the hunter, longed to leap down and punish Bruenor for his ignorance--for the ignorance of all those who had rejected Drizzt based solely on his race.
But he fought the urge.
Drizzt knew what was in his heart, Mielikki knew, Cattie-brie knew, and Montolio had known.
He would not betray them with violence.
Drizzt's sudden departure left Bruenor confused and annoyed. From what he knew of Drow, this one should have seen he was wounded and attacked. Why did the dark elf leave?
Bruenor was never much for puzzles, and so his mind quickly seized on the simplest solution--even if it was one he didn't quite believe...
NAH, NOT A DROW. CAN'T BE.

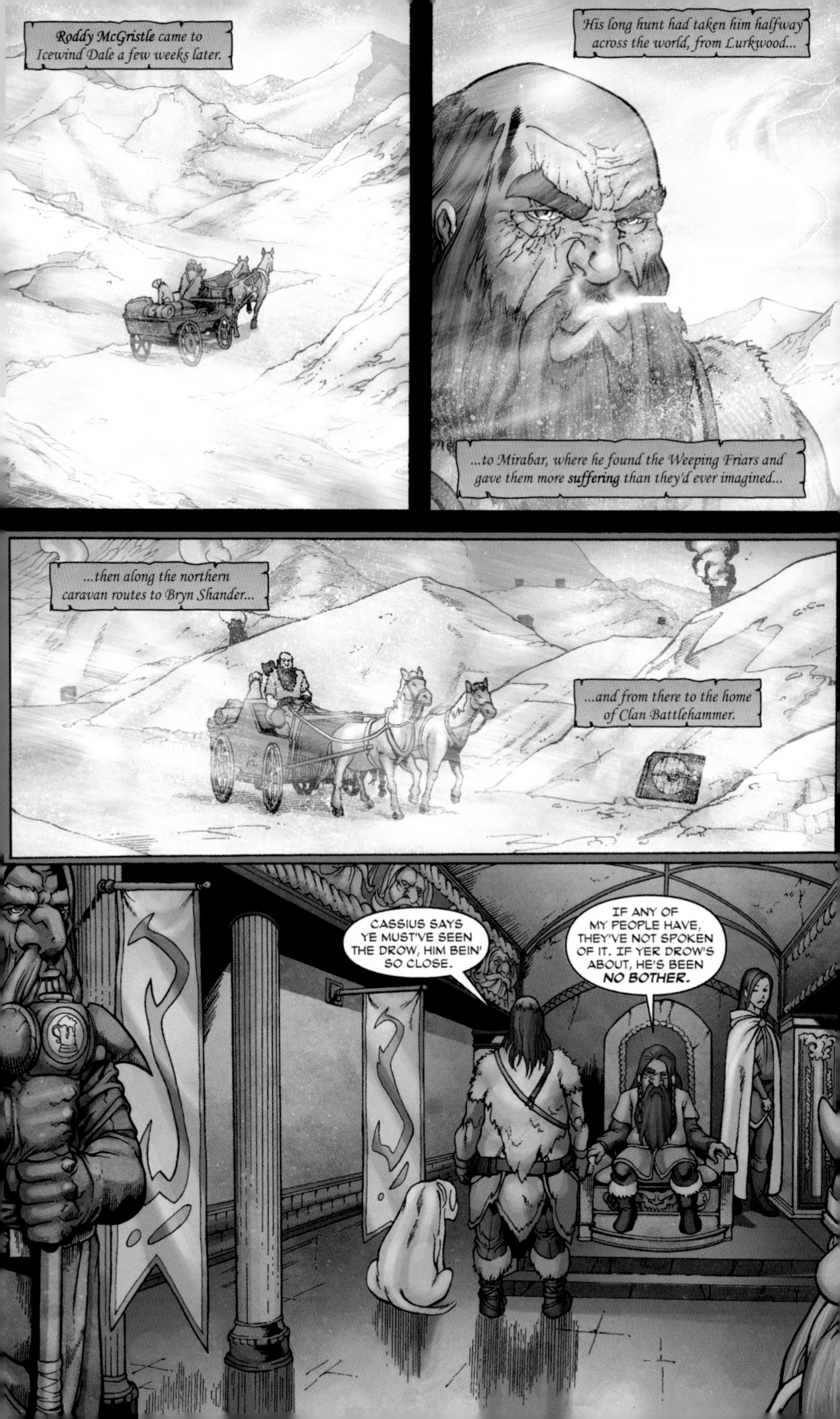

Roddy McGristle came to Icewind Dale a few weeks later.
His long hunt had taken him halfway across the world, from Lurkwood...
...to Mirabar, where he found the Weeping Friars and gave them more suffering than they'd ever imagined...
...then along the northern caravan routes to Bryn Shander...
...and from there to the home of Clan Battlehammer.
CASSIUS SAYS YE MUST'VE SEEN THE DROW, HIM BEIN' SO CLOSE.
IF ANY OF MY PEOPLE HAVE, THEY'VE NOT SPOKEN OF IT. IF YER DROW'S ABOUT, HE'S BEEN NO BOTHER.

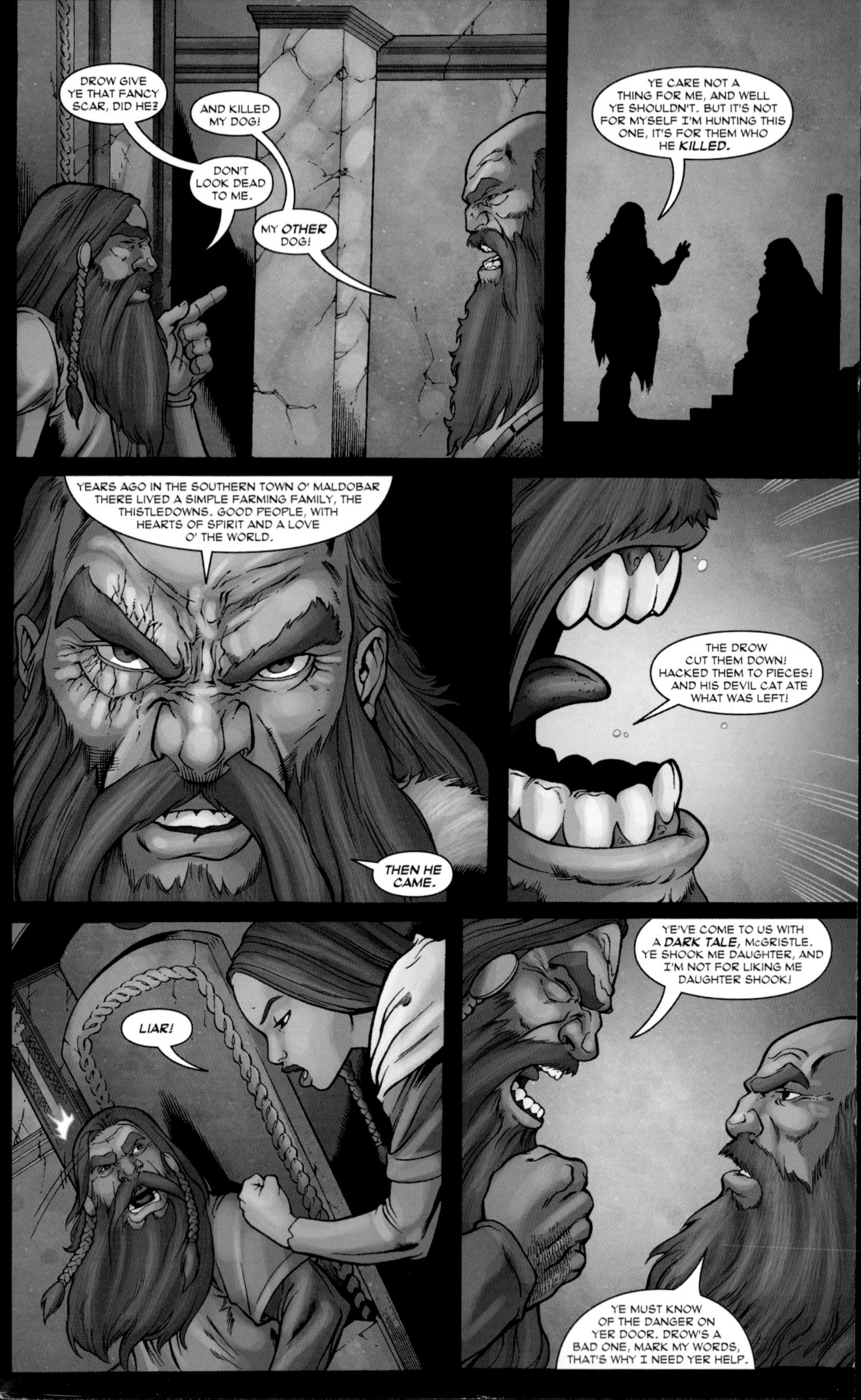
DROW GIVE YE THAT FANCY SCAR, DID HE?
AND KILLED MY DOG!
DON'T LOOK DEAD TO ME.
MY OTHER DOG!
YE CARE NOT A THING FOR ME, AND WELL YE SHOULDN'T. BUT IT'S NOT FOR MYSELF I'M HUNTING THIS ONE, IT'S FOR THEM WHO HE KILLED.
YEARS AGO IN THE SOUTHERN TOWN O' MALDOBAR THERE LIVED A SIMPLE FARMING FAMILY, THE THISTLEDOWNS. GOOD PEOPLE, WITH HEARTS OF SPIRIT AND A LOVE O' THE WORLD.
THEN HE CAME.
THE DROW CUT THEM DOWN! HACKED THEM TO PIECES! AND HIS DEVIL CAT ATE WHAT WAS LEFT!
LIAR!
YE'VE COME TO US WITH A DARK TALE, McGRISTLE. YE SHOOK ME DAUGHTER, AND I'M NOT FOR LIKING ME DAUGHTER SHOOK!
YE MUST KNOW OF THE DANGER ON YER DOOR. DROW'S A BAD ONE, MARK MY WORDS, THAT'S WHY I NEED YER HELP.

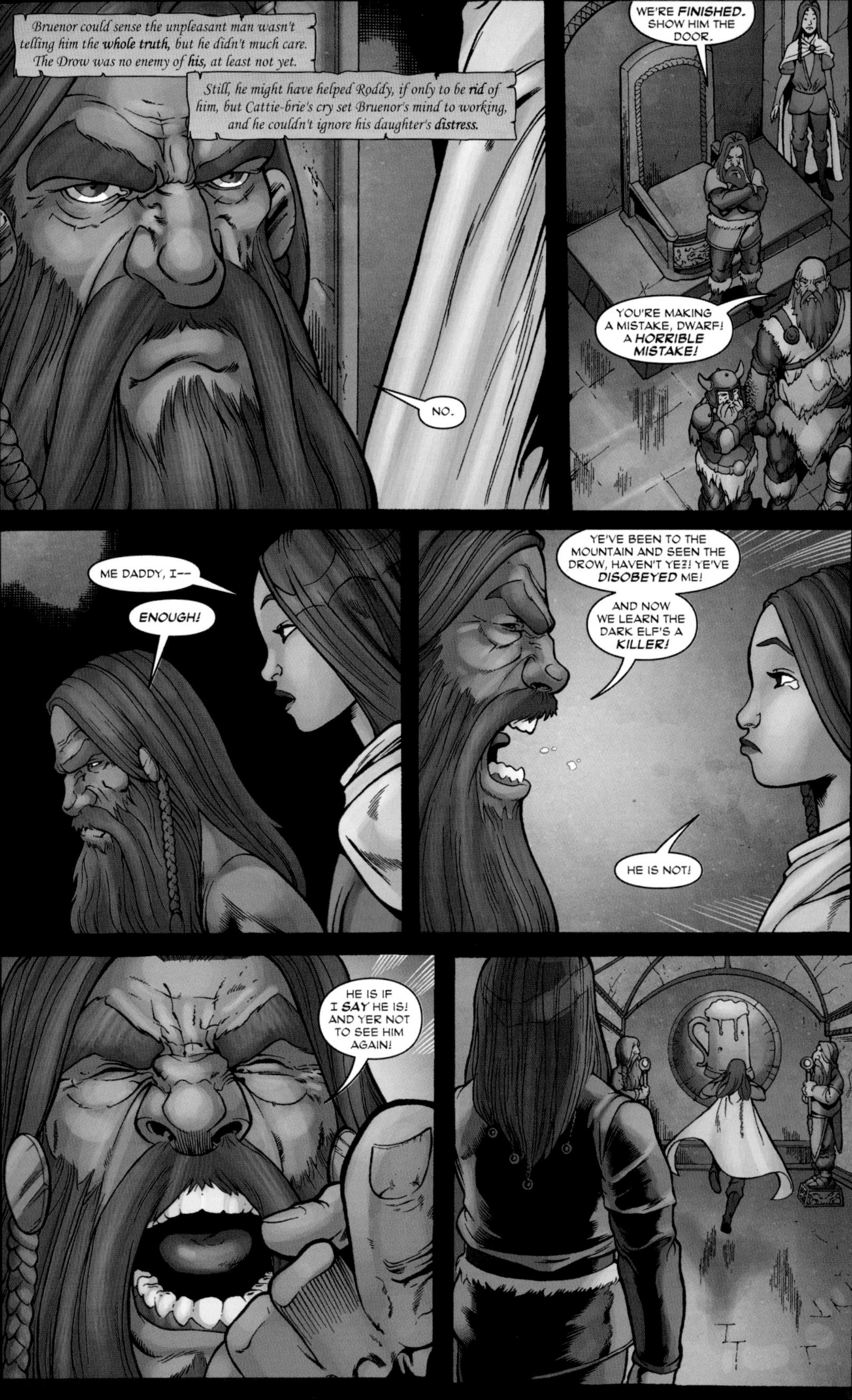
Bruenor could sense the unpleasant man wasn't telling him the whole truth, but he didn't much care. The Drow was no enemy of his, at least not yet.
Still, he might have helped Roddy, if only to be rid of him, but Cattie-brie's cry set Bruenor's mind to working, and he couldn't ignore his daughter's distress.
NO.
WE'RE FINISHED. SHOW HIM THE DOOR.
YOU'RE MAKING A MISTAKE, DWARF! A HORRIBLE MISTAKE!
ME DADDY, I--
ENOUGH!
YE'VE BEEN TO THE MOUNTAIN AND SEEN THE DROW, HAVEN'T YE?! YE'VE DISOBEYED ME!
AND NOW WE LEARN THE DARK ELF'S A KILLER!
HE IS NOT!
HE IS IF I SAY HE IS! AND YER NOT TO SEE HIM AGAIN!

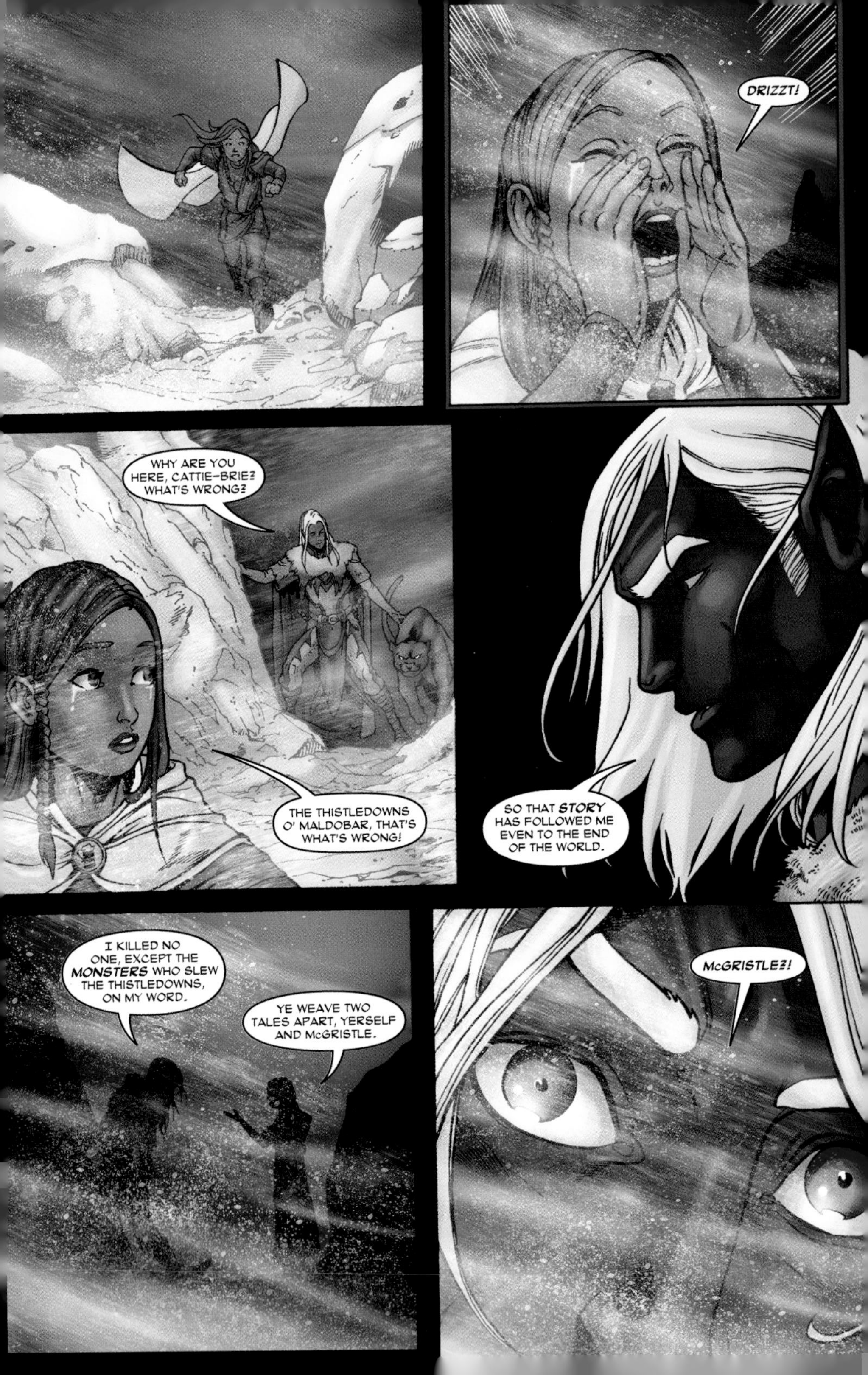
DRIZZT!
WHY ARE YOU HERE, CATTIE-BRIE? WHAT'S WRONG?
THE THISTLEDOWNS O' MALDOBAR, THAT'S WHAT'S WRONG!
SO THAT **STORY** HAS FOLLOWED ME EVEN TO THE END OF THE WORLD.
I KILLED NO ONE, EXCEPT THE **MONSTERS** WHO SLEW THE THISTLEDOWNS, ON MY WORD.
YE WEAVE TWO TALES APART, YERSELF AND McGRISTLE.
McGRISTLE?!

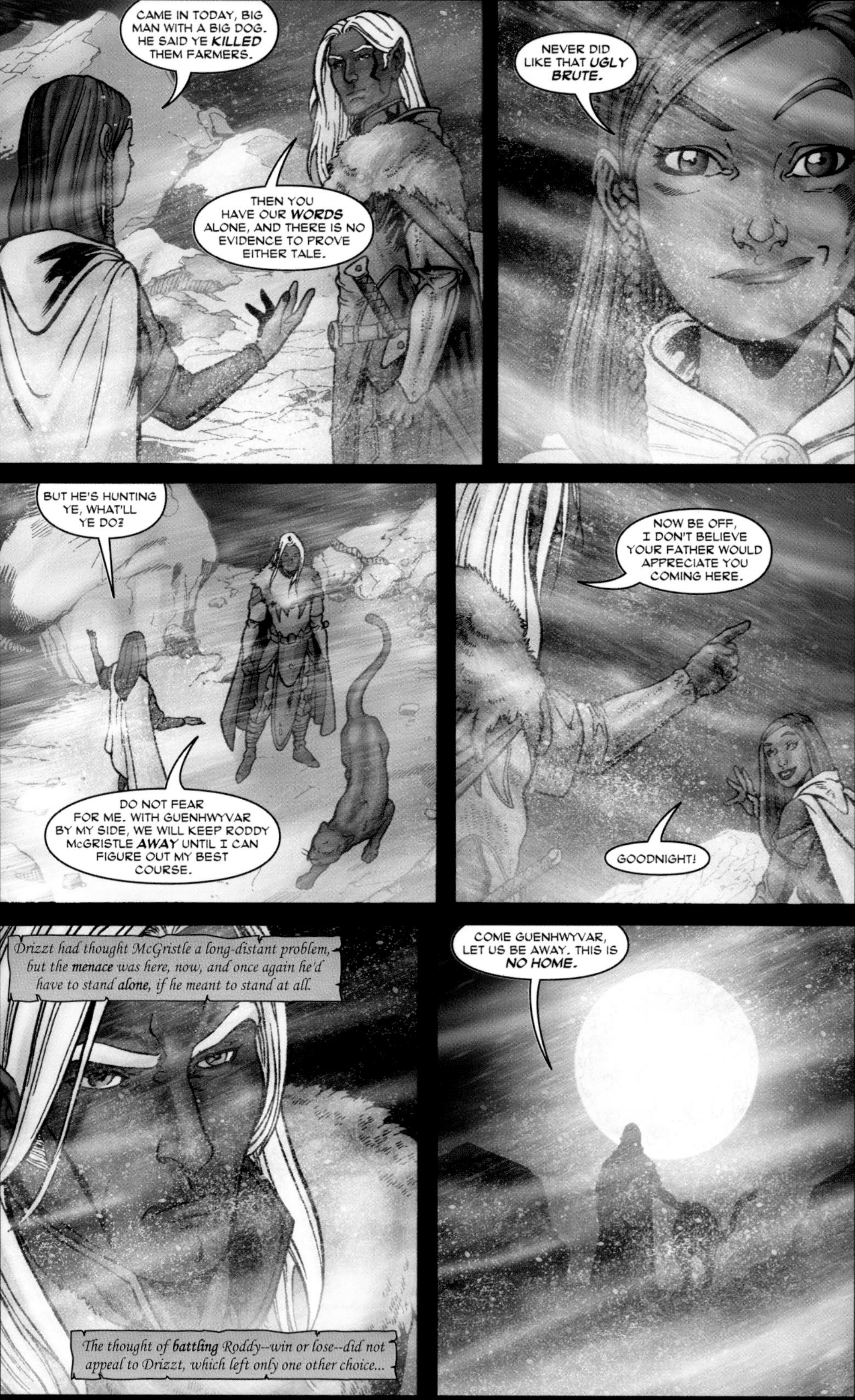
CAME IN TODAY, BIG MAN WITH A BIG DOG. HE SAID YE KILLED THEM FARMERS.
THEN YOU HAVE OUR WORDS ALONE, AND THERE IS NO EVIDENCE TO PROVE EITHER TALE.
NEVER DID LIKE THAT UGLY BRUTE.
BUT HE'S HUNTING YE, WHAT'LL YE DO?
DO NOT FEAR FOR ME. WITH GUENHWYVAR BY MY SIDE, WE WILL KEEP RODDY McGRISTLE AWAY UNTIL I CAN FIGURE OUT MY BEST COURSE.
NOW BE OFF, I DON'T BELIEVE YOUR FATHER WOULD APPRECIATE YOU COMING HERE.
GOODNIGHT!
Drizzt had thought McGristle a long-distant problem, but the menace was here, now, and once again he'd have to stand alone, if he meant to stand at all.
The thought of battling Roddy--win or lose--did not appeal to Drizzt, which left only one other choice...
COME GUENHWYVAR, LET US BE AWAY. THIS IS NO HOME.

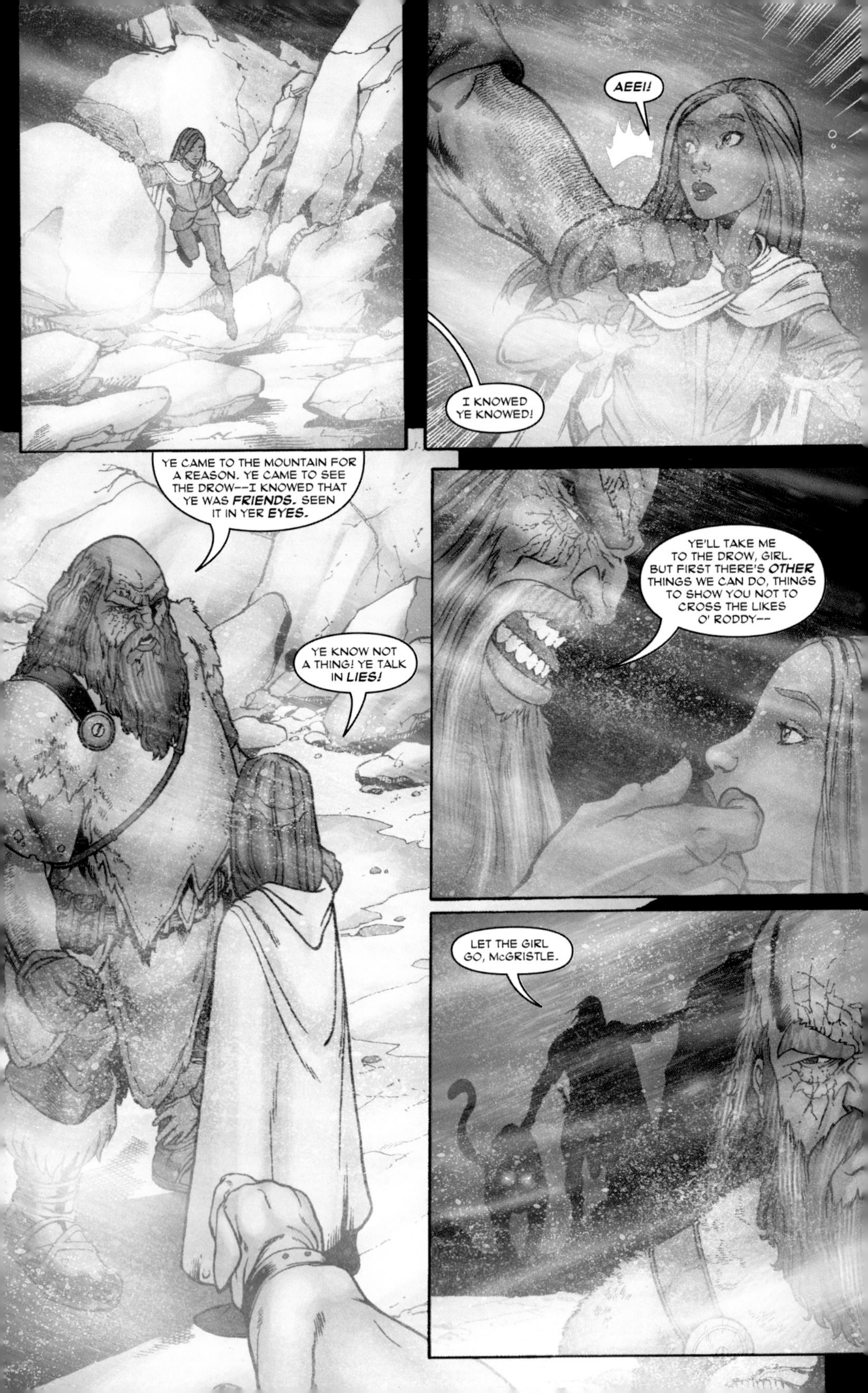
AEEI!
I KNOWED YE KNOWED!
YE CAME TO THE MOUNTAIN FOR A REASON. YE CAME TO SEE THE DROW--I KNOWED THAT YE WAS FRIENDS. SEEN IT IN YER EYES.
YE KNOW NOT A THING! YE TALK IN LIES!
YE'LL TAKE ME TO THE DROW, GIRL. BUT FIRST THERE'S OTHER THINGS WE CAN DO, THINGS TO SHOW YOU NOT TO CROSS THE LIKES O' RODDY--
LET THE GIRL GO, McGRISTLE.

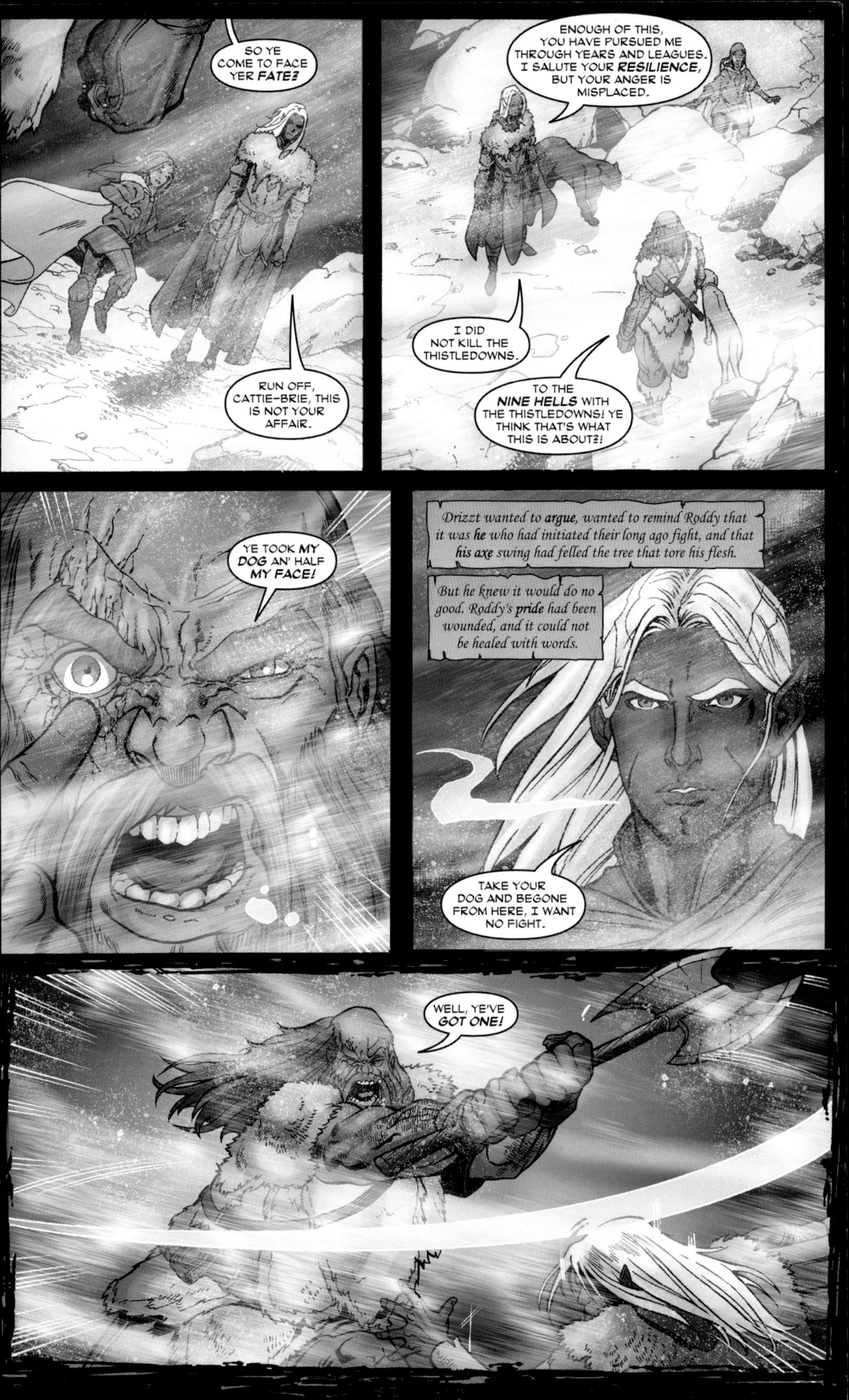
SO YE COME TO FACE YER FATE?
RUN OFF, CATTIE-BRIE, THIS IS NOT YOUR AFFAIR.
ENOUGH OF THIS, YOU HAVE PURSUED ME THROUGH YEARS AND LEAGUES. I SALUTE YOUR RESILIENCE, BUT YOUR ANGER IS MISPLACED.
I DID NOT KILL THE THISTLEDOWNS.
TO THE NINE HELLS WITH THE THISTLEDOWNS! YE THINK THAT'S WHAT THIS IS ABOUT?!
YE TOOK MY DOG AN' HALF MY FACE!
Drizzt wanted to argue, wanted to remind Roddy that it was he who had initiated their long ago fight, and that his axe swing had felled the tree that tore his flesh.
But he knew it would do no good. Roddy's pride had been wounded, and it could not be healed with words.
TAKE YOUR DOG AND BEGONE FROM HERE, I WANT NO FIGHT.
WELL, YE'VE GOT ONE!

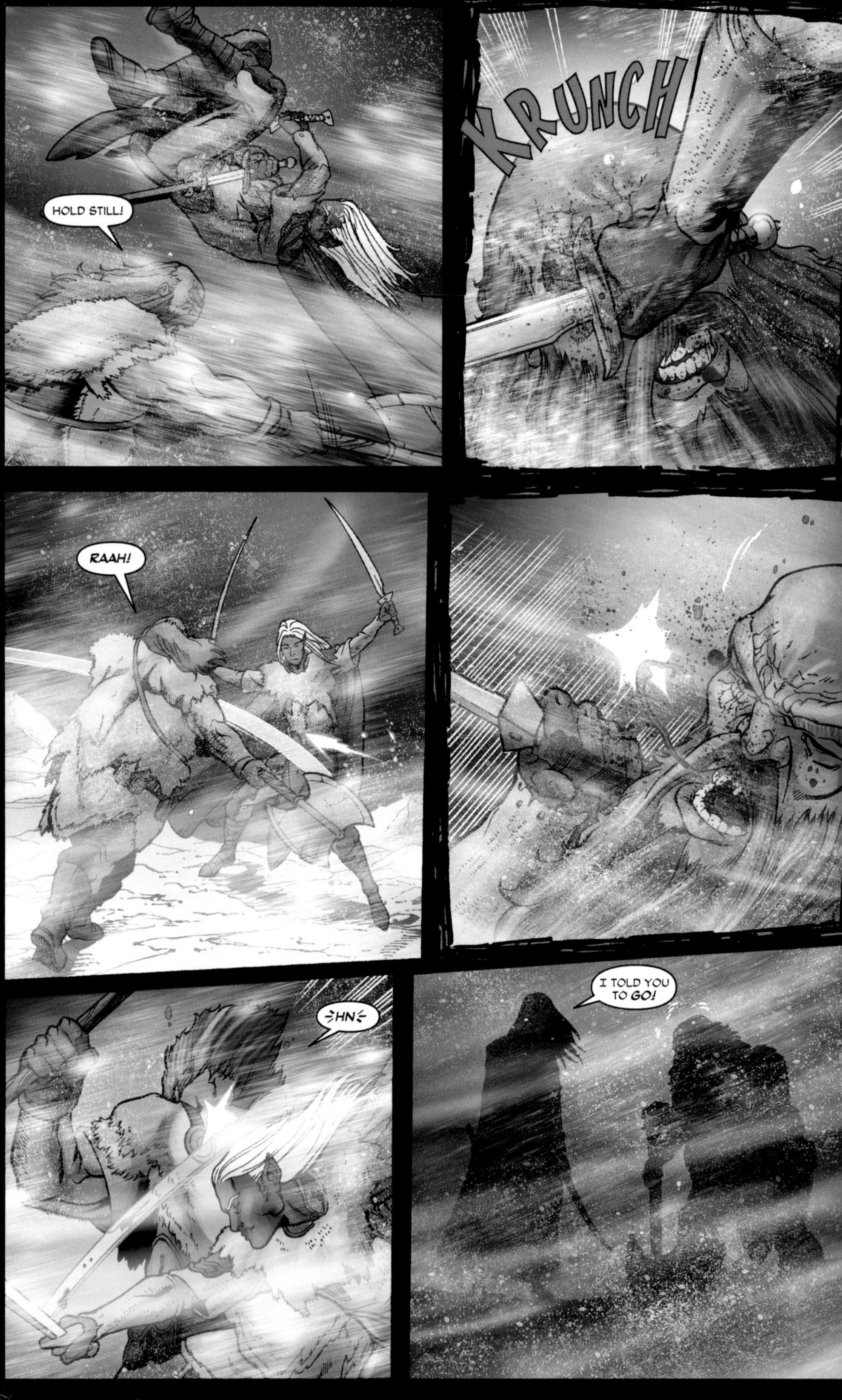
HOLD STILL!
KRUNCH
RAAH!
HN
I TOLD YOU TO GO!

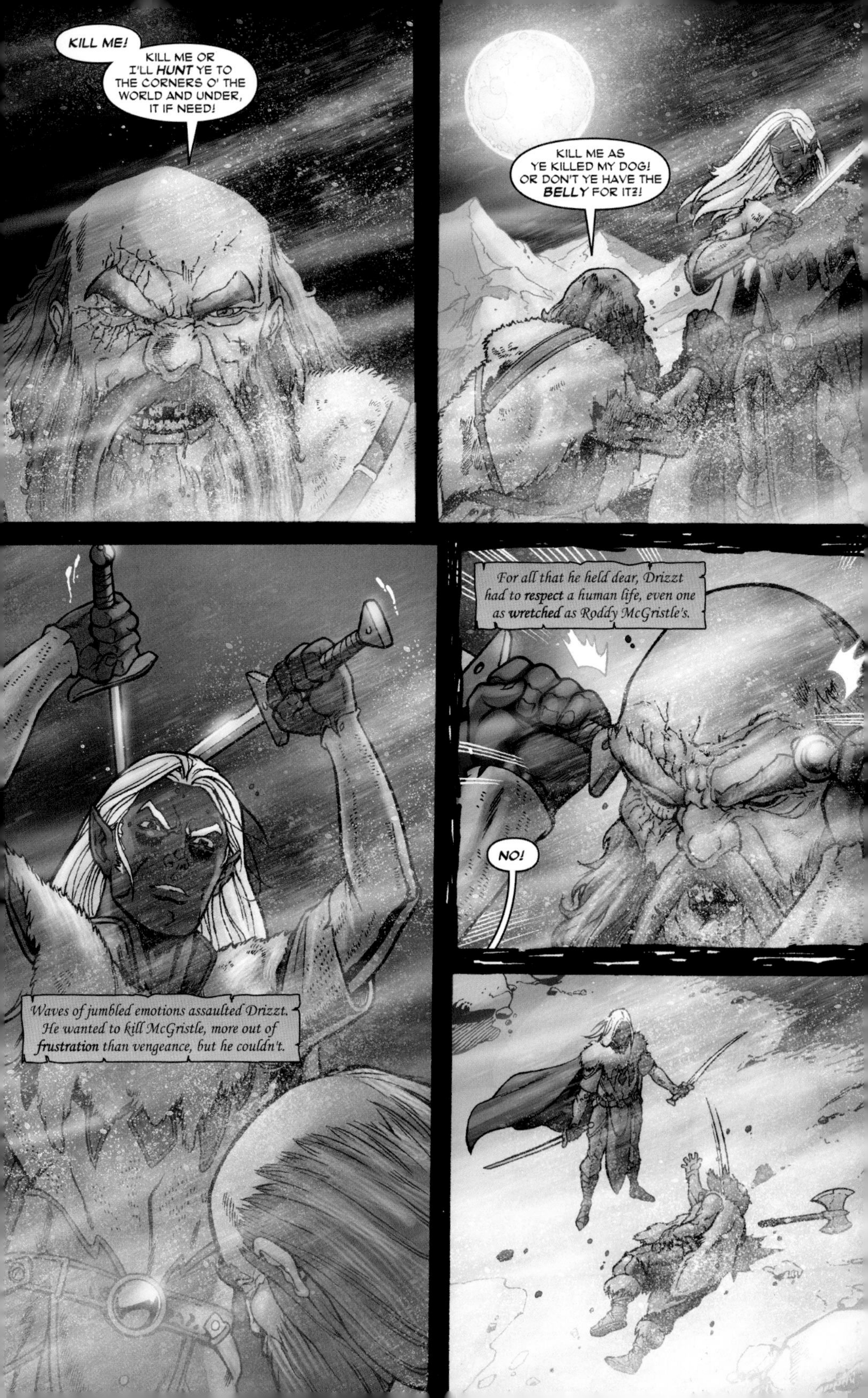

KILL ME!
KILL ME OR I'LL HUNT YE TO THE CORNERS O' THE WORLD AND UNDER, IT IF NEED!
KILL ME AS YE KILLED MY DOG! OR DON'T YE HAVE THE BELLY FOR IT?!
Waves of jumbled emotions assaulted Drizzt. He wanted to kill McGristle, more out of frustration than vengeance, but he couldn't.
For all that he held dear, Drizzt had to respect a human life, even one as wretched as Roddy McGristle's.
NO!

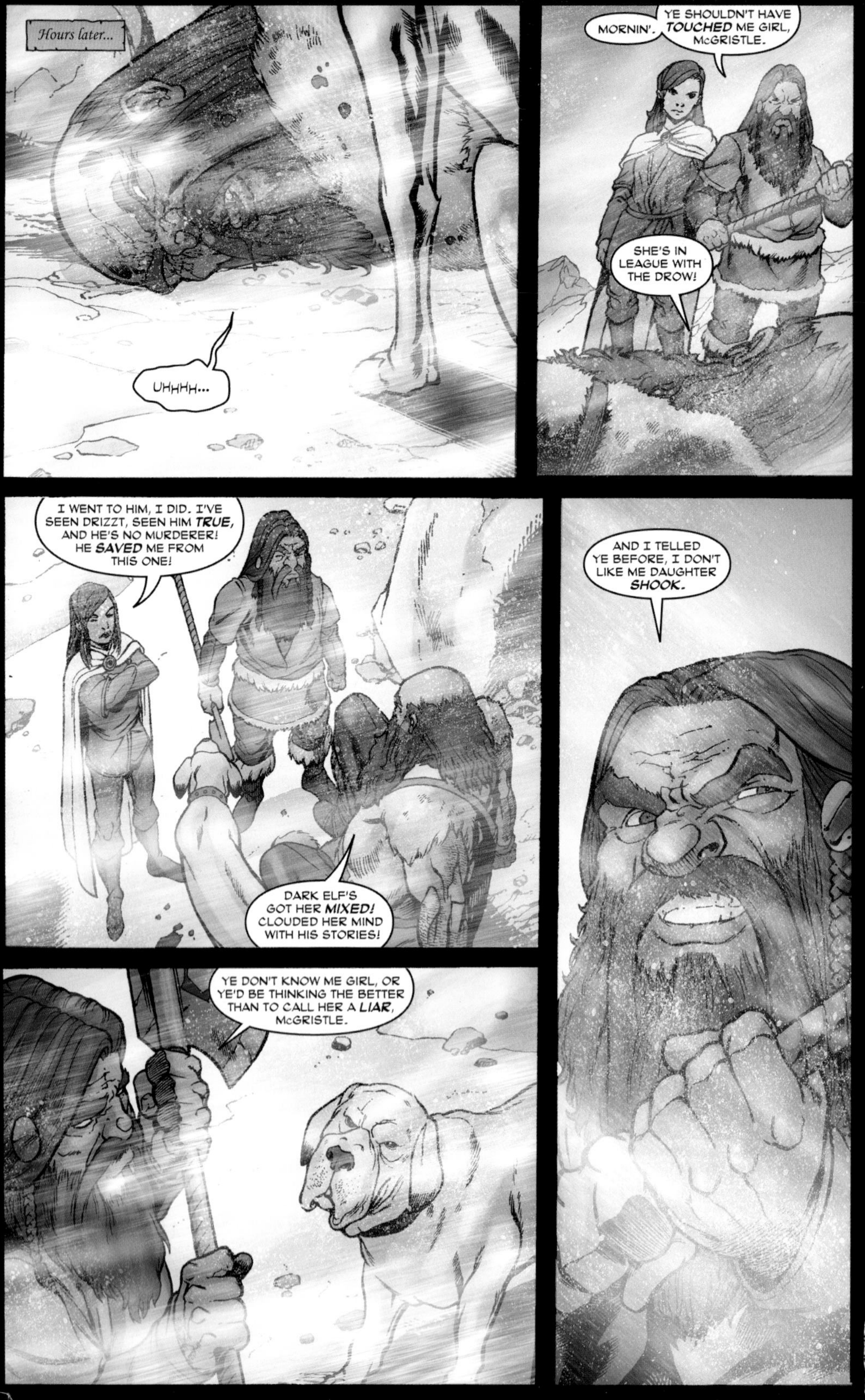

Hours later...
UHHHH...
MORNIN'.
YE SHOULDN'T HAVE TOUCHED ME GIRL, McGRISTLE.
SHE'S IN LEAGUE WITH THE DROW!
I WENT TO HIM, I DID. I'VE SEEN DRIZZT, SEEN HIM TRUE, AND HE'S NO MURDERER! HE SAVED ME FROM THIS ONE!
DARK ELF'S GOT HER MIXED! CLOUDED HER MIND WITH HIS STORIES!
YE DON'T KNOW ME GIRL, OR YE'D BE THINKING THE BETTER THAN TO CALL HER A LIAR, McGRISTLE.
AND I TELLED YE BEFORE, I DON'T LIKE ME DAUGHTER SHOOK.

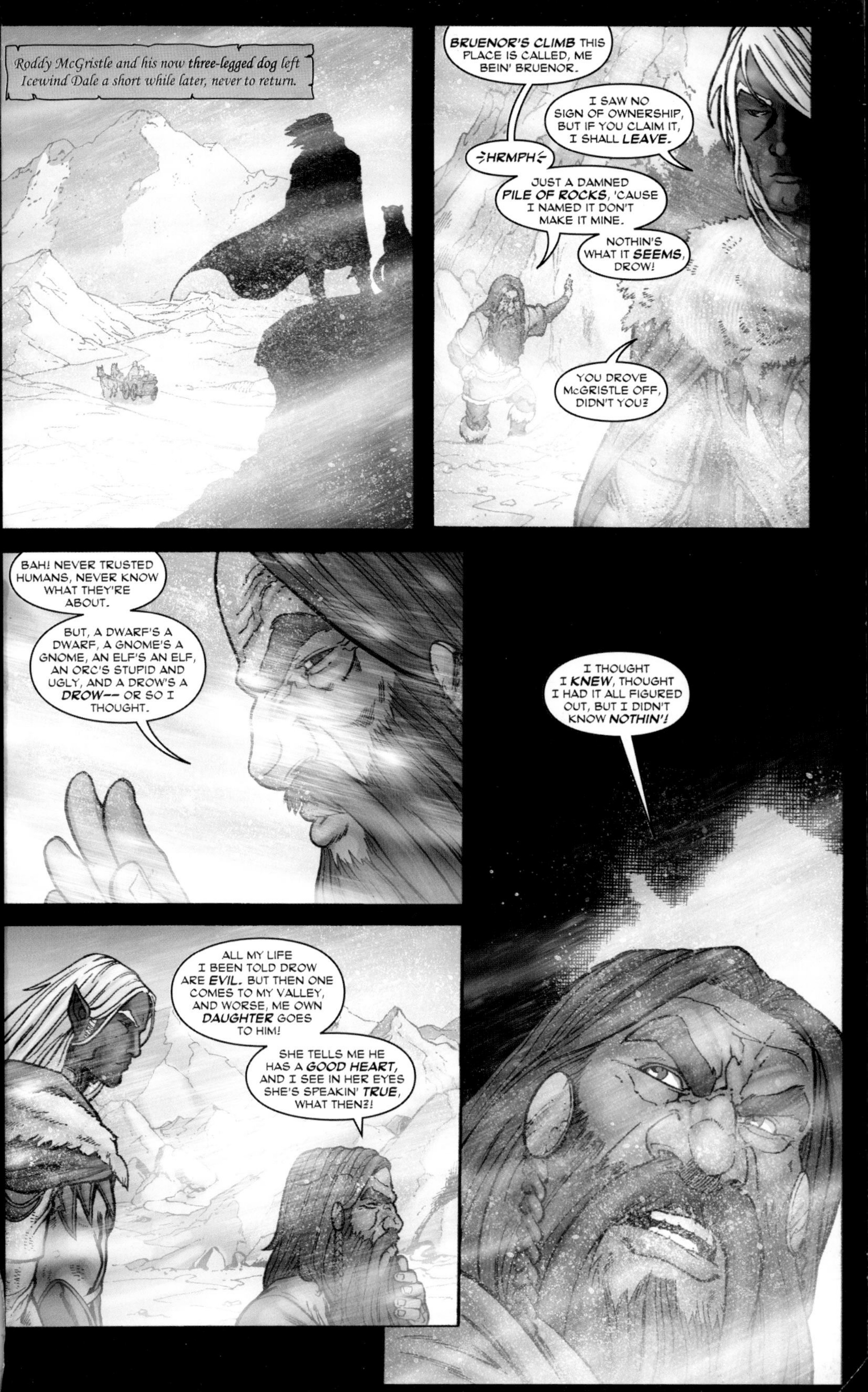

Roddy McGristle and his now **three-legged dog** left Icewind Dale a short while later, never to return.
BRUENOR'S CLIMB THIS PLACE IS CALLED, ME BEIN' BRUENOR.
I SAW NO SIGN OF OWNERSHIP, BUT IF YOU CLAIM IT, I SHALL LEAVE.
HRMPH
JUST A DAMNED PILE OF ROCKS, 'CAUSE I NAMED IT DON'T MAKE IT MINE.
NOTHIN'S WHAT IT SEEMS, DROW!
YOU DROVE McGRISTLE OFF, DIDN'T YOU?
BAH! NEVER TRUSTED HUMANS, NEVER KNOW WHAT THEY'RE ABOUT.
BUT, A DWARF'S A DWARF, A GNOME'S A GNOME, AN ELF'S AN ELF, AN ORC'S STUPID AND UGLY, AND A DROW'S A DROW-- OR SO I THOUGHT.
I THOUGHT I KNEW, THOUGHT I HAD IT ALL FIGURED OUT, BUT I DIDN'T KNOW NOTHIN'!
ALL MY LIFE I BEEN TOLD DROW ARE EVIL. BUT THEN ONE COMES TO MY VALLEY, AND WORSE, ME OWN DAUGHTER GOES TO HIM!
SHE TELLS ME HE HAS A GOOD HEART, AND I SEE IN HER EYES SHE'S SPEAKIN' TRUE, WHAT THEN?!

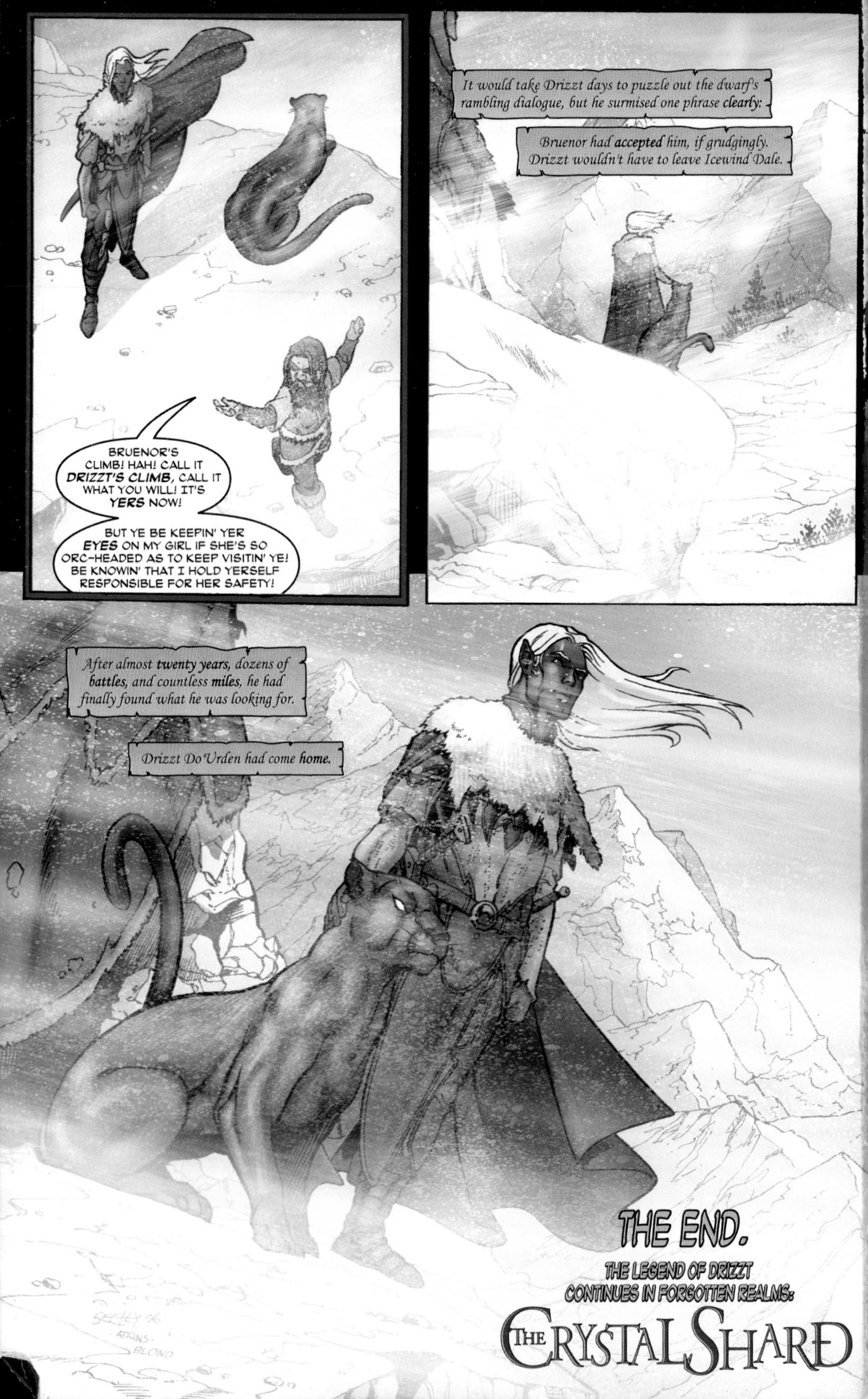
BRUENOR'S CLIMB! HAH! CALL IT DRIZZT'S CLIMB, CALL IT WHAT YOU WILL! IT'S YERS NOW!
BUT YE BE KEEPIN' YER EYES ON MY GIRL IF SHE'S SO ORC-HEADED AS TO KEEP VISITIN' YE! BE KNOWIN' THAT I HOLD YERSELF RESPONSIBLE FOR HER SAFETY!
It would take Drizzt days to puzzle out the dwarf's rambling dialogue, but he surmised one phrase clearly:
Bruenor had accepted him, if grudgingly. Drizzt wouldn't have to leave Icewind Dale.
After almost twenty years, dozens of battles, and countless miles, he had finally found what he was looking for.
Drizzt Do'Urden had come home.
THE END.
THE LEGEND OF DRIZZT CONTINUES IN FORGOTTEN REALMS:
THE CRYSTAL SHARD